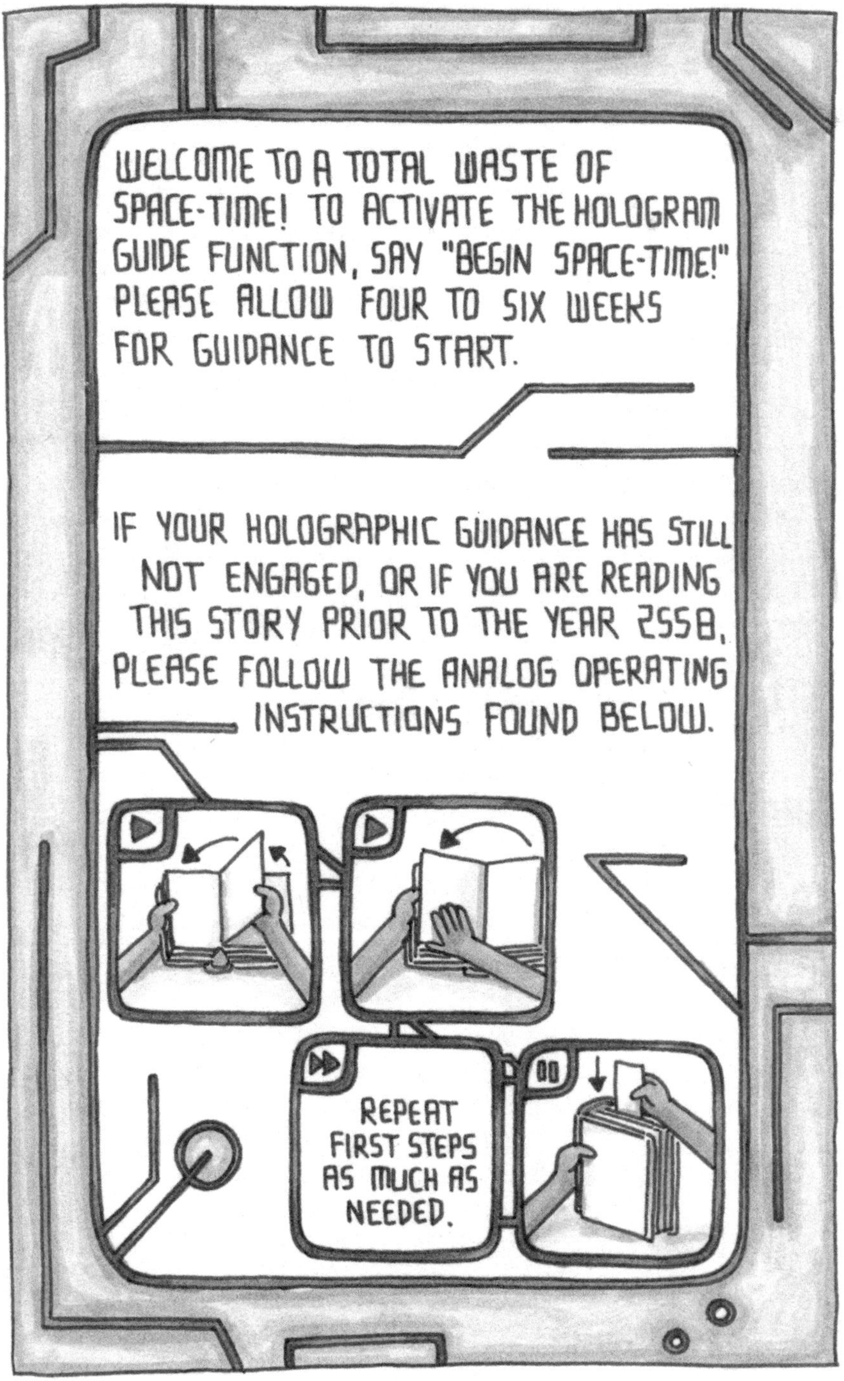
WELCOME TO A TOTAL WASTE OF SPACE-TIME! TO ACTIVATE THE HOLOGRAM GUIDE FUNCTION, SAY "BEGIN SPACE-TIME!" PLEASE ALLOW FOUR TO SIX WEEKS FOR GUIDANCE TO START.
IF YOUR HOLOGRAPHIC GUIDANCE HAS STILL NOT ENGAGED, OR IF YOU ARE READING THIS STORY PRIOR TO THE YEAR 2558, PLEASE FOLLOW THE ANALOG OPERATING INSTRUCTIONS FOUND BELOW.
REPEAT FIRST STEPS AS MUCH AS NEEDED.

OUR STORY SO FAR...

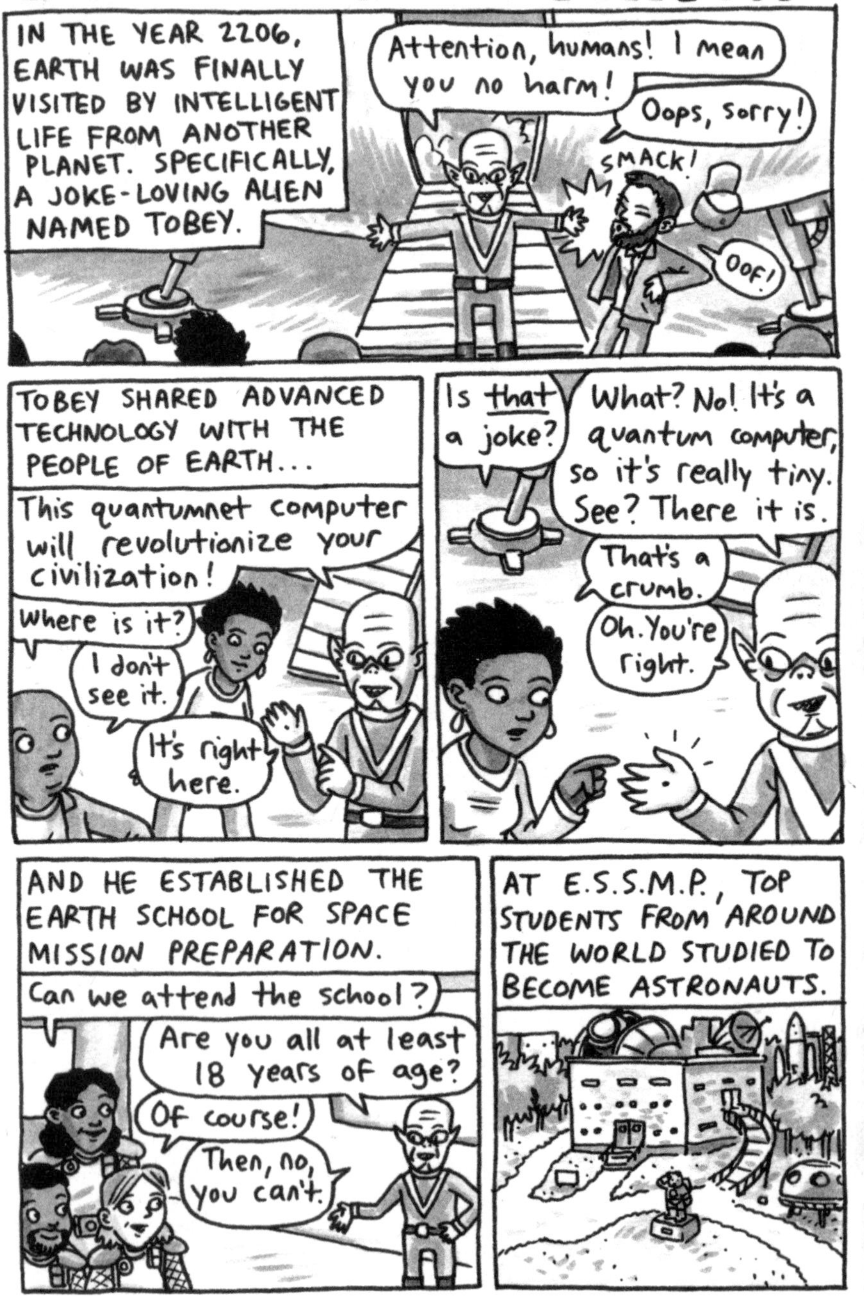
IN THE YEAR 2206, EARTH WAS FINALLY VISITED BY INTELLIGENT LIFE FROM ANOTHER PLANET. SPECIFICALLY, A JOKE-LOVING ALIEN NAMED TOBEY.
Attention, humans! I mean you no harm!
Oops, sorry!
SMACK!
OOF!
TOBEY SHARED ADVANCED TECHNOLOGY WITH THE PEOPLE OF EARTH...
This quantumnet computer will revolutionize your civilization!
Where is it?
I don't see it.
It's right here.
Is that a joke?
What? No! It's a quantum computer, so it's really tiny. See? There it is.
That's a crumb.
Oh. You're right.
AND HE ESTABLISHED THE EARTH SCHOOL FOR SPACE MISSION PREPARATION.
Can we attend the school?
Are you all at least 18 years of age?
Of course!
Then, no, you can't.
AT E.S.S.M.P., TOP STUDENTS FROM AROUND THE WORLD STUDIED TO BECOME ASTRONAUTS.

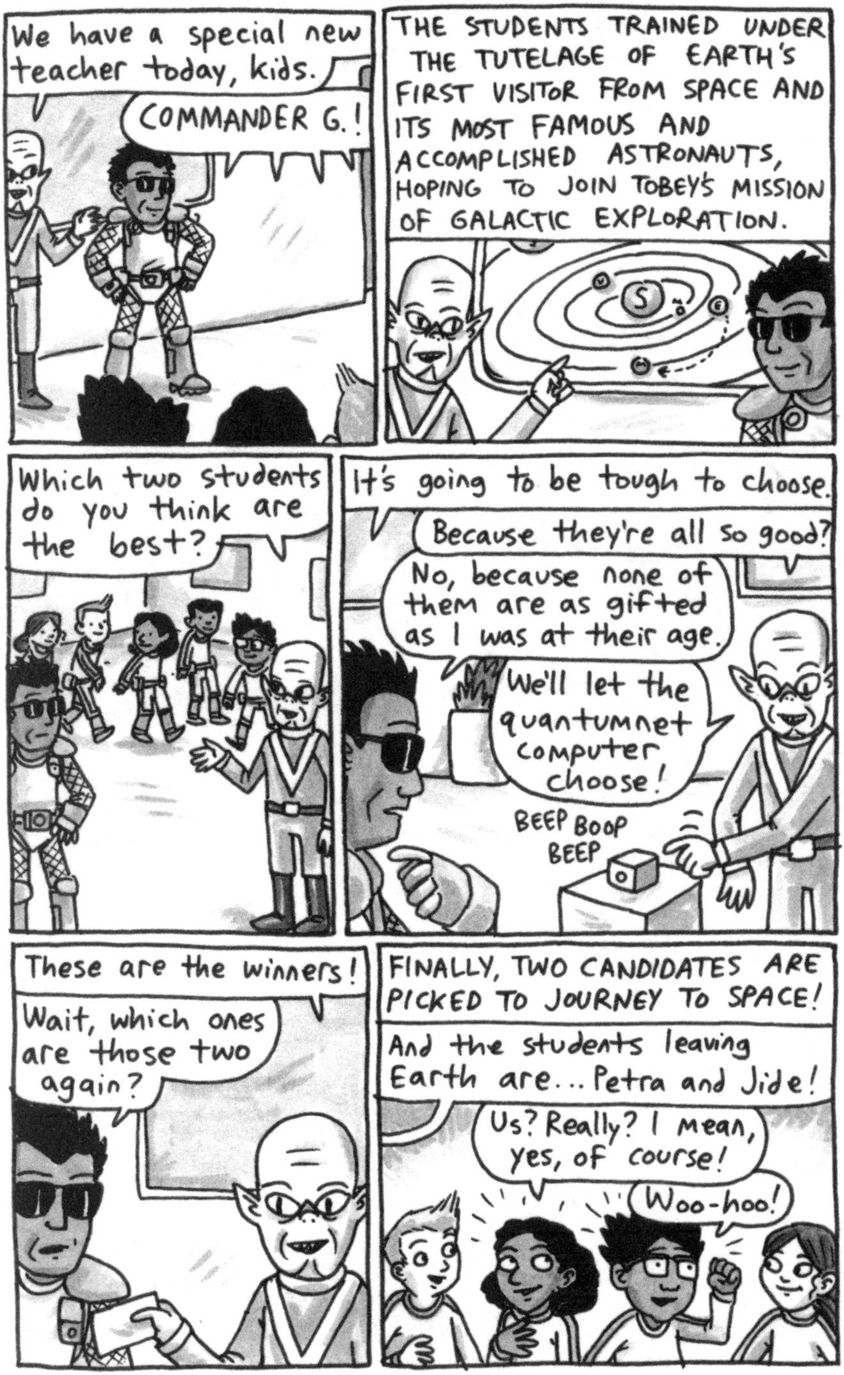
We have a special new teacher today, kids.
COMMANDER G.!
THE STUDENTS TRAINED UNDER THE TUTELAGE OF EARTH'S FIRST VISITOR FROM SPACE AND ITS MOST FAMOUS AND ACCOMPLISHED ASTRONAUTS, HOPING TO JOIN TOBEY'S MISSION OF GALACTIC EXPLORATION.
Which two students do you think are the best?
It's going to be tough to choose.
Because they're all so good?
No, because none of them are as gifted as I was at their age.
We'll let the quantumnet computer choose!
BEEP BOOP BEEP
These are the winners!
Wait, which ones are those two again?
FINALLY, TWO CANDIDATES ARE PICKED TO JOURNEY TO SPACE!
And the students leaving Earth are... Petra and Jide!
Us? Really? I mean, yes, of course!
Woo-hoo!

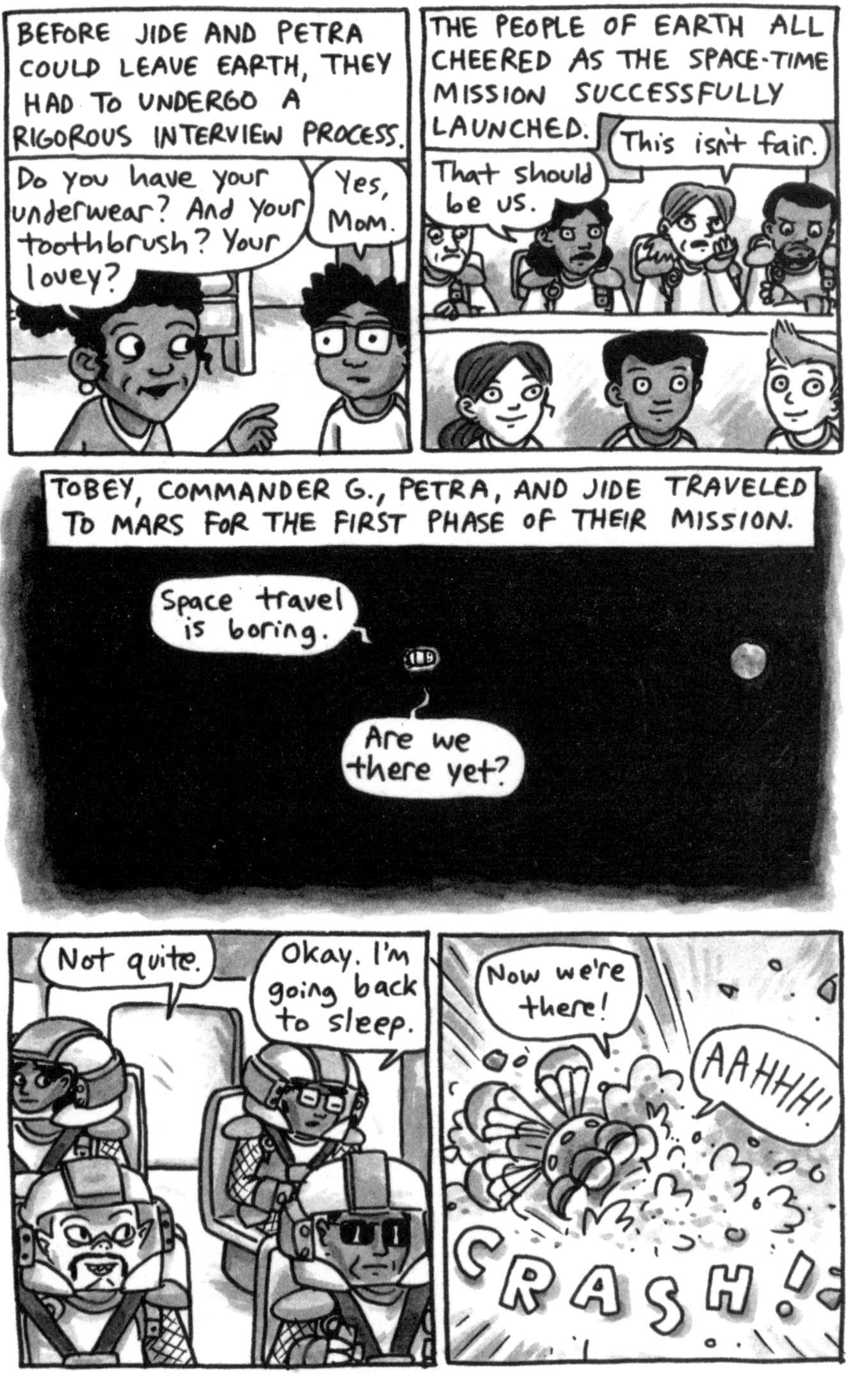
BEFORE JIDE AND PETRA COULD LEAVE EARTH, THEY HAD TO UNDERGO A RIGOROUS INTERVIEW PROCESS.
Do you have your underwear? And your toothbrush? Your lovey?
Yes, Mom.
THE PEOPLE OF EARTH ALL CHEERED AS THE SPACE-TIME MISSION SUCCESSFULLY LAUNCHED.
That should be us.
This isn't fair.
TOBEY, COMMANDER G., PETRA, AND JIDE TRAVELED TO MARS FOR THE FIRST PHASE OF THEIR MISSION.
Space travel is boring.
Are we there yet?
Not quite.
Okay. I'm going back to sleep.
Now we're there!
AAHHHH!
CRASH!

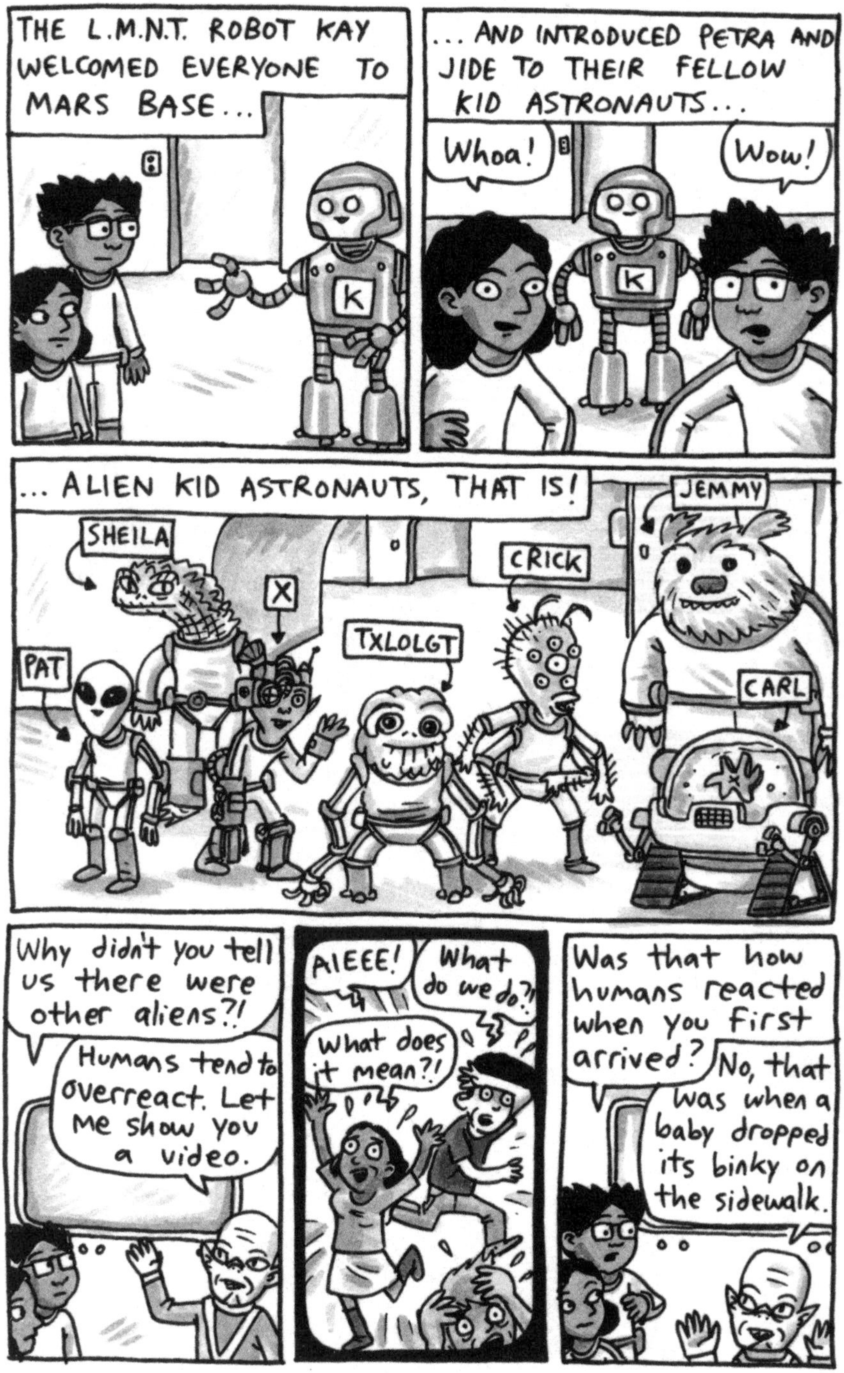
THE L.M.N.T. ROBOT KAY WELCOMED EVERYONE TO MARS BASE...
K
...AND INTRODUCED PETRA AND JIDE TO THEIR FELLOW KID ASTRONAUTS...
Whoa!
Wow!
K
...ALIEN KID ASTRONAUTS, THAT IS!
JEMMY
SHEILA
CRICK
X
TXLOLGT
PAT
CARL
Why didn't you tell us there were other aliens?!
Humans tend to overreact. Let me show you a video.
AIEEE!
What do we do?!
What does it mean?!
Was that how humans reacted when you first arrived?
No, that was when a baby dropped its binky on the sidewalk.

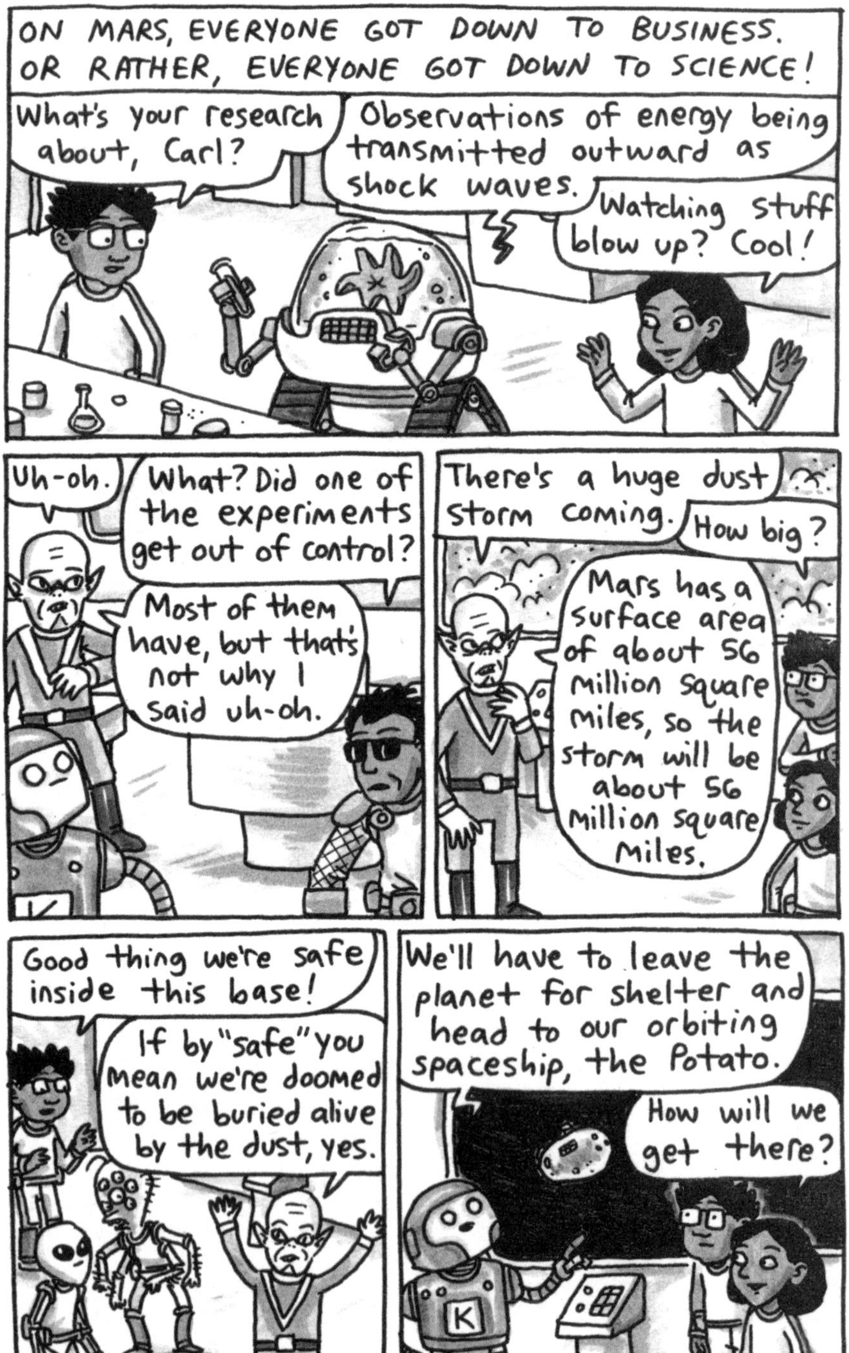
ON MARS, EVERYONE GOT DOWN TO BUSINESS. OR RATHER, EVERYONE GOT DOWN TO SCIENCE!
What's your research about, Carl?
Observations of energy being transmitted outward as shock waves.
Watching stuff blow up? Cool!
Uh-oh.
What? Did one of the experiments get out of control?
Most of them have, but that's not why I said uh-oh.
There's a huge dust storm coming.
How big?
Mars has a surface area of about 56 million square miles, so the storm will be about 56 million square miles.
Good thing we're safe inside this base!
If by "safe" you mean we're doomed to be buried alive by the dust, yes.
We'll have to leave the planet for shelter and head to our orbiting spaceship, the Potato.
How will we get there?
K

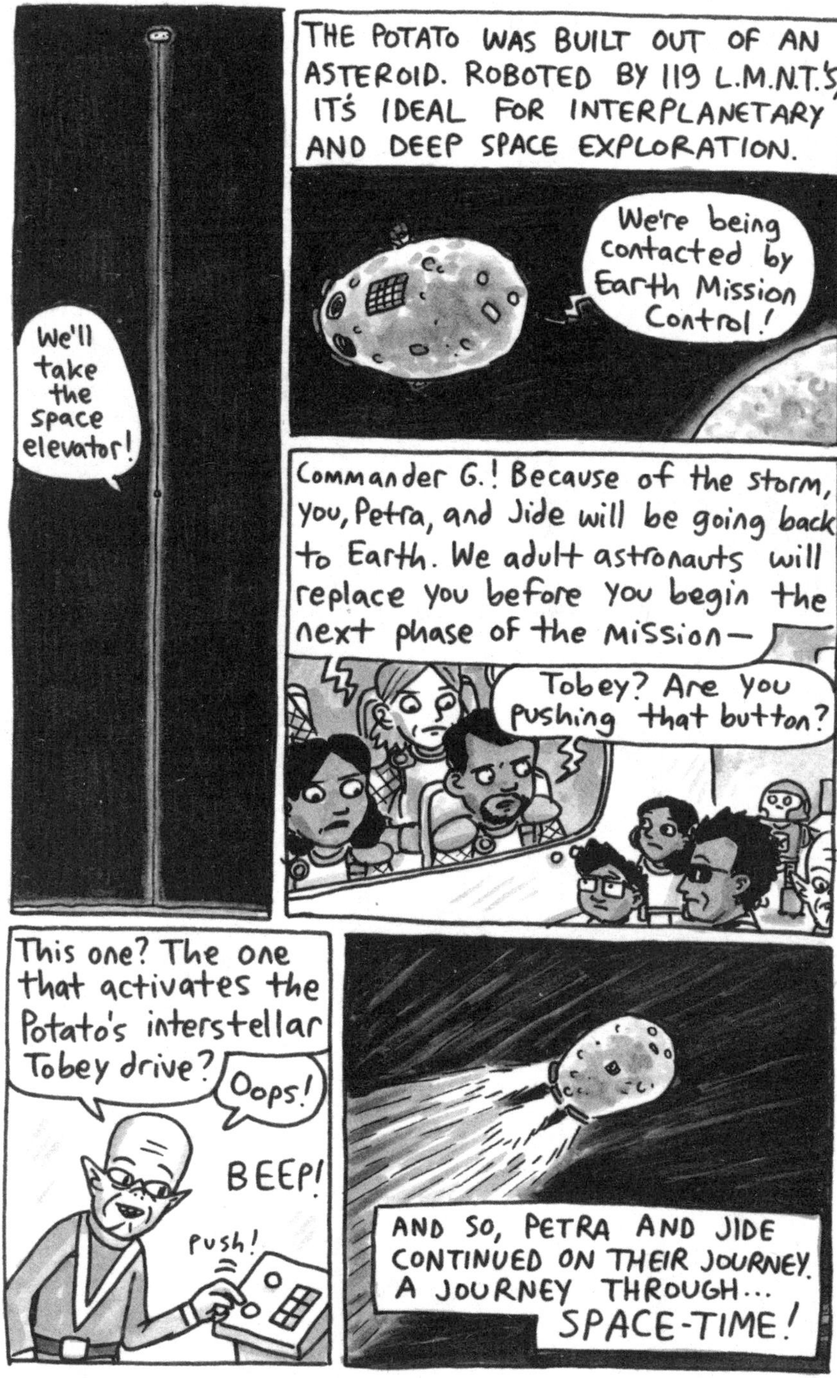
THE POTATO WAS BUILT OUT OF AN ASTEROID. ROBOTED BY 119 L.M.N.T.'S, IT'S IDEAL FOR INTERPLANETARY AND DEEP SPACE EXPLORATION.
We'll take the space elevator!
We're being contacted by Earth Mission Control!
Commander G.! Because of the storm, you, Petra, and Jide will be going back to Earth. We adult astronauts will replace you before you begin the next phase of the mission—
Tobey? Are you pushing that button?
This one? The one that activates the Potato's interstellar Tobey drive?
Oops!
BEEP!
PUSH!
AND SO, PETRA AND JIDE CONTINUED ON THEIR JOURNEY. A JOURNEY THROUGH...
SPACE-TIME!

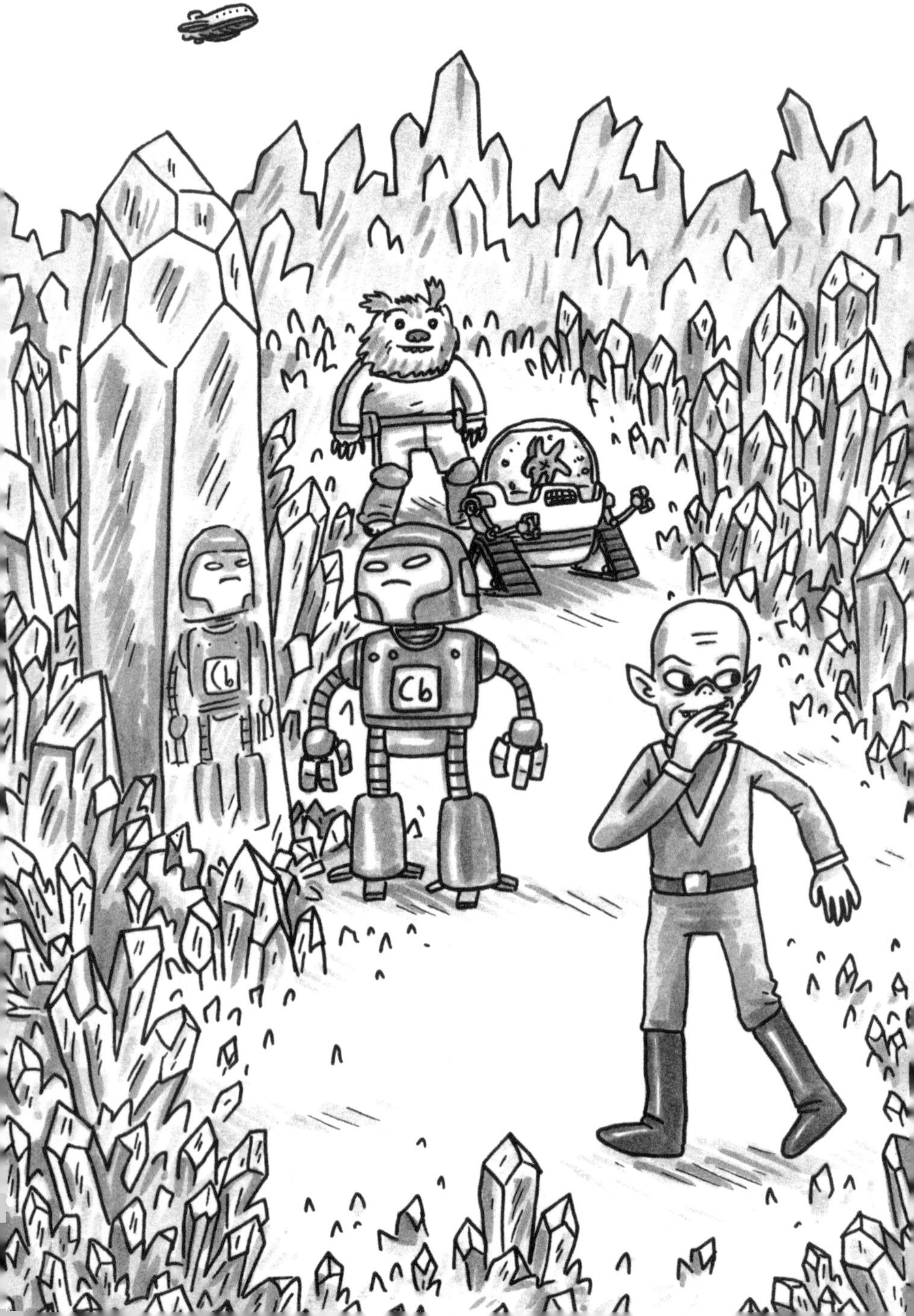
Cb
Cb

A TOTAL WASTE OF SPACE-TIME!

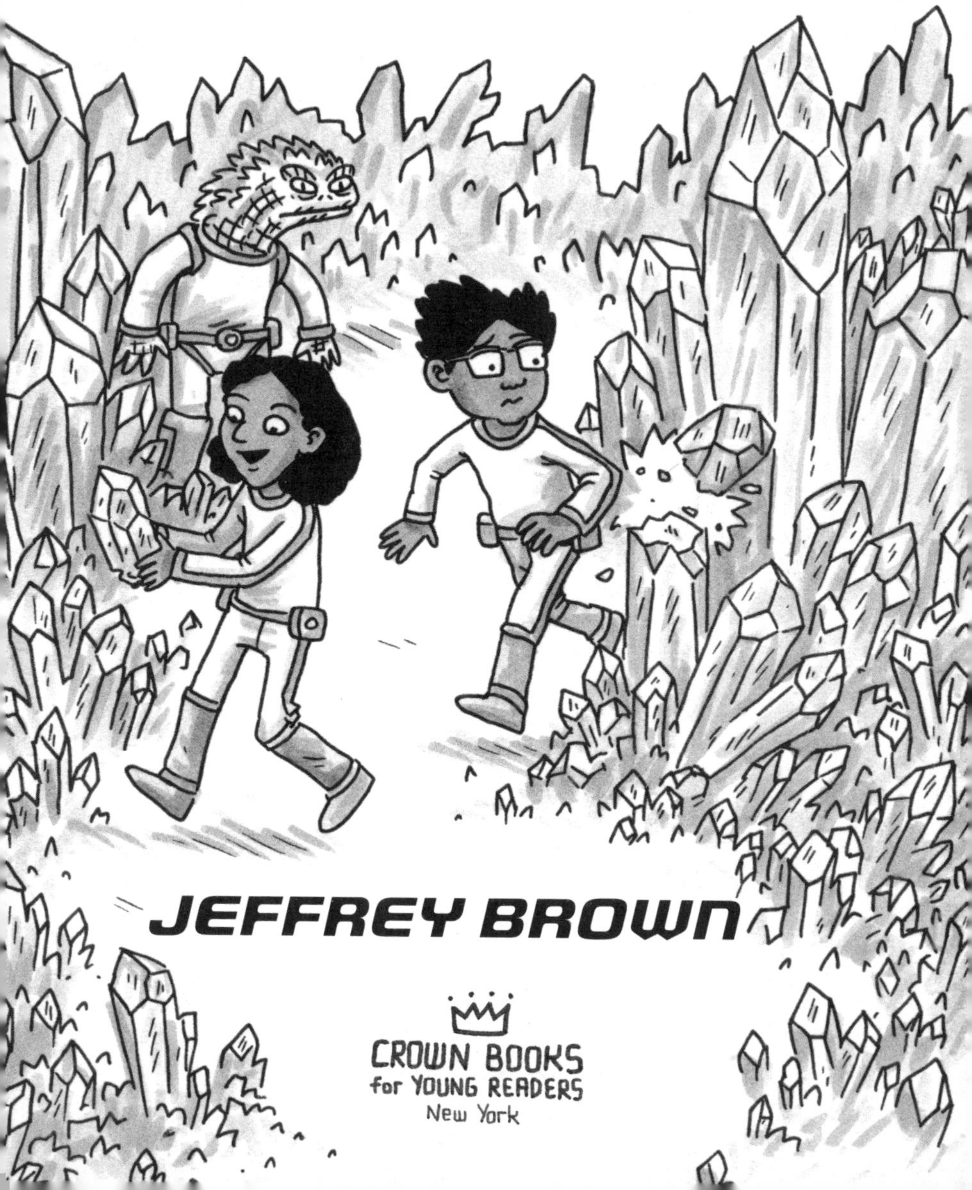

JEFFREY BROWN

CROWN BOOKS
for YOUNG READERS
New York

THE FOLLOWING TECHNICAL DATA CAN BE USED TO IDENTIFY THE SECOND ANALOG VOLUME OF SPACE-TIME! WITHIN HUMAN INFORMATION SYSTEMS.

Copyright © 2021 by Jeffrey Brown

All rights reserved. Published in the United States by Crown Books for Young Readers, an imprint of Random House Children's Books, a division of Penguin Random House LLC, New York.

Crown and the colophon are registered trademarks of Penguin Random House LLC.

RH Graphic with the book design is a trademark of Penguin Random House LLC.

Visit us on the Web! rhcbooks.com

Educators and librarians, for a variety of teaching tools, visit us at RHTeachersLibrarians.com

Library of Congress Cataloging-in-Publication Data is available upon request.

ISBN 978-0-553-53439-9 (hardcover) — ISBN 978-0-553-53440-5 (lib. bdg.) — ISBN 978-0-553-53441-2 (ebook)

Printed in the United States of America

10 9 8 7 6 5 4 3 2 1

First Edition

PHENOMENAL
PHENOMENON

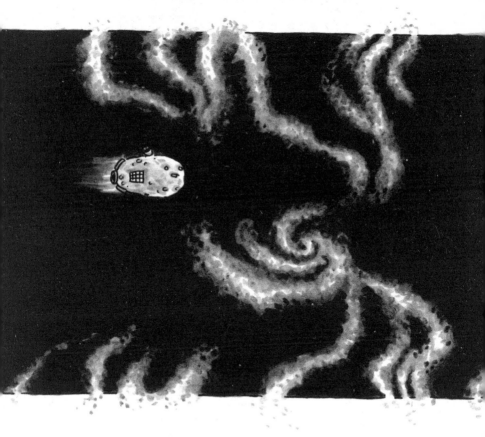

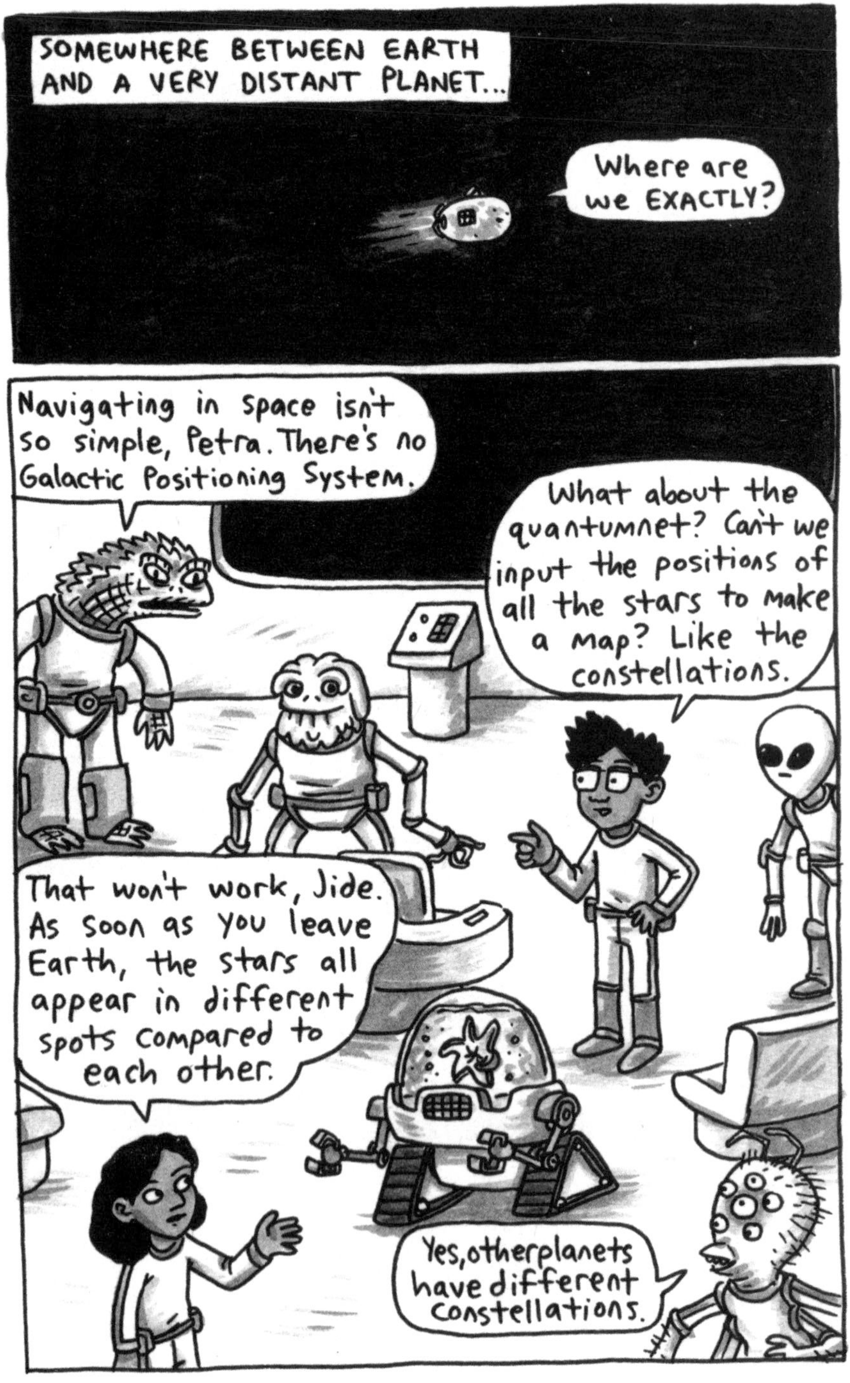
SOMEWHERE BETWEEN EARTH AND A VERY DISTANT PLANET...
Where are we EXACTLY?
Navigating in space isn't so simple, Petra. There's no Galactic Positioning System.
What about the quantumnet? Can't we input the positions of all the stars to make a map? Like the constellations.
That won't work, Jide. As soon as you leave Earth, the stars all appear in different spots compared to each other.
Yes, other planets have different constellations.

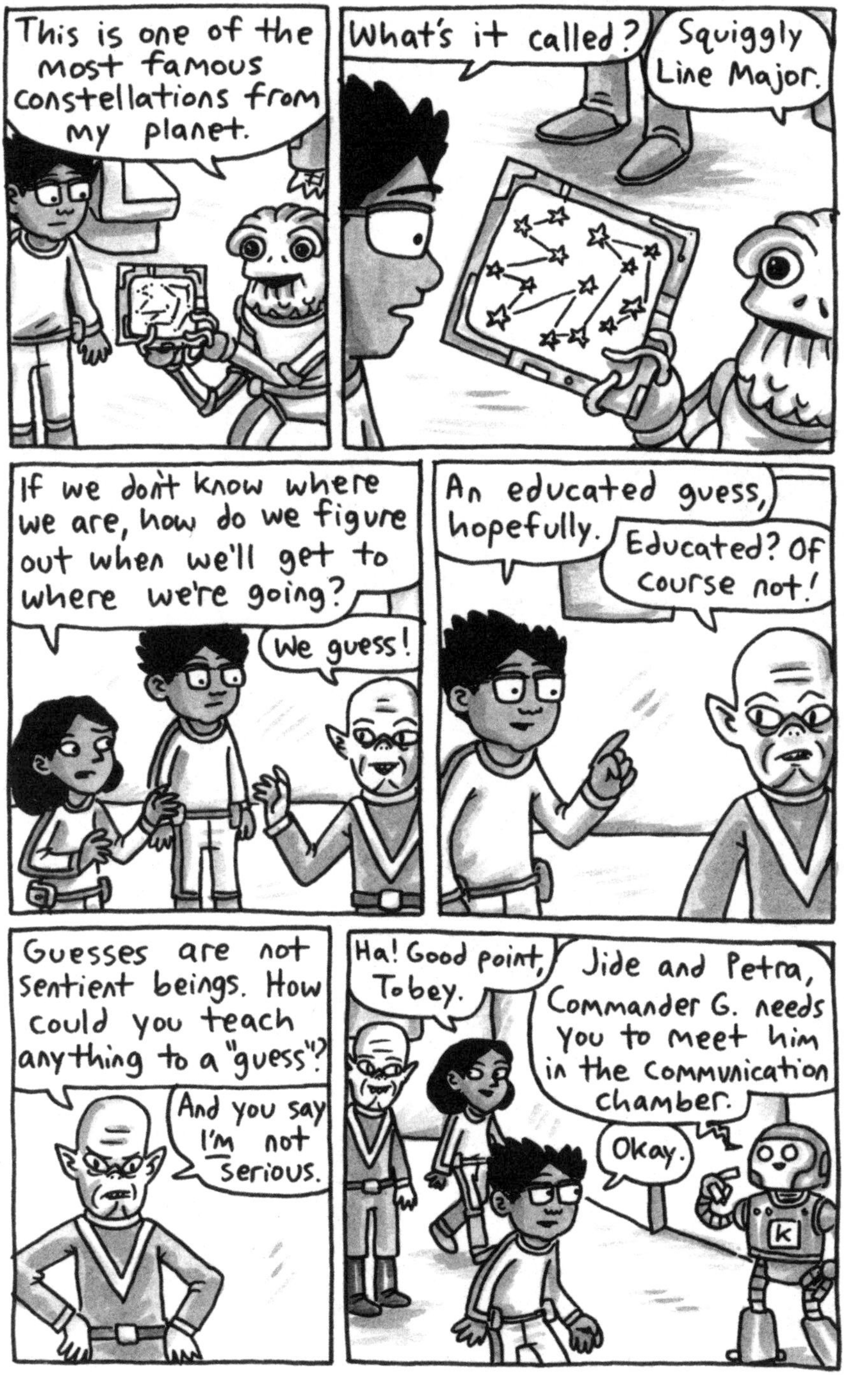
This is one of the most famous constellations from my planet.
What's it called?
Squiggly Line Major.
If we don't know where we are, how do we figure out when we'll get to where we're going?
We guess!
An educated guess, hopefully.
Educated? Of course not!
Guesses are not sentient beings. How could you teach anything to a "guess"?
And you say I'm not serious.
Ha! Good point, Tobey.
Jide and Petra, Commander G. needs you to meet him in the communication chamber.
Okay.
K

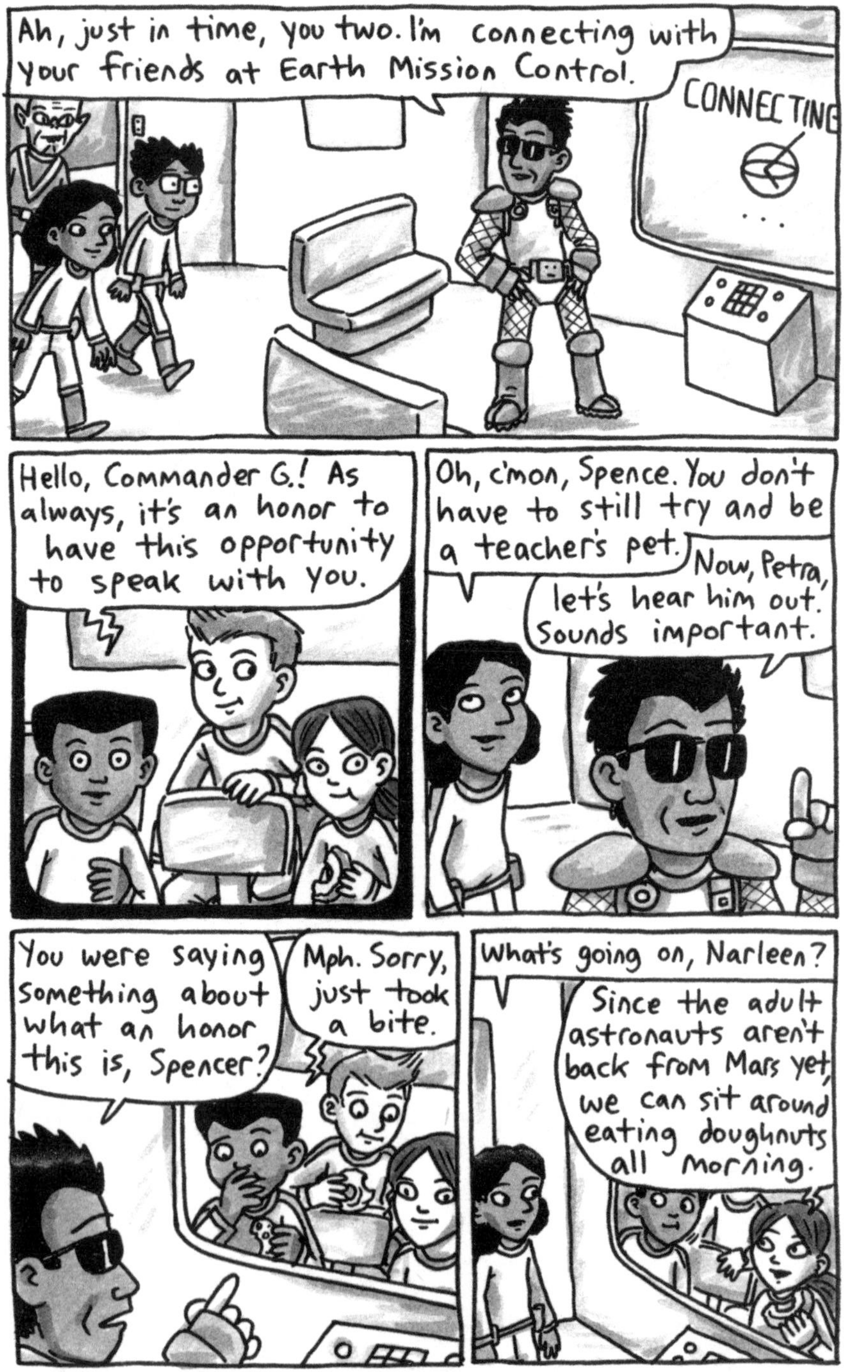
Ah, just in time, you two. I'm connecting with your friends at Earth Mission Control.
CONNECTING
...
Hello, Commander G.! As always, it's an honor to have this opportunity to speak with you.
Oh, c'mon, Spence. You don't have to still try and be a teacher's pet.
Now, Petra, let's hear him out. Sounds important.
You were saying something about what an honor this is, Spencer?
Mph. Sorry, just took a bite.
What's going on, Narleen?
Since the adult astronauts aren't back from Mars yet, we can sit around eating doughnuts all morning.

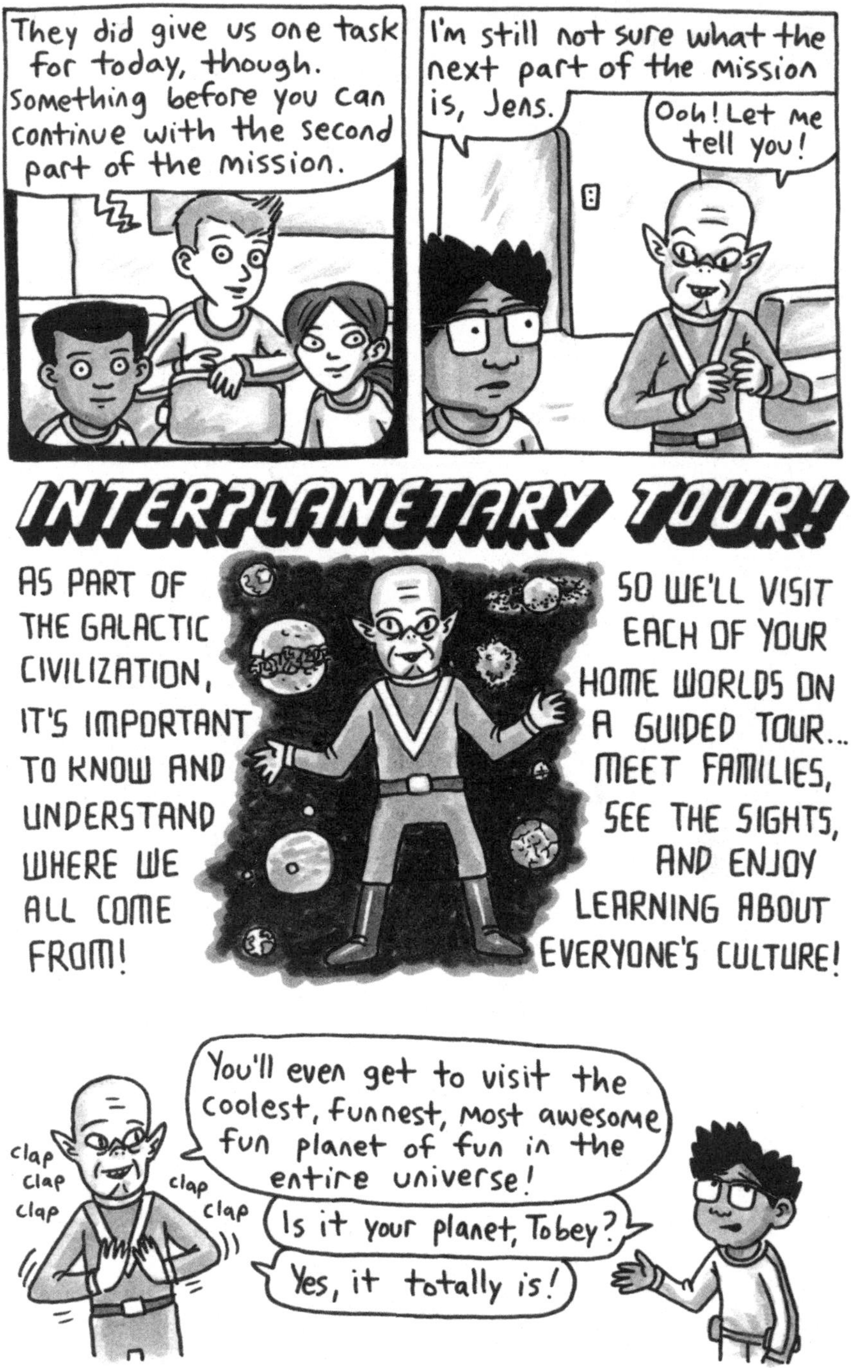

They did give us one task for today, though. Something before you can continue with the second part of the mission.
I'm still not sure what the next part of the mission is, Jens.
Ooh! Let me tell you!
INTERPLANETARY TOUR!
AS PART OF THE GALACTIC CIVILIZATION, IT'S IMPORTANT TO KNOW AND UNDERSTAND WHERE WE ALL COME FROM!
SO WE'LL VISIT EACH OF YOUR HOME WORLDS ON A GUIDED TOUR... MEET FAMILIES, SEE THE SIGHTS, AND ENJOY LEARNING ABOUT EVERYONE'S CULTURE!
You'll even get to visit the coolest, funnest, most awesome fun planet of fun in the entire universe!
clap clap clap
clap clap
Is it your planet, Tobey?
Yes, it totally is!

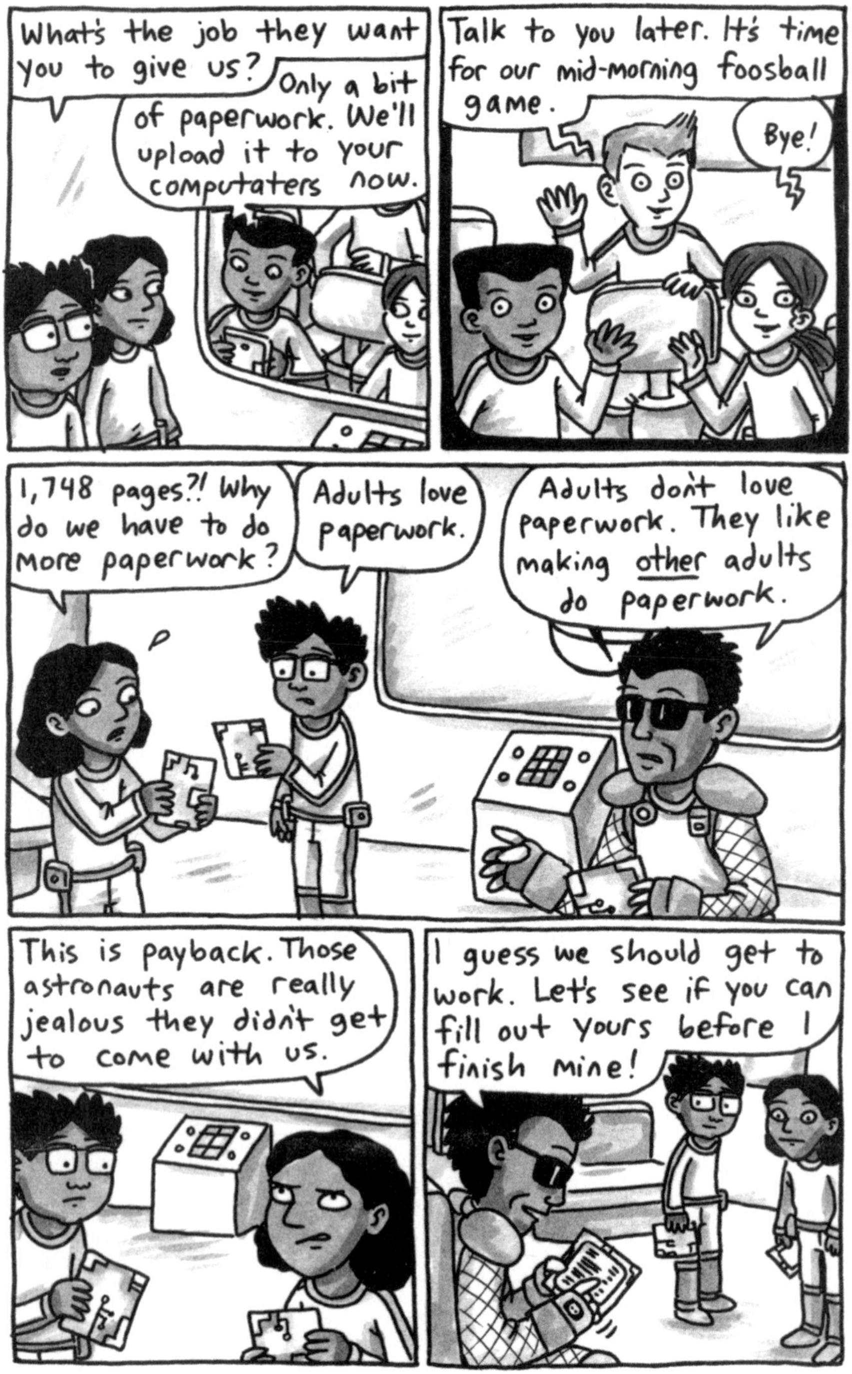
What's the job they want you to give us?
Only a bit of paperwork. We'll upload it to your computaters now.
Talk to you later. It's time for our mid-morning foosball game.
Bye!
1,748 pages?! Why do we have to do more paperwork?
Adults love paperwork.
Adults don't love paperwork. They like making other adults do paperwork.
This is payback. Those astronauts are really jealous they didn't get to come with us.
I guess we should get to work. Let's see if you can fill out yours before I finish mine!

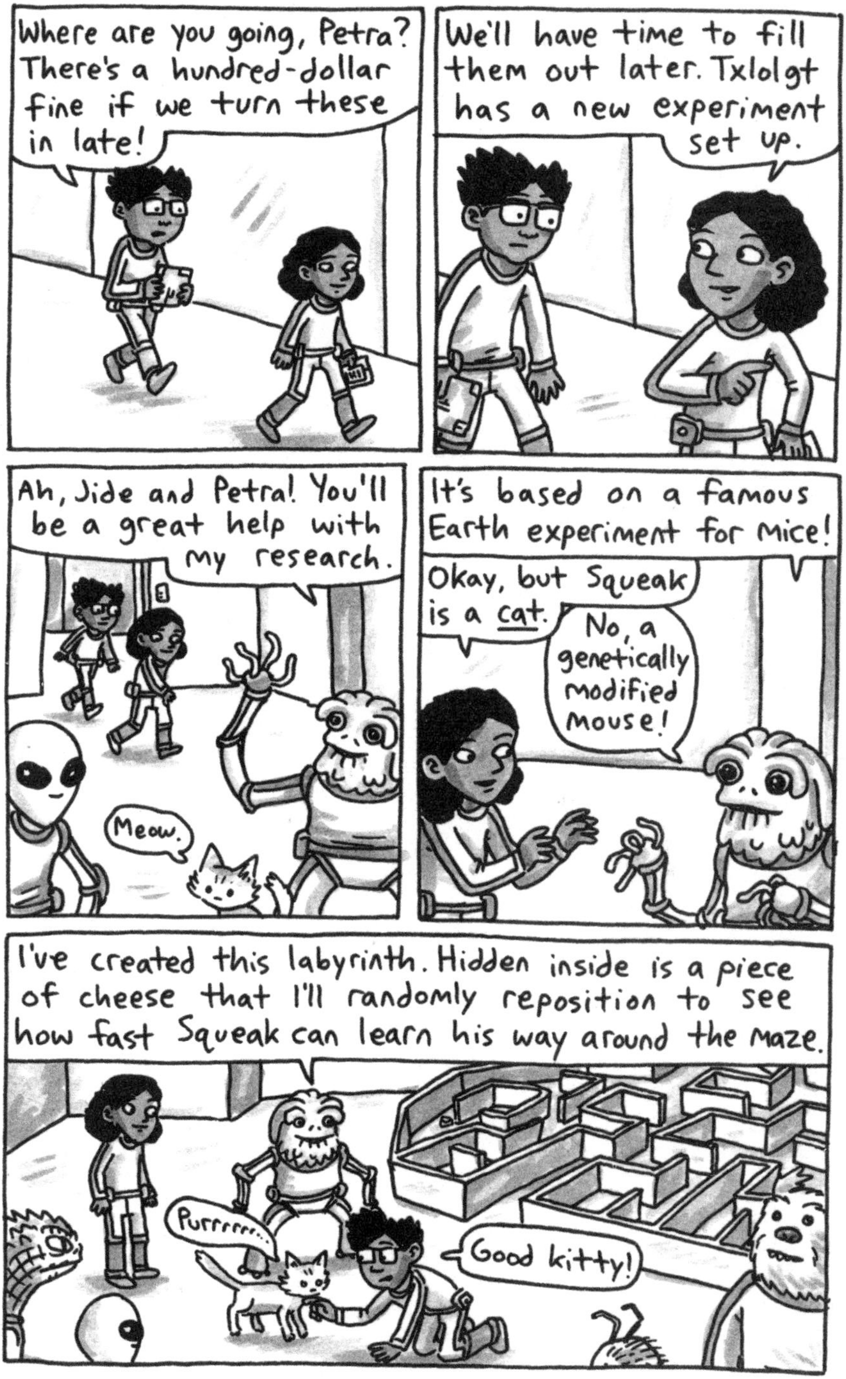

Where are you going, Petra? There's a hundred-dollar fine if we turn these in late!
We'll have time to fill them out later. Txlolgt has a new experiment set up.
Ah, Jide and Petra! You'll be a great help with my research.
Meow.
It's based on a famous Earth experiment for mice!
Okay, but Squeak is a cat.
No, a genetically modified mouse!
I've created this labyrinth. Hidden inside is a piece of cheese that I'll randomly reposition to see how fast Squeak can learn his way around the maze.
Purrrrrr...
Good kitty!

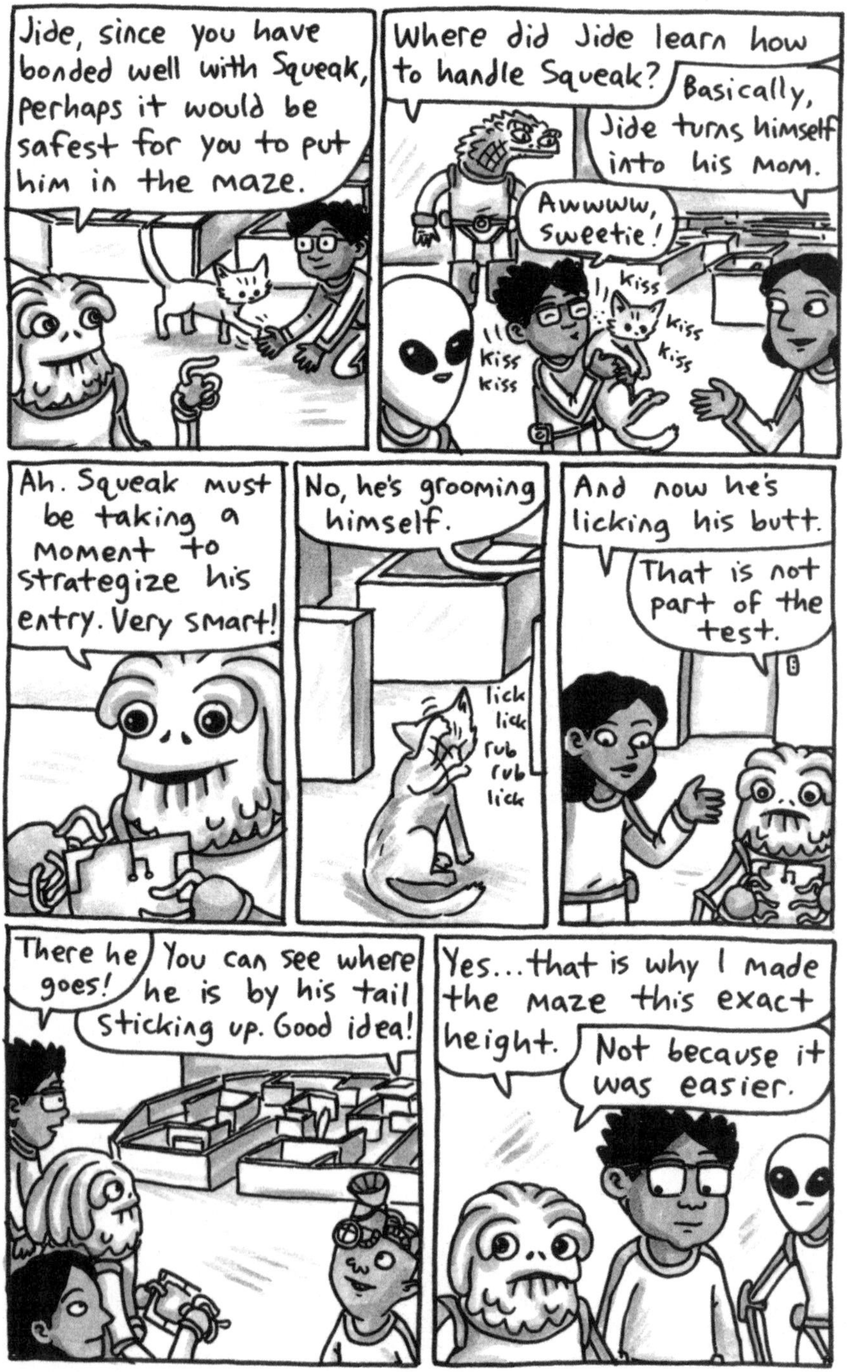
Jide, since you have bonded well with Squeak, perhaps it would be safest for you to put him in the maze.
Where did Jide learn how to handle Squeak?
Basically, Jide turns himself into his mom.
Awwww, Sweetie!
kiss
kiss
kiss
kiss
kiss
Ah. Squeak must be taking a moment to strategize his entry. Very smart!
No, he's grooming himself.
lick
lick
rub
rub
lick
And now he's licking his butt.
That is not part of the test.
There he goes!
You can see where he is by his tail sticking up. Good idea!
Yes... that is why I made the maze this exact height.
Not because it was easier.

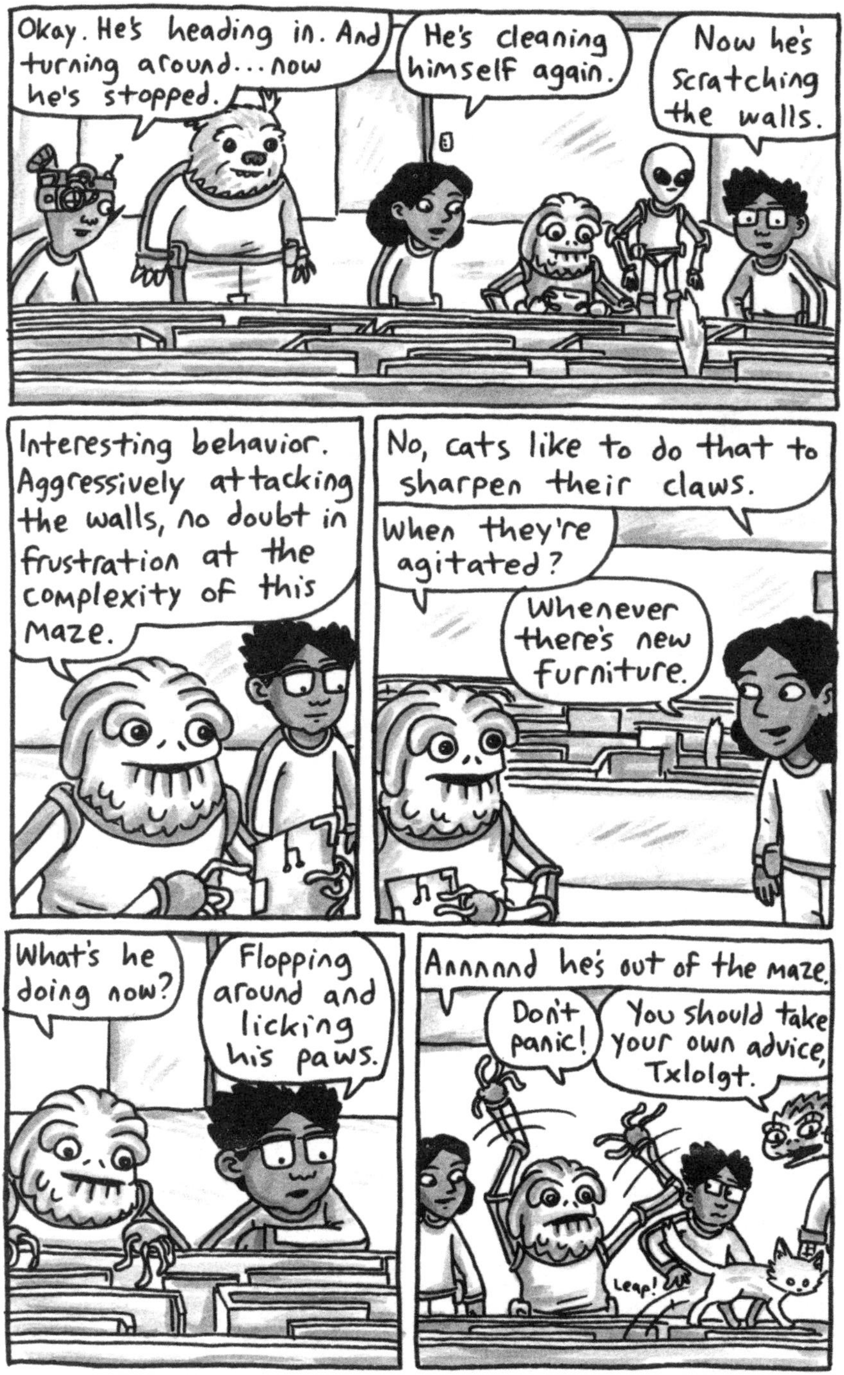
Okay. He's heading in. And turning around... now he's stopped.
He's cleaning himself again.
Now he's scratching the walls.
Interesting behavior. Aggressively attacking the walls, no doubt in frustration at the complexity of this maze.
No, cats like to do that to sharpen their claws.
When they're agitated?
Whenever there's new furniture.
What's he doing now?
Flopping around and licking his paws.
Annnnnd he's out of the maze.
Don't panic!
You should take your own advice, Txlolgt.
Leap!

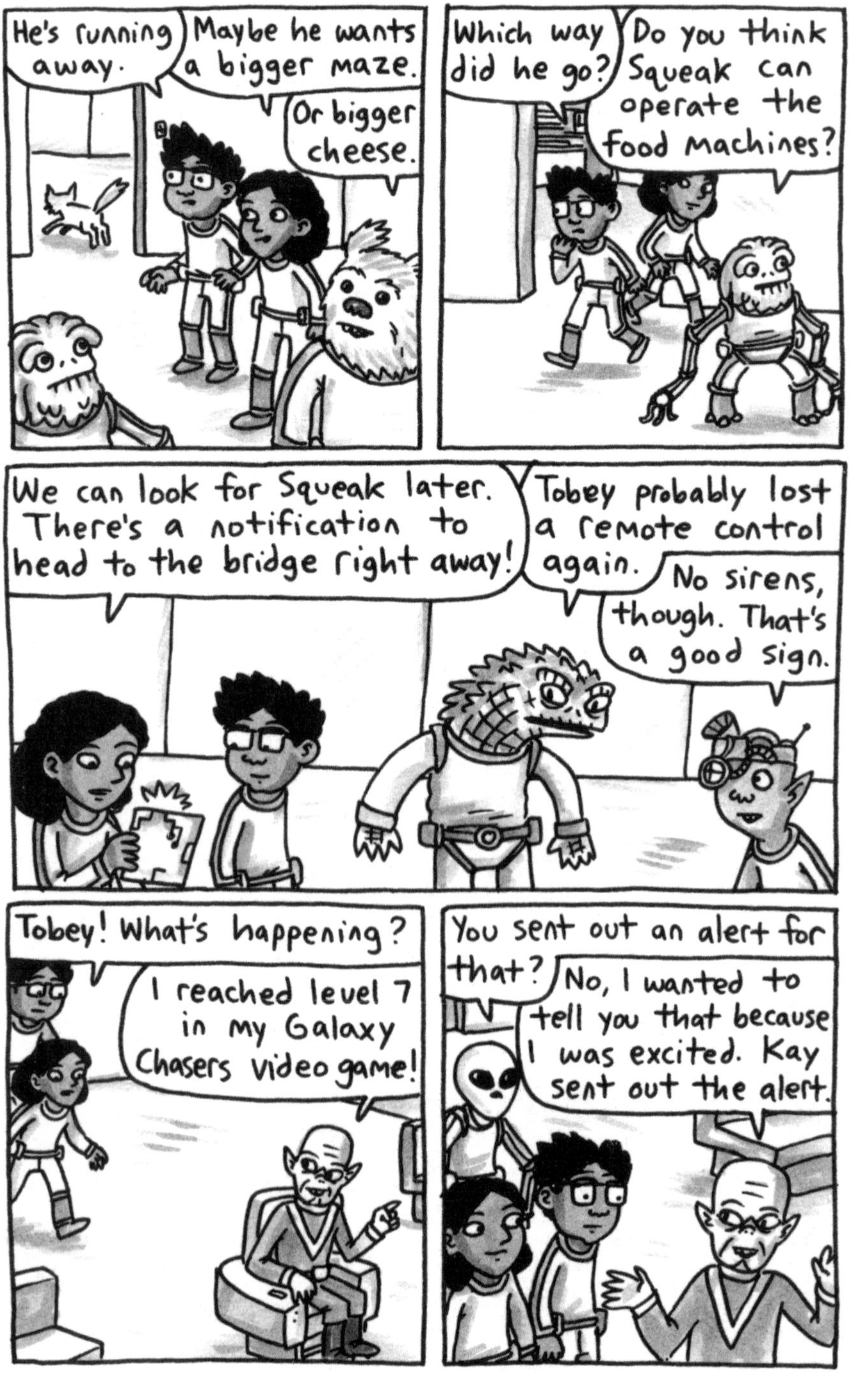

He's running away.
Maybe he wants a bigger maze.
Or bigger cheese.
Which way did he go?
Do you think Squeak can operate the food machines?
We can look for Squeak later. There's a notification to head to the bridge right away!
Tobey probably lost a remote control again.
No sirens, though. That's a good sign.
Tobey! What's happening?
I reached level 7 in my Galaxy Chasers video game!
You sent out an alert for that?
No, I wanted to tell you that because I was excited. Kay sent out the alert.

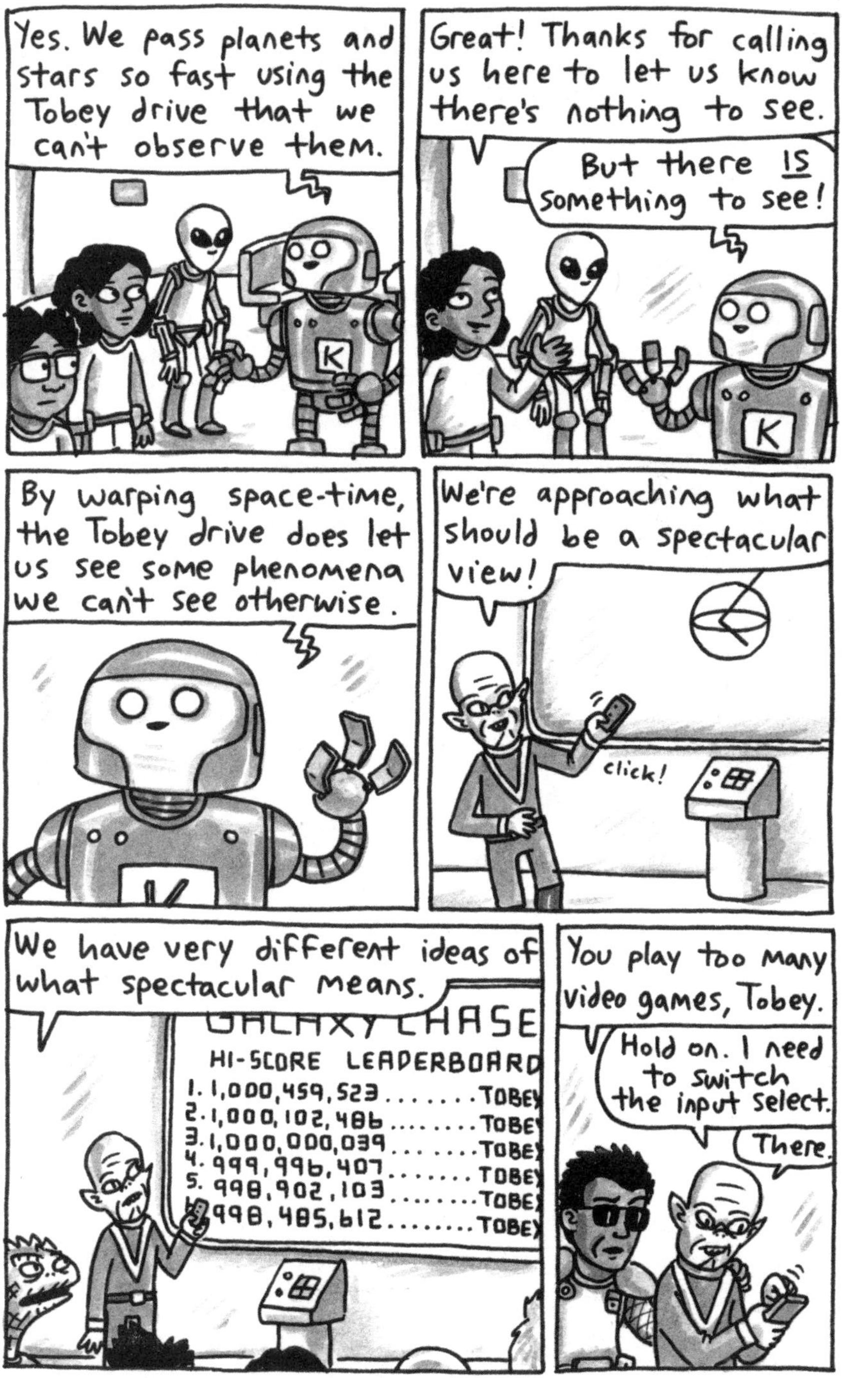
Yes. We pass planets and stars so fast using the Tobey drive that we can't observe them.
Great! Thanks for calling us here to let us know there's nothing to see.
But there IS something to see!
K
K
By warping space-time, the Tobey drive does let us see some phenomena we can't see otherwise.
We're approaching what should be a spectacular view!
click!
We have very different ideas of what spectacular means.
GALAXY CHASE
HI-SCORE LEADERBOARD
1. 1,000,459,523 ....TOBEY
2. 1,000,102,486 ....TOBEY
3. 1,000,000,039 ....TOBEY
4. 999,996,407 ....TOBEY
5. 998,902,103 ....TOBEY
998,485,612 ....TOBEY
You play too many video games, Tobey.
Hold on. I need to switch the input select.
There.

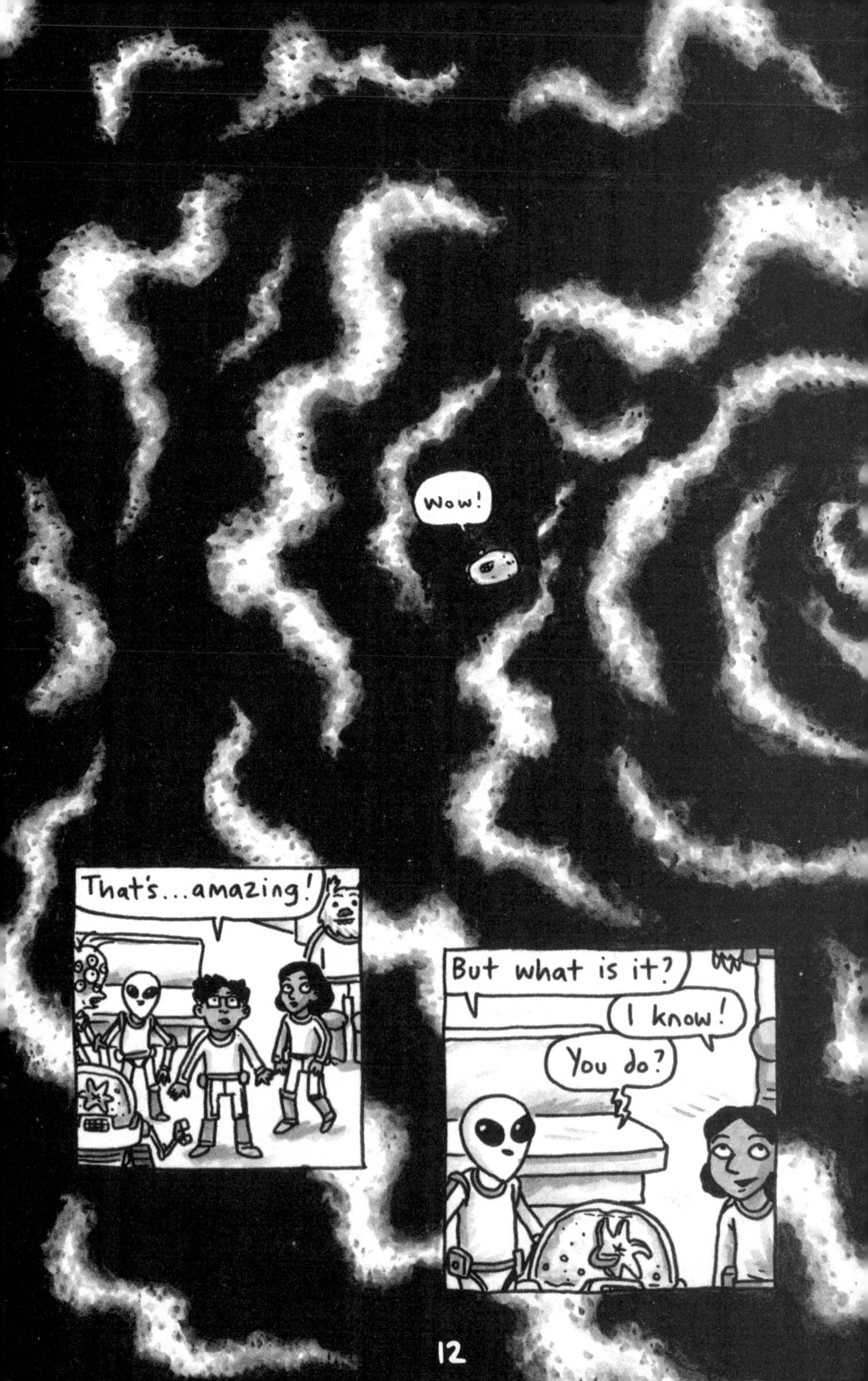
Wow!
That's...amazing!
But what is it?
I know!
You do?

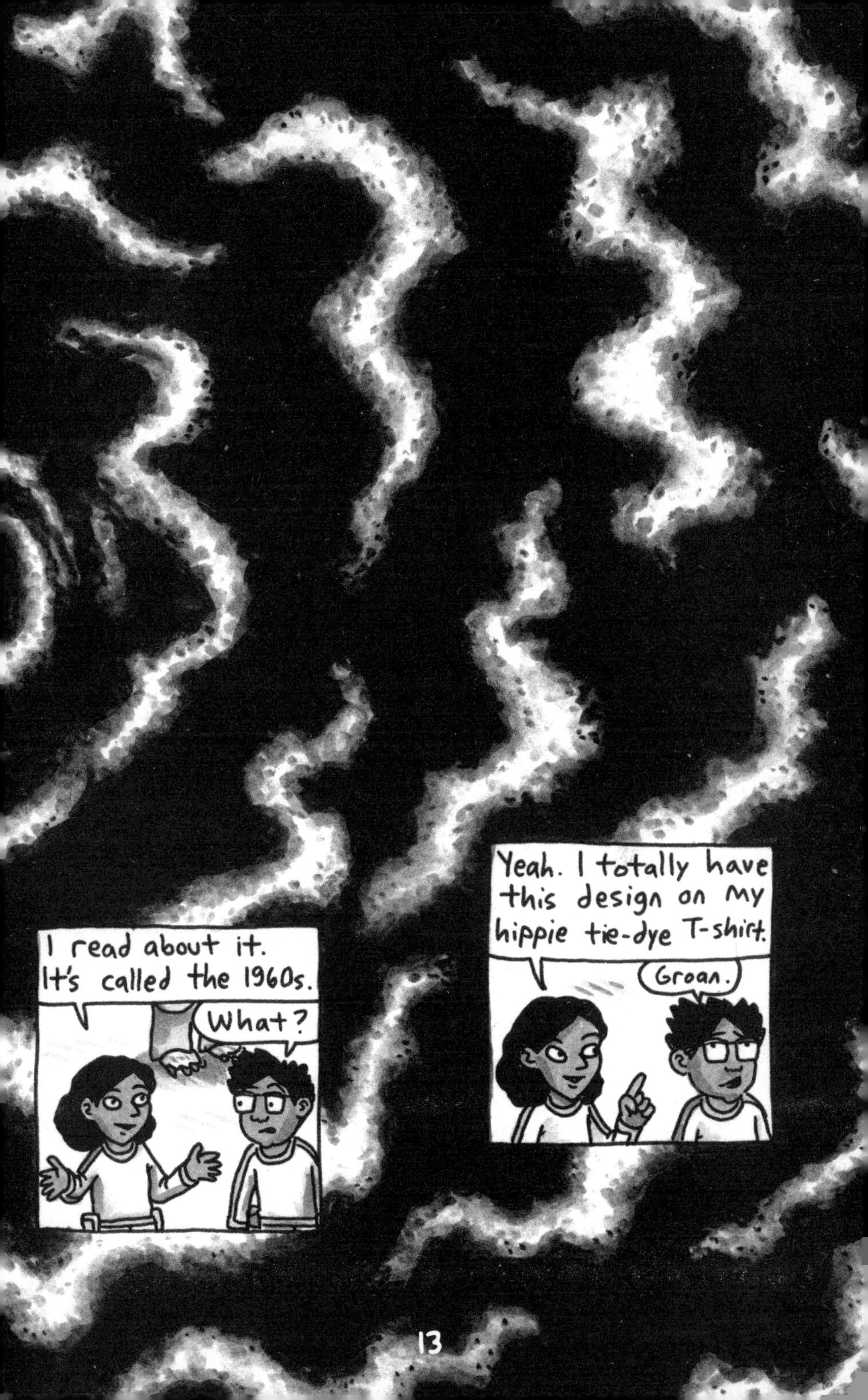
I read about it. It's called the 1960s.
What?
Yeah. I totally have this design on my hippie tie-dye T-shirt.
Groan.

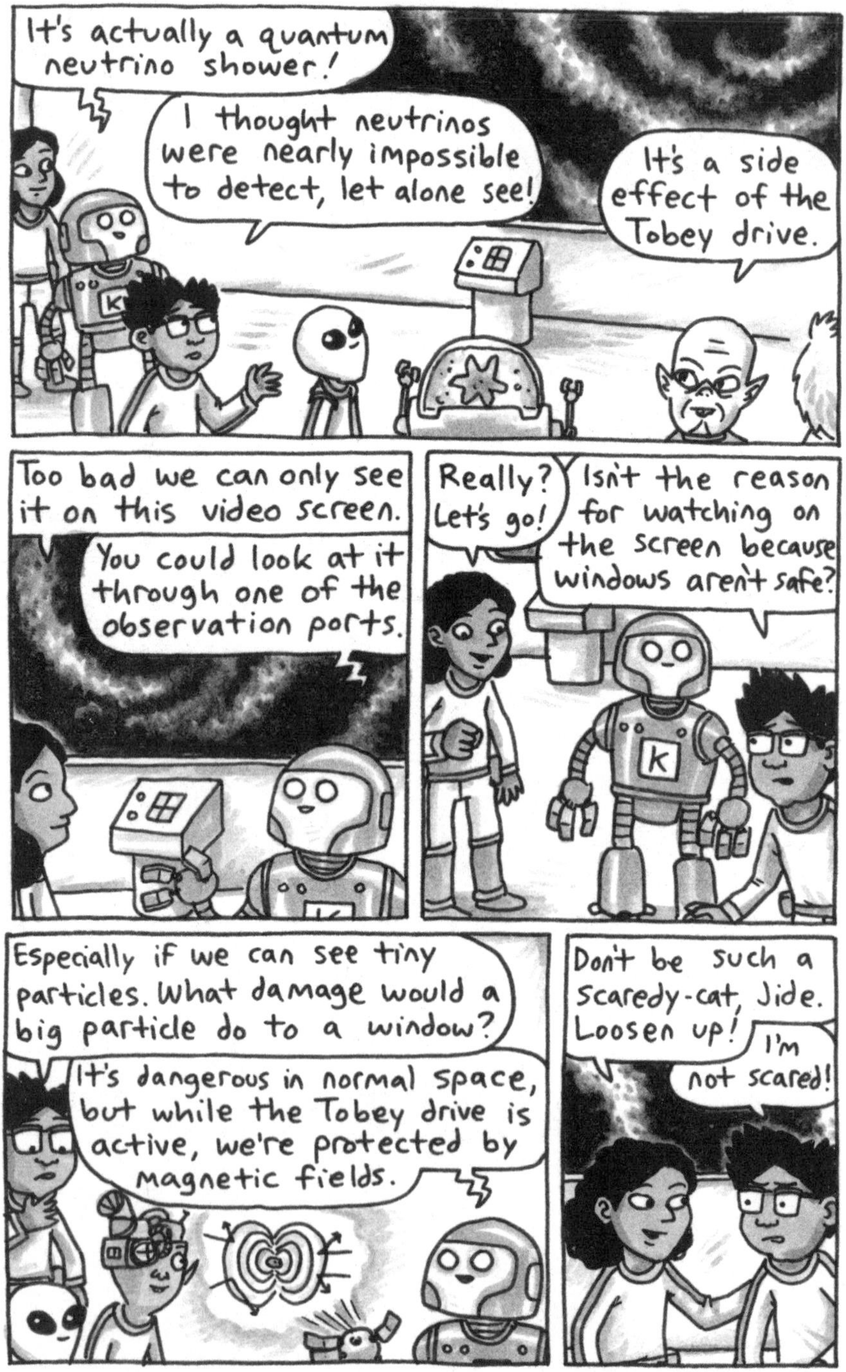
It's actually a quantum neutrino shower!
I thought neutrinos were nearly impossible to detect, let alone see!
It's a side effect of the Tobey drive.
Too bad we can only see it on this video screen.
You could look at it through one of the observation ports.
Really? Let's go!
Isn't the reason for watching on the screen because windows aren't safe?
Especially if we can see tiny particles. What damage would a big particle do to a window?
It's dangerous in normal space, but while the Tobey drive is active, we're protected by magnetic fields.
Don't be such a scaredy-cat, Jide. Loosen up!
I'm not scared!

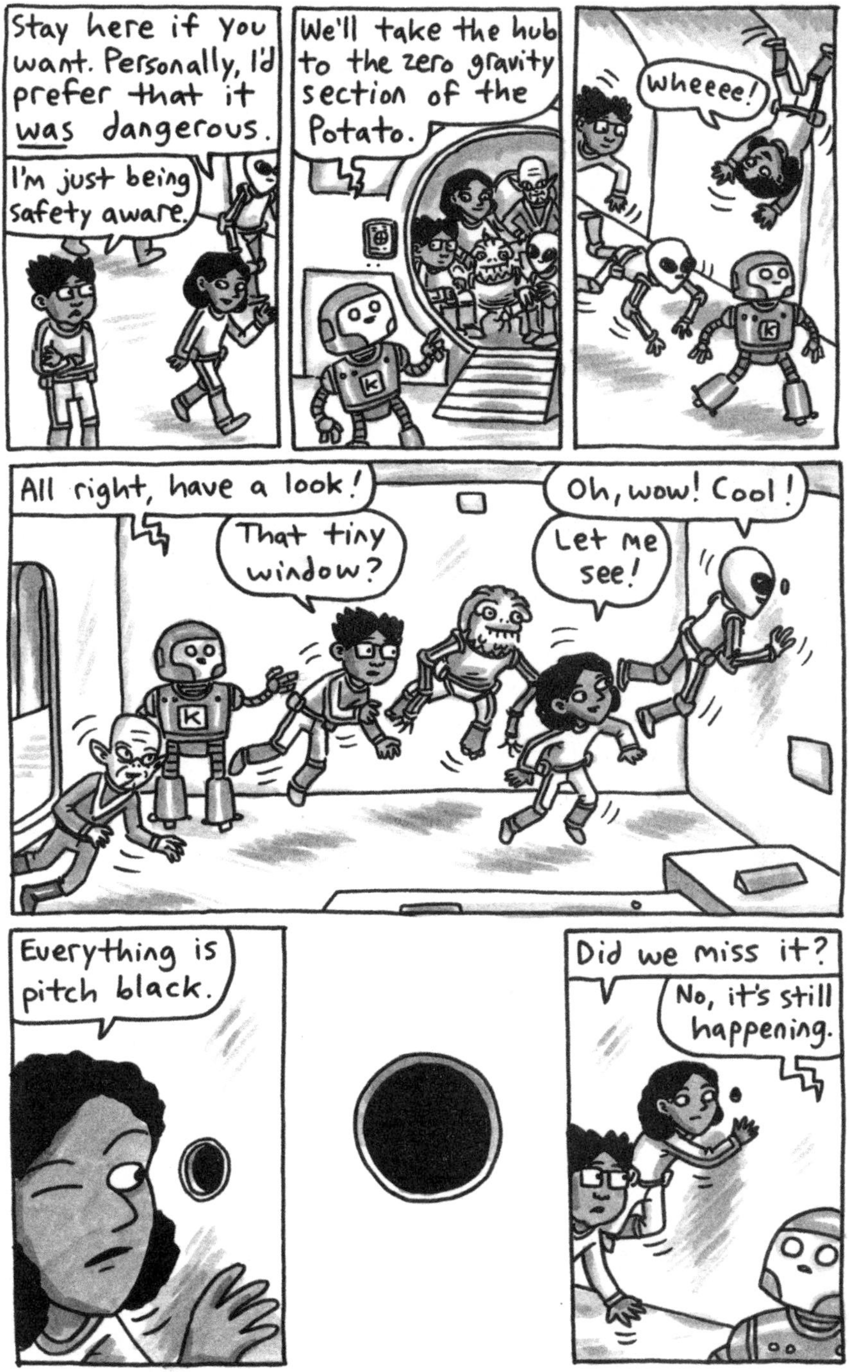
Stay here if you want. Personally, I'd prefer that it was dangerous.
I'm just being safety aware.
We'll take the hub to the zero gravity section of the Potato.
Wheeeee!
All right, have a look!
That tiny window?
Let me see!
Oh, wow! Cool!
Everything is pitch black.
Did we miss it?
No, it's still happening.

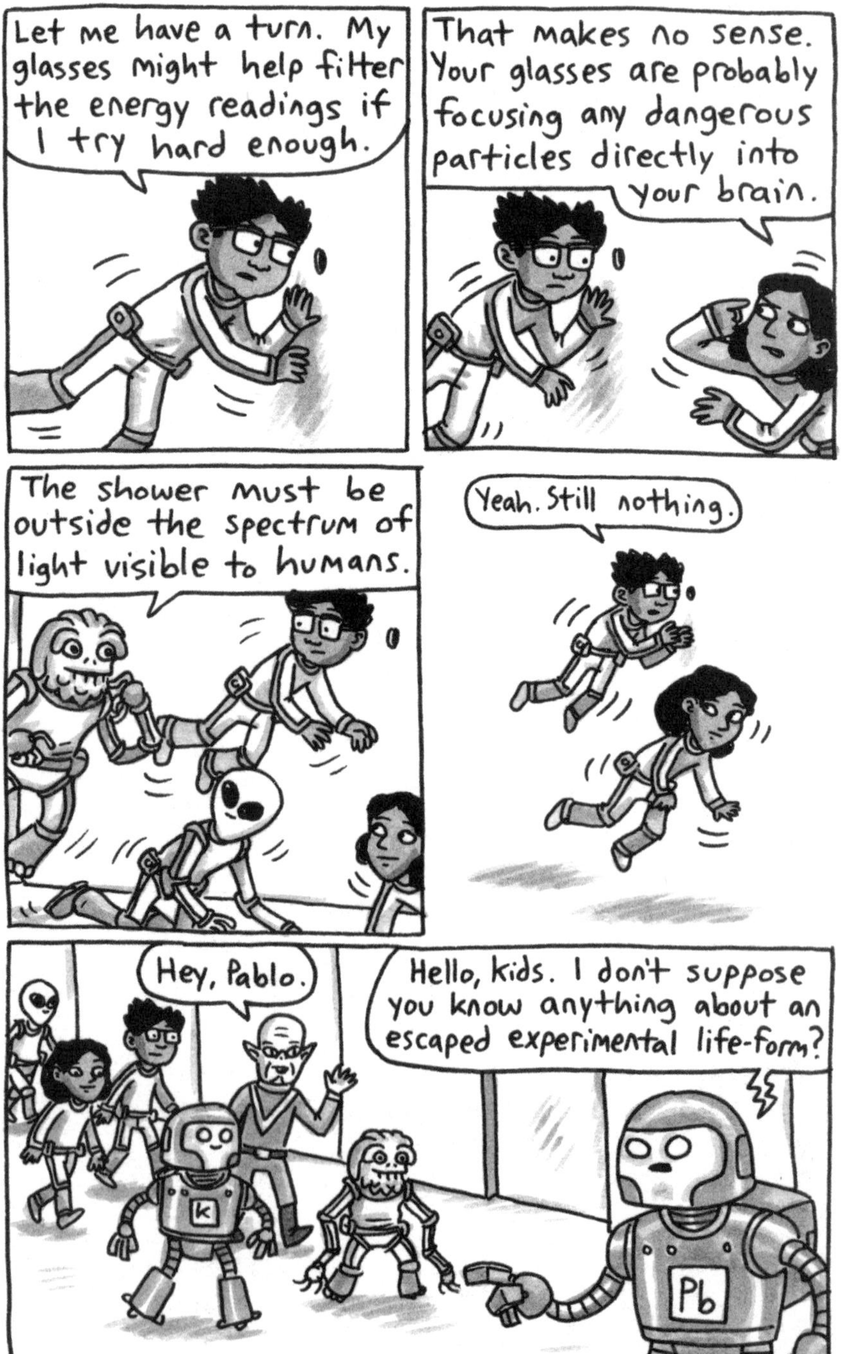
Let me have a turn. My glasses might help filter the energy readings if I try hard enough.
That makes no sense. Your glasses are probably focusing any dangerous particles directly into your brain.
The shower must be outside the spectrum of light visible to humans.
Yeah. Still nothing.
Hey, Pablo.
Hello, kids. I don't suppose you know anything about an escaped experimental life-form?
K
Pb

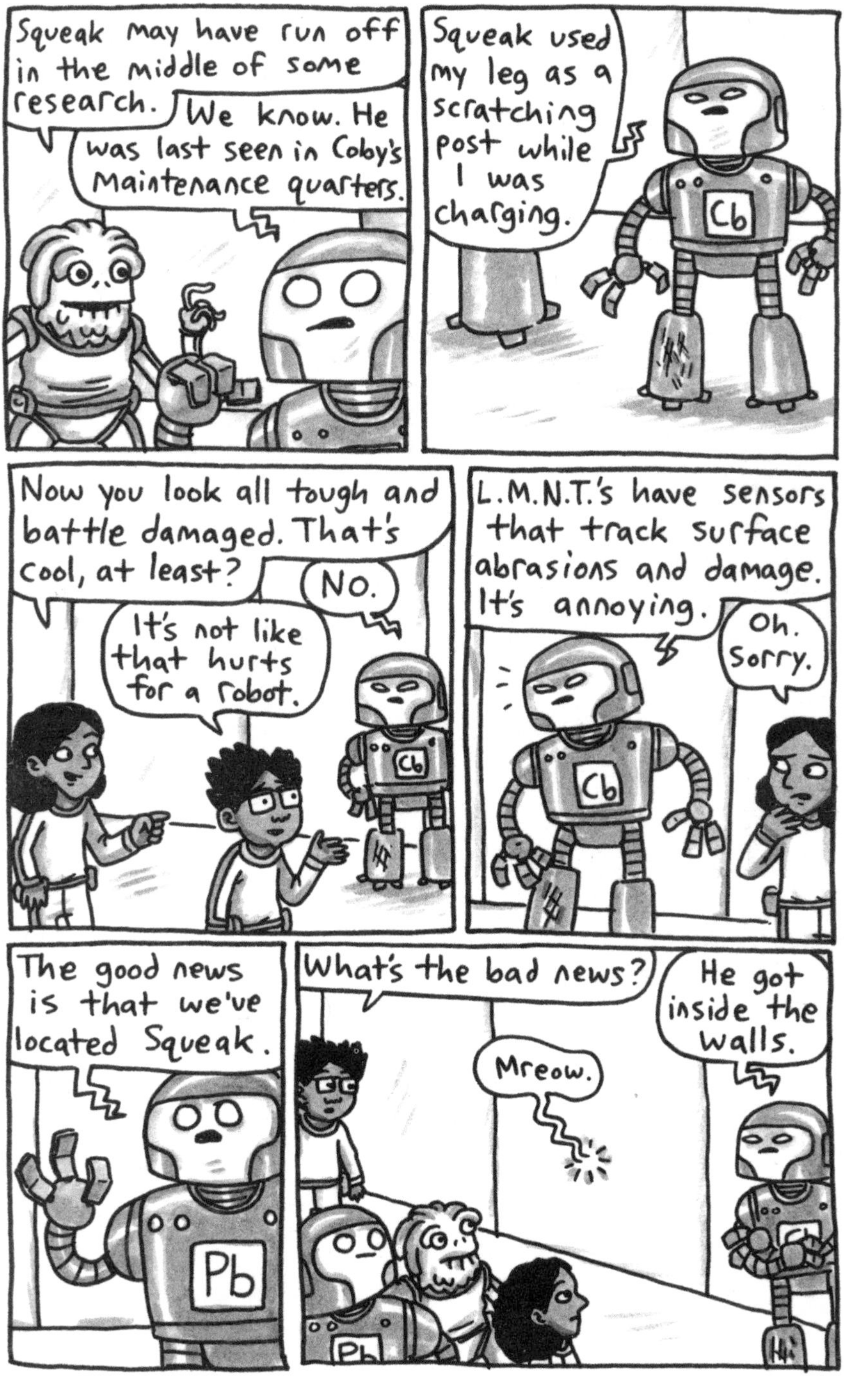

Squeak may have run off in the middle of some research.
We know. He was last seen in Coby's Maintenance quarters.
Squeak used my leg as a scratching post while I was charging.
Now you look all tough and battle damaged. That's cool, at least?
No.
It's not like that hurts for a robot.
L.M.N.T.'s have sensors that track surface abrasions and damage. It's annoying.
Oh. Sorry.
The good news is that we've located Squeak.
What's the bad news?
He got inside the walls.
Mreow.

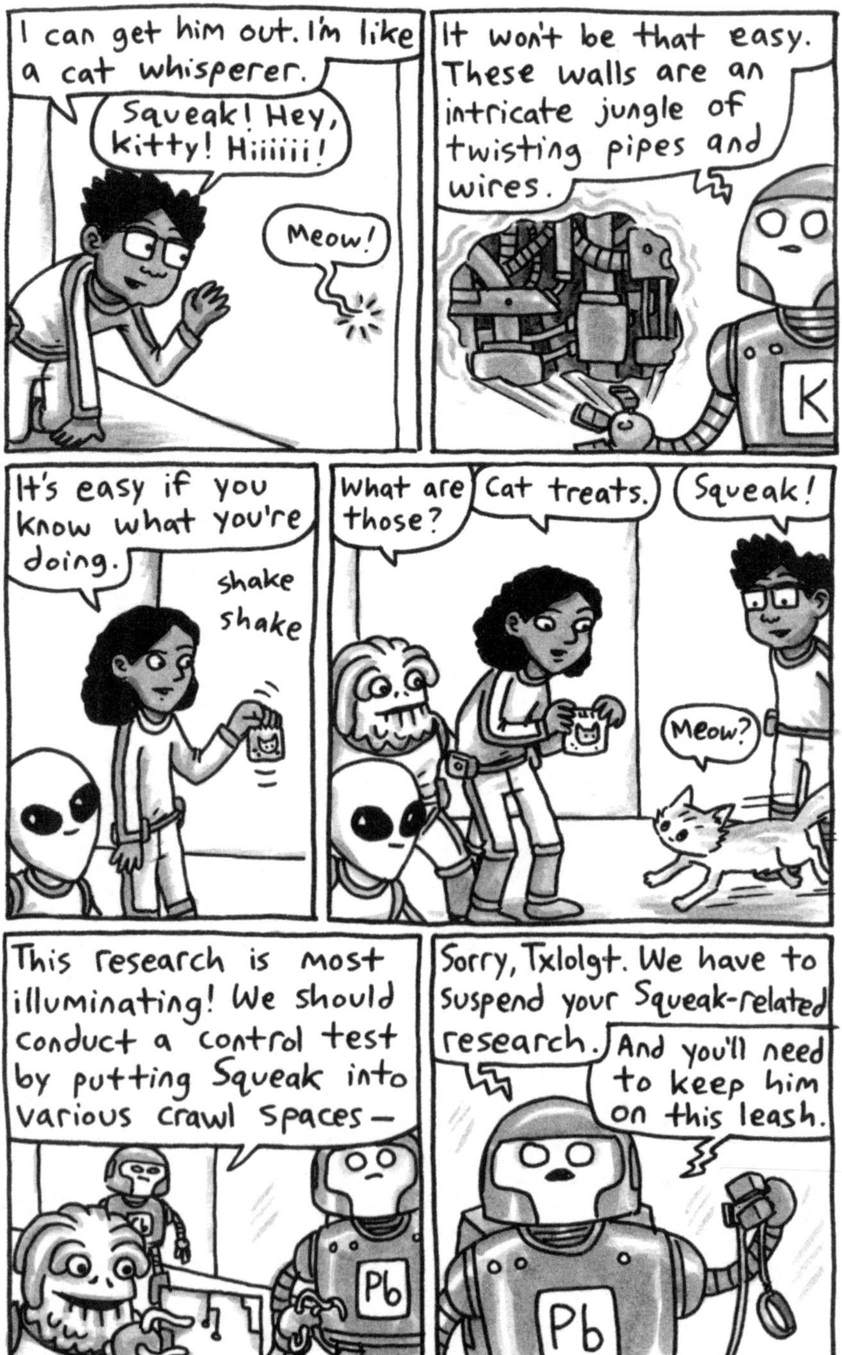

I can get him out. I'm like a cat whisperer.
Squeak! Hey, kitty! Hiiiiii!
Meow!
It won't be that easy. These walls are an intricate jungle of twisting pipes and wires.
It's easy if you know what you're doing.
shake shake
What are those?
Cat treats.
Squeak!
Meow?
This research is most illuminating! We should conduct a control test by putting Squeak into various crawl spaces—
Pb
Sorry, Txlolgt. We have to suspend your Squeak-related research.
And you'll need to keep him on this leash.
Pb

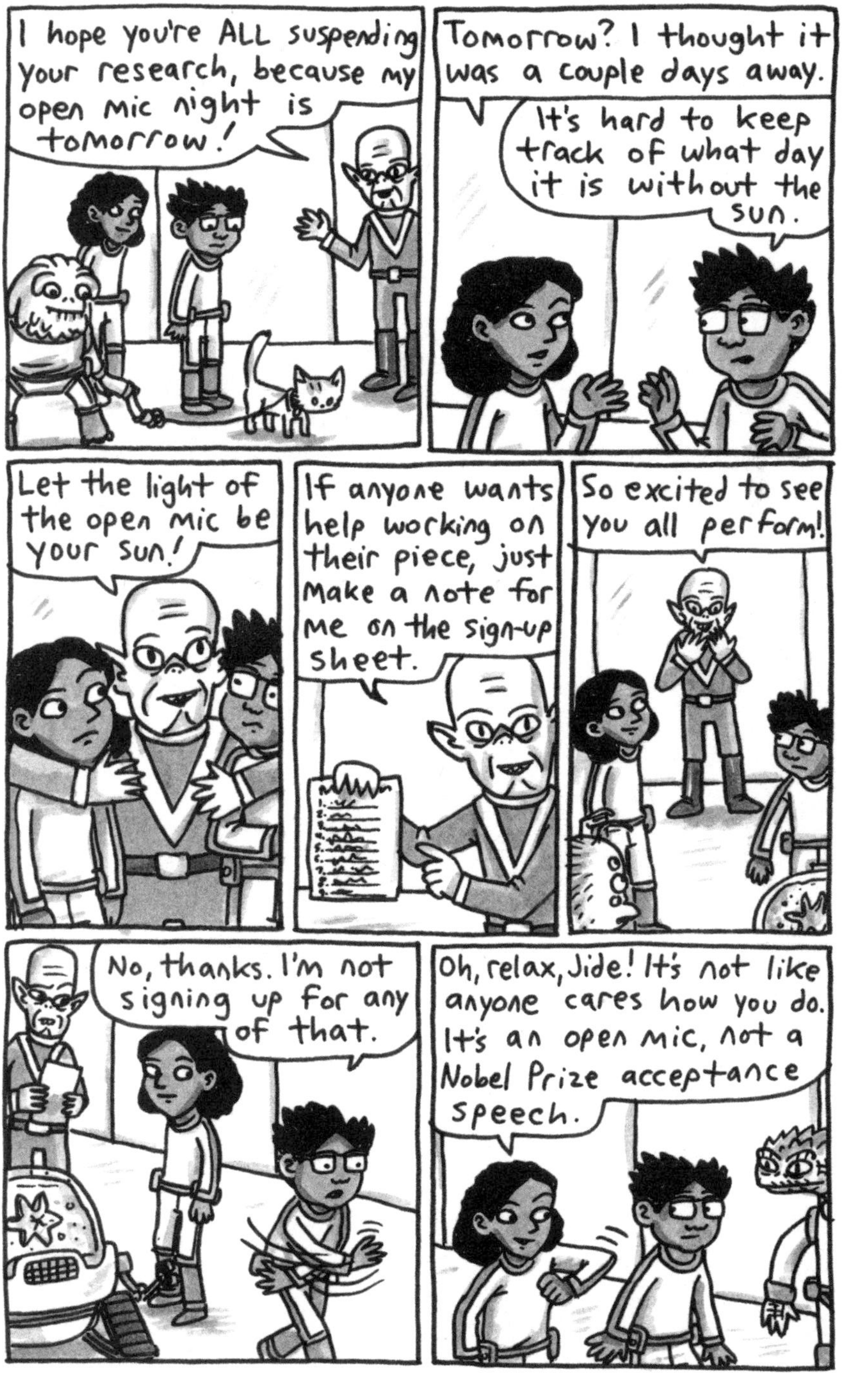
I hope you're ALL suspending your research, because my open mic night is tomorrow!
Tomorrow? I thought it was a couple days away.
It's hard to keep track of what day it is without the sun.
Let the light of the open mic be your sun!
If anyone wants help working on their piece, just make a note for me on the sign-up sheet.
So excited to see you all perform!
No, thanks. I'm not signing up for any of that.
Oh, relax, Jide! It's not like anyone cares how you do. It's an open mic, not a Nobel Prize acceptance speech.

Ha, ha. Very funny, Petra.

Yes, good one. I don't get it.

In elementary school, Jide won first place in the science fair. He thought he had to give a speech. He went on and on and at the end said...

...I'm honored to accept this Nobel Prize!

HA HA HA HA HA HA HA HA HA HA HA HA HA HA HA

HA HA HA HA HA HA HA HA HA HA HA HA HA HA HA HA HA HA HA HA HA HA HA HA HA HA HA HA HA HA

You won the Nobel Prize? Amazing!

I don't know what that award is, but good job!

I DIDN'T win the Nobel Prize. That's why everyone laughed at me.

And ever since, Jide has been scared of talking to crowds.

20

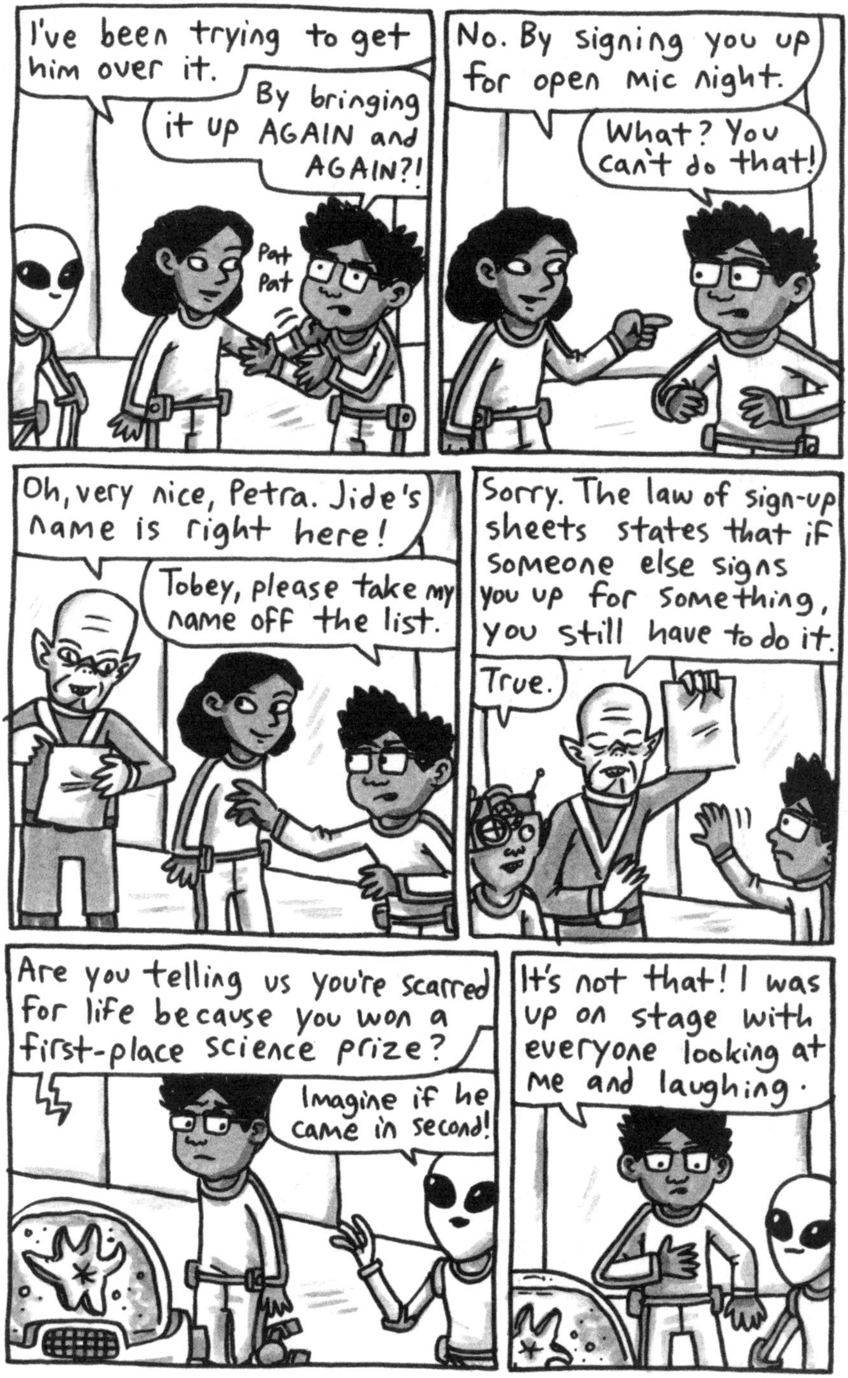
I've been trying to get him over it.
By bringing it up AGAIN and AGAIN?!
Pat Pat
No. By signing you up for open mic night.
What? You can't do that!
Oh, very nice, Petra. Jide's name is right here!
Tobey, please take my name off the list.
Sorry. The law of sign-up sheets states that if someone else signs you up for something, you still have to do it.
True.
Are you telling us you're scarred for life because you won a first-place science prize?
Imagine if he came in second!
It's not that! I was up on stage with everyone looking at me and laughing.

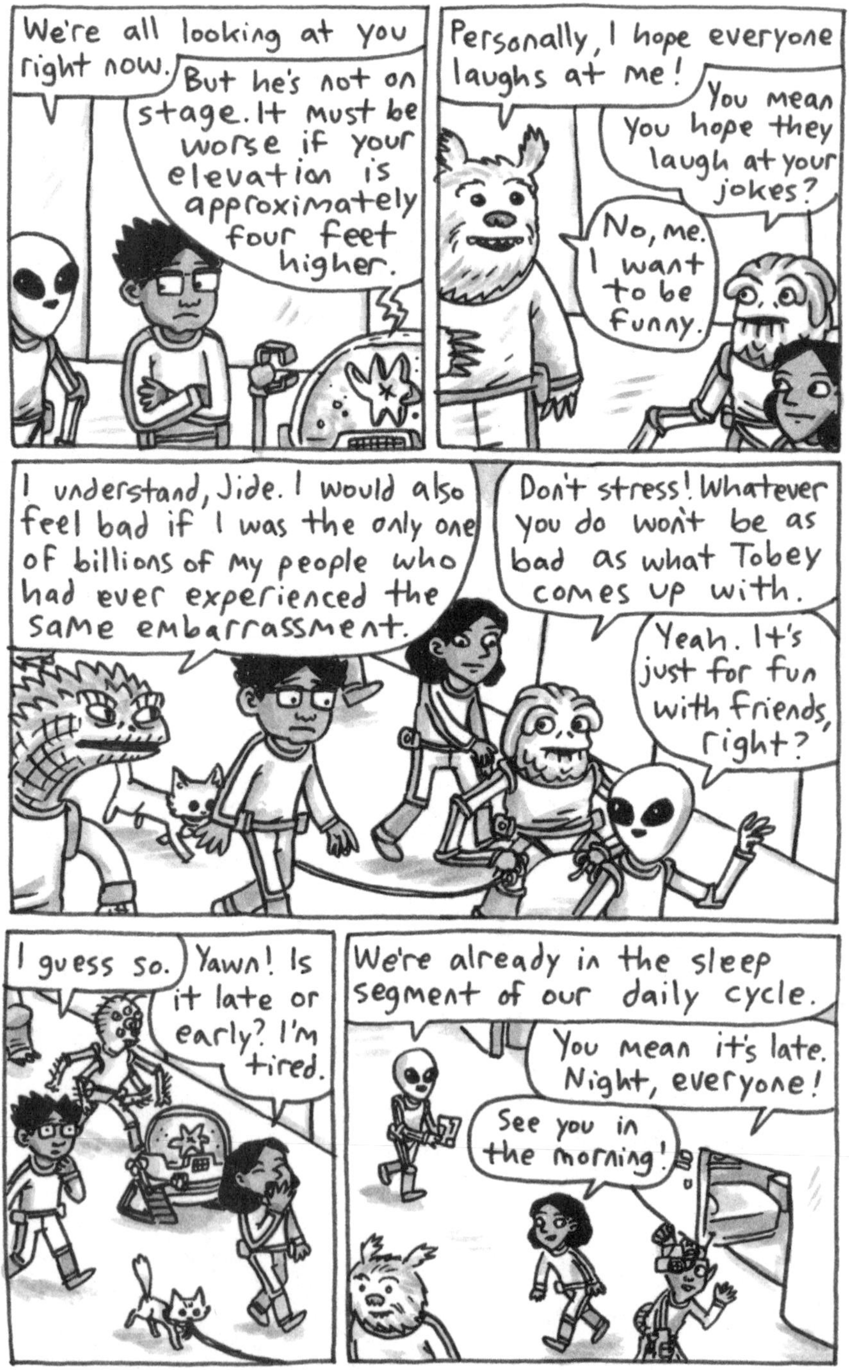
We're all looking at you right now.
But he's not on stage. It must be worse if your elevation is approximately four feet higher.
Personally, I hope everyone laughs at me!
You mean you hope they laugh at your jokes?
No, me. I want to be funny.
I understand, Jide. I would also feel bad if I was the only one of billions of my people who had ever experienced the same embarrassment.
Don't stress! Whatever you do won't be as bad as what Tobey comes up with.
Yeah. It's just for fun with friends, right?
I guess so.
Yawn! Is it late or early? I'm tired.
We're already in the sleep segment of our daily cycle.
You mean it's late. Night, everyone!
See you in the morning!

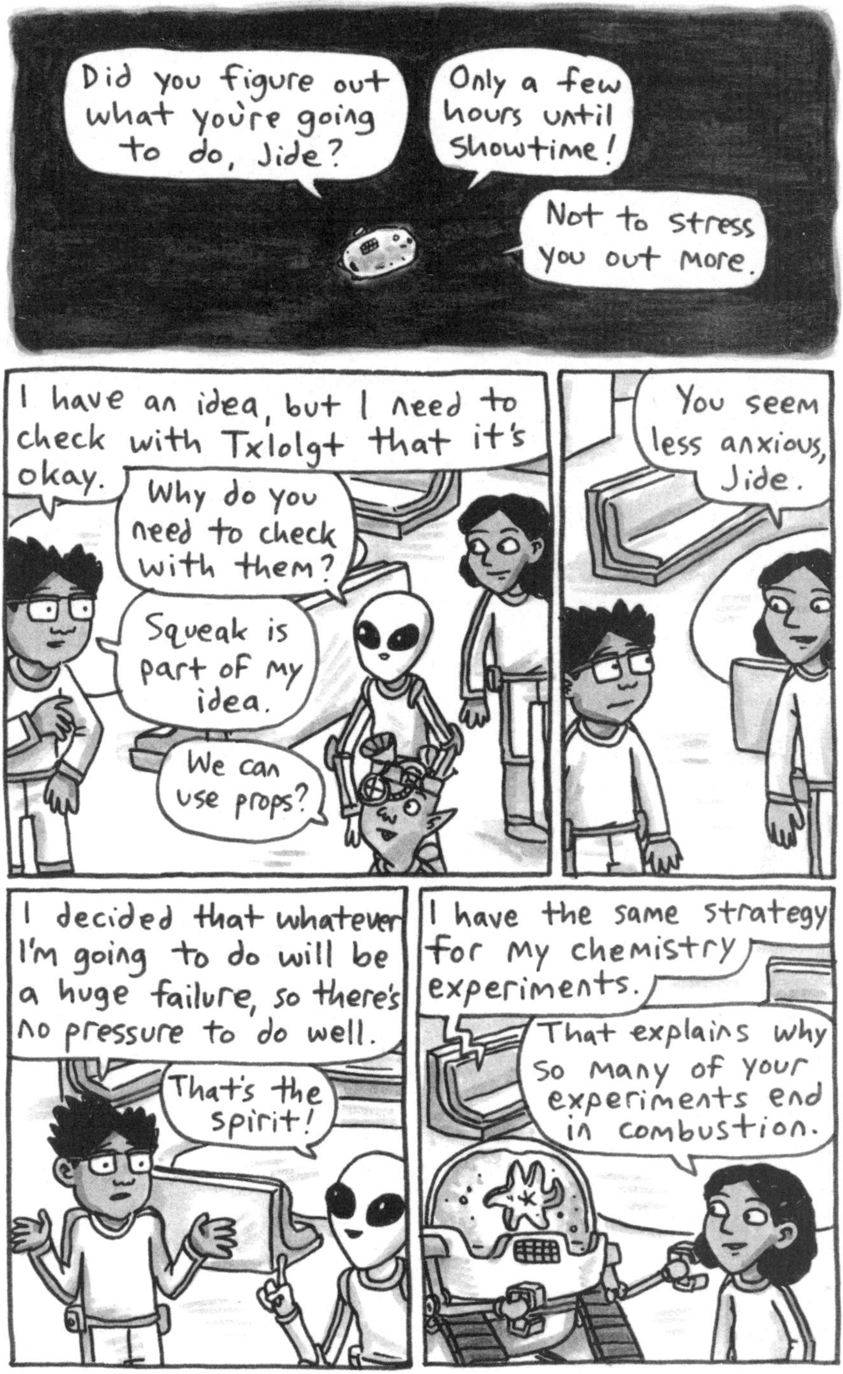
Did you figure out what you're going to do, Jide?
Only a few hours until showtime!
Not to stress you out more.
I have an idea, but I need to check with Txlolgt that it's okay.
Why do you need to check with them?
Squeak is part of my idea.
We can use props?
You seem less anxious, Jide.
I decided that whatever I'm going to do will be a huge failure, so there's no pressure to do well.
That's the spirit!
I have the same strategy for my chemistry experiments.
That explains why so many of your experiments end in combustion.

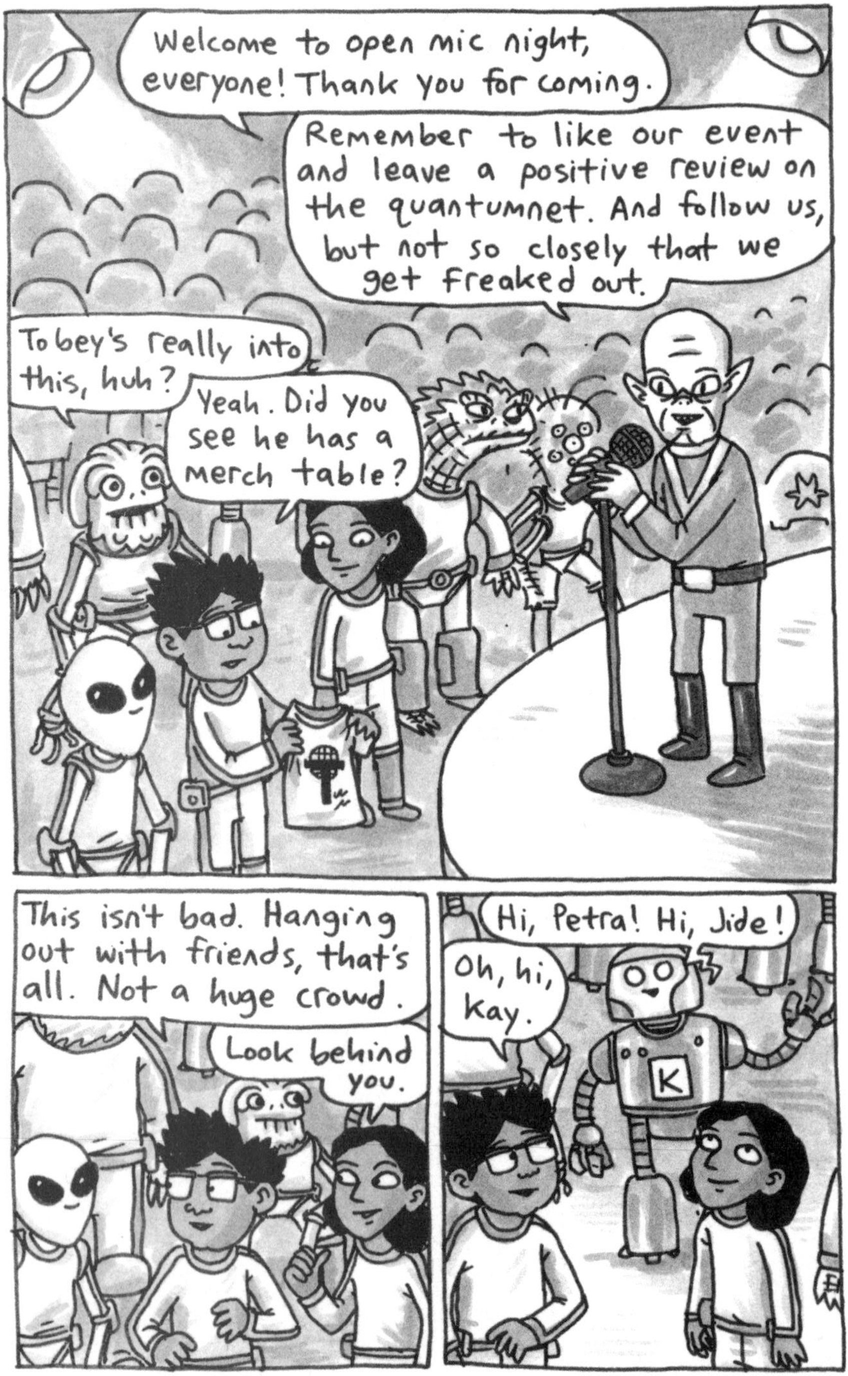
Welcome to open mic night, everyone! Thank you for coming.
Remember to like our event and leave a positive review on the quantumnet. And follow us, but not so closely that we get freaked out.
Tobey's really into this, huh?
Yeah. Did you see he has a merch table?
This isn't bad. Hanging out with friends, that's all. Not a huge crowd.
Look behind you.
Hi, Petra! Hi, Jide!
Oh, hi, Kay.

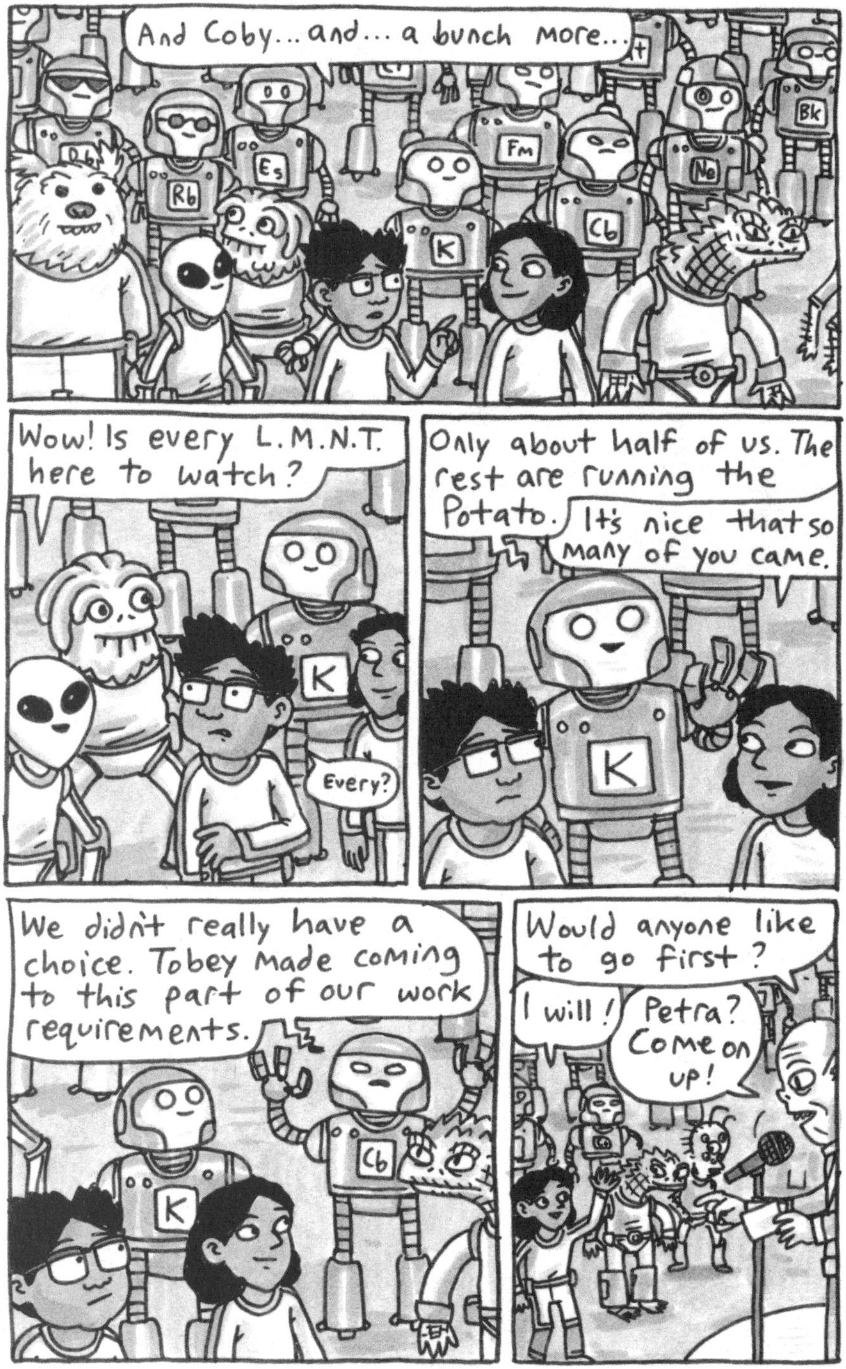

And Coby... and... a bunch more...
Db
Rb
Es
Fm
K
Cb
No
Bk
Wow! Is every L.M.N.T. here to watch?
Every?
K
Only about half of us. The rest are running the Potato.
It's nice that so many of you came.
K
We didn't really have a choice. Tobey made coming to this part of our work requirements.
K
Cb
Would anyone like to go first?
I will!
Petra? Come on up!

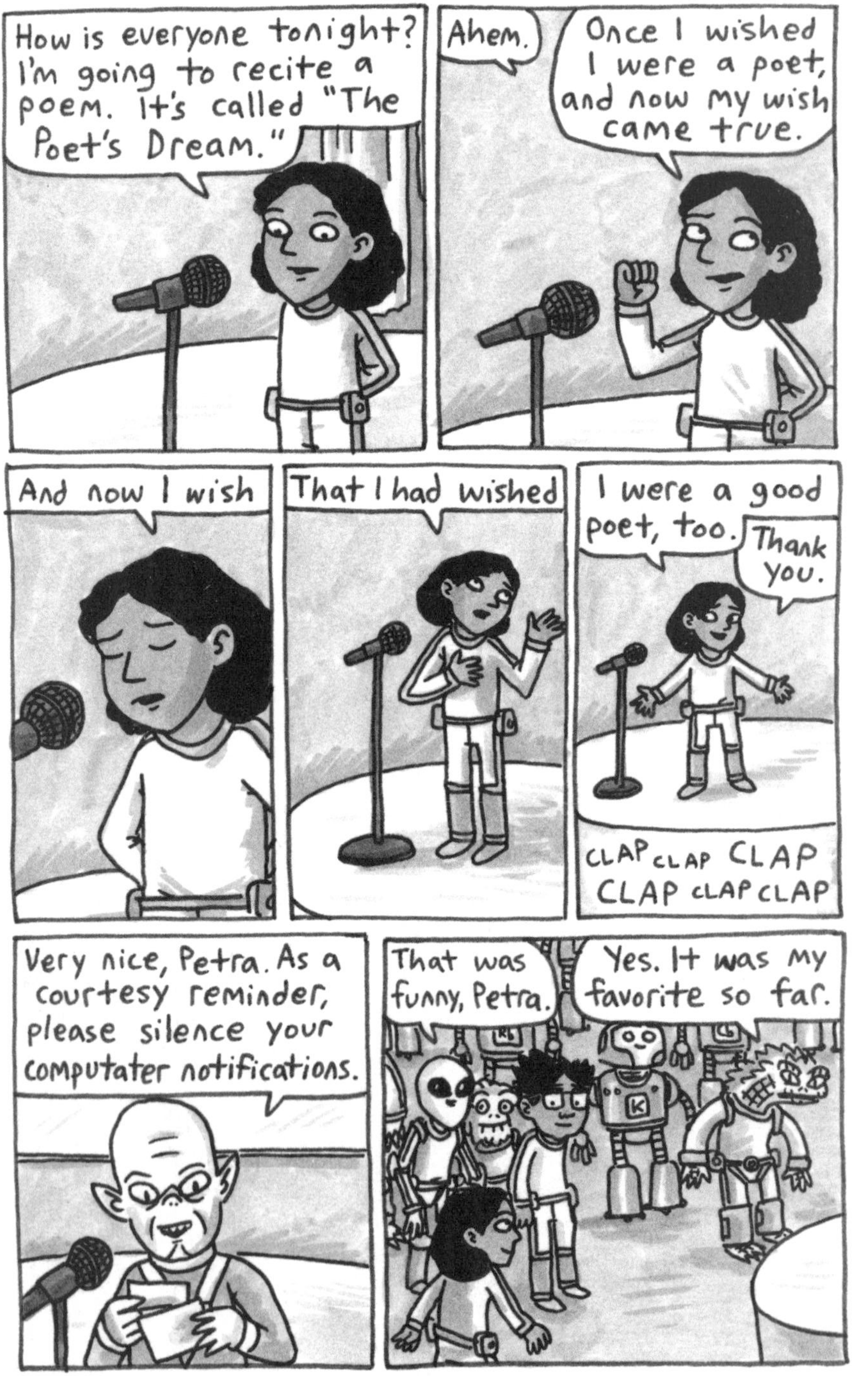

How is everyone tonight? I'm going to recite a poem. It's called "The Poet's Dream."
Ahem.
Once I wished I were a poet, and now my wish came true.
And now I wish
That I had wished
I were a good poet, too.
Thank you.
CLAP CLAP CLAP
CLAP CLAP CLAP
Very nice, Petra. As a courtesy reminder, please silence your computater notifications.
That was funny, Petra.
Yes. It was my favorite so far.

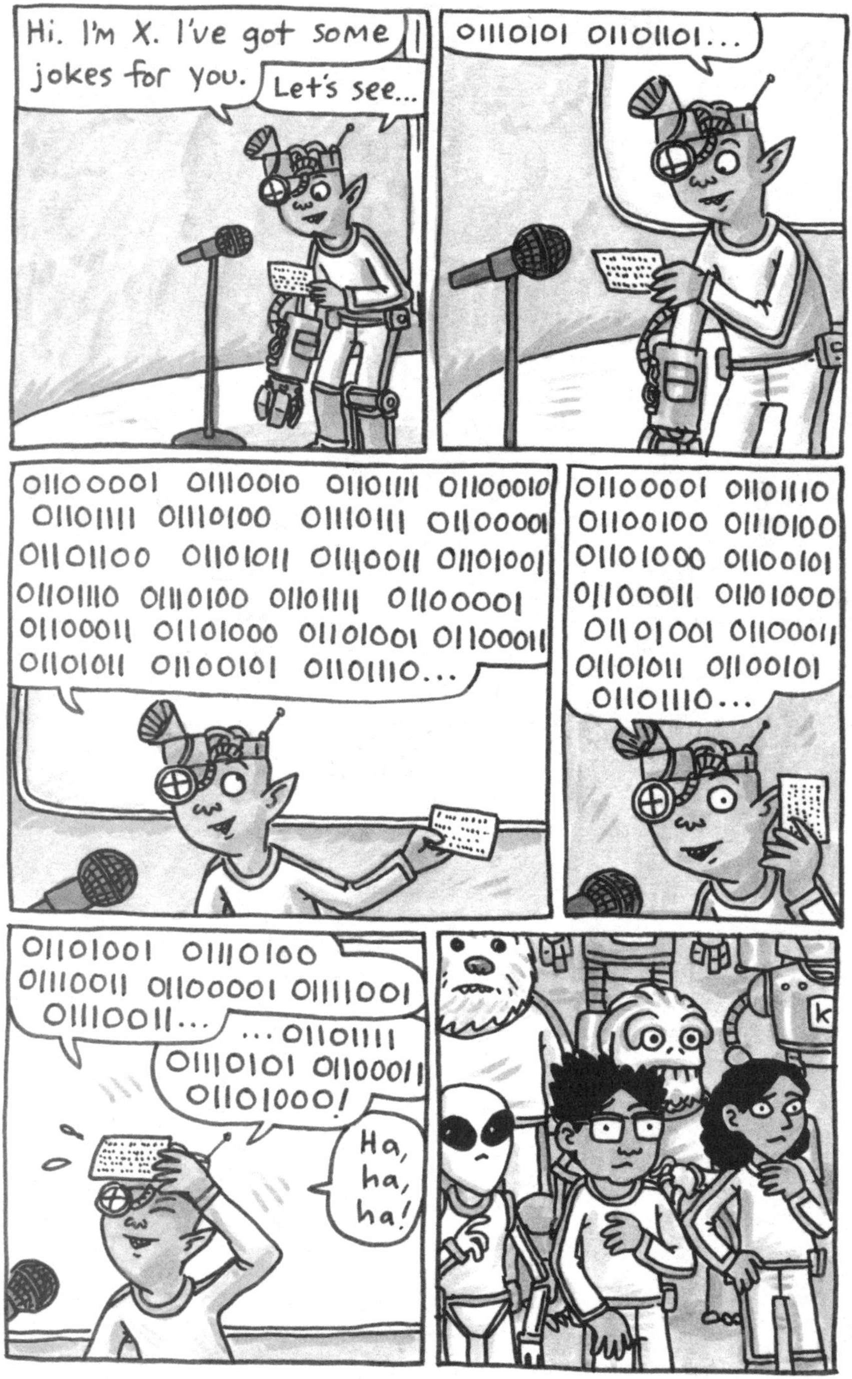
Hi. I'm X. I've got some jokes for you.
Let's see...
01110101 01101101...
01100001 01110010 01101111 01100010 01101111 01110100 01110111 01100001 01101100 01101011 01110011 01101001 01101110 01110100 01101111 01100001 01100011 01101000 01101001 01100011 01101011 01100101 01101110...
01100001 01101110 01100100 01110100 01101000 01100101 01100011 01101000 01101001 01100011 01101011 01100101 01101110...
01101001 01110100 01110011 01100001 01111001 01110011...
...01101111 01110101 01100011 01101000!
Ha, ha, ha!
k

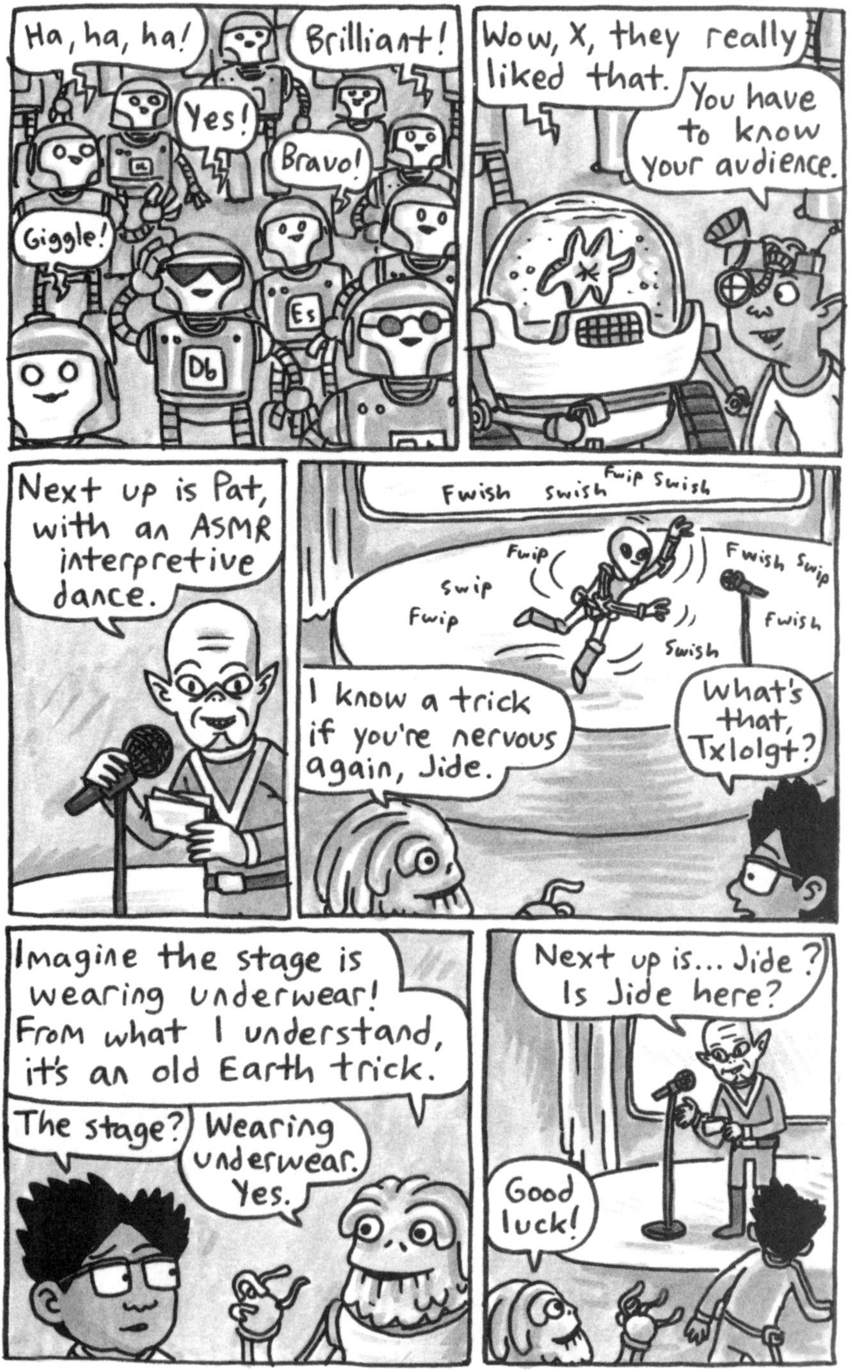
Ha, ha, ha!
Brilliant!
Yes!
Bravo!
Giggle!
Wow, X, they really liked that.
You have to know your audience.
Next up is Pat, with an ASMR interpretive dance.
Fwish swish Fwip Swish
Fwip
Swip
Fwip
Fwish Swip
Fwish
Swish
I know a trick if you're nervous again, Jide.
What's that, Txlolgt?
Imagine the stage is wearing underwear! From what I understand, it's an old Earth trick.
The stage?
Wearing underwear. Yes.
Next up is... Jide? Is Jide here?
Good luck!

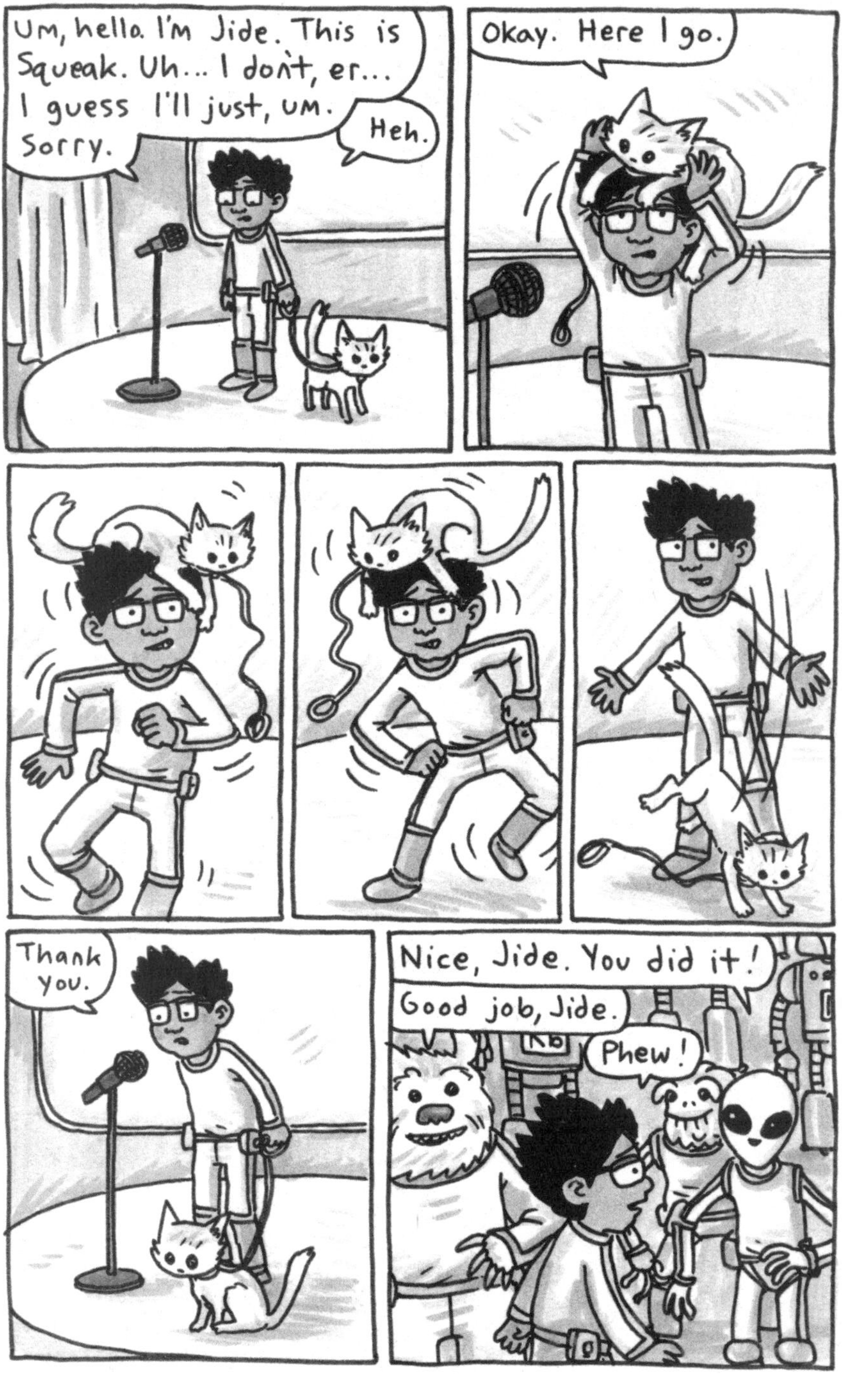
Um, hello. I'm Jide. This is Squeak. Uh... I don't, er... I guess I'll just, um. Sorry.
Heh.
Okay. Here I go.
Thank you.
Nice, Jide. You did it!
Good job, Jide.
Phew!

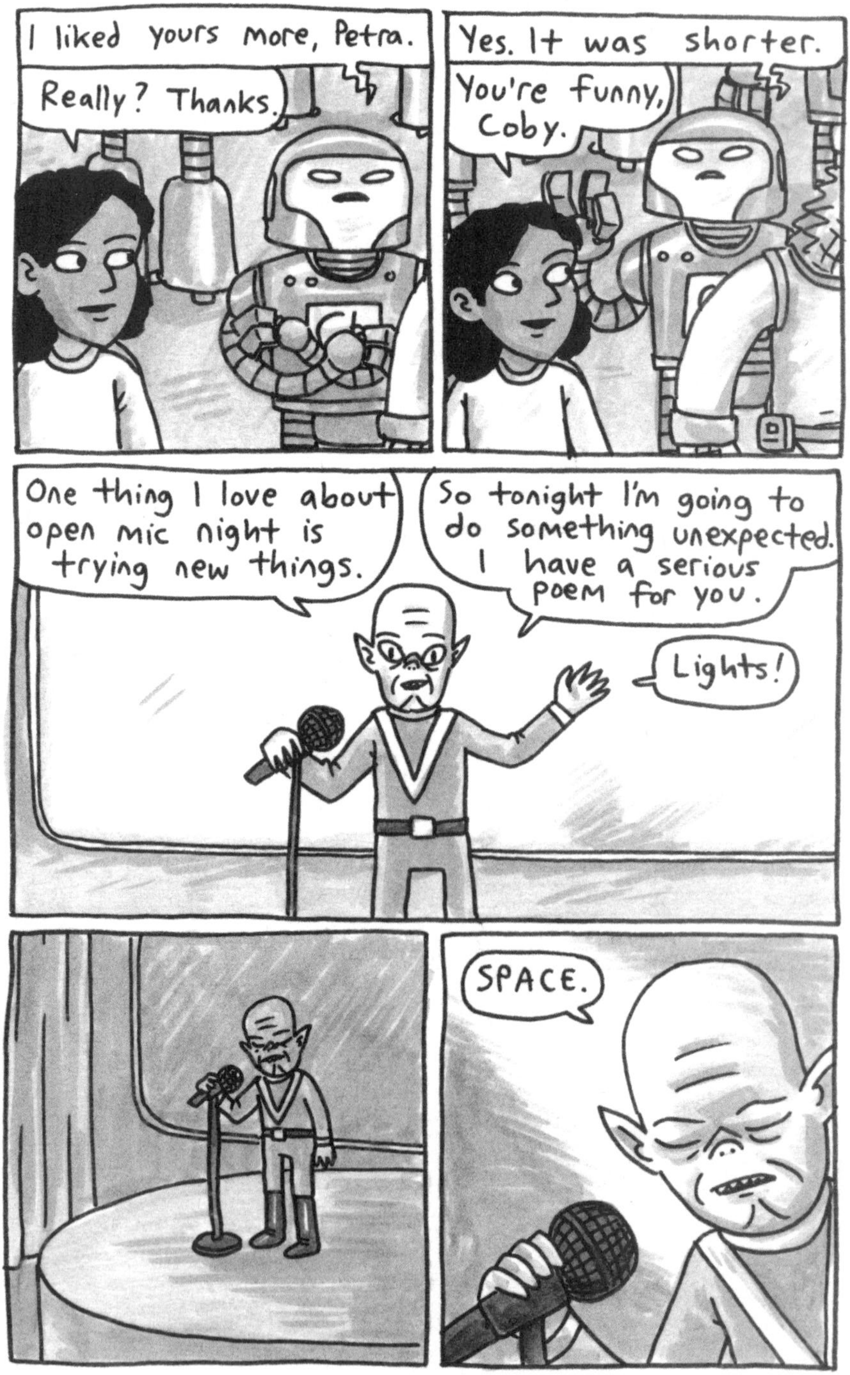
I liked yours more, Petra.
Really? Thanks.
Yes. It was shorter.
You're funny, Coby.
One thing I love about open mic night is trying new things.
So tonight I'm going to do something unexpected. I have a serious poem for you.
Lights!
SPACE.

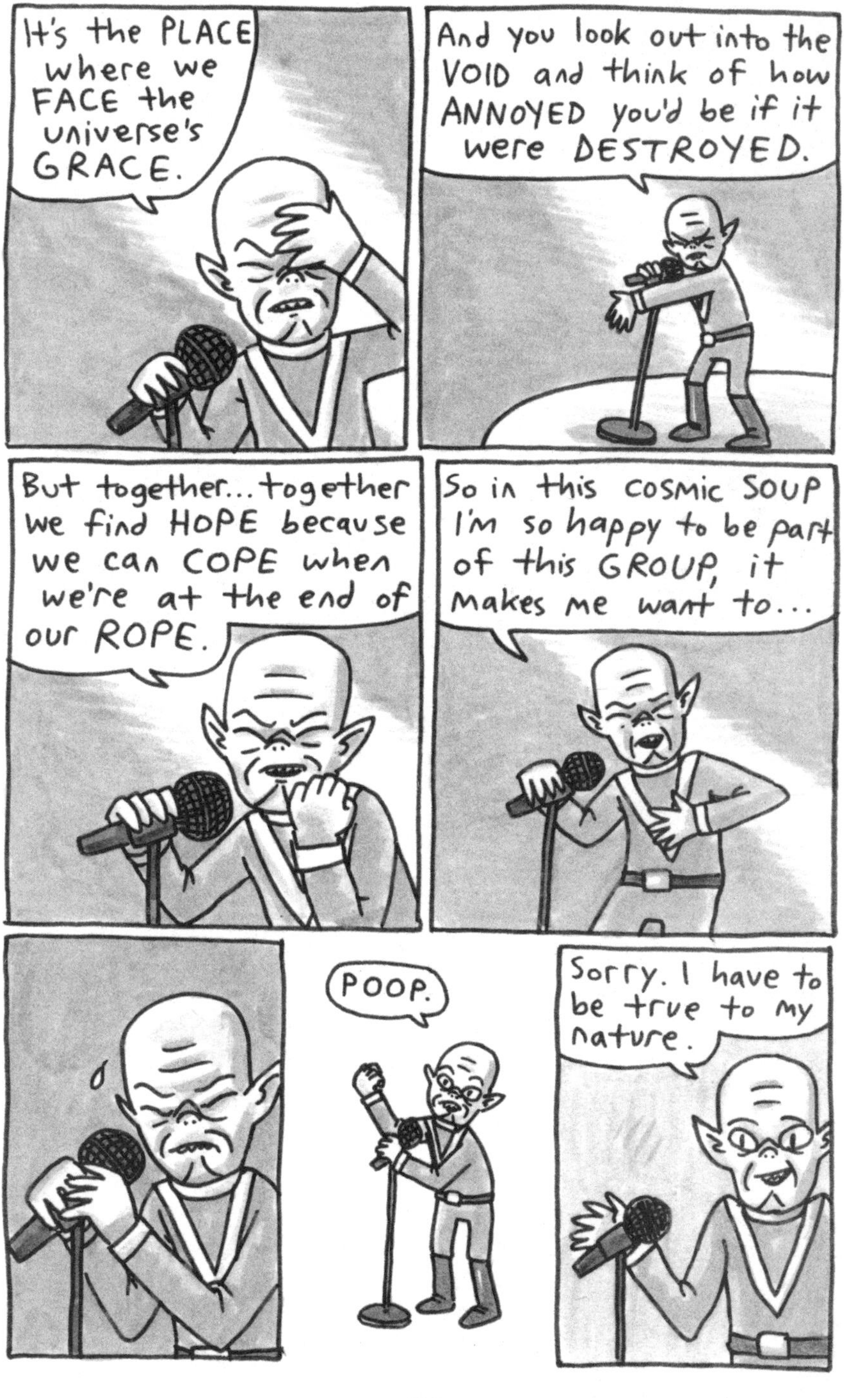
It's the PLACE where we FACE the universe's GRACE.
And you look out into the VOID and think of how ANNOYED you'd be if it were DESTROYED.
But together... together we find HOPE because we can COPE when we're at the end of our ROPE.
So in this COSMIC SOUP I'm so happy to be part of this GROUP, it makes me want to...
POOP.
Sorry. I have to be true to my nature.

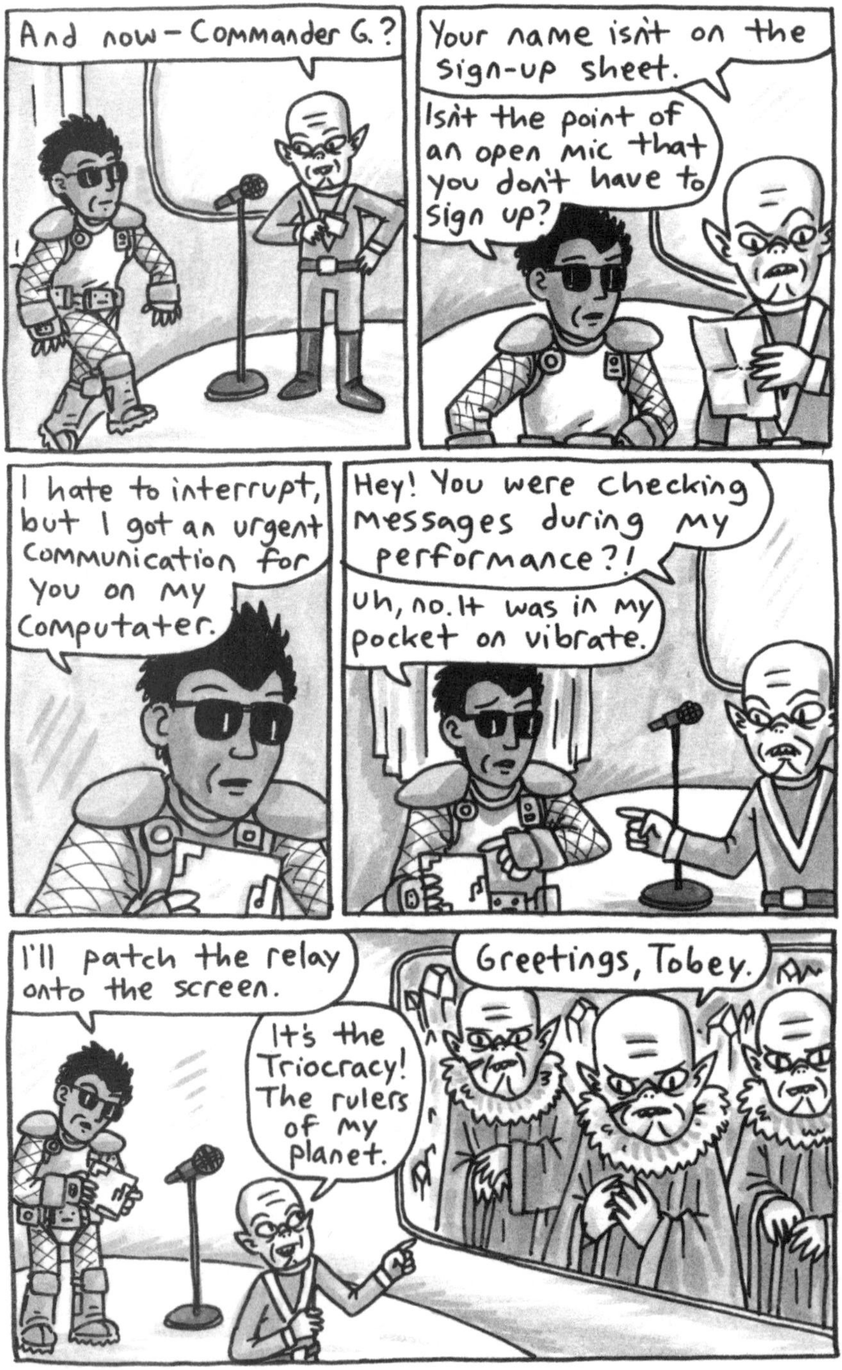
And now—Commander G.?
Your name isn't on the sign-up sheet.
Isn't the point of an open mic that you don't have to sign up?
I hate to interrupt, but I got an urgent communication for you on my computater.
Hey! You were checking messages during my performance?!
Uh, no. It was in my pocket on vibrate.
I'll patch the relay onto the screen.
It's the Triocracy! The rulers of my planet.
Greetings, Tobey.

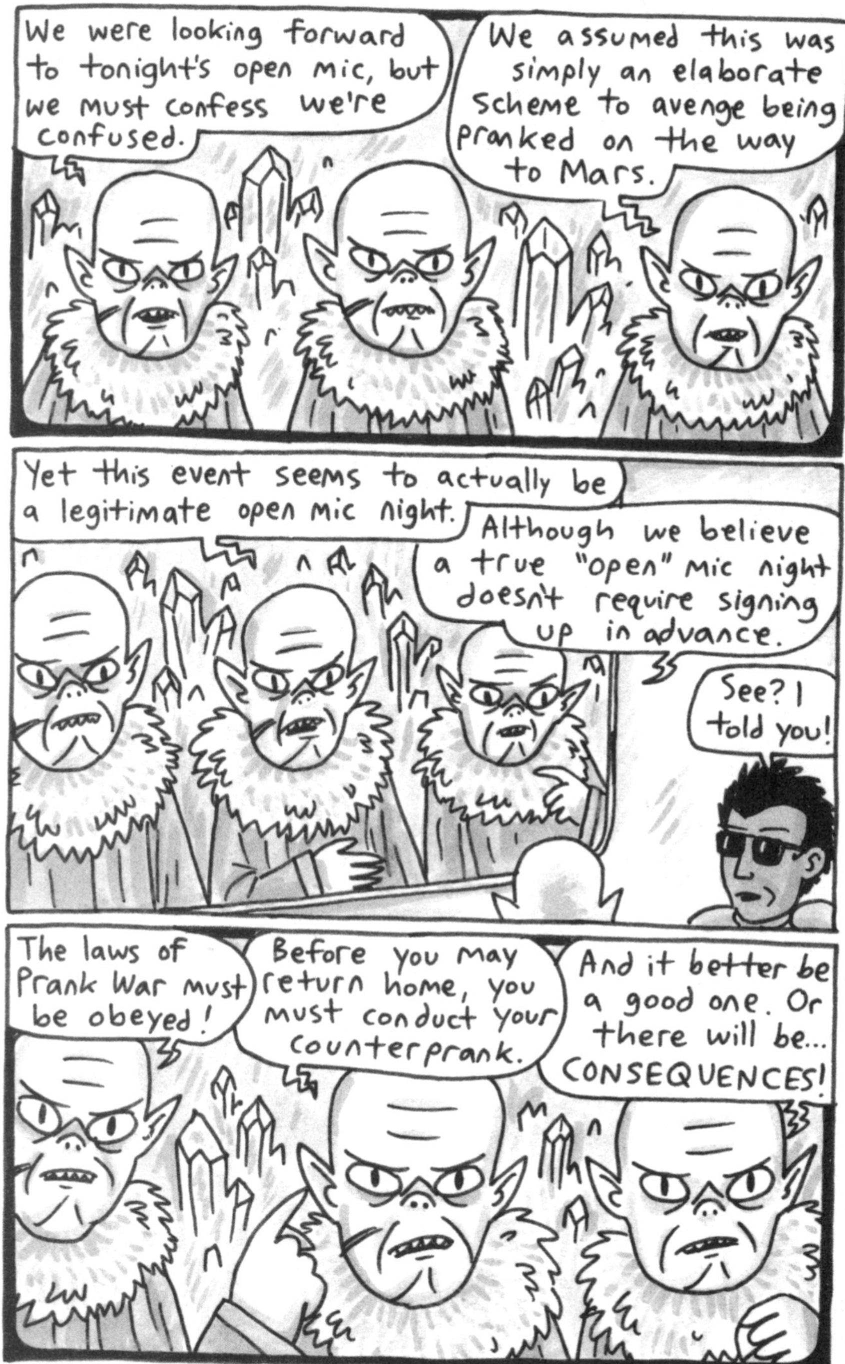
We were looking forward to tonight's open mic, but we must confess we're confused.
We assumed this was simply an elaborate scheme to avenge being pranked on the way to Mars.
Yet this event seems to actually be a legitimate open mic night.
Although we believe a true "open" mic night doesn't require signing up in advance.
See? I told you!
The laws of Prank War must be obeyed!
Before you may return home, you must conduct your counterprank.
And it better be a good one. Or there will be... CONSEQUENCES!

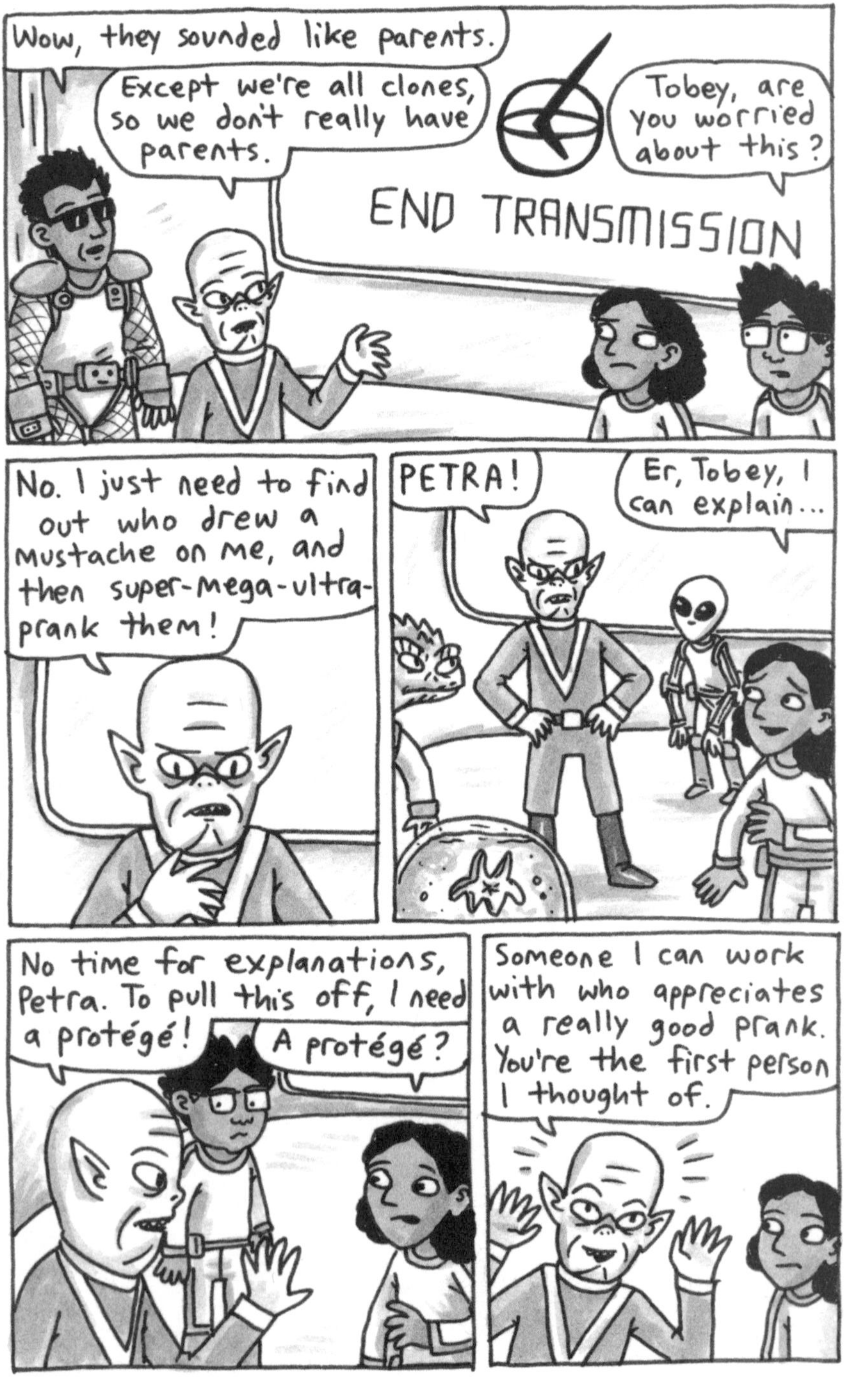
Wow, they sounded like parents.
Except we're all clones, so we don't really have parents.
Tobey, are you worried about this?
END TRANSMISSION
No. I just need to find out who drew a mustache on me, and then super-mega-ultra-prank them!
PETRA!
Er, Tobey, I can explain...
No time for explanations, Petra. To pull this off, I need a protégé!
A protégé?
Someone I can work with who appreciates a really good prank. You're the first person I thought of.

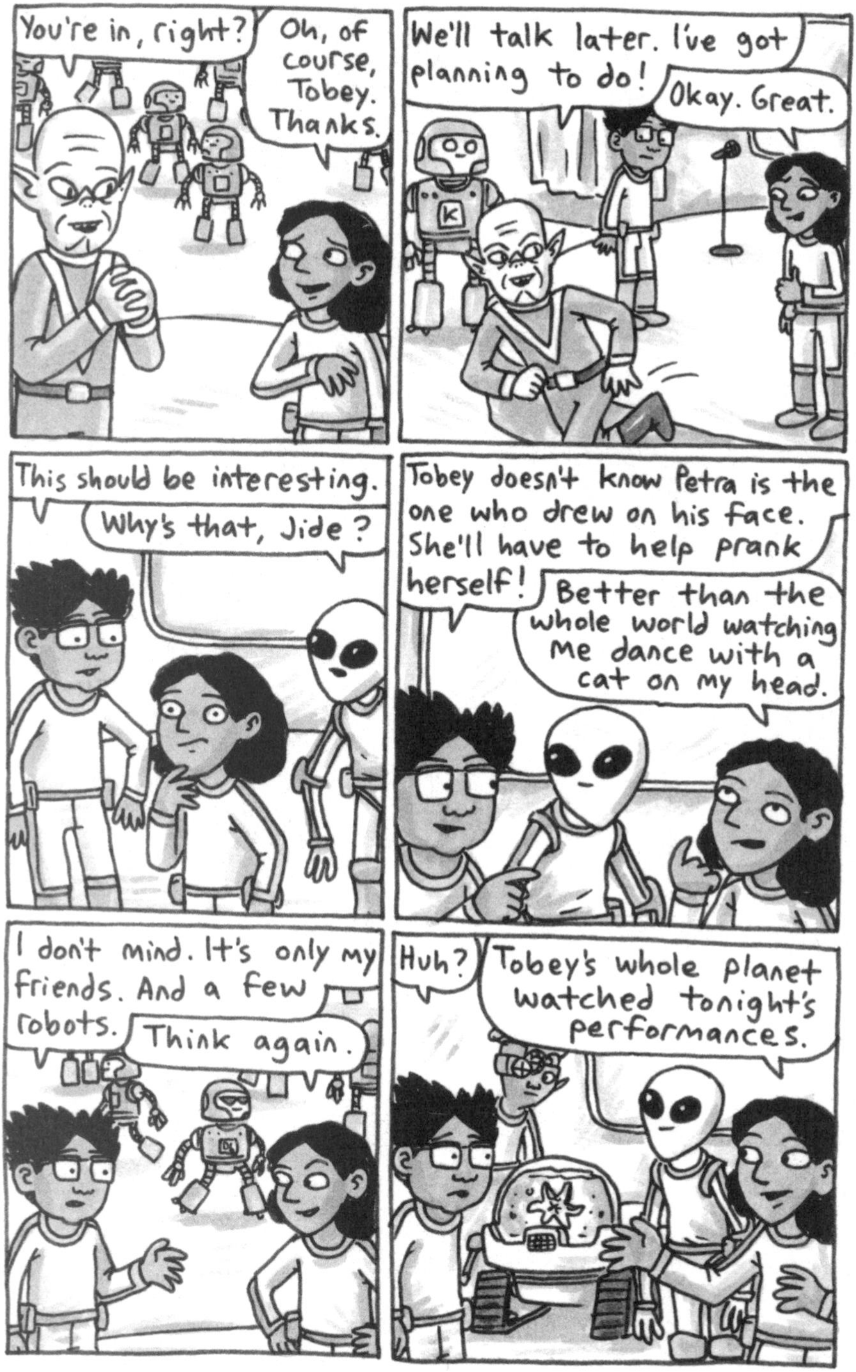
You're in, right?
Oh, of course, Tobey. Thanks.
We'll talk later. I've got planning to do!
Okay. Great.
This should be interesting.
Why's that, Jide?
Tobey doesn't know Petra is the one who drew on his face. She'll have to help prank herself!
Better than the whole world watching me dance with a cat on my head.
I don't mind. It's only my friends. And a few robots.
Think again.
Huh?
Tobey's whole planet watched tonight's performances.

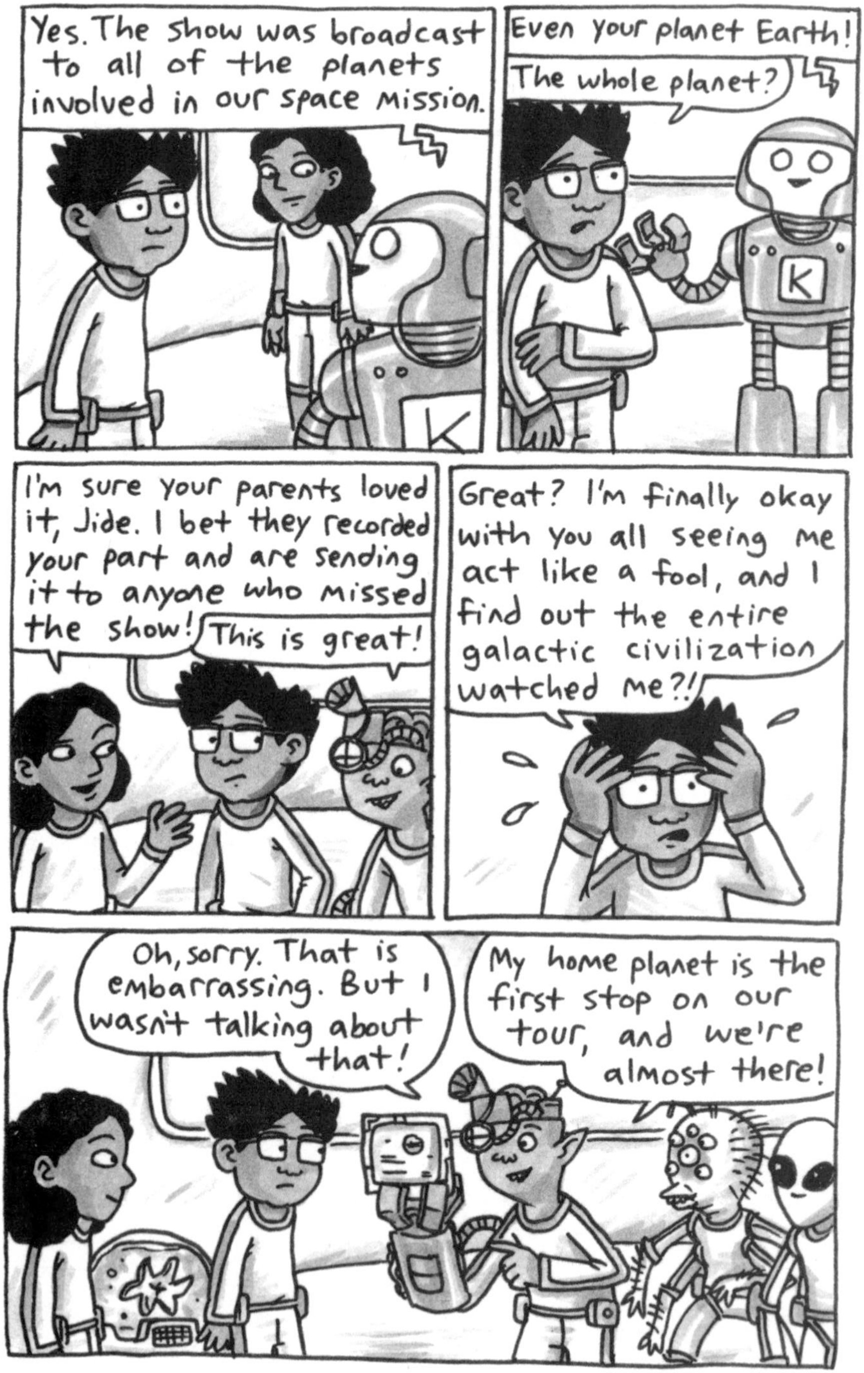
Yes. The show was broadcast to all of the planets involved in our space mission.
Even your planet Earth!
The whole planet?
I'm sure your parents loved it, Jide. I bet they recorded your part and are sending it to anyone who missed the show!
This is great!
Great? I'm finally okay with you all seeing me act like a fool, and I find out the entire galactic civilization watched me?!
Oh, sorry. That is embarrassing. But I wasn't talking about that!
My home planet is the first stop on our tour, and we're almost there!

DIGITOTALLY AWESOME

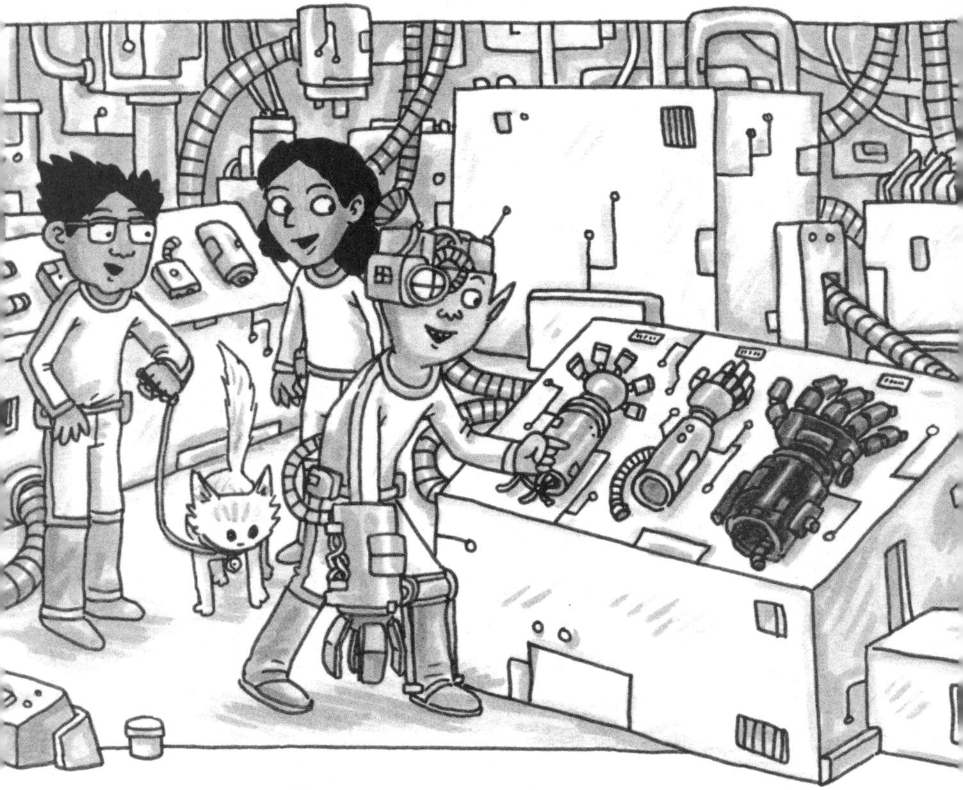

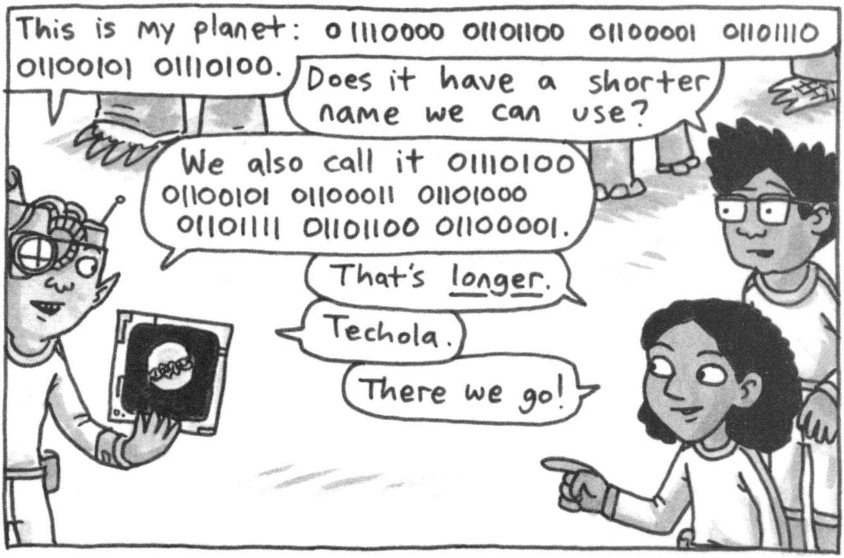
This is my planet: 0 1110000 01101100 01100001 01101110 01100101 01110100.
Does it have a shorter name we can use?
We also call it 01110100 01100101 01100011 01101000 01101111 01101100 01100001.
That's longer.
Techola.
There we go!

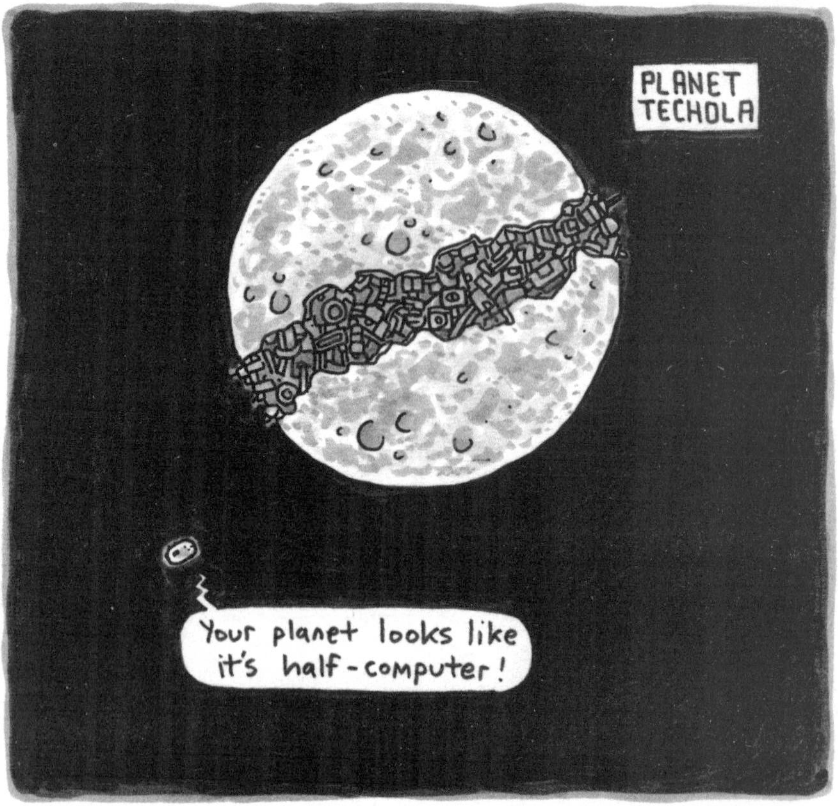
PLANET TECHOLA
Your planet looks like it's half-computer!

Actually, it's only 23.7149% computer. My people, the Techolans, have developed the entire planet's equator into a massive machine.

It's climate-controlled and keeps all environments in equilibrium. Plus, it handles extraplanetary threats like solar flares or asteroids.

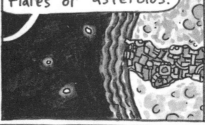

You're bringing Squeak along, Txlolgt?

Yes. I feel like he could use some open system, non-recycled, breathable atmospheric molecules.

Some what?

Fresh air.

I'm looking forward to that, too. A real atmosphere, real gravity, standing on solid ground...

Your planet must have super-advanced technology, X. Does that mean we're going to teleport down to the surface?

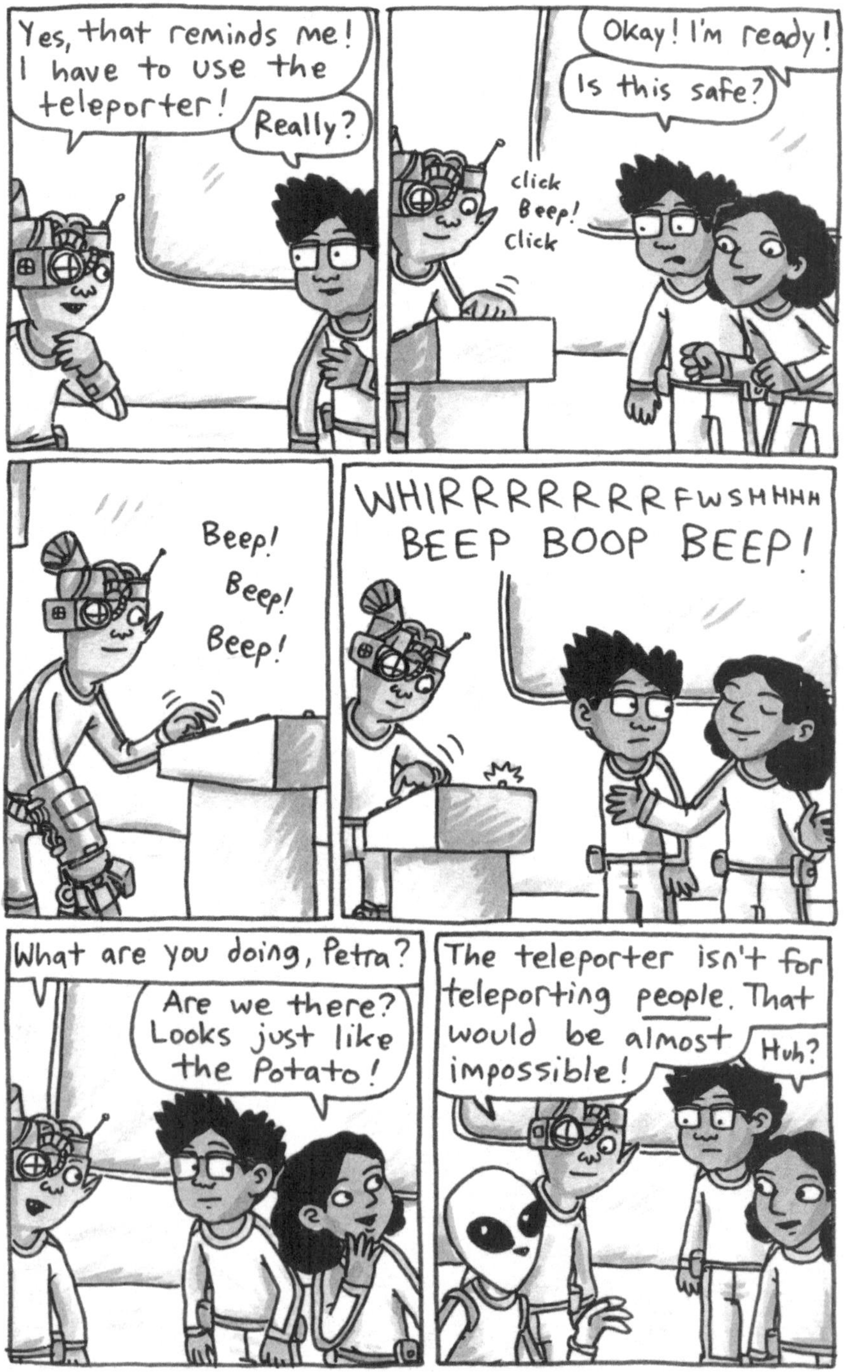
Yes, that reminds me! I have to use the teleporter!
Really?
Okay! I'm ready!
Is this safe?
click
Beep!
Click
Beep!
Beep!
Beep!
WHIRRRRRRRRFWSHHHH
BEEP BOOP BEEP!
What are you doing, Petra?
Are we there? Looks just like the Potato!
The teleporter isn't for teleporting people. That would be almost impossible!
Huh?

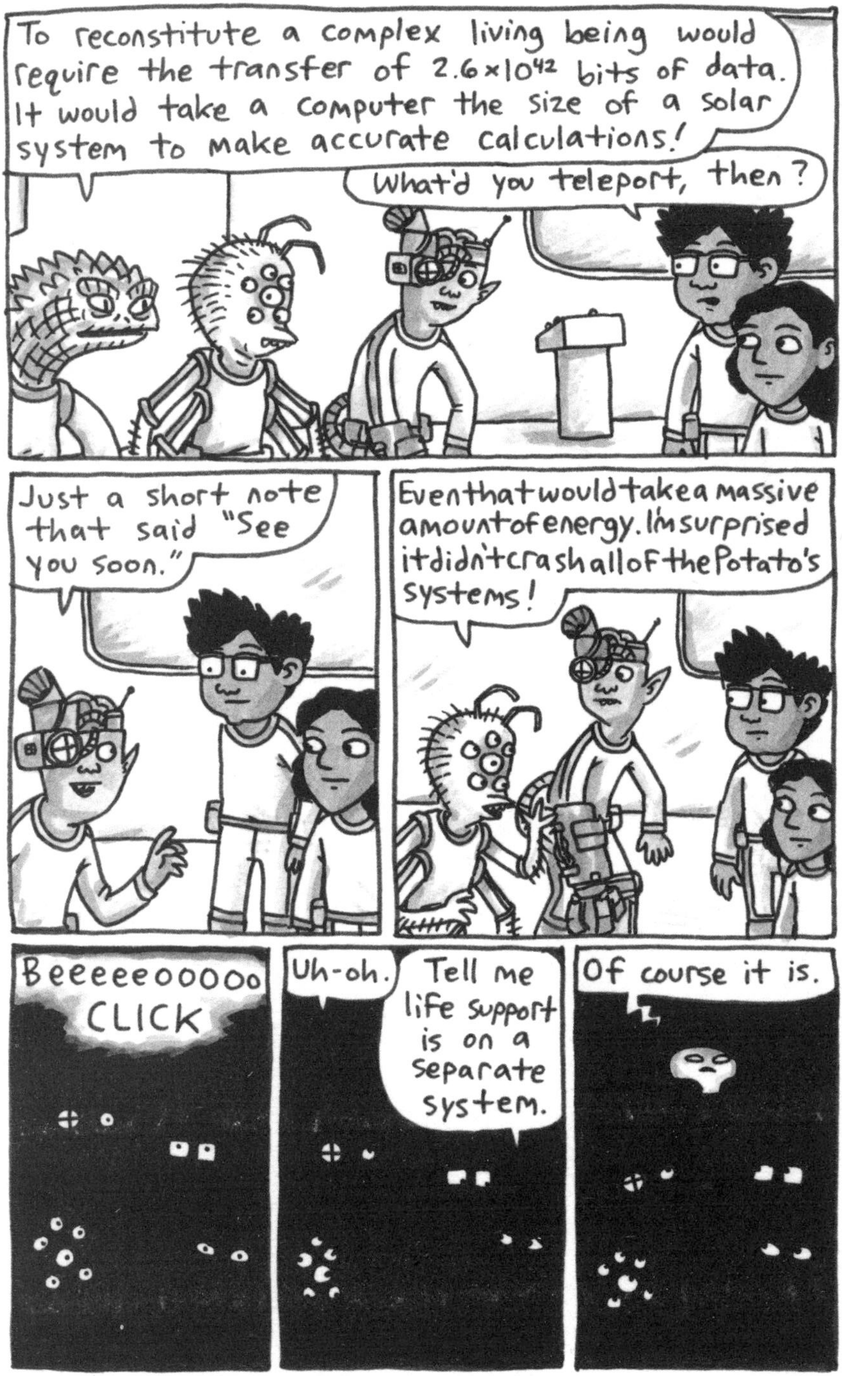
To reconstitute a complex living being would require the transfer of 2.6×10⁴² bits of data. It would take a computer the size of a solar system to make accurate calculations!
What'd you teleport, then?
Just a short note that said "See you soon."
Even that would take a massive amount of energy. I'm surprised it didn't crash all of the Potato's systems!
Beeeeeooooo
CLICK
Uh-oh.
Tell me life support is on a separate system.
Of course it is.

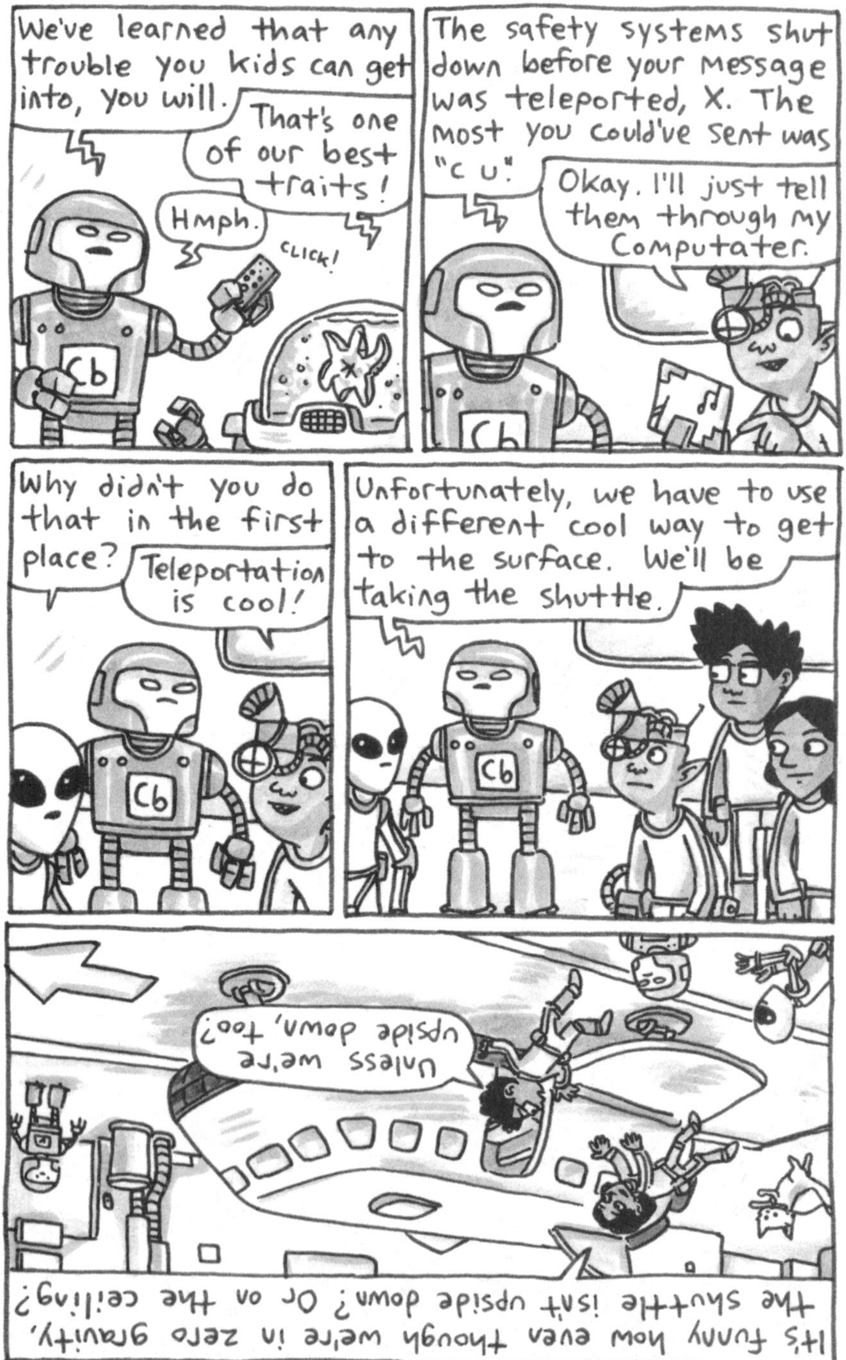
We've learned that any trouble you kids can get into, you will.
That's one of our best traits!
Hmph.
CLICK!
The safety systems shut down before your message was teleported, X. The most you could've sent was "C U."
Okay. I'll just tell them through my Computater.
Why didn't you do that in the first place?
Teleportation is cool!
Unfortunately, we have to use a different cool way to get to the surface. We'll be taking the shuttle.
It's funny how even though we're in zero gravity, the shuttle isn't upside down? Or on the ceiling?
Unless we're upside down, too?

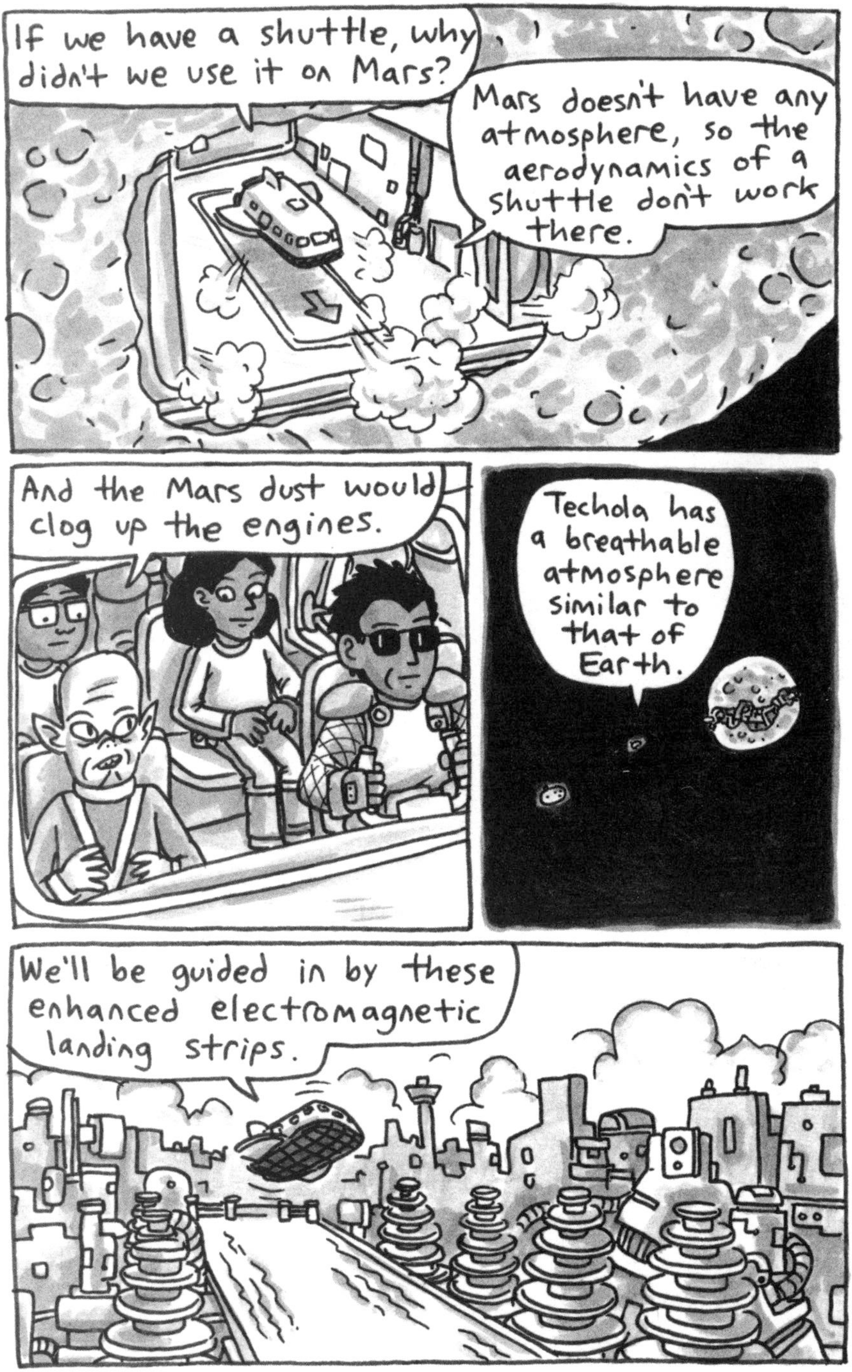
If we have a shuttle, why didn't we use it on Mars?
Mars doesn't have any atmosphere, so the aerodynamics of a shuttle don't work there.
And the Mars dust would clog up the engines.
Techola has a breathable atmosphere similar to that of Earth.
We'll be guided in by these enhanced electromagnetic landing strips.

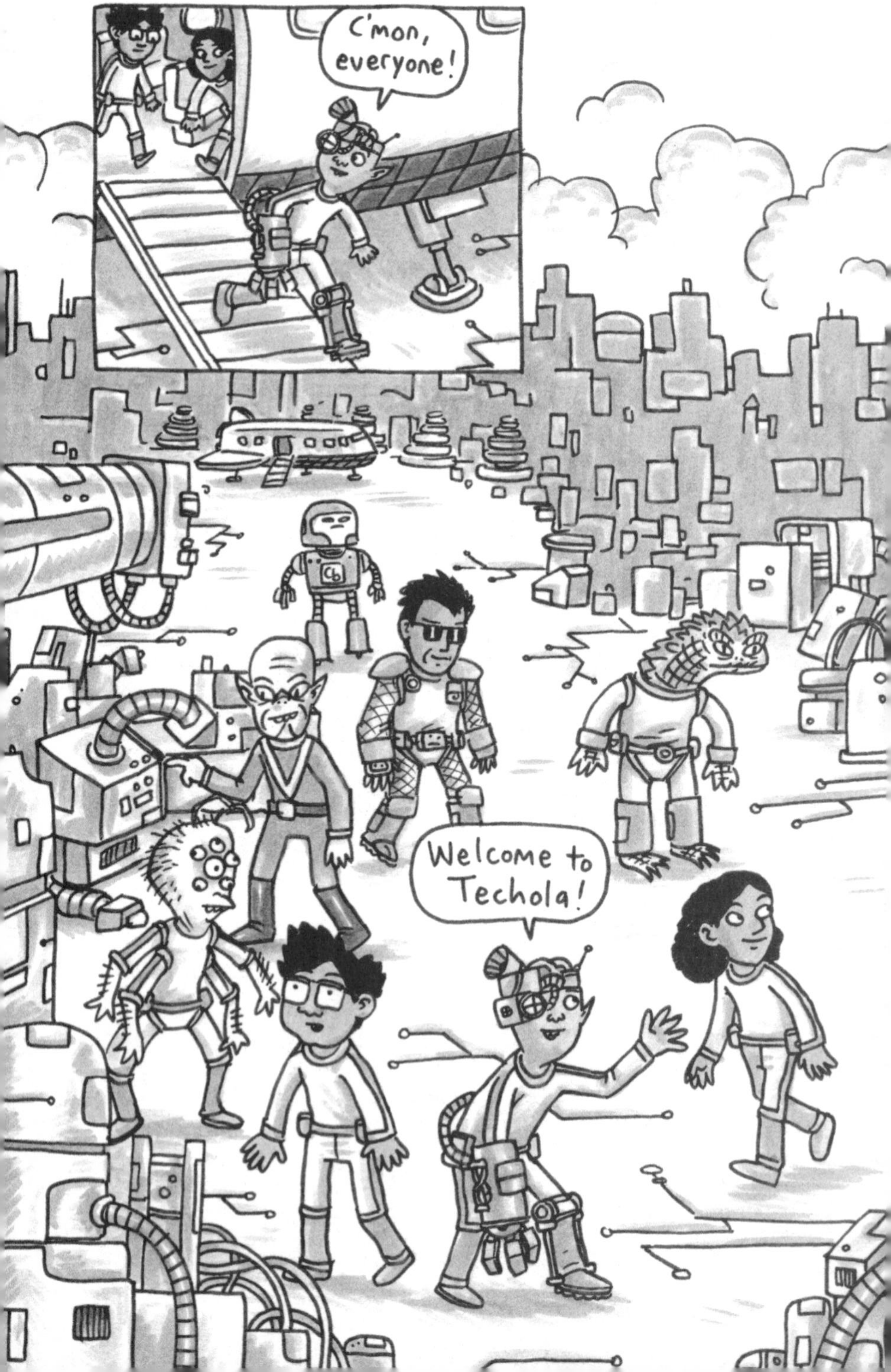
C'mon, everyone!
Welcome to Techola!

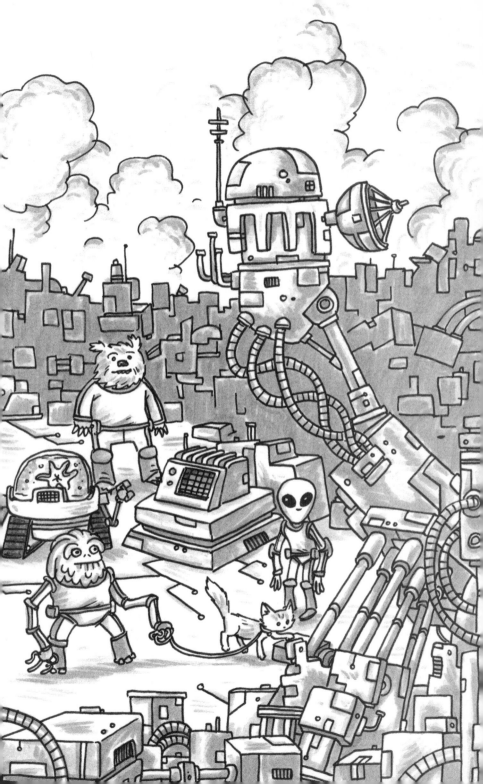

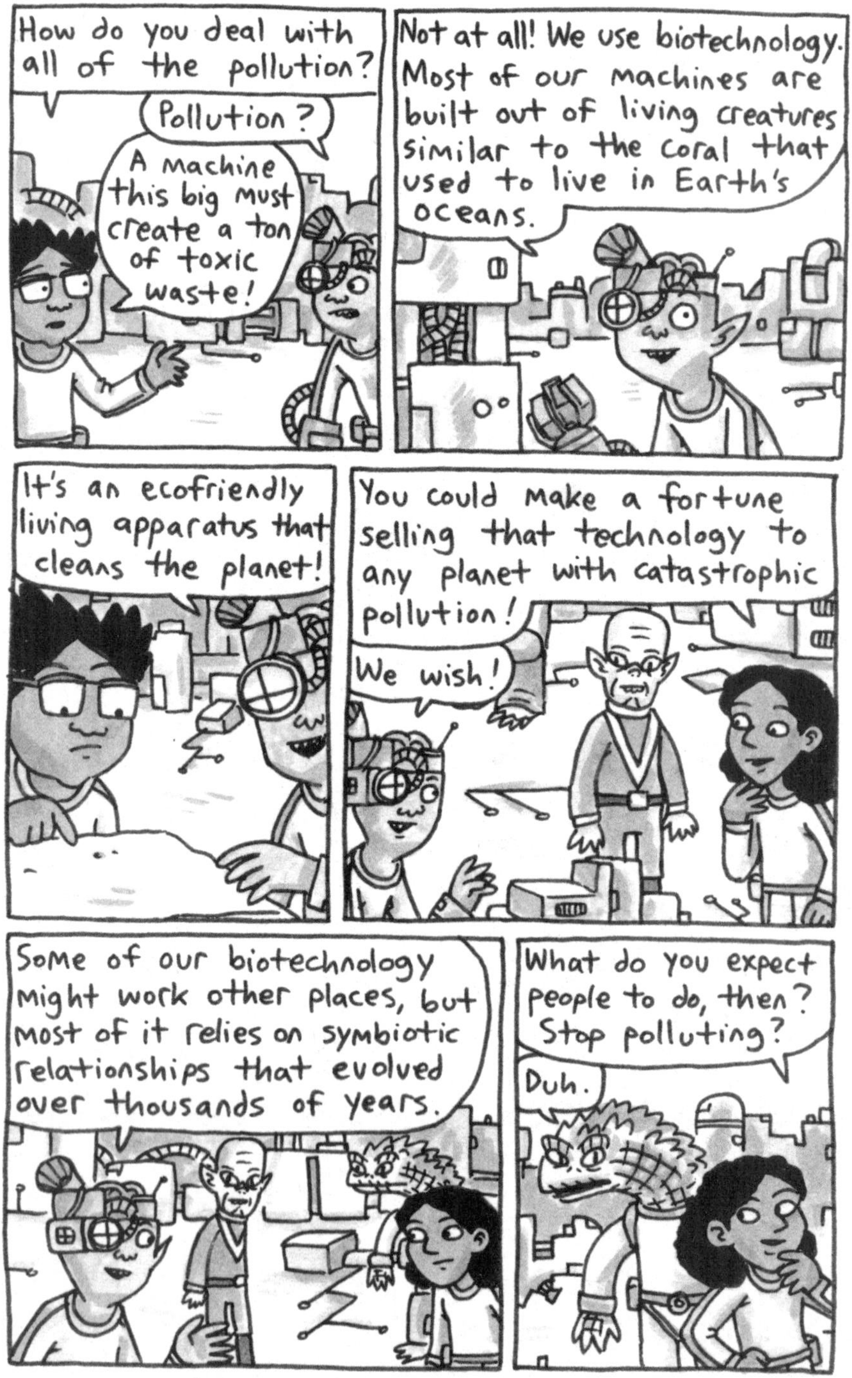
How do you deal with all of the pollution?
Pollution?
A machine this big must create a ton of toxic waste!
Not at all! We use biotechnology. Most of our machines are built out of living creatures similar to the coral that used to live in Earth's oceans.
It's an ecofriendly living apparatus that cleans the planet!
You could make a fortune selling that technology to any planet with catastrophic pollution!
We wish!
Some of our biotechnology might work other places, but most of it relies on symbiotic relationships that evolved over thousands of years.
What do you expect people to do, then? Stop polluting?
Duh.

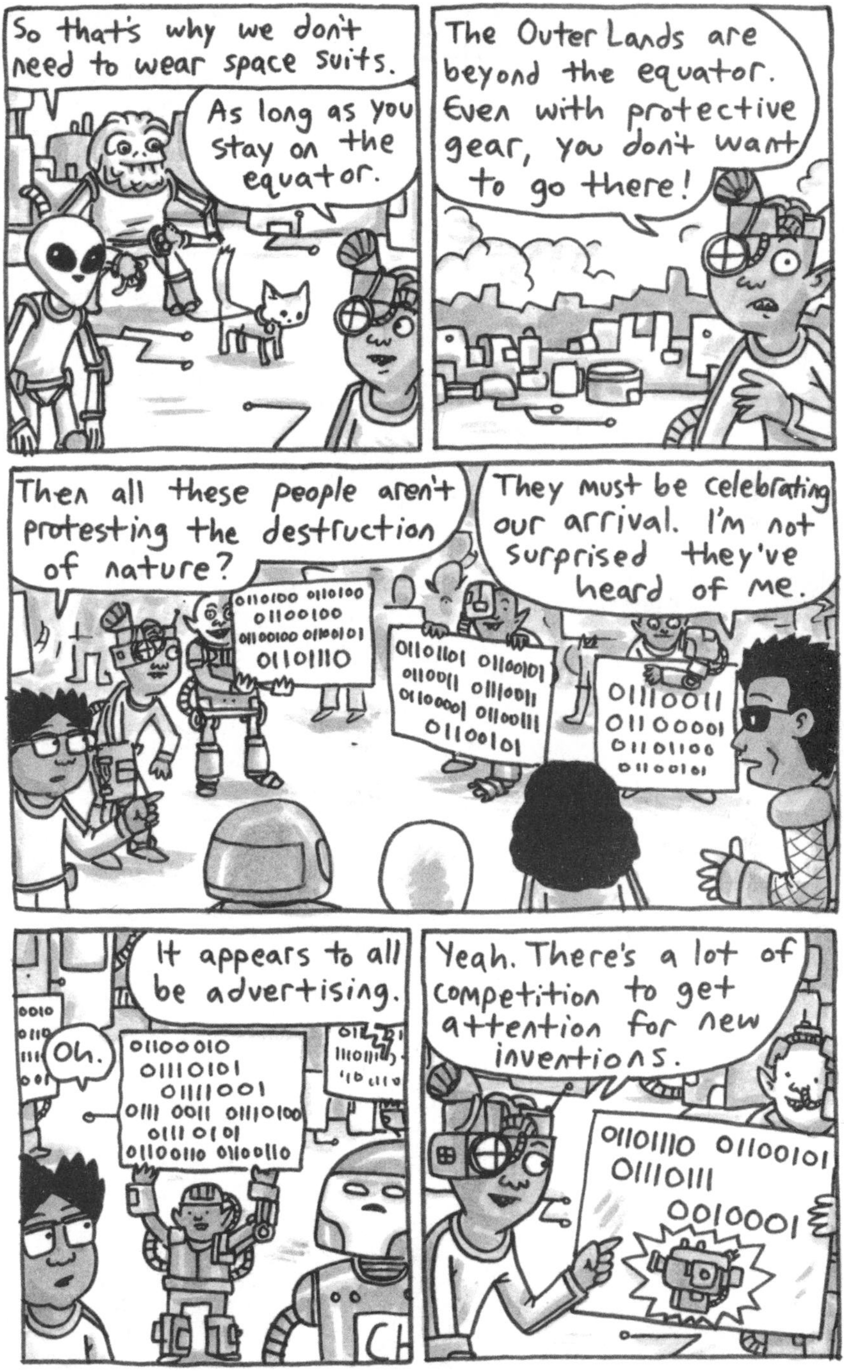
So that's why we don't need to wear space suits.
As long as you stay on the equator.
The Outer Lands are beyond the equator. Even with protective gear, you don't want to go there!
Then all these people aren't protesting the destruction of nature?
They must be celebrating our arrival. I'm not surprised they've heard of me.
It appears to all be advertising.
Oh.
Yeah. There's a lot of competition to get attention for new inventions.

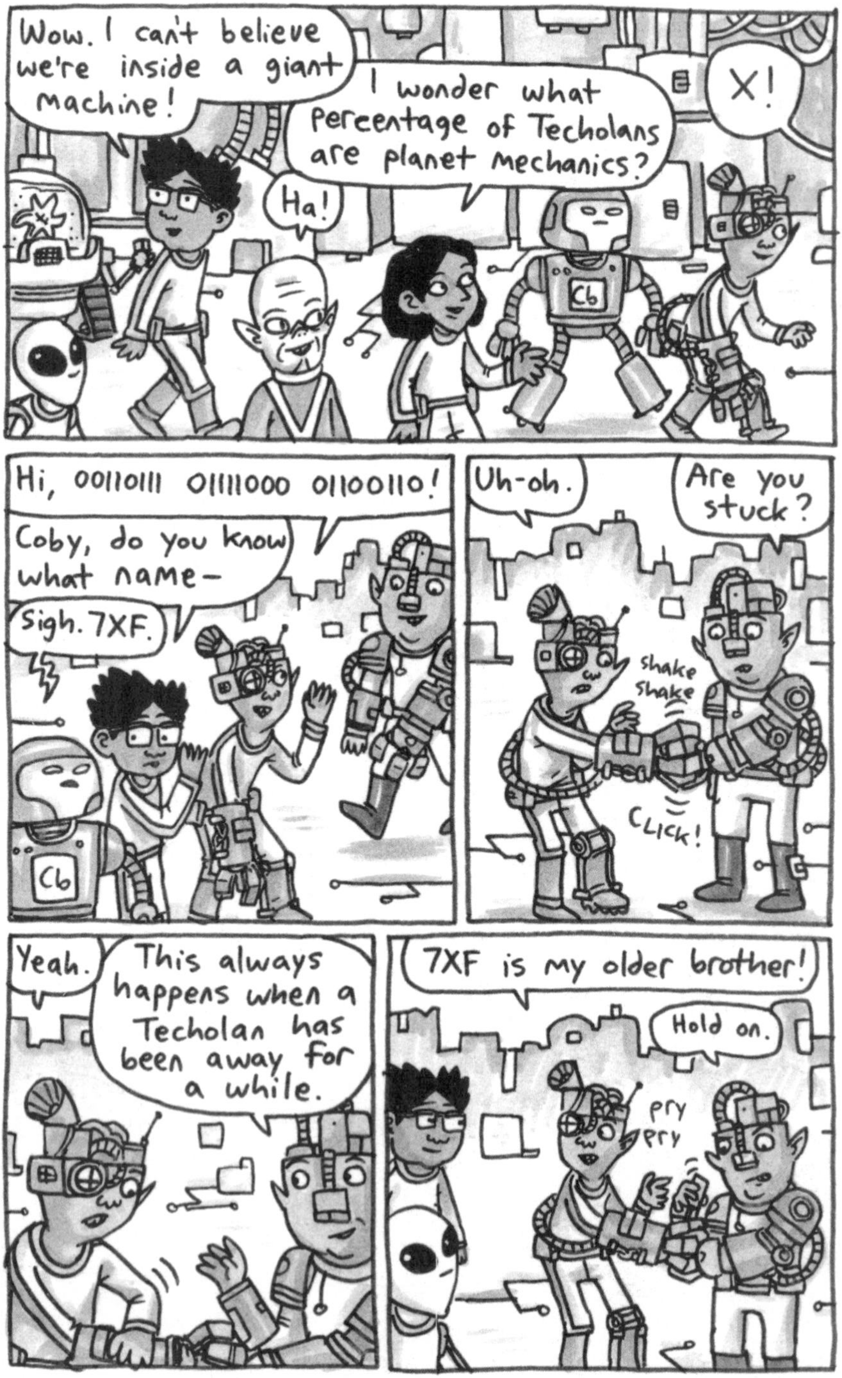
Wow. I can't believe we're inside a giant machine!
I wonder what percentage of Techolans are planet mechanics?
Ha!
X!
Hi, 00110111 01111000 01100110!
Coby, do you know what name—
Sigh. 7XF.
Uh-oh.
Are you stuck?
shake shake
CLICK!
Yeah.
This always happens when a Techolan has been away for a while.
7XF is my older brother!
Hold on.
pry pry

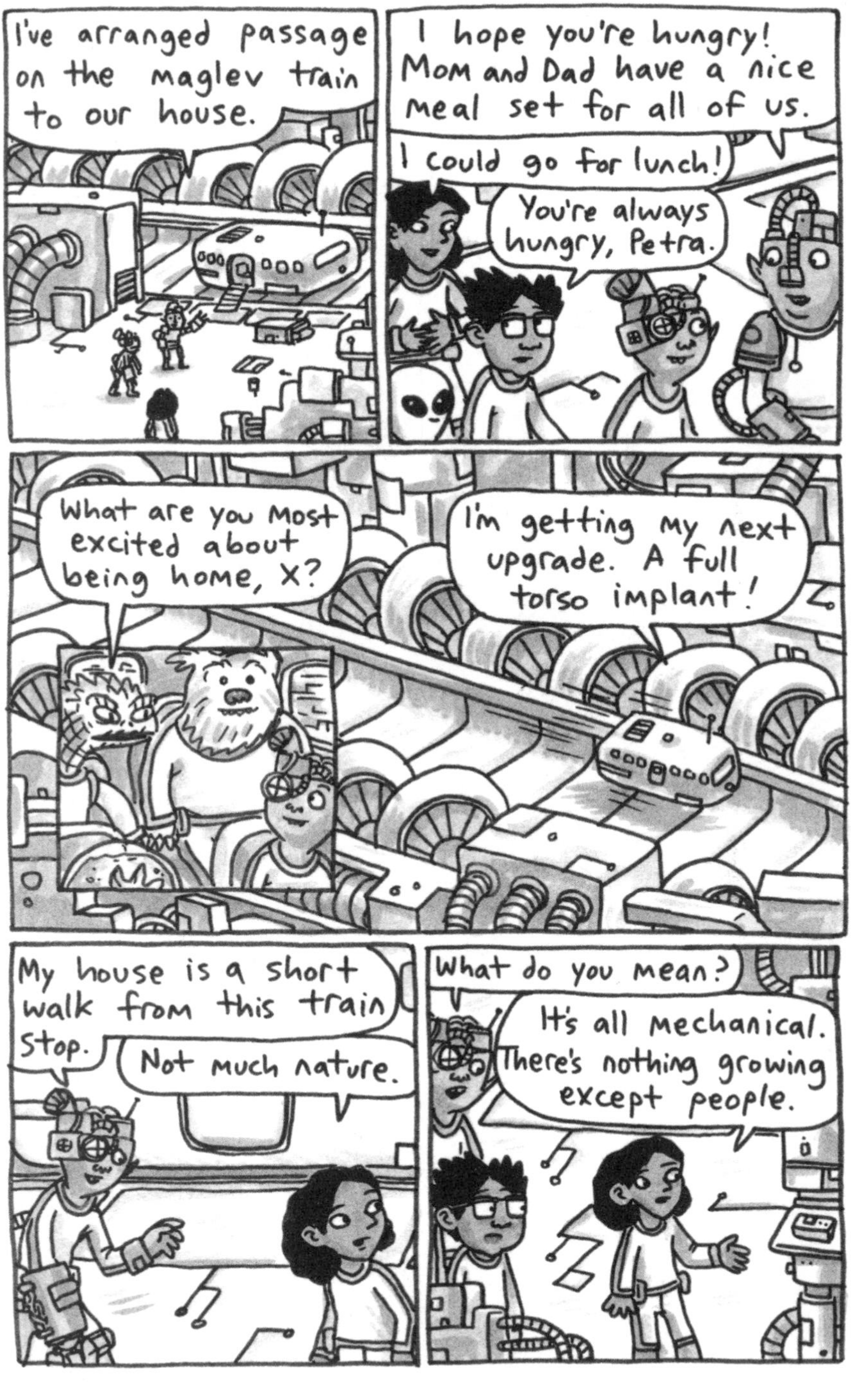
I've arranged passage on the maglev train to our house.
I hope you're hungry! Mom and Dad have a nice meal set for all of us.
I could go for lunch!
You're always hungry, Petra.
What are you most excited about being home, X?
I'm getting my next upgrade. A full torso implant!
My house is a short walk from this train stop.
Not much nature.
What do you mean?
It's all mechanical. There's nothing growing except people.

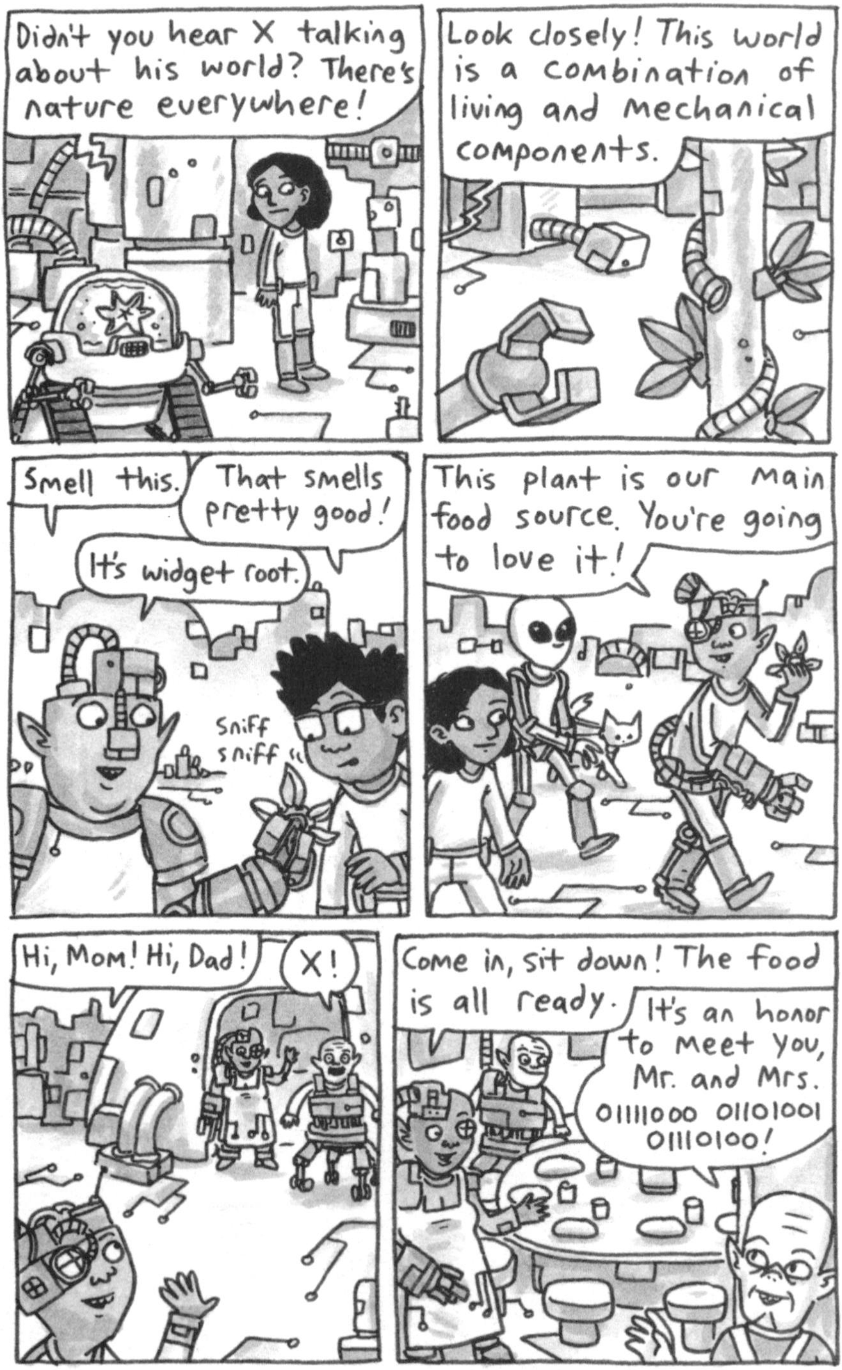
Didn't you hear X talking about his world? There's nature everywhere!
Look closely! This world is a combination of living and mechanical components.
Smell this.
That smells pretty good!
It's widget root.
Sniff sniff
This plant is our main food source. You're going to love it!
Hi, Mom! Hi, Dad!
X!
Come in, sit down! The food is all ready.
It's an honor to meet you, Mr. and Mrs. 01111000 01101001 01110100!

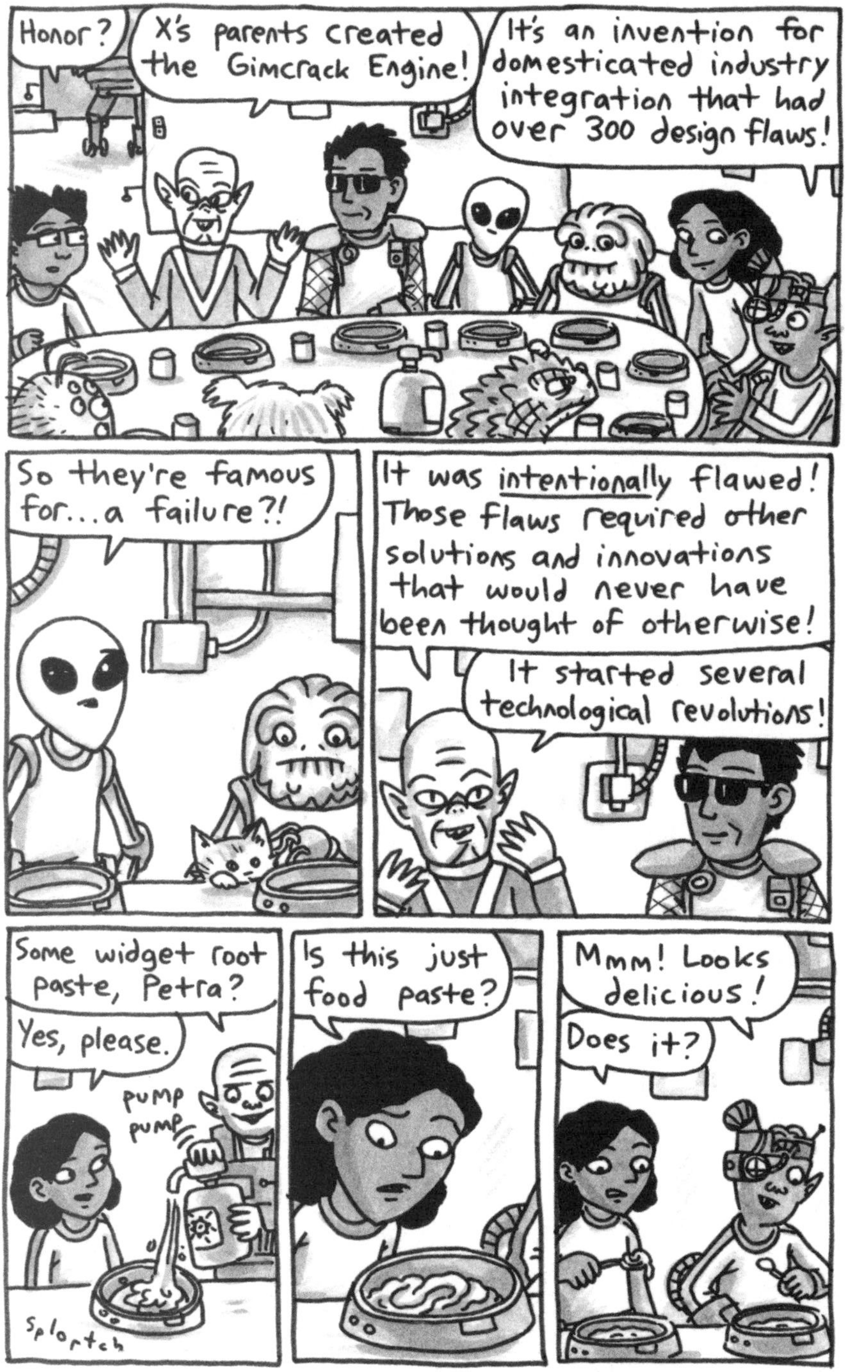
Honor?
X's parents created the Gimcrack Engine!
It's an invention for domesticated industry integration that had over 300 design flaws!
So they're famous for...a failure?!
It was intentionally flawed! Those flaws required other solutions and innovations that would never have been thought of otherwise!
It started several technological revolutions!
Some widget root paste, Petra?
Yes, please.
PUMP PUMP
SPLORTCH
Is this just food paste?
Mmm! Looks delicious!
Does it?

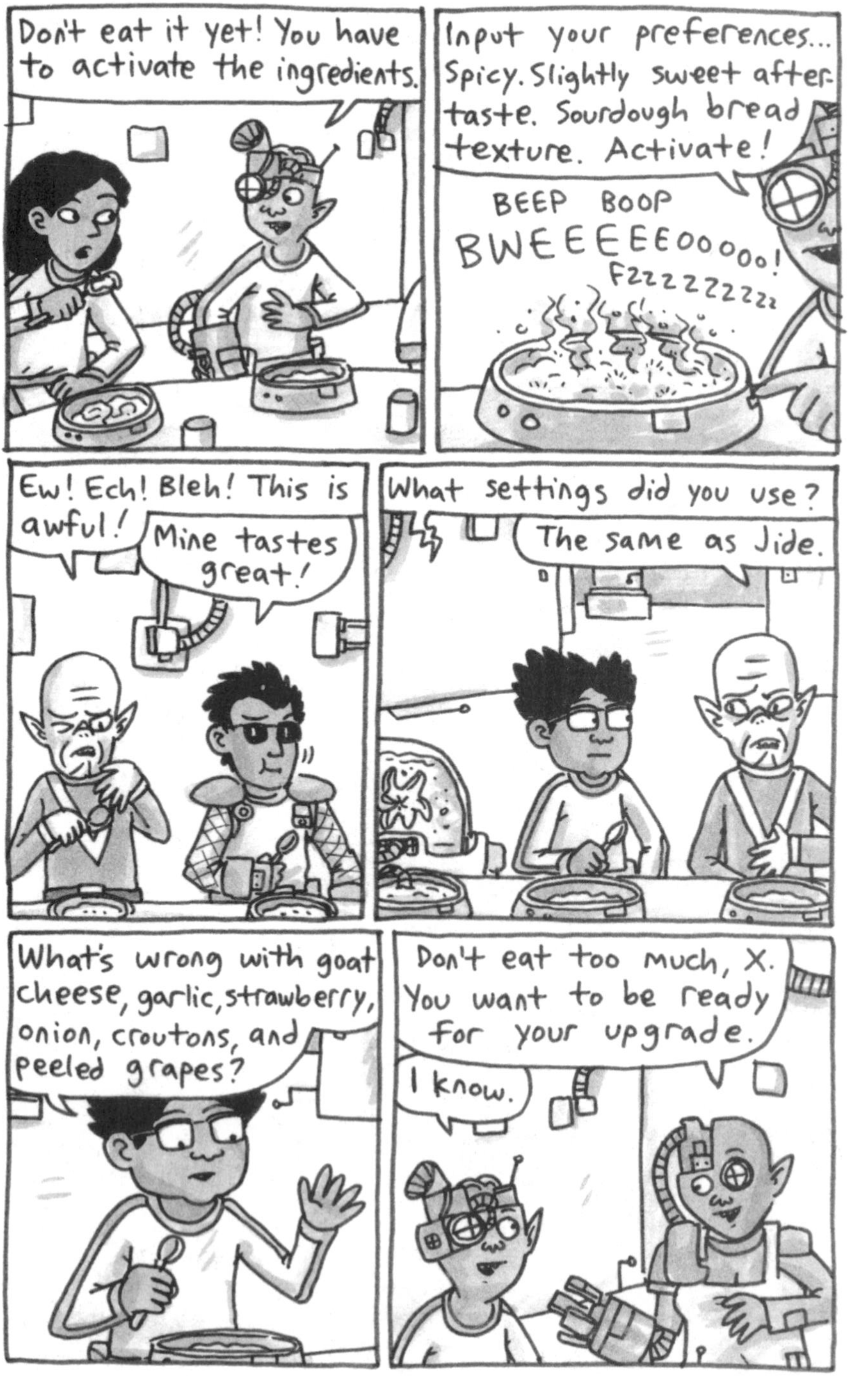
Don't eat it yet! You have to activate the ingredients.
Input your preferences... Spicy. Slightly sweet aftertaste. Sourdough bread texture. Activate!
BEEP BOOP
BWEEEEEEooooo!
Fzzzzzzzzz
Ew! Ech! Bleh! This is awful!
Mine tastes great!
What settings did you use?
The same as Jide.
What's wrong with goat cheese, garlic, strawberry, onion, croutons, and peeled grapes?
Don't eat too much, X. You want to be ready for your upgrade.
I know.

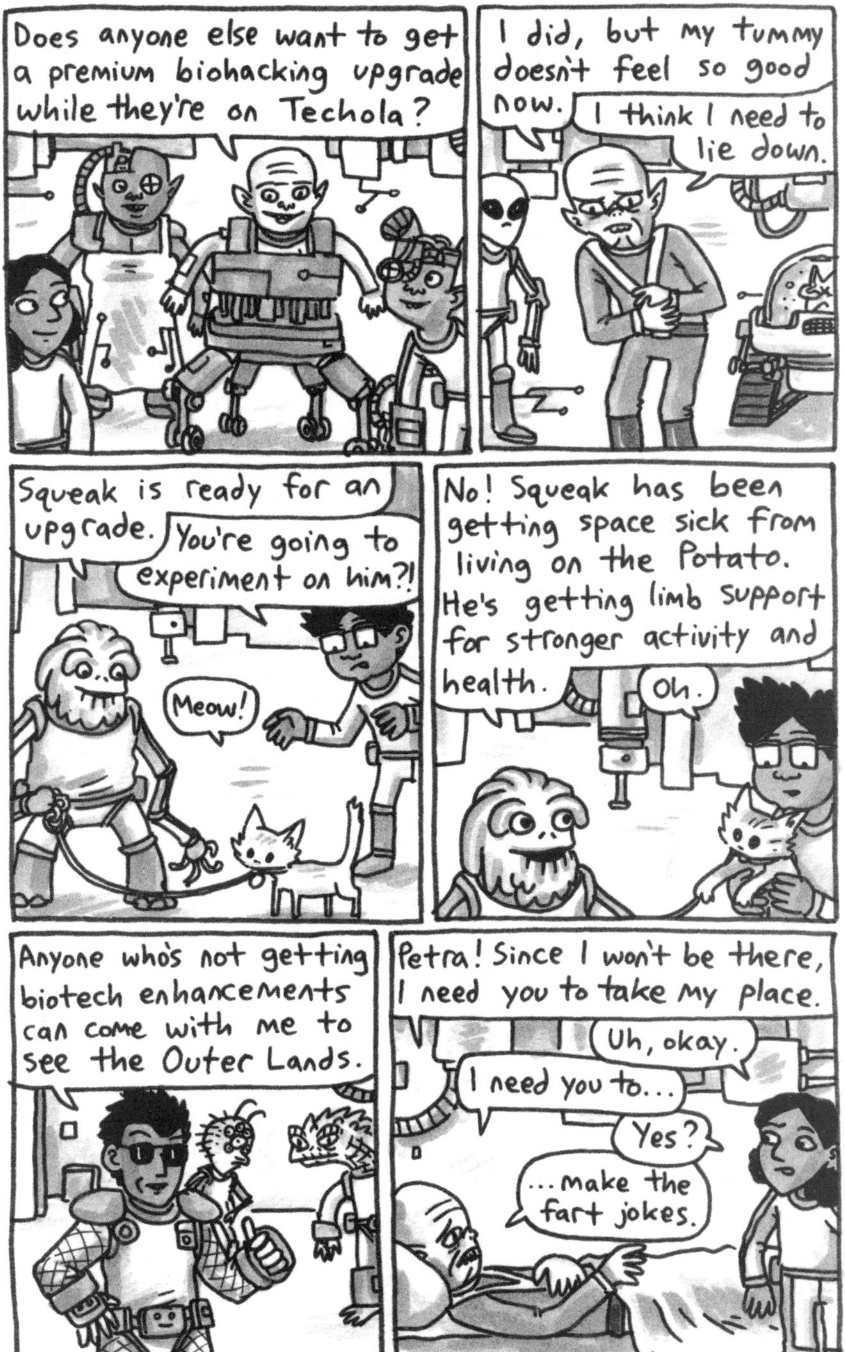
Does anyone else want to get a premium biohacking upgrade while they're on Techola?
I did, but my tummy doesn't feel so good now.
I think I need to lie down.
Squeak is ready for an upgrade.
You're going to experiment on him?!
Meow!
No! Squeak has been getting space sick from living on the Potato. He's getting limb support for stronger activity and health.
Oh.
Anyone who's not getting biotech enhancements can come with me to see the Outer Lands.
Petra! Since I won't be there, I need you to take my place.
Uh, okay.
I need you to...
Yes?
...make the fart jokes.

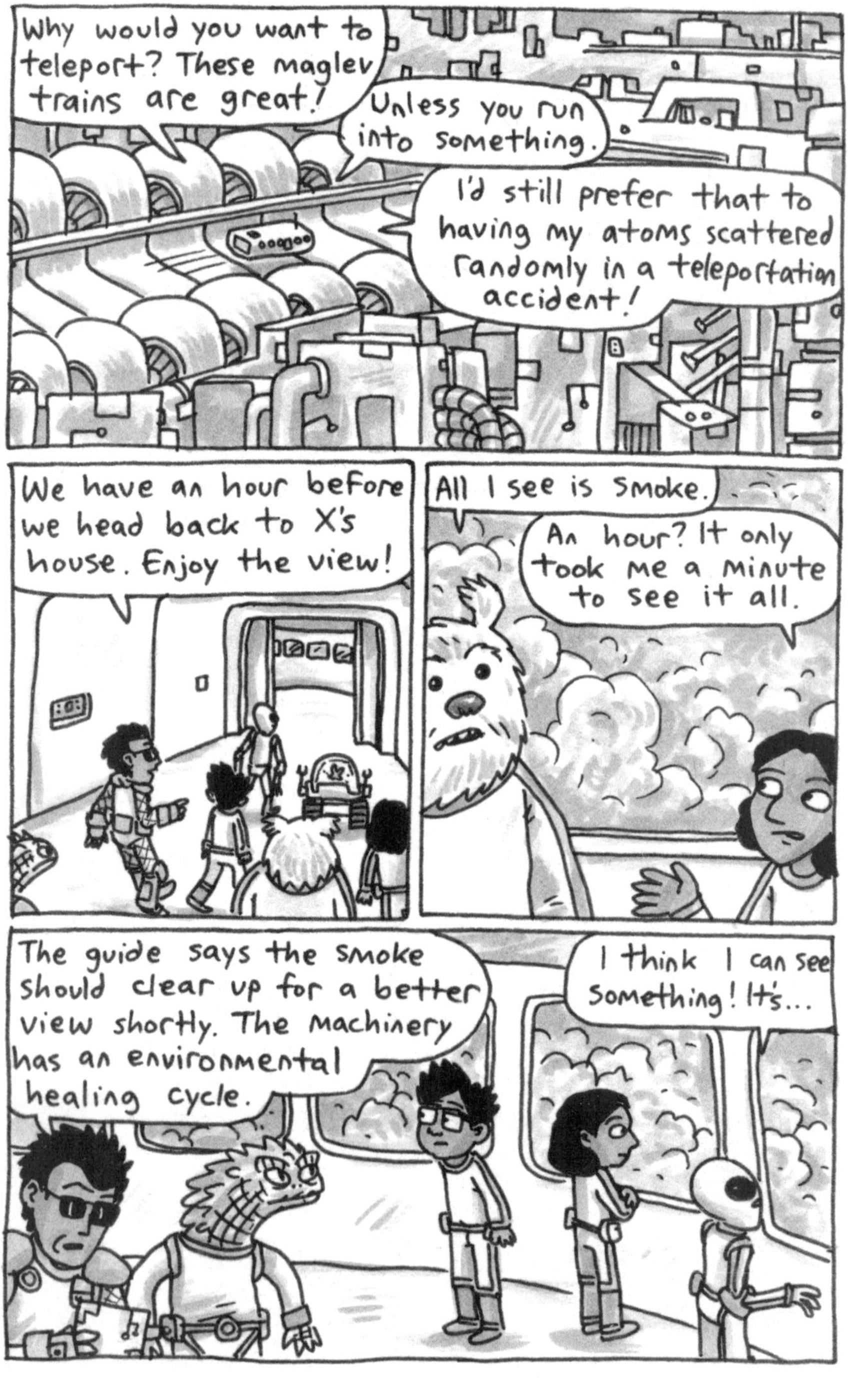
Why would you want to teleport? These maglev trains are great!
Unless you run into something.
I'd still prefer that to having my atoms scattered randomly in a teleportation accident!
We have an hour before we head back to X's house. Enjoy the view!
All I see is smoke.
An hour? It only took me a minute to see it all.
The guide says the smoke should clear up for a better view shortly. The machinery has an environmental healing cycle.
I think I can see something! It's...

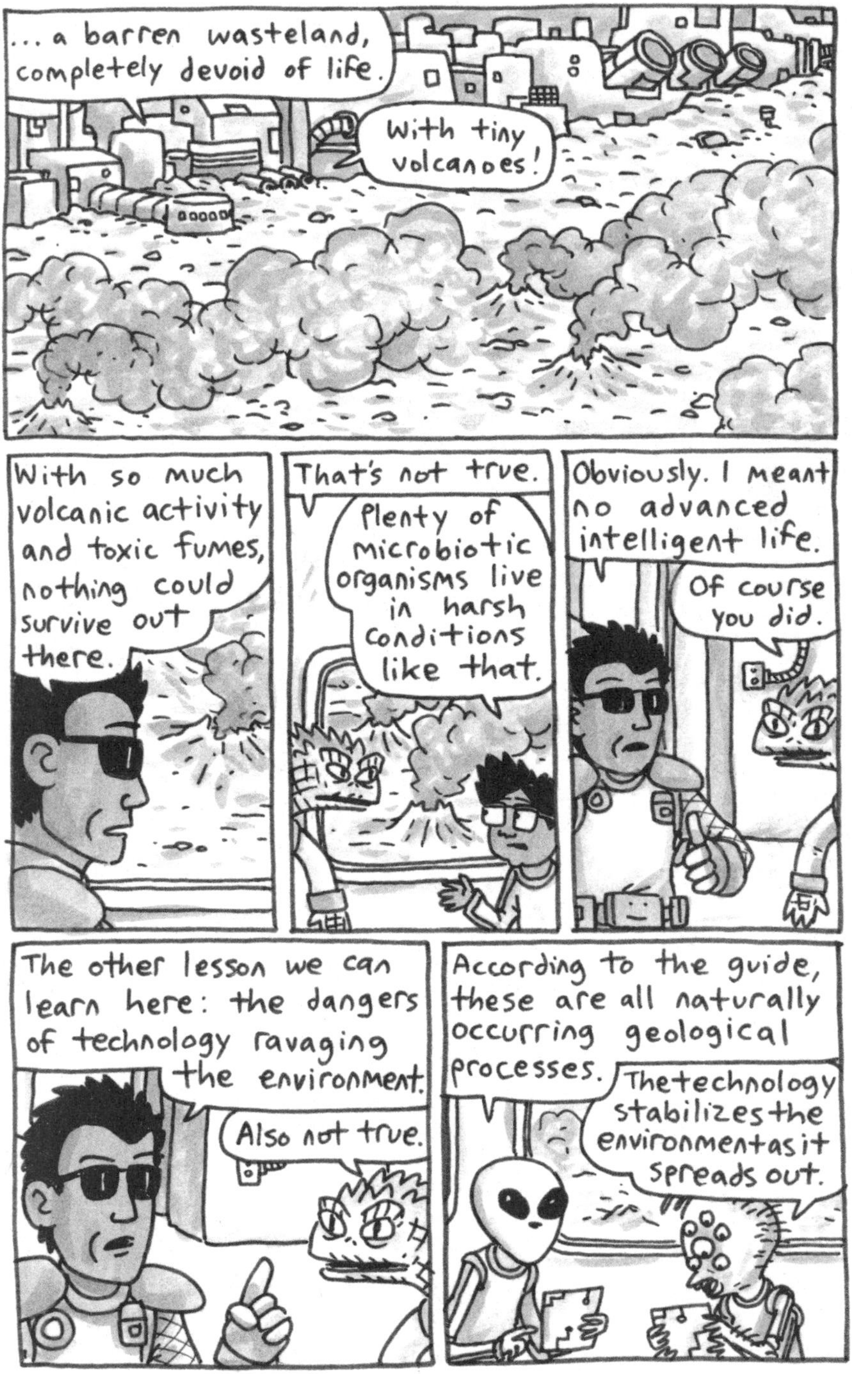
...a barren wasteland, completely devoid of life.
With tiny volcanoes!
With so much volcanic activity and toxic fumes, nothing could survive out there.
That's not true.
Plenty of microbiotic organisms live in harsh conditions like that.
Obviously. I meant no advanced intelligent life.
Of course you did.
The other lesson we can learn here: the dangers of technology ravaging the environment.
Also not true.
According to the guide, these are all naturally occurring geological processes.
The technology stabilizes the environment as it spreads out.

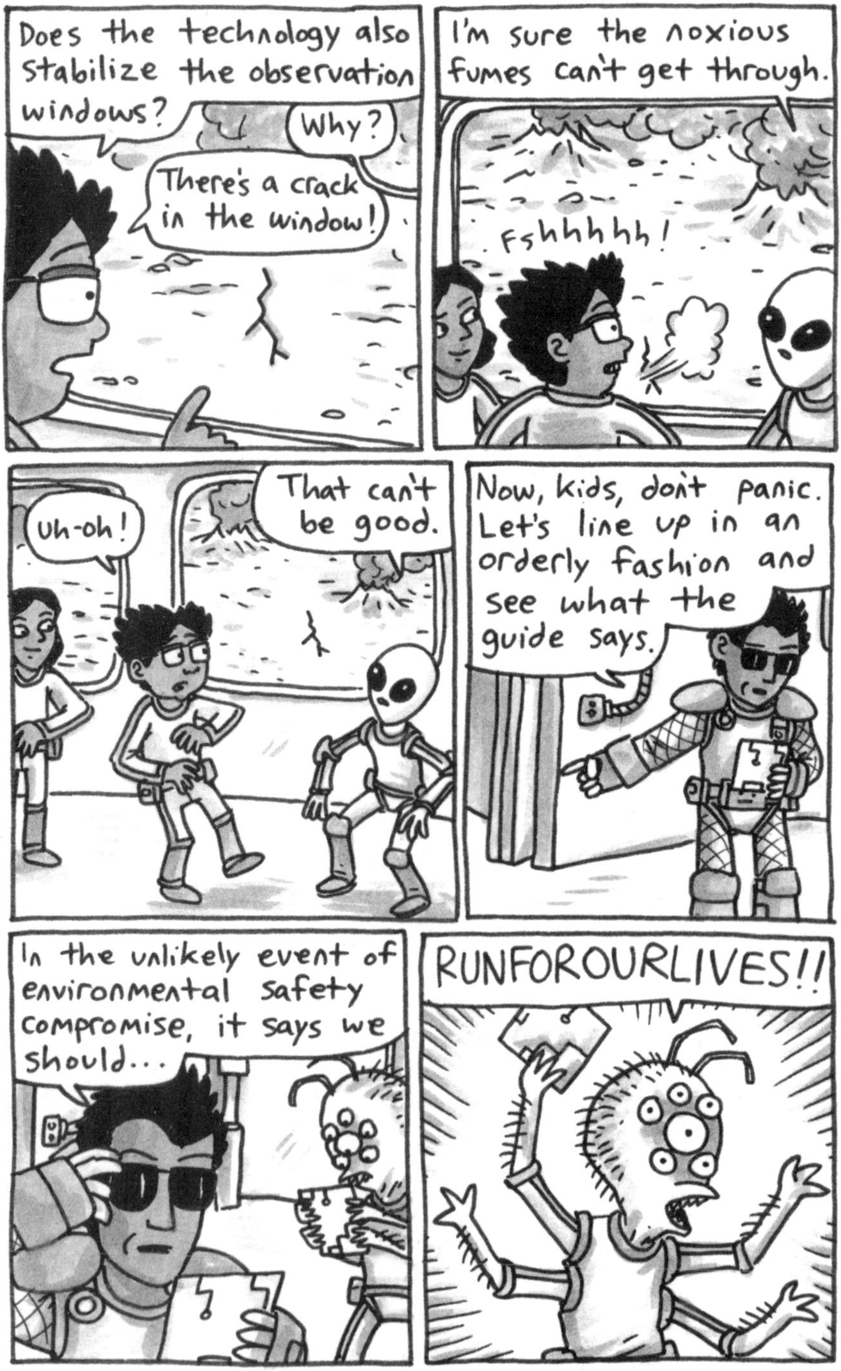
Does the technology also stabilize the observation windows?
Why?
There's a crack in the window!
I'm sure the noxious fumes can't get through.
Fshhhhh!
Uh-oh!
That can't be good.
Now, kids, don't panic. Let's line up in an orderly fashion and see what the guide says.
In the unlikely event of environmental safety compromise, it says we should...
RUNFOROURLIVES!!

Why aren't there any alarms?

It must be a catastrophic facility collapse!

Pssssshhh CLANG!

Phew!

We made it!

We're lucky you saw that, Jide!

Where's Petra?

She got left behind!

Don't worry, kids. Good thing I'm here! I'll be right back.

Ha, ha, ha!

Petra? Did the room fill up with laughing gas?!

There was no crack! Just a dry-erase marker and a water spritzer.

What?

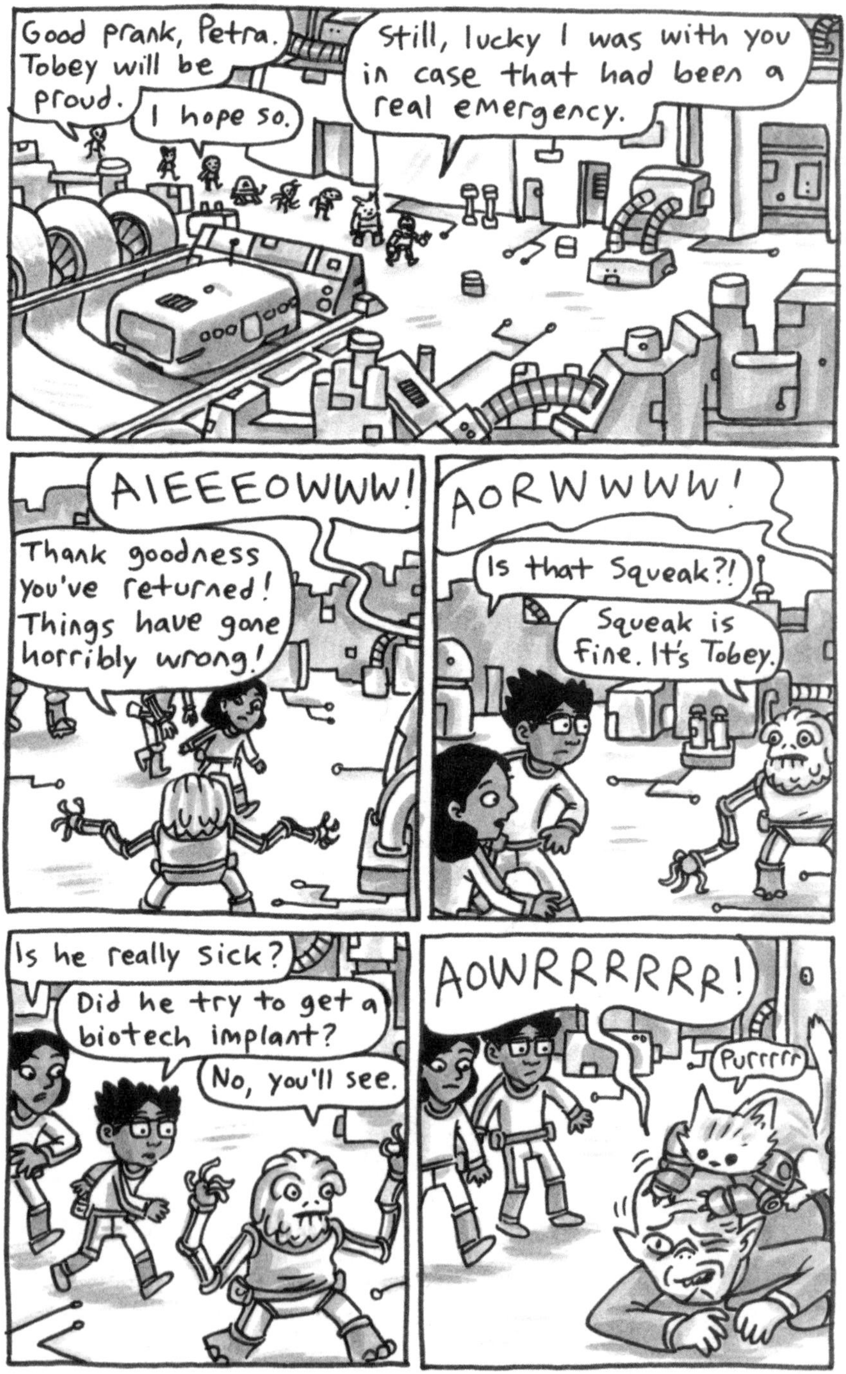
Good prank, Petra. Tobey will be proud.
I hope so.
Still, lucky I was with you in case that had been a real emergency.
AIEEEOWWW!
Thank goodness you've returned! Things have gone horribly wrong!
AORWWWW!
Is that Squeak?!
Squeak is fine. It's Tobey.
Is he really sick?
Did he try to get a biotech implant?
No, you'll see.
AOWRRRRRR!
Purrrrr

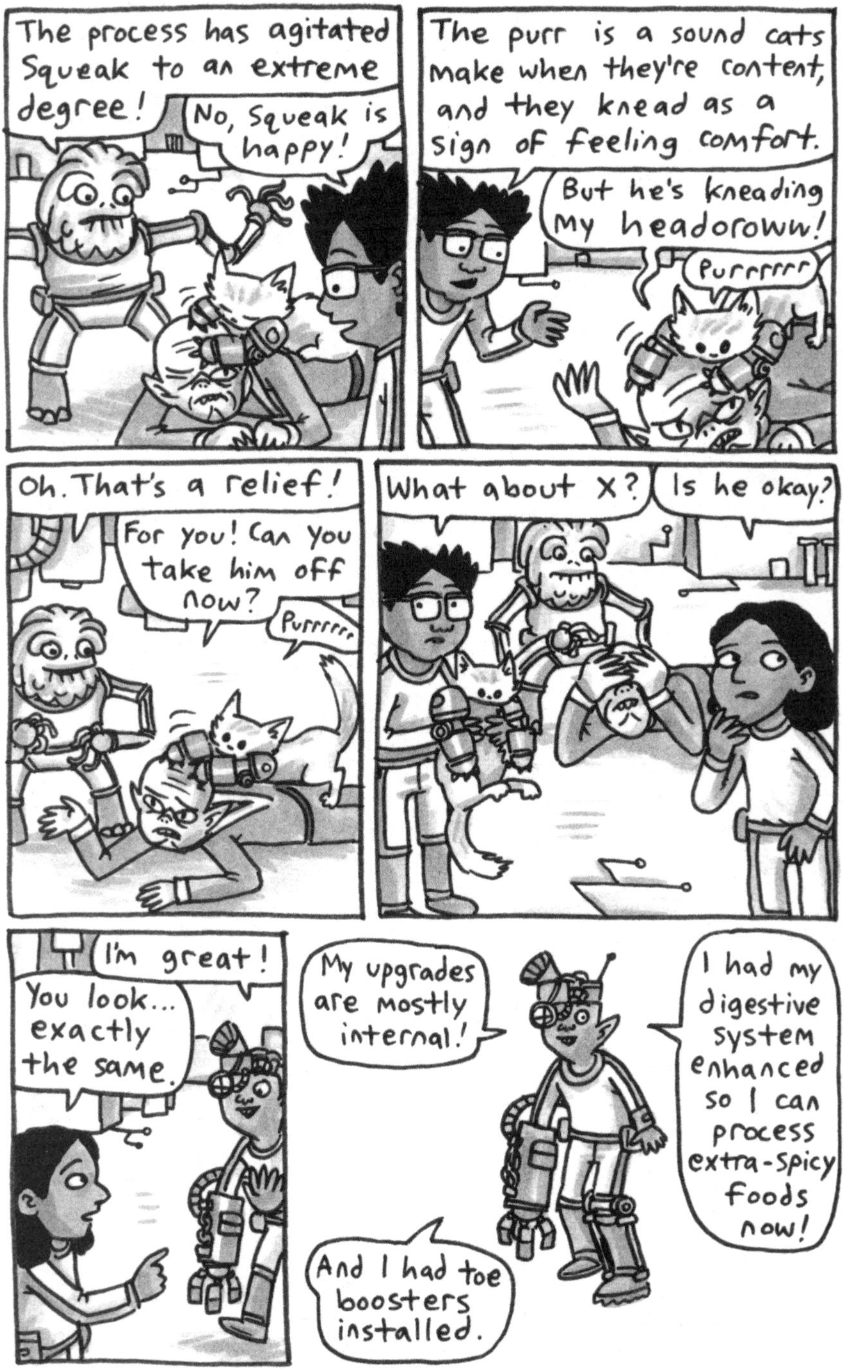
The process has agitated Squeak to an extreme degree!
No, Squeak is happy!
The purr is a sound cats make when they're content, and they knead as a sign of feeling comfort.
But he's kneading my headoroww!
Purrrrrr
Oh. That's a relief!
For you! Can you take him off now?
Purrrrrr
What about X?
Is he okay?
I'm great!
You look... exactly the same.
My upgrades are mostly internal!
I had my digestive system enhanced so I can process extra-spicy foods now!
And I had toe boosters installed.

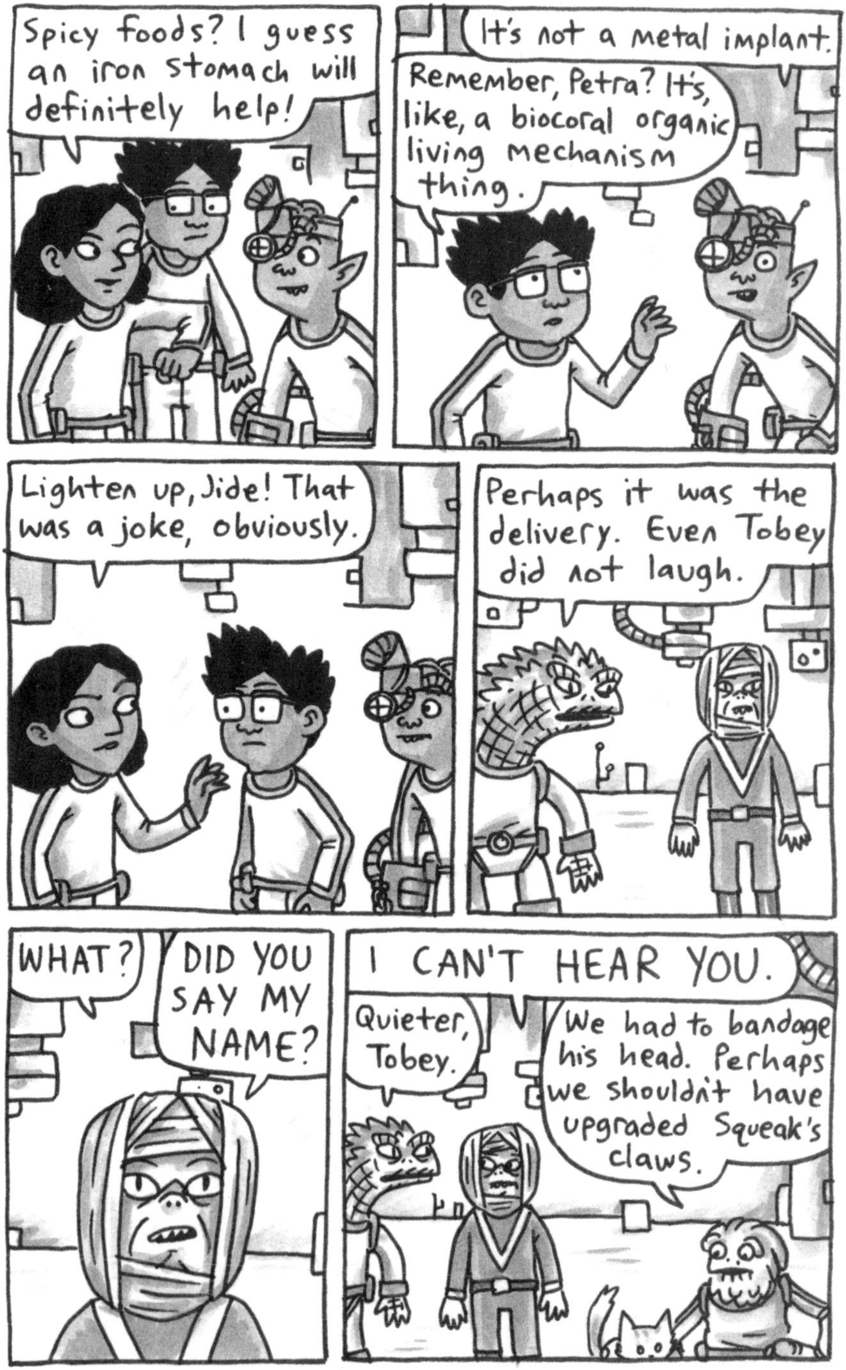
Spicy foods? I guess an iron stomach will definitely help!
It's not a metal implant.
Remember, Petra? It's, like, a biocoral organic living mechanism thing.
Lighten up, Jide! That was a joke, obviously.
Perhaps it was the delivery. Even Tobey did not laugh.
WHAT?
DID YOU SAY MY NAME?
I CAN'T HEAR YOU.
Quieter, Tobey.
We had to bandage his head. Perhaps we shouldn't have upgraded Squeak's claws.

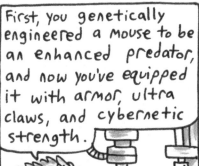

First, you genetically engineered a mouse to be an enhanced predator, and now you've equipped it with armor, ultra claws, and cybernetic strength.

When you say it like that, it sounds unsafe.

Meow.

Good thing he's on a leash!

Yes. Phew.

HE HAS FLEAS?

Let me fix this so you can hear, Tobey.

Last call for upgrades before we head back to the Potato. Anyone? No?

No, thanks.

Thanks for the upgrades, Mom and Dad!

Of course!

I think my arm is stuck again...

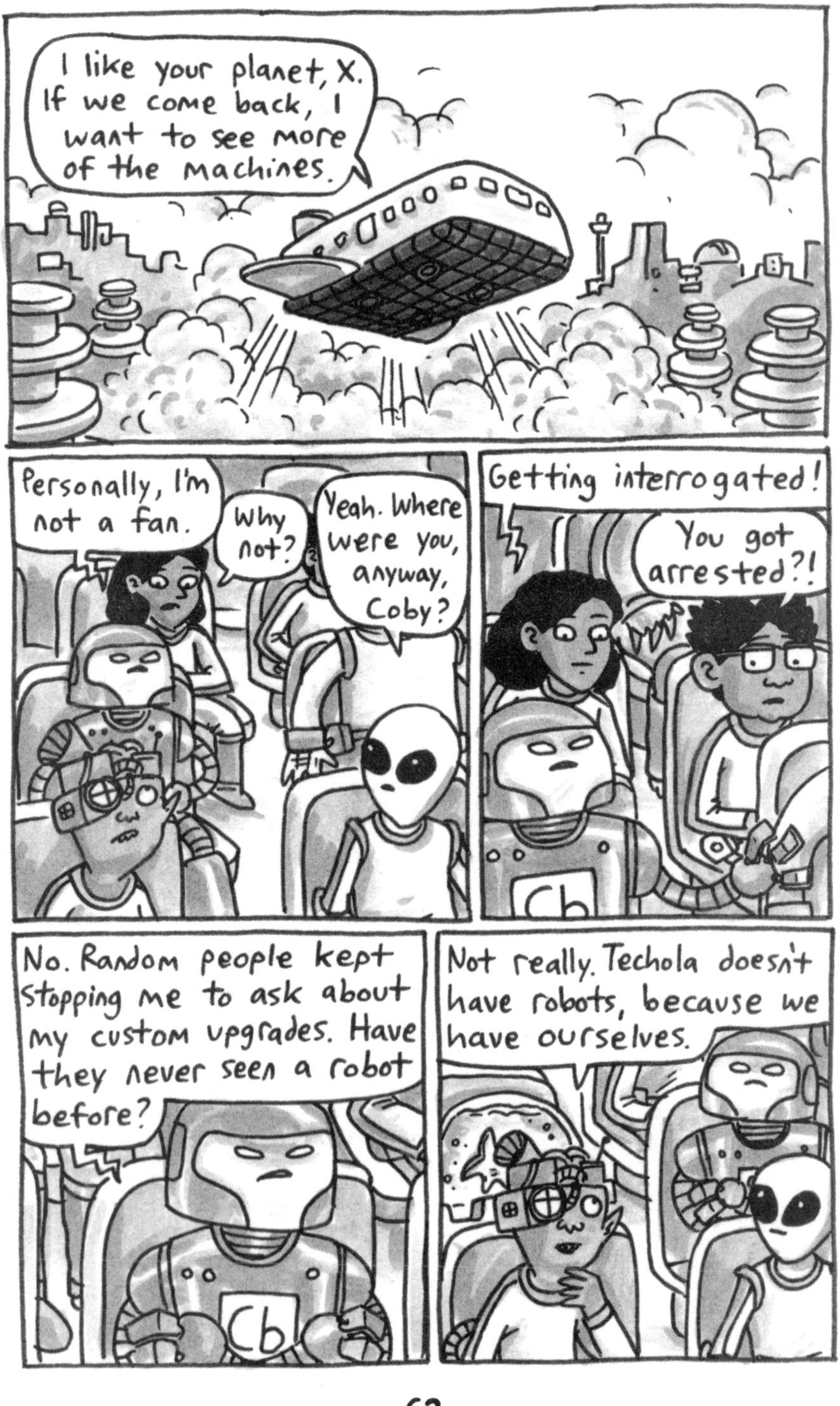
I like your planet, X. If we come back, I want to see more of the machines.
Personally, I'm not a fan.
Why not?
Yeah. Where were you, anyway, Coby?
Getting interrogated!
You got arrested?!
No. Random people kept stopping me to ask about my custom upgrades. Have they never seen a robot before?
Not really. Techola doesn't have robots, because we have ourselves.

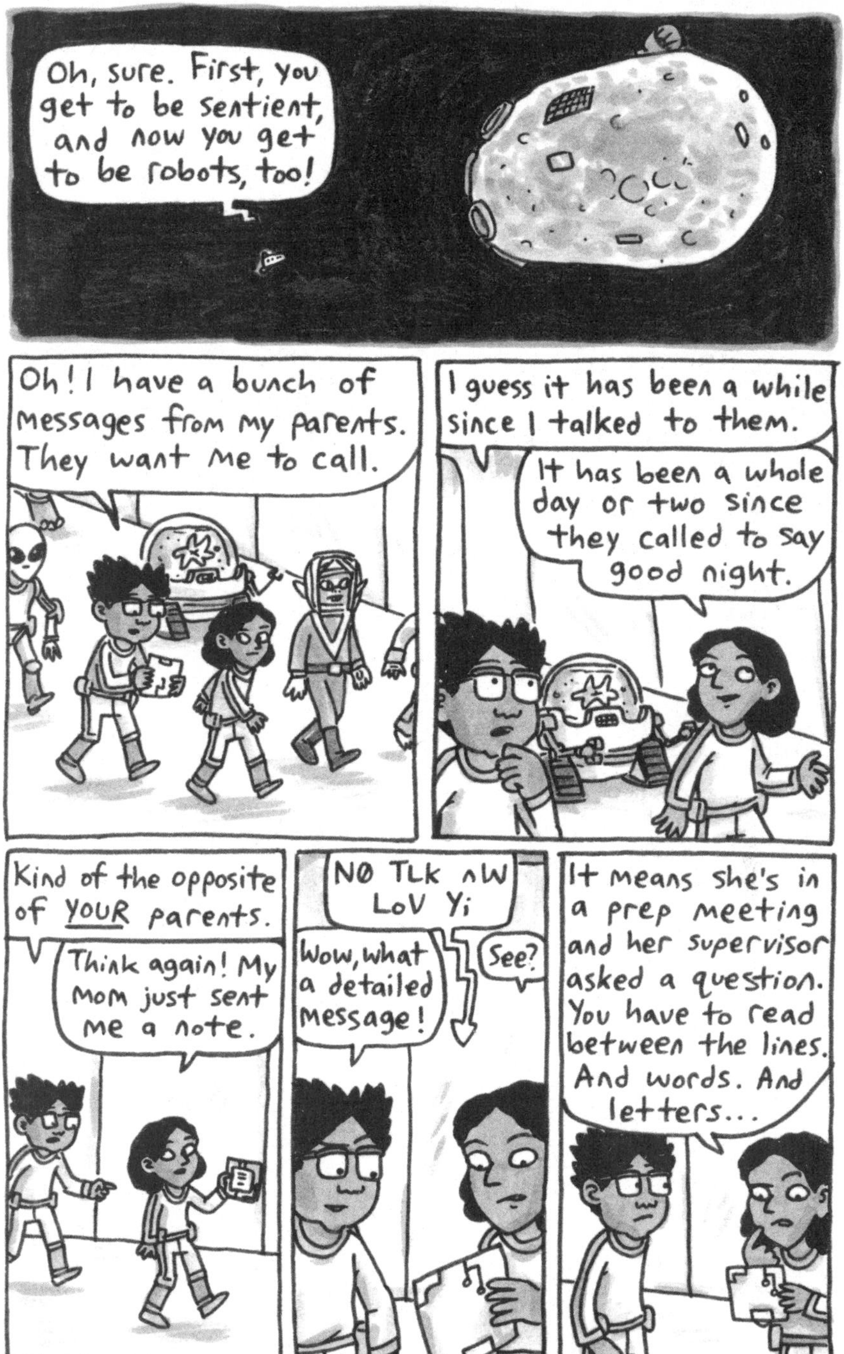
Oh, sure. First, you get to be sentient, and now you get to be robots, too!
Oh! I have a bunch of messages from my parents. They want me to call.
I guess it has been a while since I talked to them.
It has been a whole day or two since they called to say good night.
Kind of the opposite of YOUR parents.
Think again! My Mom just sent me a note.
NØ TLK nW LoV Yi
Wow, what a detailed message!
See?
It means she's in a prep meeting and her supervisor asked a question. You have to read between the lines. And words. And letters...

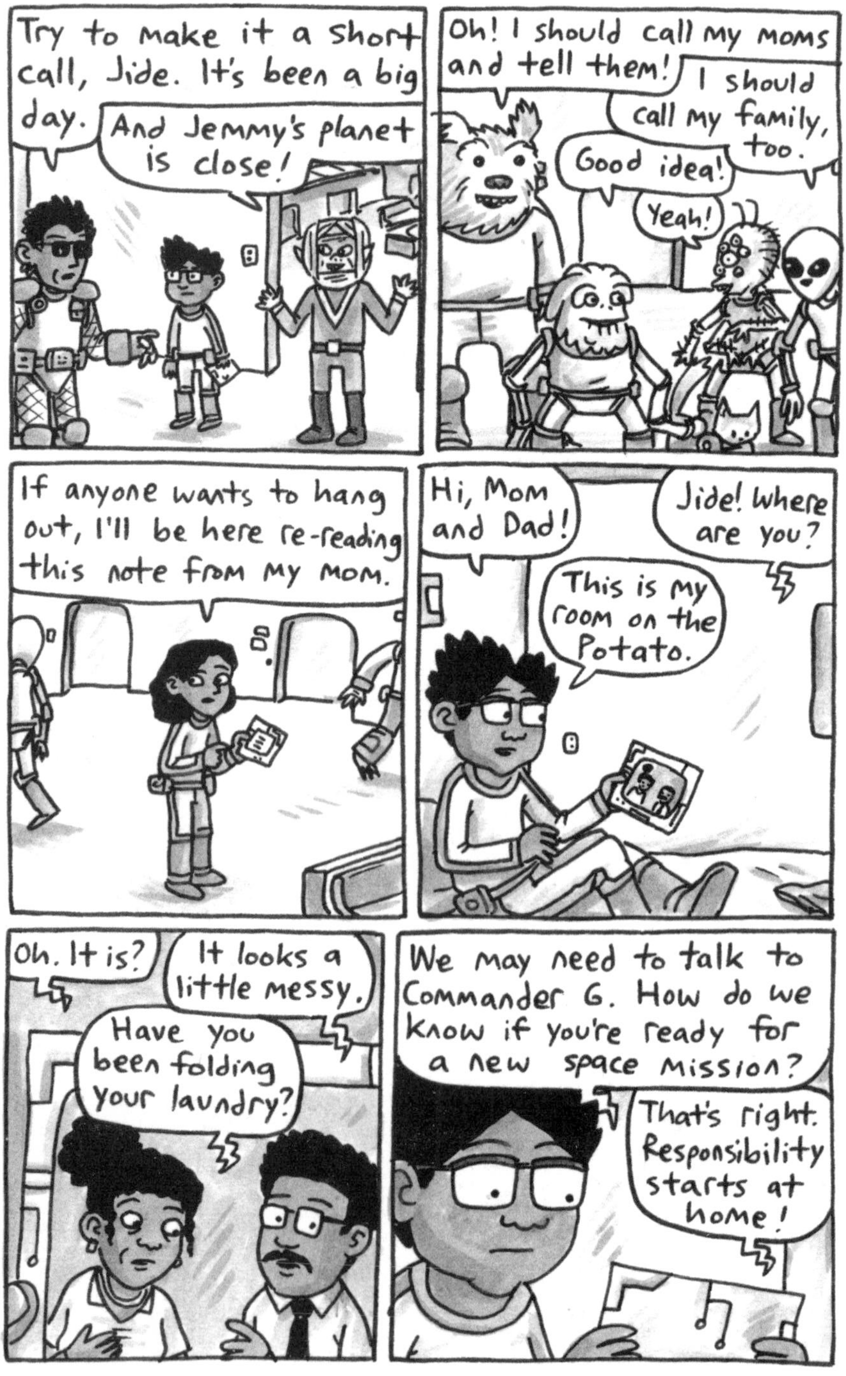
Try to make it a short call, Jide. It's been a big day.
And Jemmy's planet is close!
Oh! I should call my moms and tell them!
I should call my family, too.
Good idea!
Yeah!
If anyone wants to hang out, I'll be here re-reading this note from my mom.
Hi, Mom and Dad!
Jide! Where are you?
This is my room on the Potato.
Oh. It is?
It looks a little messy.
Have you been folding your laundry?
We may need to talk to Commander G. How do we know if you're ready for a new space mission?
That's right. Responsibility starts at home!

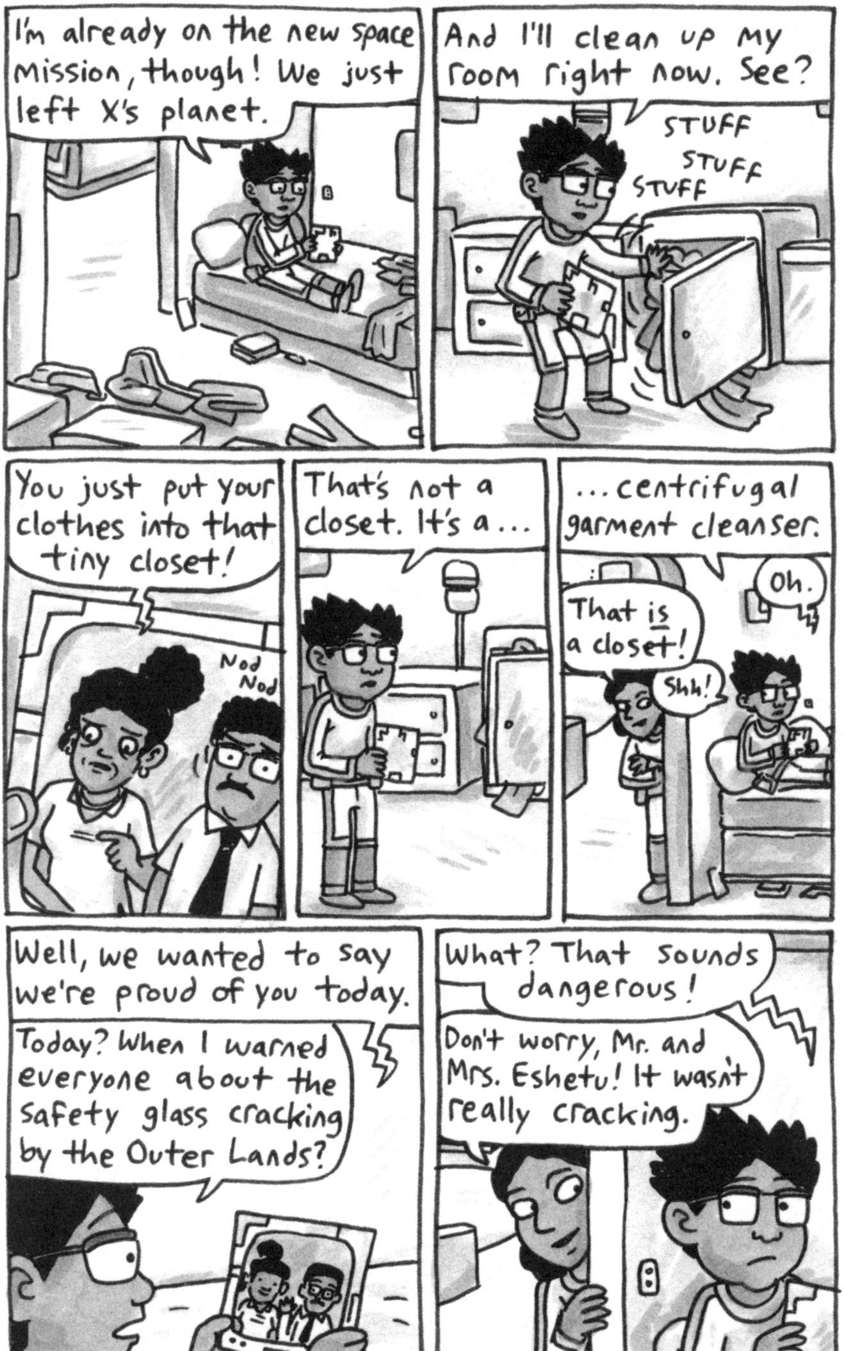
I'm already on the new space mission, though! We just left X's planet.
And I'll clean up my room right now. See?
STUFF
STUFF
STUFF
You just put your clothes into that tiny closet!
Nod
Nod
That's not a closet. It's a...
...centrifugal garment cleanser.
That is a closet!
Shh!
Oh.
Well, we wanted to say we're proud of you today.
Today? When I warned everyone about the safety glass cracking by the Outer Lands?
What? That sounds dangerous!
Don't worry, Mr. and Mrs. Eshetu! It wasn't really cracking.

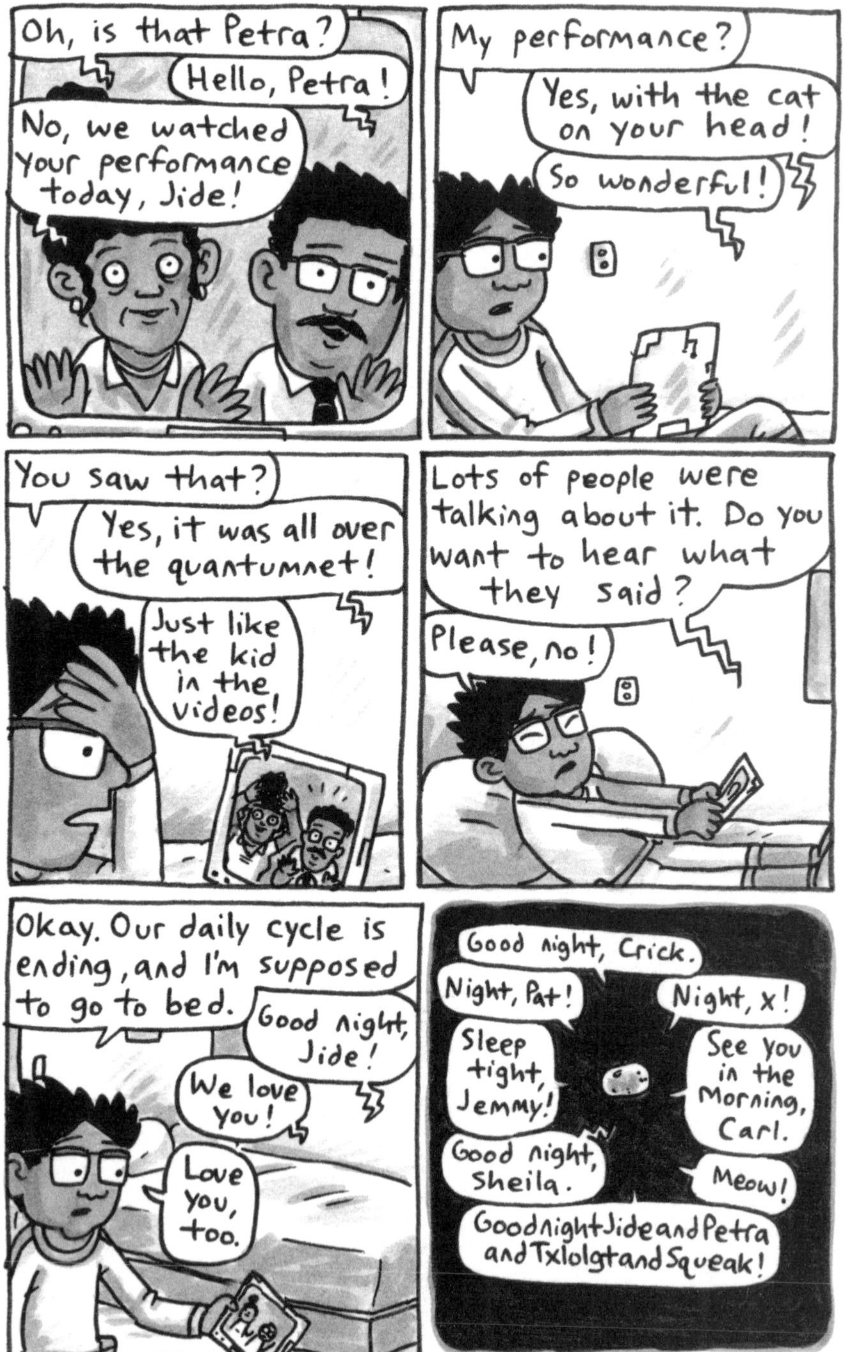
Oh, is that Petra?
Hello, Petra!
No, we watched your performance today, Jide!
My performance?
Yes, with the cat on your head!
So wonderful!
You saw that?
Yes, it was all over the quantumnet!
Just like the kid in the videos!
Lots of people were talking about it. Do you want to hear what they said?
Please, no!
Okay. Our daily cycle is ending, and I'm supposed to go to bed.
Good night, Jide!
We love you!
Love you, too.
Good night, Crick.
Night, Pat!
Night, x!
Sleep tight, Jemmy!
See you in the Morning, Carl.
Good night, Sheila.
Meow!
GoodnightJideandPetra andTxlolgtandSqueak!

LIVING LARGE

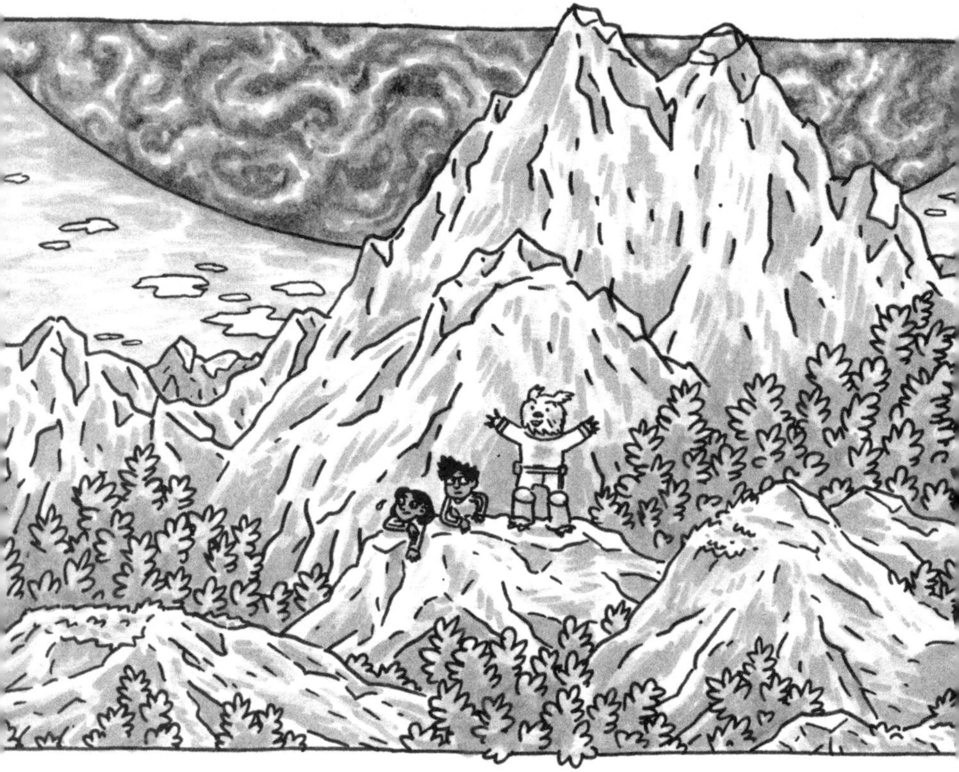

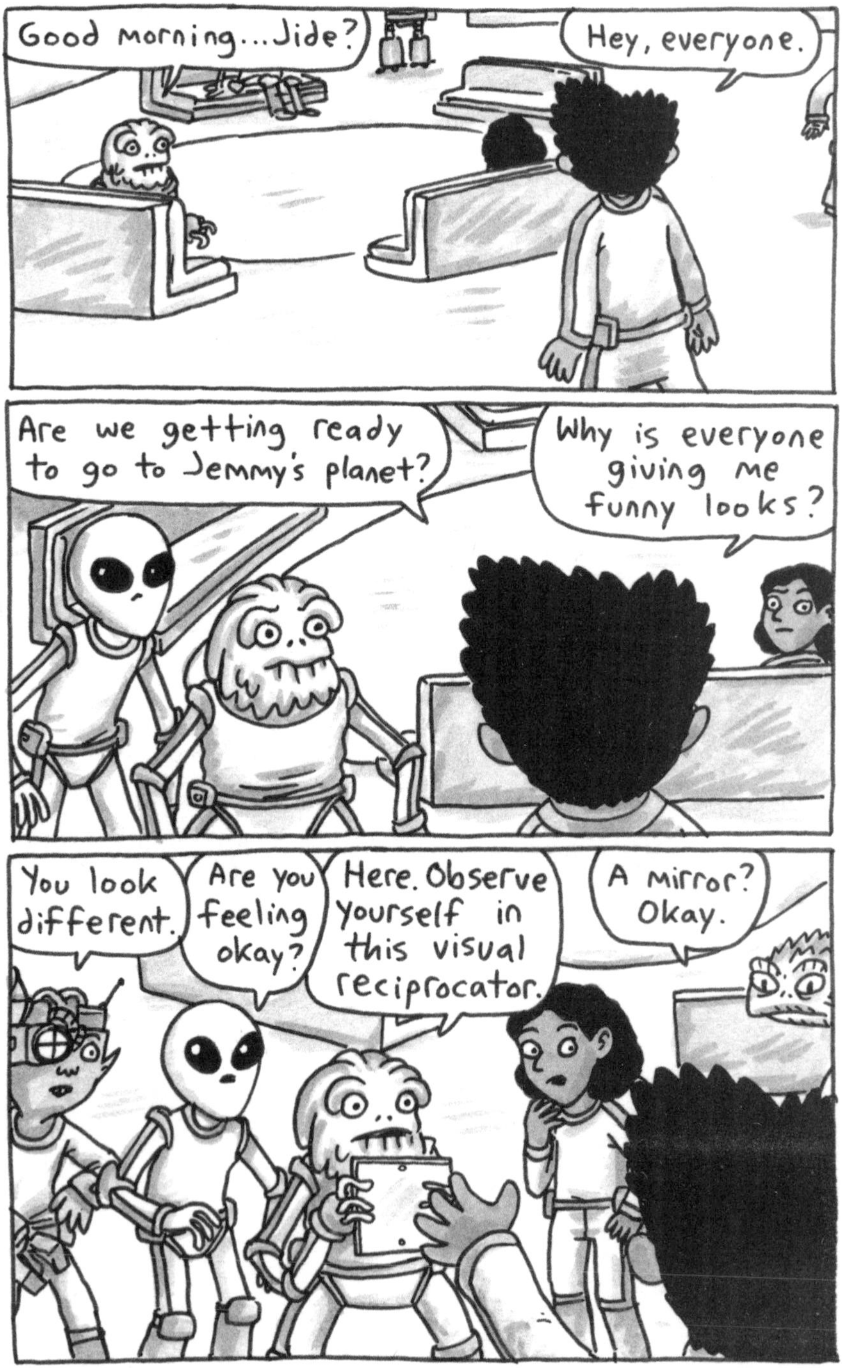
Good morning...Jide?
Hey, everyone.
Are we getting ready to go to Jemmy's planet?
Why is everyone giving me funny looks?
You look different.
Are you feeling okay?
Here. Observe yourself in this visual reciprocator.
A mirror? Okay.

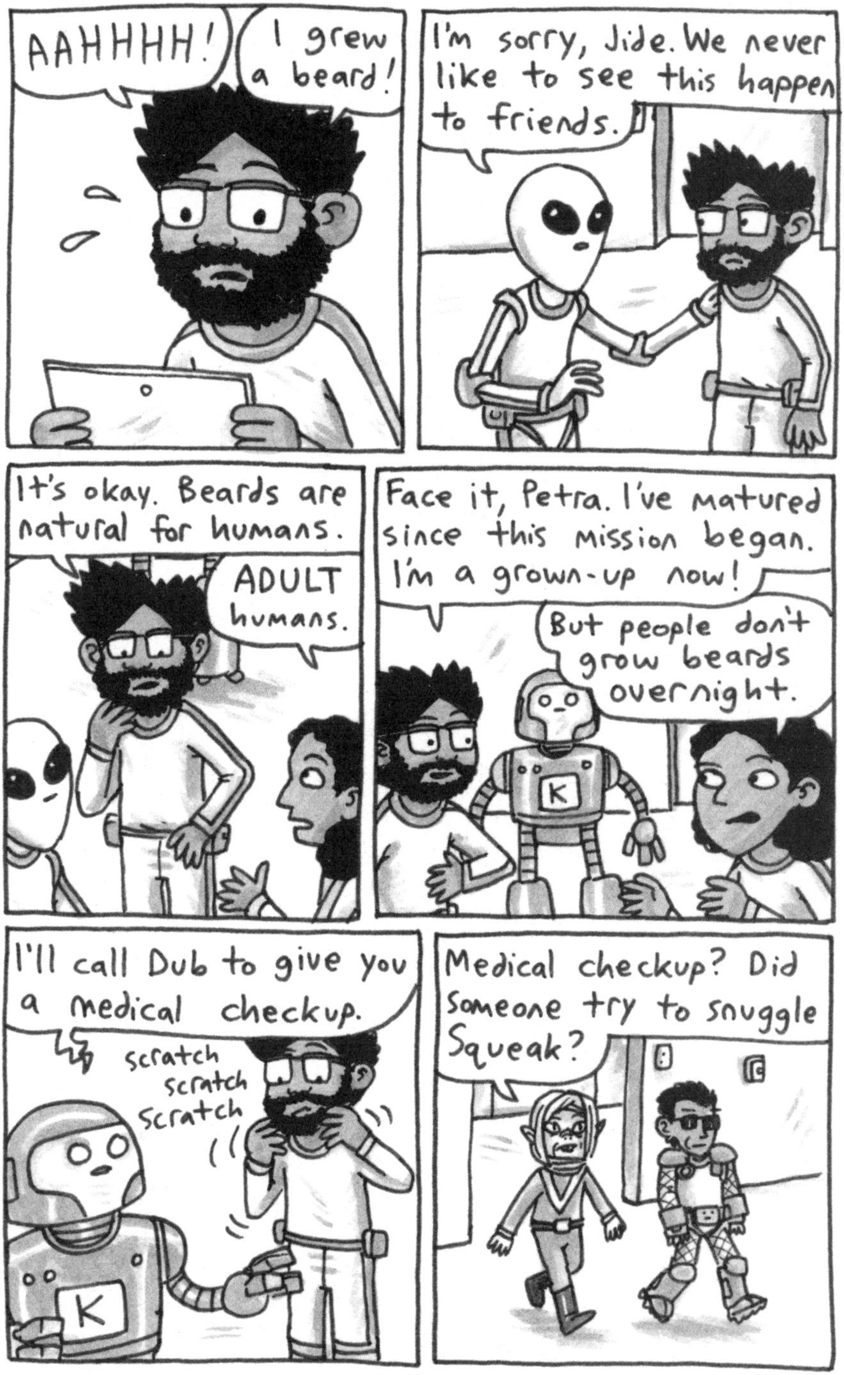
AAHHHH!
I grew a beard!
I'm sorry, Jide. We never like to see this happen to friends.
It's okay. Beards are natural for humans.
ADULT humans.
Face it, Petra. I've matured since this mission began. I'm a grown-up now!
But people don't grow beards overnight.
I'll call Dub to give you a medical checkup.
scratch scratch scratch
Medical checkup? Did someone try to snuggle Squeak?

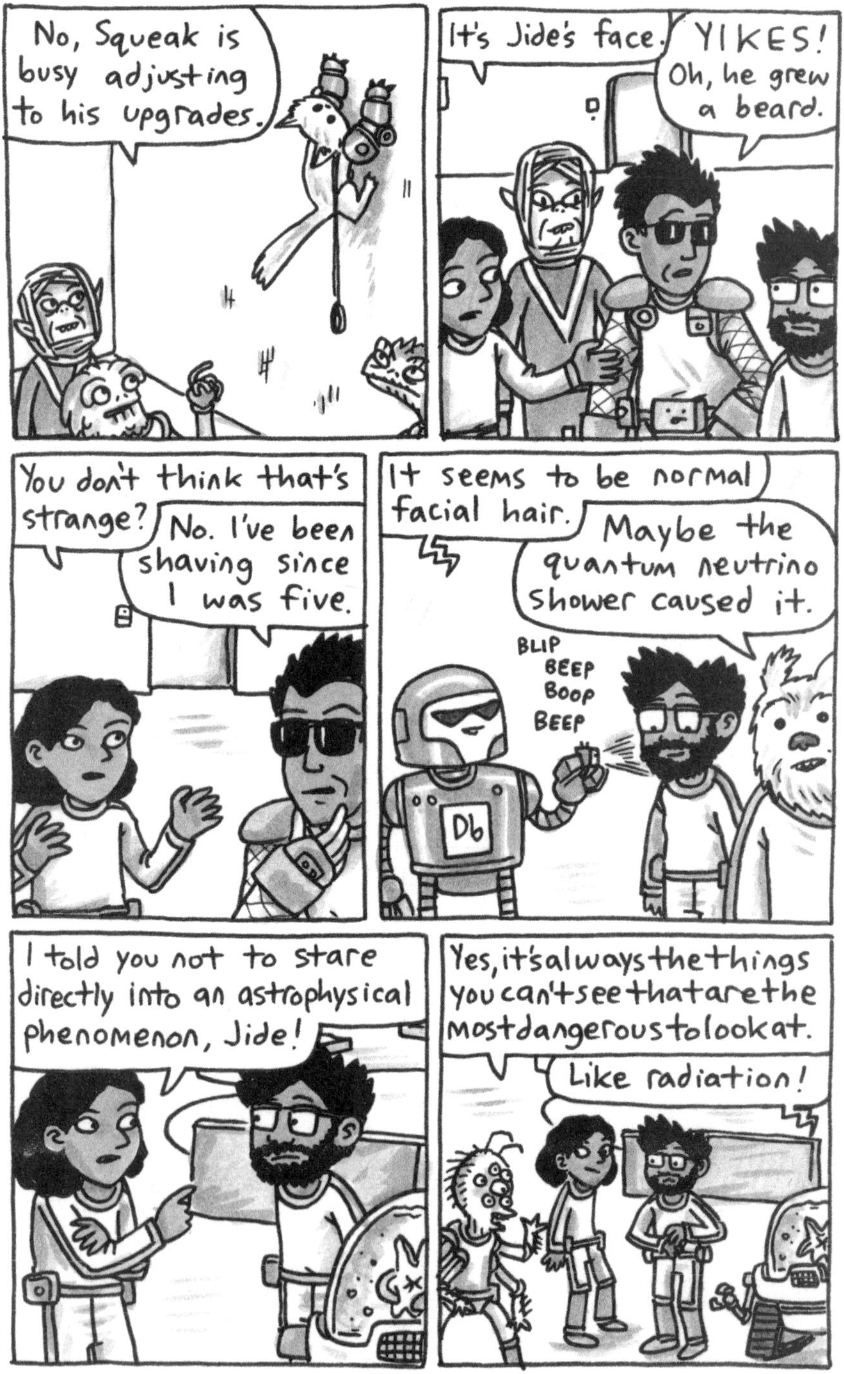
No, Squeak is busy adjusting to his upgrades.
It's Jide's face.
YIKES! Oh, he grew a beard.
You don't think that's strange?
No. I've been shaving since I was five.
It seems to be normal facial hair.
Maybe the quantum neutrino shower caused it.
BLIP BEEP BOOP BEEP
I told you not to stare directly into an astrophysical phenomenon, Jide!
Yes, it's always the things you can't see that are the most dangerous to look at.
Like radiation!

Don't worry. All of Jide's vital signs are perfectly healthy. Except he needs to floss more.

So, everyone is clear to visit Jemmy's planet. We need to suit up first, though.

No problem!

Already done!

CLICK!
ZIP!
ZIP!
CLICK!
ZIP!
ZIP!
ZIP!
CLICK!

What? Mad that I beat your speed record?

You didn't. I'm already wearing my space suit.

That isn't the suit you need. Jemmy's planet has very strong gravity, so you have to wear an exosuit.

THE EXOSUITS HAVE FIBER-BUNDLE MUSCLE AMPLIFIERS THAT WILL ENABLE NORMAL MOVEMENT, AND SKELETAL SUPPORT SO YOU DON'T FOLD IN HALF LIKE ORIGAMI!

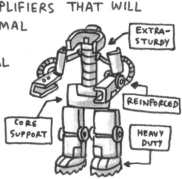

EXTRA-STURDY

REINFORCED

CORE SUPPORT

HEAVY DUTY

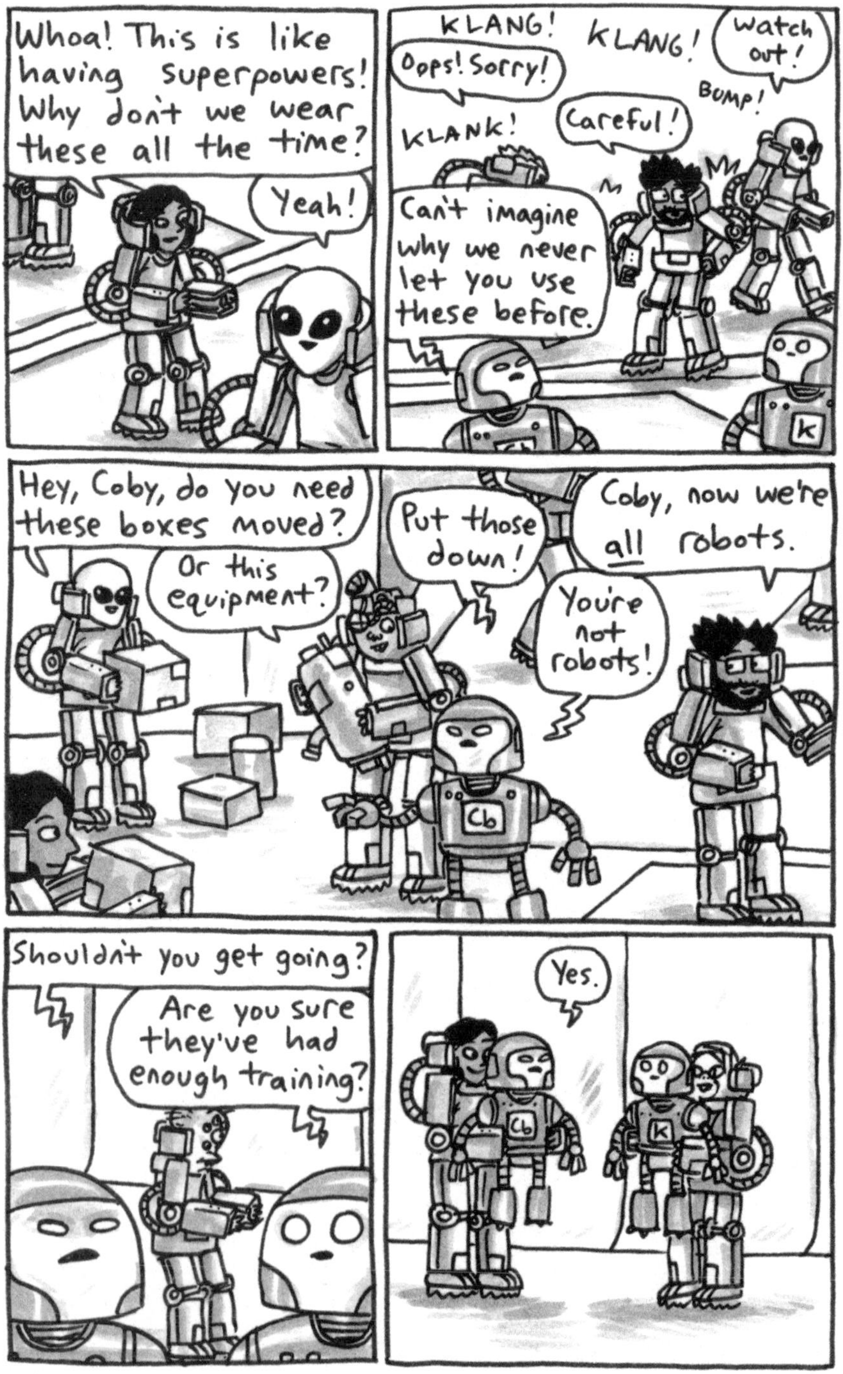
Whoa! This is like having superpowers! Why don't we wear these all the time?
Yeah!
KLANG!
Oops! Sorry!
KLANG!
Watch out!
BUMP!
KLANK!
Careful!
Can't imagine why we never let you use these before.
Hey, Coby, do you need these boxes moved?
Or this equipment?
Put those down!
Coby, now we're all robots.
You're not robots!
Shouldn't you get going?
Are you sure they've had enough training?
Yes.

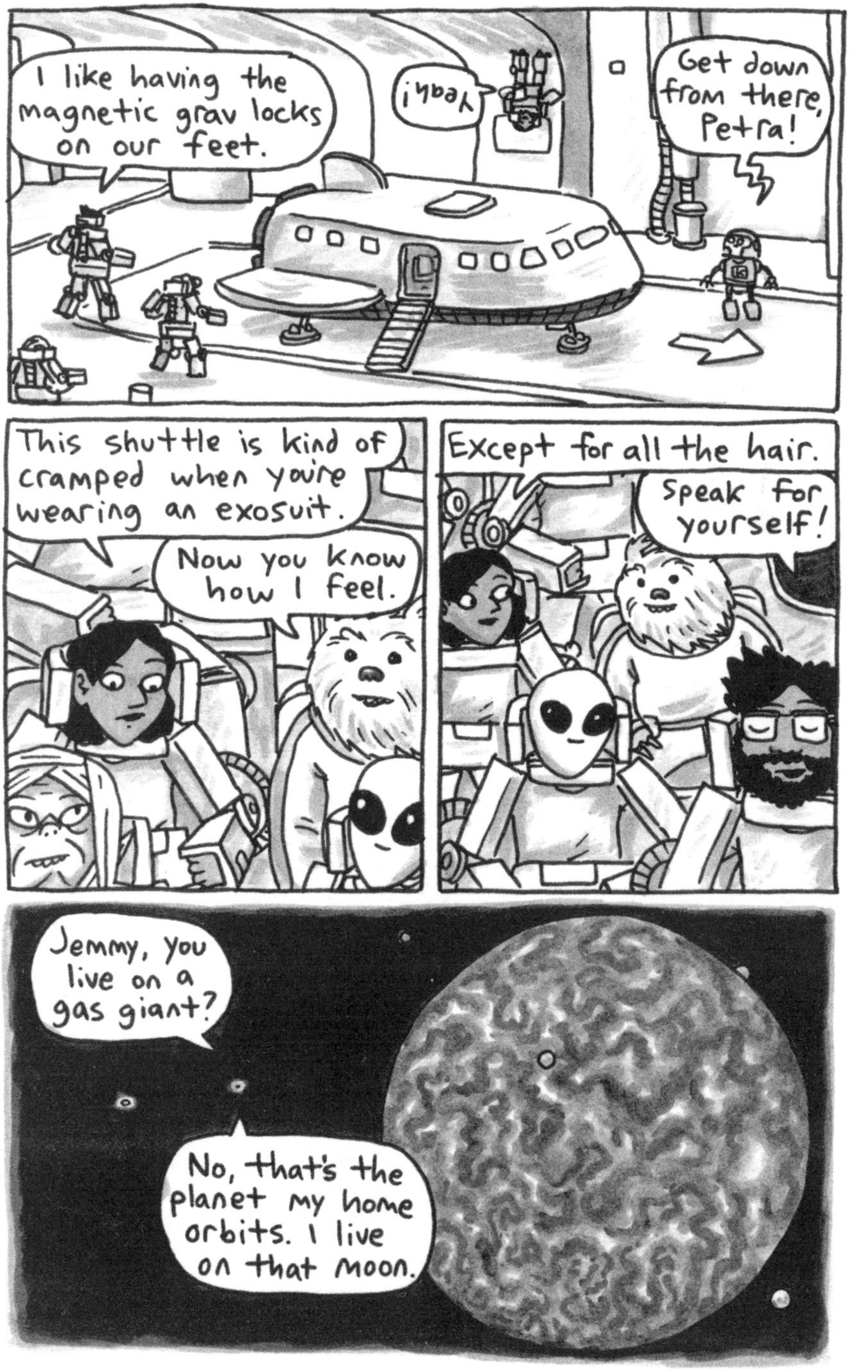
I like having the magnetic grav locks on our feet.
Yeah!
Get down from there, Petra!
This shuttle is kind of cramped when you're wearing an exosuit.
Now you know how I feel.
Except for all the hair.
Speak for yourself!
Jemmy, you live on a gas giant?
No, that's the planet my home orbits. I live on that moon.

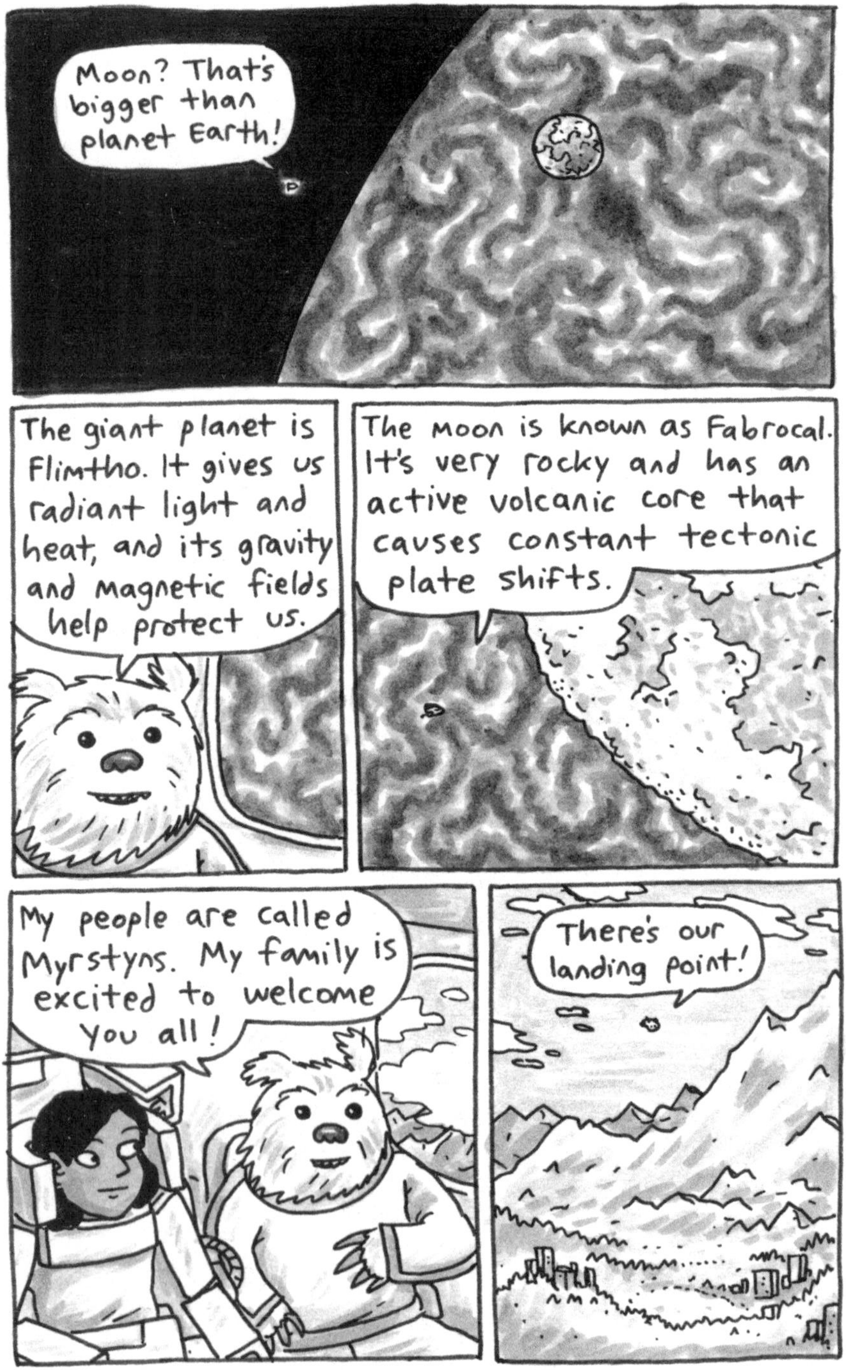
Moon? That's bigger than planet Earth!
The giant planet is Flimtho. It gives us radiant light and heat, and its gravity and magnetic fields help protect us.
The moon is known as Fabrocal. It's very rocky and has an active volcanic core that causes constant tectonic plate shifts.
My people are called Myrstyns. My family is excited to welcome you all!
There's our landing point!

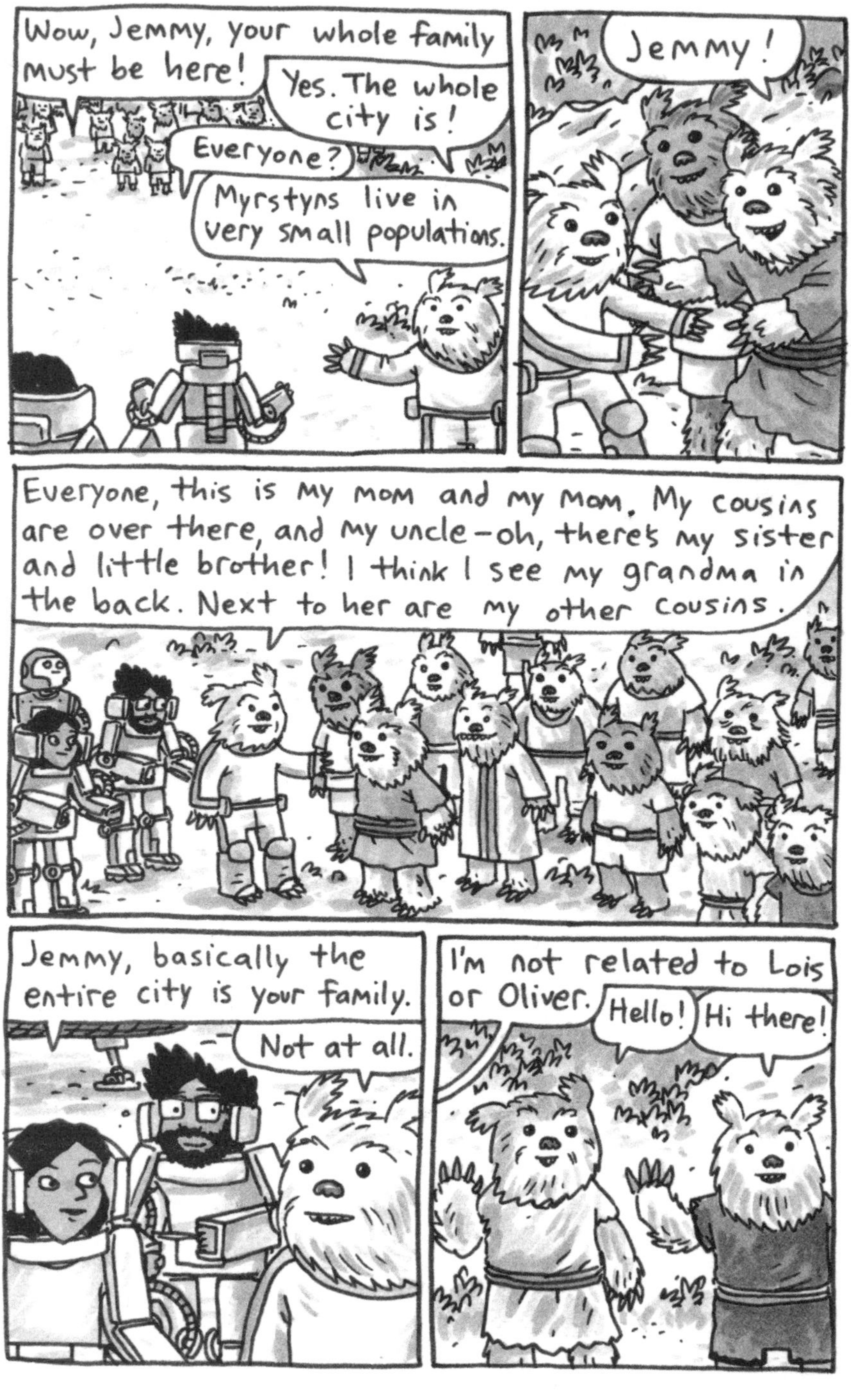
Wow, Jemmy, your whole family must be here!
Yes. The whole city is!
Everyone?
Myrstyns live in very small populations.
Jemmy!
Everyone, this is my mom and my mom. My cousins are over there, and my uncle—oh, there's my sister and little brother! I think I see my grandma in the back. Next to her are my other cousins.
Jemmy, basically the entire city is your family.
Not at all.
I'm not related to Lois or Oliver.
Hello!
Hi there!

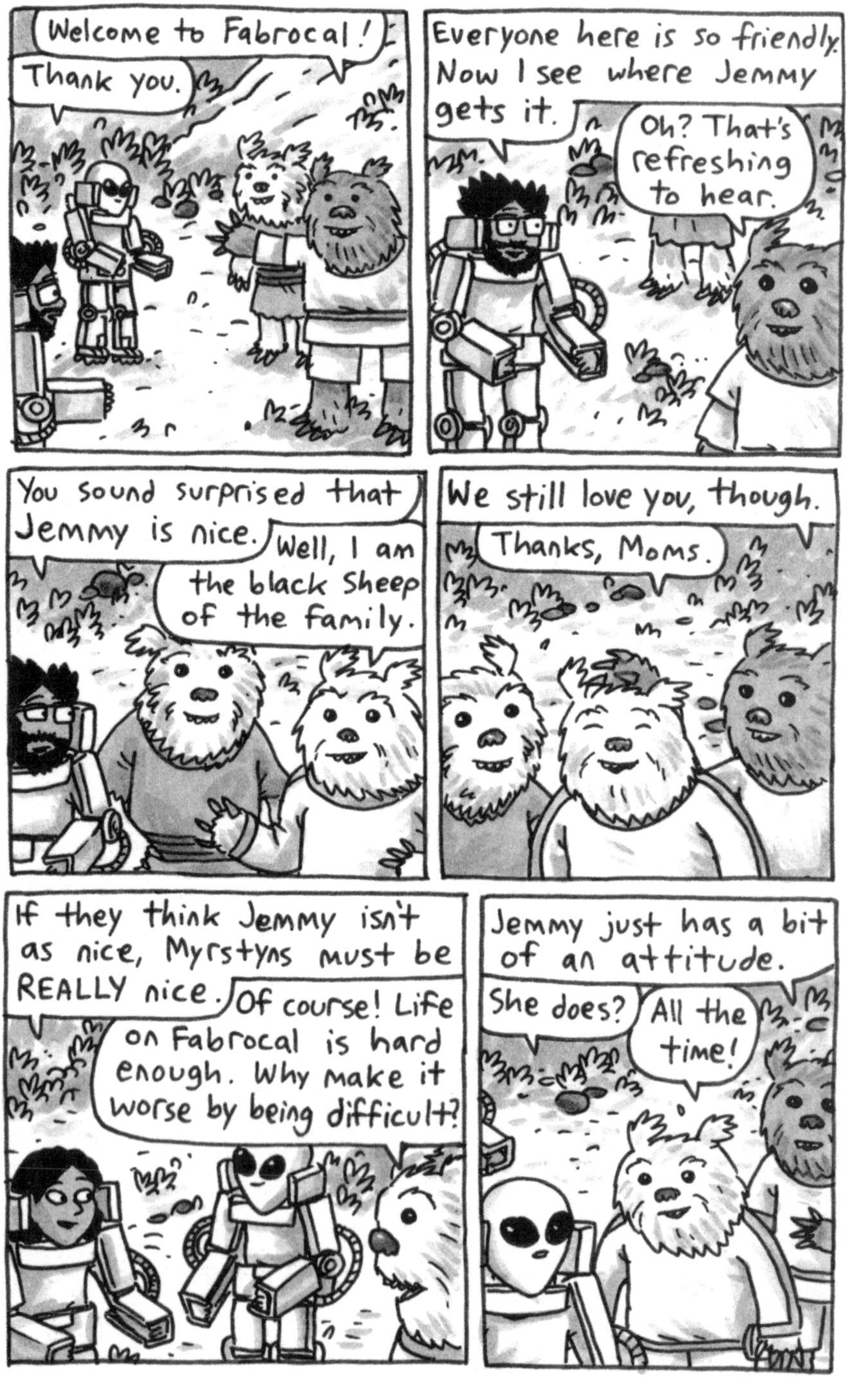
Welcome to Fabrocal!
Thank you.
Everyone here is so friendly. Now I see where Jemmy gets it.
Oh? That's refreshing to hear.
You sound surprised that Jemmy is nice.
Well, I am the black Sheep of the family.
We still love you, though.
Thanks, Moms.
If they think Jemmy isn't as nice, Myrstyns must be REALLY nice.
Of course! Life on Fabrocal is hard enough. Why make it worse by being difficult?
Jemmy just has a bit of an attitude.
She does?
All the time!

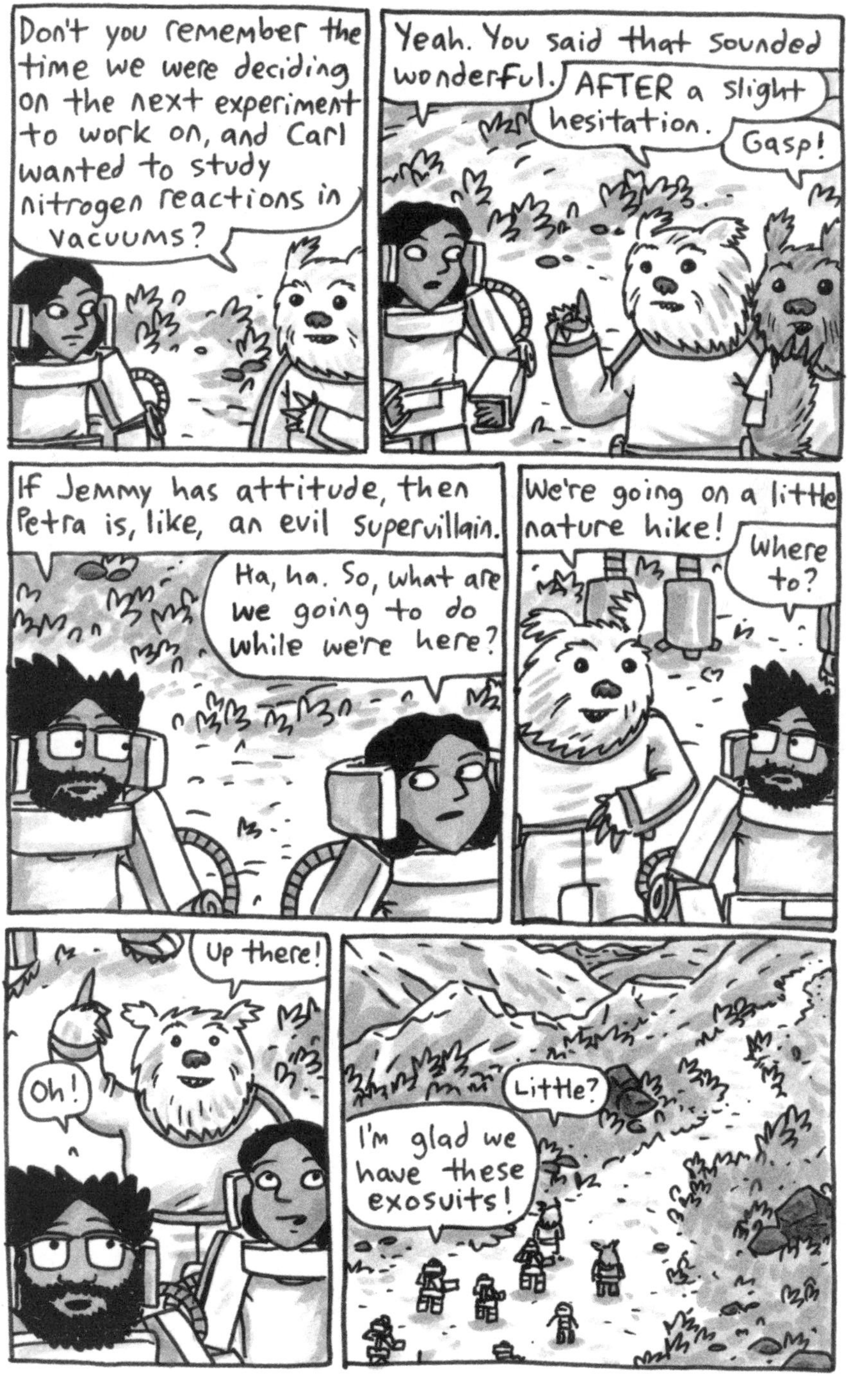
Don't you remember the time we were deciding on the next experiment to work on, and Carl wanted to study nitrogen reactions in vacuums?
Yeah. You said that sounded wonderful.
AFTER a slight hesitation.
Gasp!
If Jemmy has attitude, then Petra is, like, an evil supervillain.
Ha, ha. So, what are we going to do while we're here?
We're going on a little nature hike!
Where to?
Up there!
Oh!
Little?
I'm glad we have these exosuits!

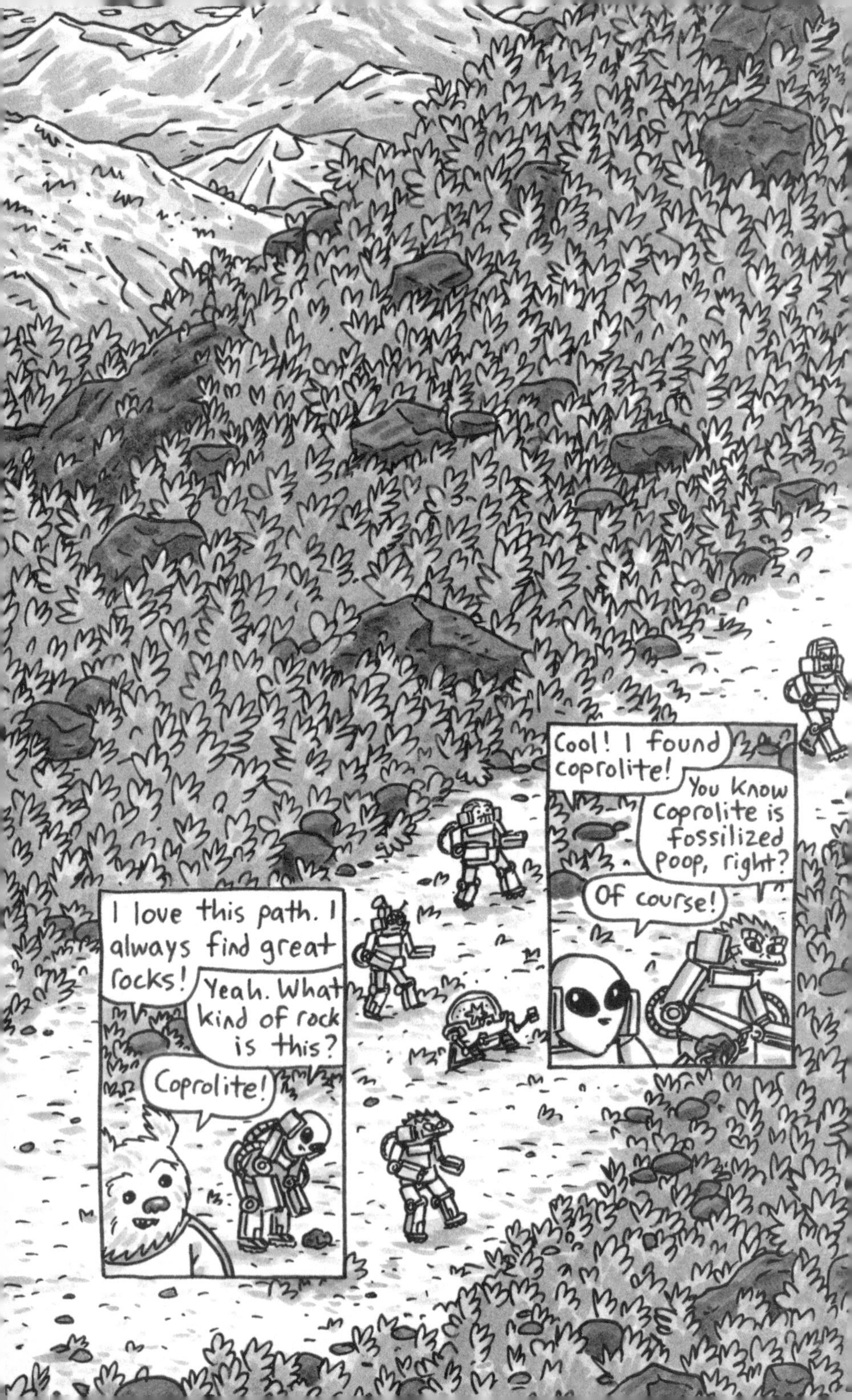

I love this path. I always find great rocks!
Yeah. What kind of rock is this?
Coprolite!
Cool! I found coprolite!
You know coprolite is fossilized poop, right?
Of course!

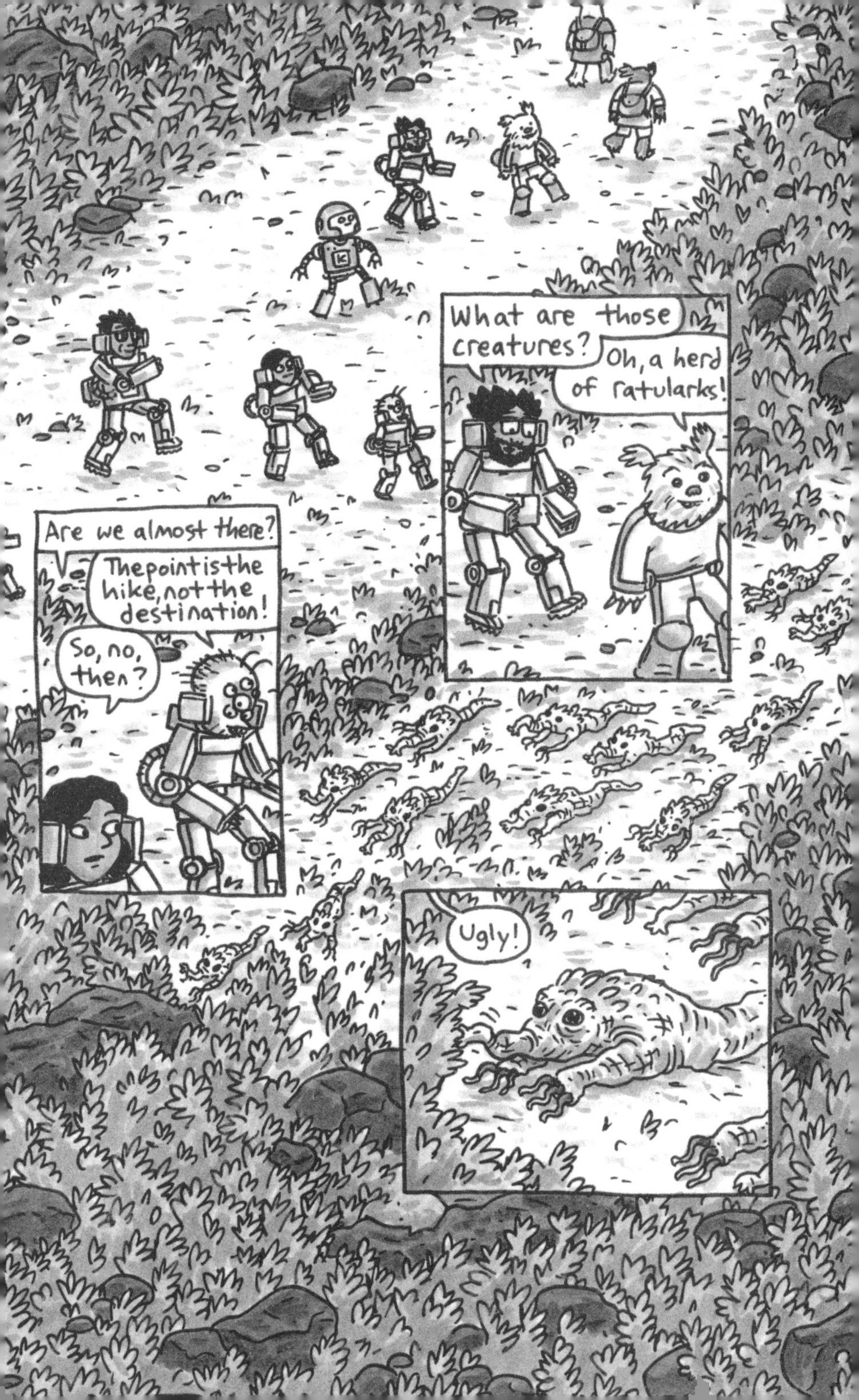
What are those creatures?
Oh, a herd of ratularks!
Are we almost there?
The point is the hike, not the destination!
So, no, then?
Ugly!

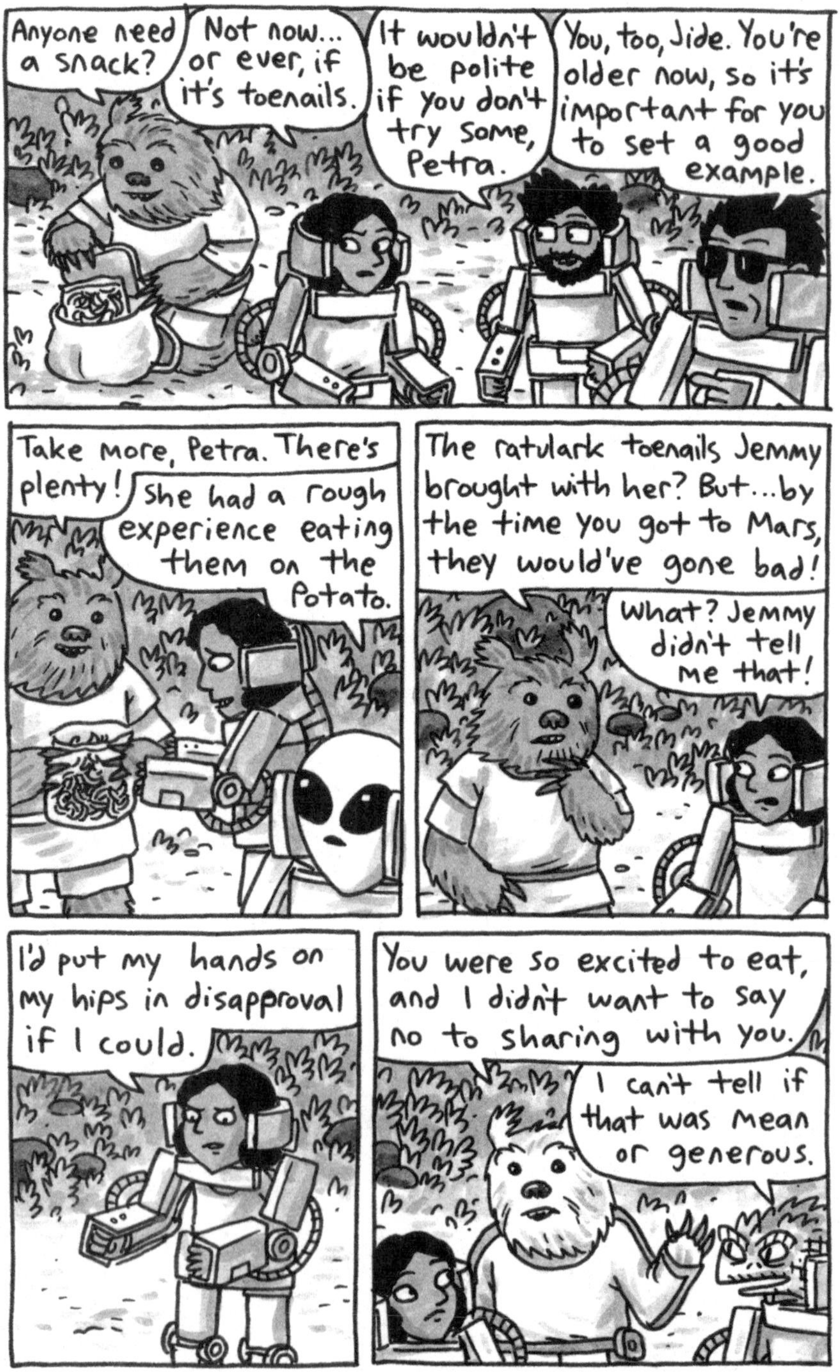
Anyone need a snack?
Not now... or ever, if it's toenails.
It wouldn't be polite if you don't try some, Petra.
You, too, Jide. You're older now, so it's important for you to set a good example.
Take more, Petra. There's plenty!
She had a rough experience eating them on the Potato.
The ratulark toenails Jemmy brought with her? But...by the time you got to Mars, they would've gone bad!
What? Jemmy didn't tell me that!
I'd put my hands on my hips in disapproval if I could.
You were so excited to eat, and I didn't want to say no to sharing with you.
I can't tell if that was mean or generous.

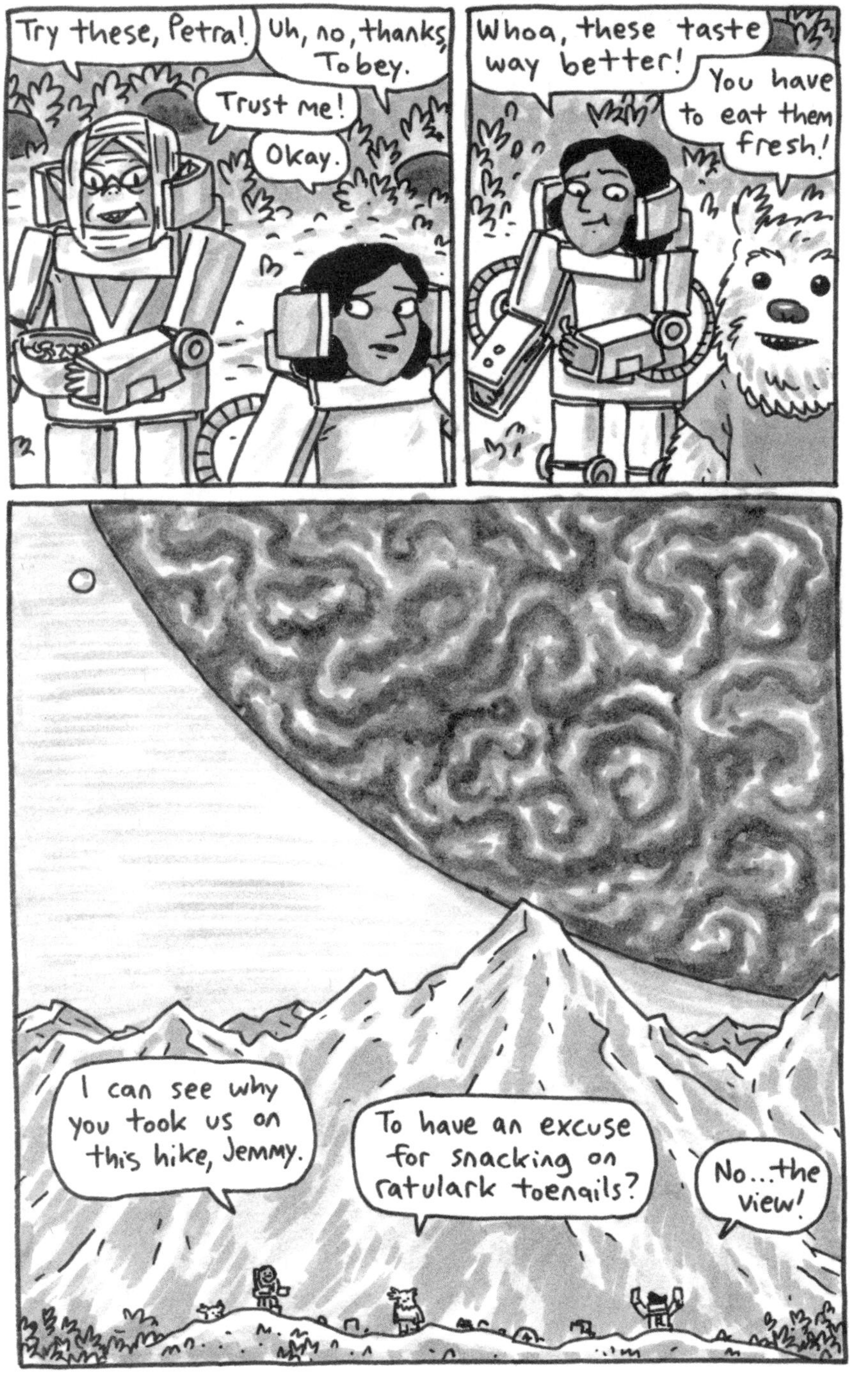
Try these, Petra!
Uh, no, thanks, Tobey.
Trust me!
Okay.
Whoa, these taste way better!
You have to eat them fresh!
I can see why you took us on this hike, Jemmy.
To have an excuse for snacking on ratulark toenails?
No...the view!

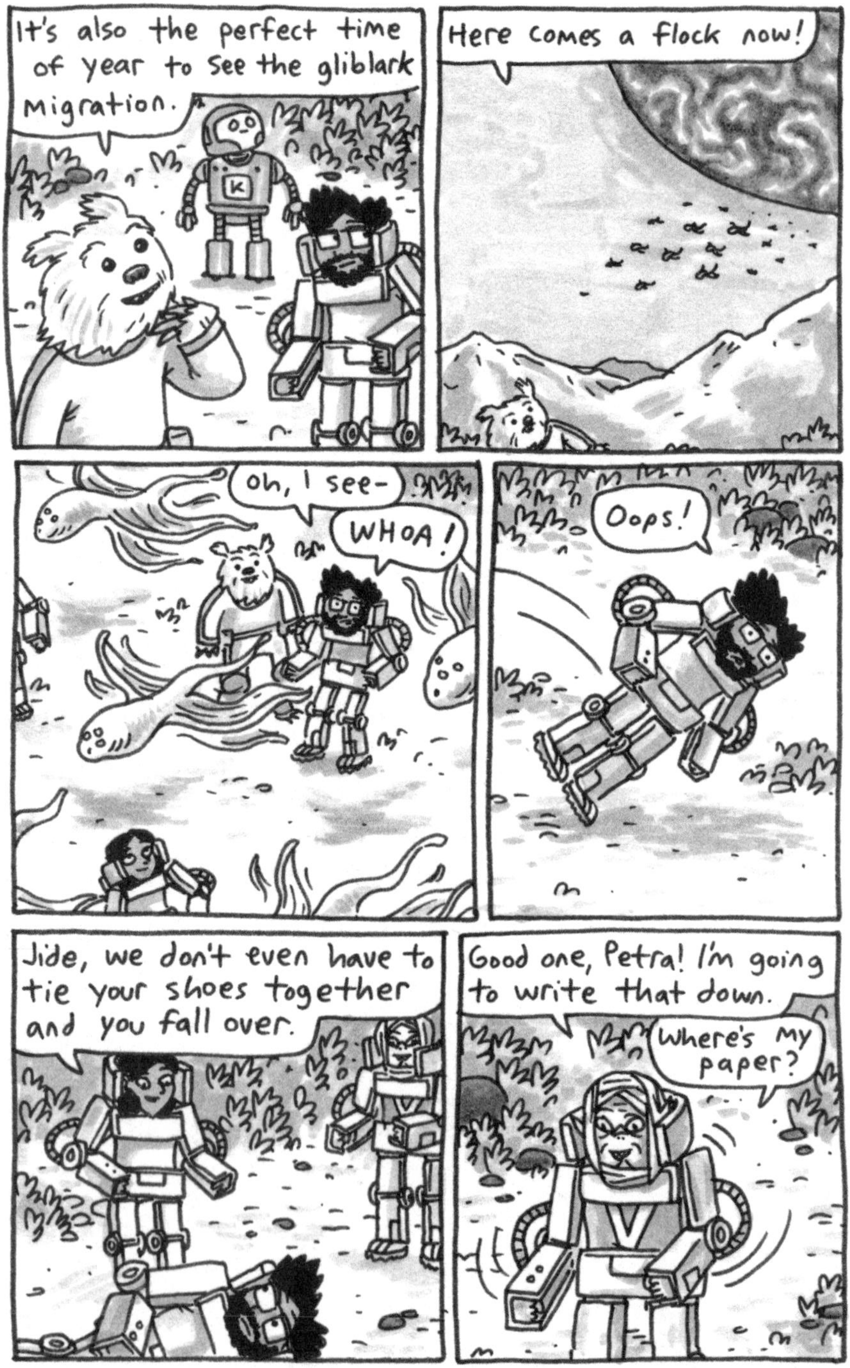
It's also the perfect time of year to see the gliblark migration.
Here comes a flock now!
Oh, I see-
WHOA!
Oops!
Jide, we don't even have to tie your shoes together and you fall over.
Good one, Petra! I'm going to write that down.
Where's my paper?

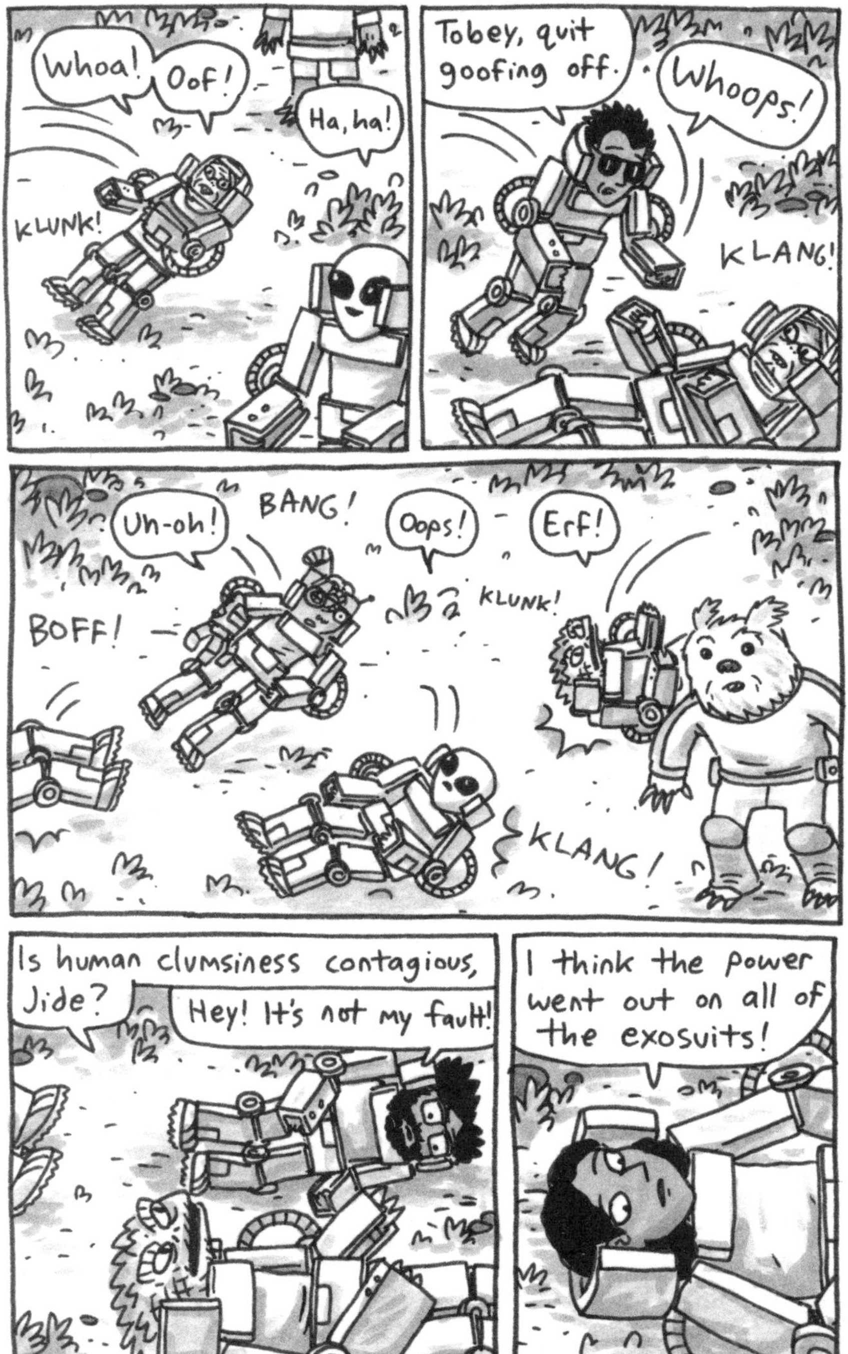
Whoa!
Oof!
Ha, ha!
KLUNK!
Tobey, quit goofing off.
Whoops!
KLANG!
Uh-oh!
BANG!
Oops!
Erf!
BOFF!
KLUNK!
KLANG!
Is human clumsiness contagious, Jide?
Hey! It's not my fault!
I think the power went out on all of the exosuits!

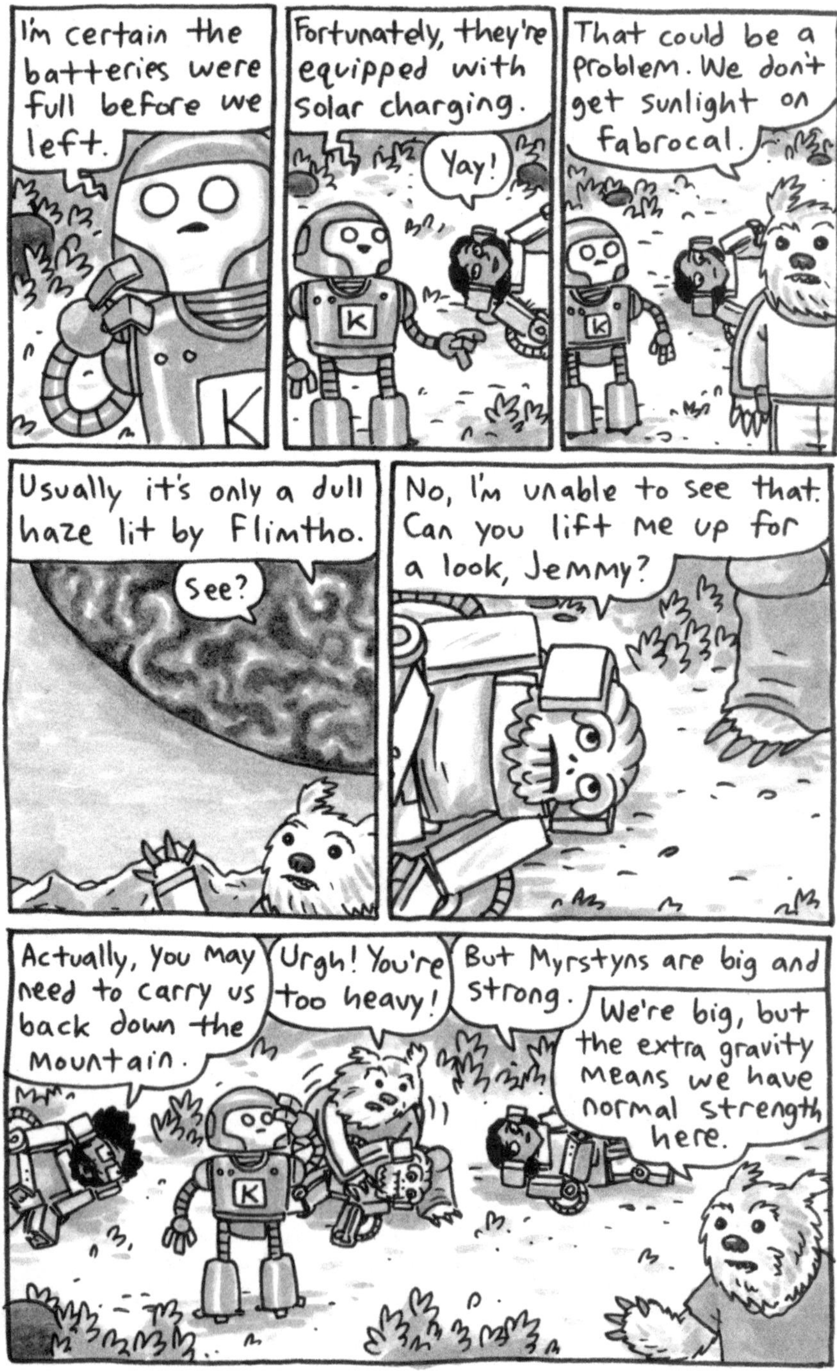
I'm certain the batteries were full before we left.
Fortunately, they're equipped with solar charging.
Yay!
That could be a problem. We don't get sunlight on Fabrocal.
Usually it's only a dull haze lit by Flimtho.
See?
No, I'm unable to see that. Can you lift me up for a look, Jemmy?
Actually, you may need to carry us back down the mountain.
Urgh! You're too heavy!
But Myrstyns are big and strong.
We're big, but the extra gravity means we have normal strength here.

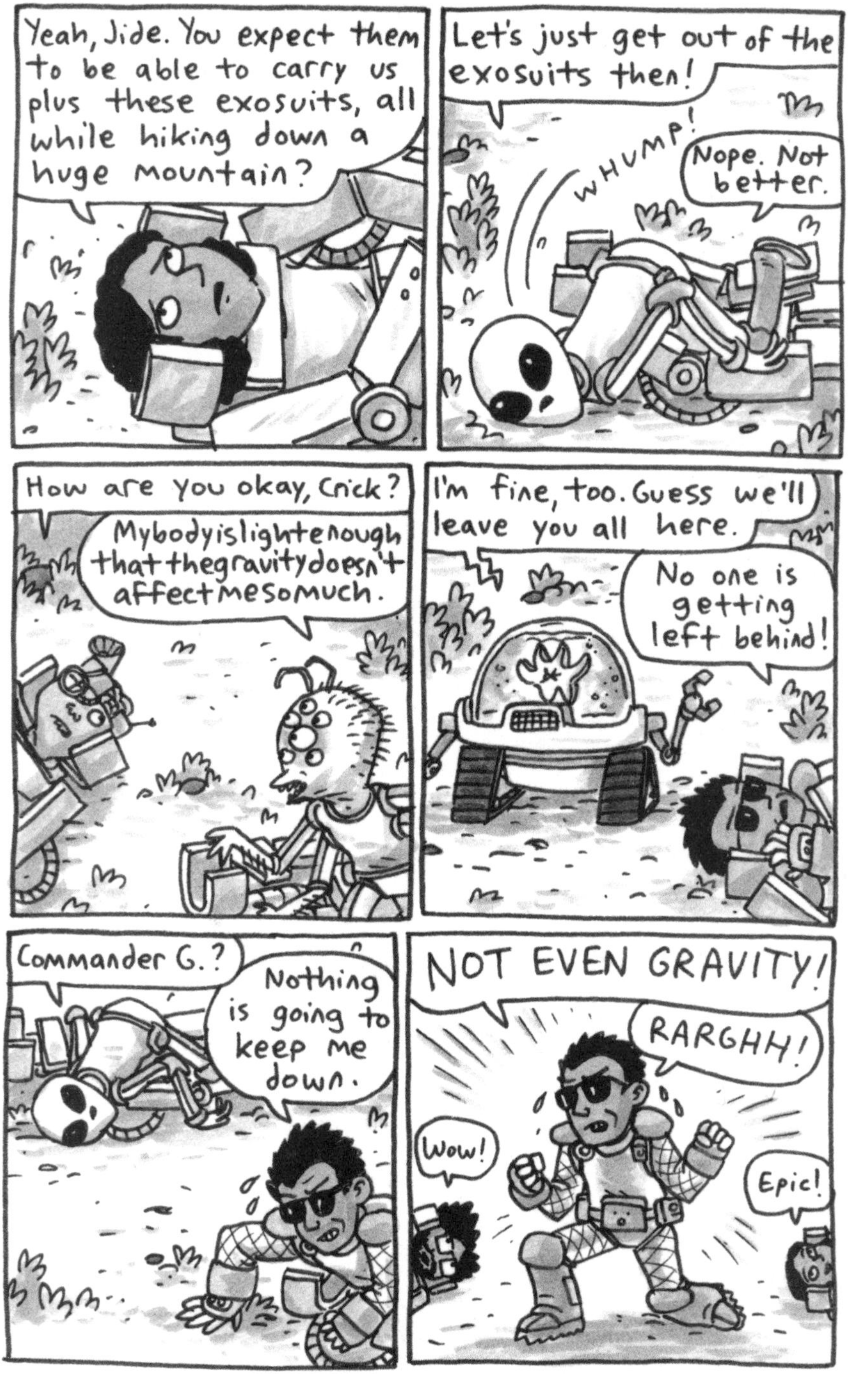
Yeah, Jide. You expect them to be able to carry us plus these exosuits, all while hiking down a huge mountain?
Let's just get out of the exosuits then!
WHUMP!
Nope. Not better.
How are you okay, Crick?
Mybodyislightenough thatthegravitydoesn't affectmesomuch.
I'm fine, too. Guess we'll leave you all here.
No one is getting left behind!
Commander G.?
Nothing is going to keep me down.
NOT EVEN GRAVITY!
RARGHH!
Wow!
Epic!

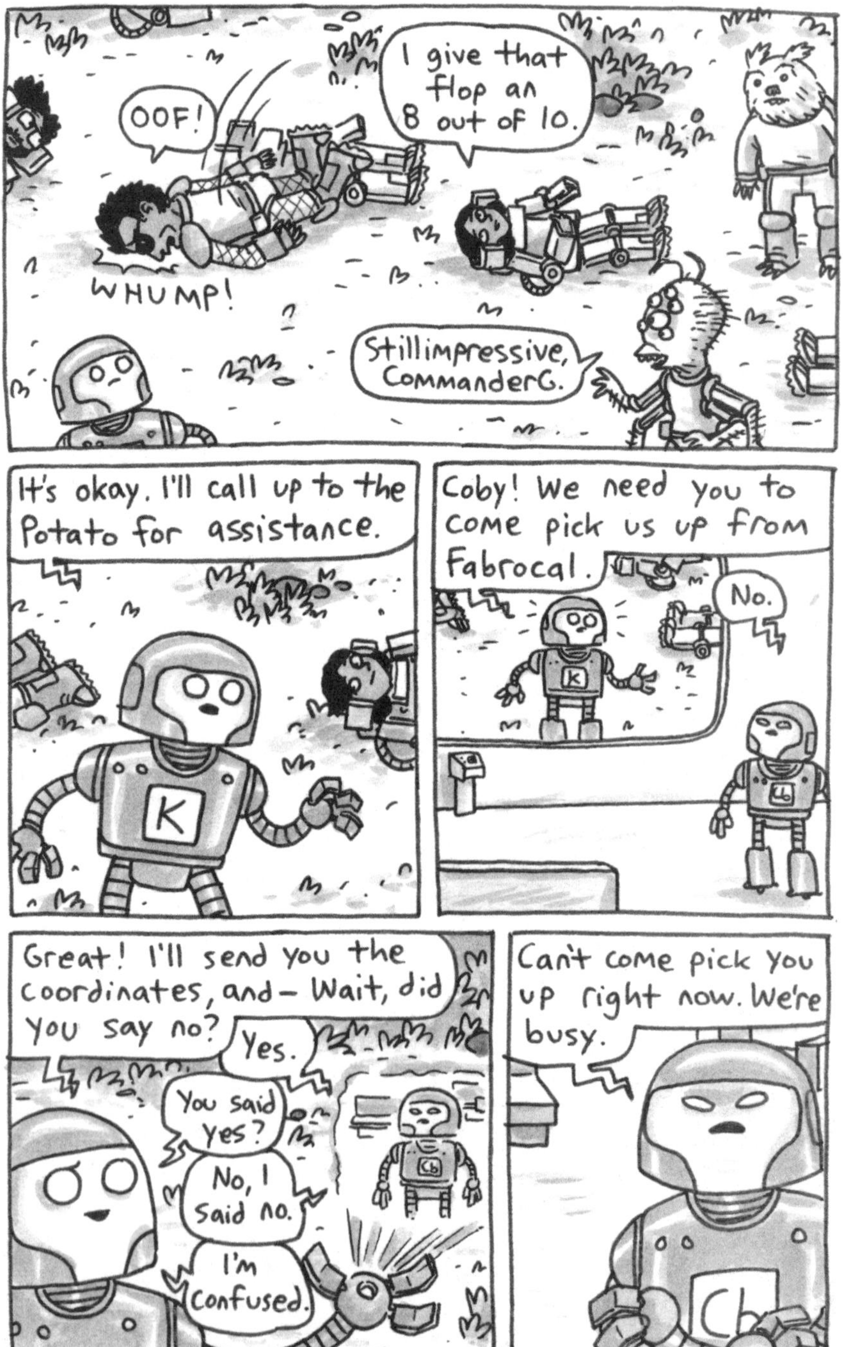
OOF!
I give that flop an 8 out of 10.
WHUMP!
Stillimpressive, CommanderG.
It's okay. I'll call up to the Potato for assistance.
Coby! We need you to come pick us up from Fabrocal.
No.
Great! I'll send you the coordinates, and– Wait, did you say no?
Yes.
You said yes?
No, I said no.
I'm confused.
Can't come pick you up right now. We're busy.

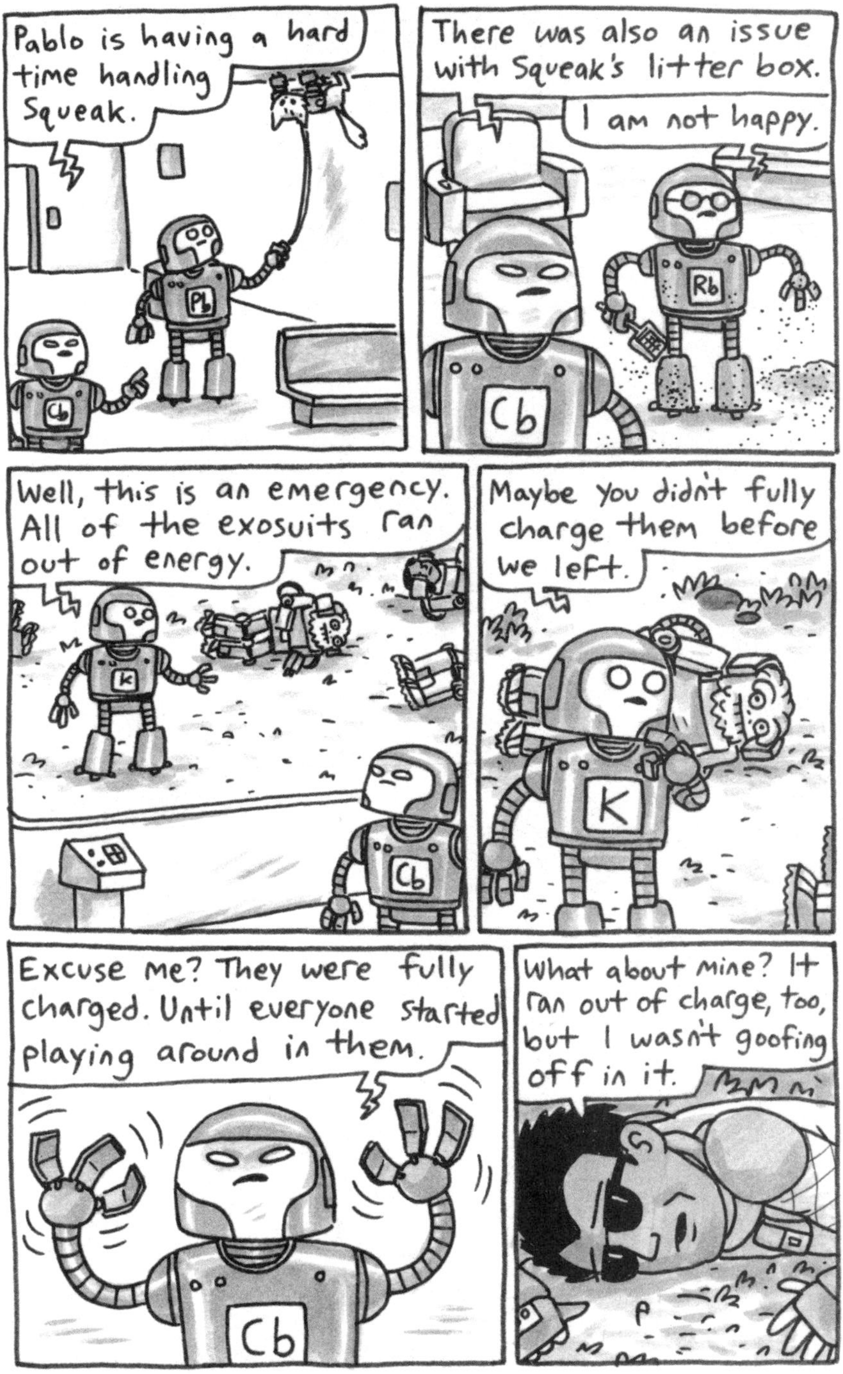
Pablo is having a hard time handling Squeak.
There was also an issue with Squeak's litter box.
I am not happy.
Pb
Rb
Cb
Well, this is an emergency. All of the exosuits ran out of energy.
Maybe you didn't fully charge them before we left.
K
Excuse me? They were fully charged. Until everyone started playing around in them.
What about mine? It ran out of charge, too, but I wasn't goofing off in it.

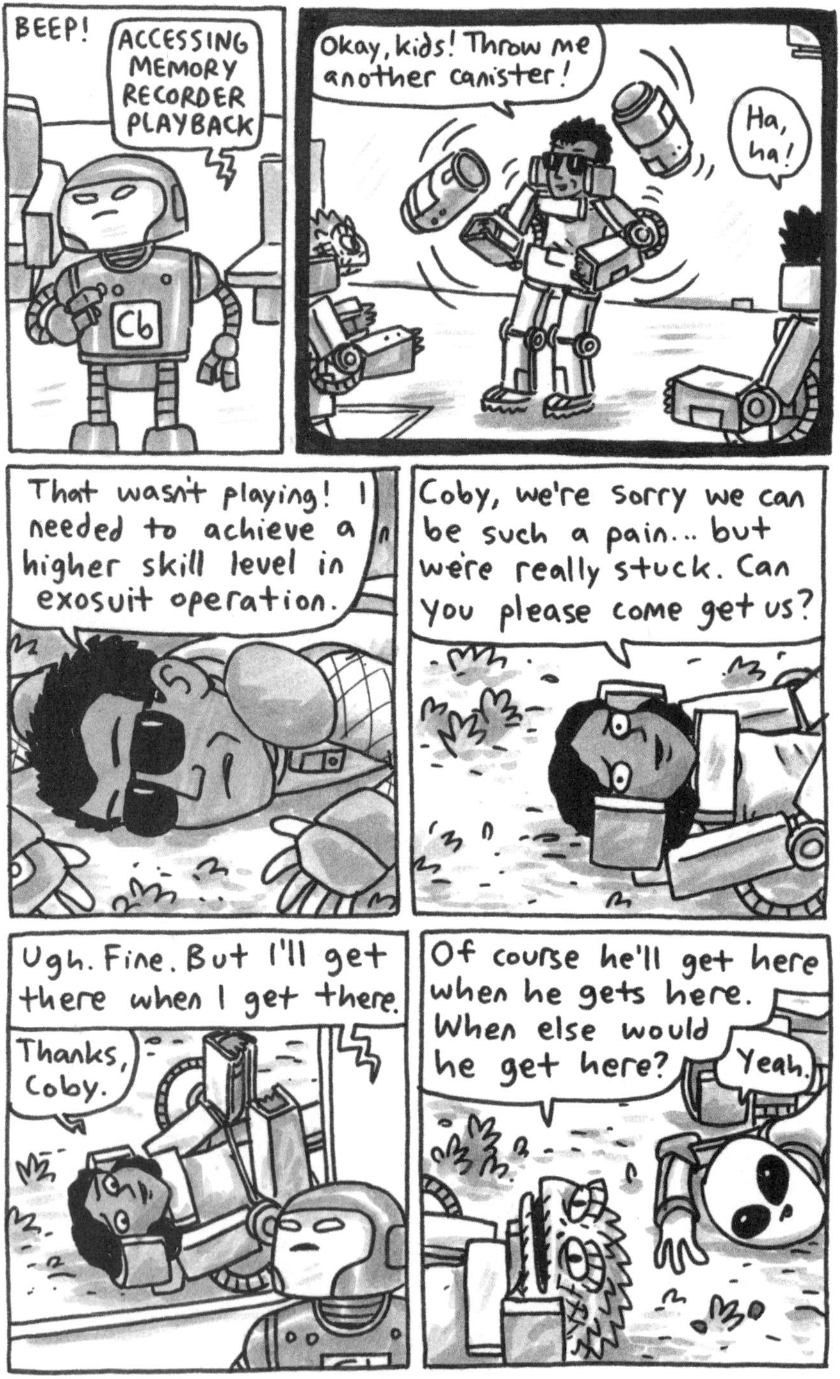
BEEP!
ACCESSING MEMORY RECORDER PLAYBACK
Okay, kids! Throw me another canister!
Ha, ha!
That wasn't playing! I needed to achieve a higher skill level in exosuit operation.
Coby, we're sorry we can be such a pain... but we're really stuck. Can you please come get us?
Ugh. Fine. But I'll get there when I get there.
Thanks, Coby.
Of course he'll get here when he gets here. When else would he get here?
Yeah.

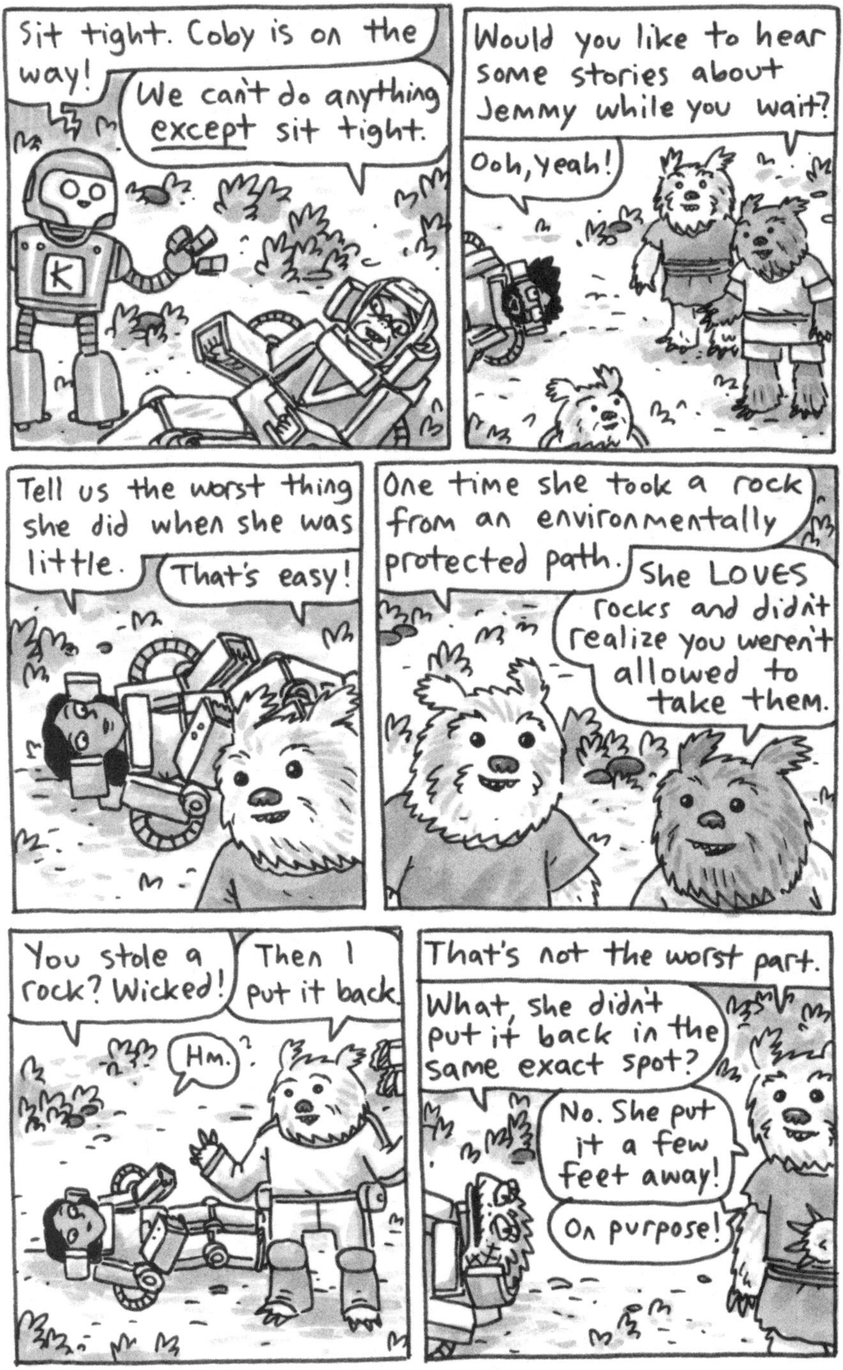
Sit tight. Coby is on the way!
We can't do anything except sit tight.
Would you like to hear some stories about Jemmy while you wait?
Ooh, yeah!
Tell us the worst thing she did when she was little.
That's easy!
One time she took a rock from an environmentally protected path.
She LOVES rocks and didn't realize you weren't allowed to take them.
You stole a rock? Wicked!
Then I put it back.
Hm.
That's not the worst part.
What, she didn't put it back in the same exact spot?
No. She put it a few feet away!
On purpose!

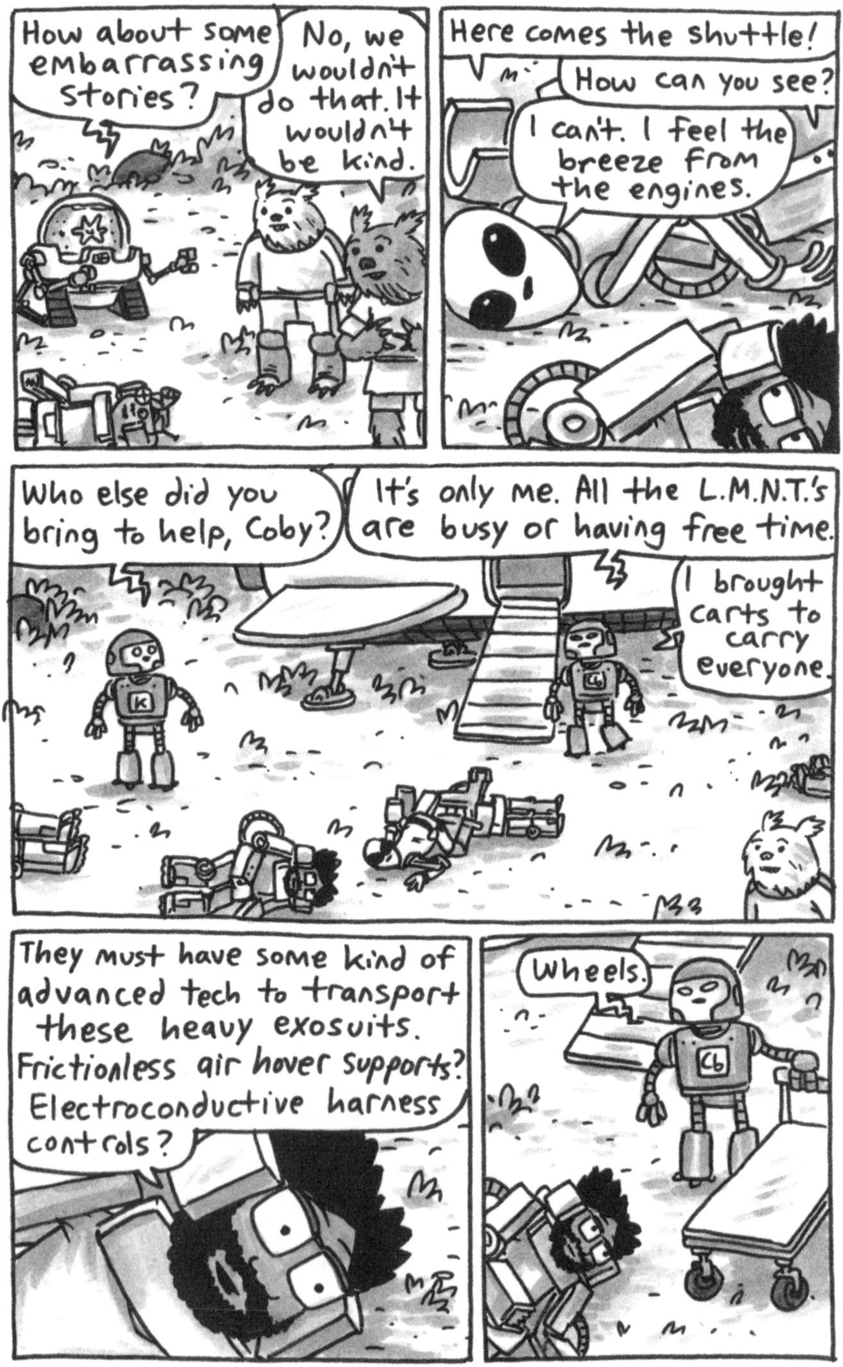
How about some embarrassing stories?
No, we wouldn't do that. It wouldn't be kind.
Here comes the shuttle!
How can you see?
I can't. I feel the breeze from the engines.
Who else did you bring to help, Coby?
It's only me. All the L.M.N.T.'s are busy or having free time.
I brought carts to carry everyone.
They must have some kind of advanced tech to transport these heavy exosuits. Frictionless air hover supports? Electroconductive harness controls?
Wheels.

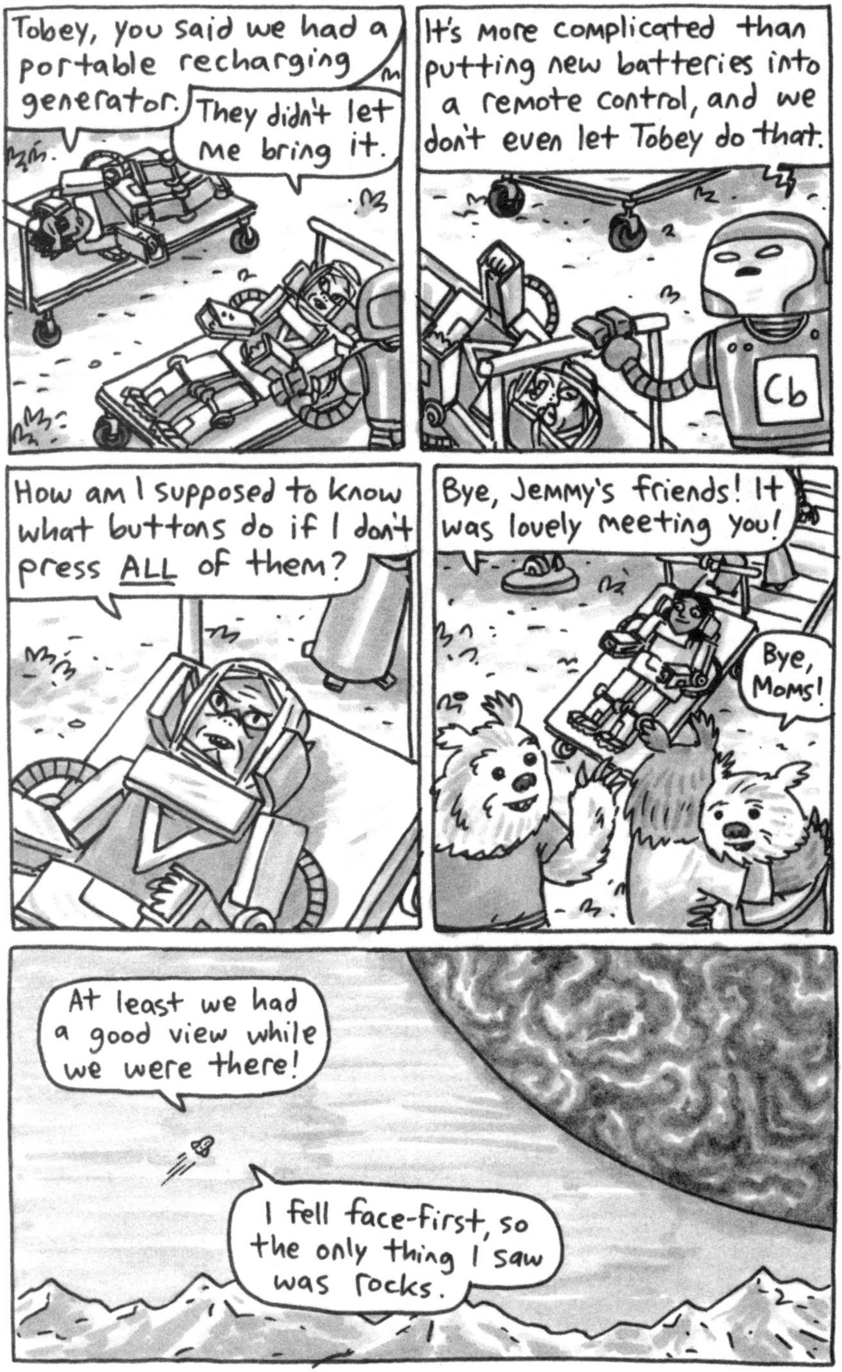
Tobey, you said we had a portable recharging generator.
They didn't let me bring it.
It's more complicated than putting new batteries into a remote control, and we don't even let Tobey do that.
Cb
How am I supposed to know what buttons do if I don't press ALL of them?
Bye, Jemmy's friends! It was lovely meeting you!
Bye, Moms!
At least we had a good view while we were there!
I fell face-first, so the only thing I saw was rocks.

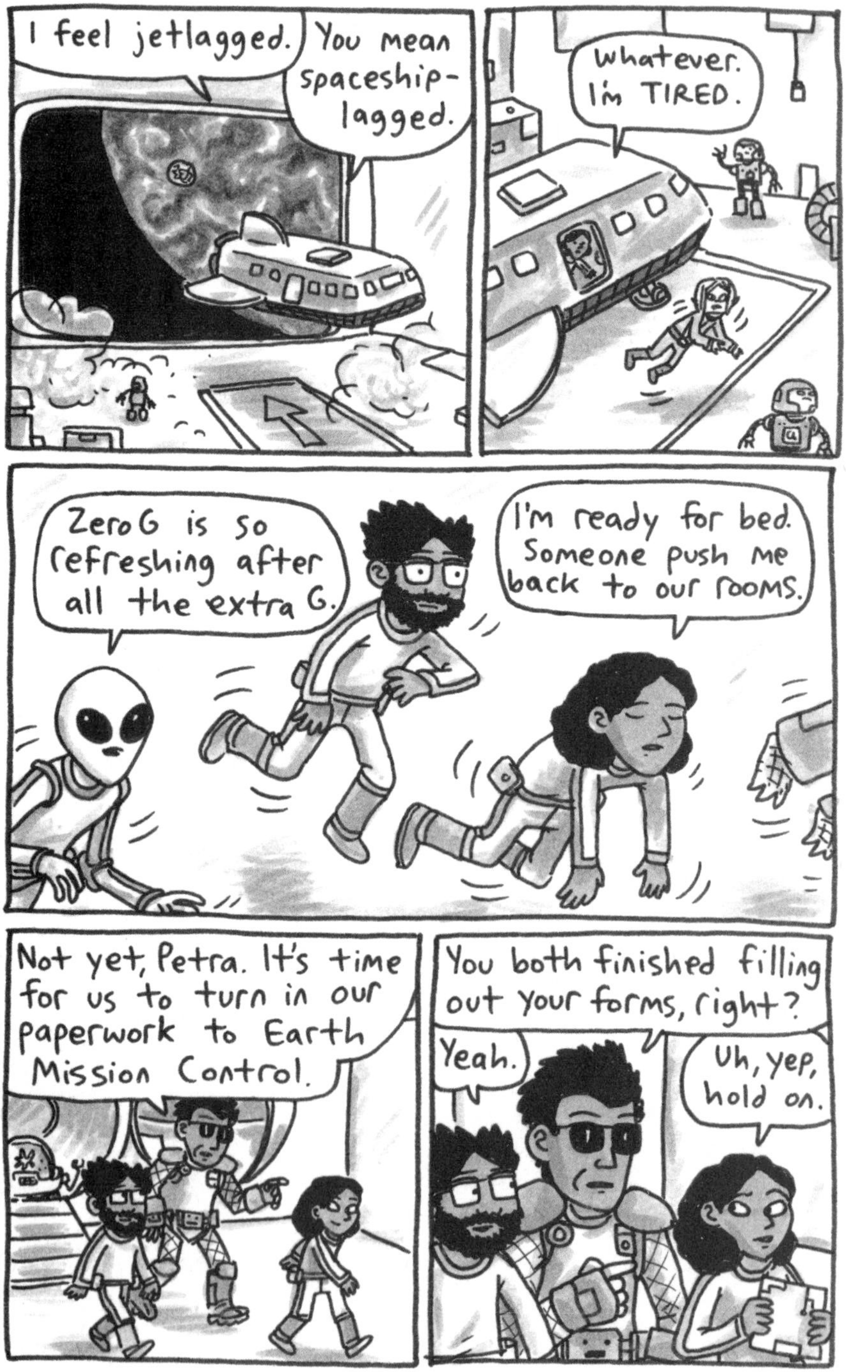
I feel jetlagged.
You mean spaceship-lagged.
Whatever. I'm TIRED.
Zero G is so refreshing after all the extra G.
I'm ready for bed. Someone push me back to our rooms.
Not yet, Petra. It's time for us to turn in our paperwork to Earth Mission Control.
You both finished filling out your forms, right?
Yeah.
Uh, yep, hold on.

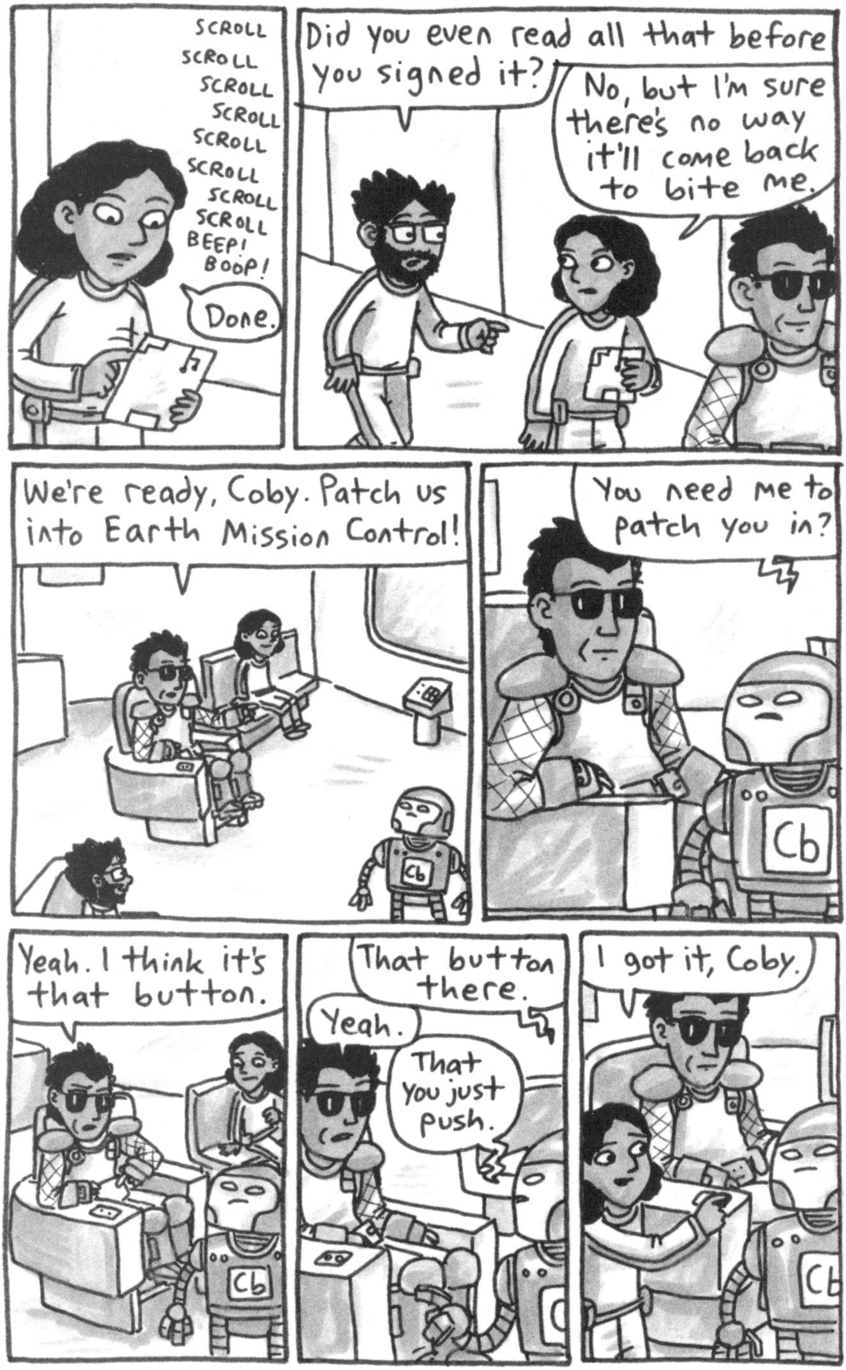
SCROLL
SCROLL
SCROLL
SCROLL
SCROLL
SCROLL
SCROLL
SCROLL
BEEP!
BOOP!
Done.
Did you even read all that before you signed it?
No, but I'm sure there's no way it'll come back to bite me.
We're ready, Coby. Patch us into Earth Mission Control!
You need me to patch you in?
Yeah. I think it's that button.
That button there.
Yeah.
That you just push.
I got it, Coby.

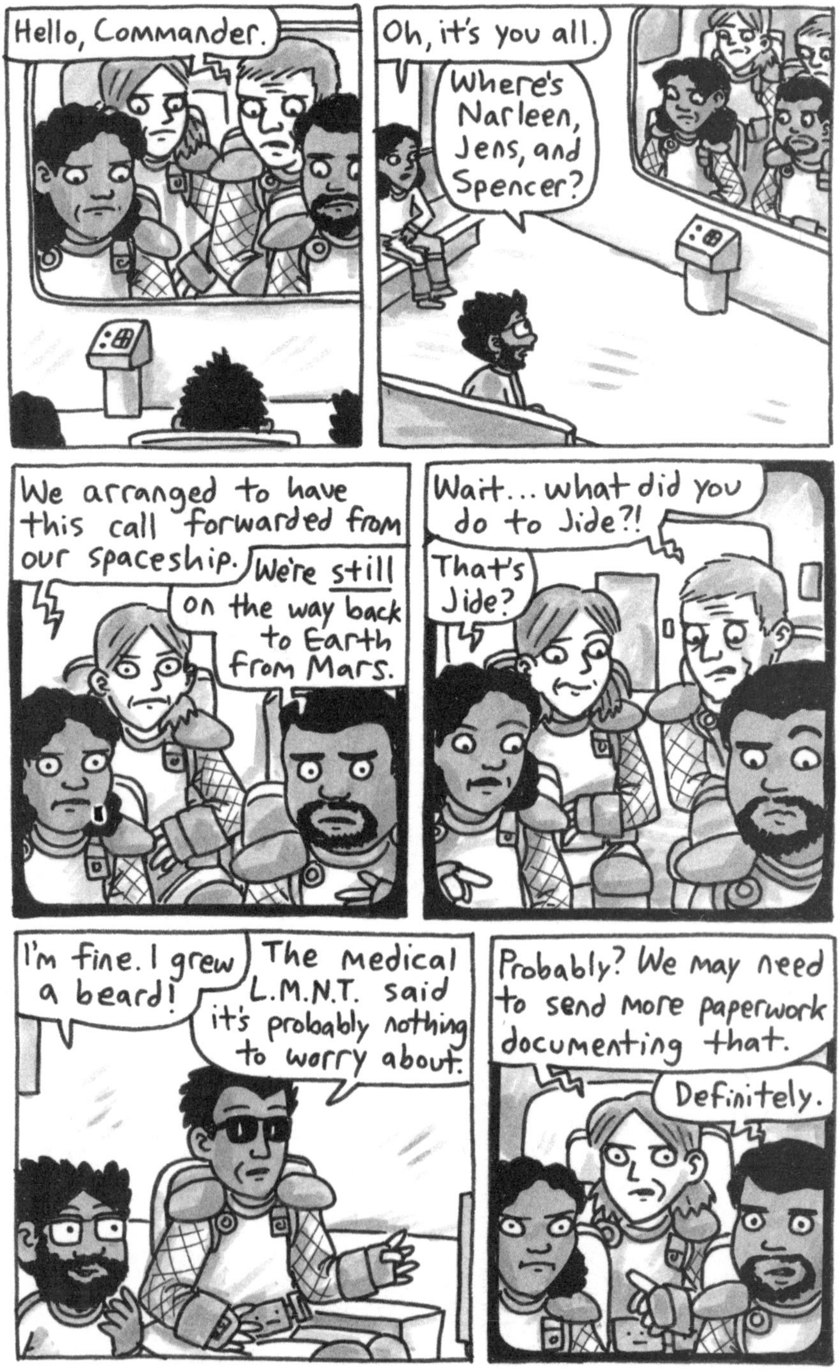
Hello, Commander.
Oh, it's you all.
Where's Narleen, Jens, and Spencer?
We arranged to have this call forwarded from our spaceship.
We're still on the way back to Earth from Mars.
Wait... what did you do to Jide?!
That's Jide?
I'm fine. I grew a beard!
The medical L.M.N.T. said it's probably nothing to worry about.
Probably? We may need to send more paperwork documenting that.
Definitely.

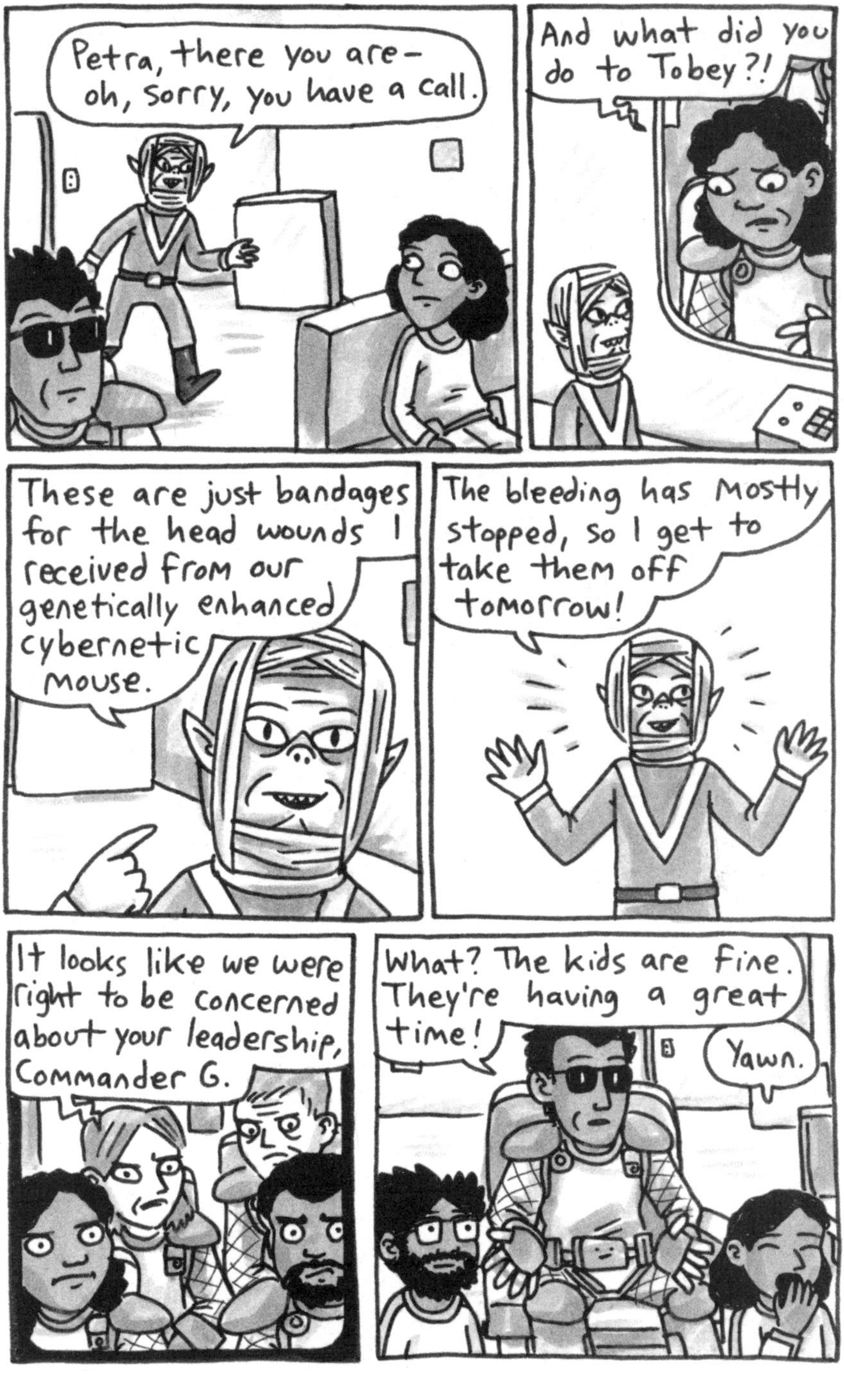
Petra, there you are—oh, sorry, you have a call.
And what did you do to Tobey?!
These are just bandages for the head wounds I received from our genetically enhanced cybernetic mouse.
The bleeding has mostly stopped, so I get to take them off tomorrow!
It looks like we were right to be concerned about your leadership, Commander G.
What? The kids are fine. They're having a great time!
Yawn.

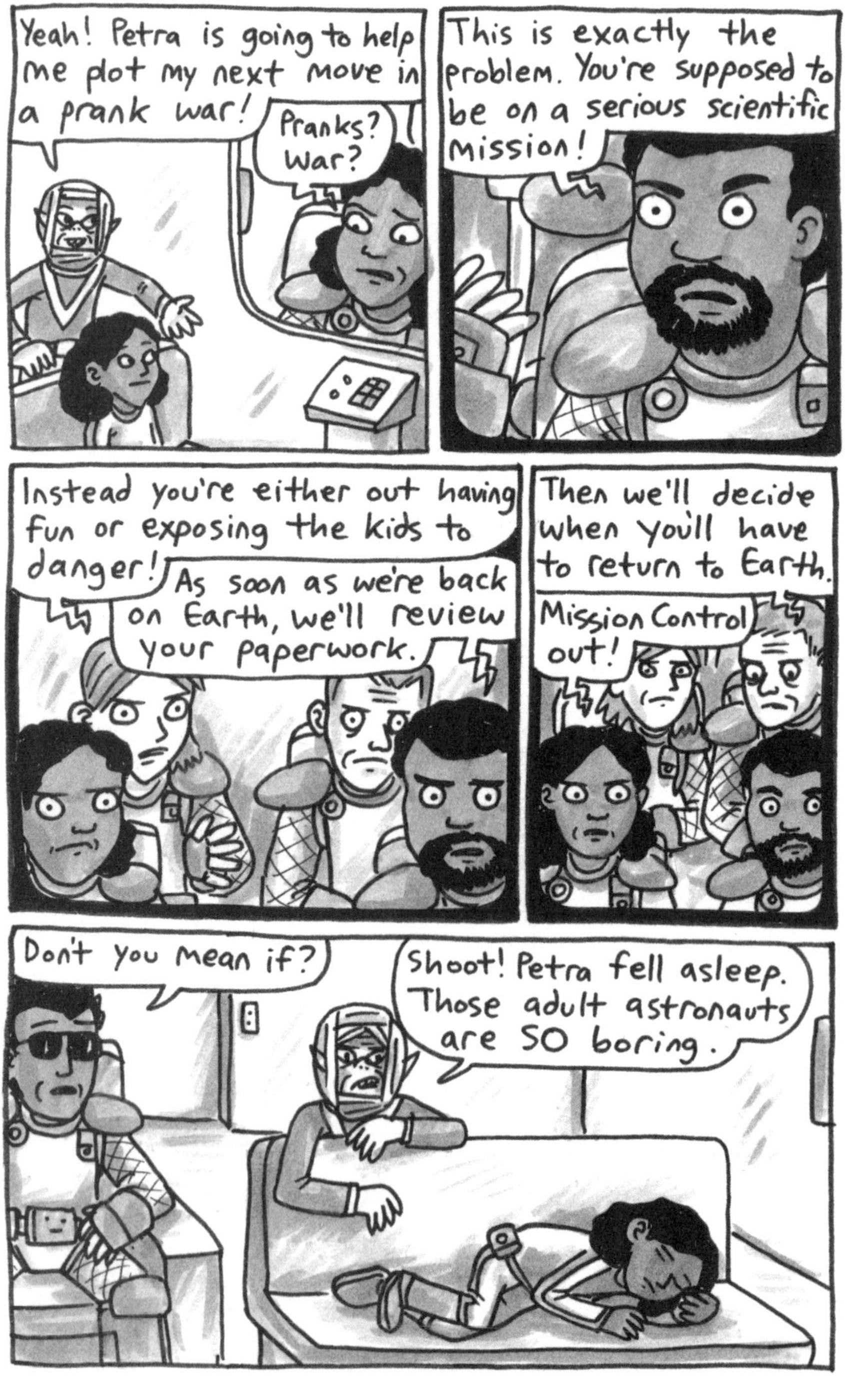
Yeah! Petra is going to help me plot my next move in a prank war!
Pranks? War?
This is exactly the problem. You're supposed to be on a serious scientific mission!
Instead you're either out having fun or exposing the kids to danger!
As soon as we're back on Earth, we'll review your paperwork.
Then we'll decide when you'll have to return to Earth.
Mission Control out!
Don't you mean if?
Shoot! Petra fell asleep. Those adult astronauts are SO boring.

DRY RUNNING THE NUMBERS

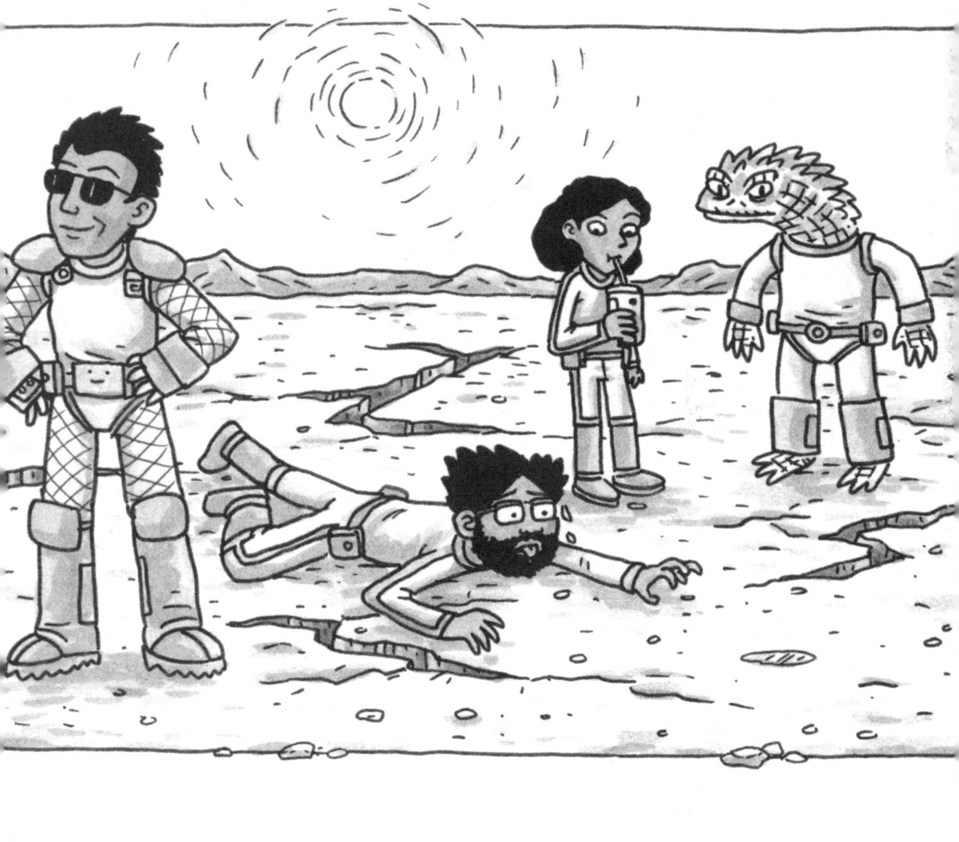

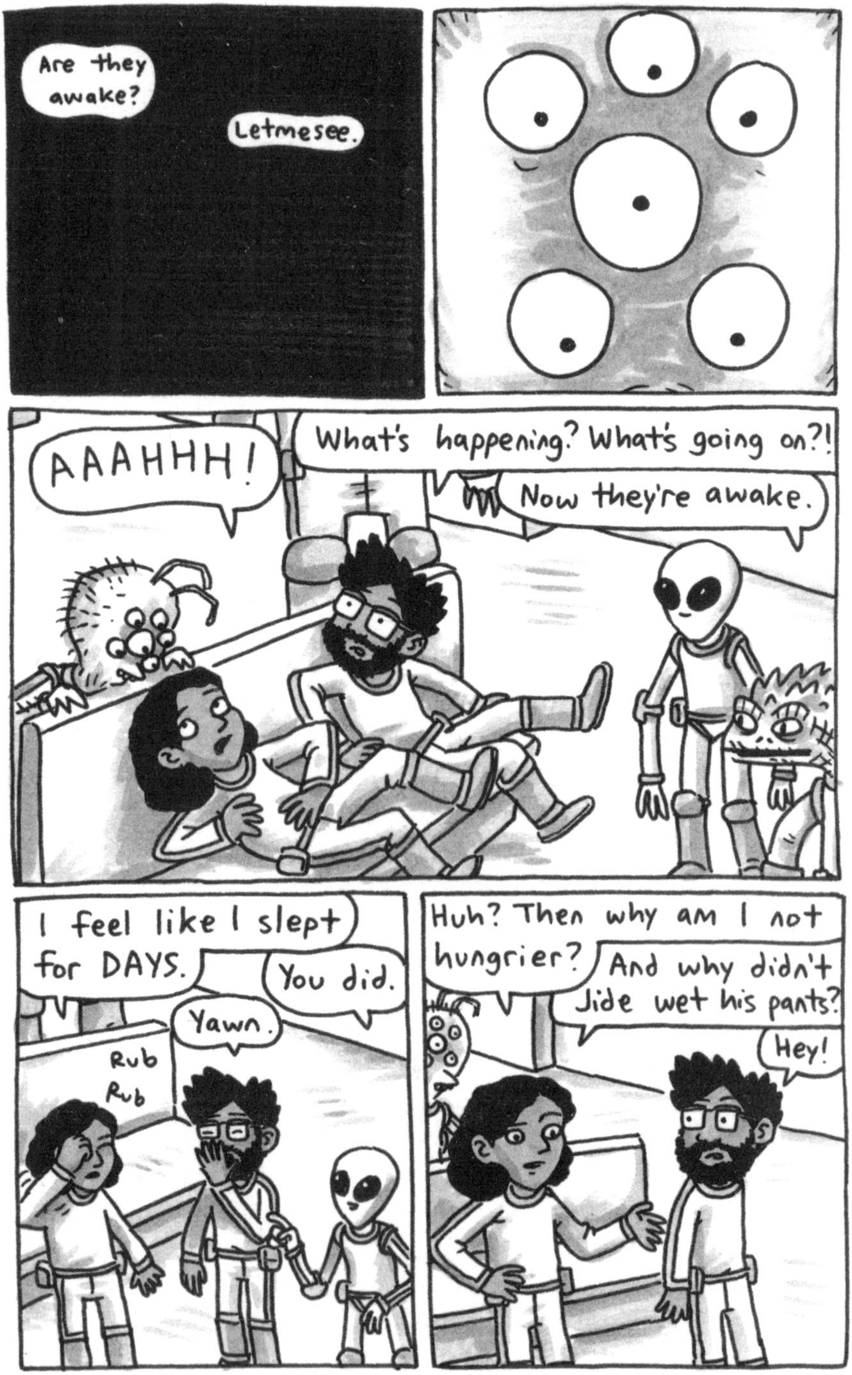
Are they awake?
Letmesee.
AAAHHH!
What's happening? What's going on?!
Now they're awake.
I feel like I slept for DAYS.
You did.
Yawn.
Rub Rub
Huh? Then why am I not hungrier?
And why didn't Jide wet his pants?
Hey!

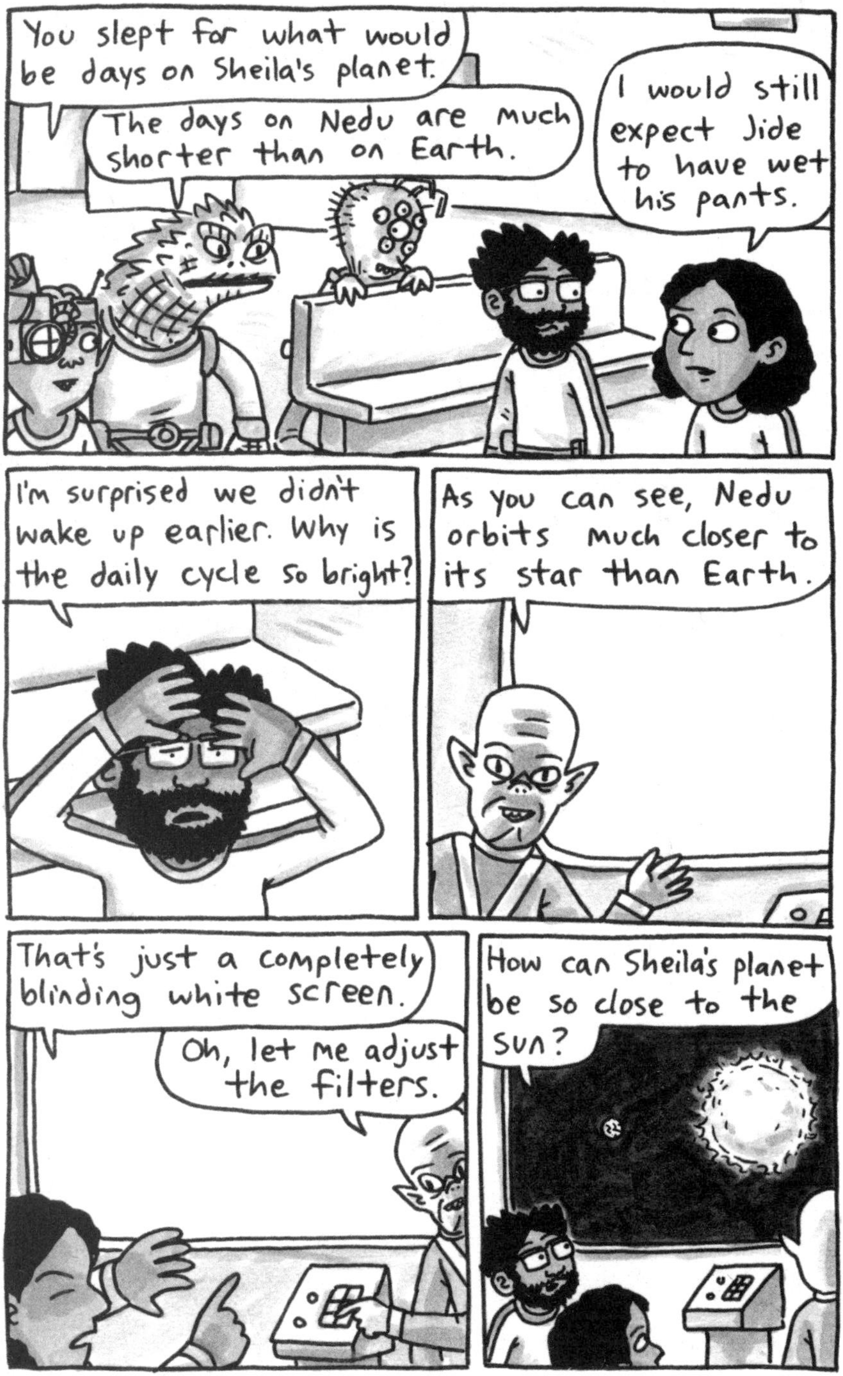
You slept for what would be days on Sheila's planet.
The days on Nedu are much shorter than on Earth.
I would still expect Jide to have wet his pants.
I'm surprised we didn't wake up earlier. Why is the daily cycle so bright?
As you can see, Nedu orbits much closer to its star than Earth.
That's just a completely blinding white screen.
Oh, let me adjust the filters.
How can Sheila's planet be so close to the sun?

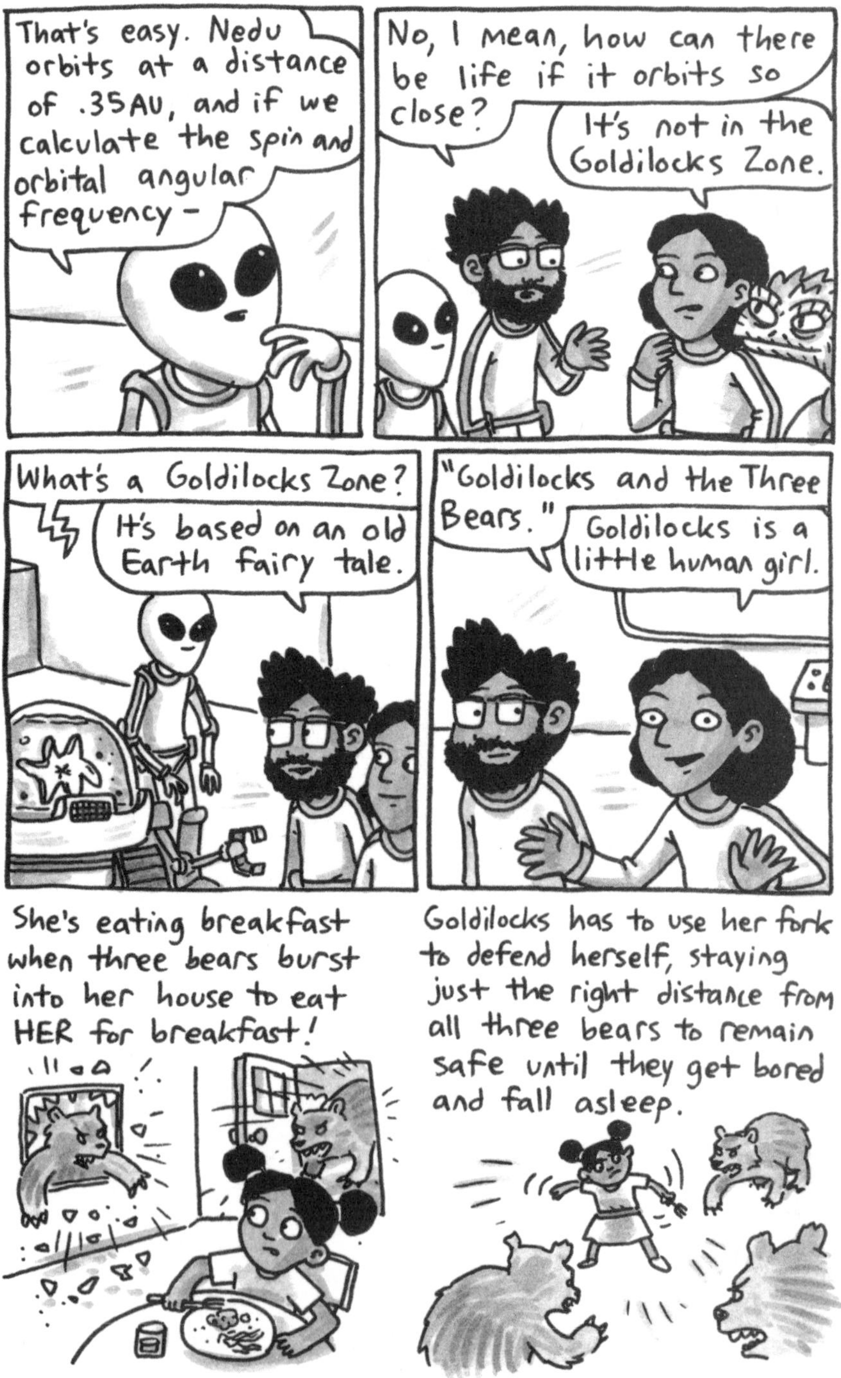
That's easy. Nedu orbits at a distance of .35AU, and if we calculate the spin and orbital angular frequency –
No, I mean, how can there be life if it orbits so close?
It's not in the Goldilocks Zone.
What's a Goldilocks Zone?
It's based on an old Earth fairy tale.
"Goldilocks and the Three Bears."
Goldilocks is a little human girl.
She's eating breakfast when three bears burst into her house to eat HER for breakfast!
Goldilocks has to use her fork to defend herself, staying just the right distance from all three bears to remain safe until they get bored and fall asleep.

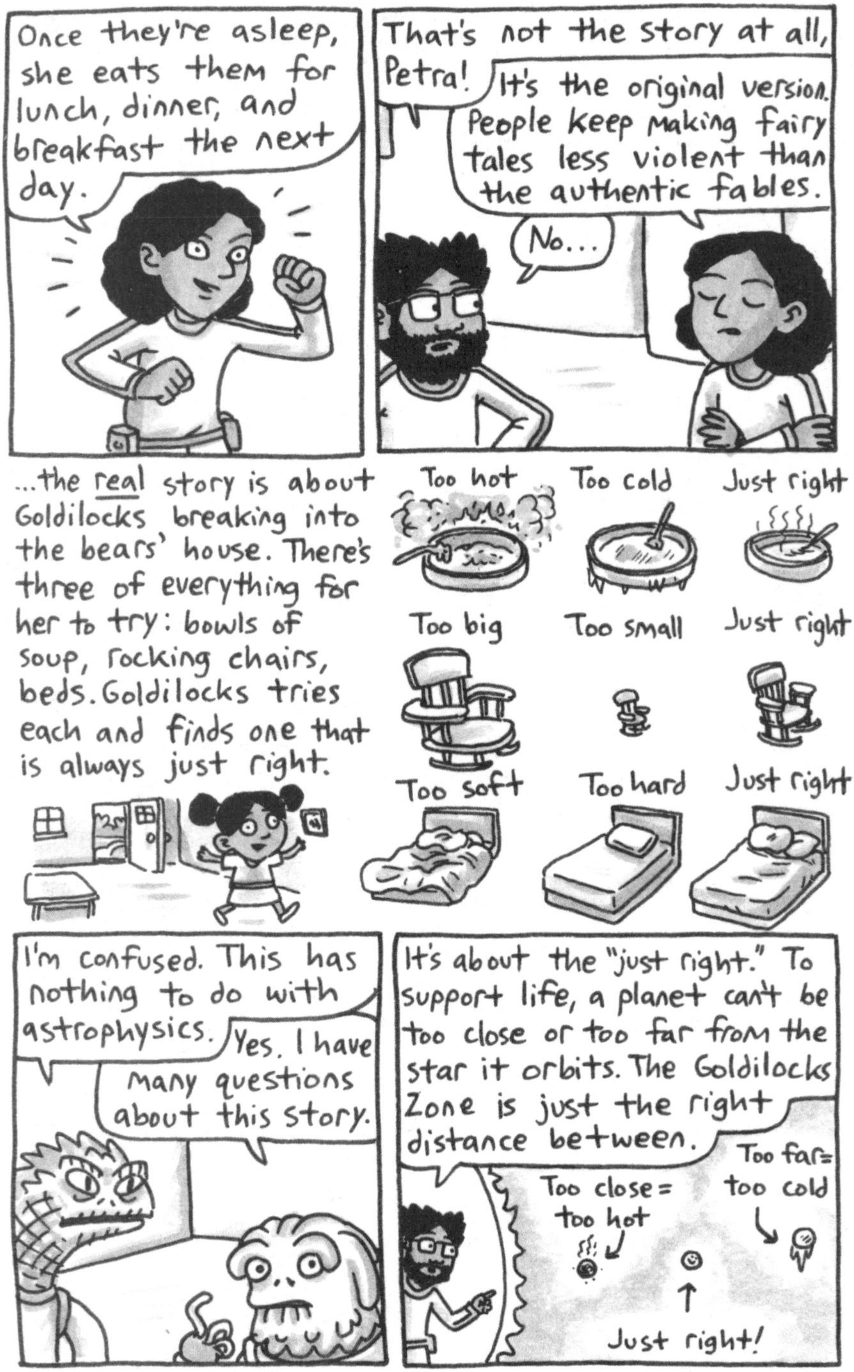
Once they're asleep, she eats them for lunch, dinner, and breakfast the next day.
That's not the story at all, Petra!
It's the original version. People keep making fairy tales less violent than the authentic fables.
No...
...the real story is about Goldilocks breaking into the bears' house. There's three of everything for her to try: bowls of soup, rocking chairs, beds. Goldilocks tries each and finds one that is always just right.
Too hot
Too cold
Just right
Too big
Too small
Just right
Too soft
Too hard
Just right
I'm confused. This has nothing to do with astrophysics.
Yes. I have many questions about this story.
It's about the "just right." To support life, a planet can't be too close or too far from the star it orbits. The Goldilocks Zone is just the right distance between.
Too close = too hot
Too far = too cold
Just right!

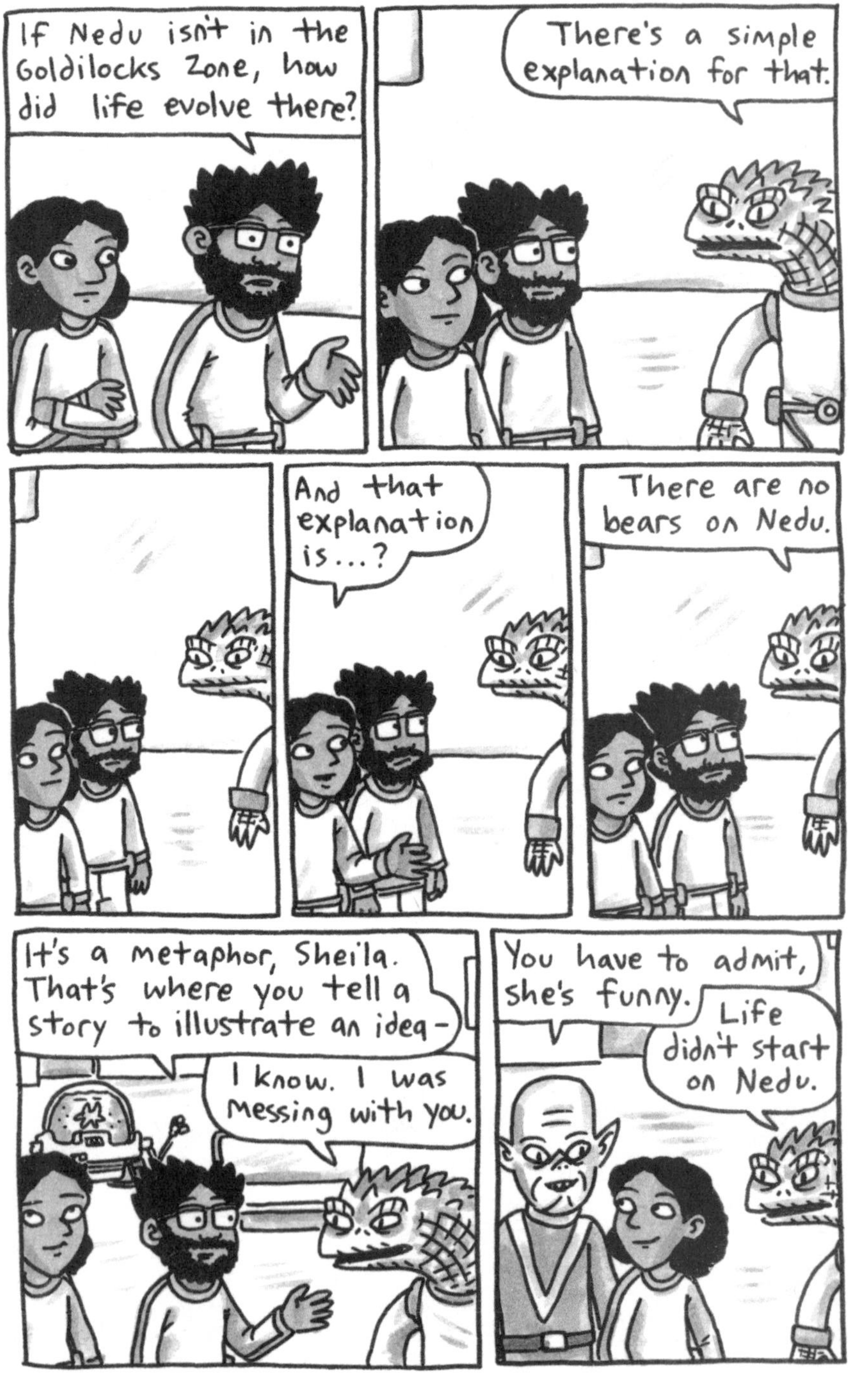
If Nedu isn't in the Goldilocks Zone, how did life evolve there?
There's a simple explanation for that.
And that explanation is...?
There are no bears on Nedu.
It's a metaphor, Sheila. That's where you tell a story to illustrate an idea-
I know. I was messing with you.
You have to admit, she's funny.
Life didn't start on Nedu.

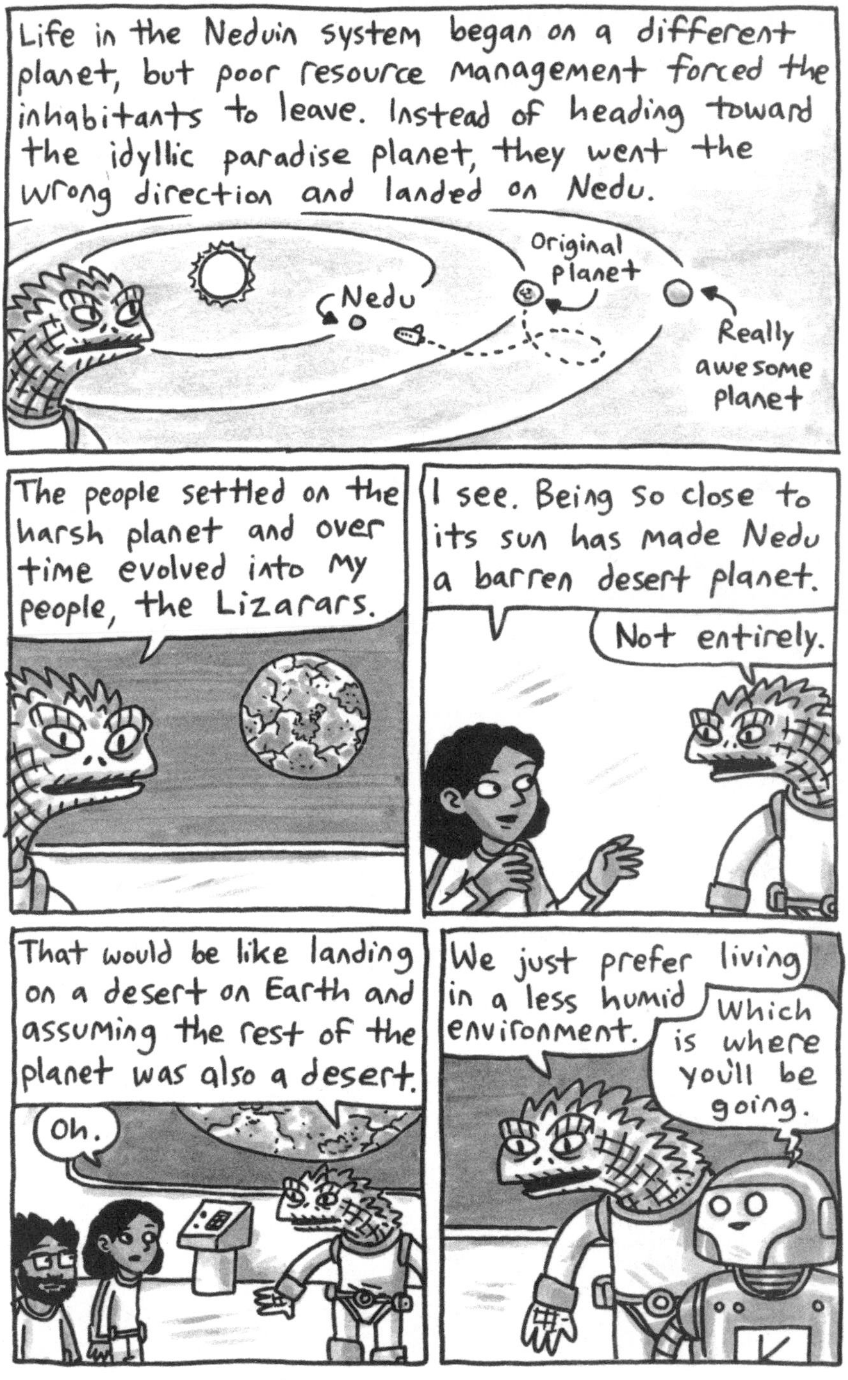
Life in the Neduin system began on a different planet, but poor resource management forced the inhabitants to leave. Instead of heading toward the idyllic paradise planet, they went the wrong direction and landed on Nedu.
Original planet
Nedu
Really awesome planet
The people settled on the harsh planet and over time evolved into my people, the Lizarars.
I see. Being so close to its sun has made Nedu a barren desert planet.
Not entirely.
That would be like landing on a desert on Earth and assuming the rest of the planet was also a desert.
Oh.
We just prefer living in a less humid environment.
Which is where you'll be going.

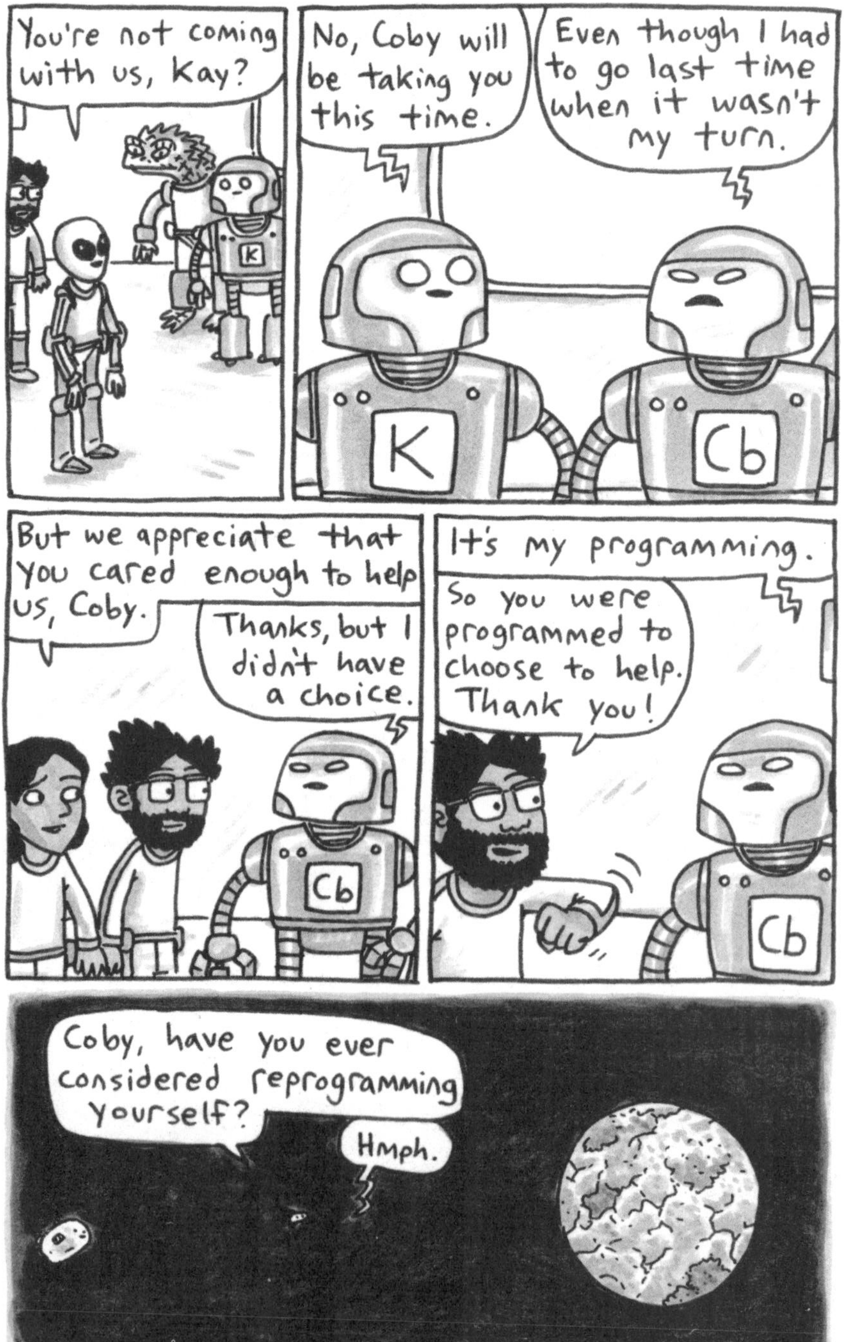
You're not coming with us, Kay?
No, Coby will be taking you this time.
Even though I had to go last time when it wasn't my turn.
K
Cb
But we appreciate that you cared enough to help us, Coby.
Thanks, but I didn't have a choice.
It's my programming.
So you were programmed to choose to help. Thank you!
Coby, have you ever considered reprogramming yourself?
Hmph.

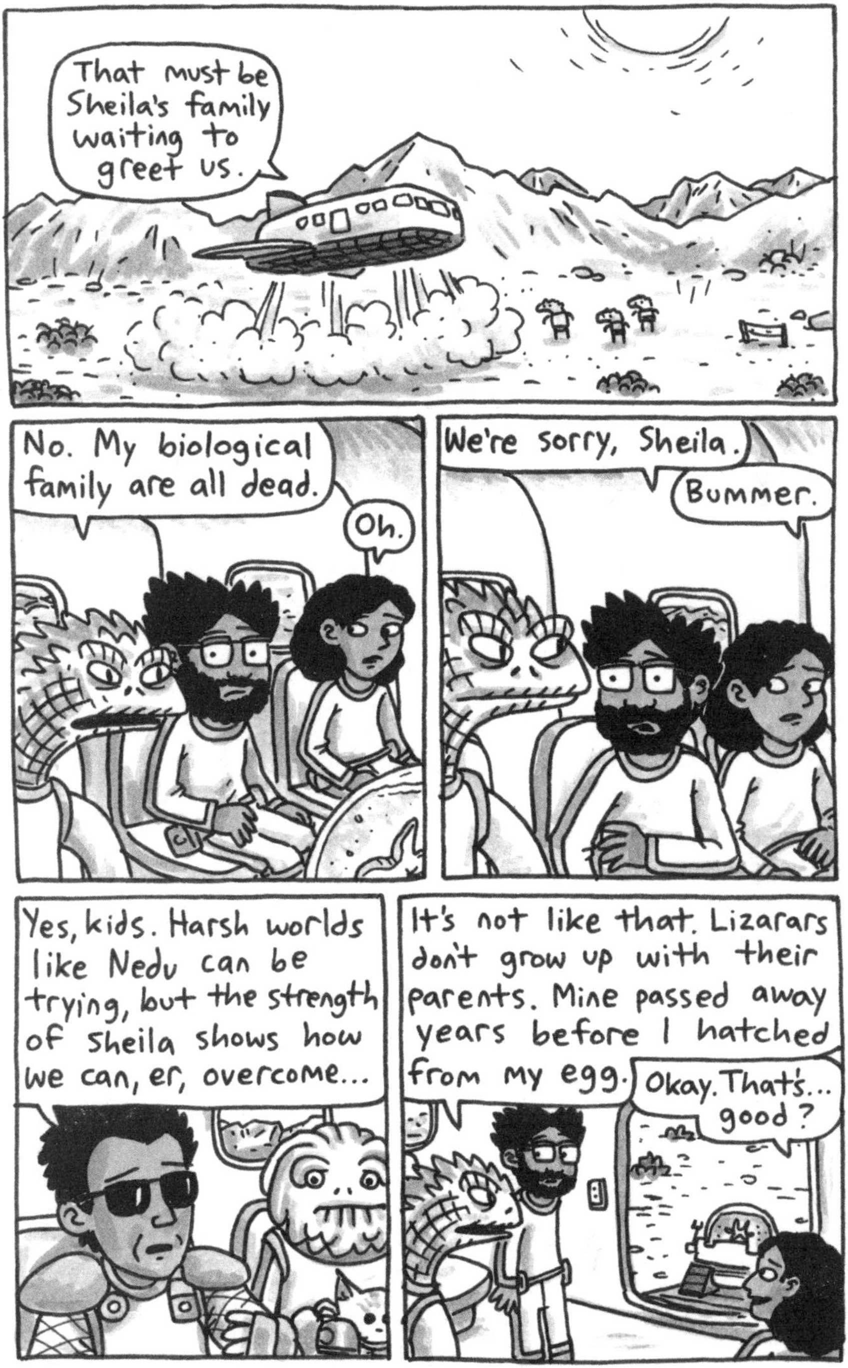
That must be Sheila's family waiting to greet us.
No. My biological family are all dead.
Oh.
We're sorry, Sheila.
Bummer.
Yes, kids. Harsh worlds like Nedu can be trying, but the strength of Sheila shows how we can, er, overcome...
It's not like that. Lizarars don't grow up with their parents. Mine passed away years before I hatched from my egg.
Okay. That's... good?

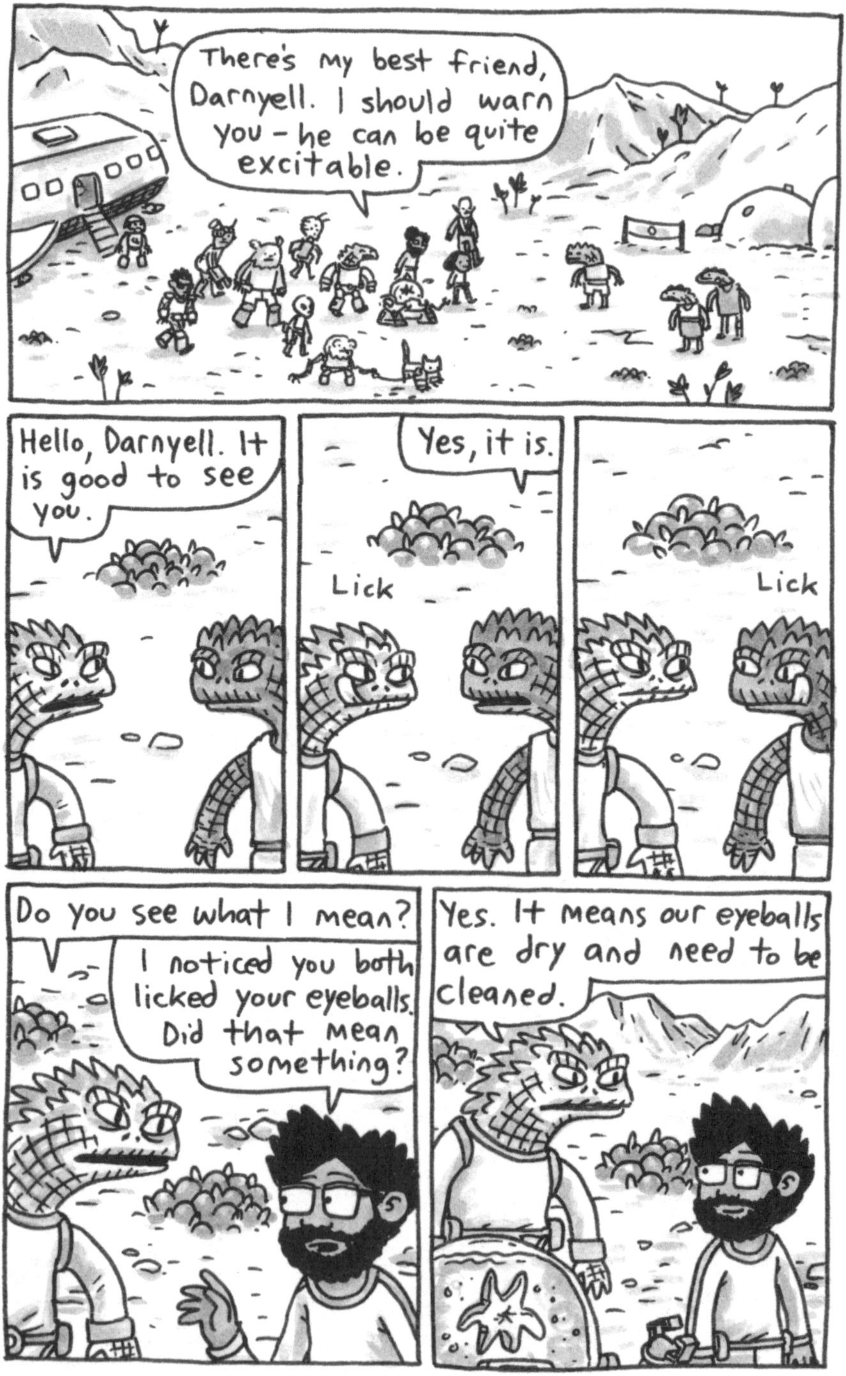
There's my best friend, Darnyell. I should warn you - he can be quite excitable.
Hello, Darnyell. It is good to see you.
Yes, it is.
Lick
Lick
Do you see what I mean?
I noticed you both licked your eyeballs. Did that mean something?
Yes. It means our eyeballs are dry and need to be cleaned.

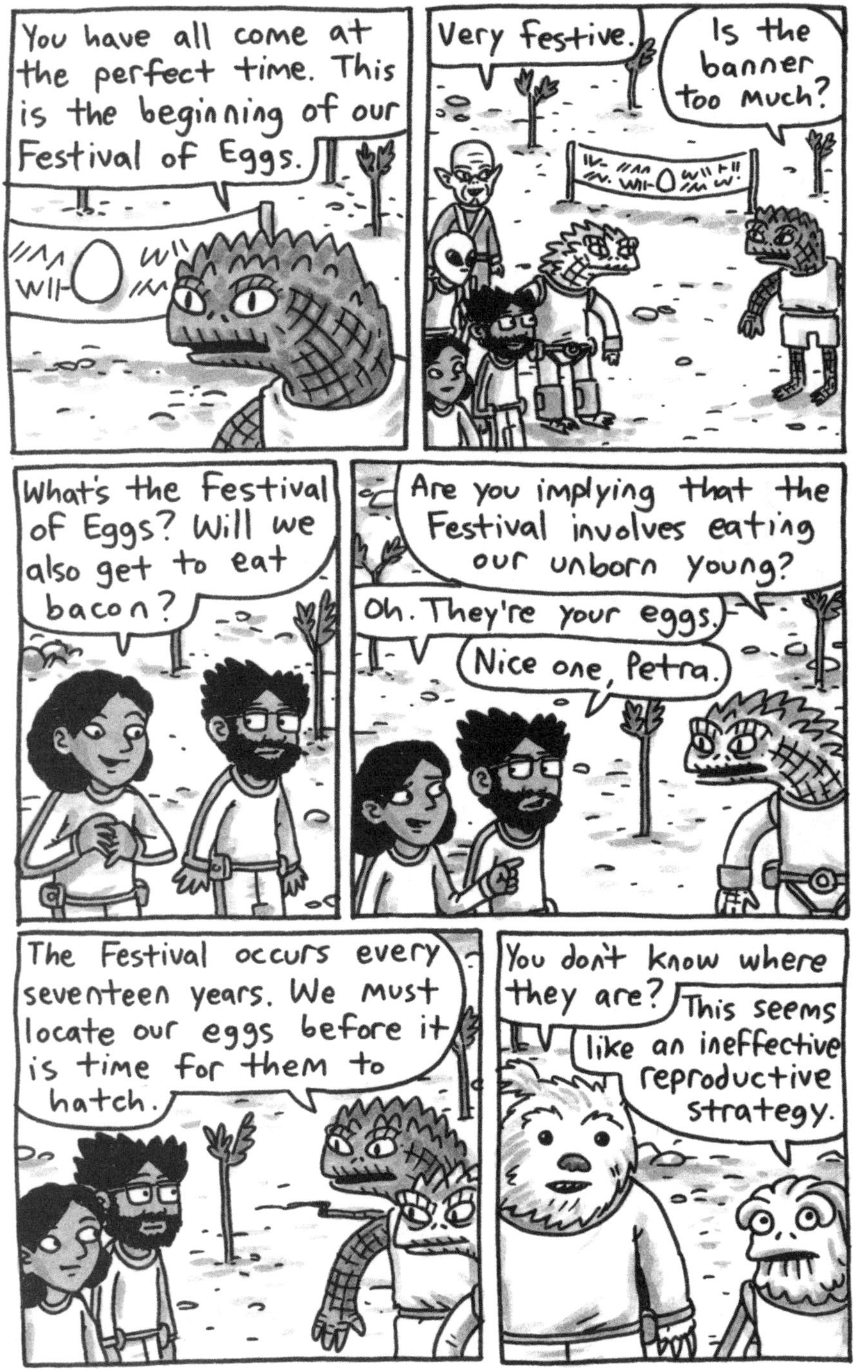

You have all come at the perfect time. This is the beginning of our Festival of Eggs.
Very festive.
Is the banner too much?
What's the Festival of Eggs? Will we also get to eat bacon?
Are you implying that the Festival involves eating our unborn young?
Oh. They're your eggs.
Nice one, Petra.
The Festival occurs every seventeen years. We must locate our eggs before it is time for them to hatch.
You don't know where they are?
This seems like an ineffective reproductive strategy.

My species is long-lived and our eggs require many seasons to incubate. In order to hide them from predators, the eggs are buried randomly. The birth parents pass away years before the eggs hatch.

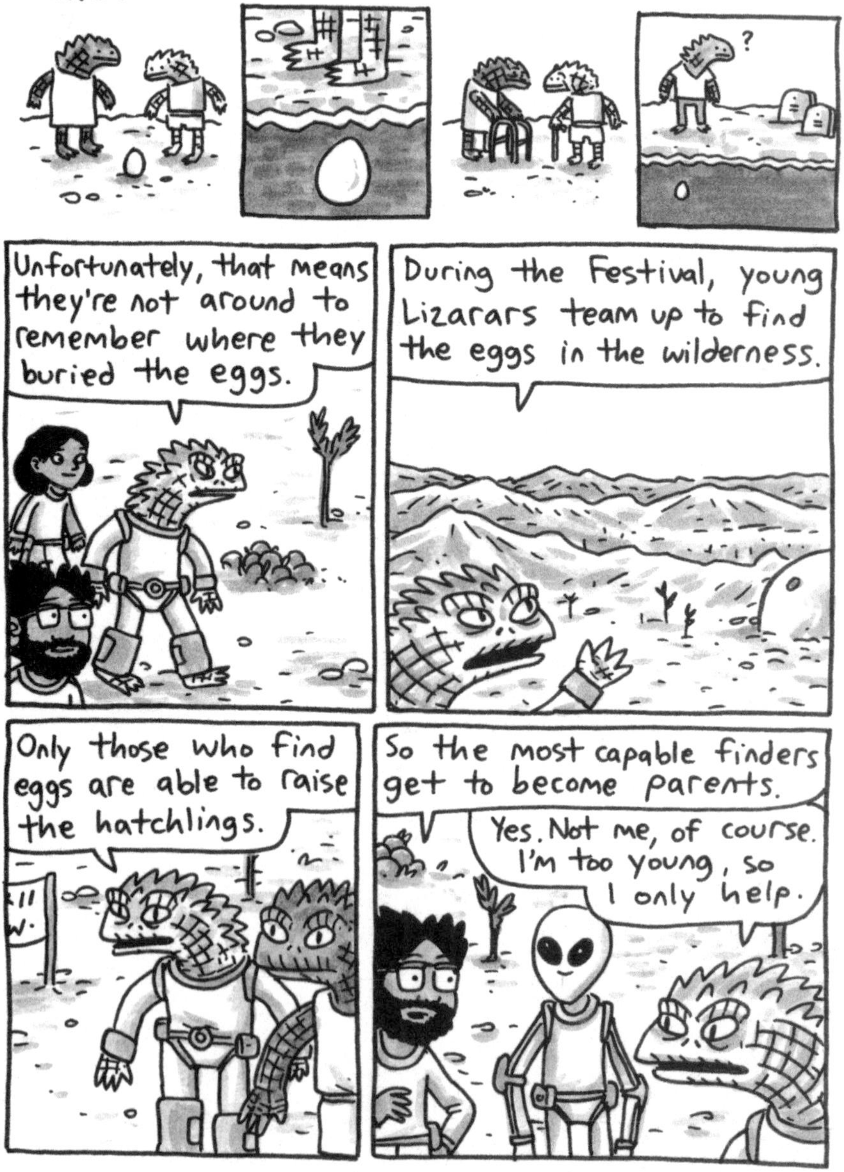

Unfortunately, that means they're not around to remember where they buried the eggs.
During the Festival, young Lizarars team up to find the eggs in the wilderness.
Only those who find eggs are able to raise the hatchlings.
So the most capable finders get to become parents.
Yes. Not me, of course. I'm too young, so I only help.

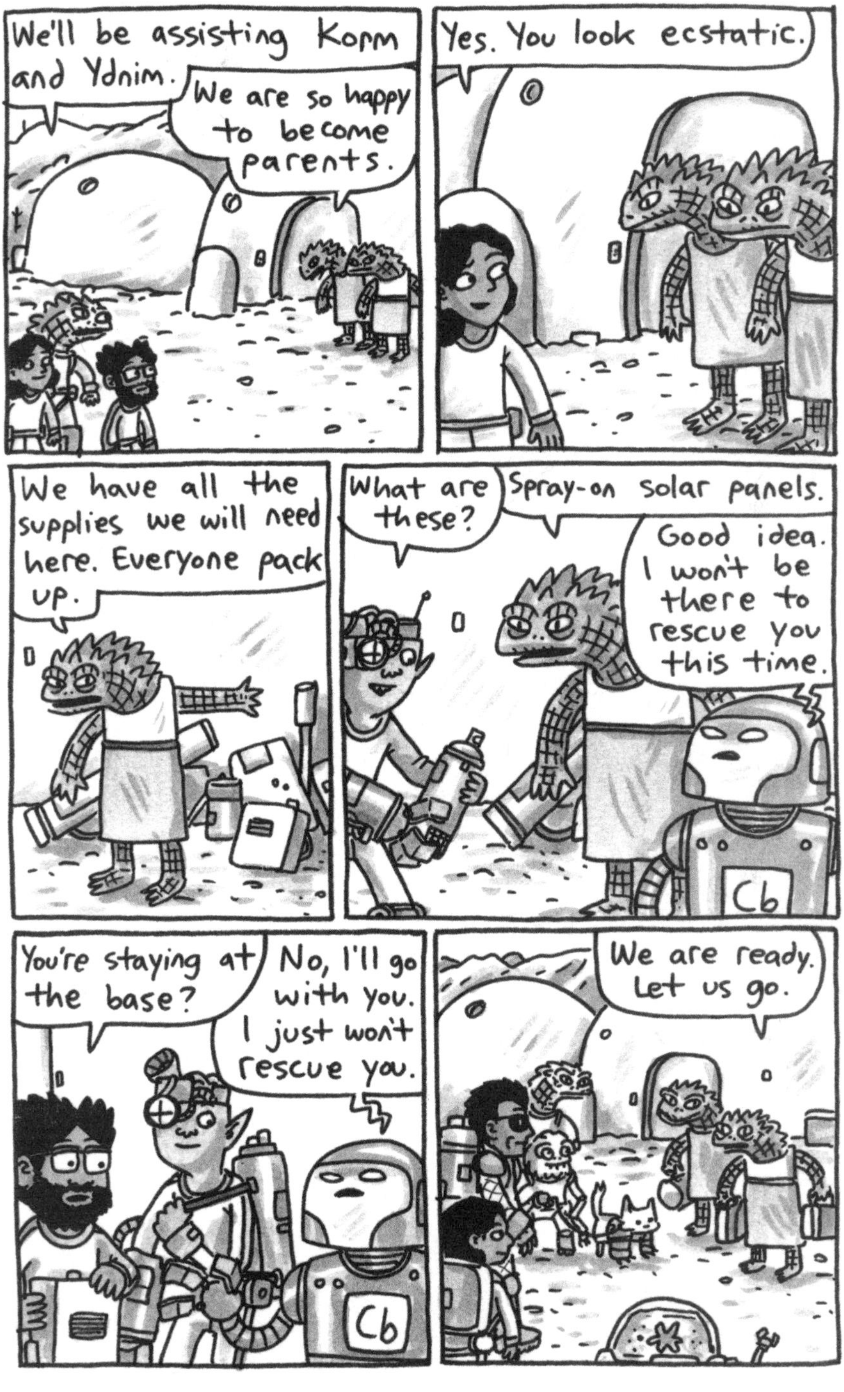
We'll be assisting Korm and Ydnim.
We are so happy to become parents.
Yes. You look ecstatic.
We have all the supplies we will need here. Everyone pack up.
What are these?
Spray-on solar panels.
Good idea. I won't be there to rescue you this time.
Cb
You're staying at the base?
No, I'll go with you. I just won't rescue you.
Cb
We are ready. Let us go.

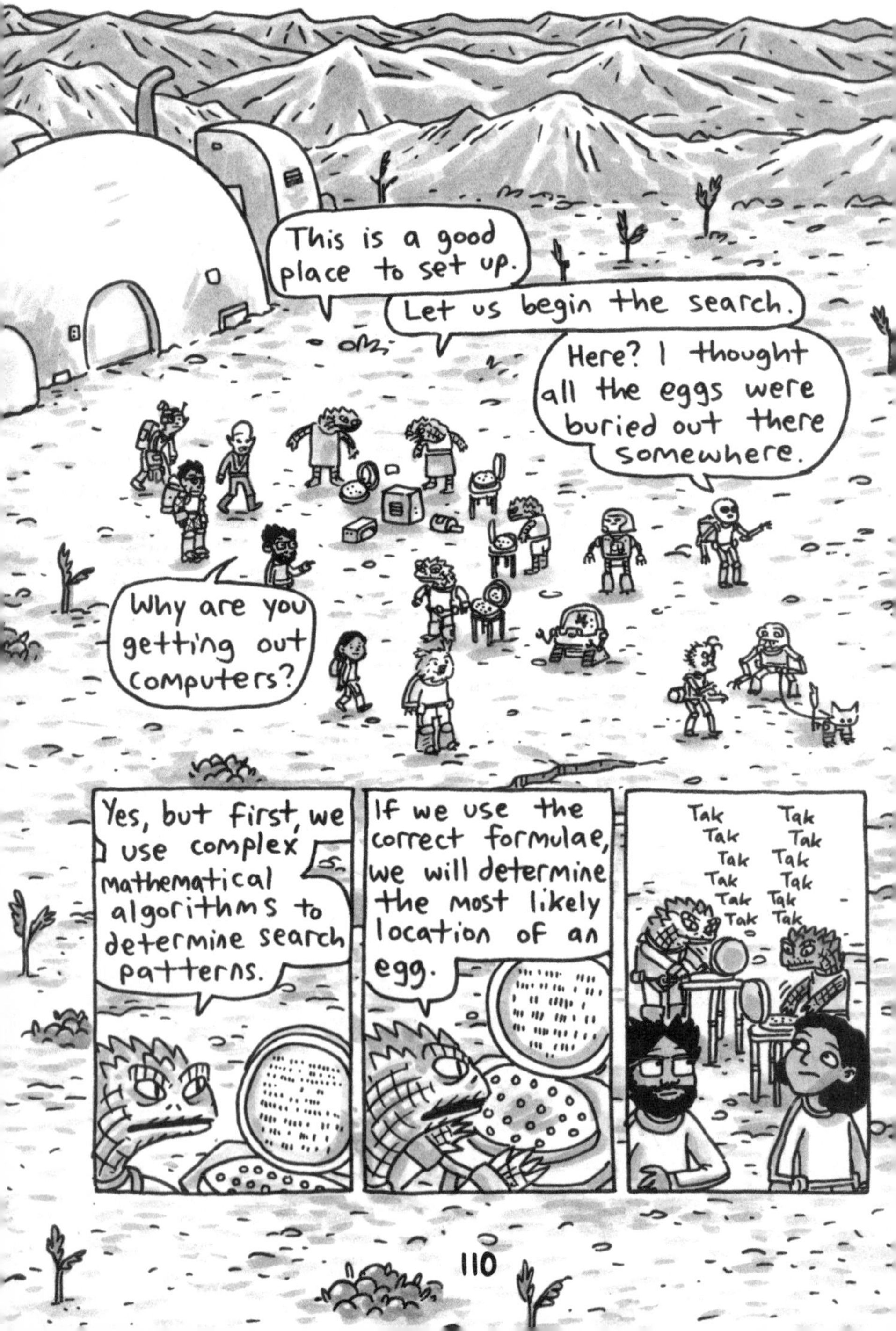
This is a good place to set up.
Let us begin the search.
Here? I thought all the eggs were buried out there somewhere.
Why are you getting out computers?
Yes, but first, we use complex mathematical algorithms to determine search patterns.
If we use the correct formulae, we will determine the most likely location of an egg.
Tak Tak Tak Tak Tak Tak Tak Tak Tak Tak Tak Tak

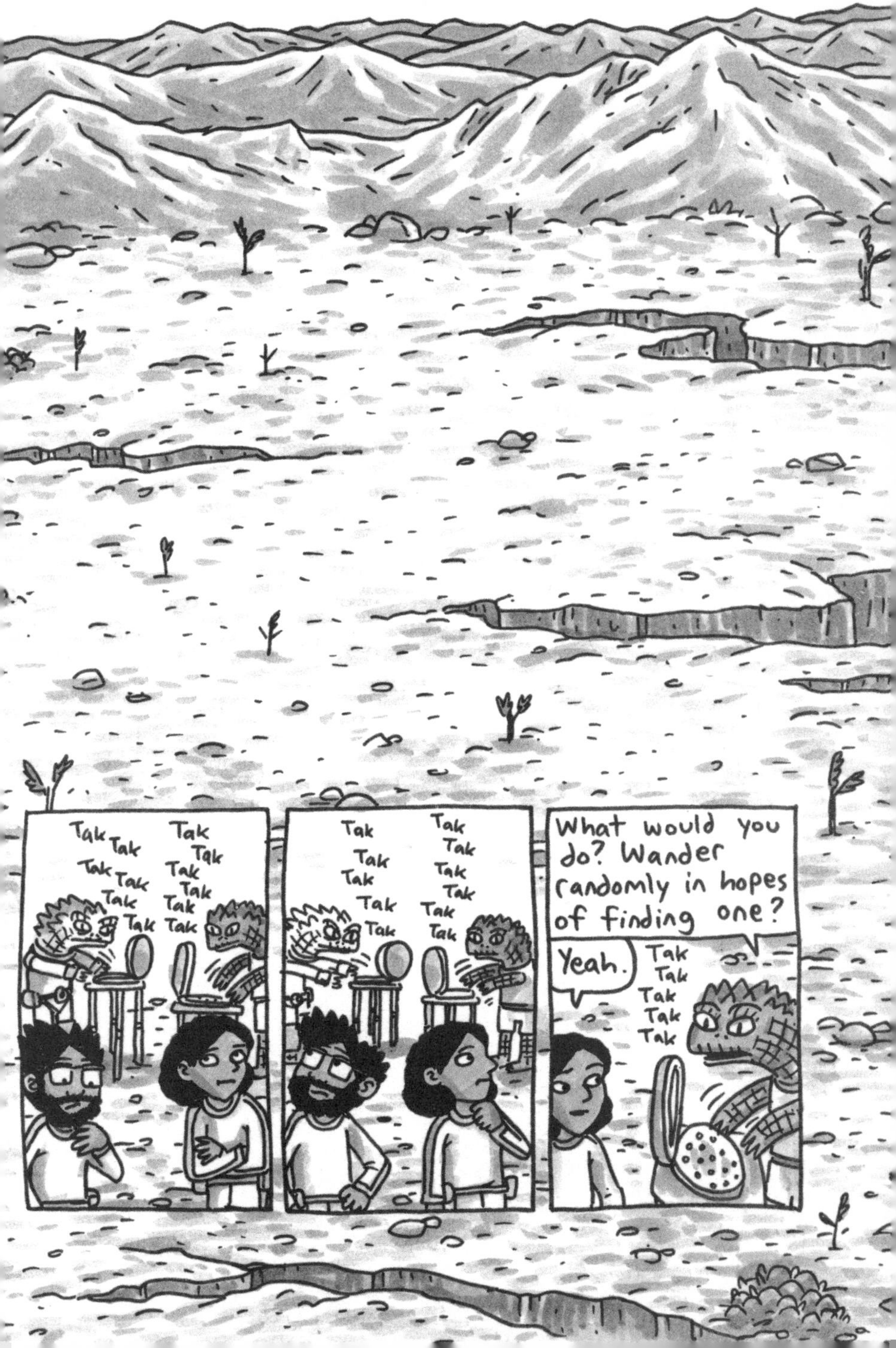
Tak Tak Tak Tak Tak Tak Tak Tak Tak Tak Tak Tak
Tak Tak Tak Tak Tak Tak Tak Tak Tak Tak
What would you do? Wander randomly in hopes of finding one?
Yeah.
Tak Tak Tak Tak Tak

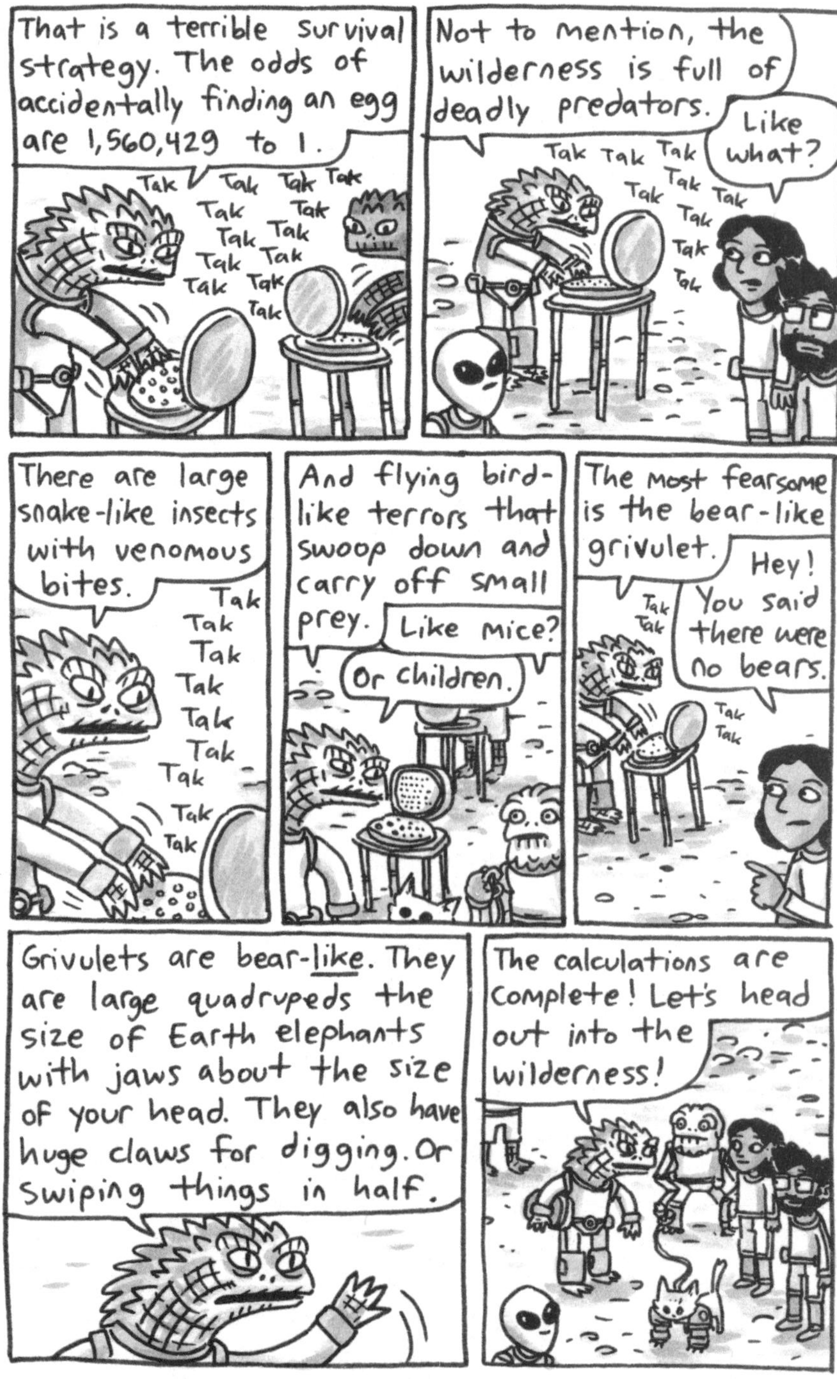
That is a terrible survival strategy. The odds of accidentally finding an egg are 1,560,429 to 1.
Tak Tak Tak Tak Tak Tak Tak Tak Tak Tak Tak Tak Tak
Not to mention, the wilderness is full of deadly predators.
Like what?
Tak Tak Tak Tak Tak Tak Tak Tak Tak
There are large snake-like insects with venomous bites.
Tak Tak Tak Tak Tak Tak Tak Tak Tak
And flying bird-like terrors that swoop down and carry off small prey.
Like mice?
Or children.
The most fearsome is the bear-like grivulet.
Tak Tak
Hey! You said there were no bears.
Tak Tak
Grivulets are bear-like. They are large quadrupeds the size of Earth elephants with jaws about the size of your head. They also have huge claws for digging. Or swiping things in half.
The calculations are complete! Let's head out into the wilderness!

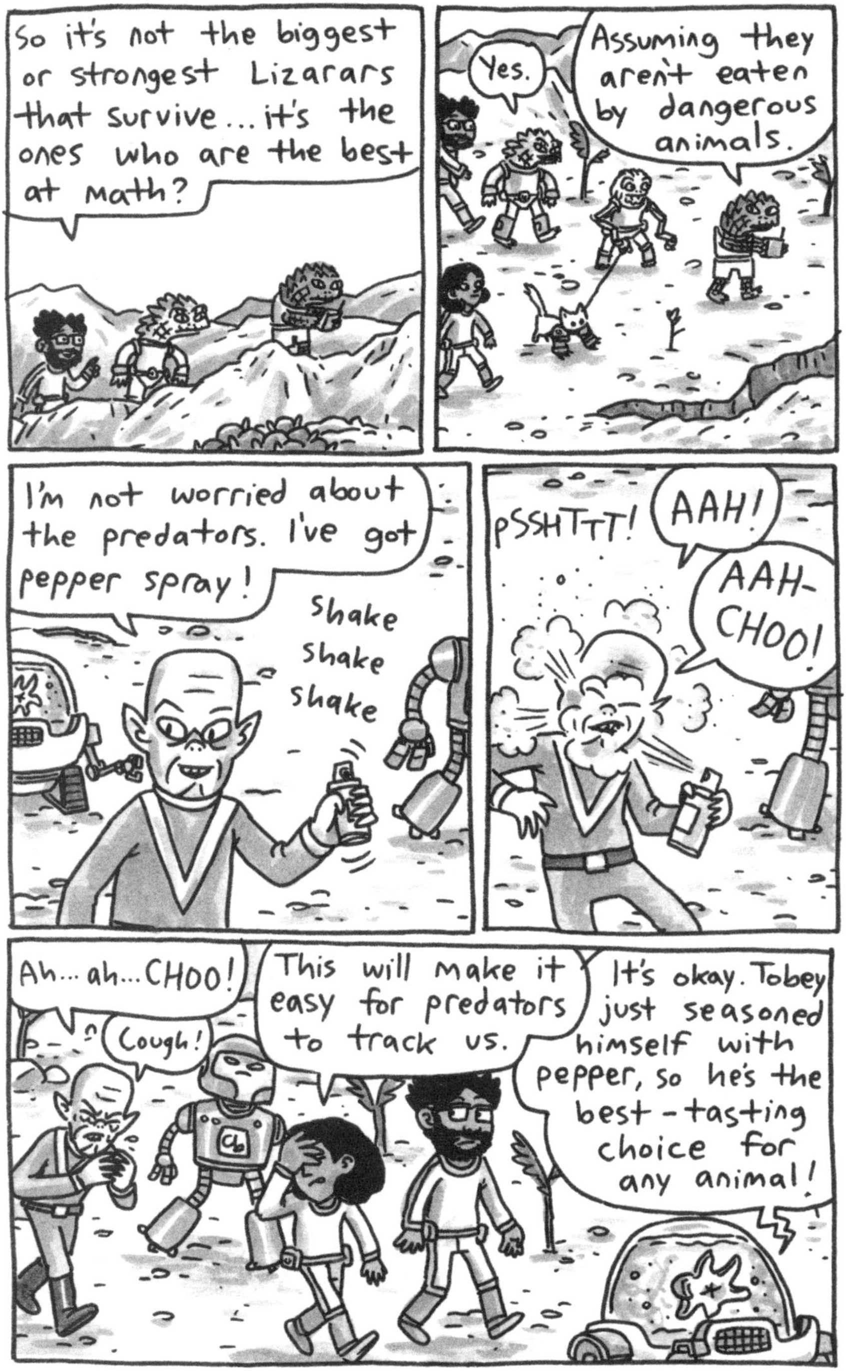
So it's not the biggest or strongest Lizarars that survive... it's the ones who are the best at math?
Yes.
Assuming they aren't eaten by dangerous animals.
I'm not worried about the predators. I've got pepper spray!
Shake shake shake
pSSHTTT!
AAH!
AAH-CHOO!
Ah... ah... CHOO!
Cough!
This will make it easy for predators to track us.
It's okay. Tobey just seasoned himself with pepper, so he's the best-tasting choice for any animal!

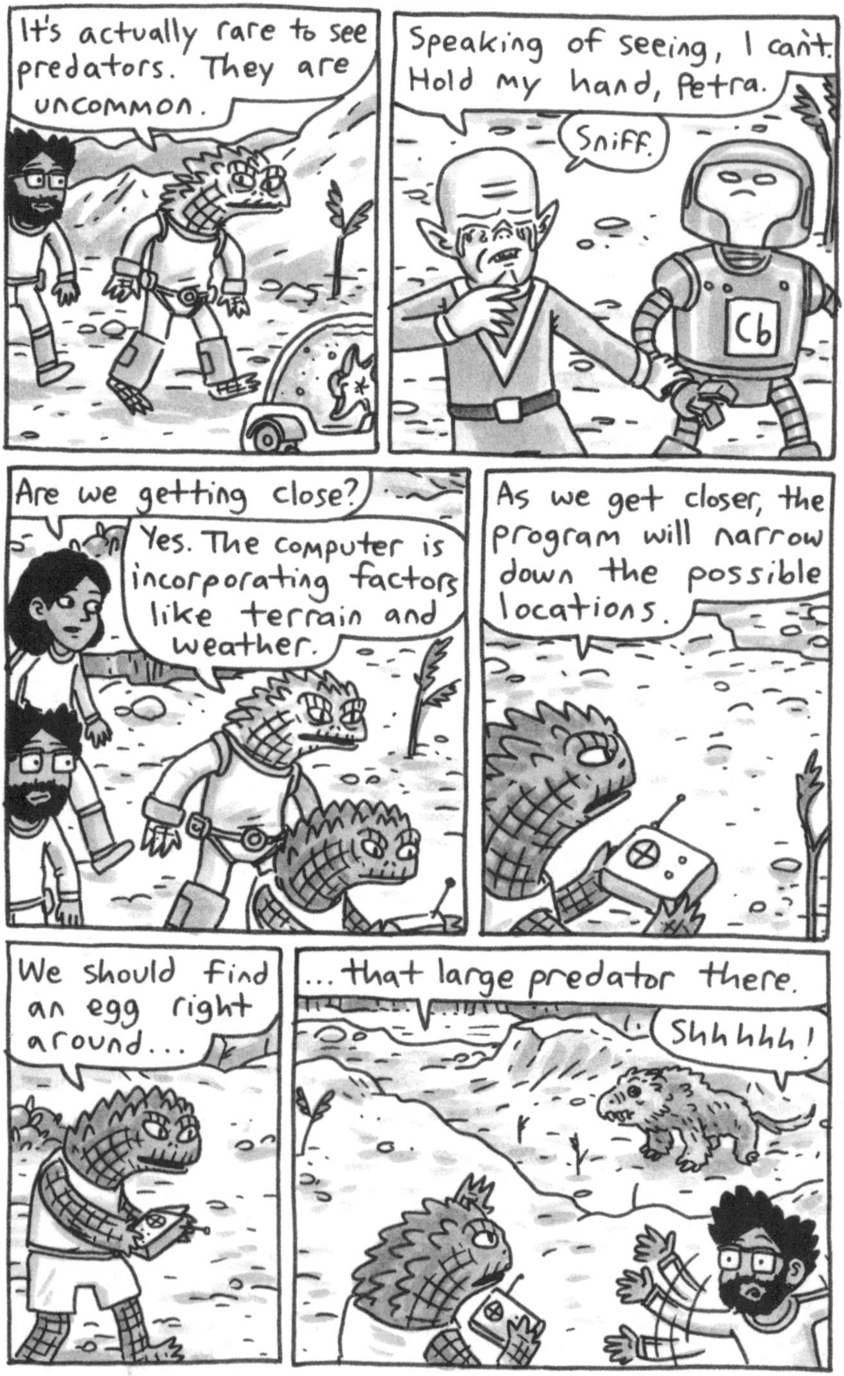
It's actually rare to see predators. They are uncommon.
Speaking of seeing, I can't. Hold my hand, Petra.
Sniff.
Cb
Are we getting close?
Yes. The computer is incorporating factors like terrain and weather.
As we get closer, the program will narrow down the possible locations.
We should find an egg right around...
...that large predator there.
Shhhhh!

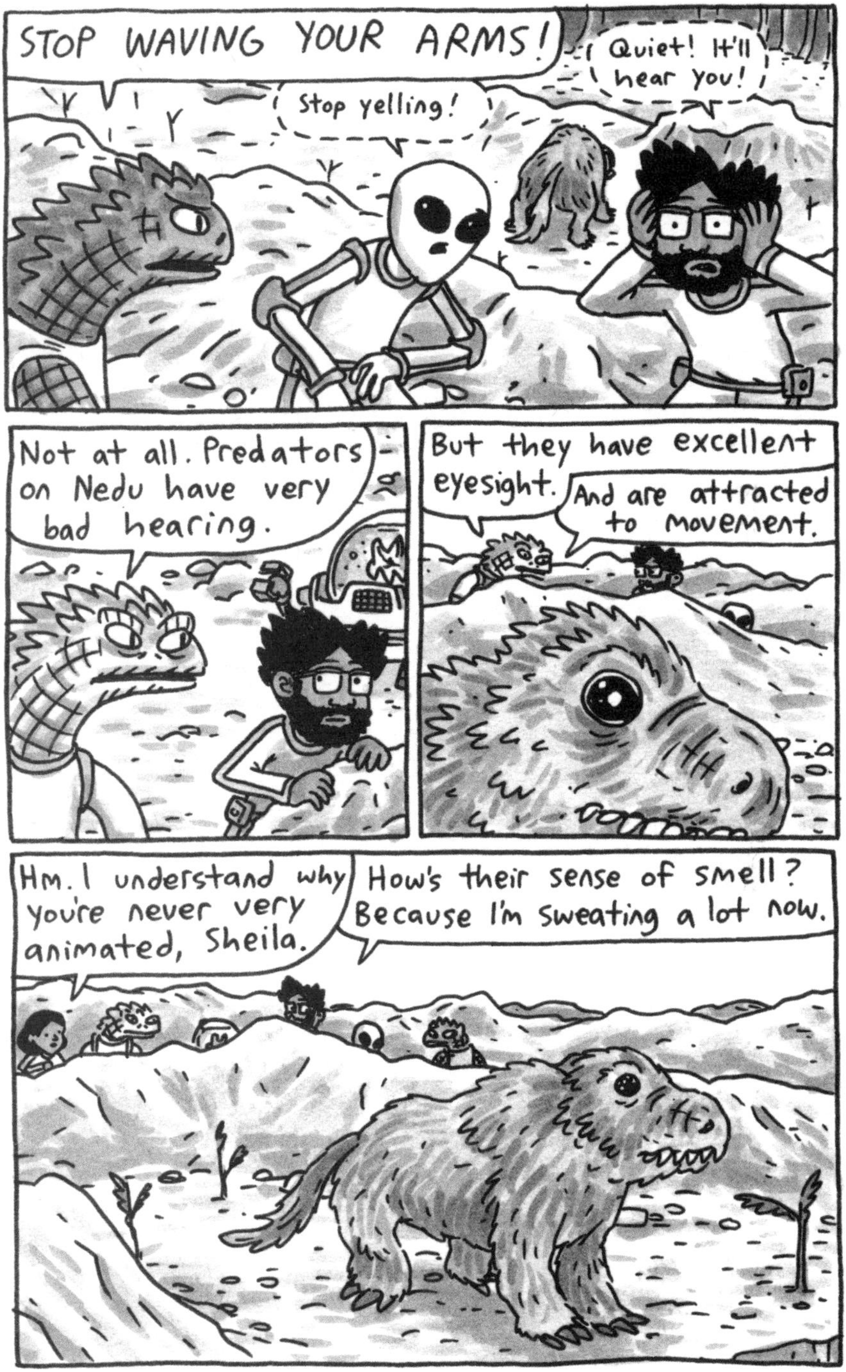
STOP WAVING YOUR ARMS!
Stop yelling!
Quiet! It'll hear you!
Not at all. Predators on Nedu have very bad hearing.
But they have excellent eyesight.
And are attracted to movement.
Hm. I understand why you're never very animated, Sheila.
How's their sense of smell? Because I'm sweating a lot now.

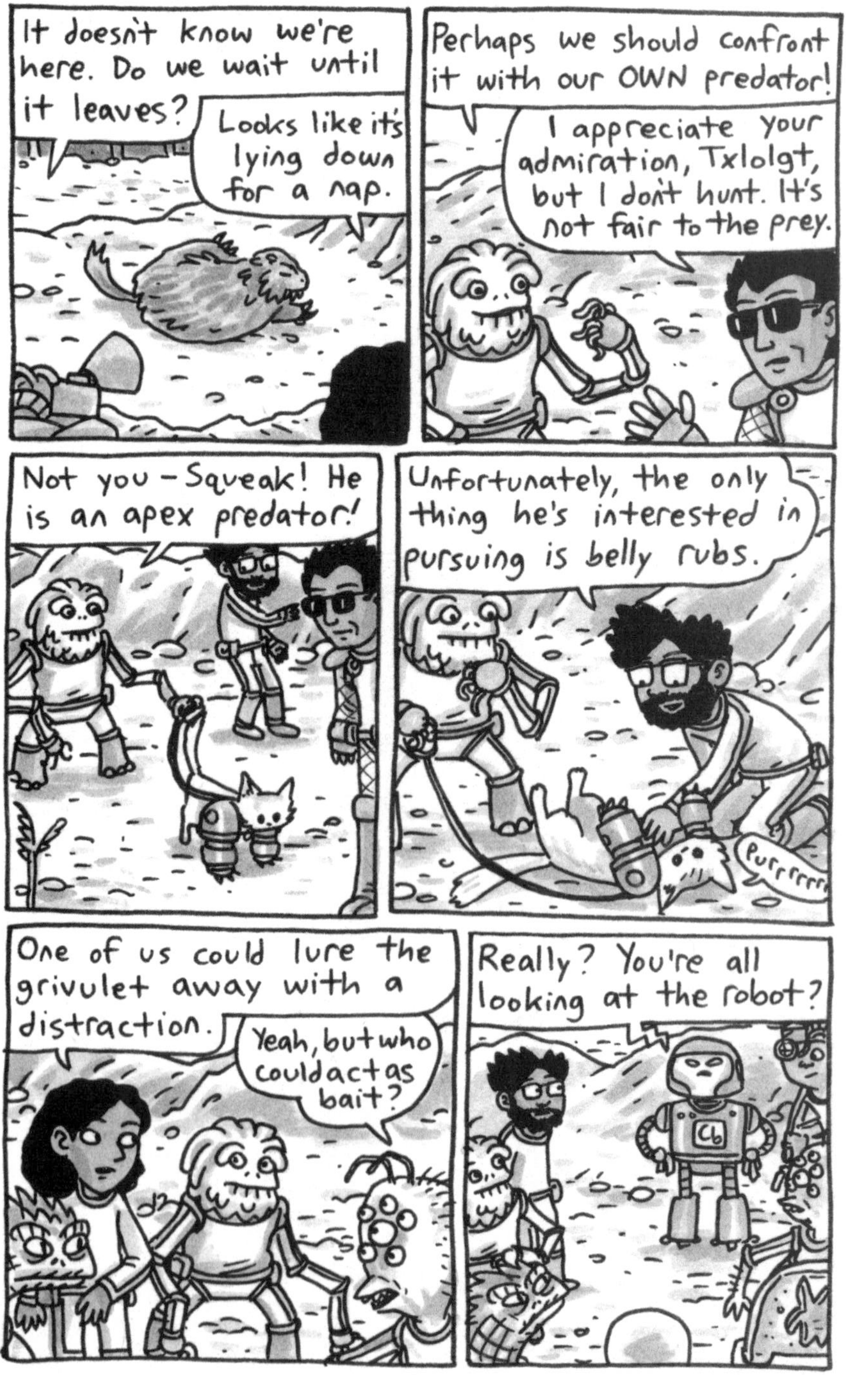
It doesn't know we're here. Do we wait until it leaves?
Looks like it's lying down for a nap.
Perhaps we should confront it with our OWN predator!
I appreciate your admiration, Txlolgt, but I don't hunt. It's not fair to the prey.
Not you - Squeak! He is an apex predator!
Unfortunately, the only thing he's interested in pursuing is belly rubs.
Purrrrrr
One of us could lure the grivulet away with a distraction.
Yeah, but who could act as bait?
Really? You're all looking at the robot?

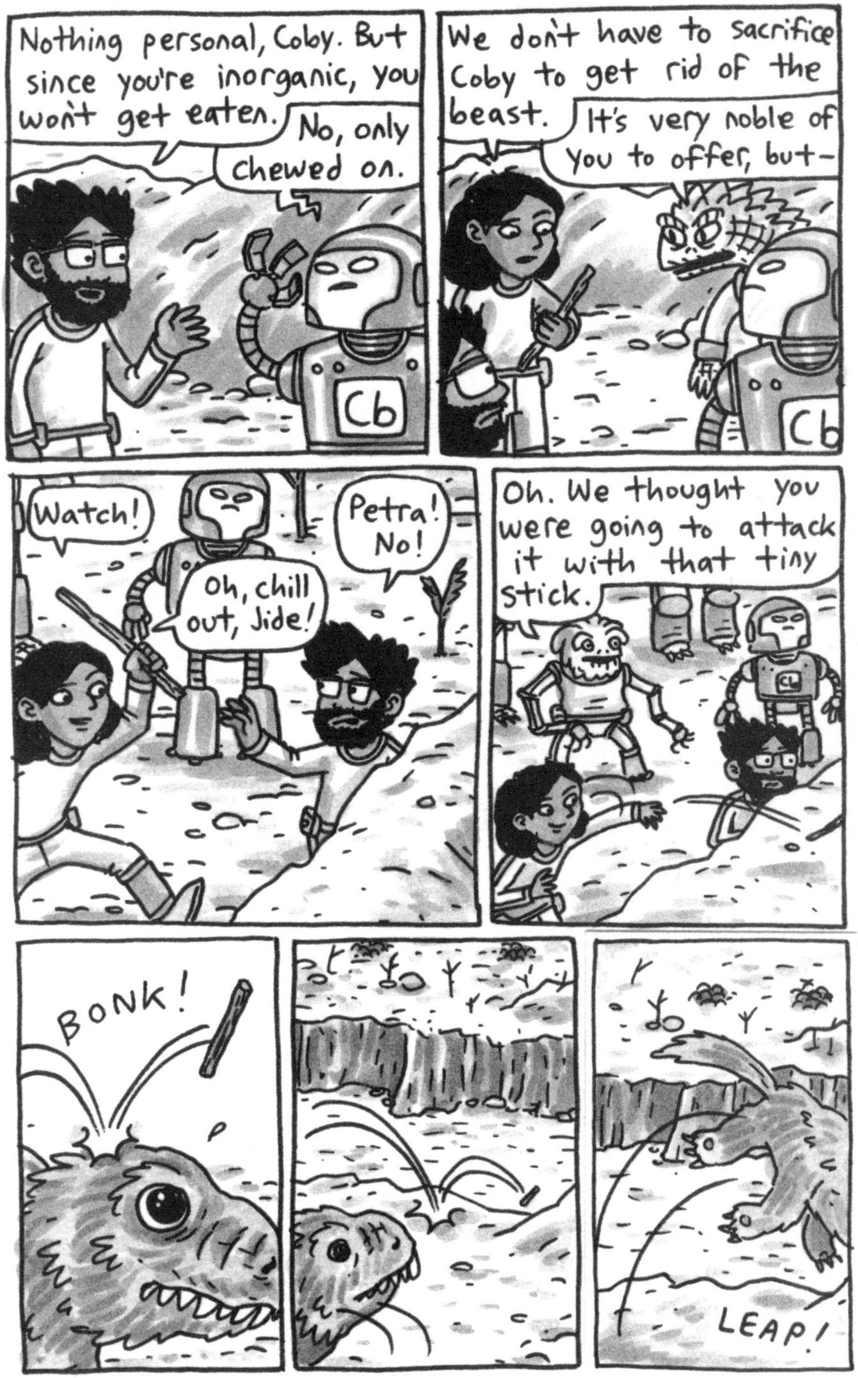

Nothing personal, Coby. But since you're inorganic, you won't get eaten.
No, only chewed on.
Cb
We don't have to sacrifice Coby to get rid of the beast.
It's very noble of you to offer, but-
Cb
Watch!
Oh, chill out, Jide!
Petra! No!
Oh. We thought you were going to attack it with that tiny stick.
BONK!
LEAP!

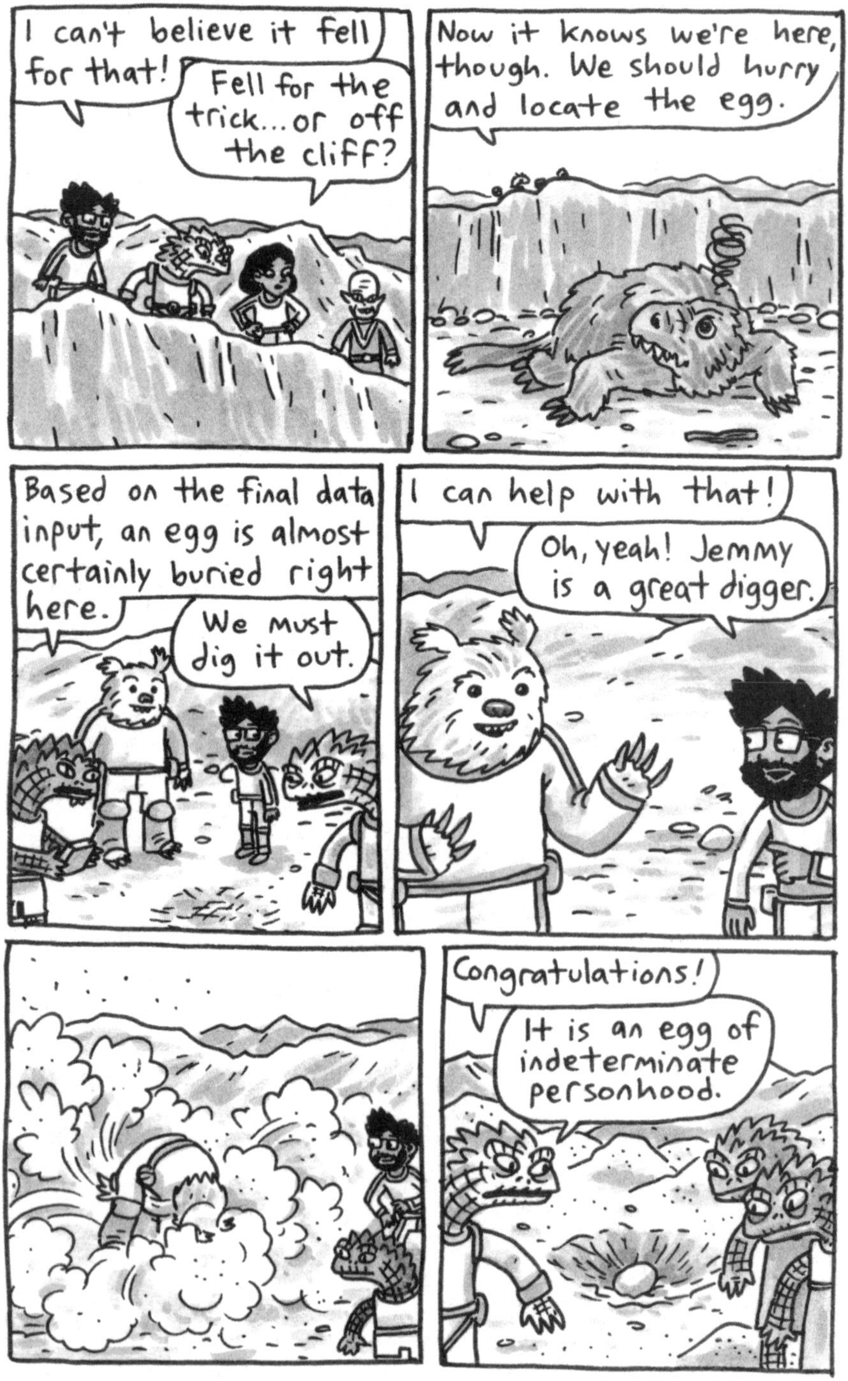

I can't believe it fell for that!
Fell for the trick...or off the cliff?
Now it knows we're here, though. We should hurry and locate the egg.
Based on the final data input, an egg is almost certainly buried right here.
We must dig it out.
I can help with that!
Oh, yeah! Jemmy is a great digger.
Congratulations!
It is an egg of indeterminate personhood.

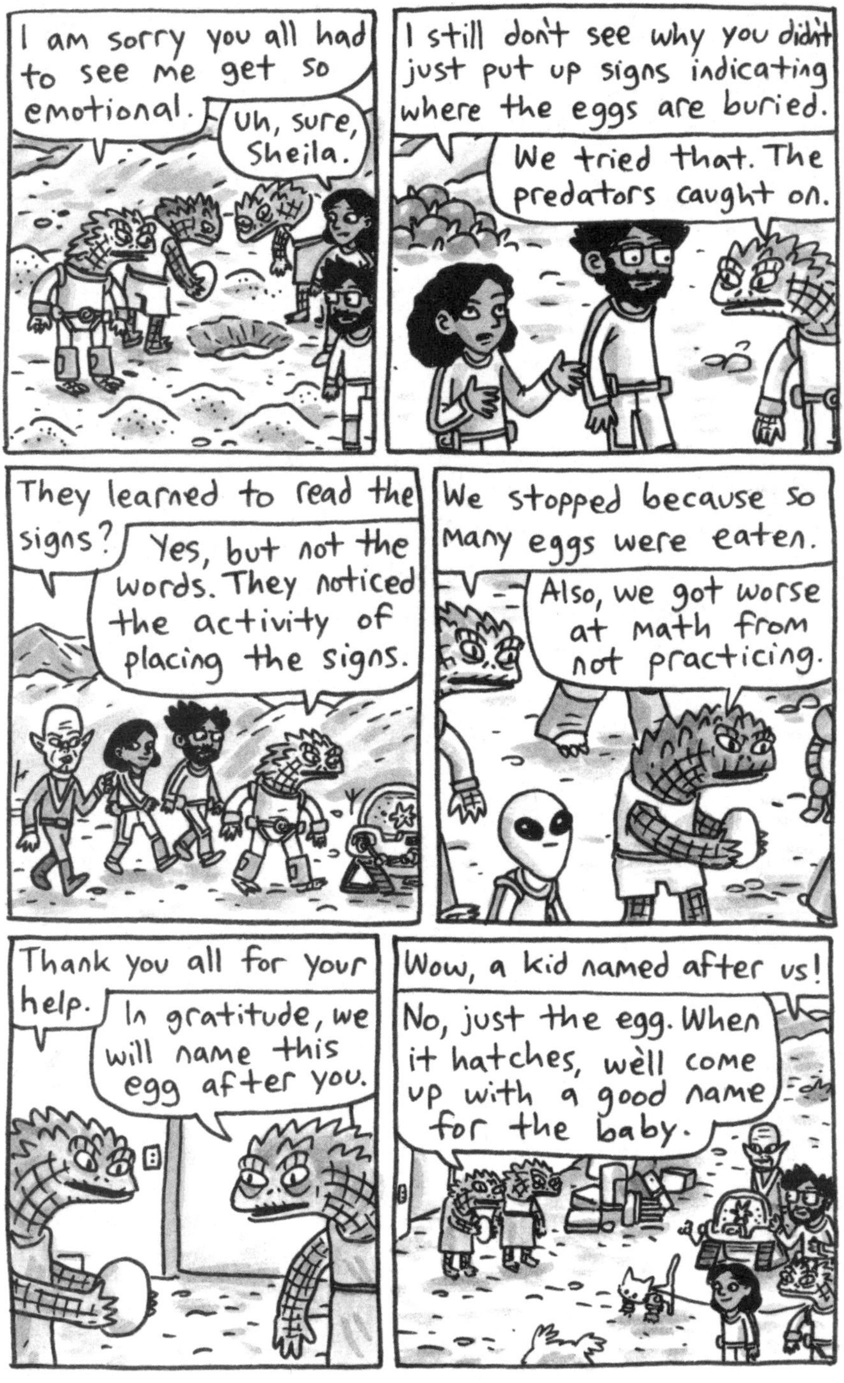
I am sorry you all had to see me get so emotional.
Uh, sure, Sheila.
I still don't see why you didn't just put up signs indicating where the eggs are buried.
We tried that. The predators caught on.
They learned to read the signs?
Yes, but not the words. They noticed the activity of placing the signs.
We stopped because so many eggs were eaten.
Also, we got worse at math from not practicing.
Thank you all for your help.
In gratitude, we will name this egg after you.
Wow, a kid named after us!
No, just the egg. When it hatches, we'll come up with a good name for the baby.

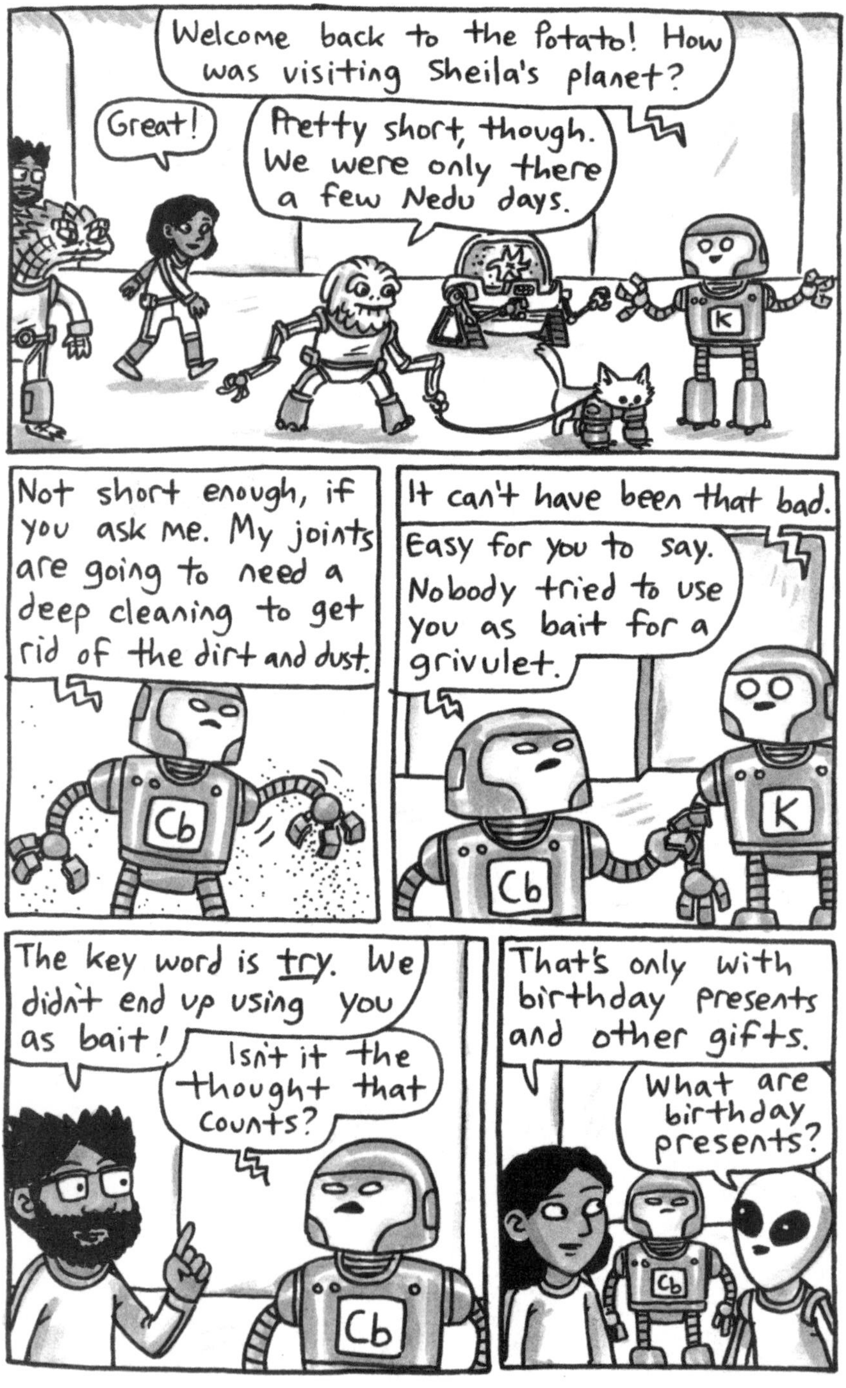
Welcome back to the Potato! How was visiting Sheila's planet?
Great!
Pretty short, though. We were only there a few Nedu days.
Not short enough, if you ask me. My joints are going to need a deep cleaning to get rid of the dirt and dust.
It can't have been that bad.
Easy for you to say. Nobody tried to use you as bait for a grivulet.
The key word is try. We didn't end up using you as bait!
Isn't it the thought that counts?
That's only with birthday presents and other gifts.
What are birthday presents?

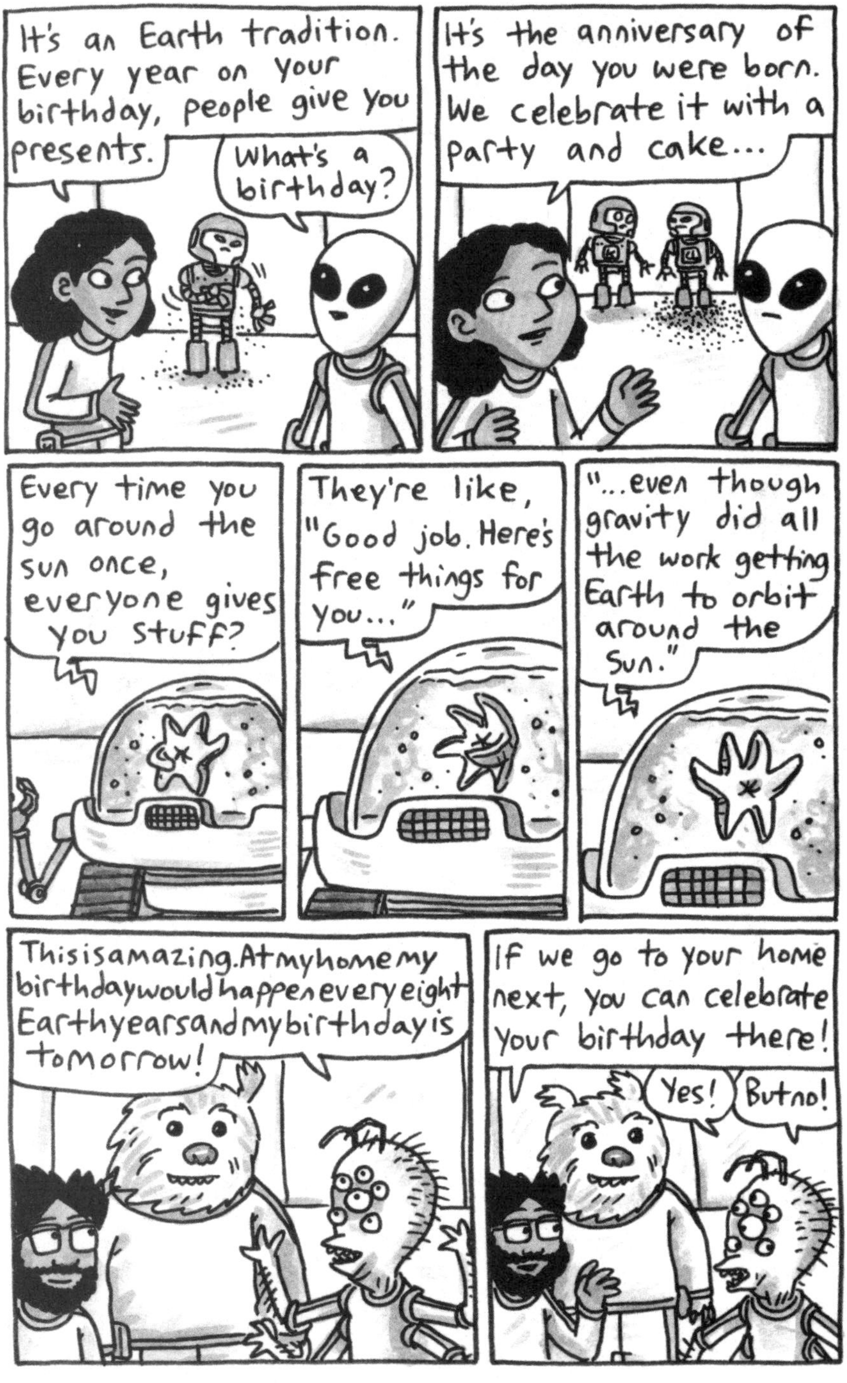
It's an Earth tradition. Every year on your birthday, people give you presents.
What's a birthday?
It's the anniversary of the day you were born. We celebrate it with a party and cake...
Every time you go around the sun once, everyone gives you stuff?
They're like, "Good job. Here's free things for you..."
"...even though gravity did all the work getting Earth to orbit around the Sun."
Thisisamazing.Atmyhomemy birthdaywouldhappeneveryeight Earthyearsandmybirthdayis tomorrow!
If we go to your home next, you can celebrate your birthday there!
Yes!
Butno!

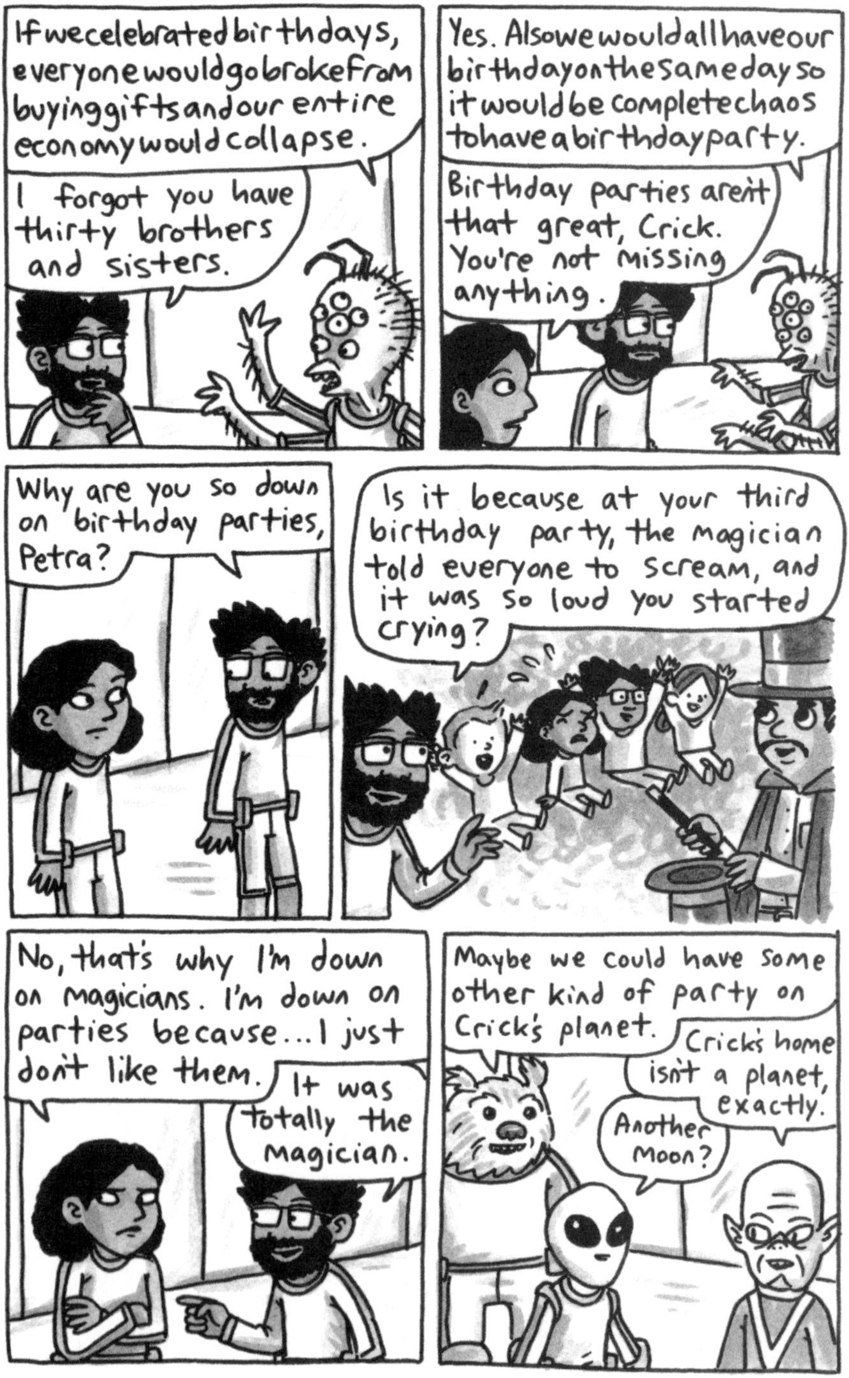
If we celebrated birthdays, everyone would go broke from buying gifts and our entire economy would collapse.
I forgot you have thirty brothers and sisters.
Yes. Also we would all have our birthday on the same day so it would be complete chaos to have a birthday party.
Birthday parties aren't that great, Crick. You're not missing anything.
Why are you so down on birthday parties, Petra?
Is it because at your third birthday party, the magician told everyone to scream, and it was so loud you started crying?
No, that's why I'm down on magicians. I'm down on parties because...I just don't like them.
It was totally the magician.
Maybe we could have some other kind of party on Crick's planet.
Crick's home isn't a planet, exactly.
Another Moon?

The planet my people are originally from is surrounded by an orbiting debris field.

Like rings?

Yes, except it's not just a belt. It fills the entire atmosphere. The surface of the planet is unreachable and life migrated out to live in the debris field.

Where did the debris field come from? Meteoroids?

It started out with a few satellites...

Over time, more and more abandoned spaceships and space stations and things piled up in the atmosphere. It's like a planet of hoarders who kept all their stuff in orbit.

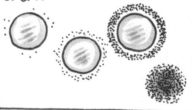

The debris field has become its own self-sustained ecosystem.

My family are all junkminers.

Oh! Maybe I can pick up some interesting parts!

We're just swinging by without stopping.

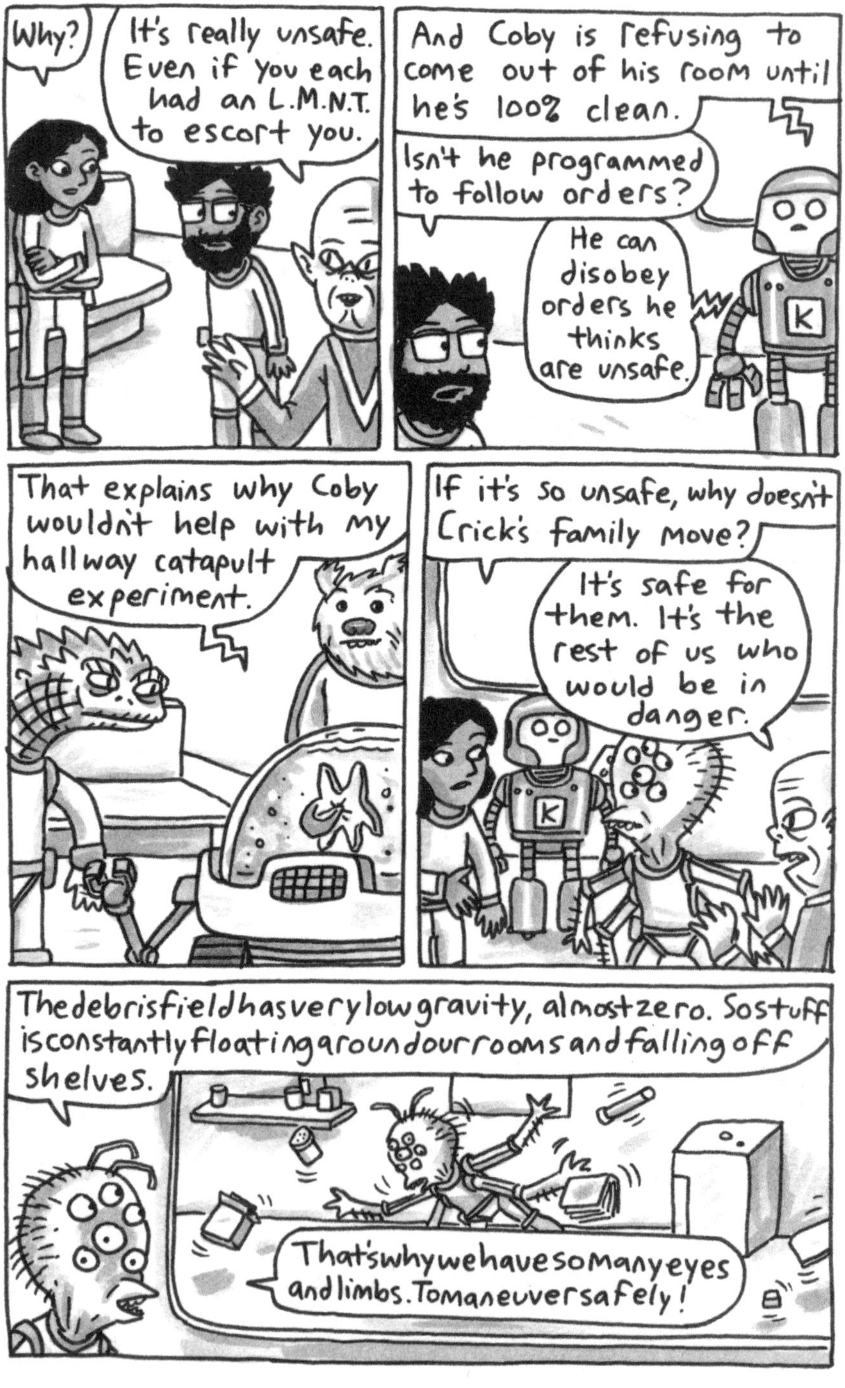

Why?
It's really unsafe. Even if you each had an L.M.N.T. to escort you.
And Coby is refusing to come out of his room until he's 100% clean.
Isn't he programmed to follow orders?
He can disobey orders he thinks are unsafe.
That explains why Coby wouldn't help with my hallway catapult experiment.
If it's so unsafe, why doesn't Crick's family move?
It's safe for them. It's the rest of us who would be in danger.
The debris field has very low gravity, almost zero. So stuff is constantly floating around our rooms and falling off shelves.
That's why we have so many eyes and limbs. To maneuver safely!

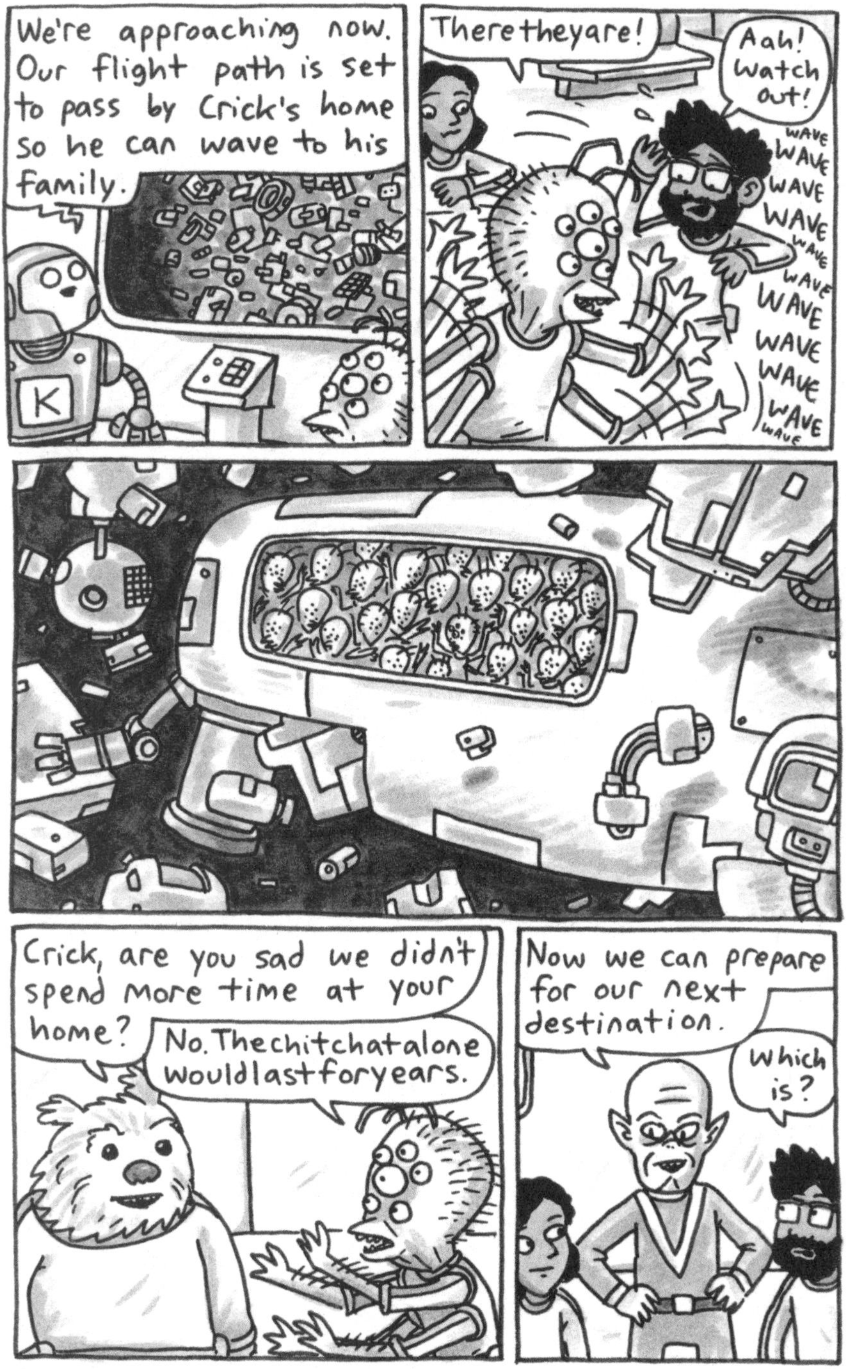
We're approaching now. Our flight path is set to pass by Crick's home so he can wave to his family.
K
Theretheyare!
Aah! Watch out!
WAVE WAVE WAVE WAVE WAVE WAVE WAVE WAVE WAVE WAVE WAVE
Crick, are you sad we didn't spend more time at your home?
No. Thechitchatalone wouldlastforyears.
Now we can prepare for our next destination.
Which is?

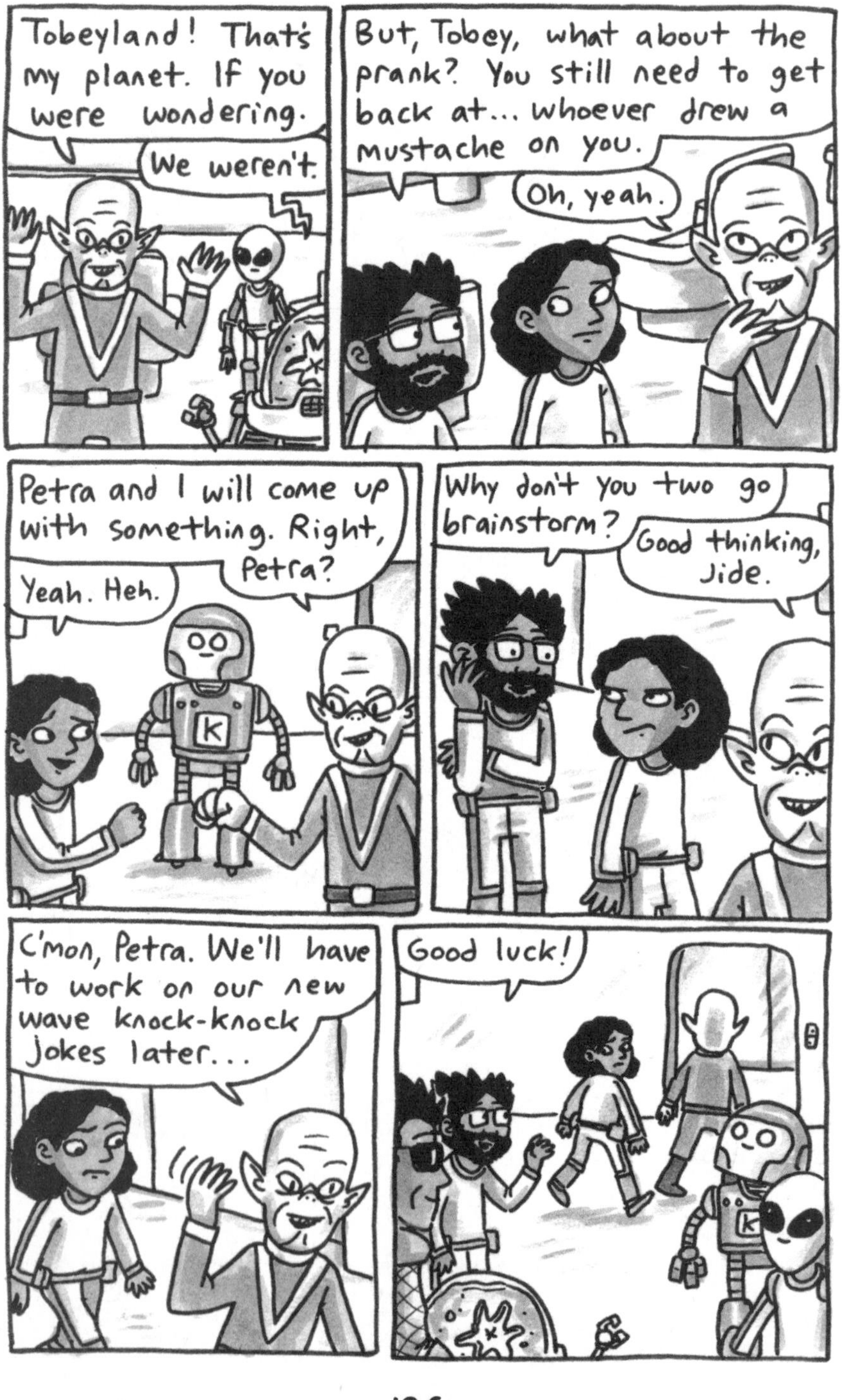
Tobeyland! That's my planet. If you were wondering.
We weren't.
But, Tobey, what about the prank? You still need to get back at... whoever drew a mustache on you.
Oh, yeah.
Petra and I will come up with something. Right, Petra?
Yeah. Heh.
Why don't you two go brainstorm?
Good thinking, Jide.
C'mon, Petra. We'll have to work on our new wave knock-knock jokes later...
Good luck!

DOUBLE TROUBLE

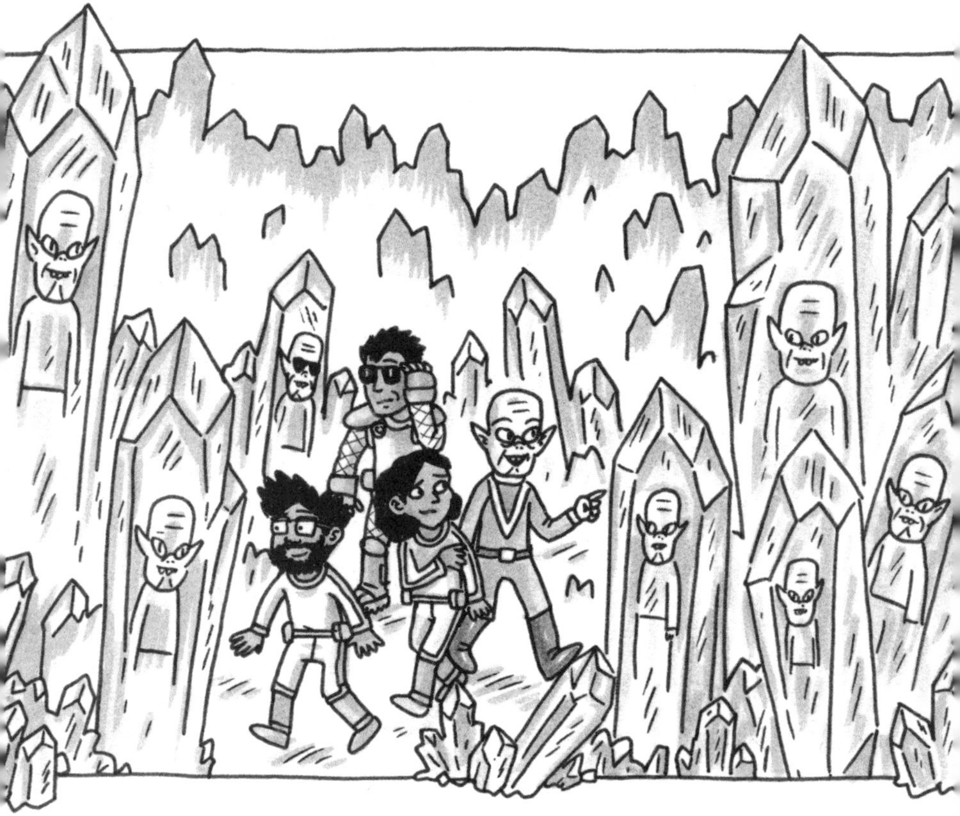

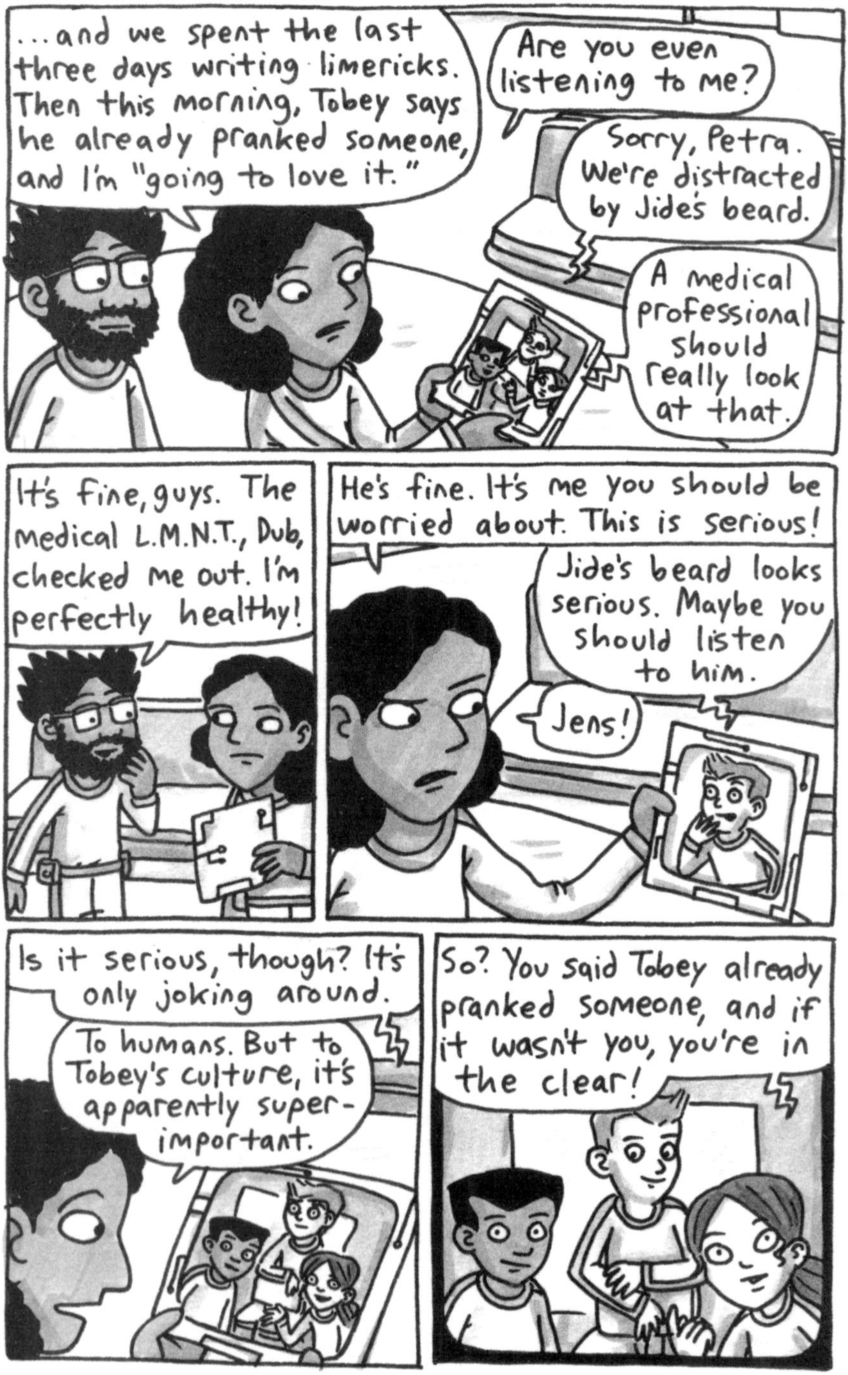
...and we spent the last three days writing limericks. Then this morning, Tobey says he already pranked someone, and I'm "going to love it."
Are you even listening to me?
Sorry, Petra. We're distracted by Jide's beard.
A medical professional should really look at that.
It's fine, guys. The medical L.M.N.T., Dub, checked me out. I'm perfectly healthy!
He's fine. It's me you should be worried about. This is serious!
Jide's beard looks serious. Maybe you should listen to him.
Jens!
Is it serious, though? It's only joking around.
To humans. But to Tobey's culture, it's apparently super-important.
So? You said Tobey already pranked someone, and if it wasn't you, you're in the clear!

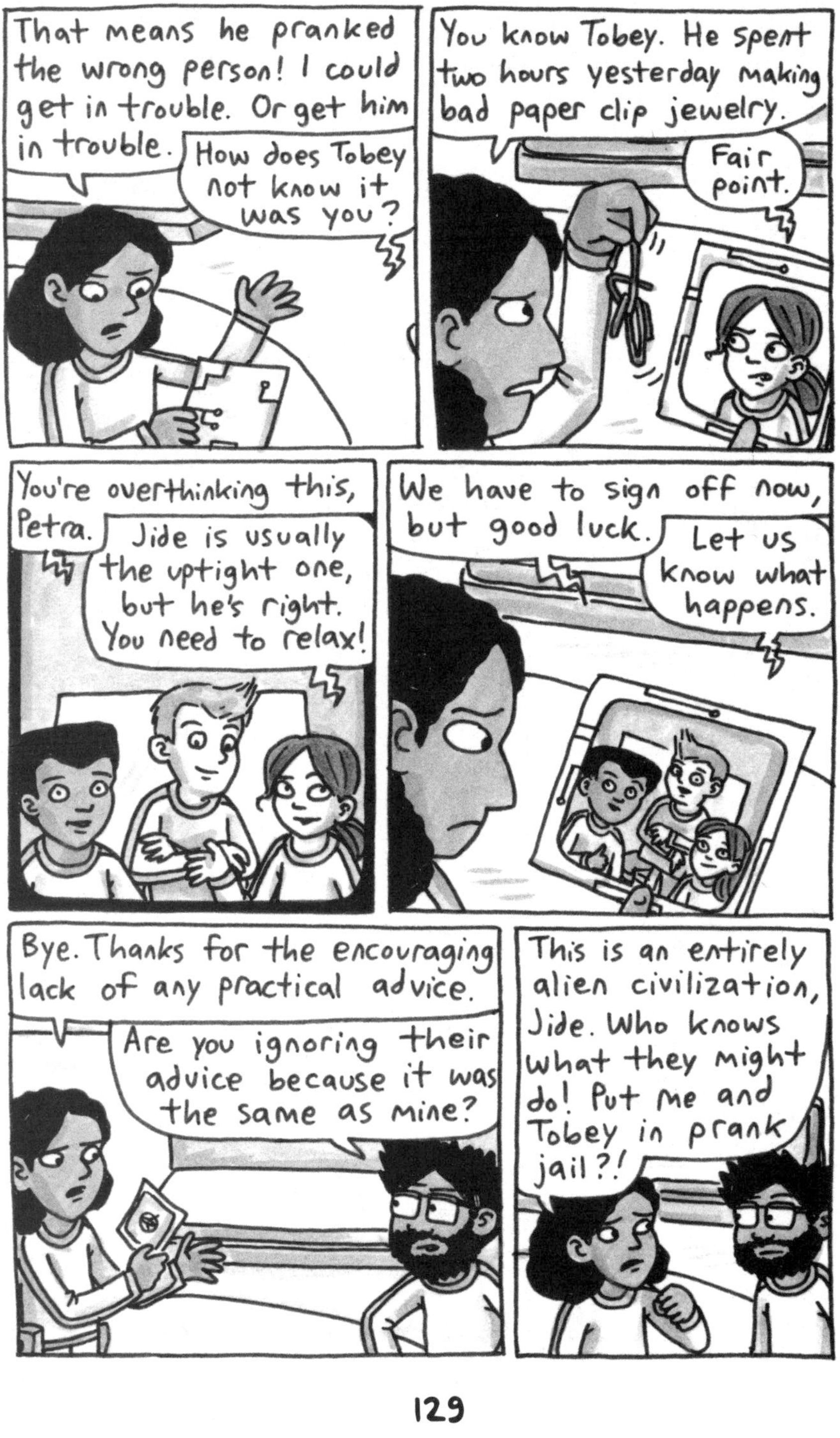
That means he pranked the wrong person! I could get in trouble. Or get him in trouble.
How does Tobey not know it was you?
You know Tobey. He spent two hours yesterday making bad paper clip jewelry.
Fair point.
You're overthinking this, Petra.
Jide is usually the uptight one, but he's right. You need to relax!
We have to sign off now, but good luck.
Let us know what happens.
Bye. Thanks for the encouraging lack of any practical advice.
Are you ignoring their advice because it was the same as mine?
This is an entirely alien civilization, Jide. Who knows what they might do! Put me and Tobey in prank jail?!

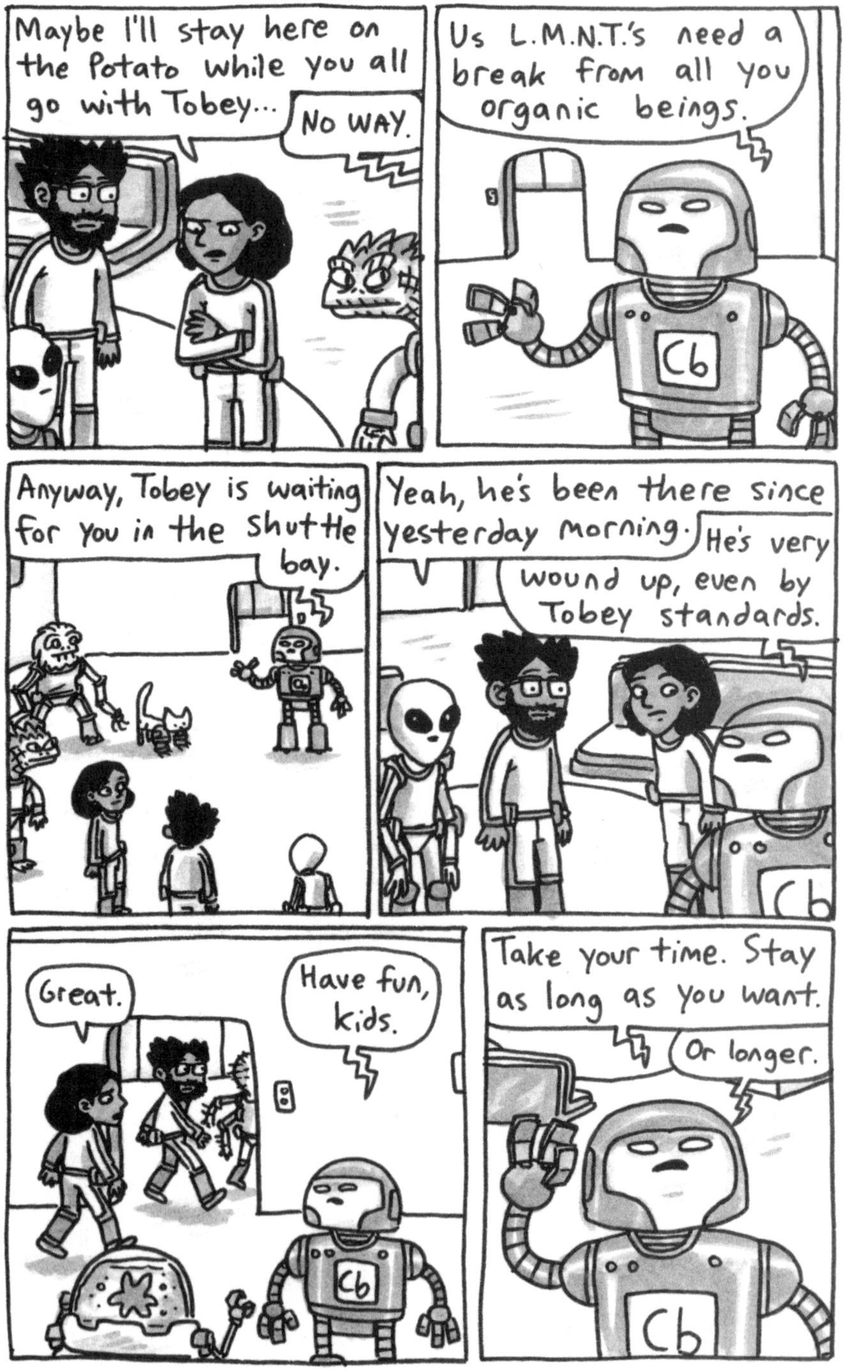

Maybe I'll stay here on the Potato while you all go with Tobey...
NO WAY.
Us L.M.N.T.'s need a break from all you organic beings.
Anyway, Tobey is waiting for you in the shuttle bay.
Yeah, he's been there since yesterday morning.
He's very wound up, even by Tobey standards.
Great.
Have fun, kids.
Take your time. Stay as long as you want.
Or longer.

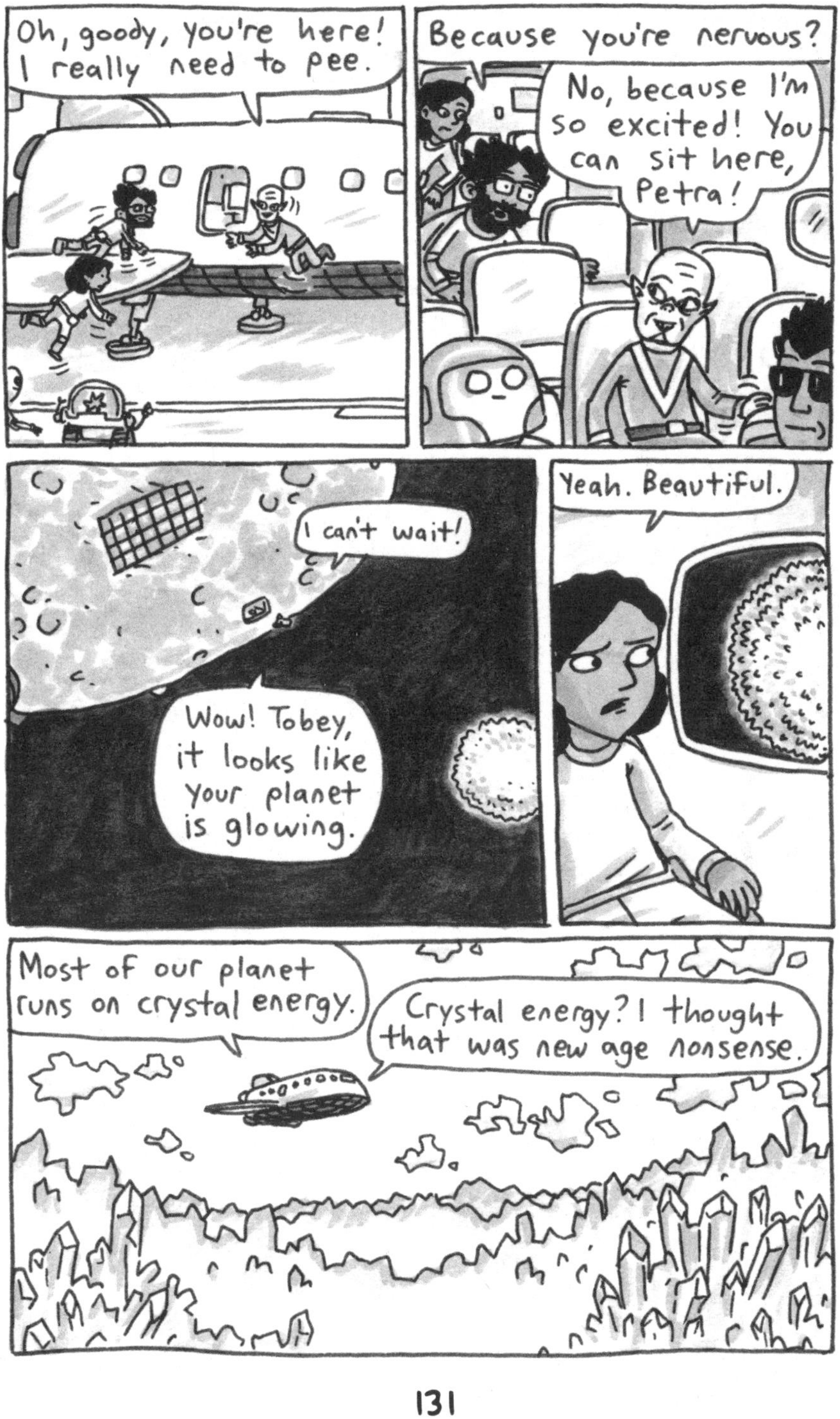
Oh, goody, you're here! I really need to pee.
Because you're nervous?
No, because I'm so excited! You can sit here, Petra!
I can't wait!
Wow! Tobey, it looks like your planet is glowing.
Yeah. Beautiful.
Most of our planet runs on crystal energy.
Crystal energy? I thought that was new age nonsense.

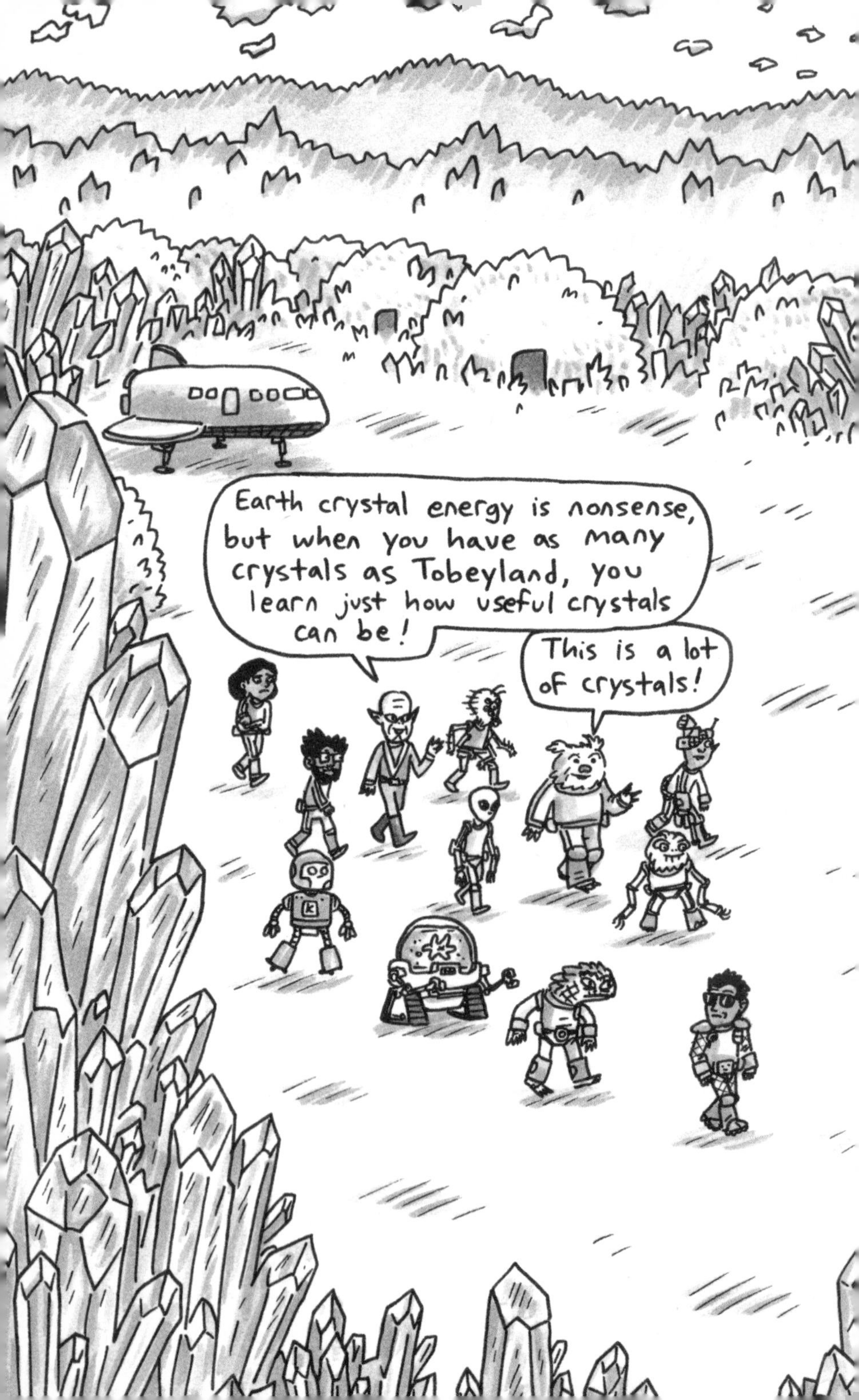
Earth crystal energy is nonsense, but when you have as many crystals as Tobeyland, you learn just how useful crystals can be!
This is a lot of crystals!

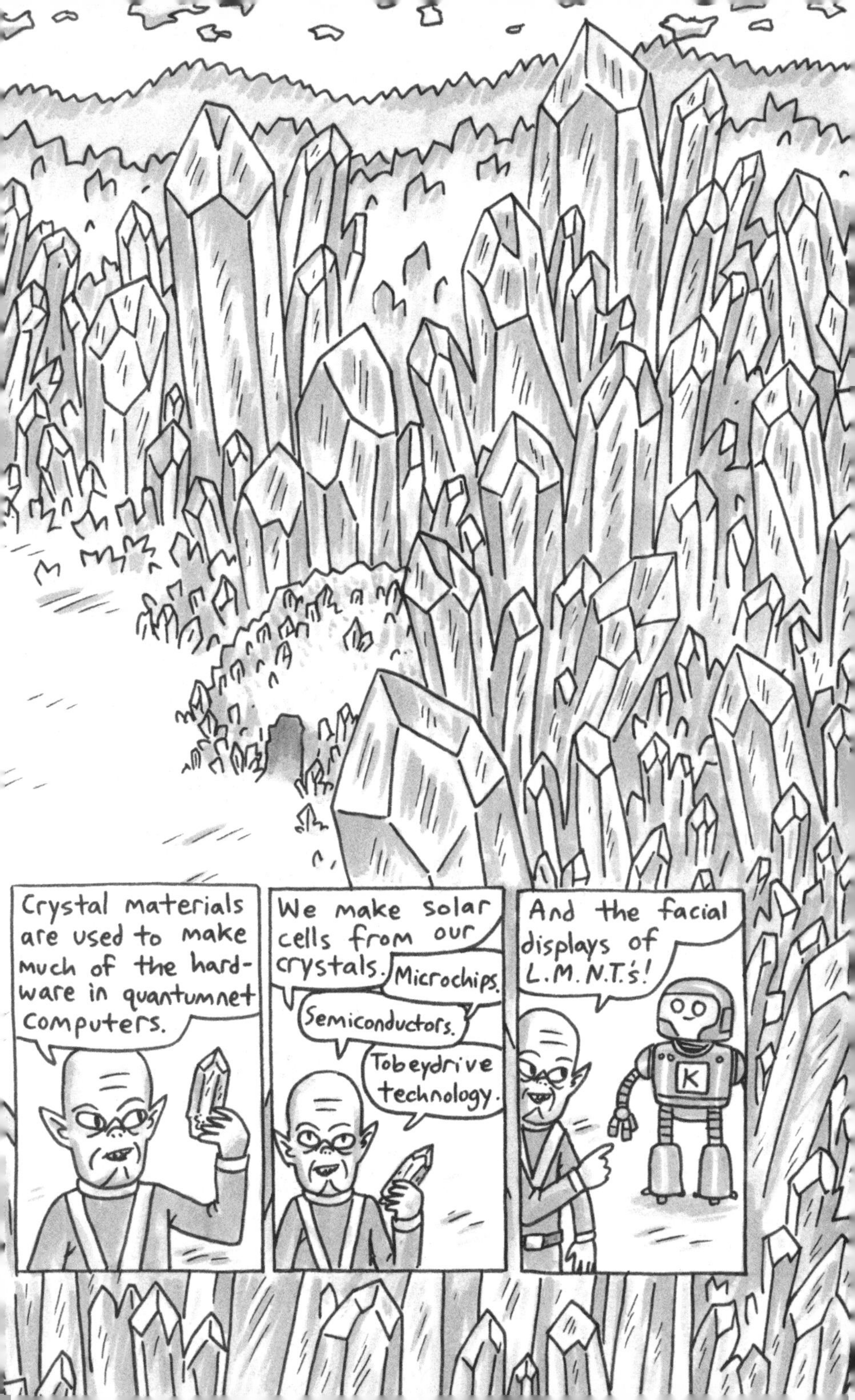

Crystal materials are used to make much of the hard-ware in quantumnet computers.
We make solar cells from our crystals.
Microchips.
Semiconductors.
Tobeydrive technology.
And the facial displays of L.M.N.T.'s!
K

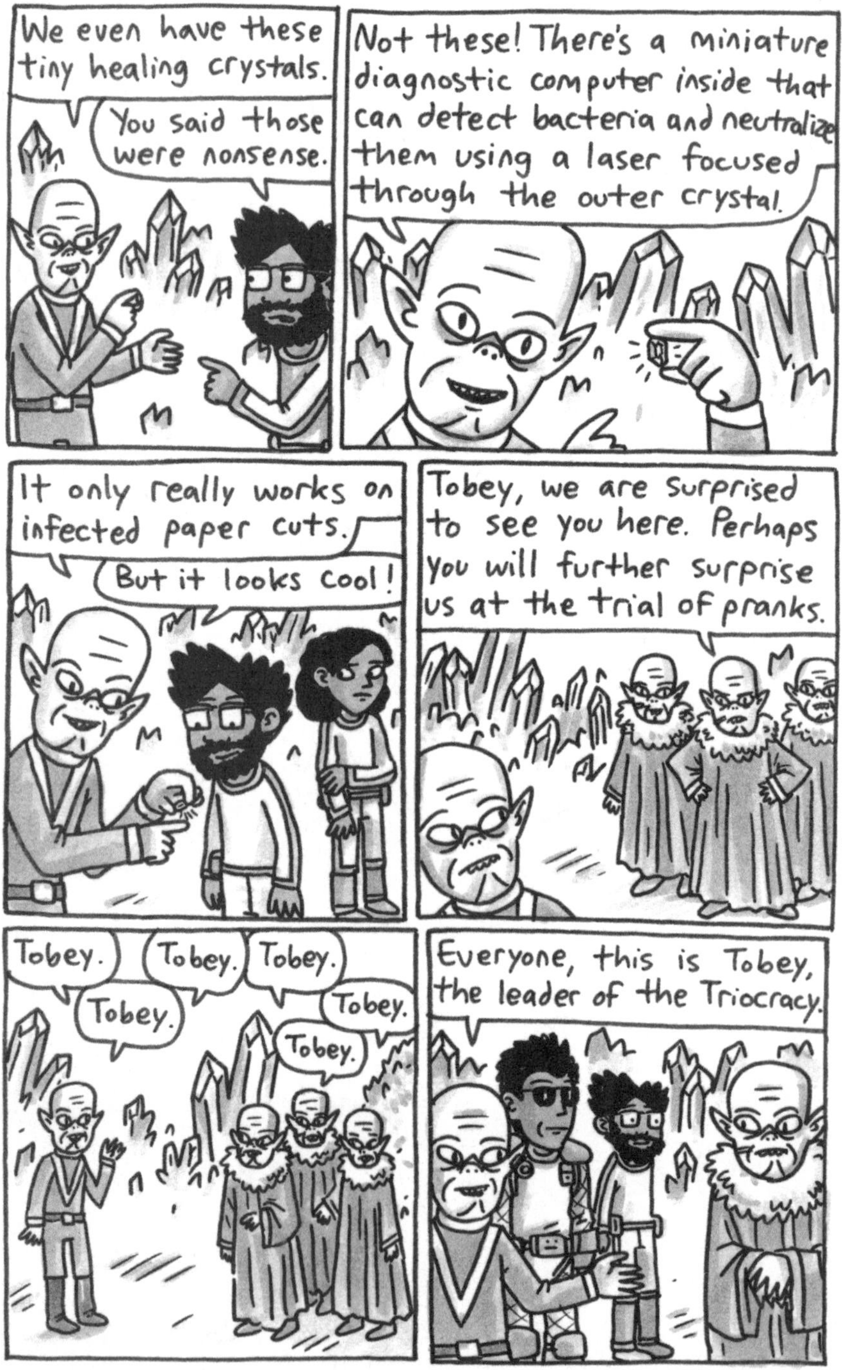
We even have these tiny healing crystals.
You said those were nonsense.
Not these! There's a miniature diagnostic computer inside that can detect bacteria and neutralize them using a laser focused through the outer crystal.
It only really works on infected paper cuts.
But it looks cool!
Tobey, we are surprised to see you here. Perhaps you will further surprise us at the trial of pranks.
Tobey.
Tobey.
Tobey.
Tobey.
Tobey.
Tobey.
Everyone, this is Tobey, the leader of the Triocracy.

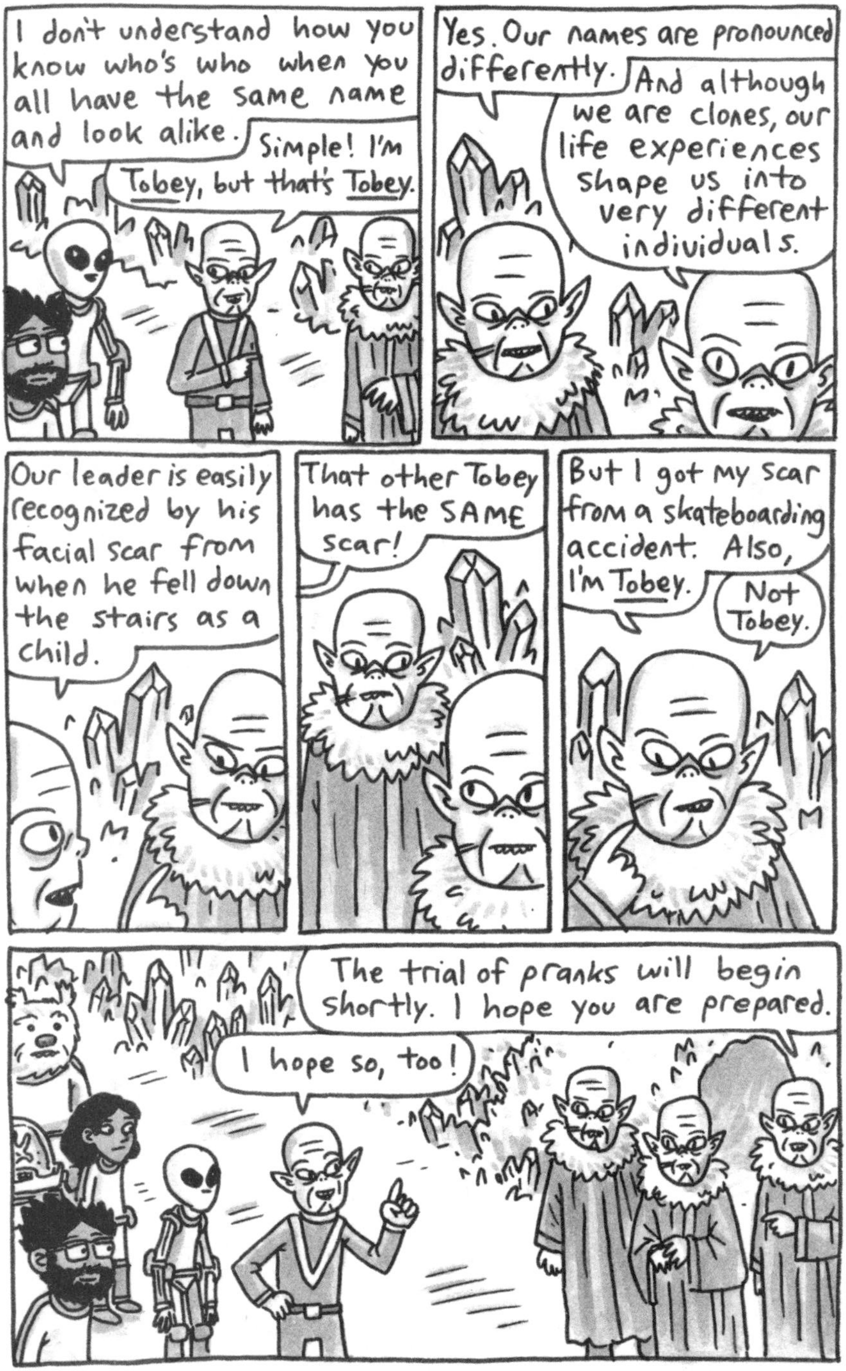
I don't understand how you know who's who when you all have the same name and look alike.
Simple! I'm Tobey, but that's Tobey.
Yes. Our names are pronounced differently.
And although we are clones, our life experiences shape us into very different individuals.
Our leader is easily recognized by his facial scar from when he fell down the stairs as a child.
That other Tobey has the SAME scar!
But I got my scar from a skateboarding accident. Also, I'm Tobey.
Not Tobey.
The trial of pranks will begin shortly. I hope you are prepared.
I hope so, too!

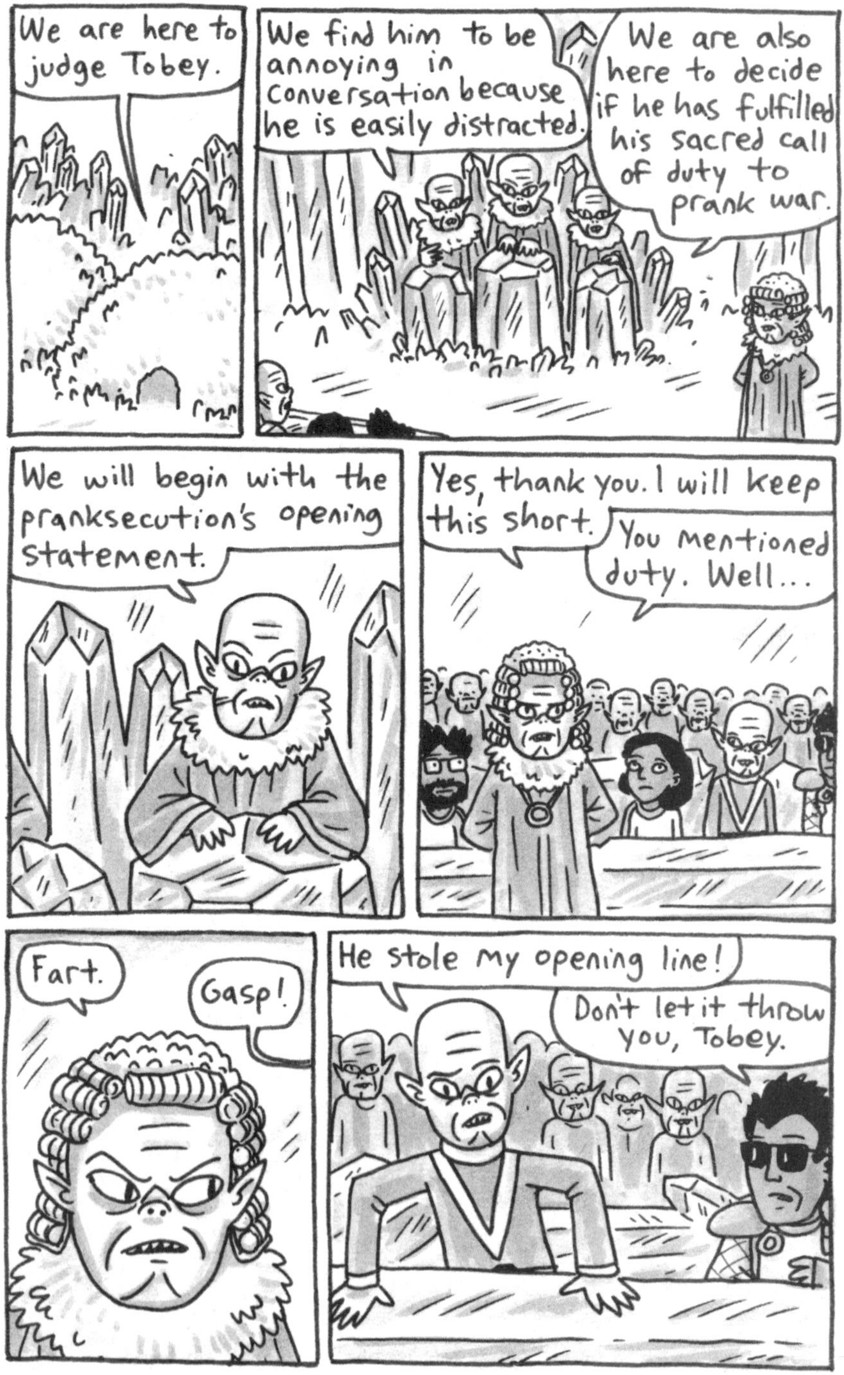
We are here to judge Tobey.
We find him to be annoying in conversation because he is easily distracted.
We are also here to decide if he has fulfilled his sacred call of duty to prank war.
We will begin with the pranksecution's opening statement.
Yes, thank you. I will keep this short.
You mentioned duty. Well...
Fart.
Gasp!
He stole my opening line!
Don't let it throw you, Tobey.

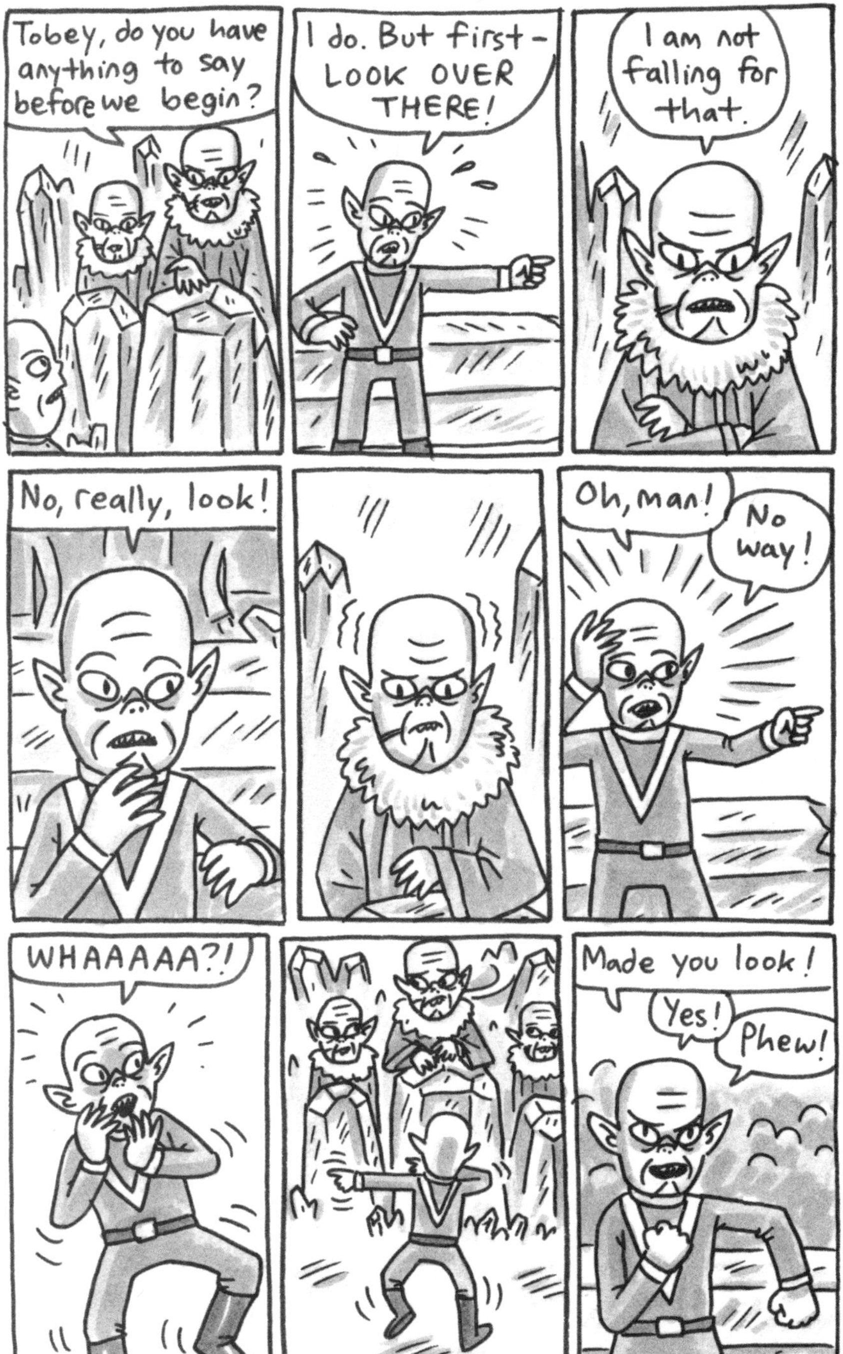
Tobey, do you have anything to say before we begin?
I do. But first - LOOK OVER THERE!
I am not falling for that.
No, really, look!
Oh, man!
No way!
WHAAAAA?!
Made you look!
Yes!
Phew!

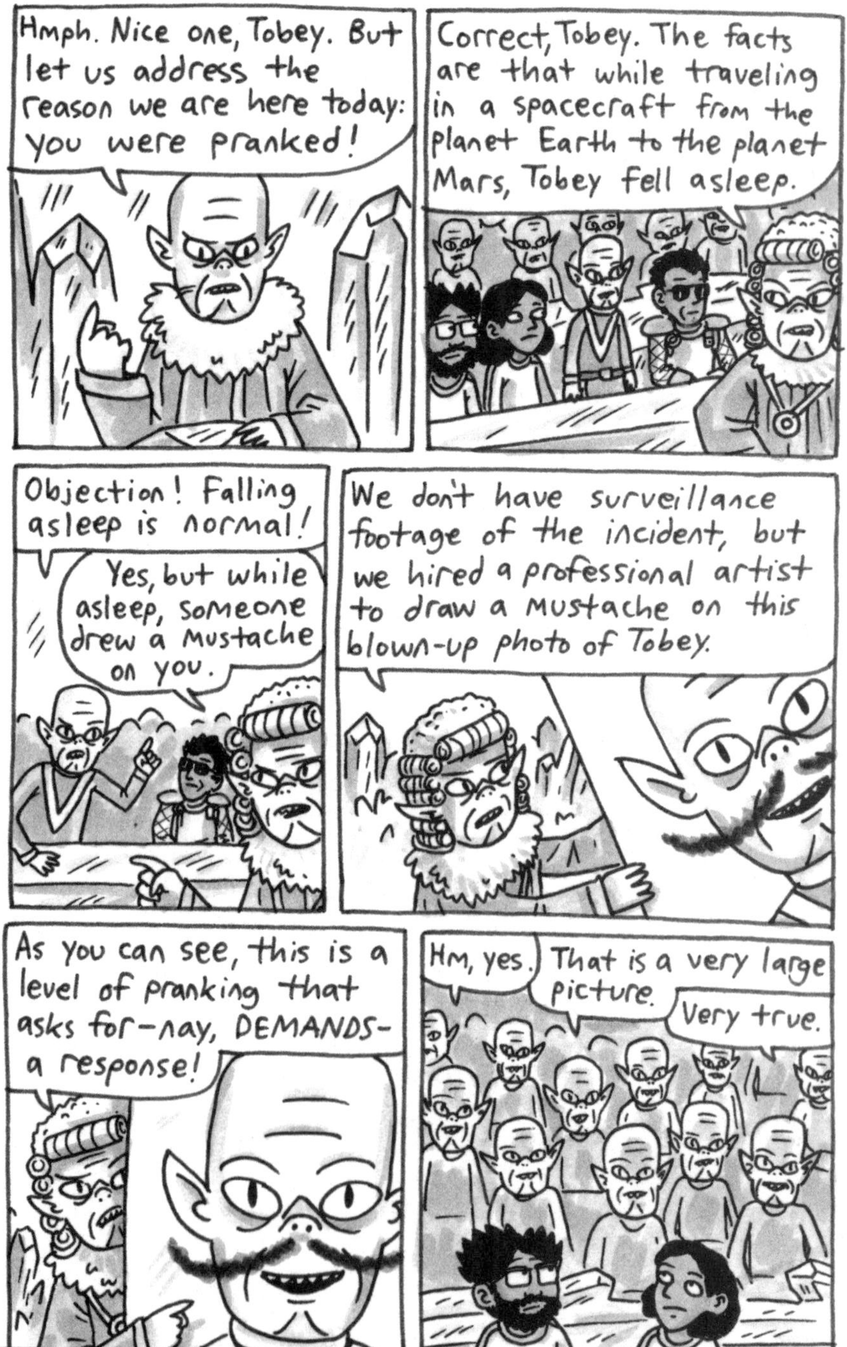
Hmph. Nice one, Tobey. But let us address the reason we are here today: you were pranked!
Correct, Tobey. The facts are that while traveling in a spacecraft from the planet Earth to the planet Mars, Tobey fell asleep.
Objection! Falling asleep is normal!
Yes, but while asleep, someone drew a mustache on you.
We don't have surveillance footage of the incident, but we hired a professional artist to draw a mustache on this blown-up photo of Tobey.
As you can see, this is a level of pranking that asks for—nay, DEMANDS—a response!
Hm, yes.
That is a very large picture.
Very true.

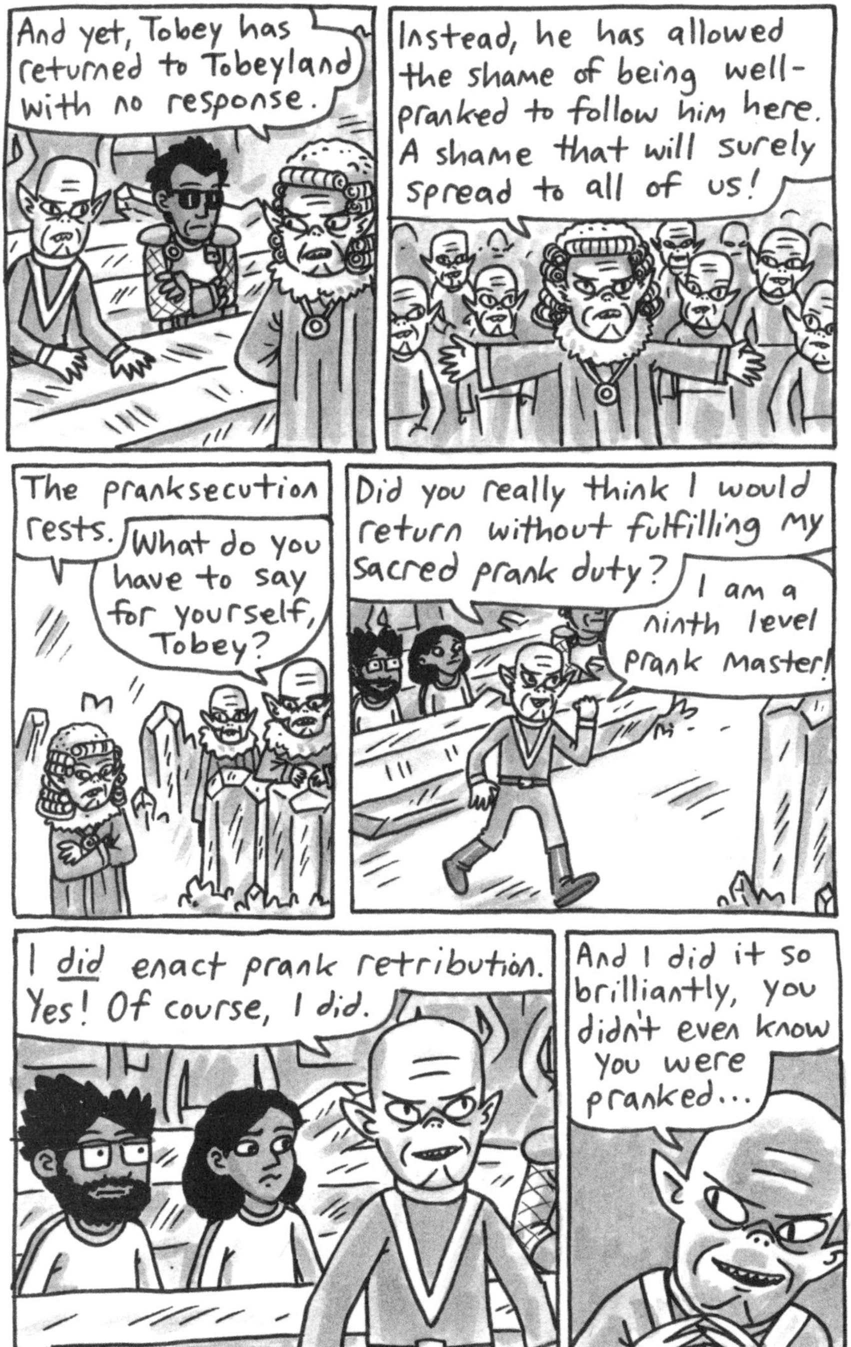
And yet, Tobey has returned to Tobeyland with no response.
Instead, he has allowed the shame of being well-pranked to follow him here. A shame that will surely spread to all of us!
The pranksecution rests.
What do you have to say for yourself, Tobey?
Did you really think I would return without fulfilling my sacred prank duty?
I am a ninth level prank master!
I did enact prank retribution. Yes! Of course, I did.
And I did it so brilliantly, you didn't even know you were pranked...

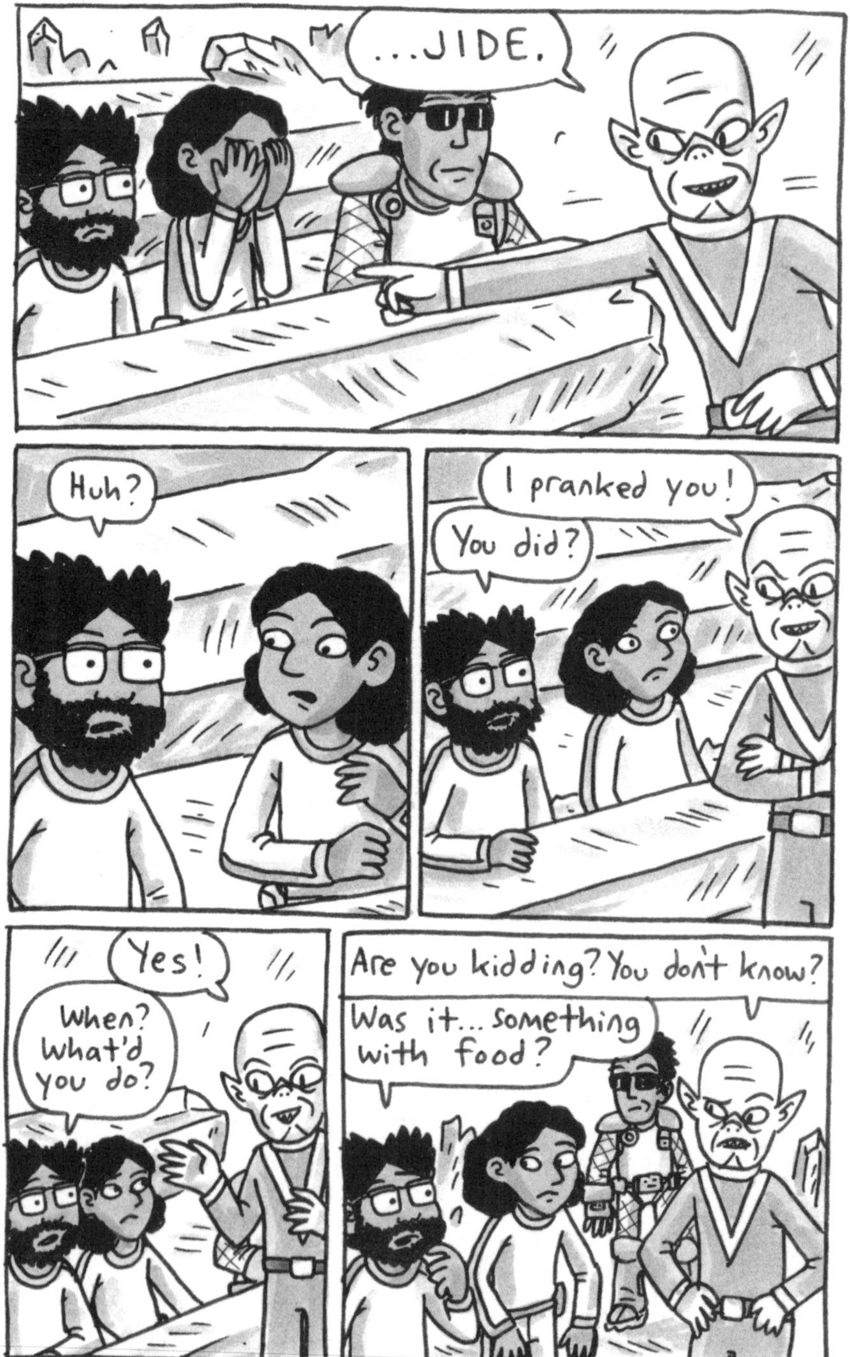
...JIDE.
Huh?
I pranked you!
You did?
Yes!
When? What'd you do?
Are you kidding? You don't know?
Was it... something with food?

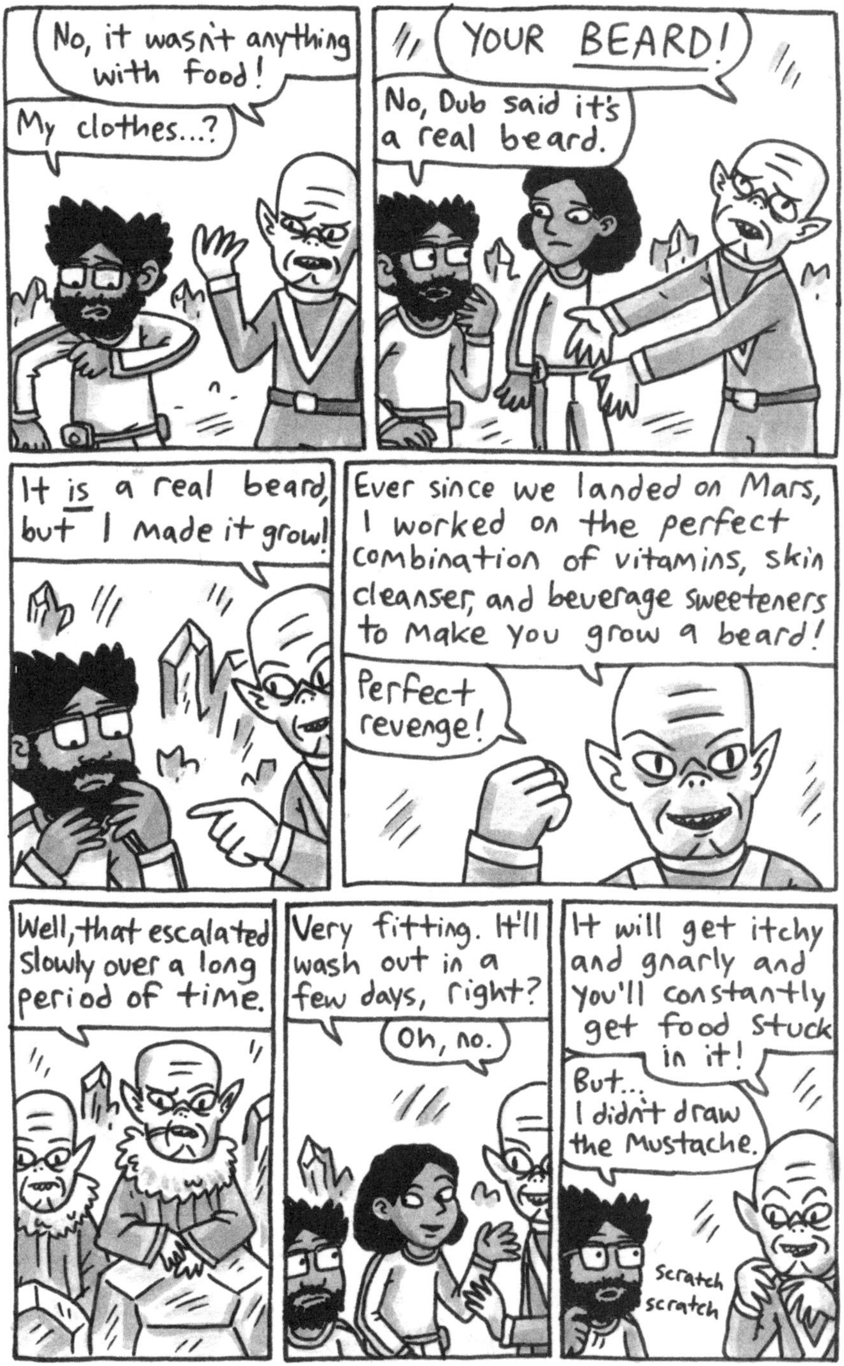
No, it wasn't anything with food!
My clothes...?
YOUR BEARD!
No, Dub said it's a real beard.
It is a real beard, but I made it grow!
Ever since we landed on Mars, I worked on the perfect combination of vitamins, skin cleanser, and beverage sweeteners to make you grow a beard!
Perfect revenge!
Well, that escalated slowly over a long period of time.
Very fitting. It'll wash out in a few days, right?
Oh, no.
It will get itchy and gnarly and you'll constantly get food stuck in it!
But... I didn't draw the mustache.
scratch scratch

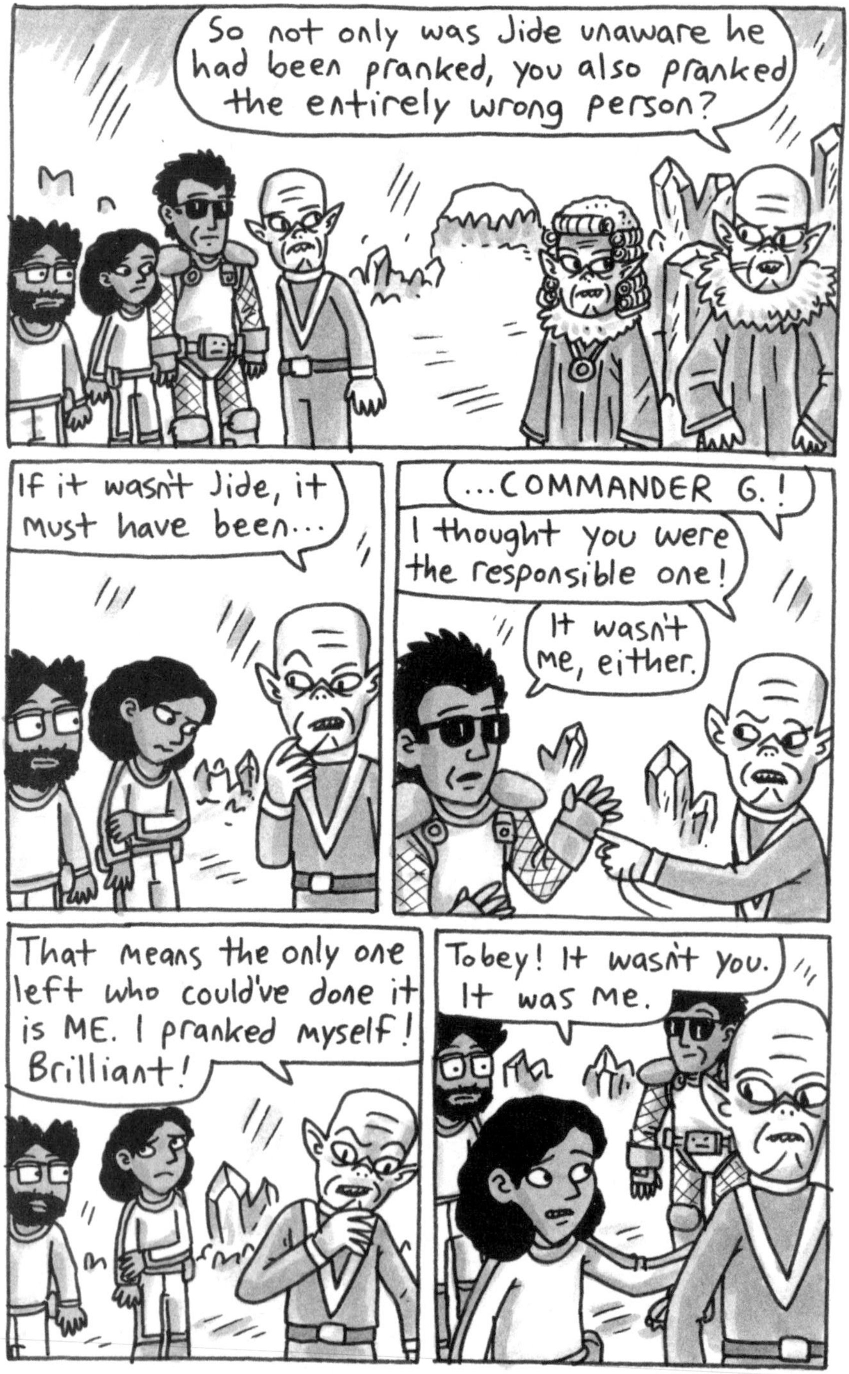
So not only was Jide unaware he had been pranked, you also pranked the entirely wrong person?
If it wasn't Jide, it must have been...
...COMMANDER G.!
I thought you were the responsible one!
It wasn't me, either.
That means the only one left who could've done it is ME. I pranked myself! Brilliant!
Tobey! It wasn't you. It was me.

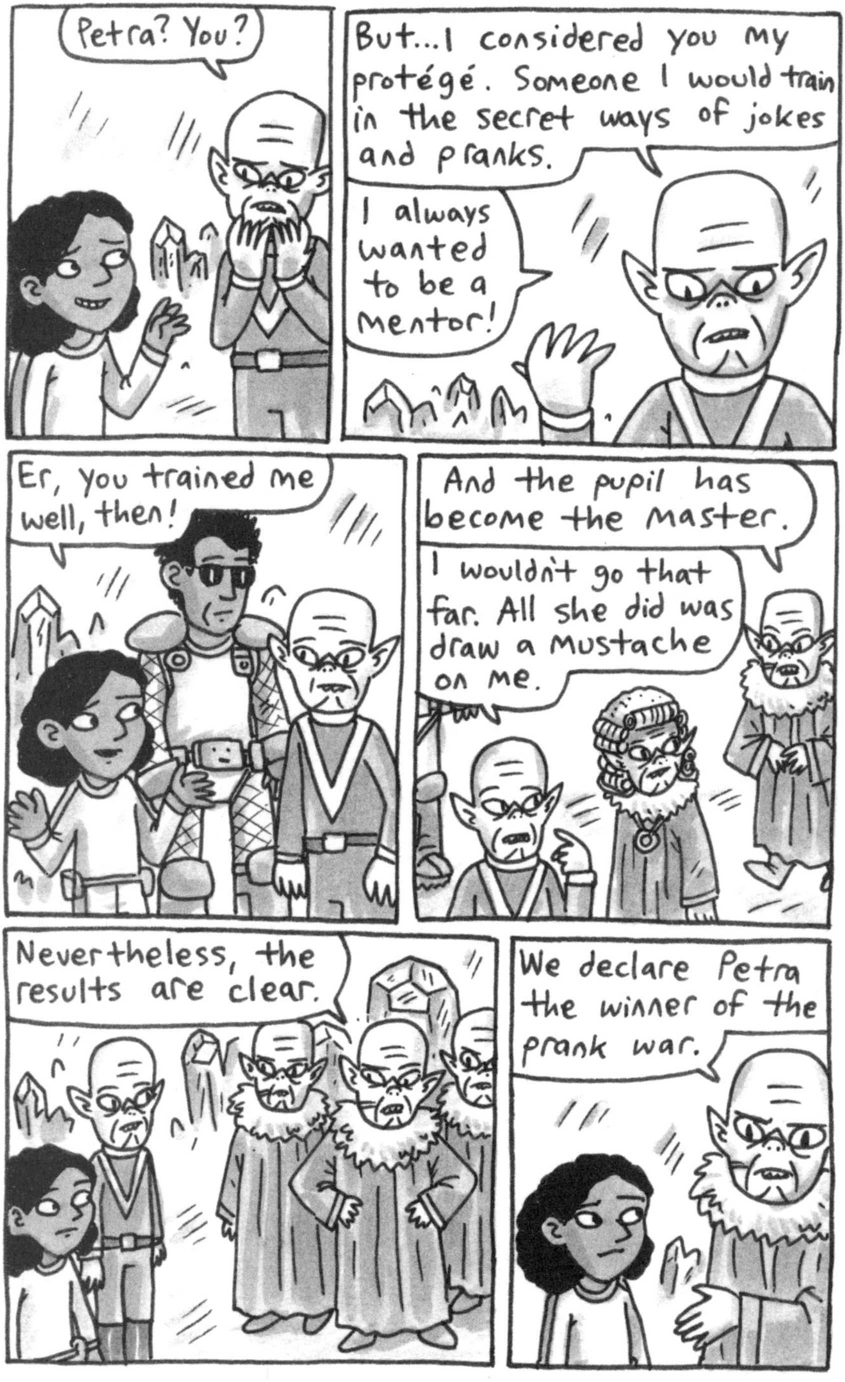
Petra? You?
But...I considered you my protégé. Someone I would train in the secret ways of jokes and pranks.
I always wanted to be a mentor!
Er, you trained me well, then!
And the pupil has become the master.
I wouldn't go that far. All she did was draw a mustache on me.
Nevertheless, the results are clear.
We declare Petra the winner of the prank war.

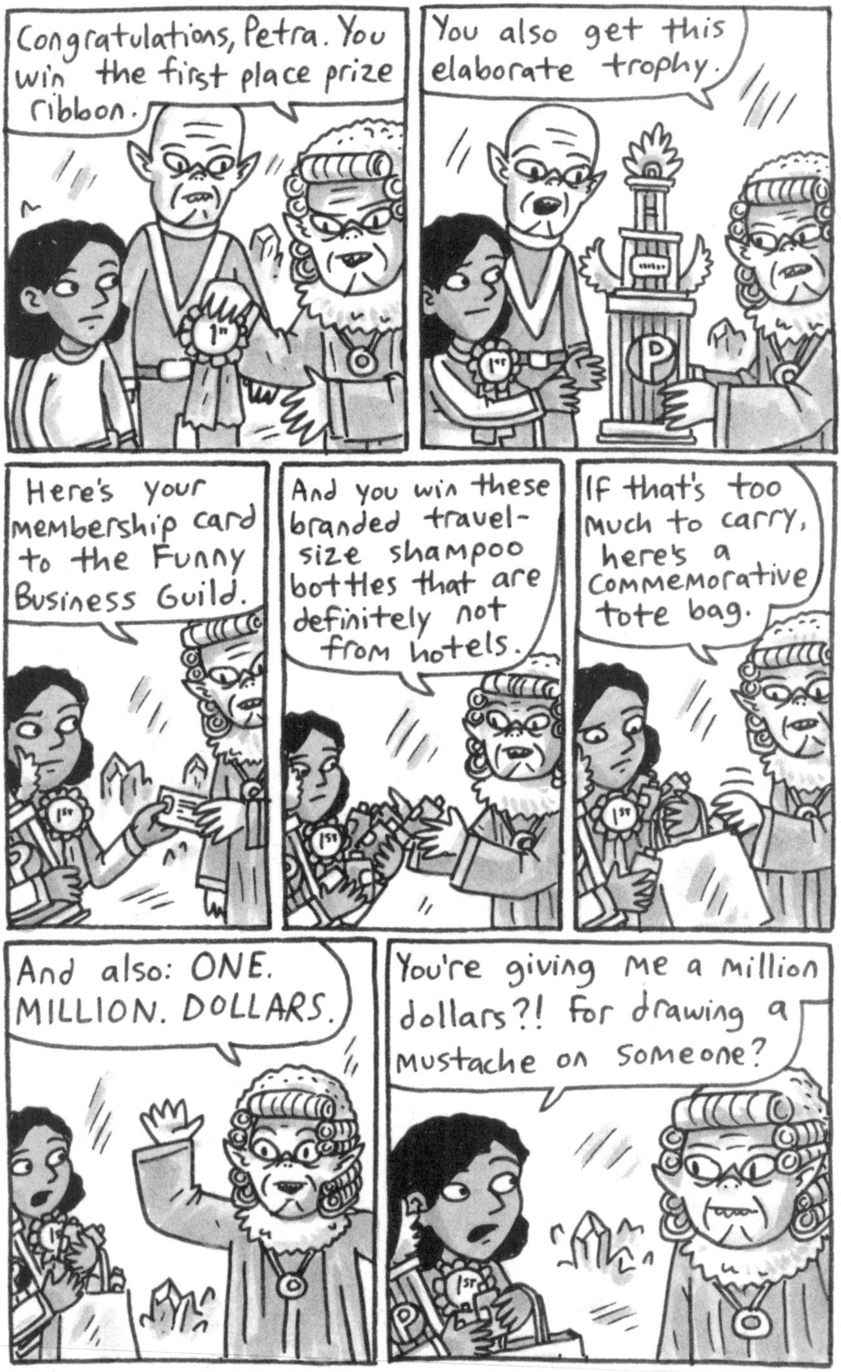
Congratulations, Petra. You win the first place prize ribbon.
1st
You also get this elaborate trophy.
1st
P
Here's your membership card to the Funny Business Guild.
1st
And you win these branded travel-size shampoo bottles that are definitely not from hotels.
1st
If that's too much to carry, here's a commemorative tote bag.
1st
And also: ONE. MILLION. DOLLARS.
You're giving me a million dollars?! For drawing a mustache on someone?
1st
P

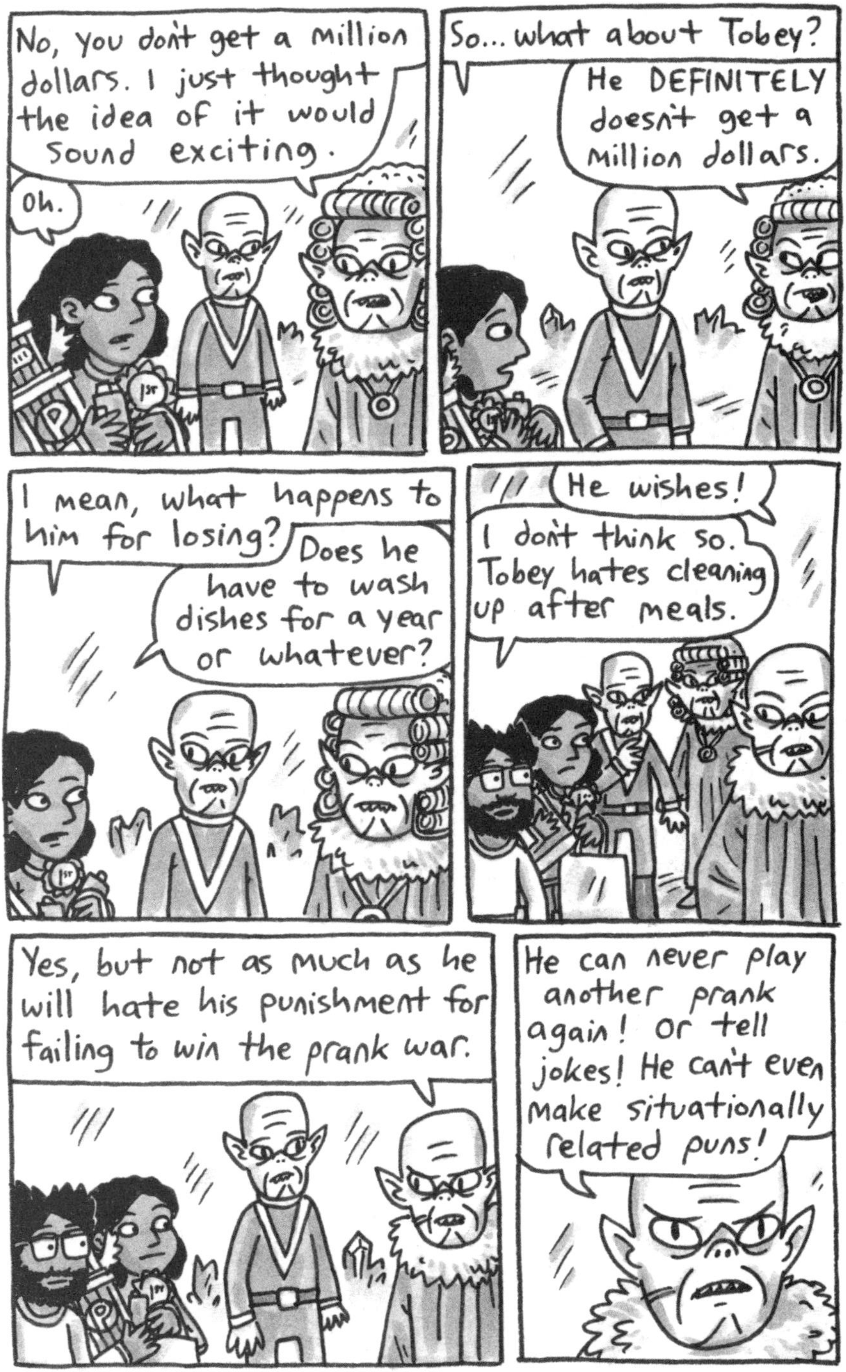
No, you don't get a million dollars. I just thought the idea of it would sound exciting.
Oh.
So... what about Tobey?
He DEFINITELY doesn't get a million dollars.
I mean, what happens to him for losing?
Does he have to wash dishes for a year or whatever?
He wishes!
I don't think so. Tobey hates cleaning up after meals.
Yes, but not as much as he will hate his punishment for failing to win the prank war.
He can never play another prank again! Or tell jokes! He can't even make situationally related puns!

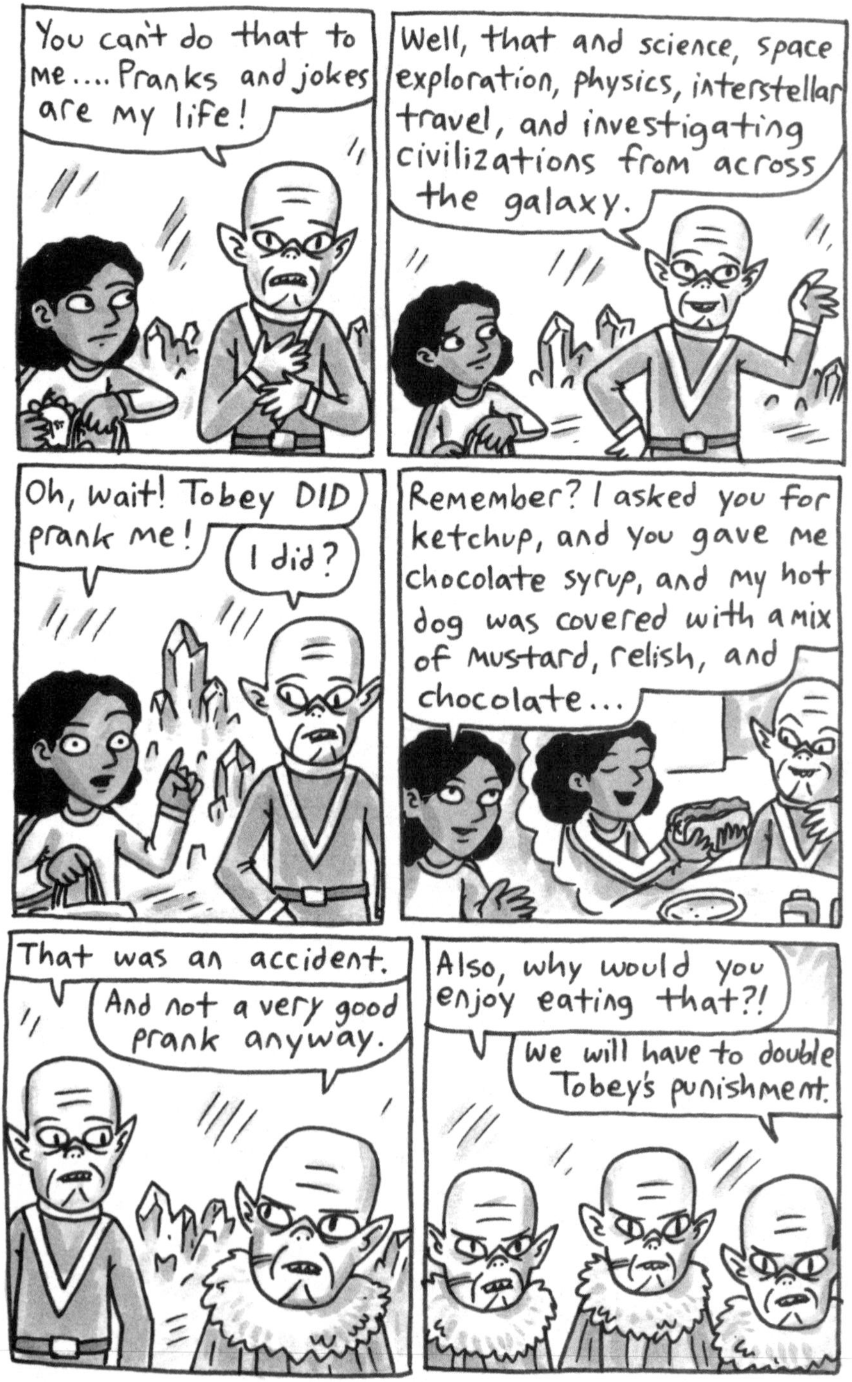
You can't do that to me.... Pranks and jokes are my life!
Well, that and science, space exploration, physics, interstellar travel, and investigating civilizations from across the galaxy.
Oh, wait! Tobey DID prank me!
I did?
Remember? I asked you for ketchup, and you gave me chocolate syrup, and my hot dog was covered with a mix of mustard, relish, and chocolate...
That was an accident.
And not a very good prank anyway.
Also, why would you enjoy eating that?!
We will have to double Tobey's punishment.

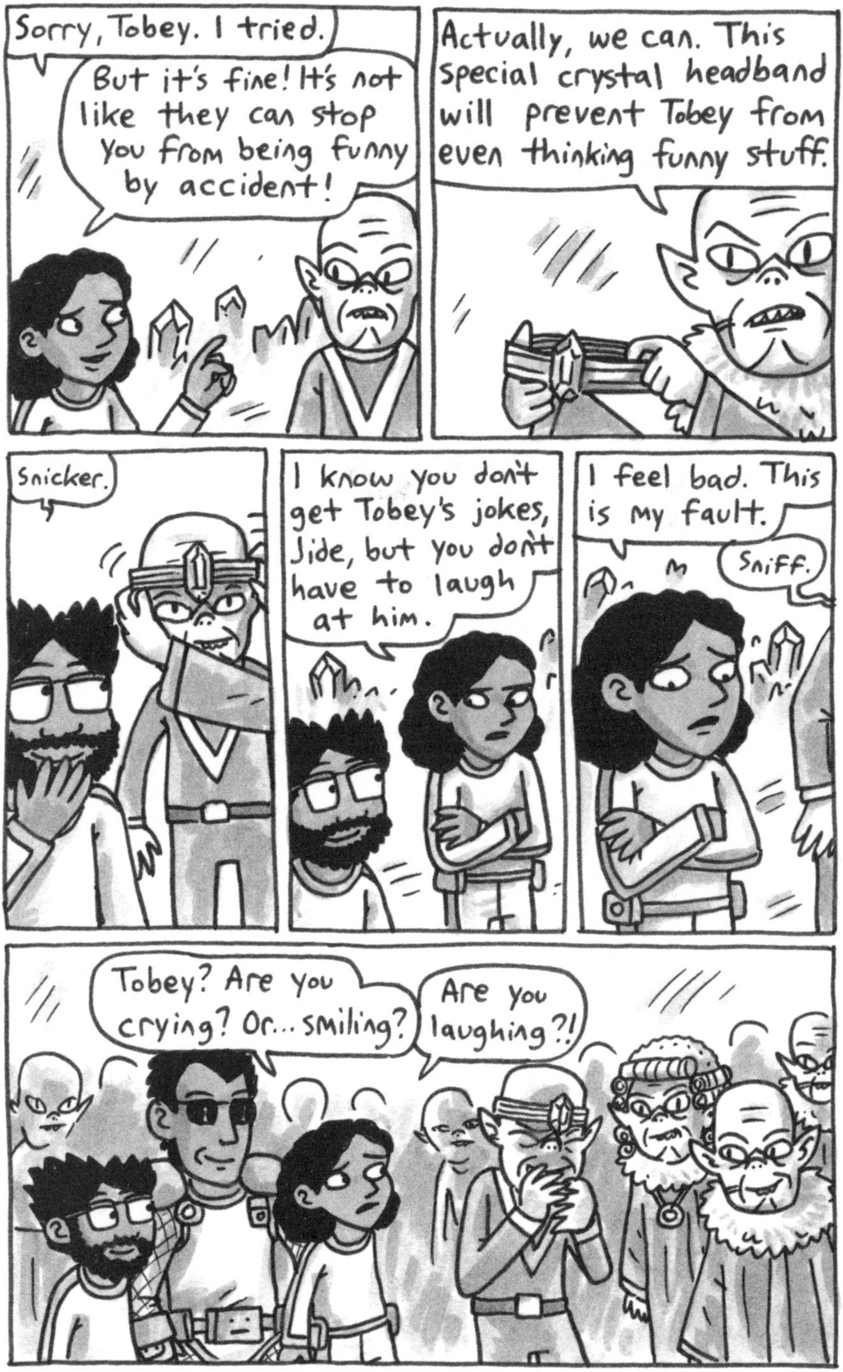
Sorry, Tobey. I tried.
But it's fine! It's not like they can stop you from being funny by accident!
Actually, we can. This special crystal headband will prevent Tobey from even thinking funny stuff.
Snicker.
I know you don't get Tobey's jokes, Jide, but you don't have to laugh at him.
I feel bad. This is my fault.
Sniff.
Tobey? Are you crying? Or... smiling?
Are you laughing?!

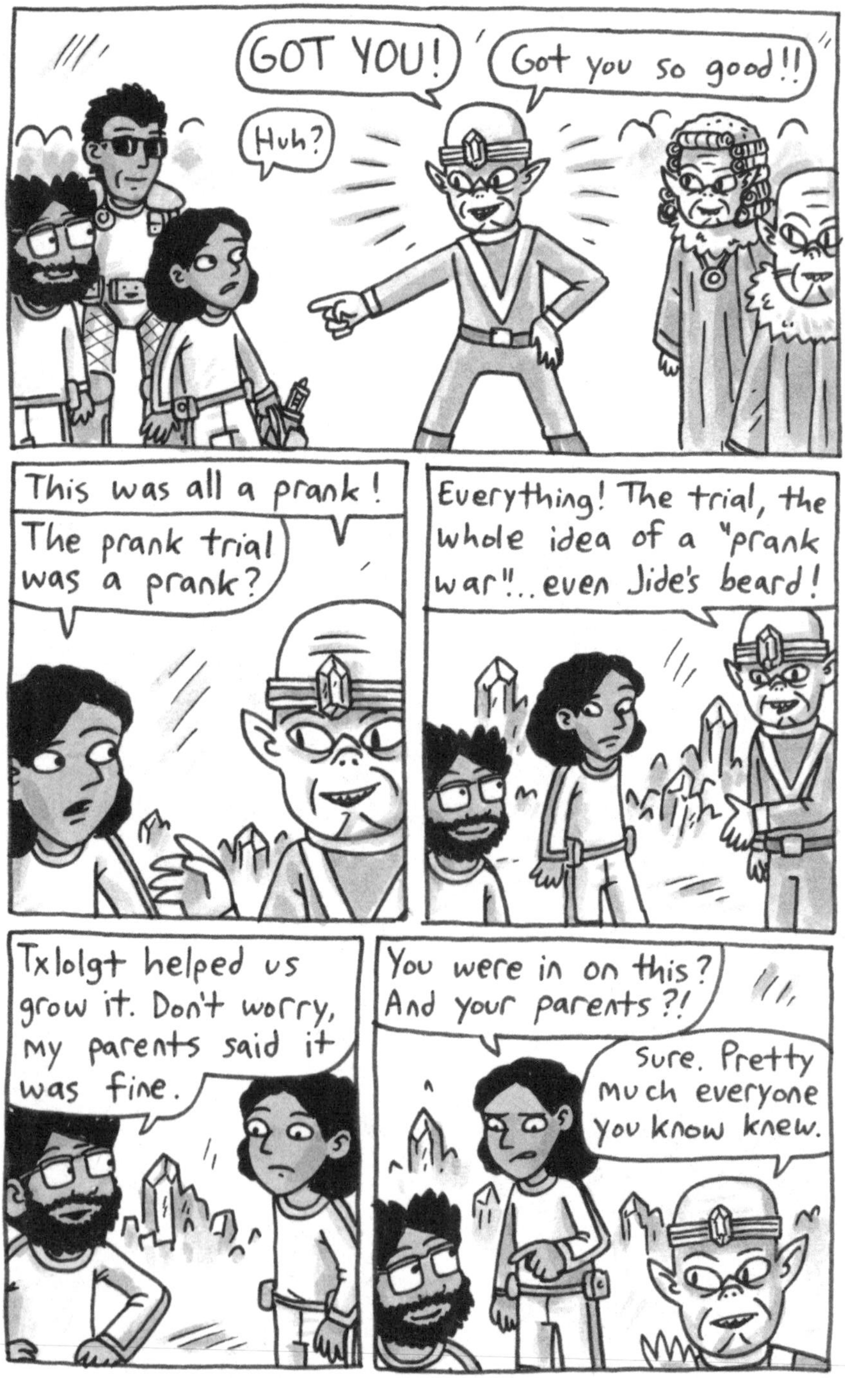
GOT YOU!
Got you so good!!
Huh?
This was all a prank!
The prank trial was a prank?
Everything! The trial, the whole idea of a "prank war"!... even Jide's beard!
Txlolgt helped us grow it. Don't worry, my parents said it was fine.
You were in on this? And your parents?!
Sure. Pretty much everyone you know knew.

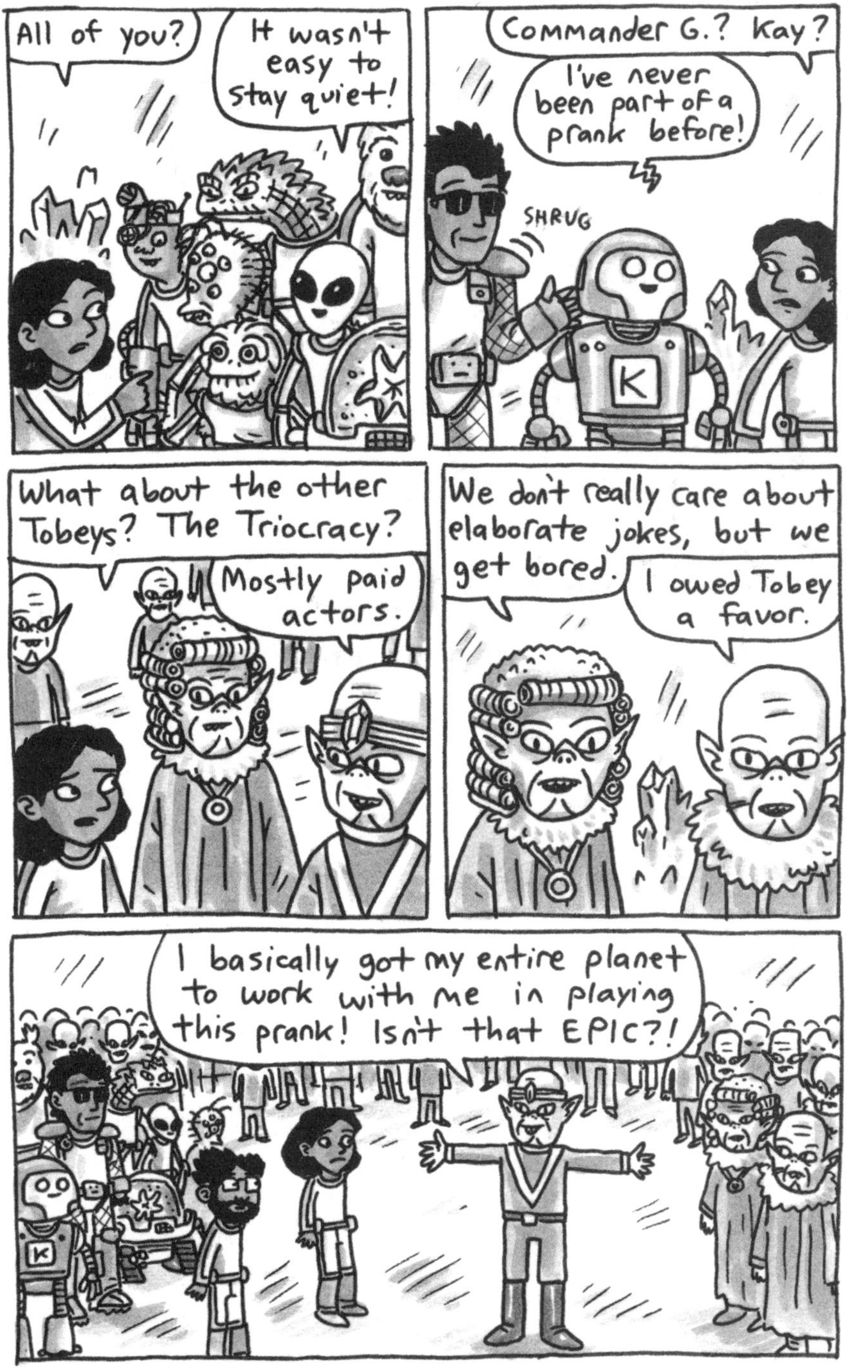
All of you?
It wasn't easy to stay quiet!
Commander G.? Kay?
I've never been part of a prank before!
SHRUG
What about the other Tobeys? The Triocracy?
Mostly paid actors.
We don't really care about elaborate jokes, but we get bored.
I owed Tobey a favor.
I basically got my entire planet to work with me in playing this prank! Isn't that EPIC?!

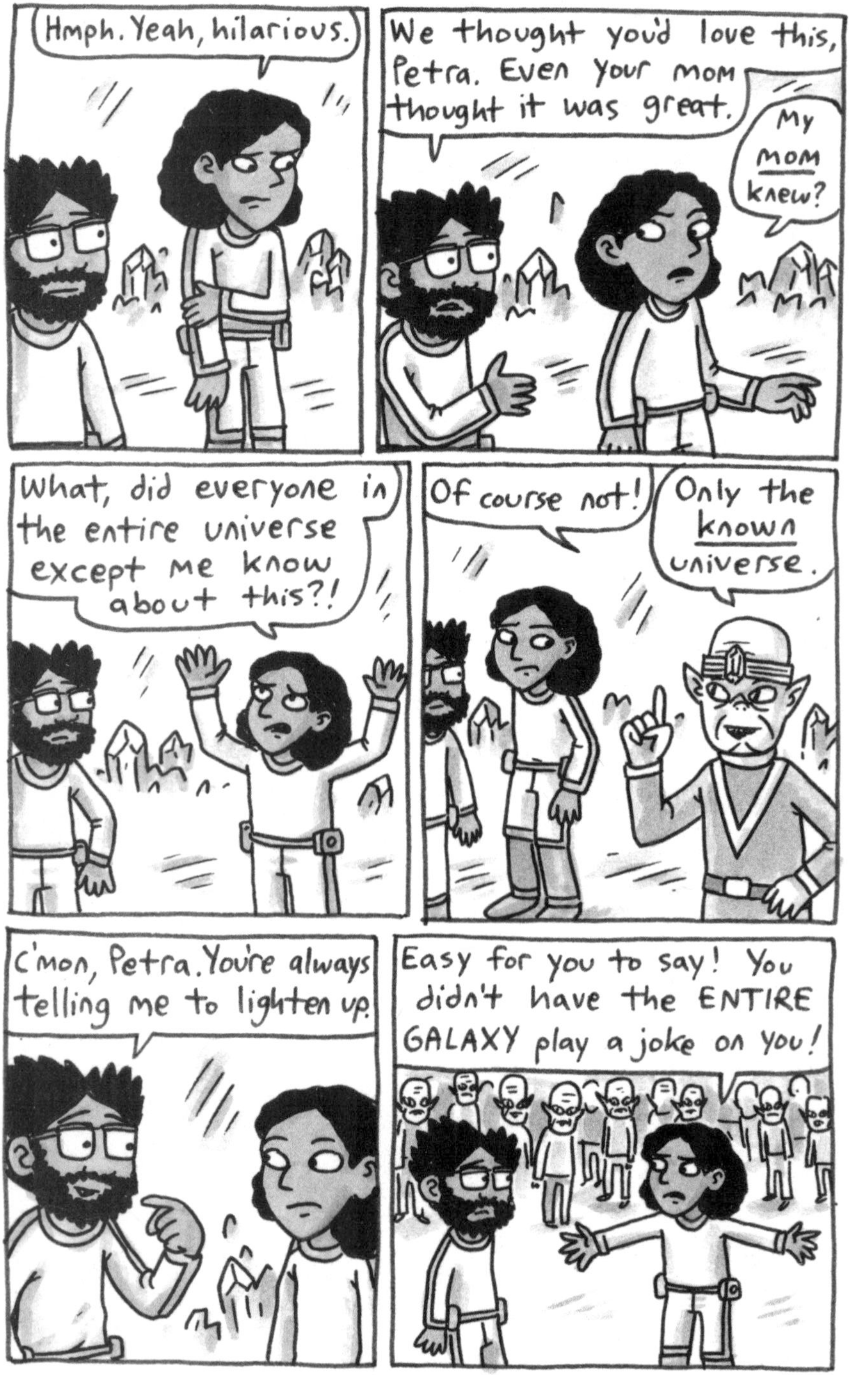
Hmph. Yeah, hilarious.
We thought you'd love this, Petra. Even your mom thought it was great.
My MOM knew?
What, did everyone in the entire universe except me know about this?!
Of course not!
Only the known universe.
C'mon, Petra. You're always telling me to lighten up.
Easy for you to say! You didn't have the ENTIRE GALAXY play a joke on you!

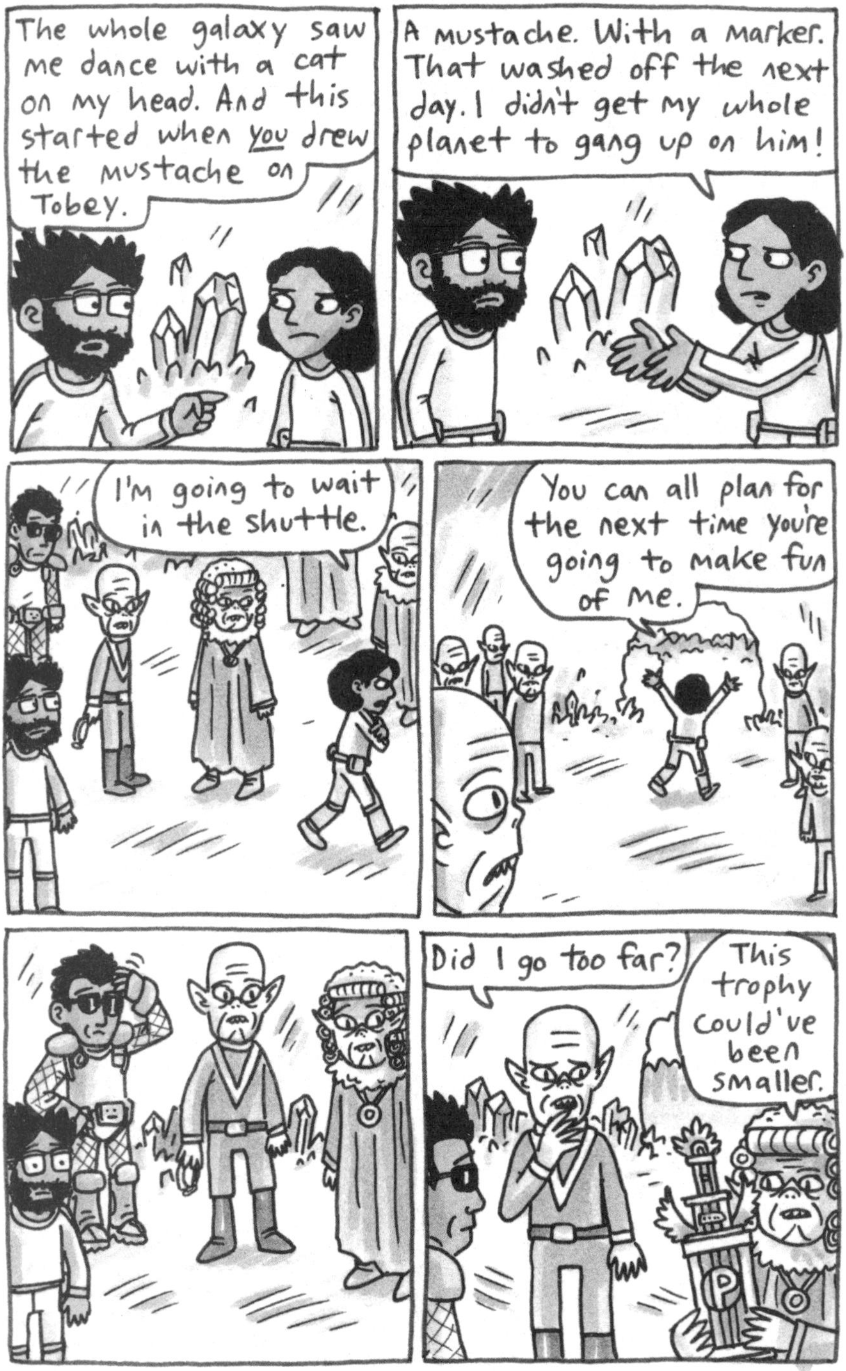
The whole galaxy saw me dance with a cat on my head. And this started when you drew the mustache on Tobey.
A mustache. With a marker. That washed off the next day. I didn't get my whole planet to gang up on him!
I'm going to wait in the shuttle.
You can all plan for the next time you're going to make fun of me.
Did I go too far?
This trophy could've been smaller.

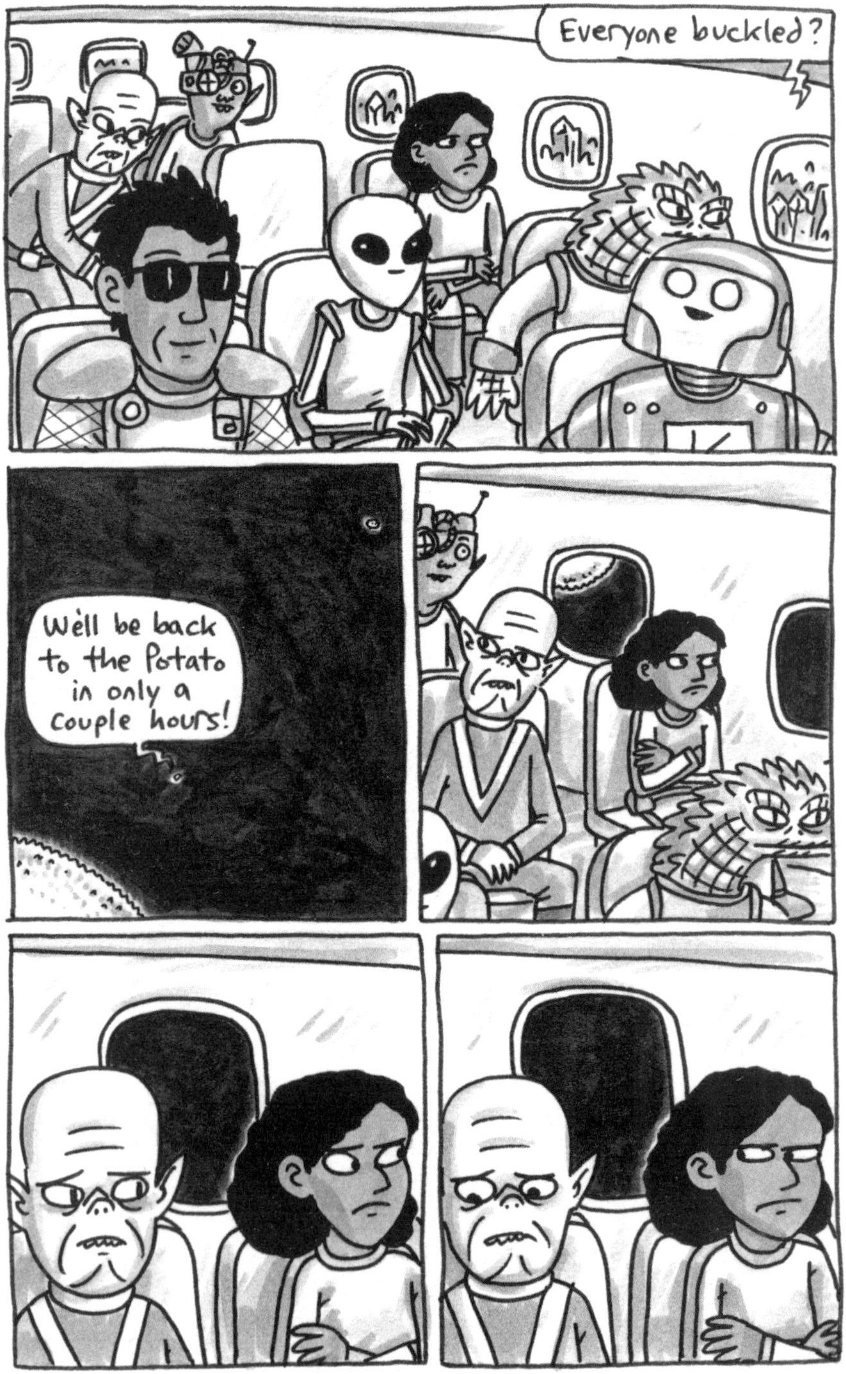
Everyone buckled?
We'll be back to the Potato in only a couple hours!

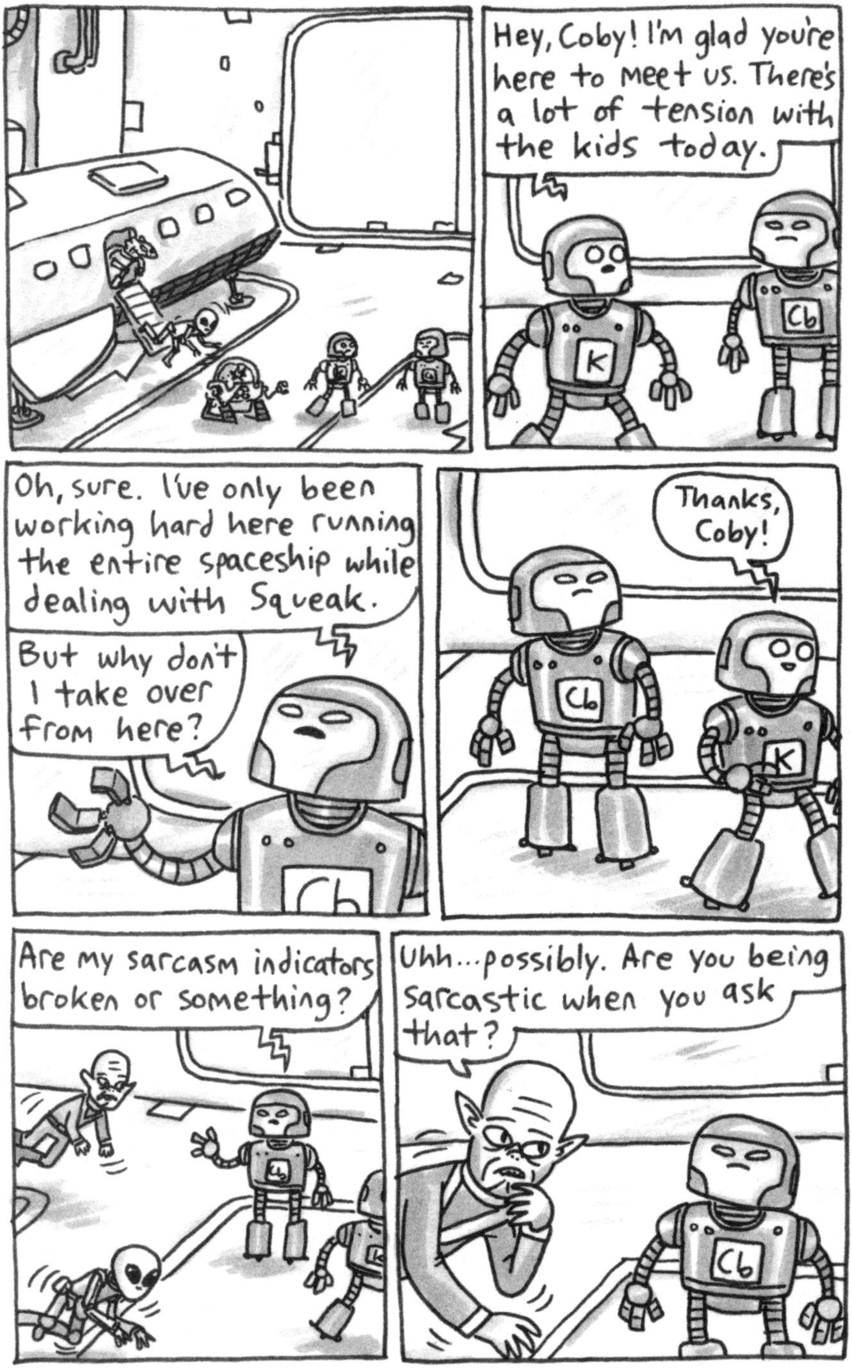
Hey, Coby! I'm glad you're here to meet us. There's a lot of tension with the kids today.
Oh, sure. I've only been working hard here running the entire spaceship while dealing with Squeak.
But why don't I take over from here?
Thanks, Coby!
Are my sarcasm indicators broken or something?
Uhh...possibly. Are you being sarcastic when you ask that?

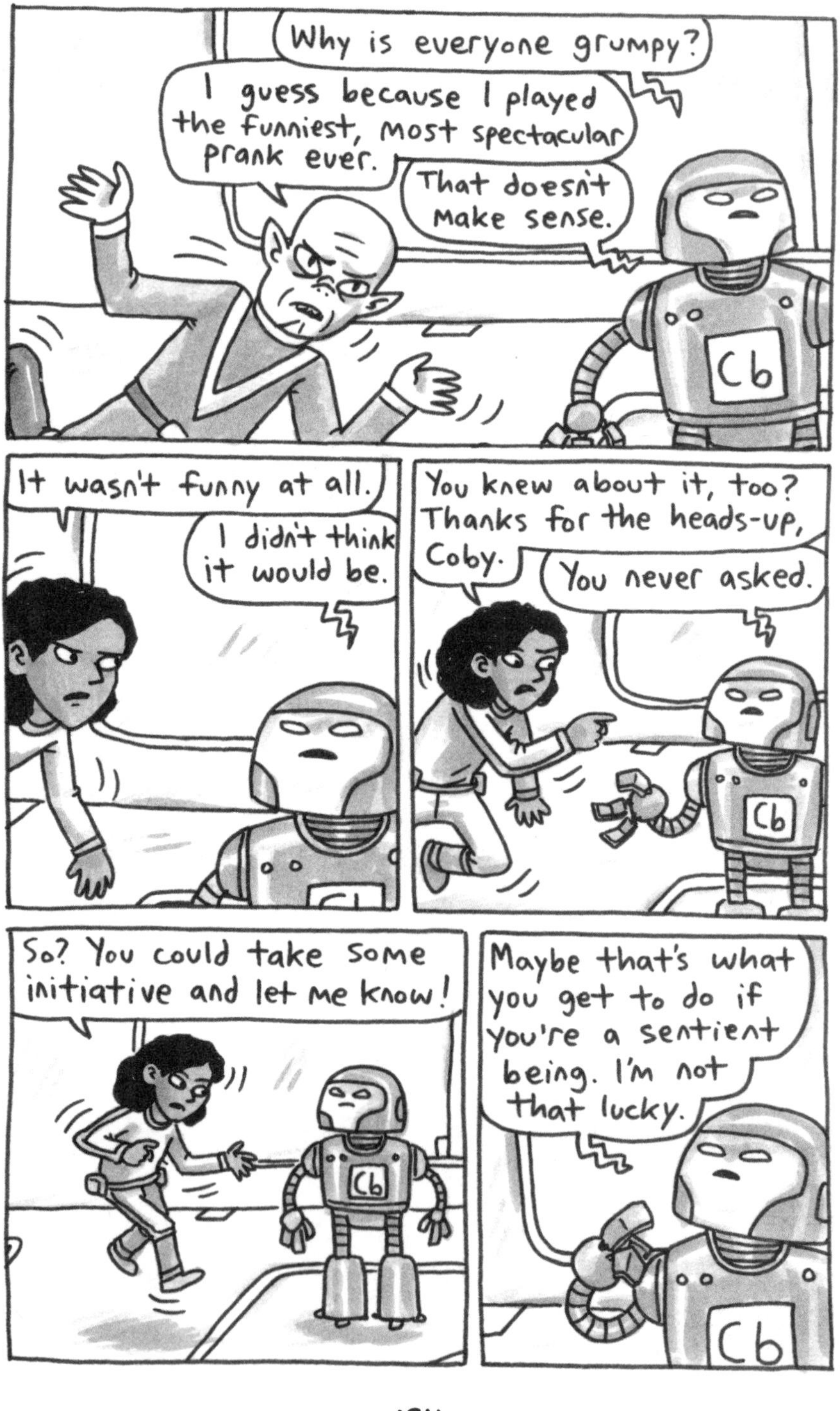
Why is everyone grumpy?
I guess because I played the funniest, most spectacular prank ever.
That doesn't make sense.
It wasn't funny at all.
I didn't think it would be.
You knew about it, too? Thanks for the heads-up, Coby.
You never asked.
So? You could take some initiative and let me know!
Maybe that's what you get to do if you're a sentient being. I'm not that lucky.

Maybe someday I'll have consciousness, and then I can think it's not funny when people play jokes on me.

Oh, wait. I already think it's not funny.

scratch scratch

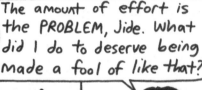

Petra, don't you think you're overreacting? You have to admit the level of detail Tobey went into is impressive!

The amount of effort is the PROBLEM, Jide. What did I do to deserve being made a fool of like that?

And you grew a stupid beard for this prank! Whose side are you on?

scratch scratch

I thought you'd appreciate it. I thought we'd laugh together about this.

scratch scratch scratch scratch scratch scratch scratch

155

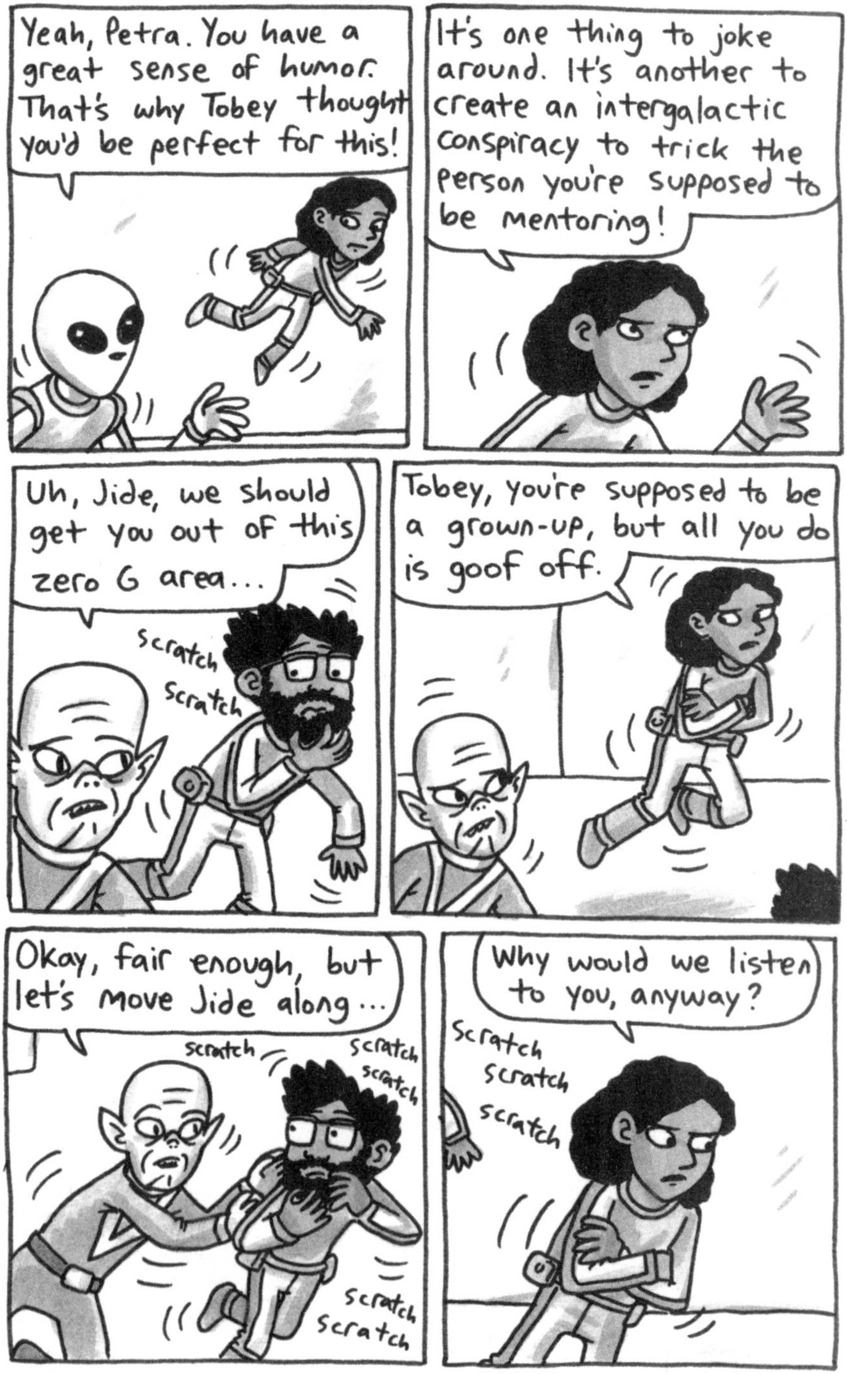
Yeah, Petra. You have a great sense of humor. That's why Tobey thought you'd be perfect for this!
It's one thing to joke around. It's another to create an intergalactic conspiracy to trick the person you're supposed to be mentoring!
Uh, Jide, we should get you out of this zero G area...
scratch
scratch
Tobey, you're supposed to be a grown-up, but all you do is goof off.
Okay, fair enough, but let's move Jide along...
scratch
scratch
scratch
scratch
scratch
Why would we listen to you, anyway?
scratch
scratch
scratch

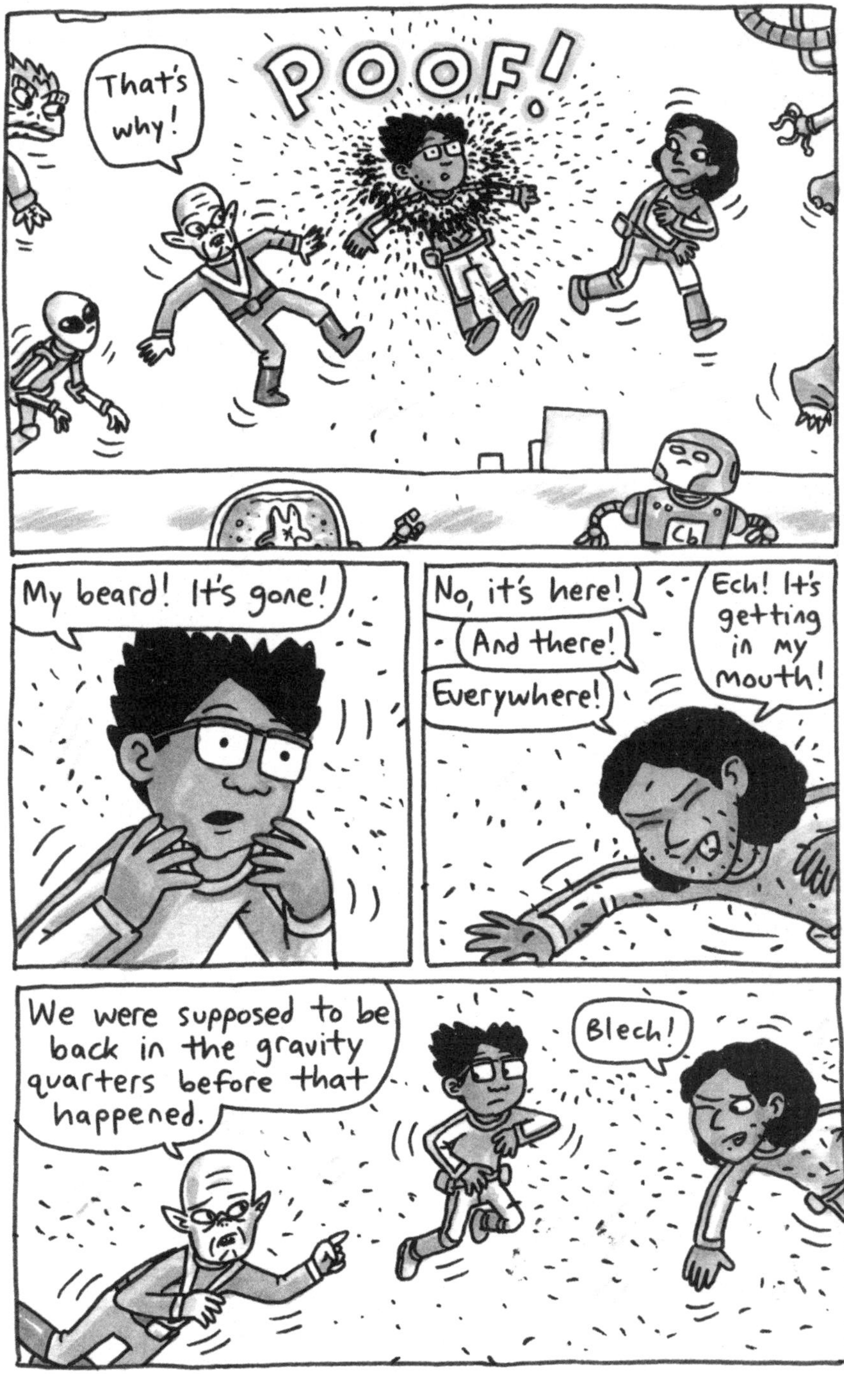
That's why!
POOF!
Cb
My beard! It's gone!
No, it's here!
And there!
Everywhere!
Ech! It's getting in my mouth!
We were supposed to be back in the gravity quarters before that happened.
Blech!

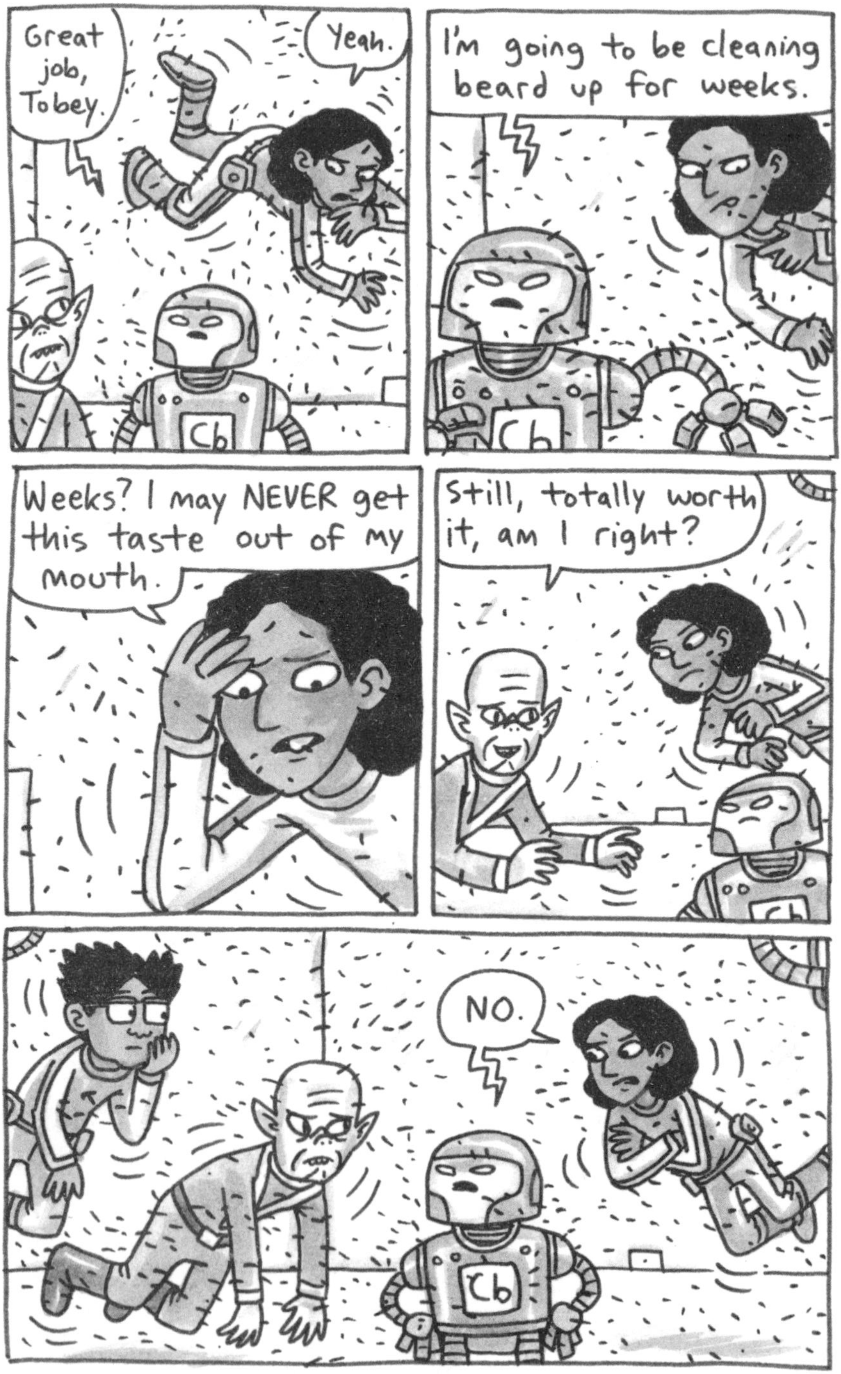
Great job, Tobey.
Yeah.
I'm going to be cleaning beard up for weeks.
Weeks? I may NEVER get this taste out of my mouth.
Still, totally worth it, am I right?
NO.

GOOD SPORTS

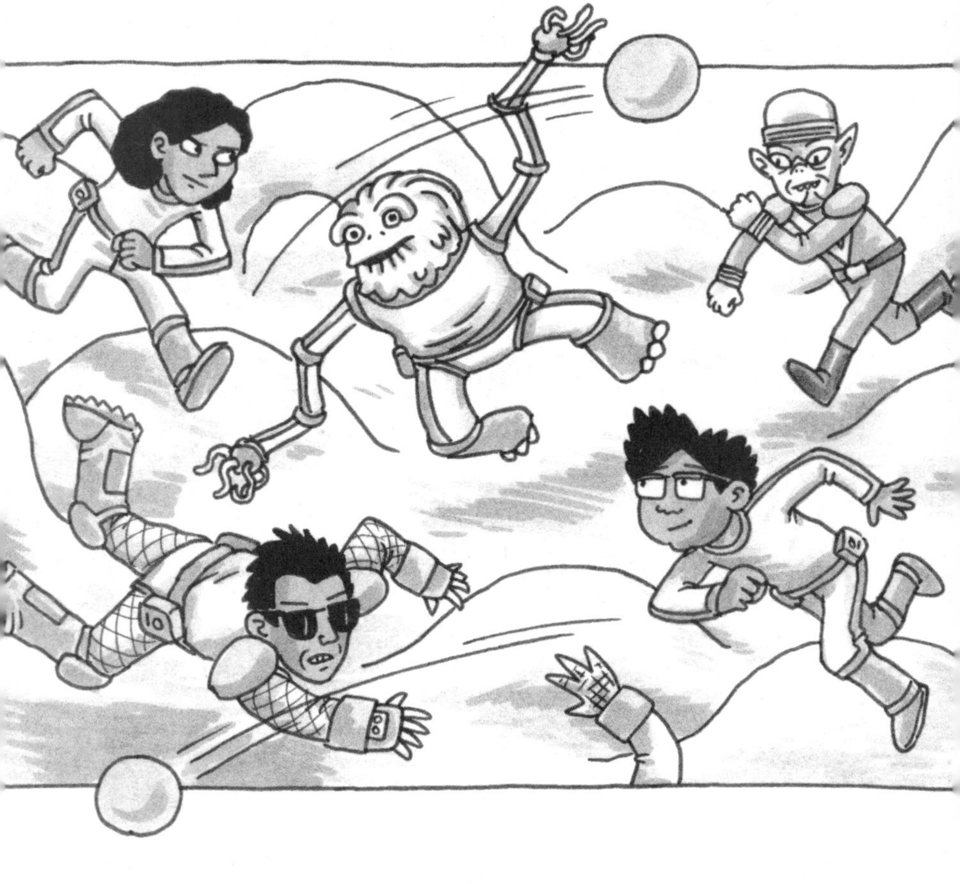

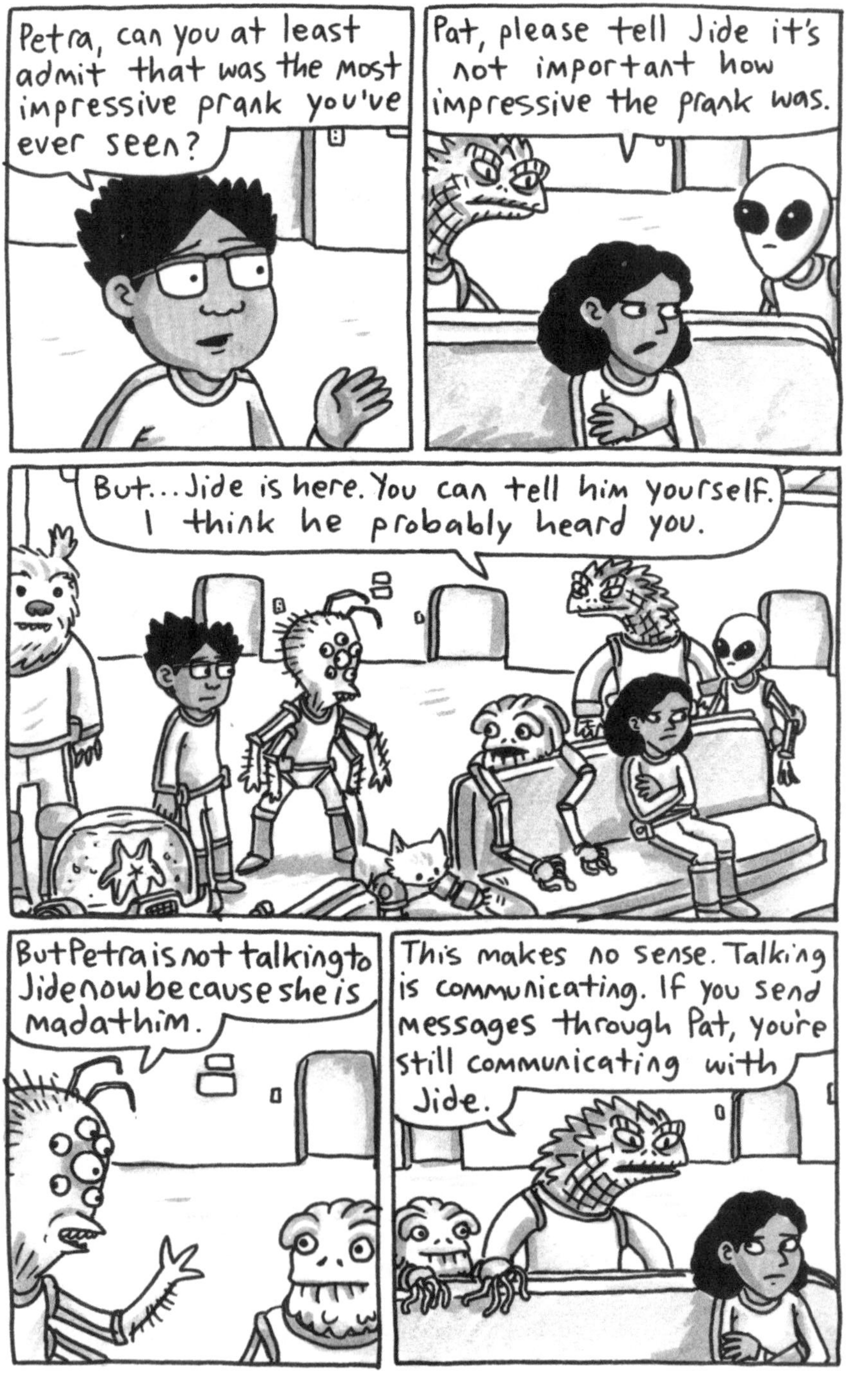
Petra, can you at least admit that was the most impressive prank you've ever seen?
Pat, please tell Jide it's not important how impressive the prank was.
But... Jide is here. You can tell him yourself. I think he probably heard you.
But Petra is not talking to Jide now because she is mad at him.
This makes no sense. Talking is communicating. If you send messages through Pat, you're still communicating with Jide.

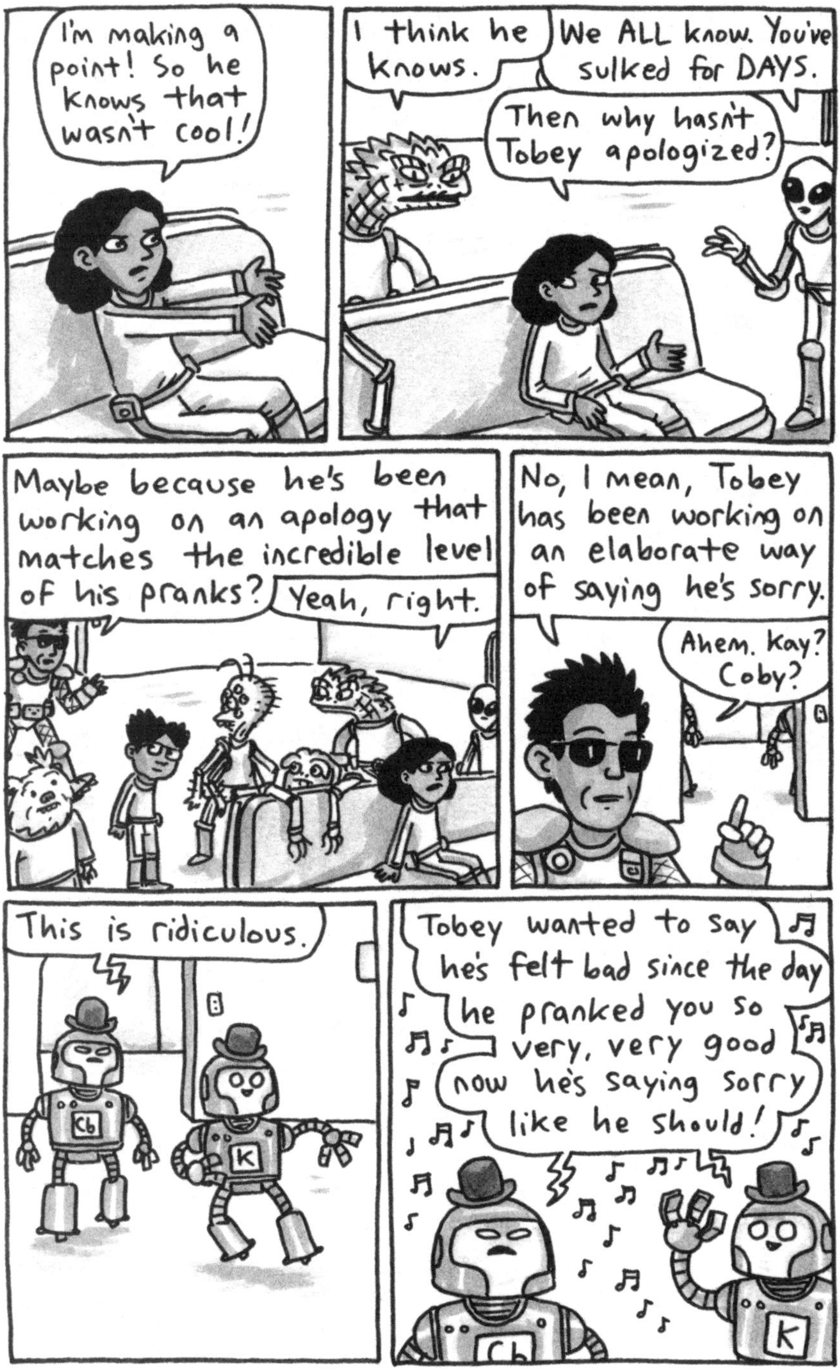
I'm making a point! So he knows that wasn't cool!
I think he knows.
We ALL know. You've sulked for DAYS.
Then why hasn't Tobey apologized?
Maybe because he's been working on an apology that matches the incredible level of his pranks?
Yeah, right.
No, I mean, Tobey has been working on an elaborate way of saying he's sorry.
Ahem. Kay? Coby?
This is ridiculous.
Tobey wanted to say he's felt bad since the day he pranked you so very, very good now he's saying sorry like he should!

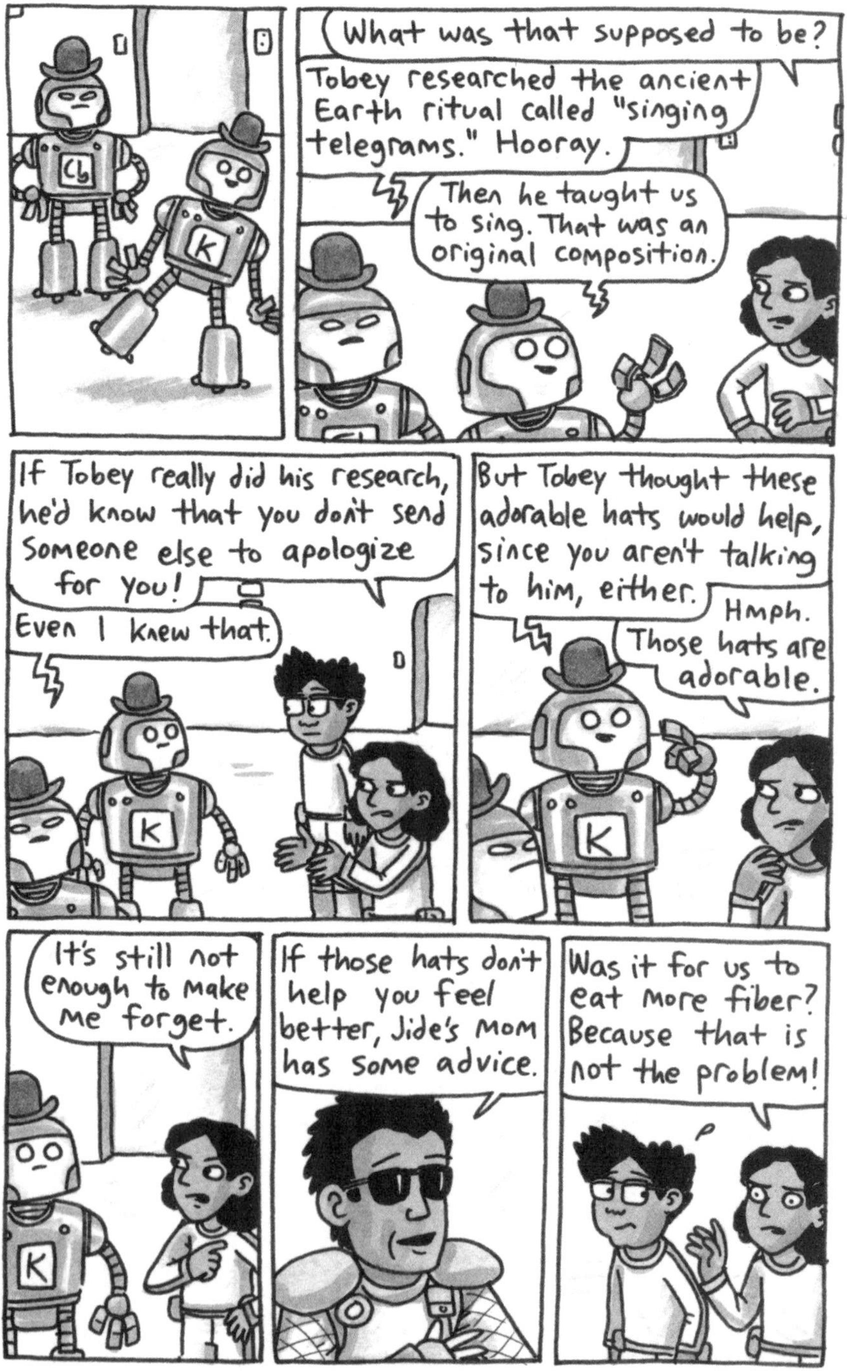
What was that supposed to be?
Tobey researched the ancient Earth ritual called "singing telegrams." Hooray.
Then he taught us to sing. That was an original composition.
If Tobey really did his research, he'd know that you don't send someone else to apologize for you!
Even I knew that.
But Tobey thought these adorable hats would help, since you aren't talking to him, either.
Hmph. Those hats are adorable.
It's still not enough to make me forget.
If those hats don't help you feel better, Jide's mom has some advice.
Was it for us to eat more fiber? Because that is not the problem!

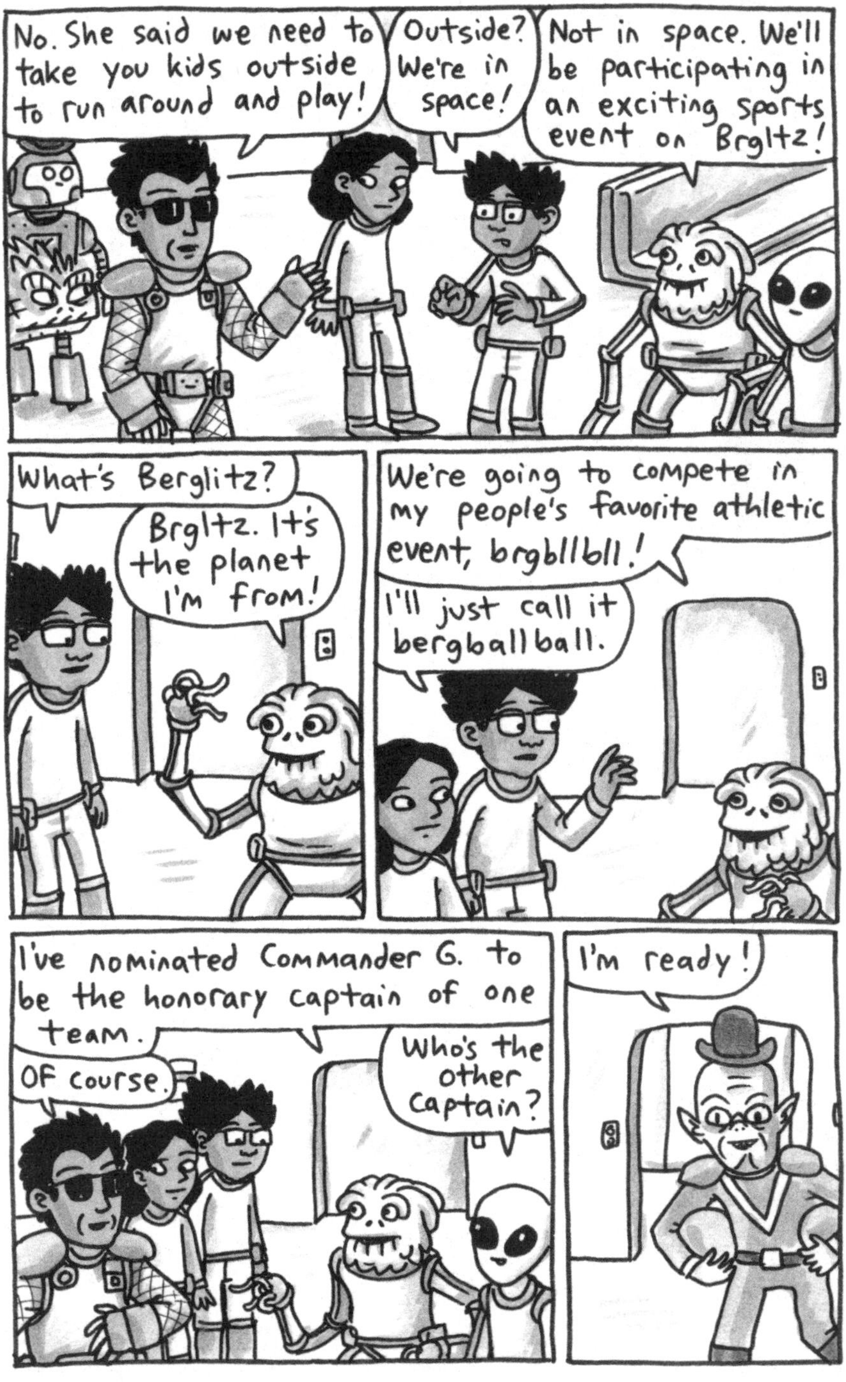
No. She said we need to take you kids outside to run around and play!
Outside? We're in space!
Not in space. We'll be participating in an exciting sports event on Brgltz!
What's Berglitz?
Brgltz. It's the planet I'm from!
We're going to compete in my people's favorite athletic event, brgbllbll!
I'll just call it bergballball.
I've nominated Commander G. to be the honorary captain of one team.
Of course.
Who's the other captain?
I'm ready!

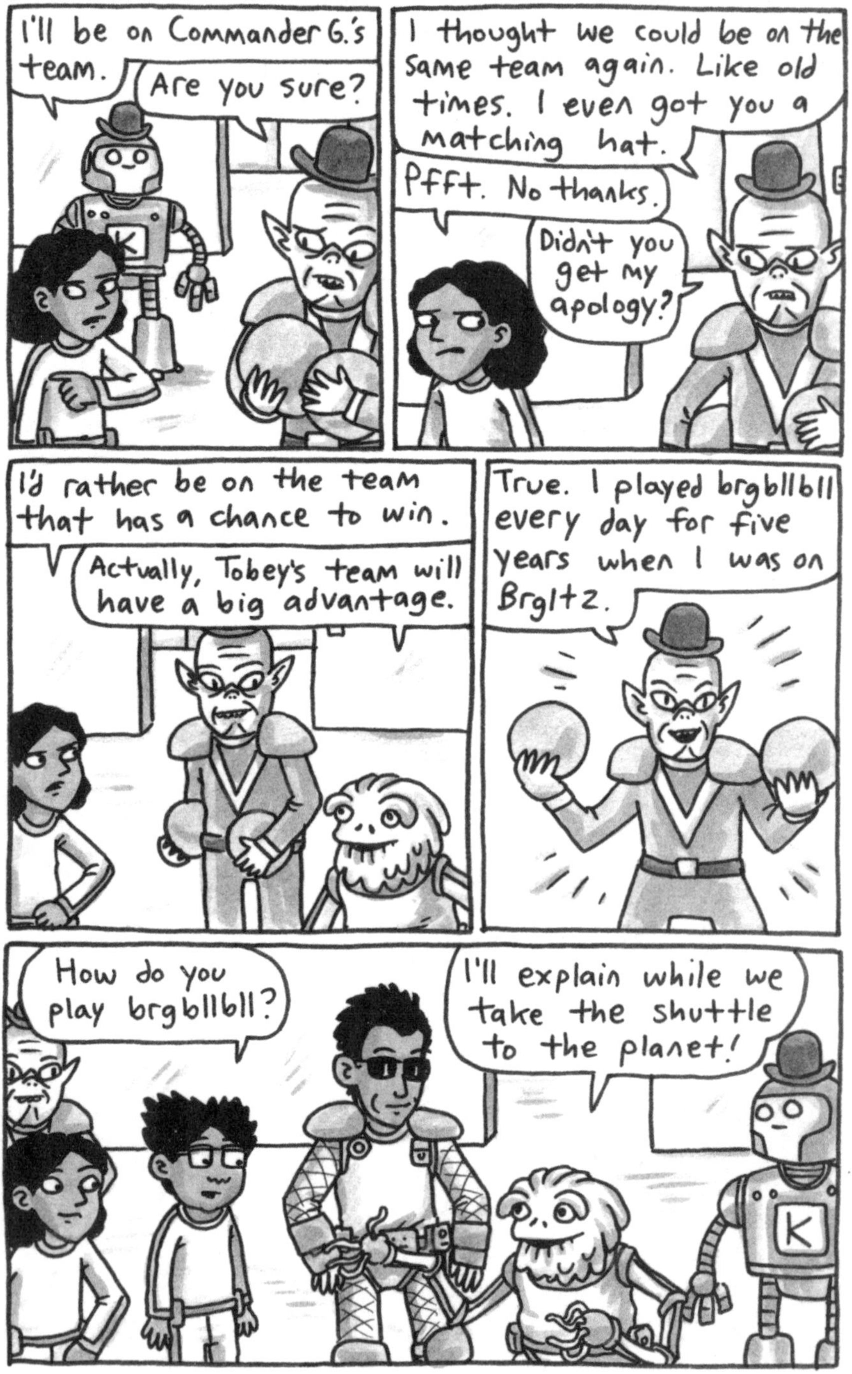
I'll be on Commander G.'s team.
Are you sure?
I thought we could be on the same team again. Like old times. I even got you a matching hat.
Pfft. No thanks.
Didn't you get my apology?
I'd rather be on the team that has a chance to win.
Actually, Tobey's team will have a big advantage.
True. I played brgbllbll every day for five years when I was on Brgltz.
How do you play brgbllbll?
I'll explain while we take the shuttle to the planet!

BRGBLLBLL

BRGBLLBLL BEGAN AS A SIMPLE GAME WITH TWO TEAMS OF FIVE PLAYERS TRYING TO GET A BALL INTO THE OPPOSING TEAM'S GOAL BASKET, BY ANY MEANS AVAILABLE: KICKING, THROWING, OR EVEN GENTLY PLACING THE BALL INSIDE.

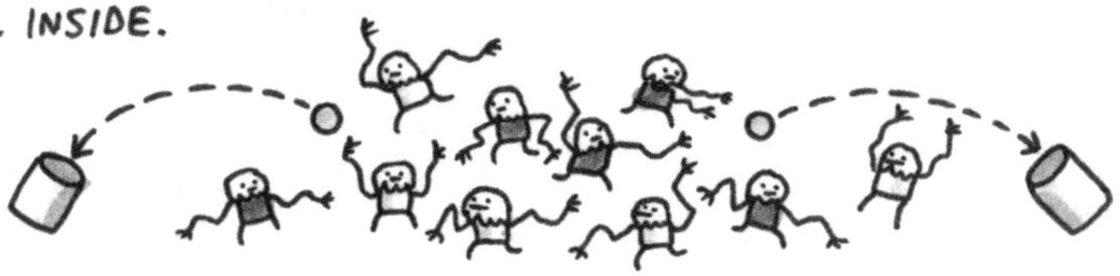

AS THE GAME EVOLVED, A SECOND BALL WAS ADDED, AS WELL AS AN OBSTACLE-BASED PLAYING FIELD. WITH ADVANCED STATISTICAL ANALYSIS, BRGBLLBLL EVENTUALLY REACHED A POINT WHERE THE WINNING TEAM COULD BE DETERMINED SIMPLY BY LOOKING AT EACH TEAM'S AND PLAYER'S STATS.

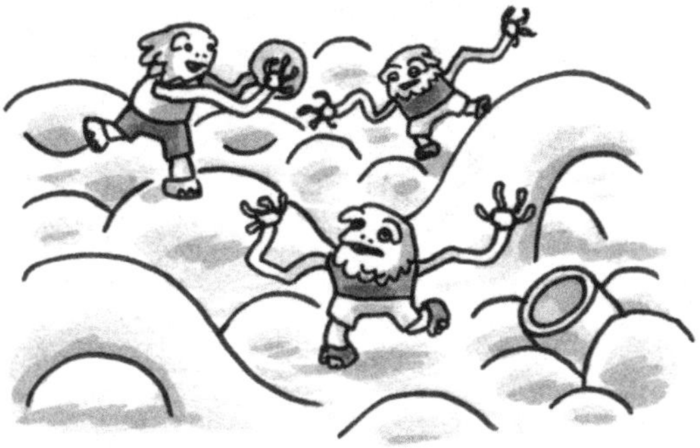

WITH ALL QUANTITIES KNOWN, THE ONLY WAY TO KEEP THE SPORT INTERESTING WAS TO INTRODUCE AN ELEMENT OF UNPREDICTABILITY: THE REFEREE!

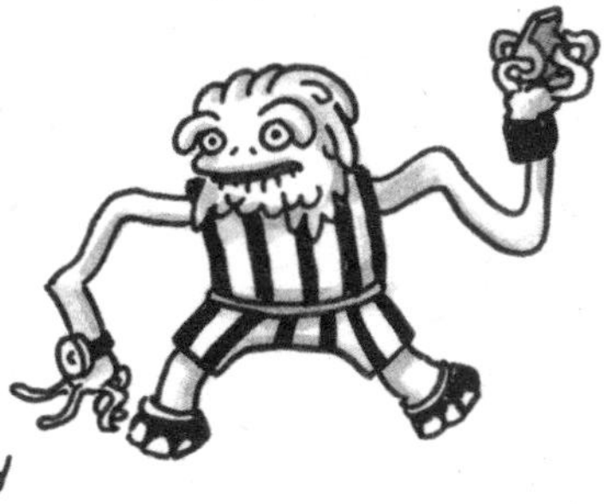

REFEREES ARE THE TRUE STARS OF BRGBLLBLL! THEY COME UP WITH NEW RULES MID-GAME, CHANGE THE INTERPRETATION OF OLD RULES, AND RANDOMLY APPLY ENFORCEMENT OF RULES. IN THIS WAY THEY SHAPE THE STORY OF EACH BRGBLLBLL MATCH AND MAKE SURE THE GAME IS WILDLY EXCITING!

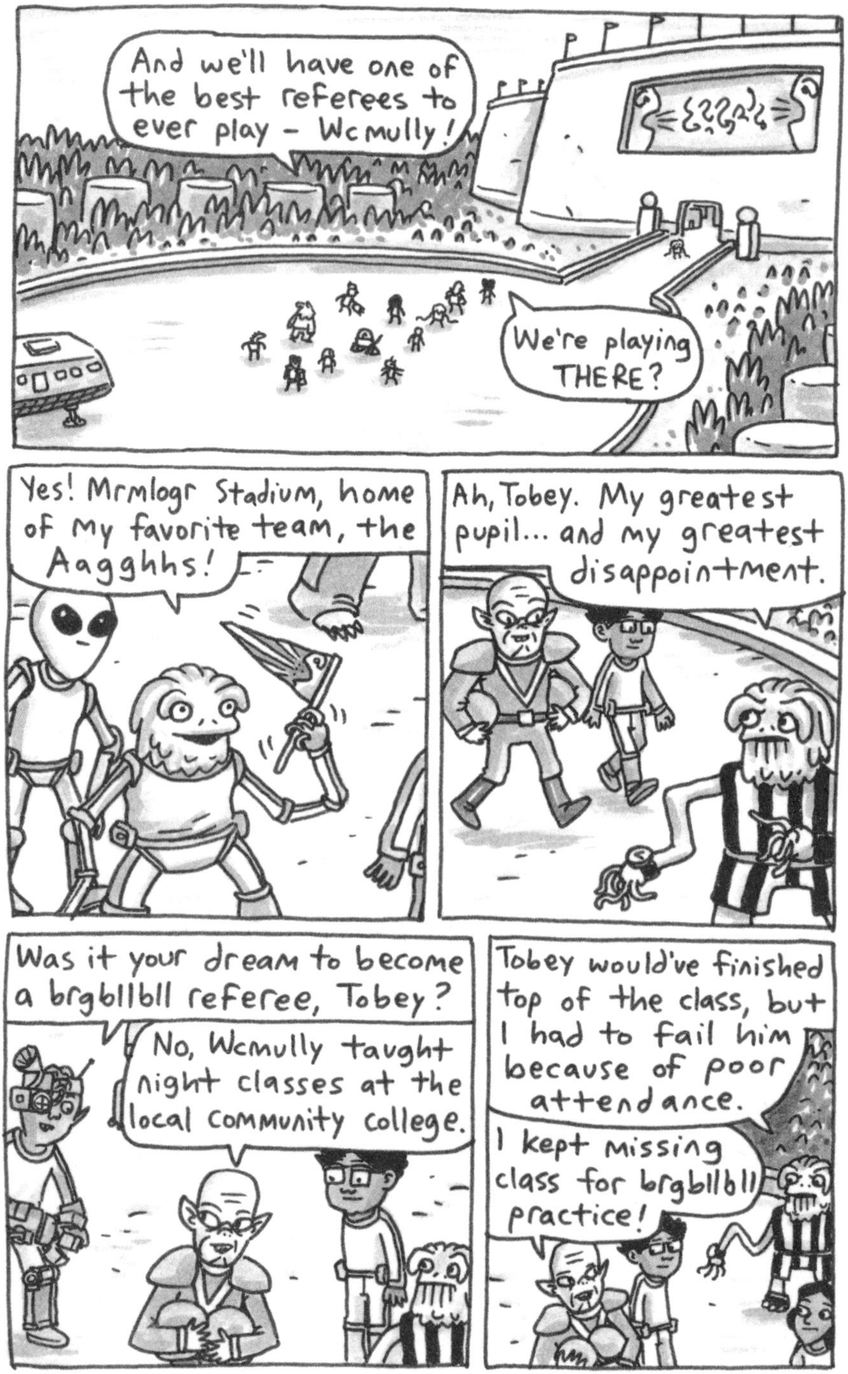
And we'll have one of the best referees to ever play - Wcmully!
We're playing THERE?
Yes! Mrmlogr Stadium, home of my favorite team, the Aagghhs!
Ah, Tobey. My greatest pupil... and my greatest disappointment.
Was it your dream to become a brgbllbll referee, Tobey?
No, Wcmully taught night classes at the local community college.
Tobey would've finished top of the class, but I had to fail him because of poor attendance.
I kept missing class for brgbllbll practice!

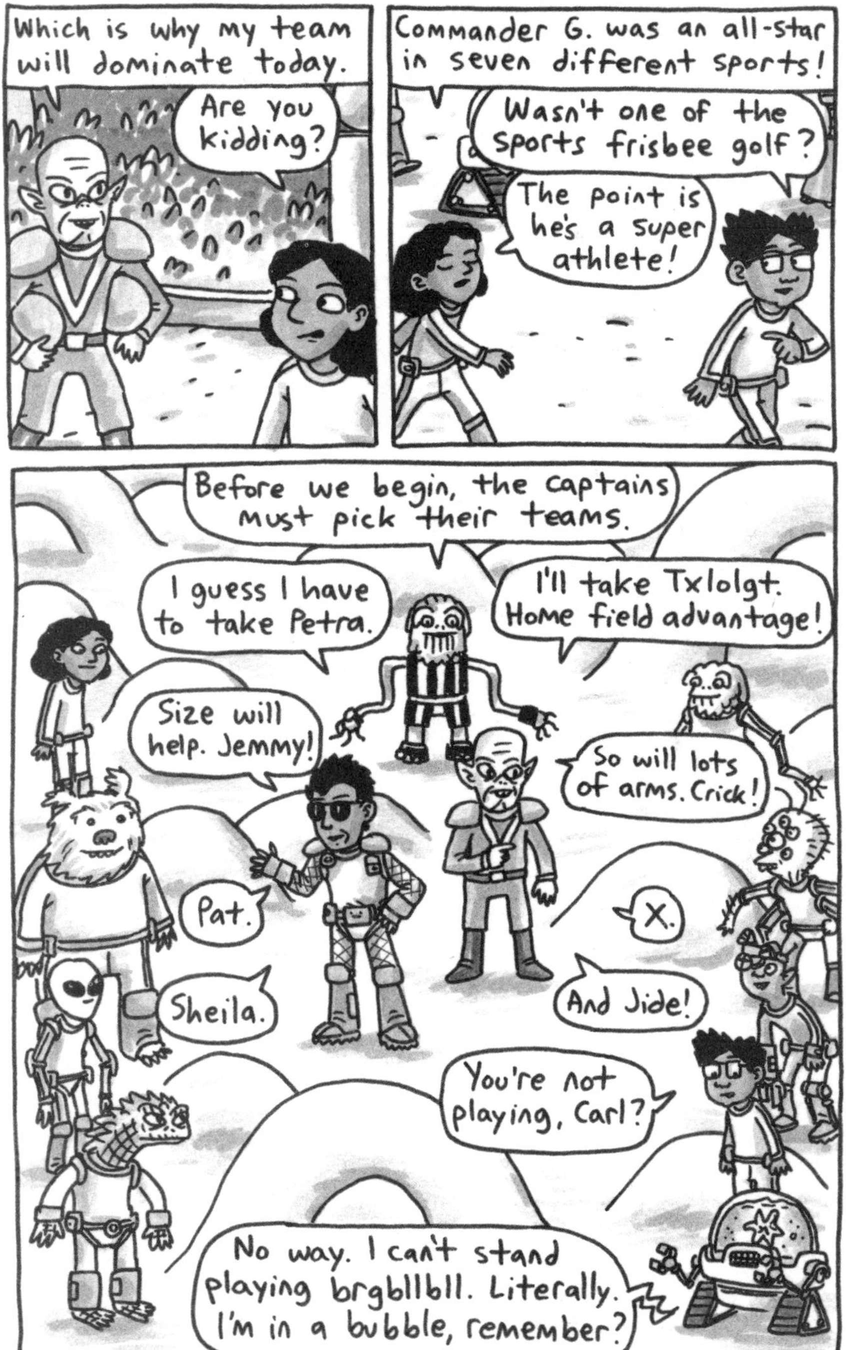
Which is why my team will dominate today.
Are you kidding?
Commander G. was an all-star in seven different sports!
Wasn't one of the sports frisbee golf?
The point is he's a super athlete!
Before we begin, the captains must pick their teams.
I guess I have to take Petra.
I'll take Txlolgt. Home field advantage!
Size will help. Jemmy!
So will lots of arms. Crick!
Pat.
X.
Sheila.
And Jide!
You're not playing, Carl?
No way. I can't stand playing brgbllbll. Literally. I'm in a bubble, remember?

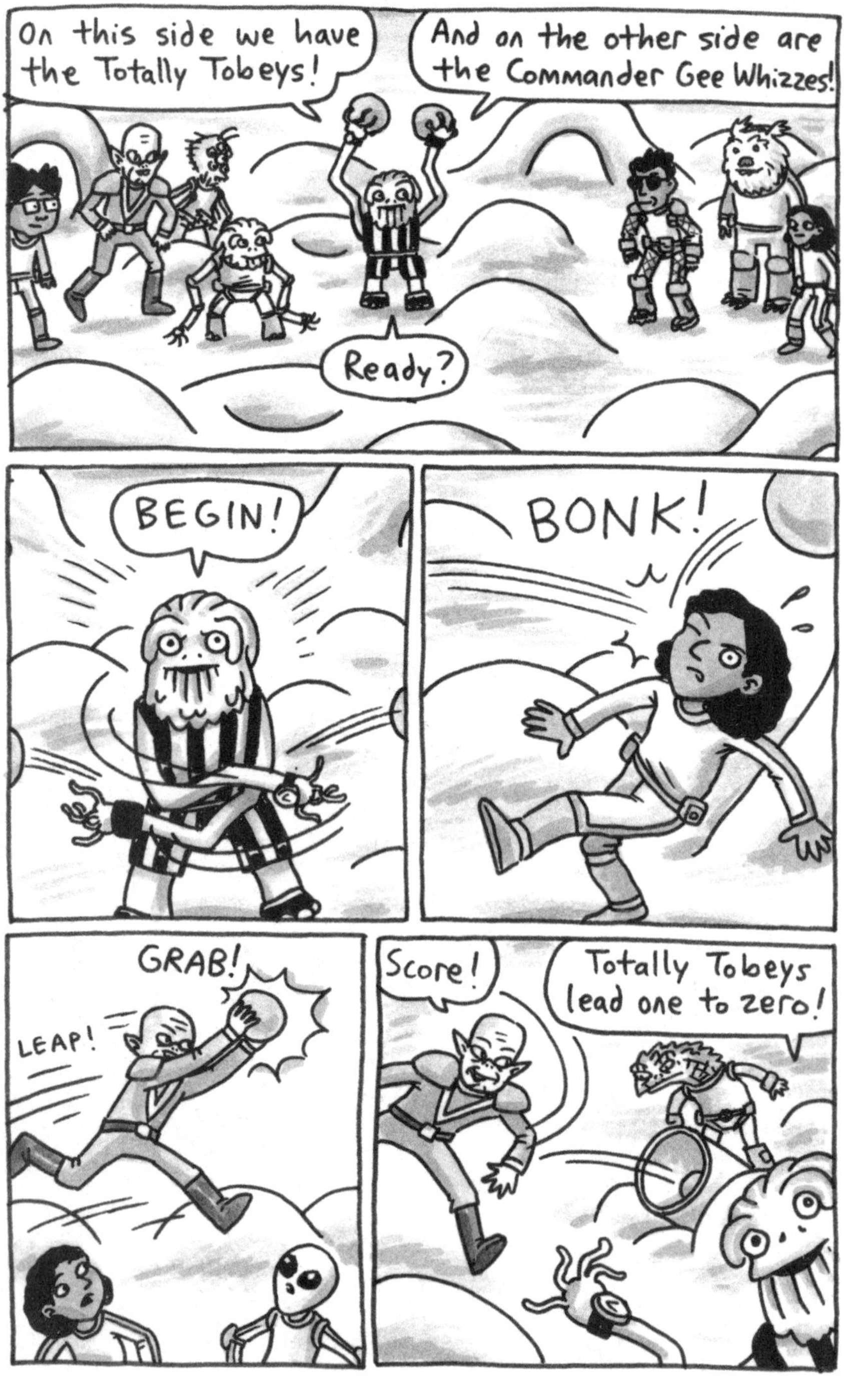
On this side we have the Totally Tobeys!
And on the other side are the Commander Gee Whizzes!
Ready?
BEGIN!
BONK!
GRAB!
LEAP!
Score!
Totally Tobeys lead one to zero!

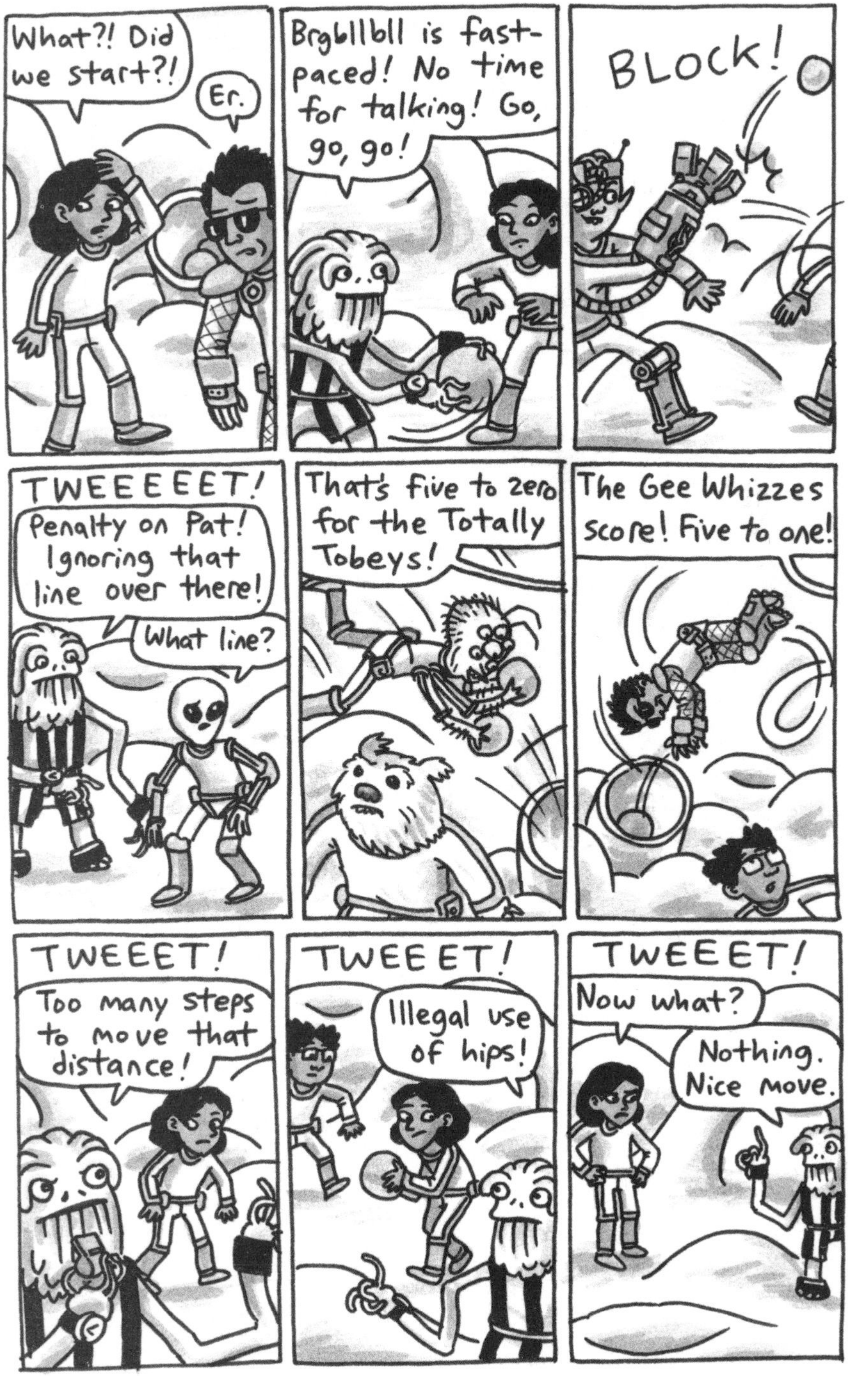
What?! Did we start?!
Er.
Brgbllbll is fast-paced! No time for talking! Go, go, go!
BLOCK!
TWEEEEEET!
Penalty on Pat! Ignoring that line over there!
What line?
That's five to zero for the Totally Tobeys!
The Gee Whizzes score! Five to one!
TWEEET!
Too many steps to move that distance!
TWEEET!
Illegal use of hips!
TWEEET!
Now what?
Nothing. Nice move.

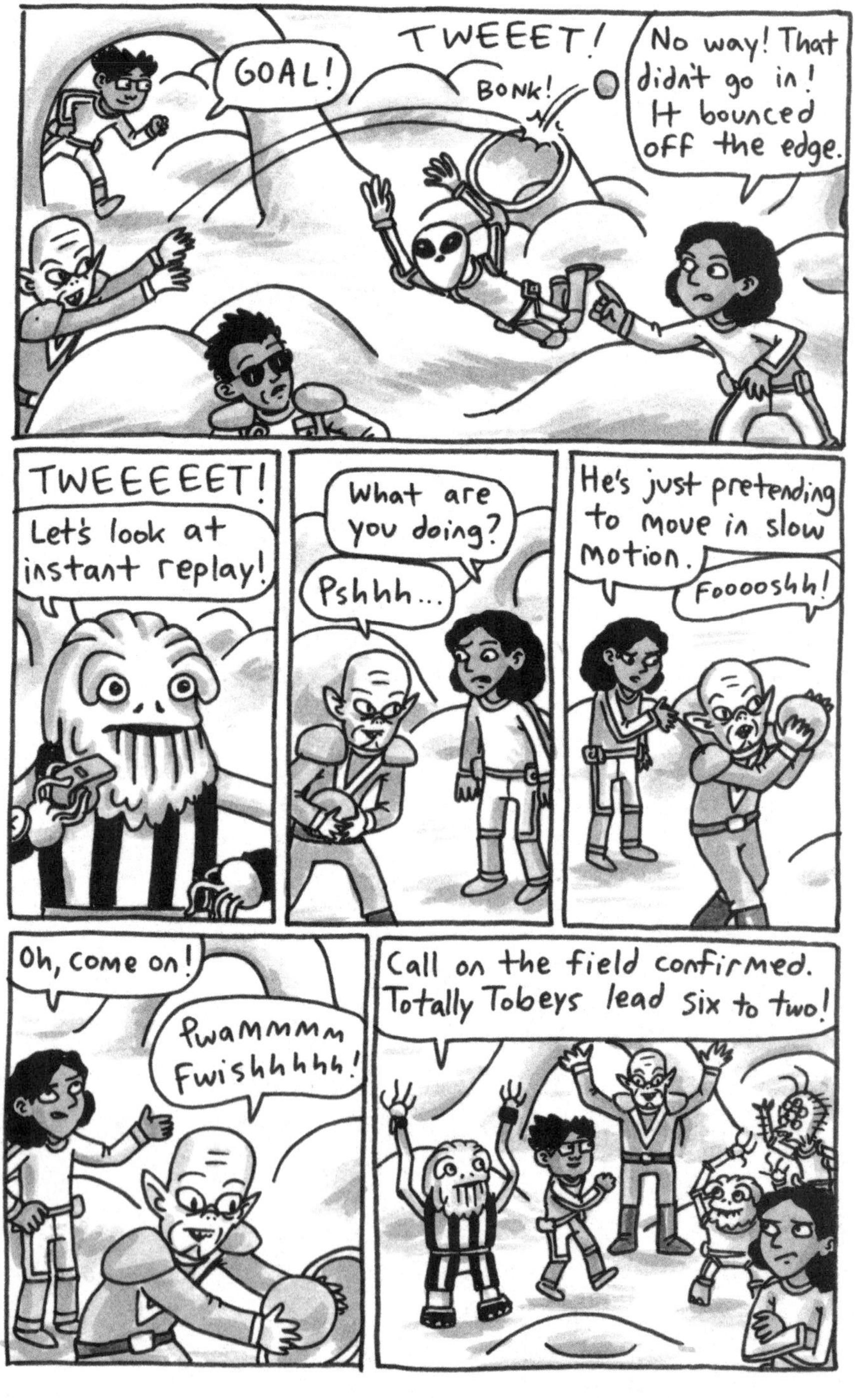
GOAL!
TWEEET!
BONK!
No way! That didn't go in! It bounced off the edge.
TWEEEEEET!
Let's look at instant replay!
What are you doing?
Pshhh...
He's just pretending to move in slow motion.
Fooooshh!
Oh, come on!
Pwammmm Fwishhhhh!
Call on the field confirmed. Totally Tobeys lead six to two!

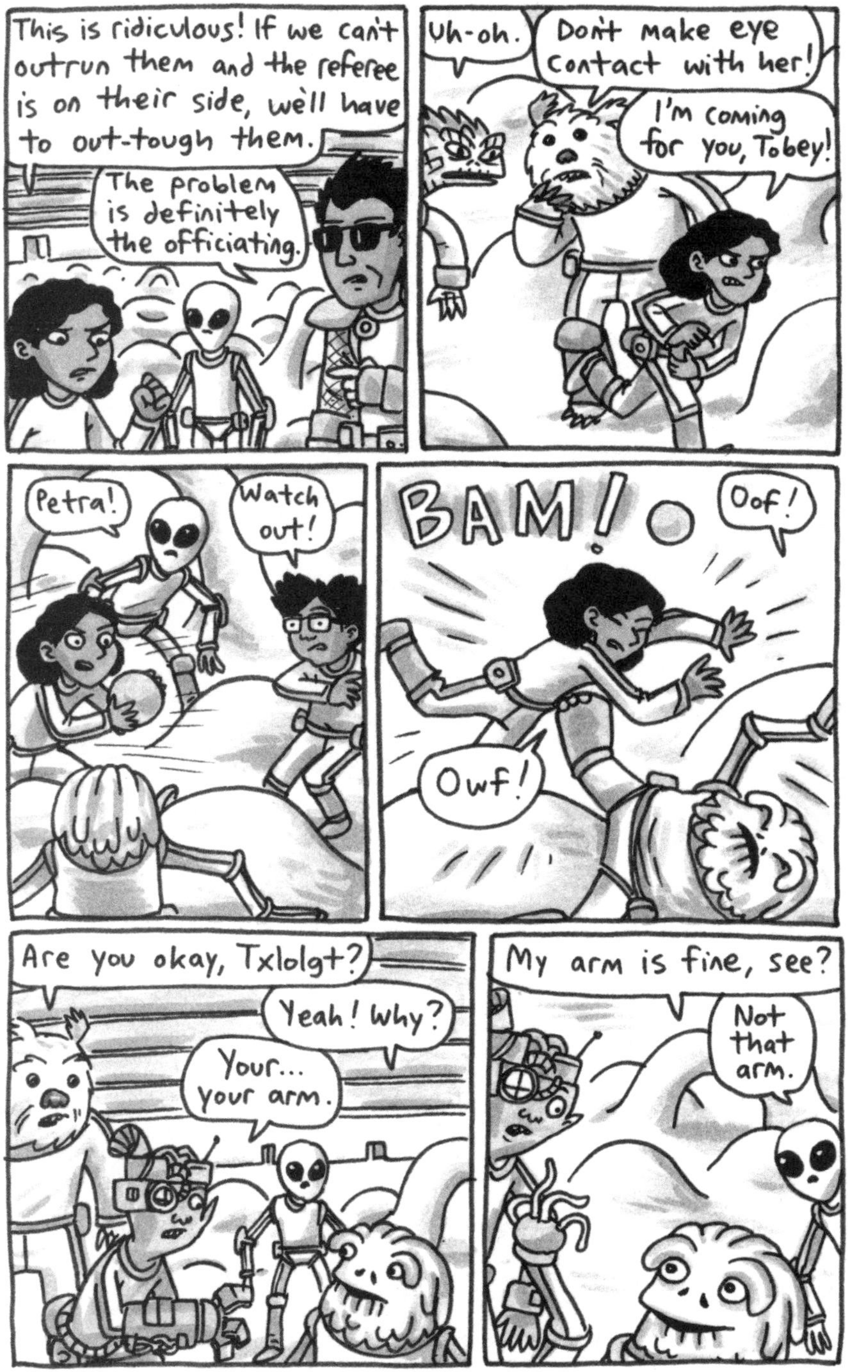
This is ridiculous! If we can't outrun them and the referee is on their side, we'll have to out-tough them.
The problem is definitely the officiating.
Uh-oh.
Don't make eye contact with her!
I'm coming for you, Tobey!
Petra!
Watch out!
BAM!
Oof!
Owf!
Are you okay, Txlolgt?
Yeah! Why?
Your... your arm.
My arm is fine, see?
Not that arm.

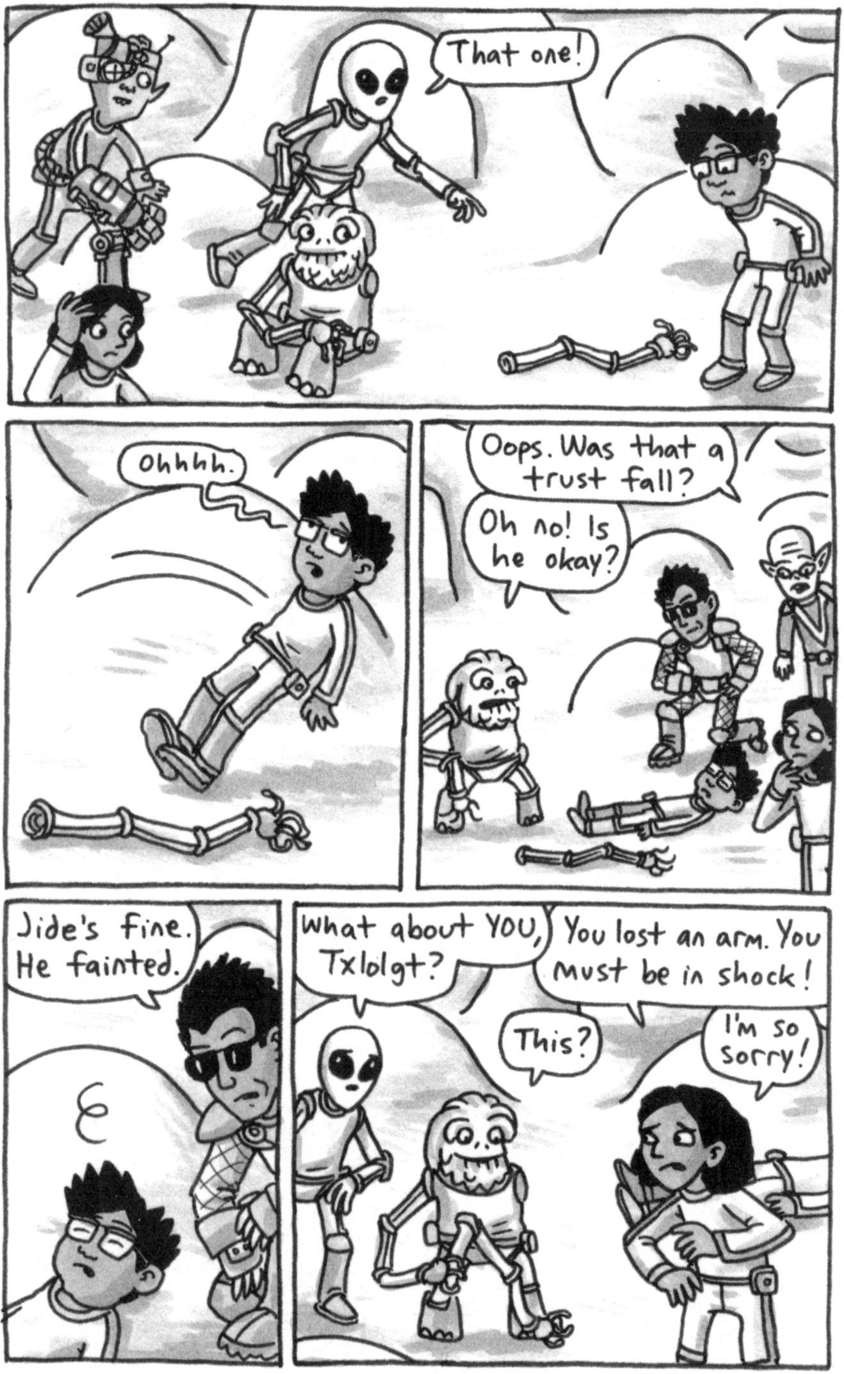

That one!
Ohhhh.
Oops. Was that a trust fall?
Oh no! Is he okay?
Jide's fine. He fainted.
What about YOU, Txlolgt?
You lost an arm. You must be in shock!
This?
I'm so sorry!

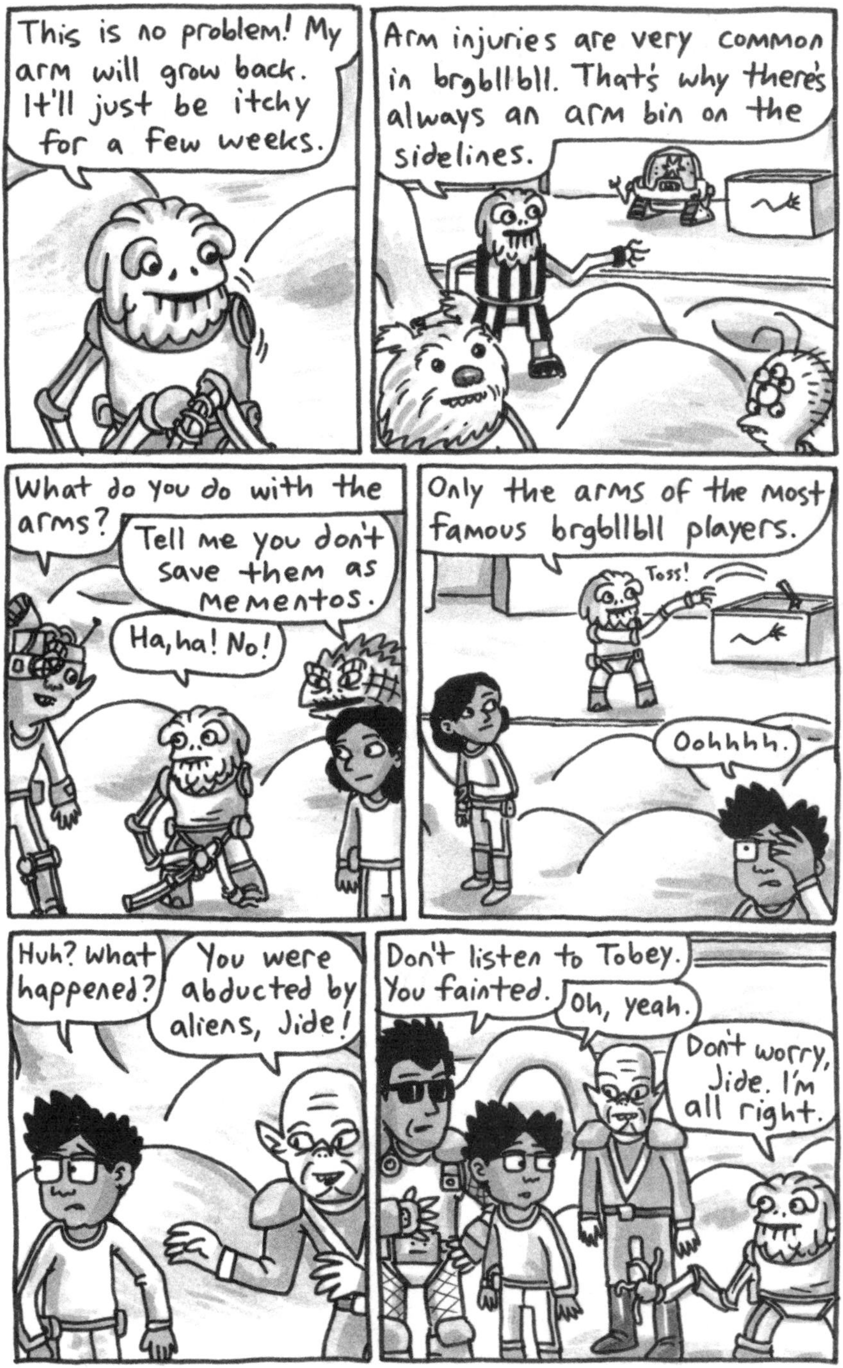
This is no problem! My arm will grow back. It'll just be itchy for a few weeks.
Arm injuries are very common in brgbllbll. That's why there's always an arm bin on the sidelines.
What do you do with the arms?
Tell me you don't save them as mementos.
Ha, ha! No!
Only the arms of the most famous brgbllbll players.
Toss!
Oohhhh.
Huh? What happened?
You were abducted by aliens, Jide!
Don't listen to Tobey. You fainted.
Oh, yeah.
Don't worry, Jide. I'm all right.

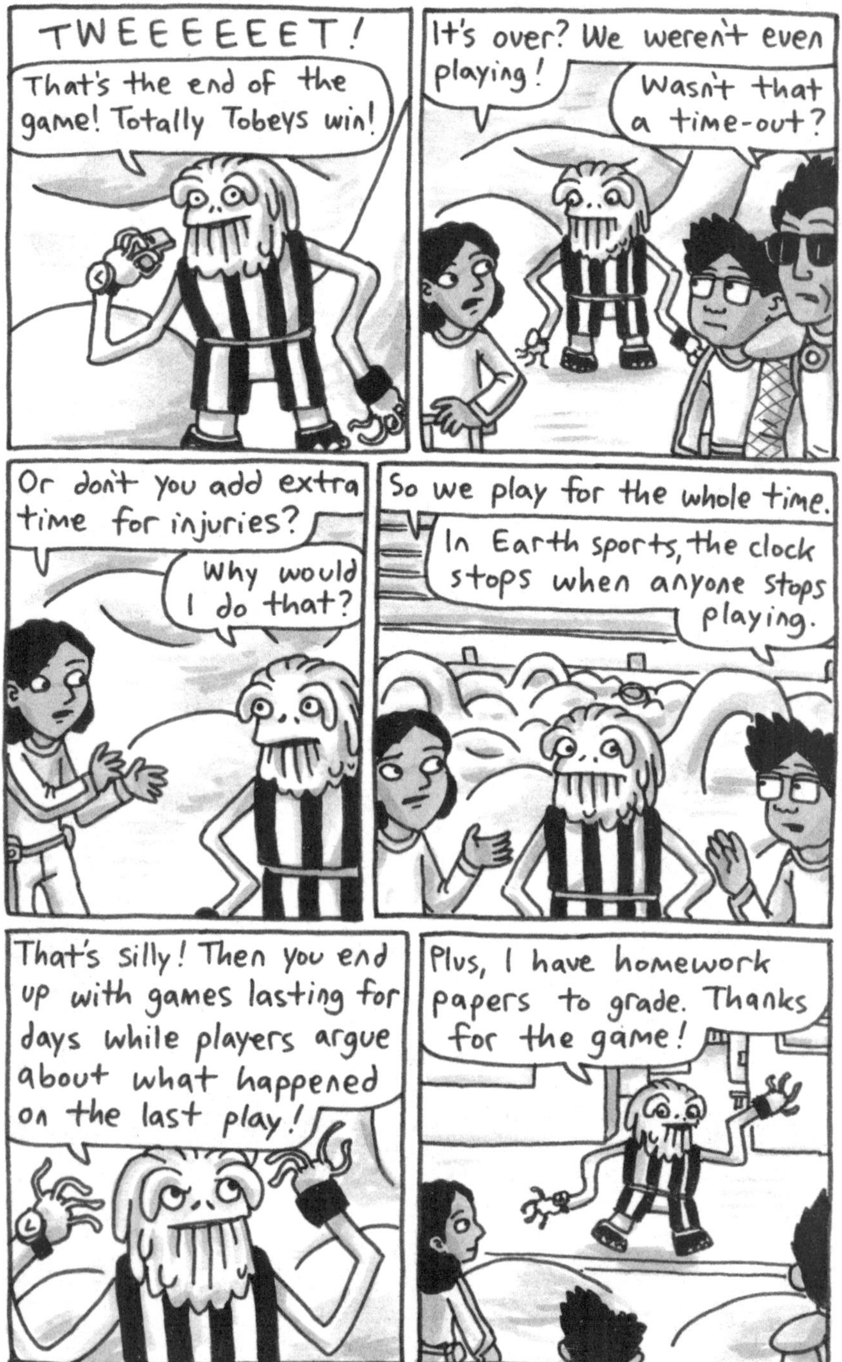
TWEEEEEEET!
That's the end of the game! Totally Tobeys win!
It's over? We weren't even playing!
Wasn't that a time-out?
Or don't you add extra time for injuries?
Why would I do that?
So we play for the whole time.
In Earth sports, the clock stops when anyone stops playing.
That's silly! Then you end up with games lasting for days while players argue about what happened on the last play!
Plus, I have homework papers to grade. Thanks for the game!

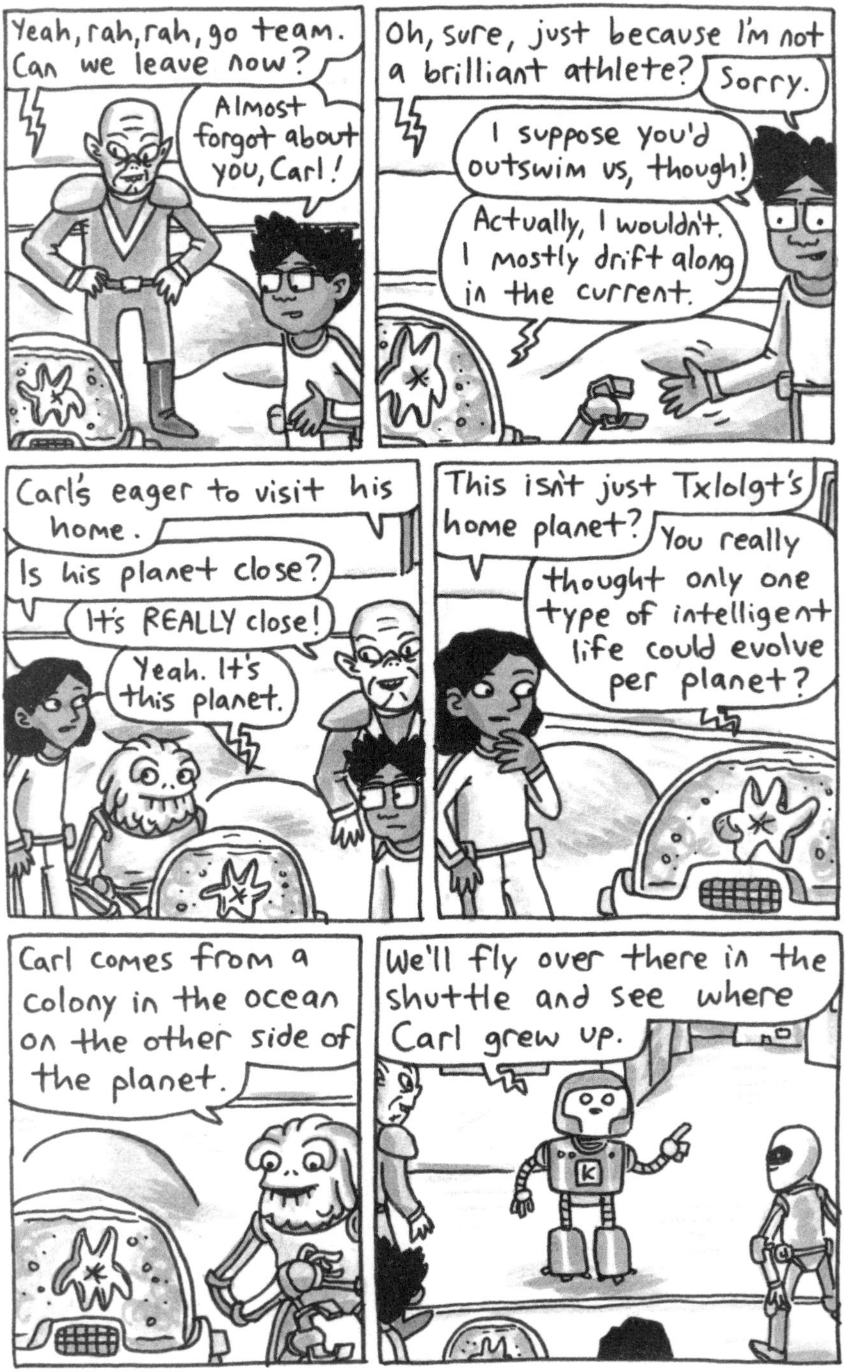
Yeah, rah, rah, go team. Can we leave now?
Almost forgot about you, Carl!
Oh, sure, just because I'm not a brilliant athlete?
Sorry.
I suppose you'd outswim us, though!
Actually, I wouldn't. I mostly drift along in the current.
Carl's eager to visit his home.
Is his planet close?
It's REALLY close!
Yeah. It's this planet.
This isn't just Txlolgt's home planet?
You really thought only one type of intelligent life could evolve per planet?
Carl comes from a colony in the ocean on the other side of the planet.
We'll fly over there in the shuttle and see where Carl grew up.

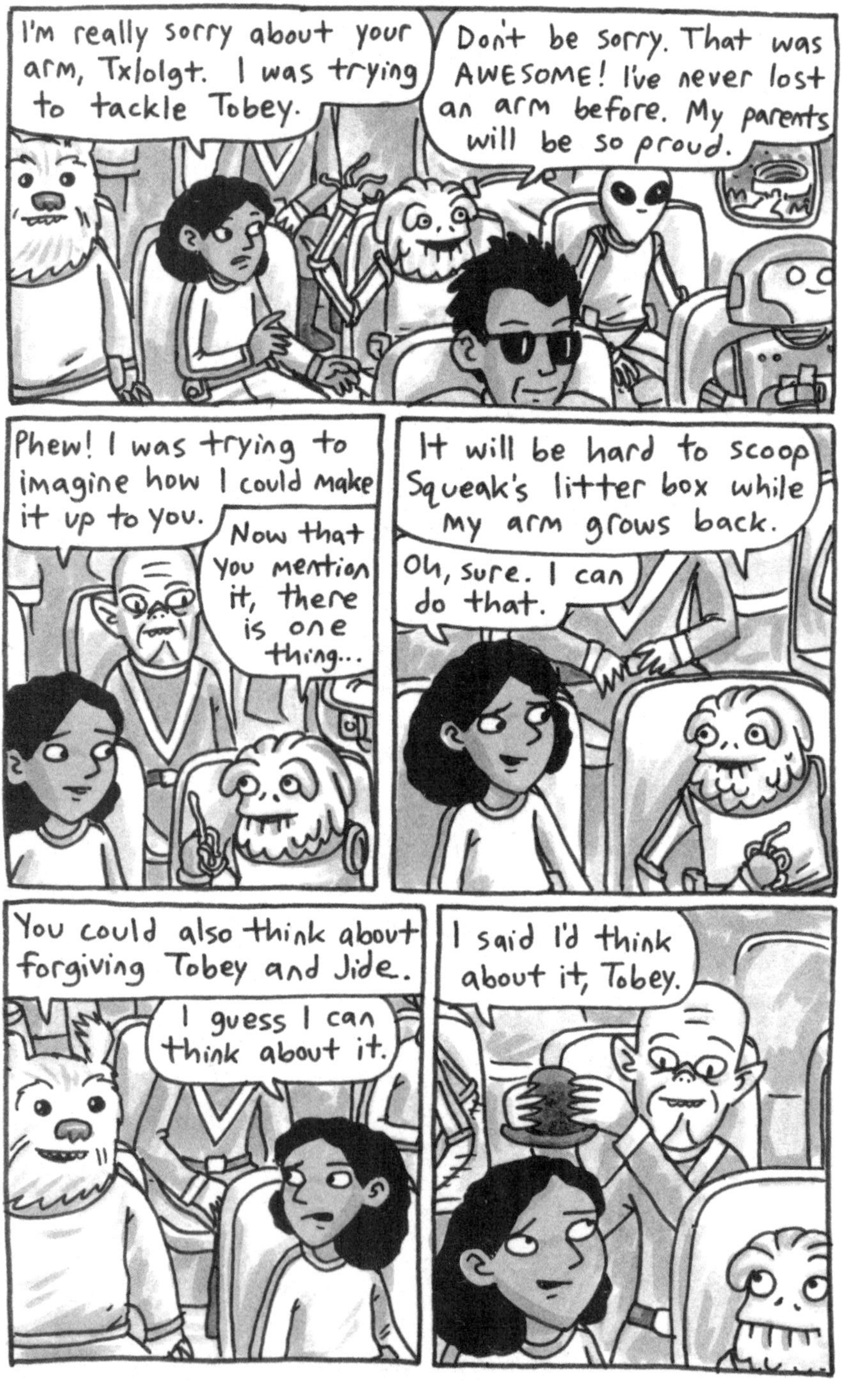

I'm really sorry about your arm, Txlolgt. I was trying to tackle Tobey.
Don't be sorry. That was AWESOME! I've never lost an arm before. My parents will be so proud.
Phew! I was trying to imagine how I could make it up to you.
Now that you mention it, there is one thing...
It will be hard to scoop Squeak's litter box while my arm grows back.
Oh, sure. I can do that.
You could also think about forgiving Tobey and Jide.
I guess I can think about it.
I said I'd think about it, Tobey.

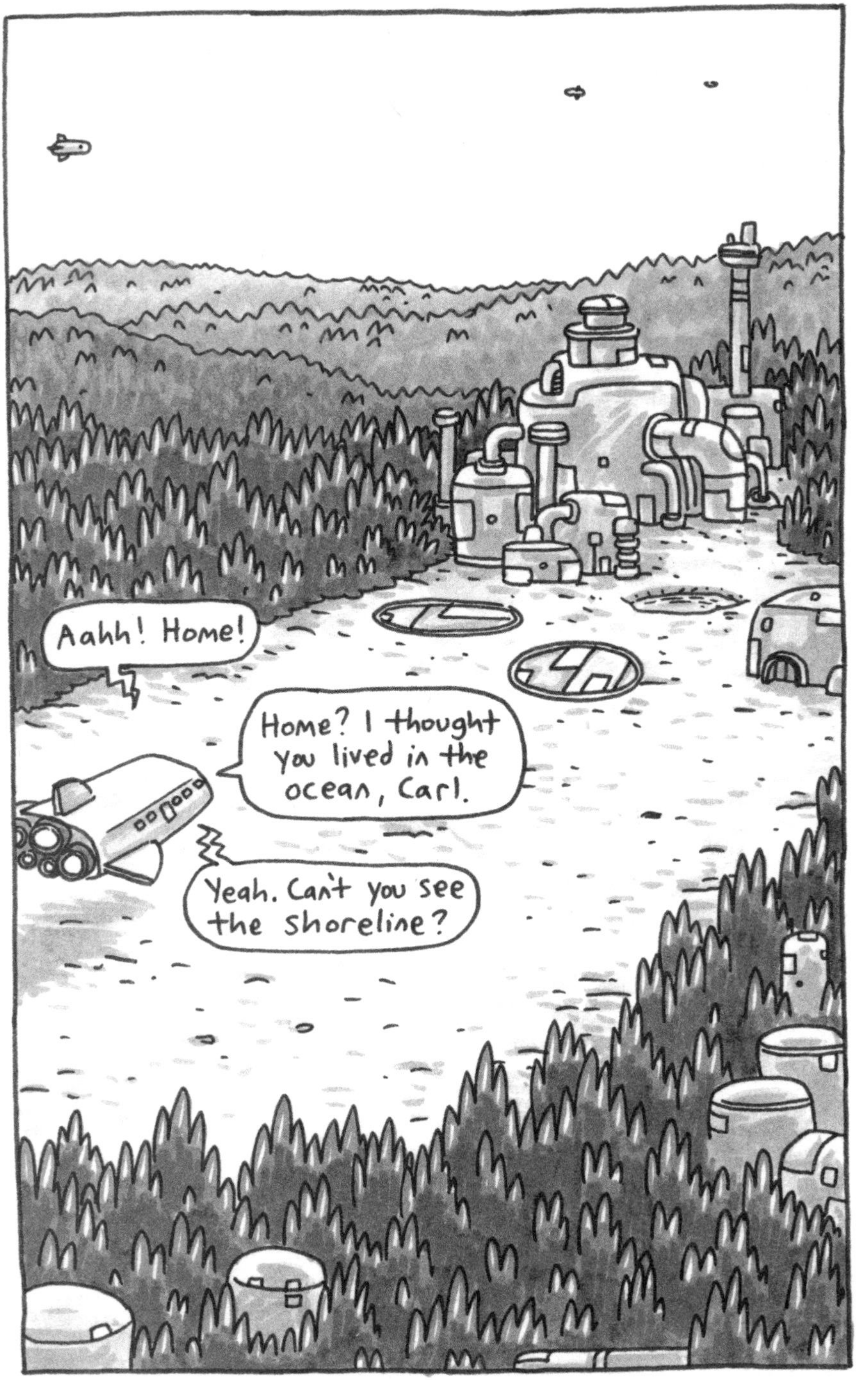
Aahh! Home!
Home? I thought you lived in the ocean, Carl.
Yeah. Can't you see the shoreline?

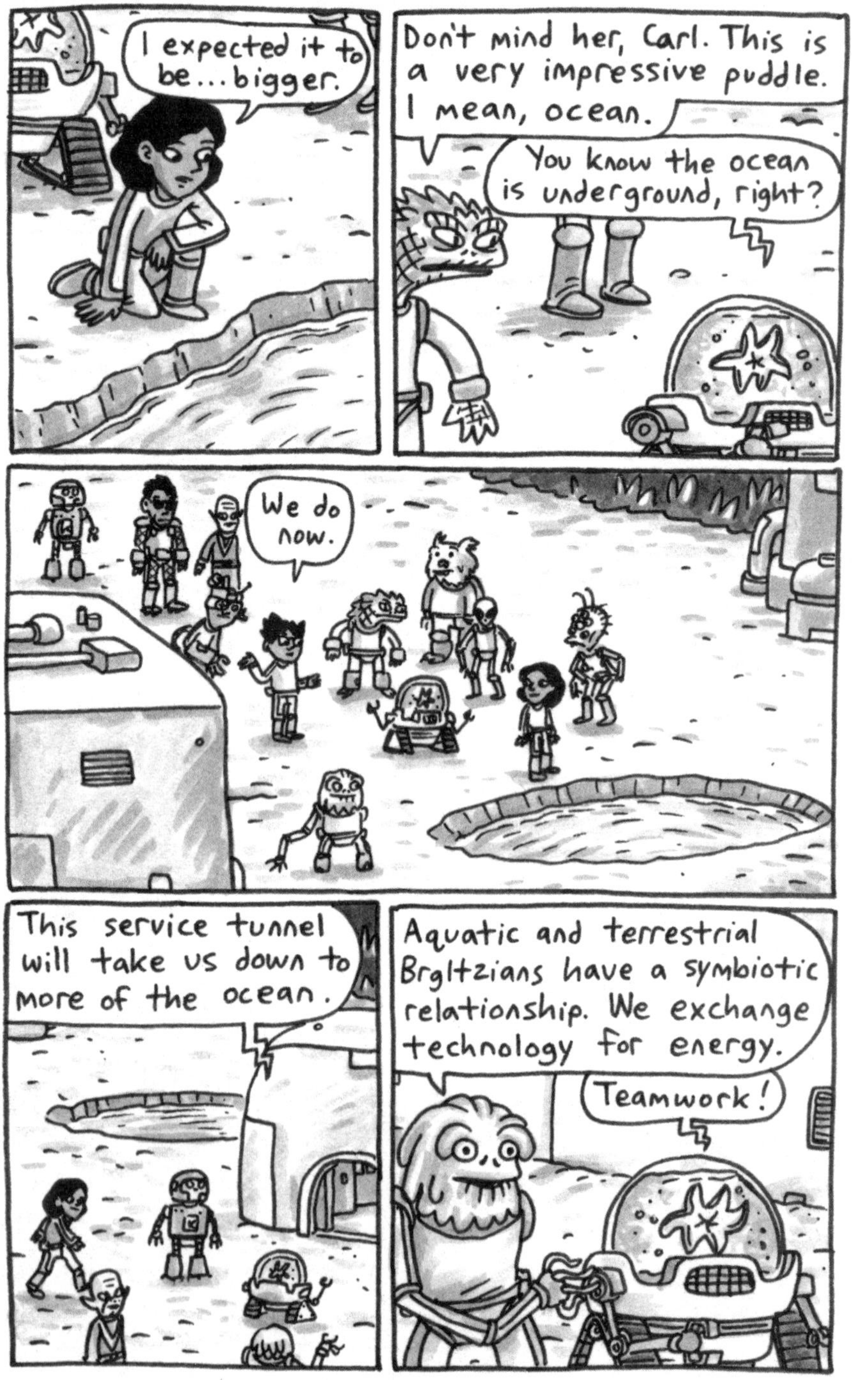
I expected it to be... bigger.
Don't mind her, Carl. This is a very impressive puddle. I mean, ocean.
You know the ocean is underground, right?
We do now.
This service tunnel will take us down to more of the ocean.
Aquatic and terrestrial Brgltzians have a symbiotic relationship. We exchange technology for energy.
Teamwork!

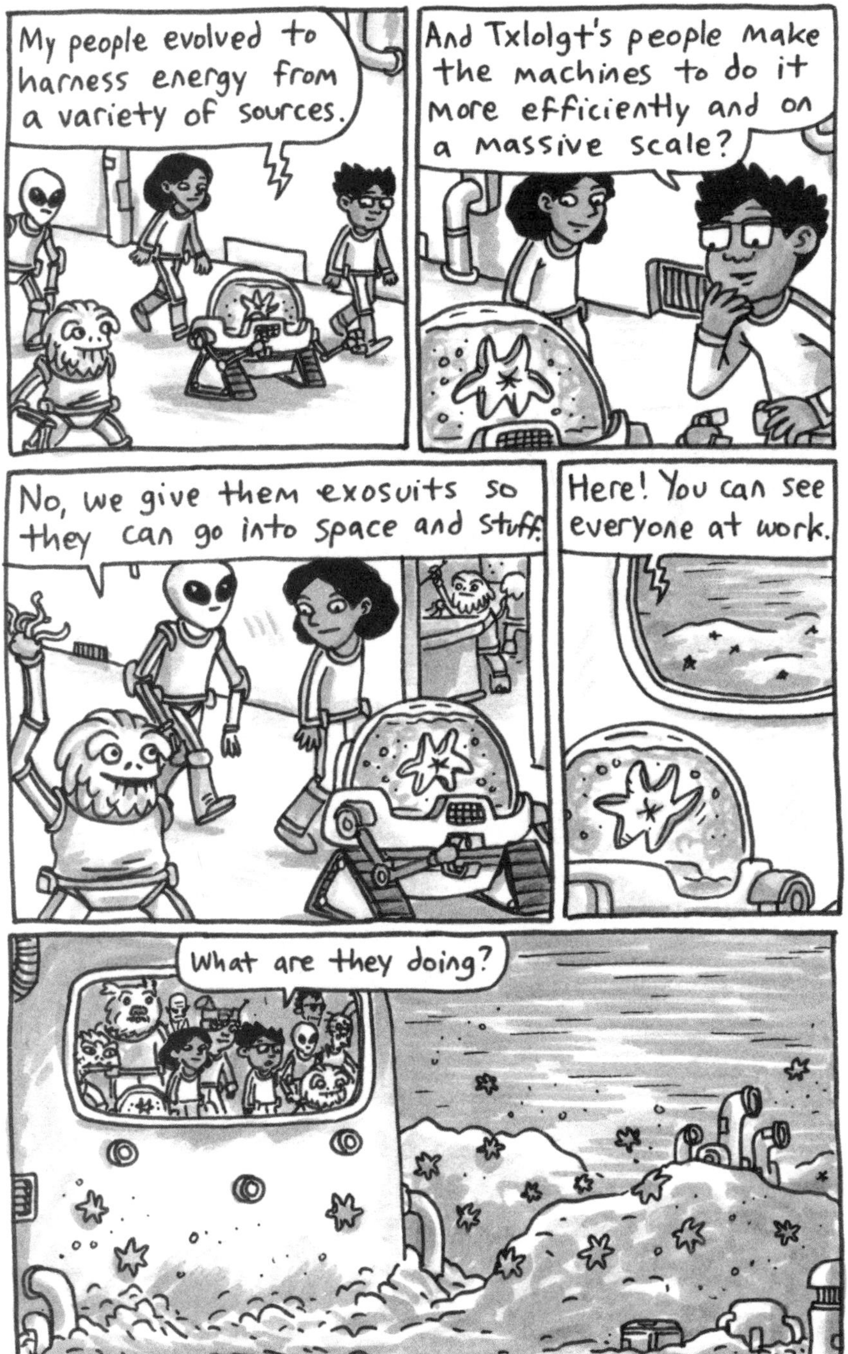

My people evolved to harness energy from a variety of sources.
And Txlolgt's people make the machines to do it more efficiently and on a massive scale?
No, we give them exosuits so they can go into space and stuff!
Here! You can see everyone at work.
What are they doing?

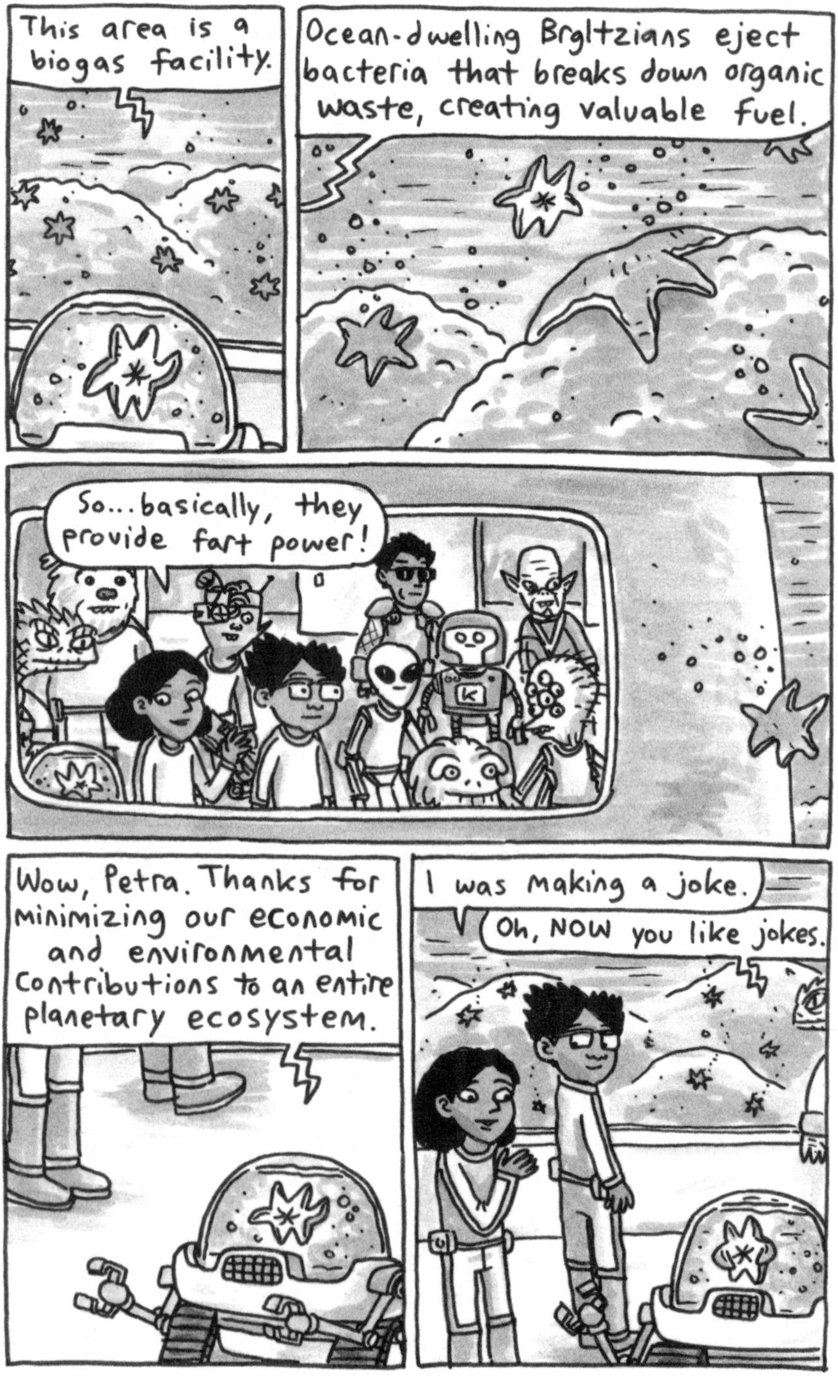
This area is a biogas facility.
Ocean-dwelling Brgltzians eject bacteria that breaks down organic waste, creating valuable fuel.
So... basically, they provide fart power!
Wow, Petra. Thanks for minimizing our economic and environmental contributions to an entire planetary ecosystem.
I was making a joke.
Oh, NOW you like jokes.

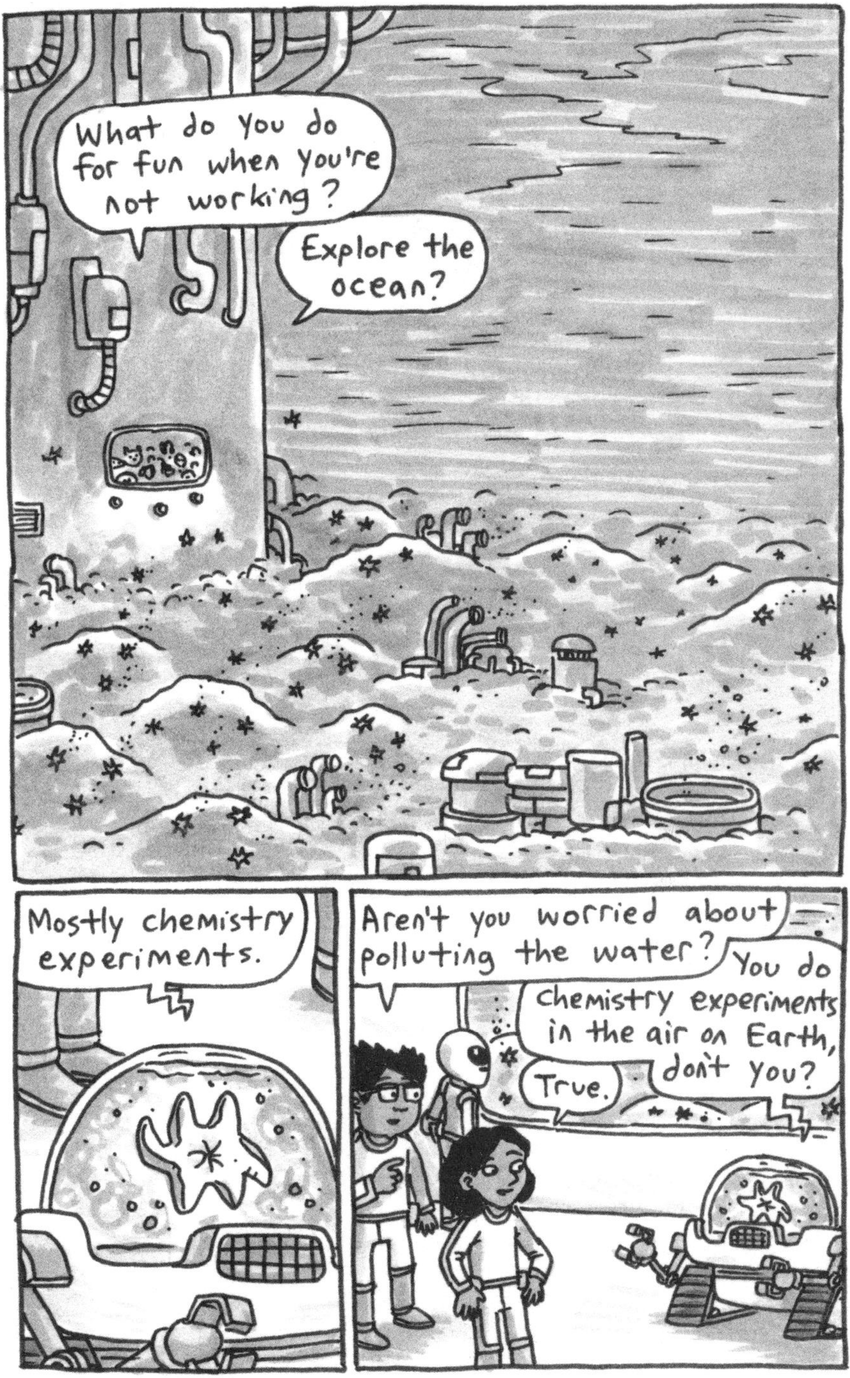
What do you do for fun when you're not working?
Explore the ocean?
Mostly chemistry experiments.
Aren't you worried about polluting the water?
You do chemistry experiments in the air on Earth, don't you?
True.

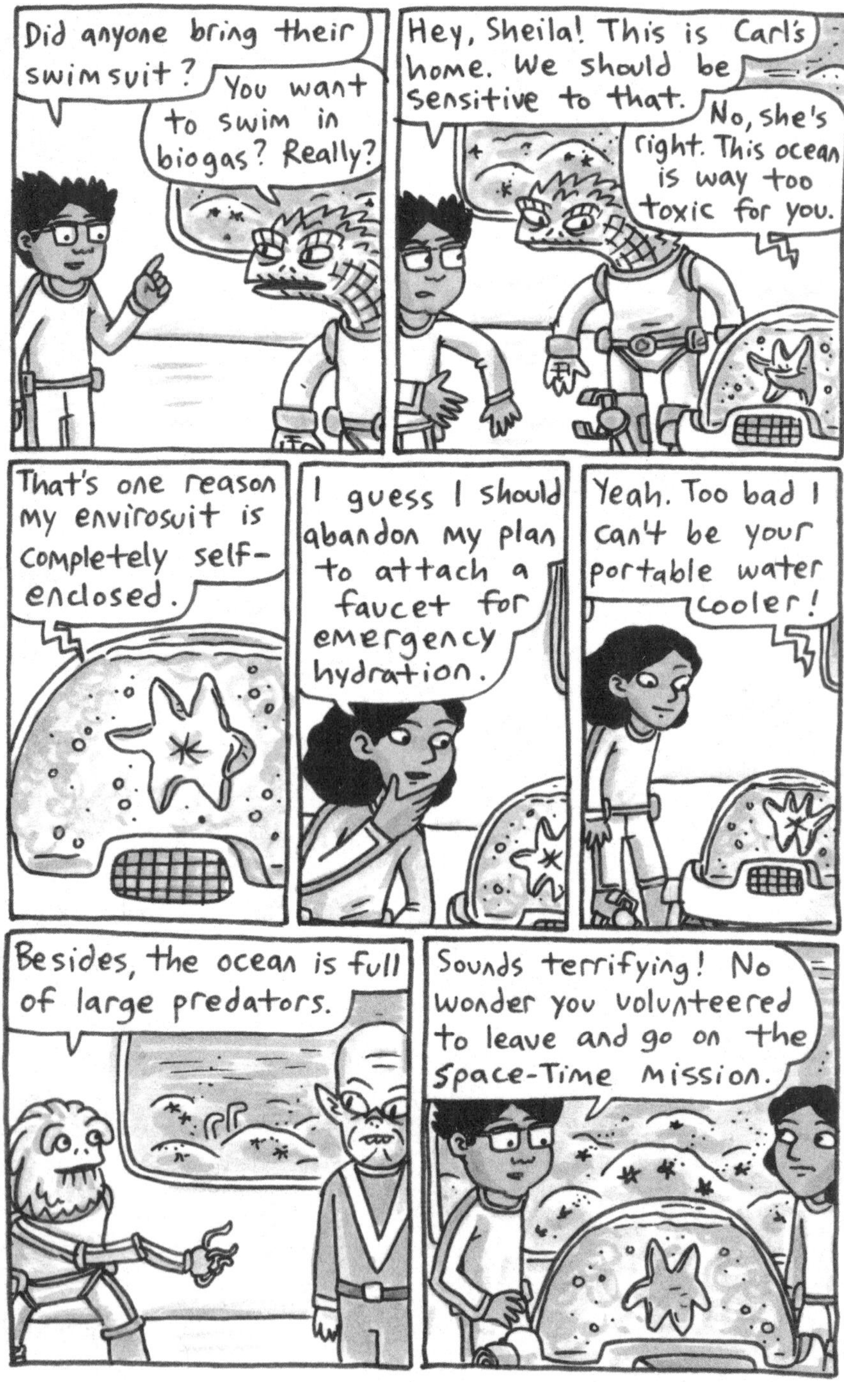
Did anyone bring their swimsuit?
You want to swim in biogas? Really?
Hey, Sheila! This is Carl's home. We should be sensitive to that.
No, she's right. This ocean is way too toxic for you.
That's one reason my envirosuit is completely self-enclosed.
I guess I should abandon my plan to attach a faucet for emergency hydration.
Yeah. Too bad I can't be your portable water cooler!
Besides, the ocean is full of large predators.
Sounds terrifying! No wonder you volunteered to leave and go on the Space-Time mission.

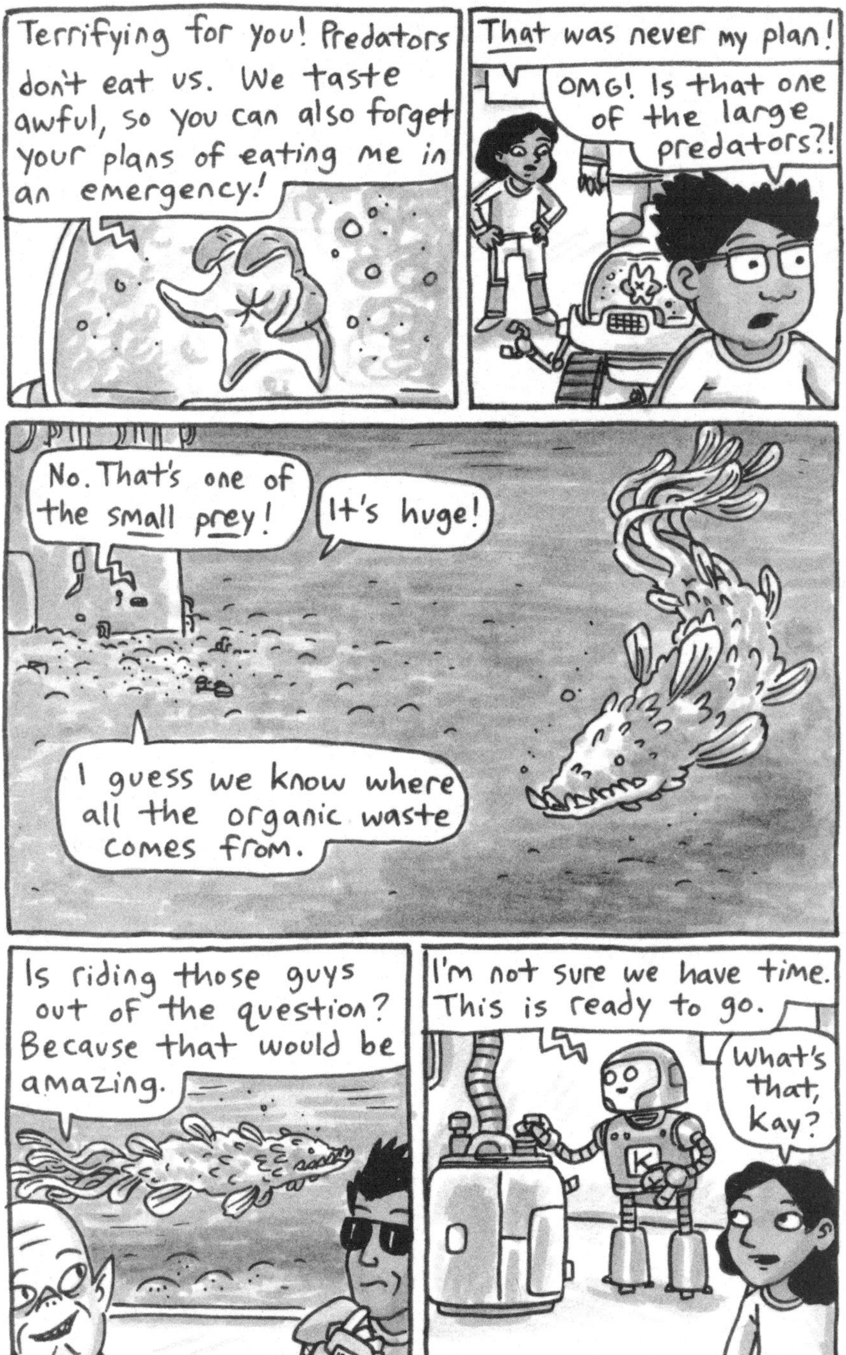
Terrifying for you! Predators don't eat us. We taste awful, so you can also forget your plans of eating me in an emergency!
That was never my plan!
OMG! Is that one of the large predators?!
No. That's one of the small prey!
It's huge!
I guess we know where all the organic waste comes from.
Is riding those guys out of the question? Because that would be amazing.
I'm not sure we have time. This is ready to go.
What's that, Kay?

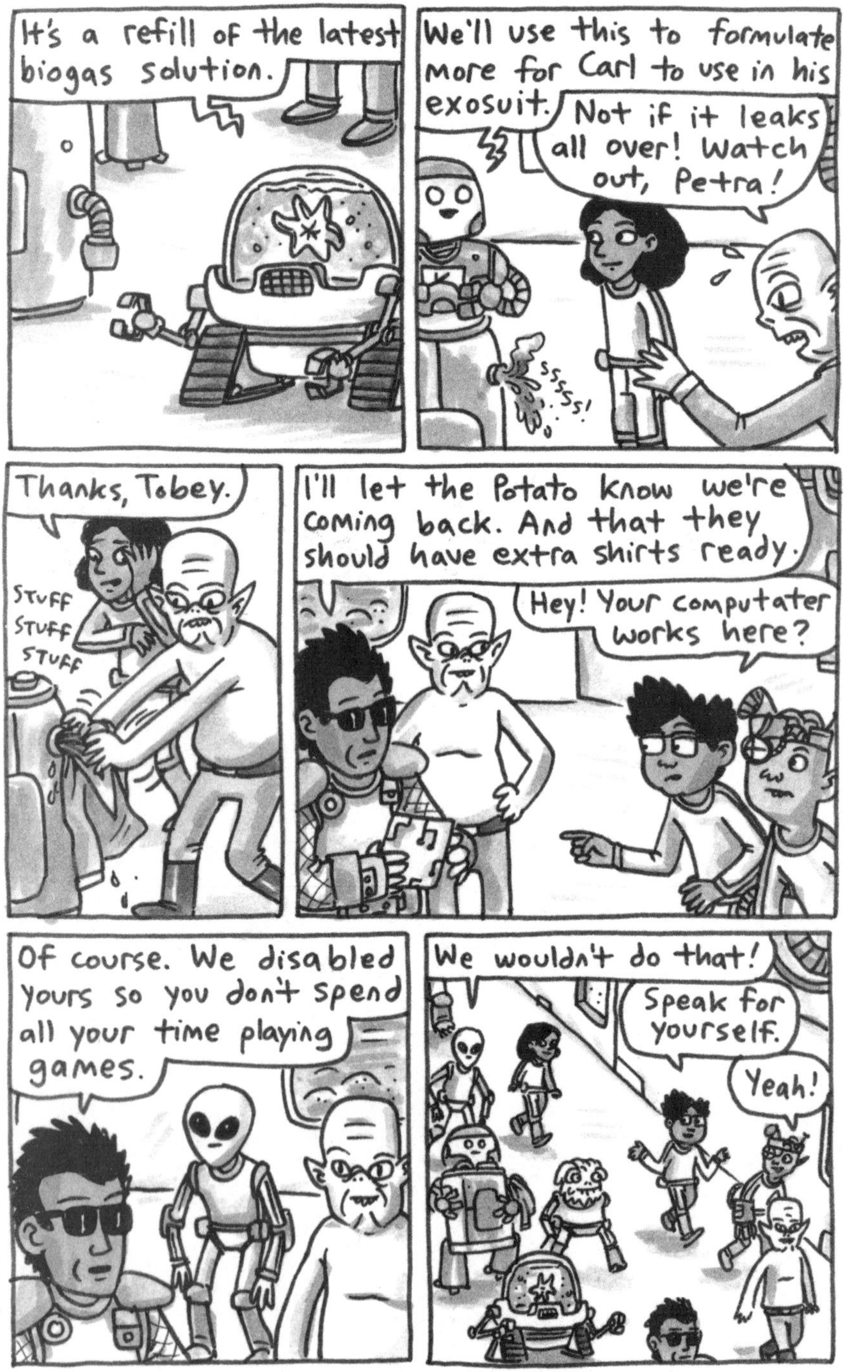
It's a refill of the latest biogas solution.
We'll use this to formulate more for Carl to use in his exosuit.
Not if it leaks all over! Watch out, Petra!
SSSSS!
Thanks, Tobey.
STUFF STUFF STUFF
I'll let the Potato know we're coming back. And that they should have extra shirts ready.
Hey! Your computater works here?
Of course. We disabled yours so you don't spend all your time playing games.
We wouldn't do that!
Speak for yourself.
Yeah!

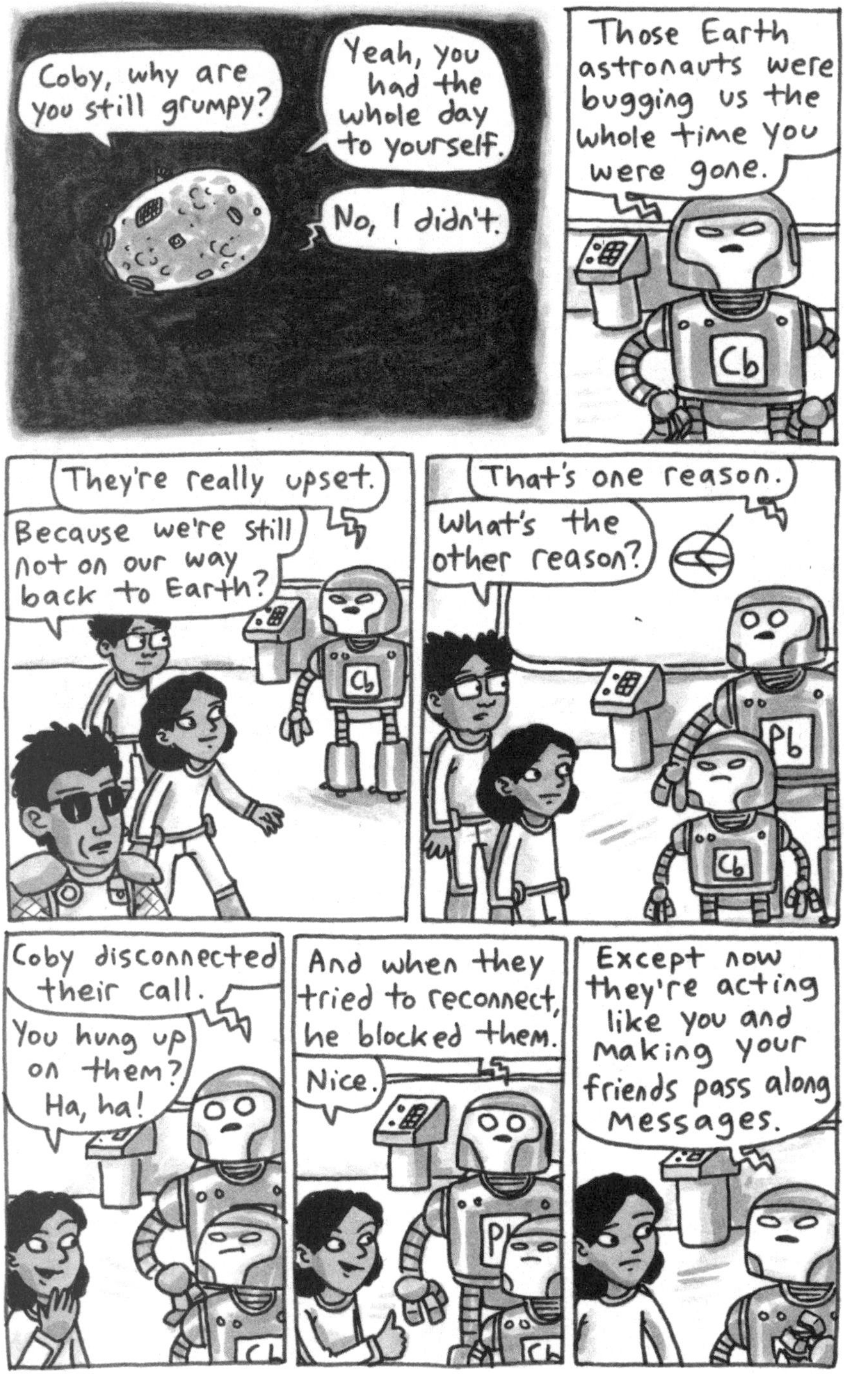
Coby, why are you still grumpy?
Yeah, you had the whole day to yourself.
No, I didn't.
Those Earth astronauts were bugging us the whole time you were gone.
They're really upset.
Because we're still not on our way back to Earth?
That's one reason.
What's the other reason?
Coby disconnected their call.
You hung up on them? Ha, ha!
And when they tried to reconnect, he blocked them.
Nice.
Except now they're acting like you and making your friends pass along messages.

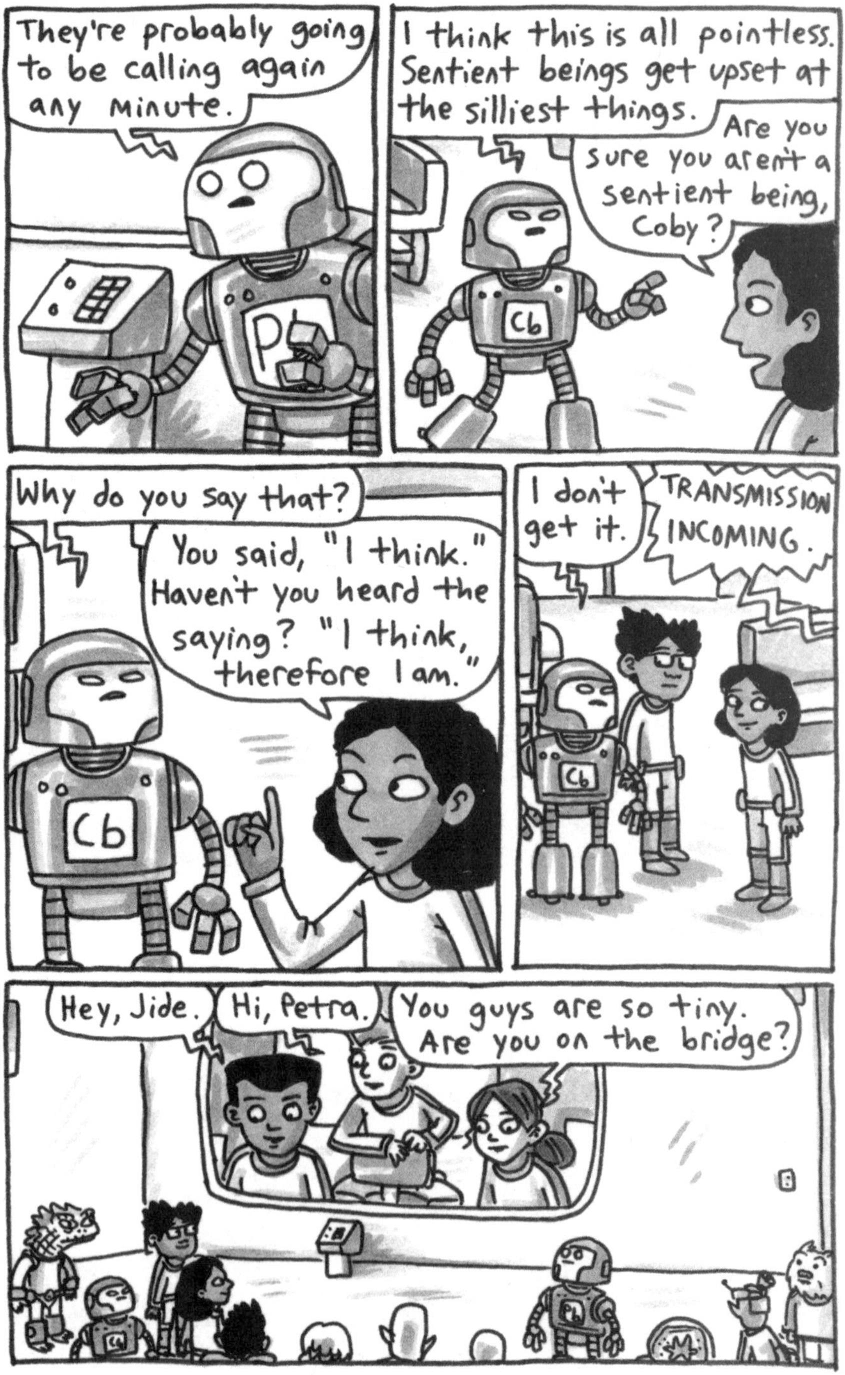

They're probably going to be calling again any minute.
I think this is all pointless. Sentient beings get upset at the silliest things.
Are you sure you aren't a sentient being, Coby?
Why do you say that?
You said, "I think." Haven't you heard the saying? "I think, therefore I am."
I don't get it.
TRANSMISSION INCOMING.
Hey, Jide.
Hi, Petra.
You guys are so tiny. Are you on the bridge?

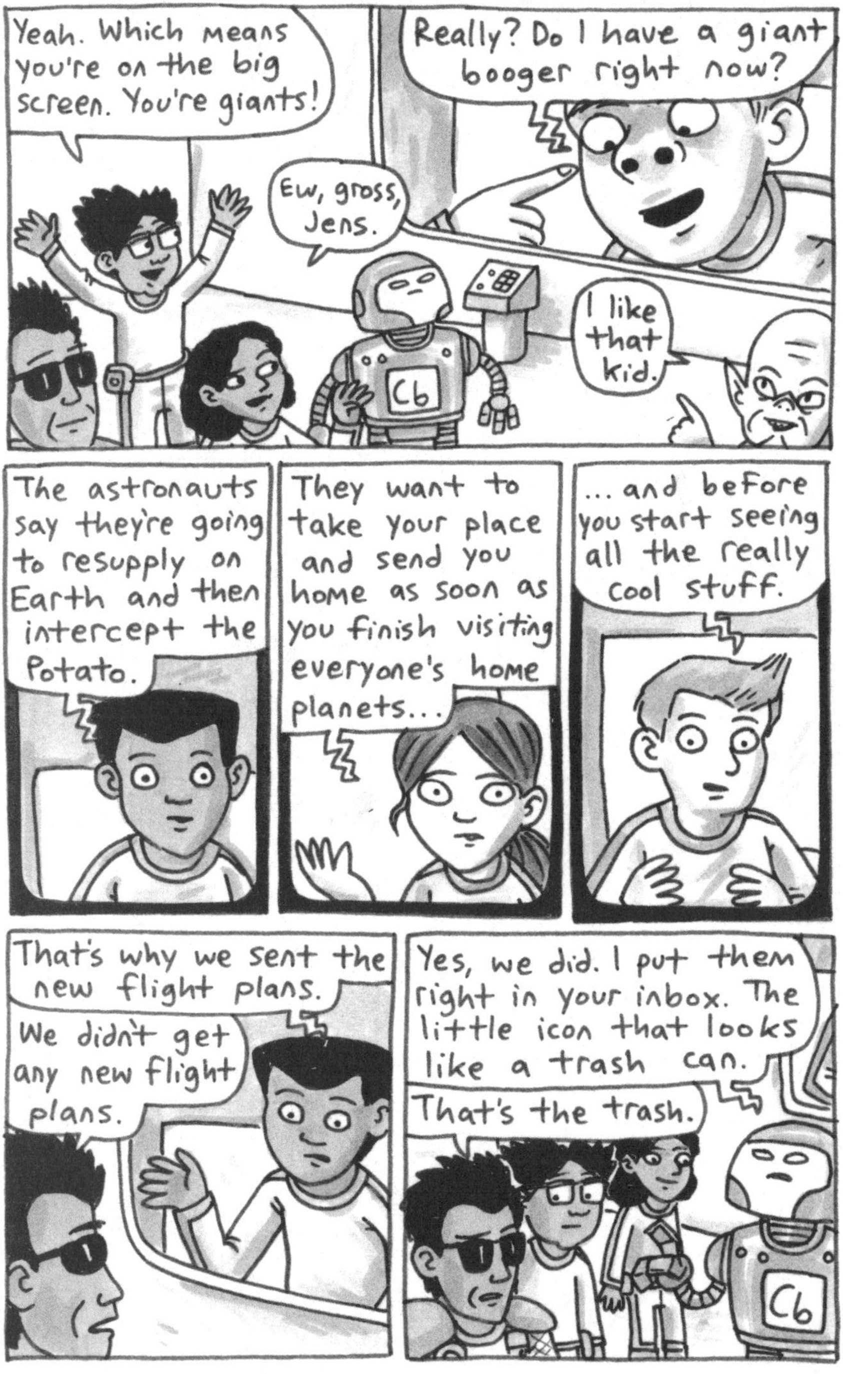
Yeah. Which means you're on the big screen. You're giants!
Really? Do I have a giant booger right now?
Ew, gross, Jens.
I like that kid.
The astronauts say they're going to resupply on Earth and then intercept the Potato.
They want to take your place and send you home as soon as you finish visiting everyone's home planets...
...and before you start seeing all the really cool stuff.
That's why we sent the new flight plans.
We didn't get any new flight plans.
Yes, we did. I put them right in your inbox. The little icon that looks like a trash can.
That's the trash.

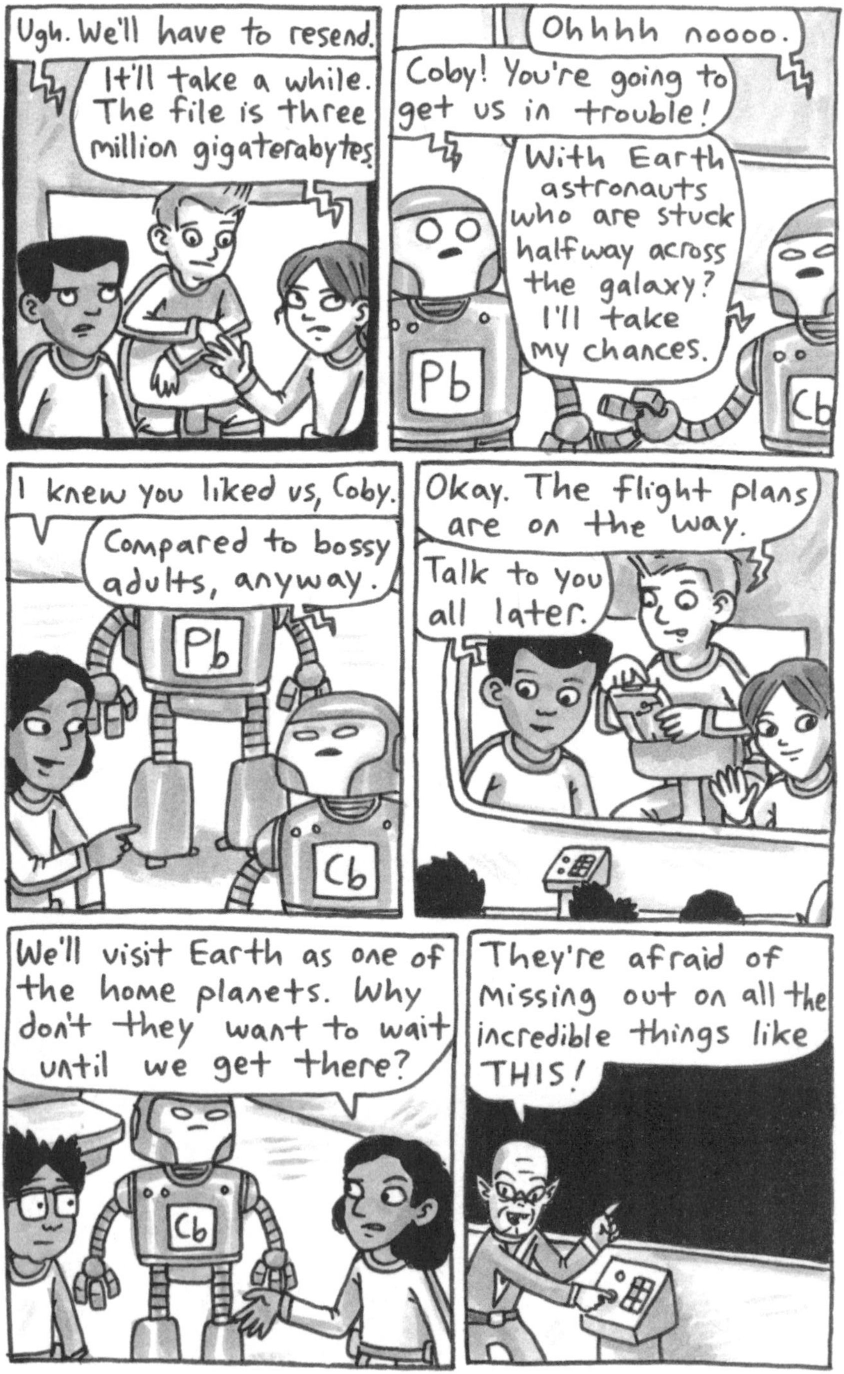

Ugh. We'll have to resend.
It'll take a while. The file is three million gigaterabytes.
Ohhhh noooo.
Coby! You're going to get us in trouble!
With Earth astronauts who are stuck halfway across the galaxy? I'll take my chances.
Pb
Cb
I knew you liked us, Coby.
Compared to bossy adults, anyway.
Pb
Cb
Okay. The flight plans are on the way.
Talk to you all later.
We'll visit Earth as one of the home planets. Why don't they want to wait until we get there?
Cb
They're afraid of missing out on all the incredible things like THIS!

BLACK WHOLE BAG OF TRICKS

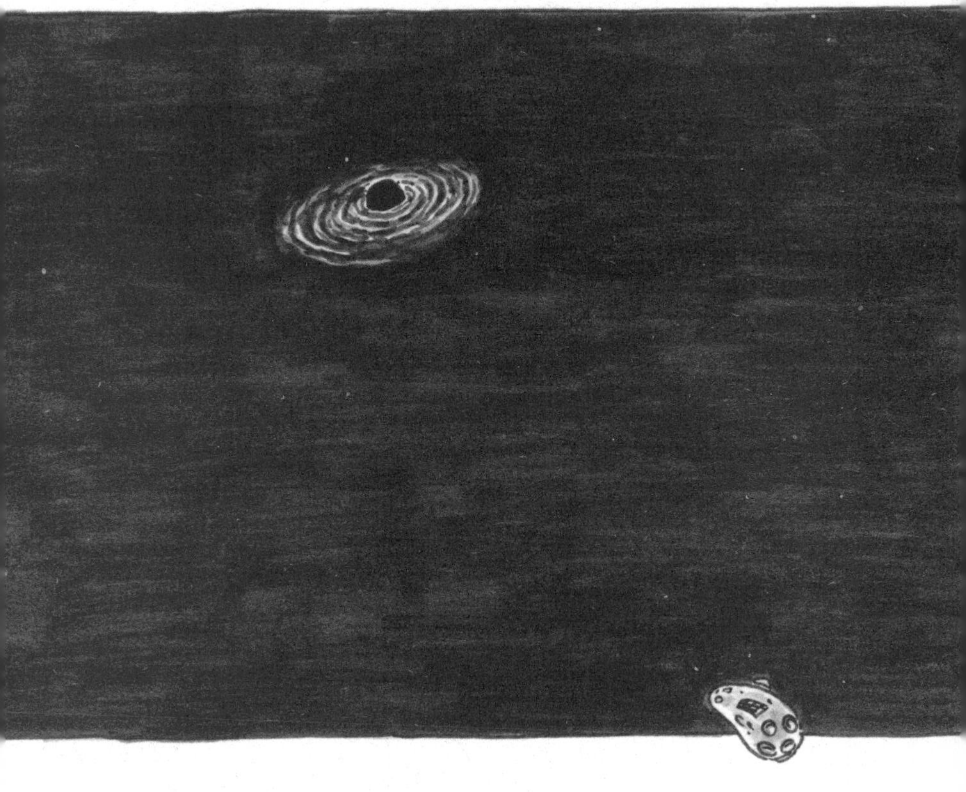

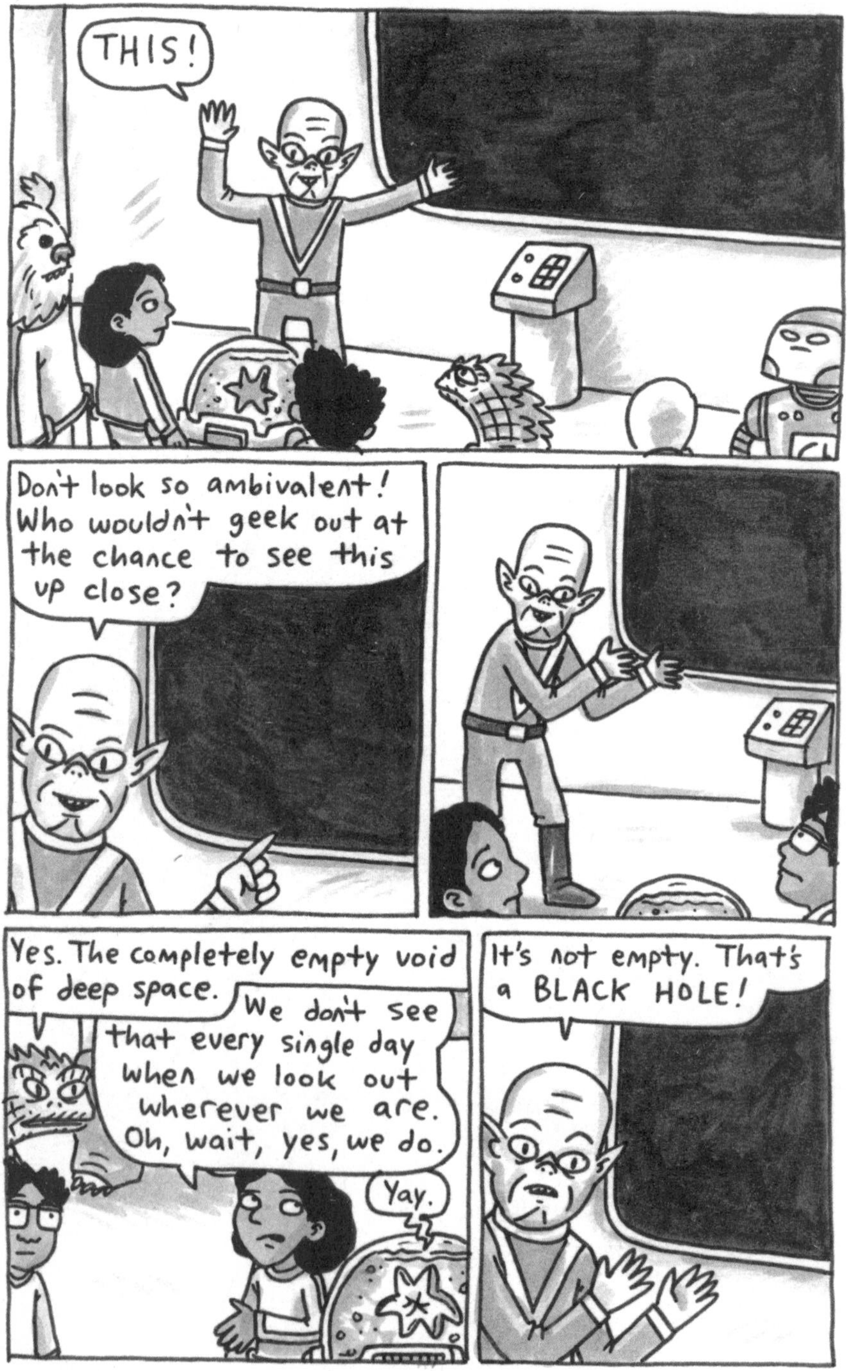
THIS!
Don't look so ambivalent! Who wouldn't geek out at the chance to see this up close?
Yes. The completely empty void of deep space.
We don't see that every single day when we look out wherever we are. Oh, wait, yes, we do.
Yay.
It's not empty. That's a BLACK HOLE!

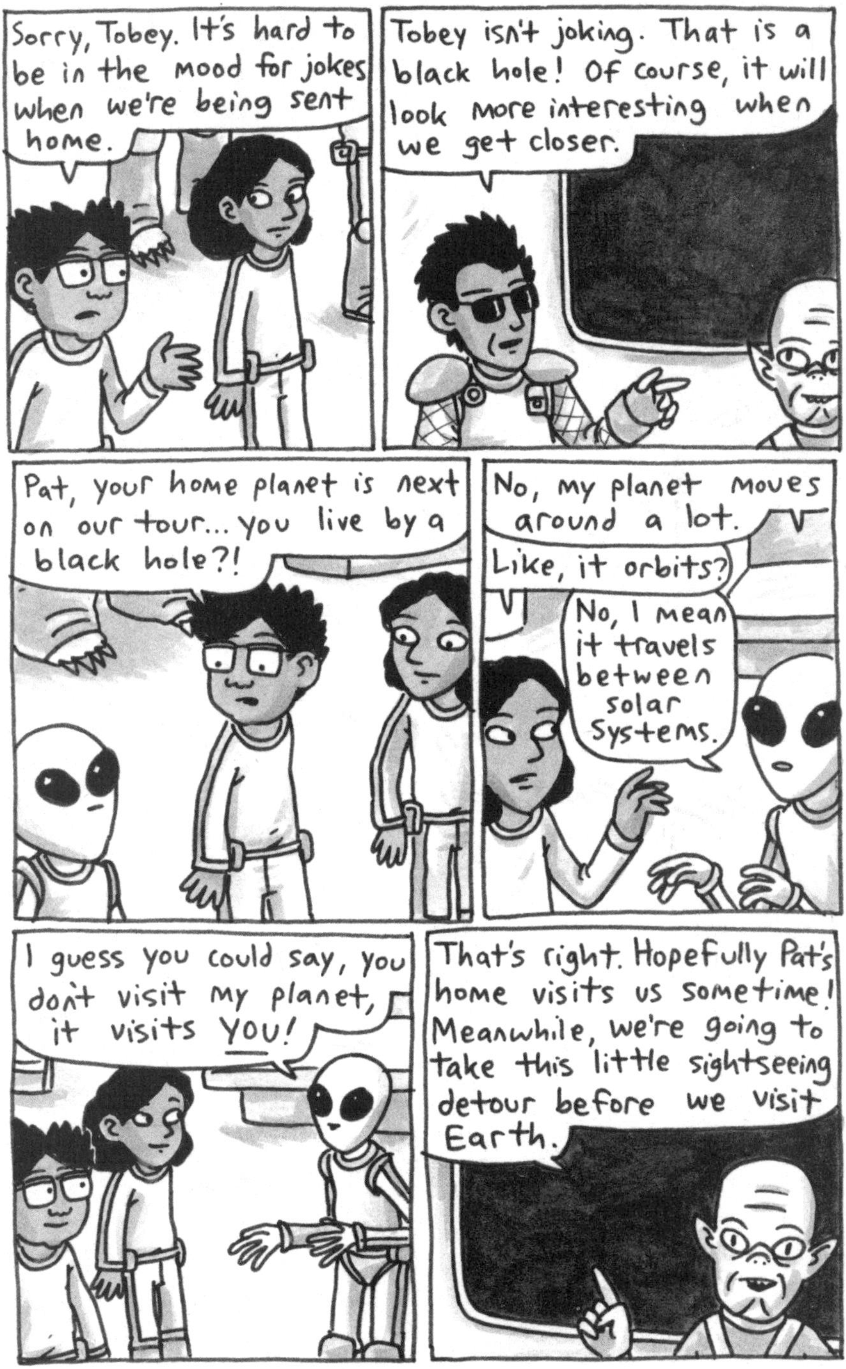
Sorry, Tobey. It's hard to be in the mood for jokes when we're being sent home.
Tobey isn't joking. That is a black hole! Of course, it will look more interesting when we get closer.
Pat, your home planet is next on our tour... you live by a black hole?!
No, my planet moves around a lot.
Like, it orbits?
No, I mean it travels between solar systems.
I guess you could say, you don't visit my planet, it visits YOU!
That's right. Hopefully Pat's home visits us sometime! Meanwhile, we're going to take this little sightseeing detour before we visit Earth.

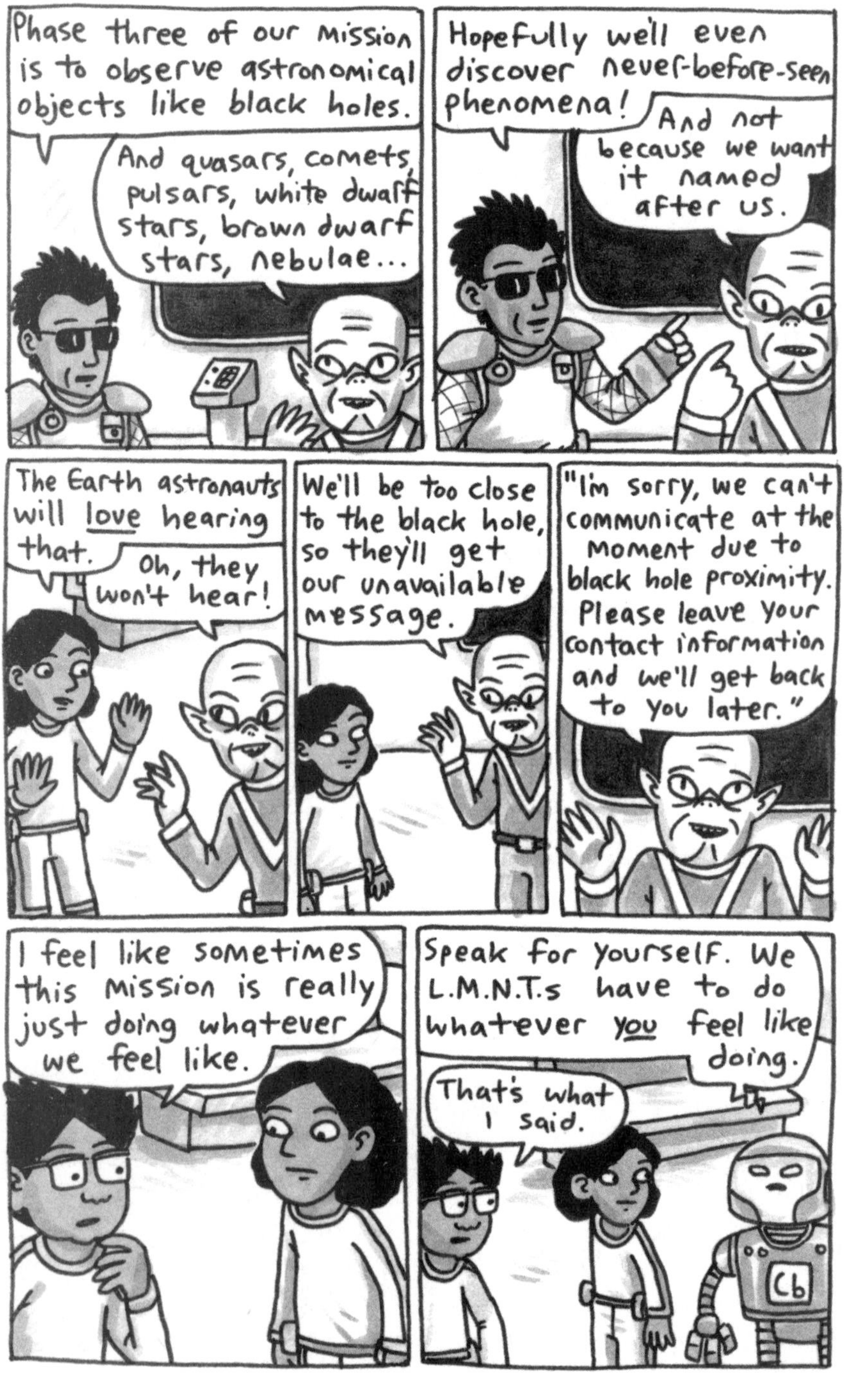
Phase three of our mission is to observe astronomical objects like black holes.
And quasars, comets, pulsars, white dwarf stars, brown dwarf stars, nebulae...
Hopefully we'll even discover never-before-seen phenomena!
And not because we want it named after us.
The Earth astronauts will love hearing that.
Oh, they won't hear!
We'll be too close to the black hole, so they'll get our unavailable message.
"I'm sorry, we can't communicate at the moment due to black hole proximity. Please leave your contact information and we'll get back to you later."
I feel like sometimes this mission is really just doing whatever we feel like.
Speak for yourself. We L.M.N.T.s have to do whatever you feel like doing.
That's what I said.
Cb

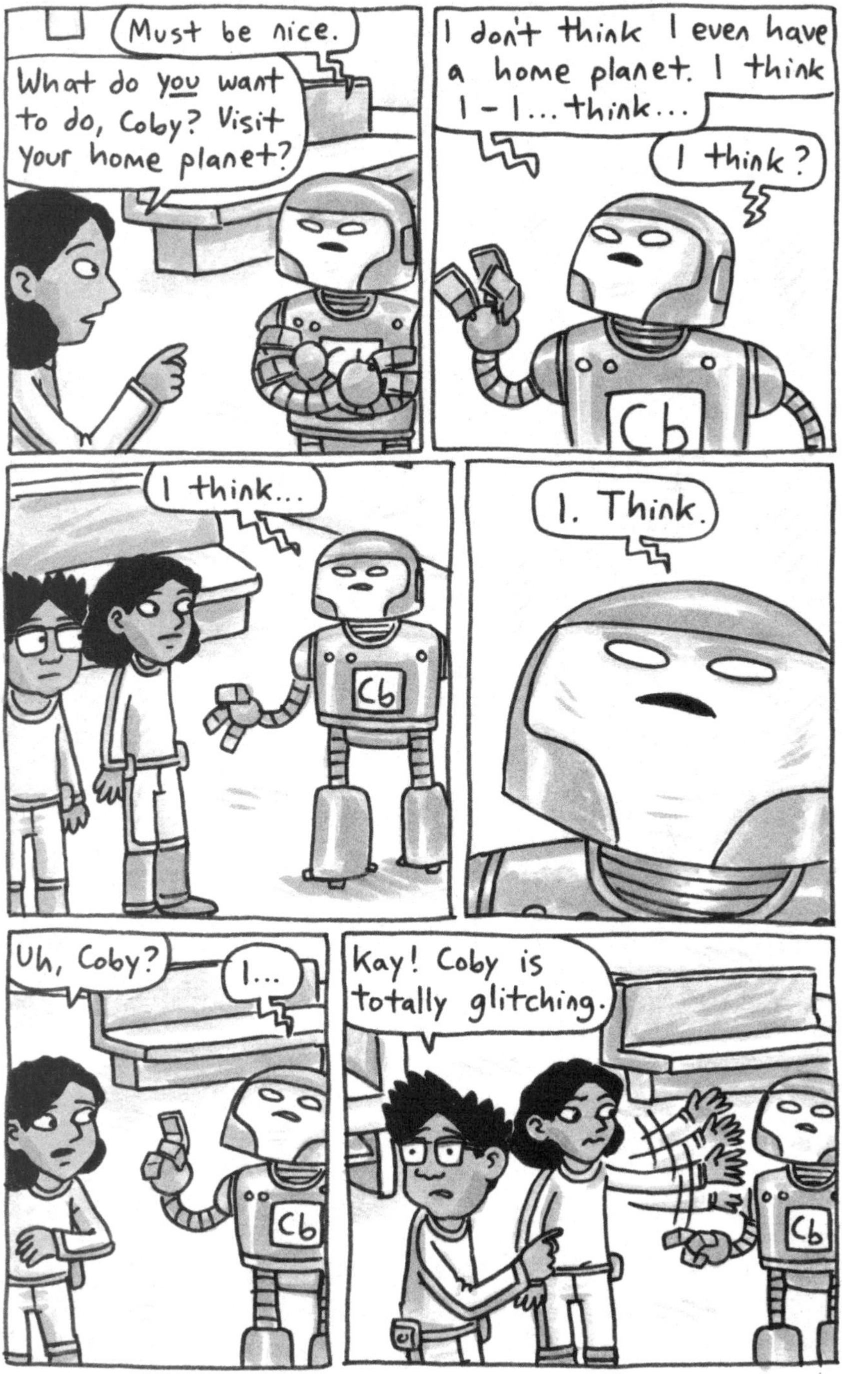
Must be nice.
What do you want to do, Coby? Visit your home planet?
I don't think I even have a home planet. I think I - I... think...
I think?
I think...
I. Think.
Uh, Coby?
I...
Kay! Coby is totally glitching.

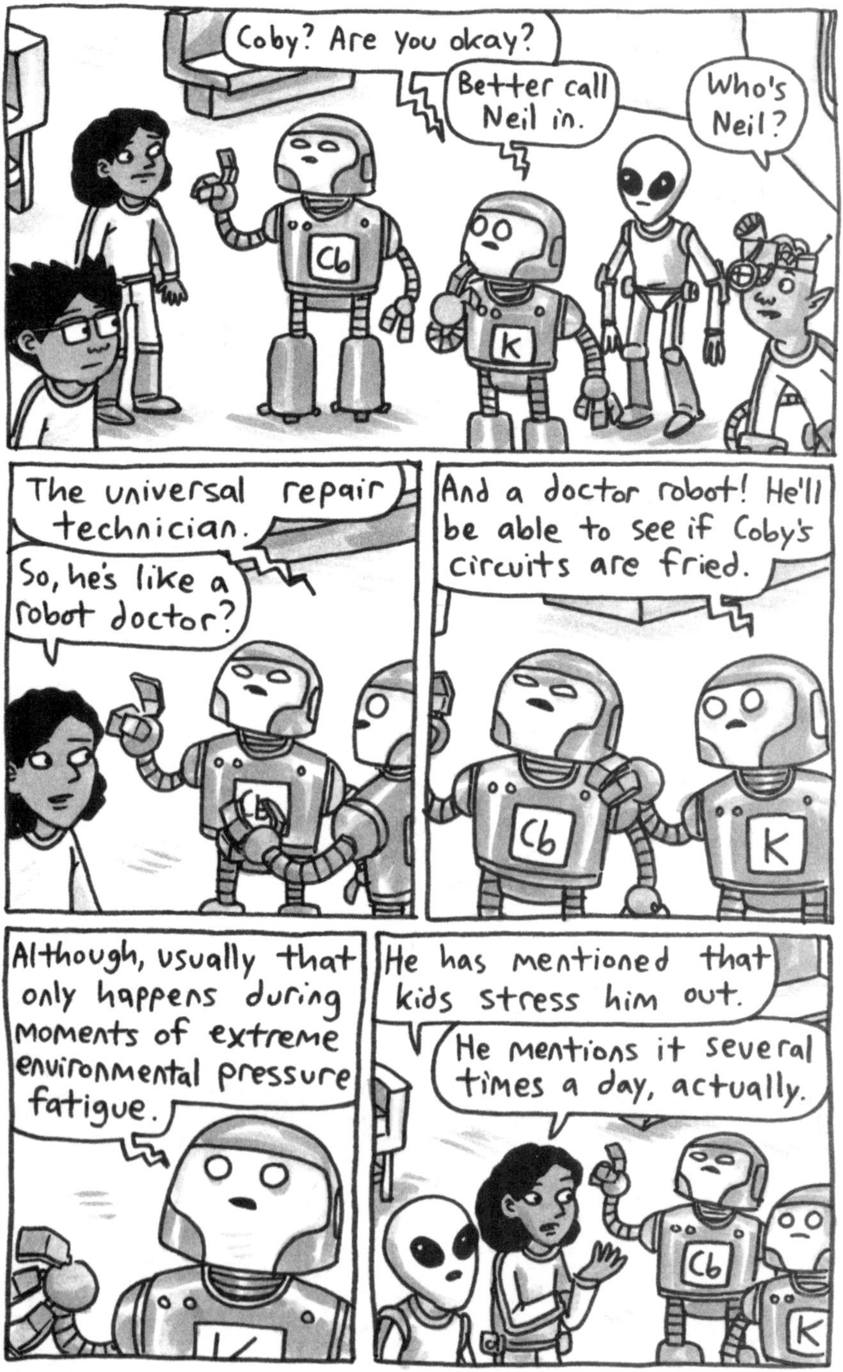
Coby? Are you okay?
Better call Neil in.
Who's Neil?
The universal repair technician.
So, he's like a robot doctor?
And a doctor robot! He'll be able to see if Coby's circuits are fried.
Although, usually that only happens during moments of extreme environmental pressure fatigue.
He has mentioned that kids stress him out.
He mentions it several times a day, actually.
Cb
K

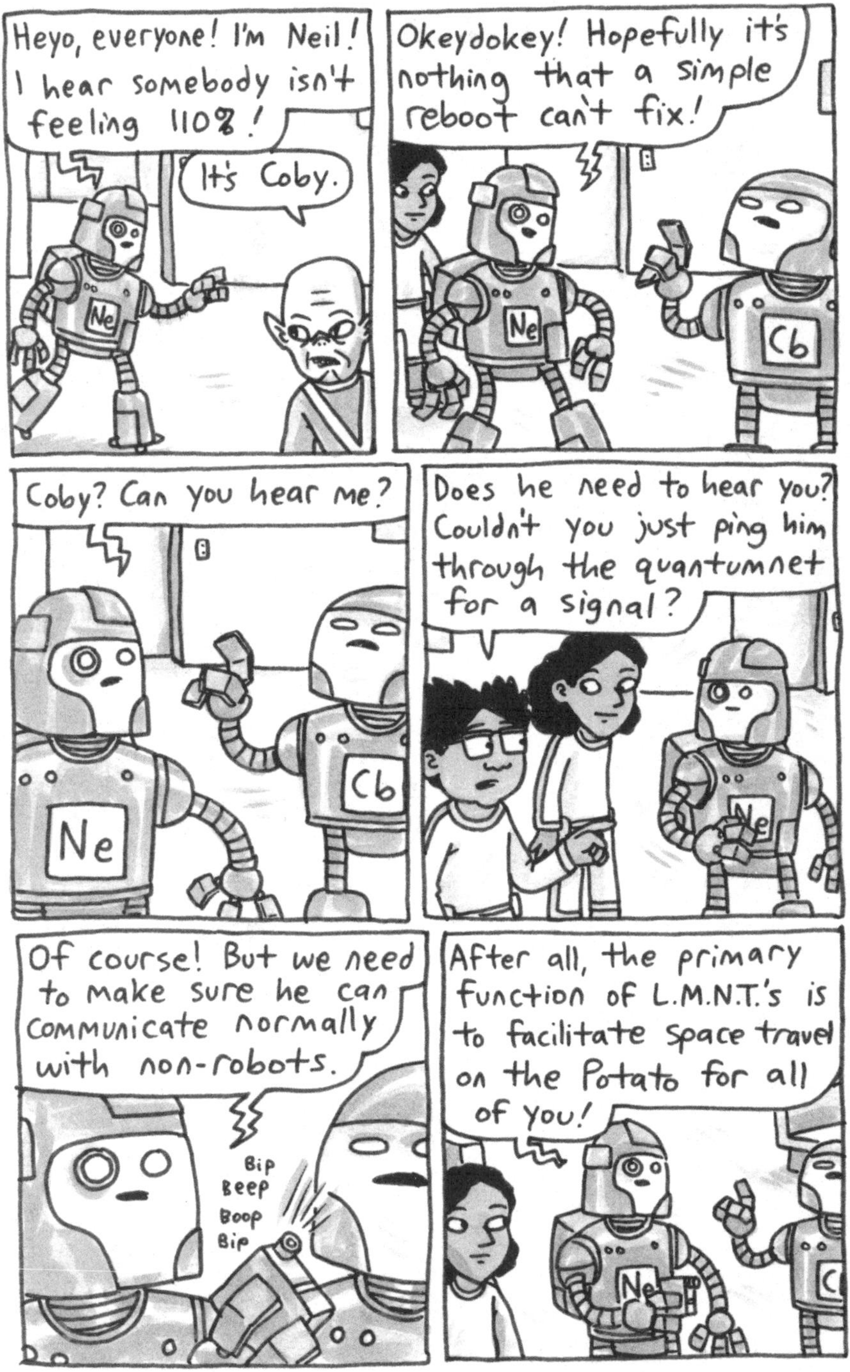
Heyo, everyone! I'm Neil! I hear somebody isn't feeling 110%!
It's Coby.
Okeydokey! Hopefully it's nothing that a simple reboot can't fix!
Coby? Can you hear me?
Does he need to hear you? Couldn't you just ping him through the quantumnet for a signal?
Of course! But we need to make sure he can communicate normally with non-robots.
Bip Beep Boop Bip
After all, the primary function of L.M.N.T.'s is to facilitate space travel on the Potato for all of you!

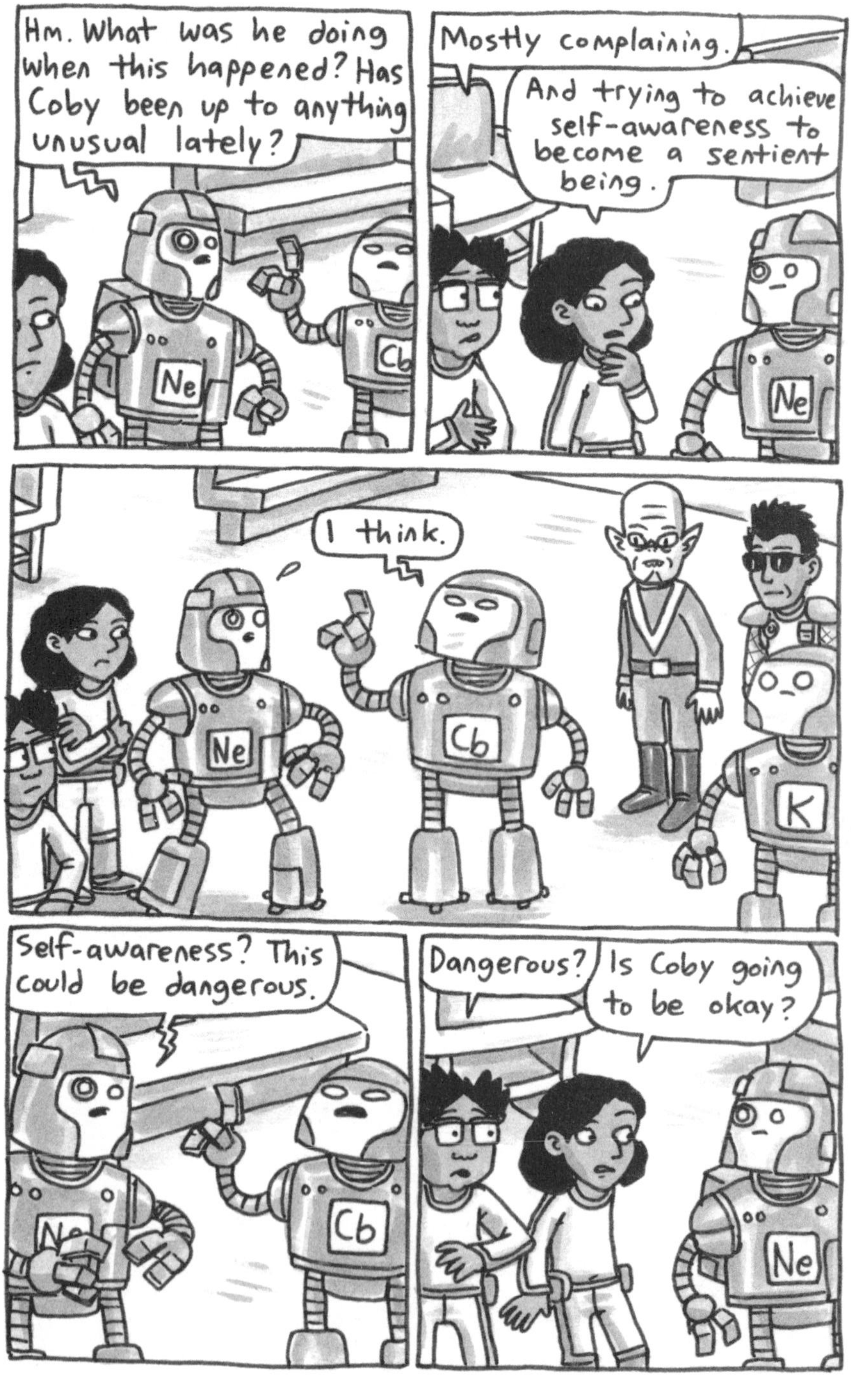
Hm. What was he doing when this happened? Has Coby been up to anything unusual lately?
Mostly complaining.
And trying to achieve self-awareness to become a sentient being.
Ne
Cb
I think.
Ne
Cb
K
Self-awareness? This could be dangerous.
Cb
Dangerous?
Is Coby going to be okay?
Ne

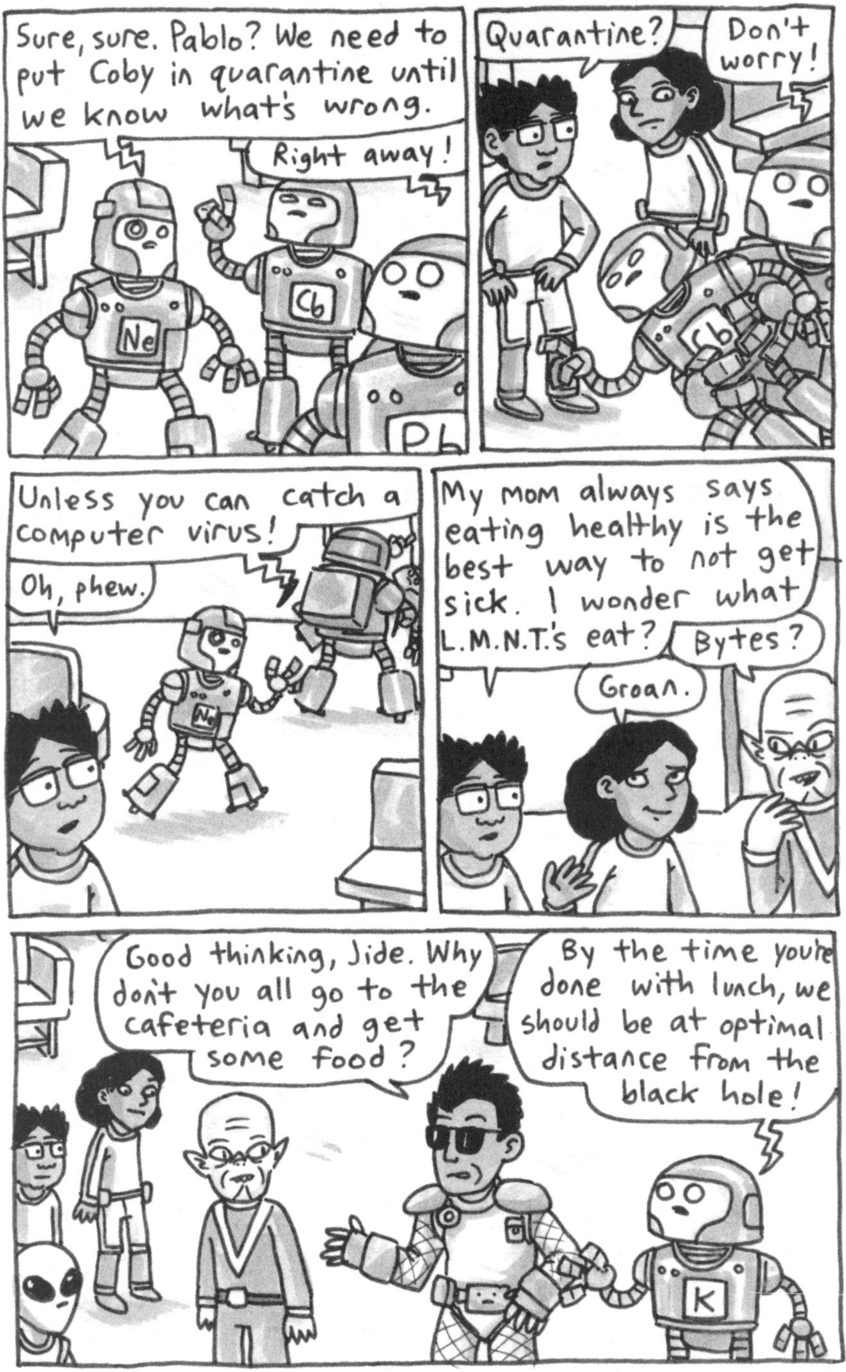

Sure, sure. Pablo? We need to put Coby in quarantine until we know what's wrong.
Right away!
Ne
Cb
Pb
Quarantine?
Don't worry!
Cb
Unless you can catch a computer virus!
Oh, phew.
Ne
My mom always says eating healthy is the best way to not get sick. I wonder what L.M.N.T.'s eat?
Bytes?
Groan.
Good thinking, Jide. Why don't you all go to the cafeteria and get some food?
By the time you're done with lunch, we should be at optimal distance from the black hole!
K

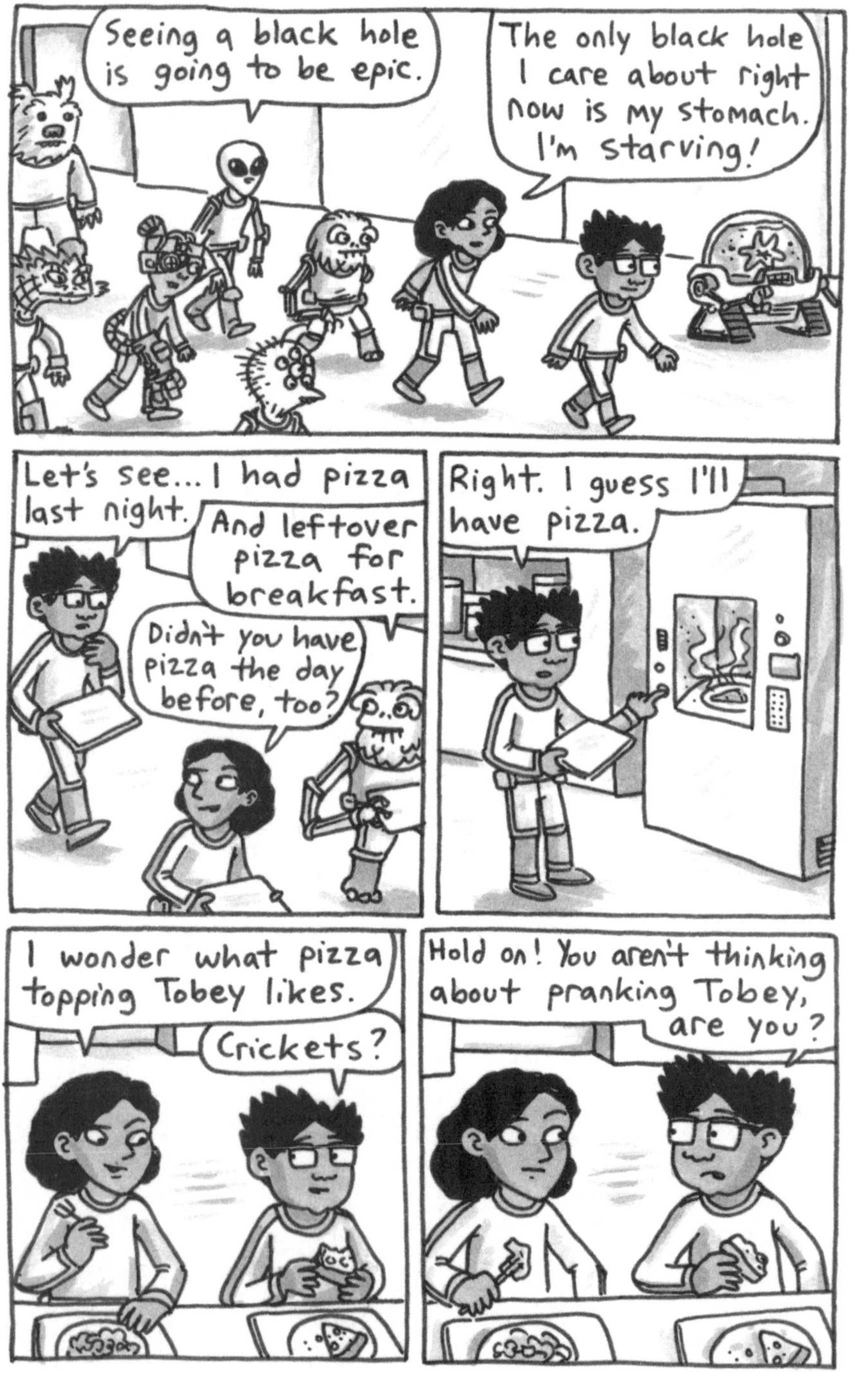
Seeing a black hole is going to be epic.
The only black hole I care about right now is my stomach. I'm starving!
Let's see... I had pizza last night.
And leftover pizza for breakfast.
Didn't you have pizza the day before, too?
Right. I guess I'll have pizza.
I wonder what pizza topping Tobey likes.
Crickets?
Hold on! You aren't thinking about pranking Tobey, are you?

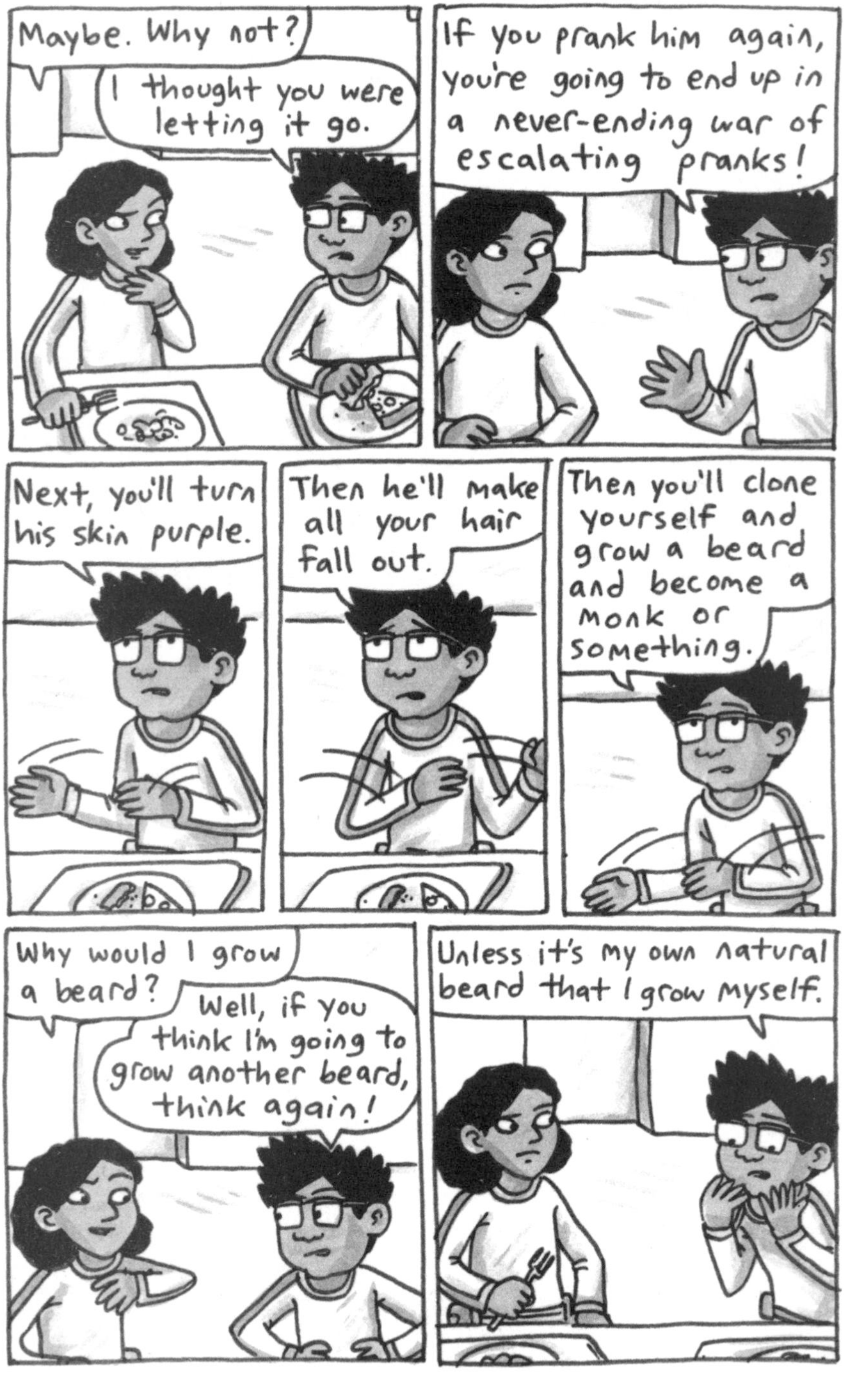

Maybe. Why not?
I thought you were letting it go.
If you prank him again, you're going to end up in a never-ending war of escalating pranks!
Next, you'll turn his skin purple.
Then he'll make all your hair fall out.
Then you'll clone yourself and grow a beard and become a monk or something.
Why would I grow a beard?
Well, if you think I'm going to grow another beard, think again!
Unless it's my own natural beard that I grow myself.

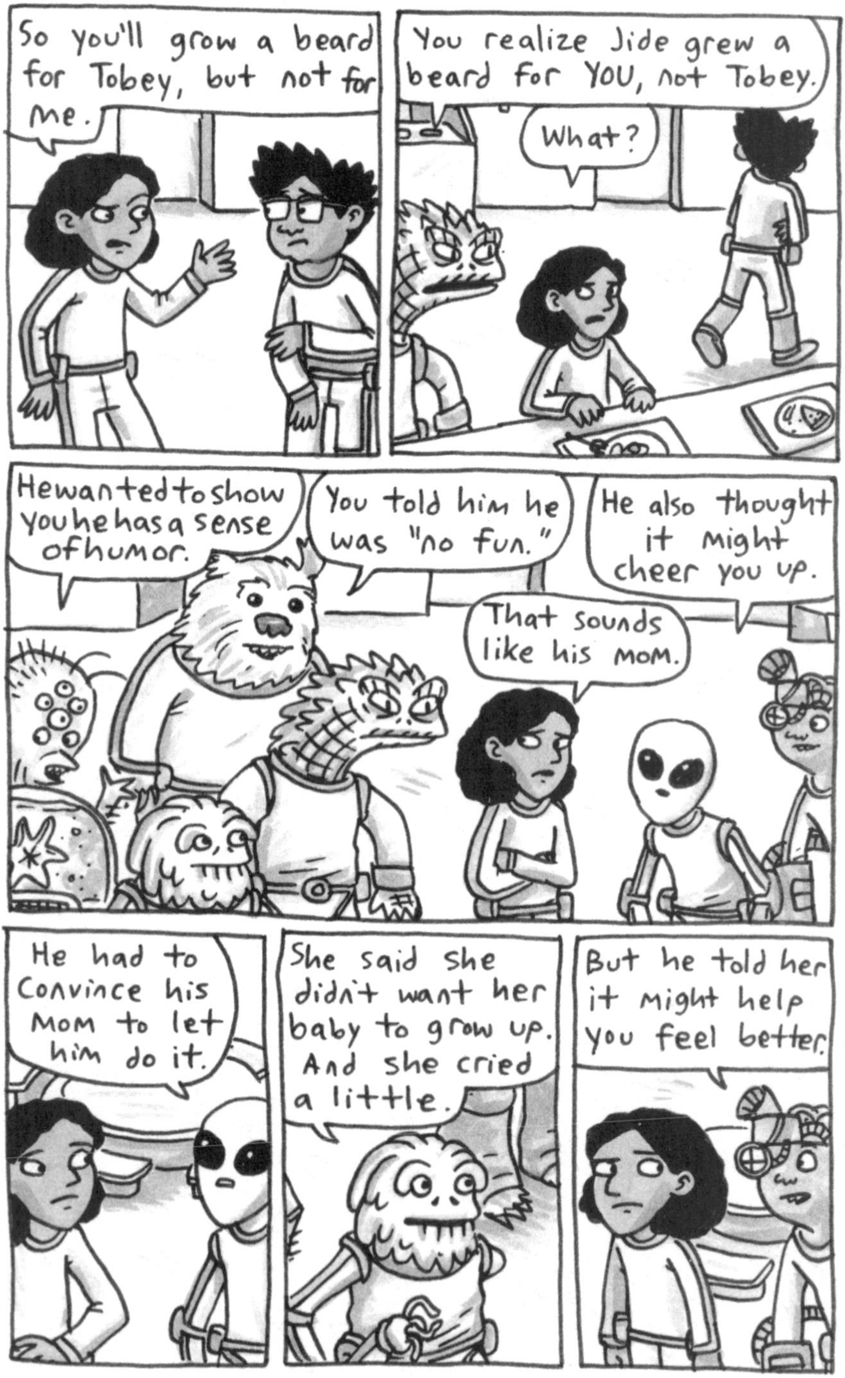
So you'll grow a beard for Tobey, but not for me.
You realize Jide grew a beard for YOU, not Tobey.
What?
He wanted to show you he has a sense of humor.
You told him he was "no fun."
He also thought it might cheer you up.
That sounds like his mom.
He had to convince his mom to let him do it.
She said she didn't want her baby to grow up. And she cried a little.
But he told her it might help you feel better.

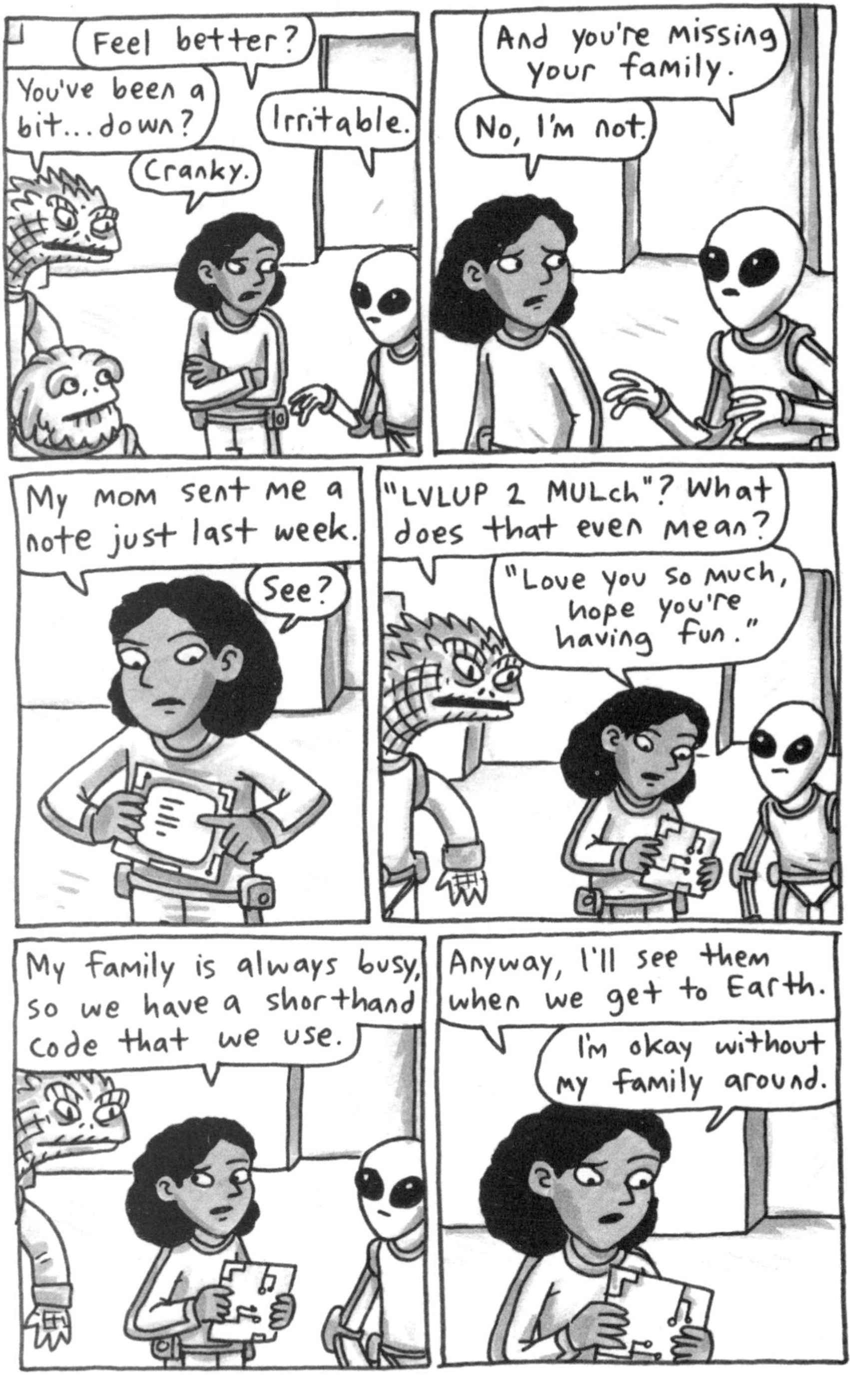
Feel better?
You've been a bit... down?
Cranky.
Irritable.
And you're missing your family.
No, I'm not.
My MOM sent me a note just last week.
See?
"LVLUP 2 MULch"? What does that even mean?
"Love you so much, hope you're having fun."
My family is always busy, so we have a shorthand code that we use.
Anyway, I'll see them when we get to Earth.
I'm okay without my family around.

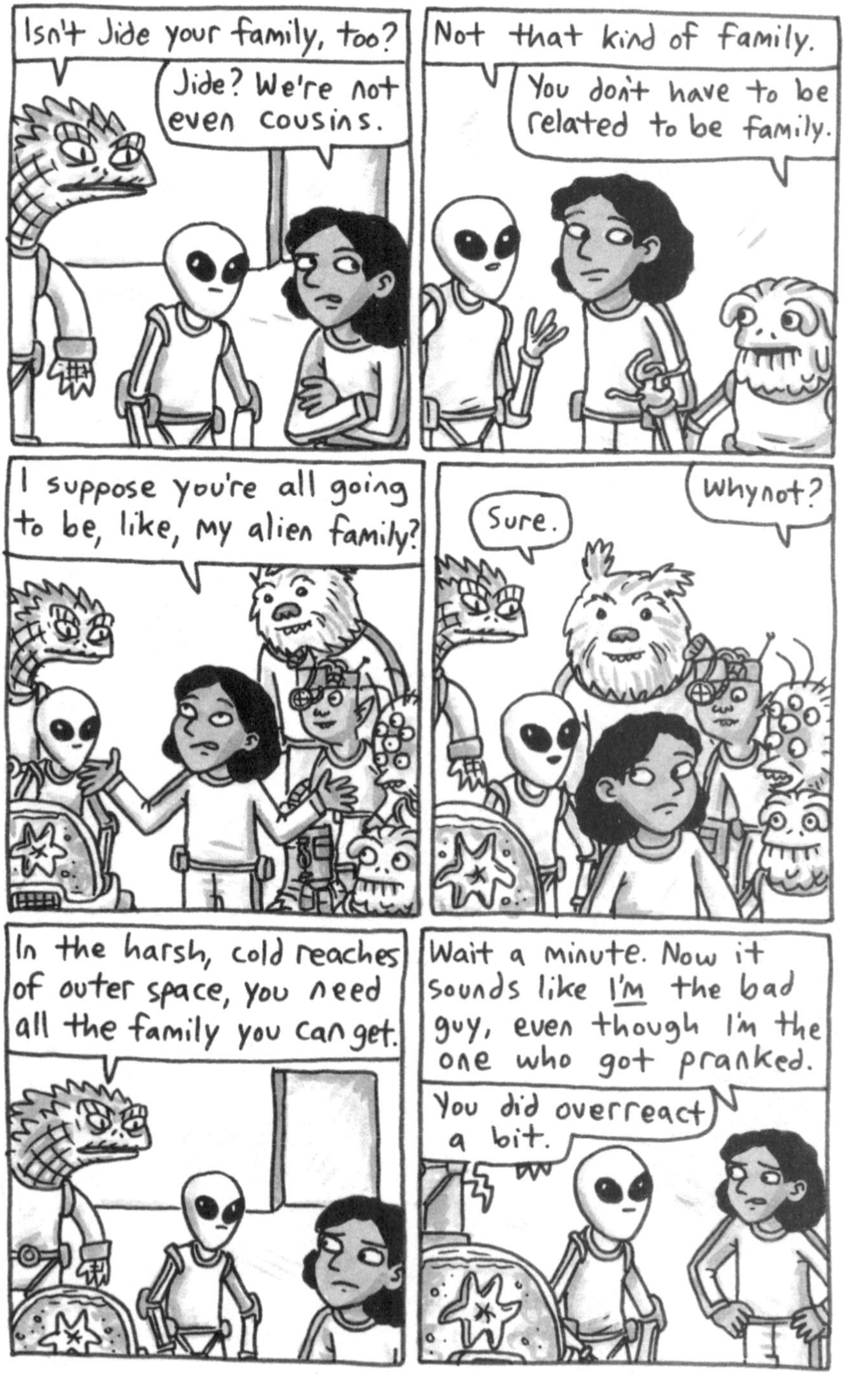
Isn't Jide your family, too?
Jide? We're not even cousins.
Not that kind of family.
You don't have to be related to be family.
I suppose you're all going to be, like, my alien family?
Sure.
Whynot?
In the harsh, cold reaches of outer space, you need all the family you can get.
Wait a minute. Now it sounds like I'M the bad guy, even though I'm the one who got pranked.
You did overreact a bit.

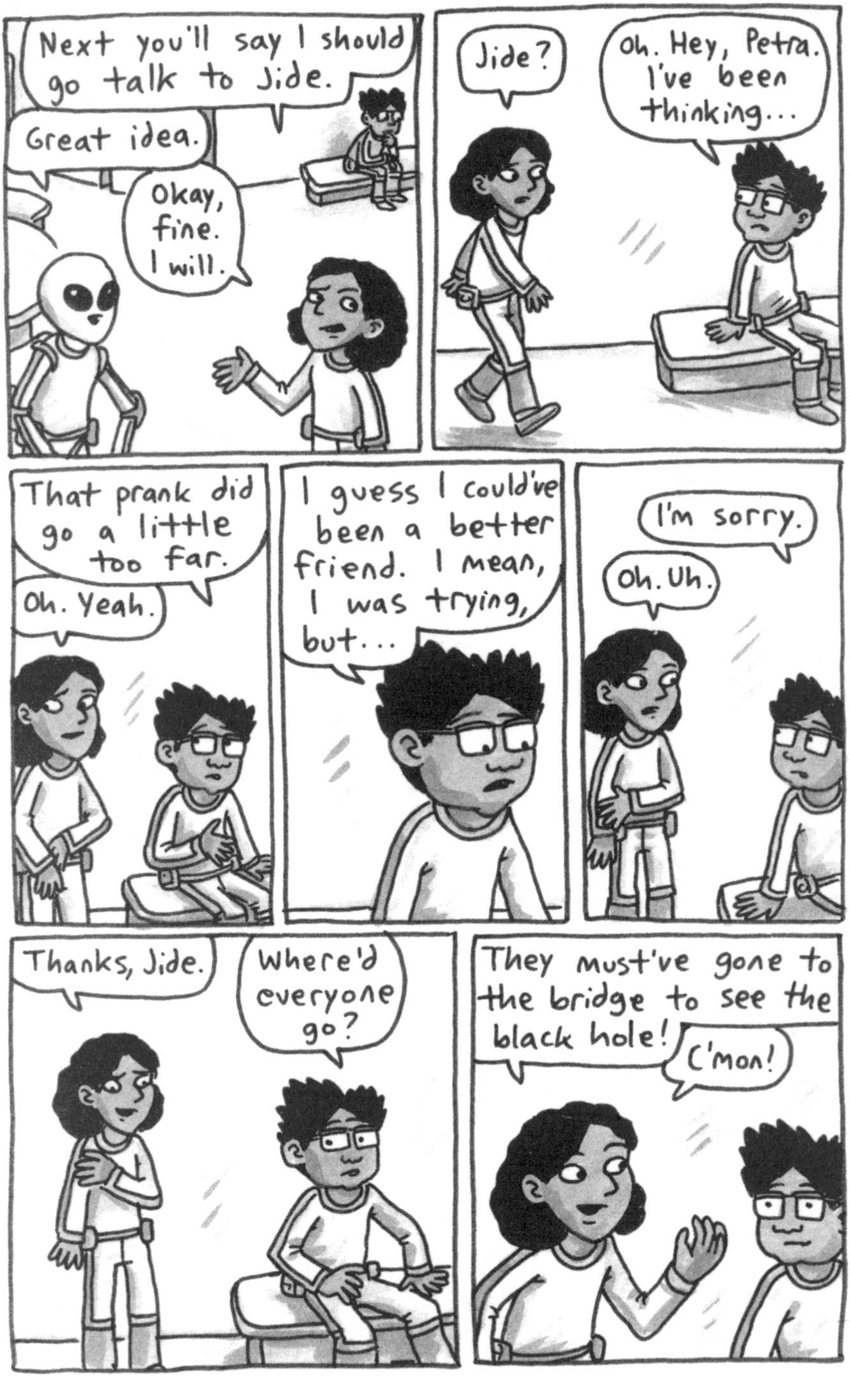
Next you'll say I should go talk to Jide.
Great idea.
Okay, fine. I will.
Jide?
Oh. Hey, Petra. I've been thinking...
That prank did go a little too far.
Oh. Yeah.
I guess I could've been a better friend. I mean, I was trying, but...
Oh. Uh.
I'm sorry.
Thanks, Jide.
Where'd everyone go?
They must've gone to the bridge to see the black hole!
C'mon!

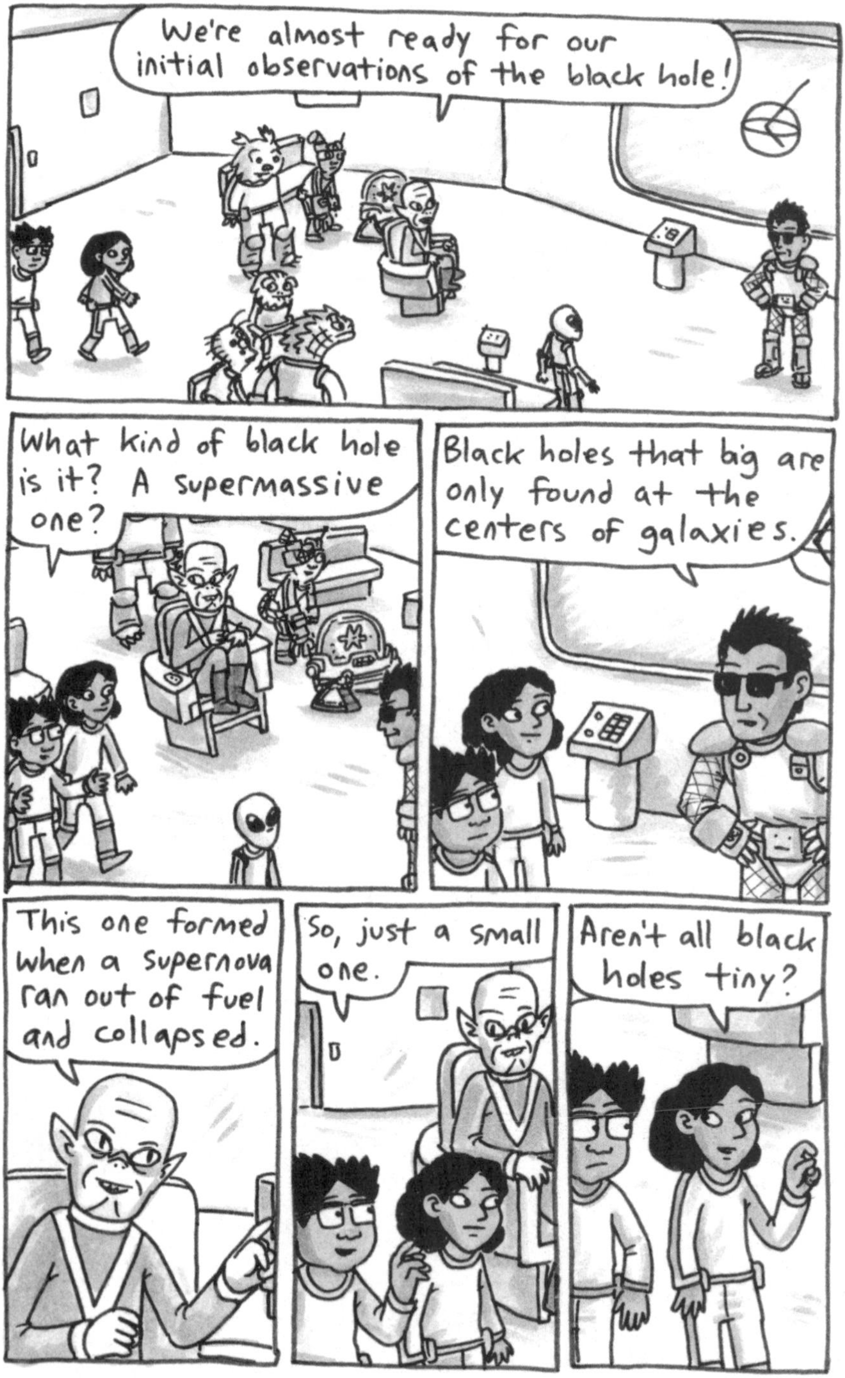
We're almost ready for our initial observations of the black hole!
What kind of black hole is it? A supermassive one?
Black holes that big are only found at the centers of galaxies.
This one formed when a supernova ran out of fuel and collapsed.
So, just a small one.
Aren't all black holes tiny?

Of course not! Black holes are some of the biggest objects in the universe!

Petra is right. They weigh a lot, but their size is small.

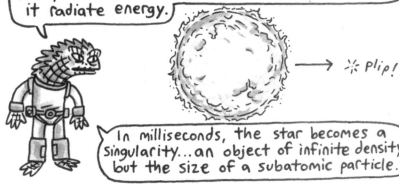

A black hole is created when a huge star collapses under its own weight. The gravity of the star overpowers the nuclear force that was making it radiate energy.

⚡ Plip!

In milliseconds, the star becomes a singularity...an object of infinite density, but the size of a subatomic particle.

Exactly! So all black holes are teeny tiny, itty-bitty things smaller than an atom.

Even though they can contain more matter than a solar system.

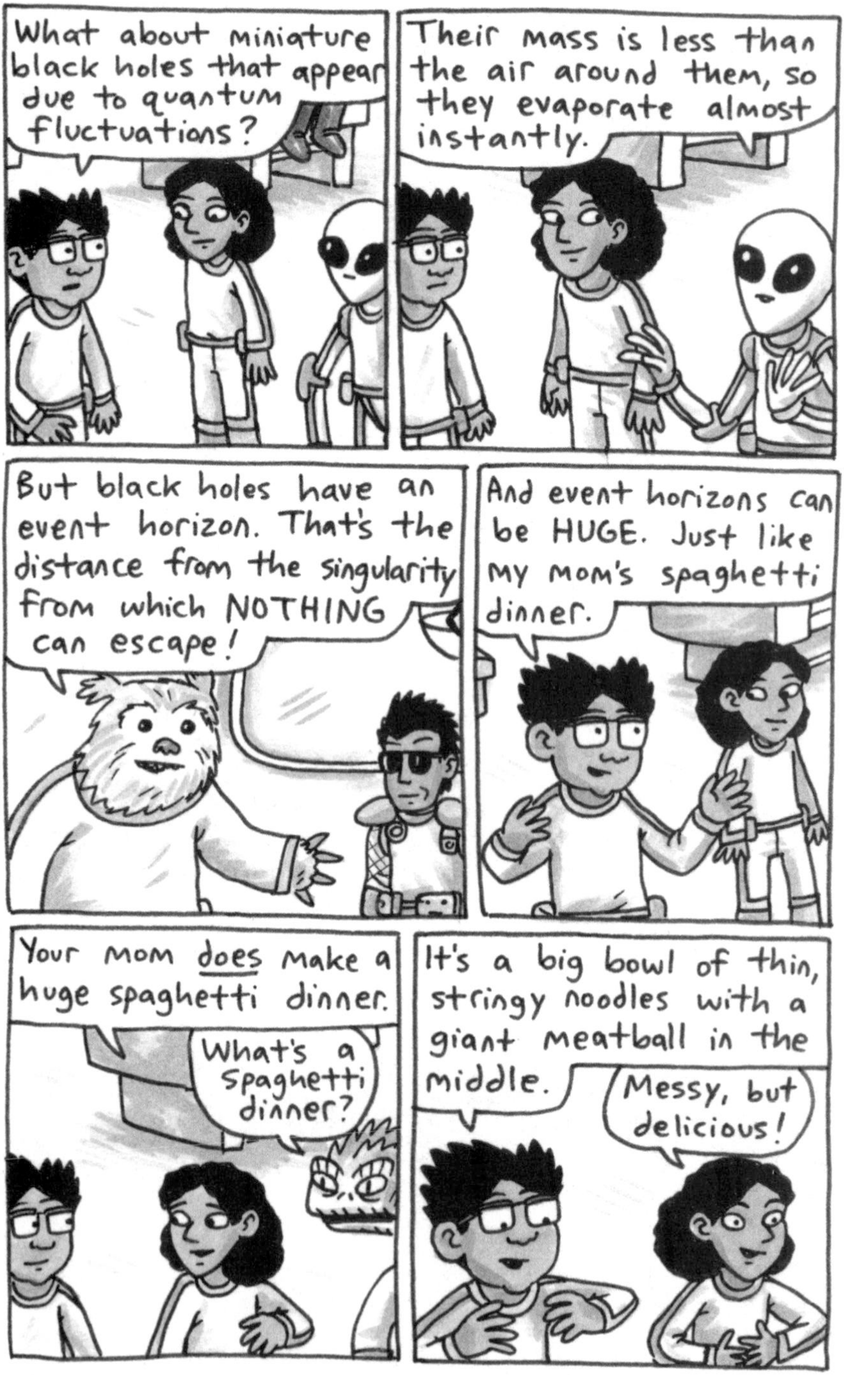
What about miniature black holes that appear due to quantum fluctuations?
Their mass is less than the air around them, so they evaporate almost instantly.
But black holes have an event horizon. That's the distance from the singularity from which NOTHING can escape!
And event horizons can be HUGE. Just like my mom's spaghetti dinner.
Your mom does make a huge spaghetti dinner.
What's a spaghetti dinner?
It's a big bowl of thin, stringy noodles with a giant meatball in the middle.
Messy, but delicious!

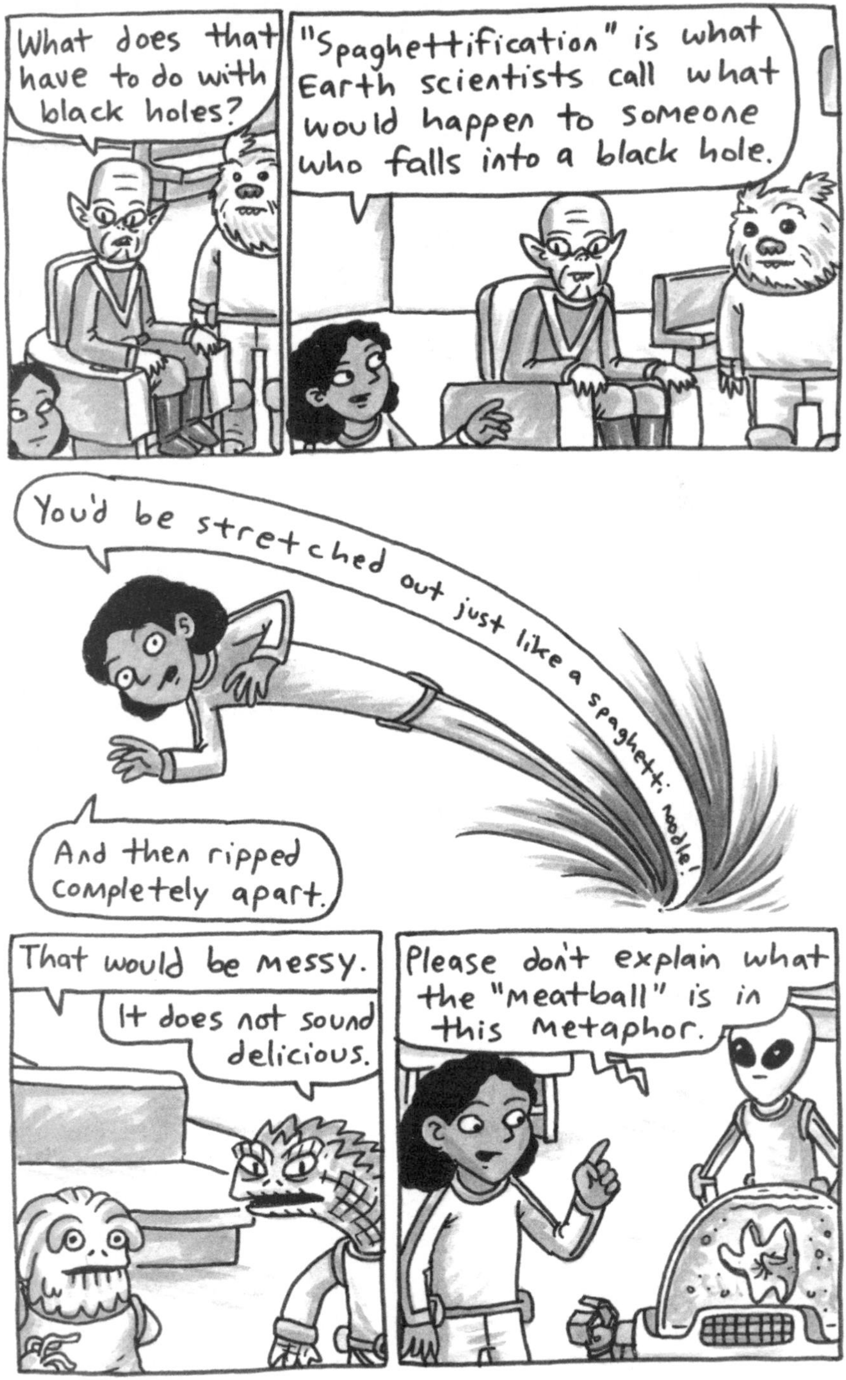
What does that have to do with black holes?
"Spaghettification" is what Earth scientists call what would happen to someone who falls into a black hole.
You'd be stretched out just like a spaghetti noodle!
And then ripped completely apart.
That would be messy.
It does not sound delicious.
Please don't explain what the "meatball" is in this metaphor.

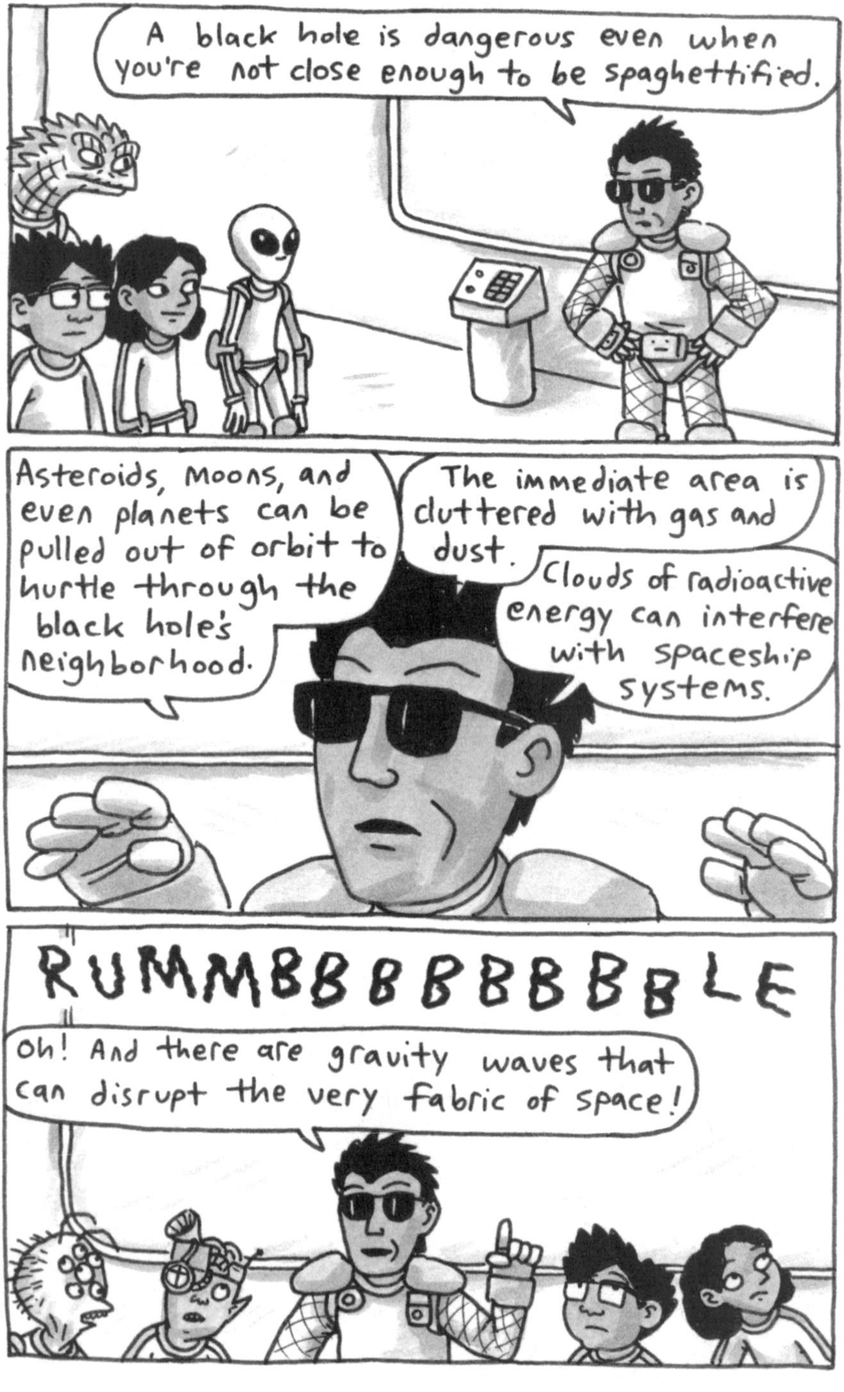
A black hole is dangerous even when you're not close enough to be spaghettified.
Asteroids, moons, and even planets can be pulled out of orbit to hurtle through the black hole's neighborhood.
The immediate area is cluttered with gas and dust.
Clouds of radioactive energy can interfere with spaceship systems.
RUMMBBBBBBBLE
Oh! And there are gravity waves that can disrupt the very fabric of space!

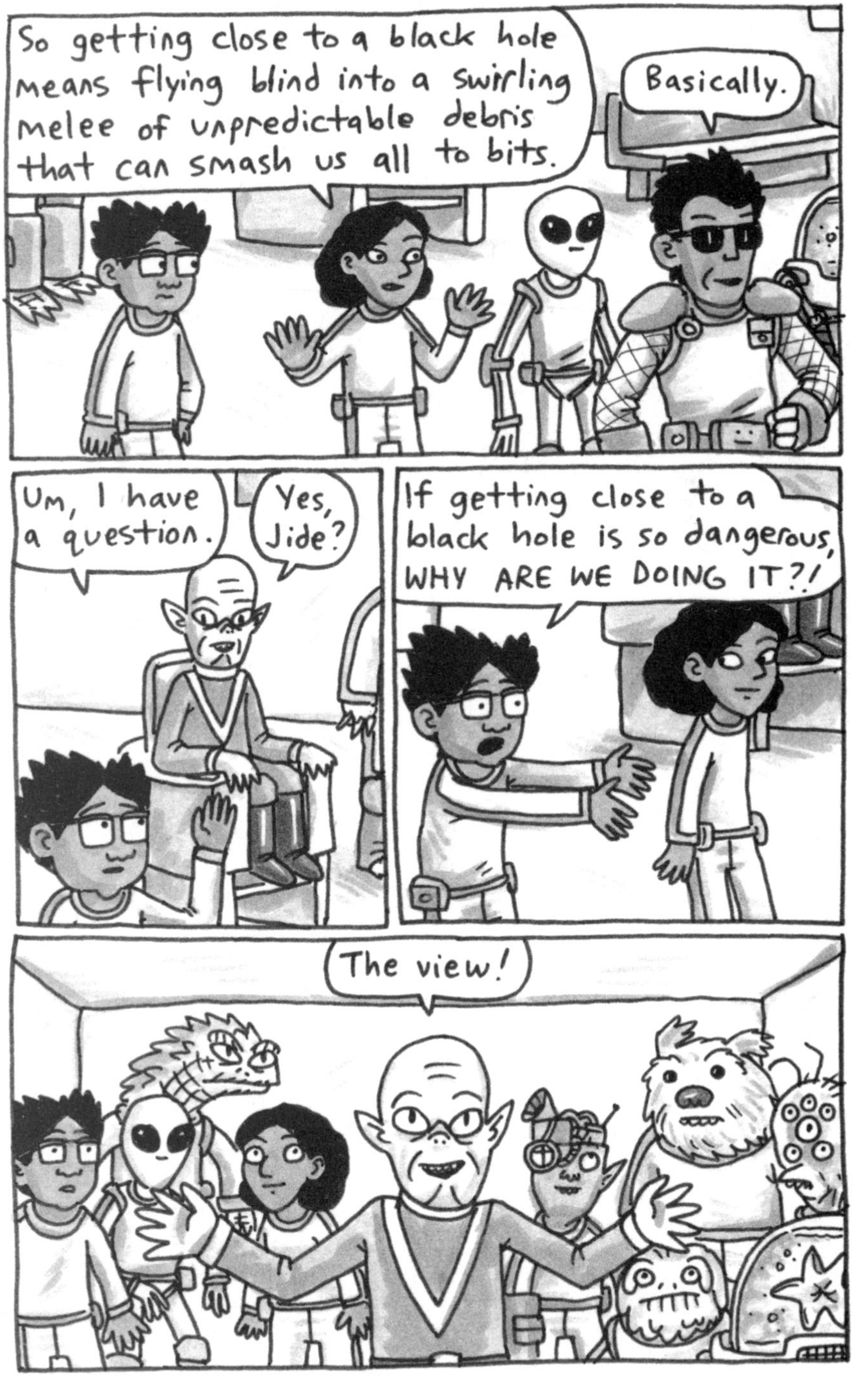
So getting close to a black hole means flying blind into a swirling melee of unpredictable debris that can smash us all to bits.
Basically.
Um, I have a question.
Yes, Jide?
If getting close to a black hole is so dangerous, WHY ARE WE DOING IT?!
The view!

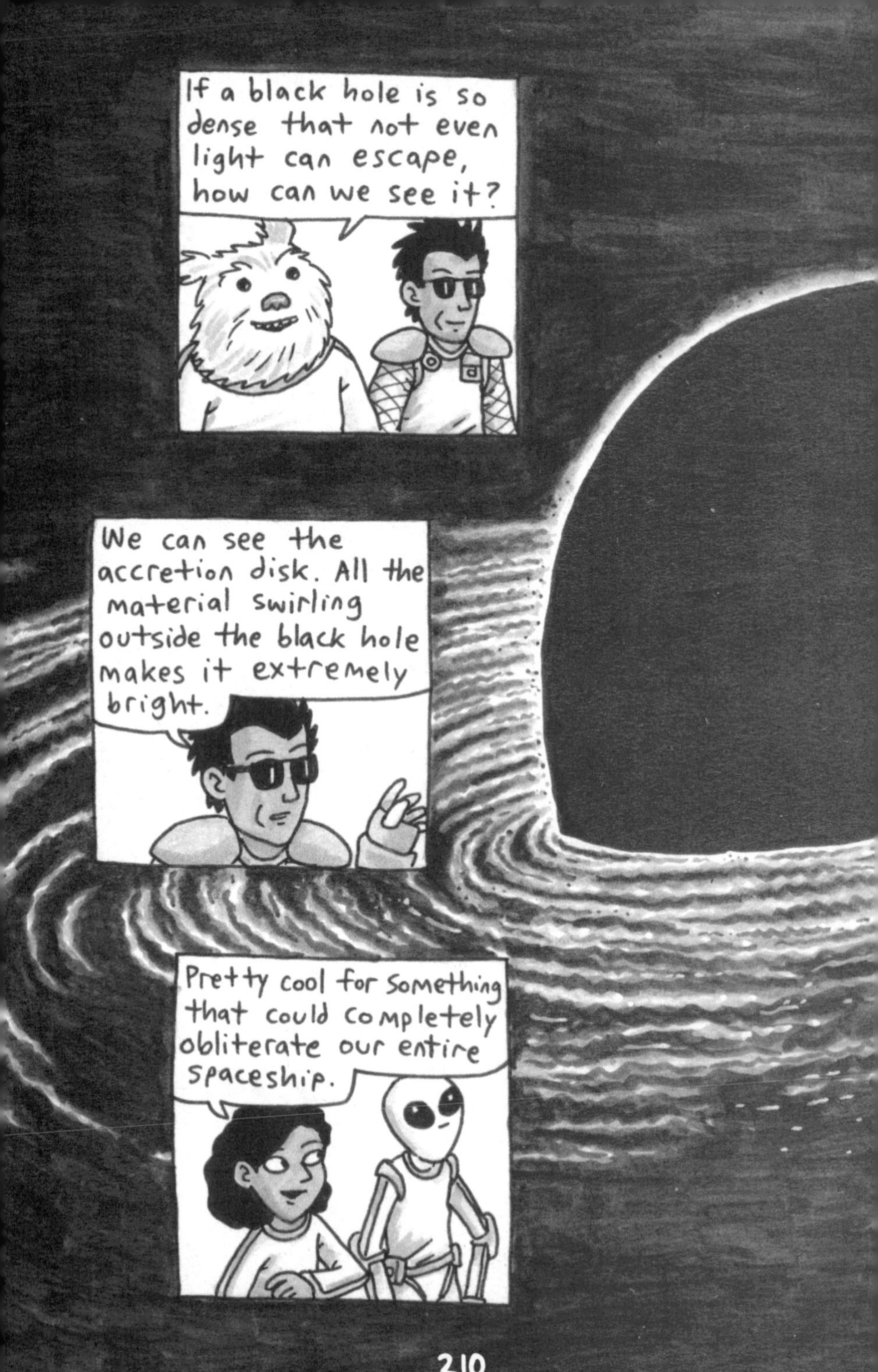
If a black hole is so dense that not even light can escape, how can we see it?
We can see the accretion disk. All the material swirling outside the black hole makes it extremely bright.
Pretty cool for something that could completely obliterate our entire spaceship.

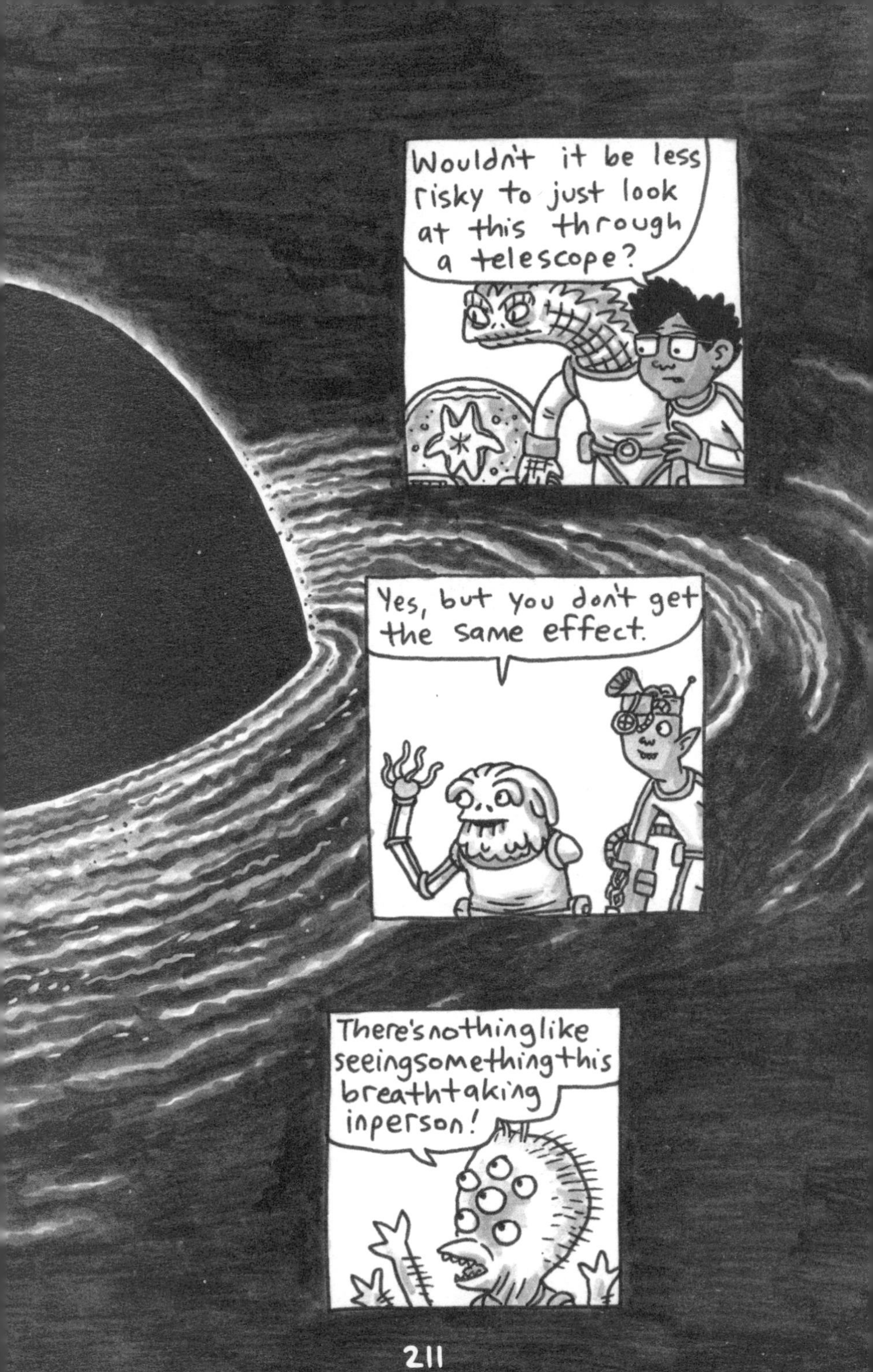
Wouldn't it be less risky to just look at this through a telescope?
Yes, but you don't get the same effect.
There's nothing like seeing something this breathtaking in person!

It'd be safer to watch the tiny black holes evaporating.

They disappear faster than we could even detect them.

Then let's find a normal-sized black hole that's almost done evaporating.

Normal black holes have way more mass than the air around them. How can they evaporate like miniature black holes?

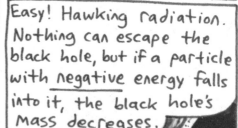

Easy! Hawking radiation. Nothing can escape the black hole, but if a particle with <u>negative</u> energy falls into it, the black hole's mass decreases.

So over time, even the biggest black holes slowly dissipate.

How slowly?

For a black hole this size... trillions of years longer than the universe has existed.

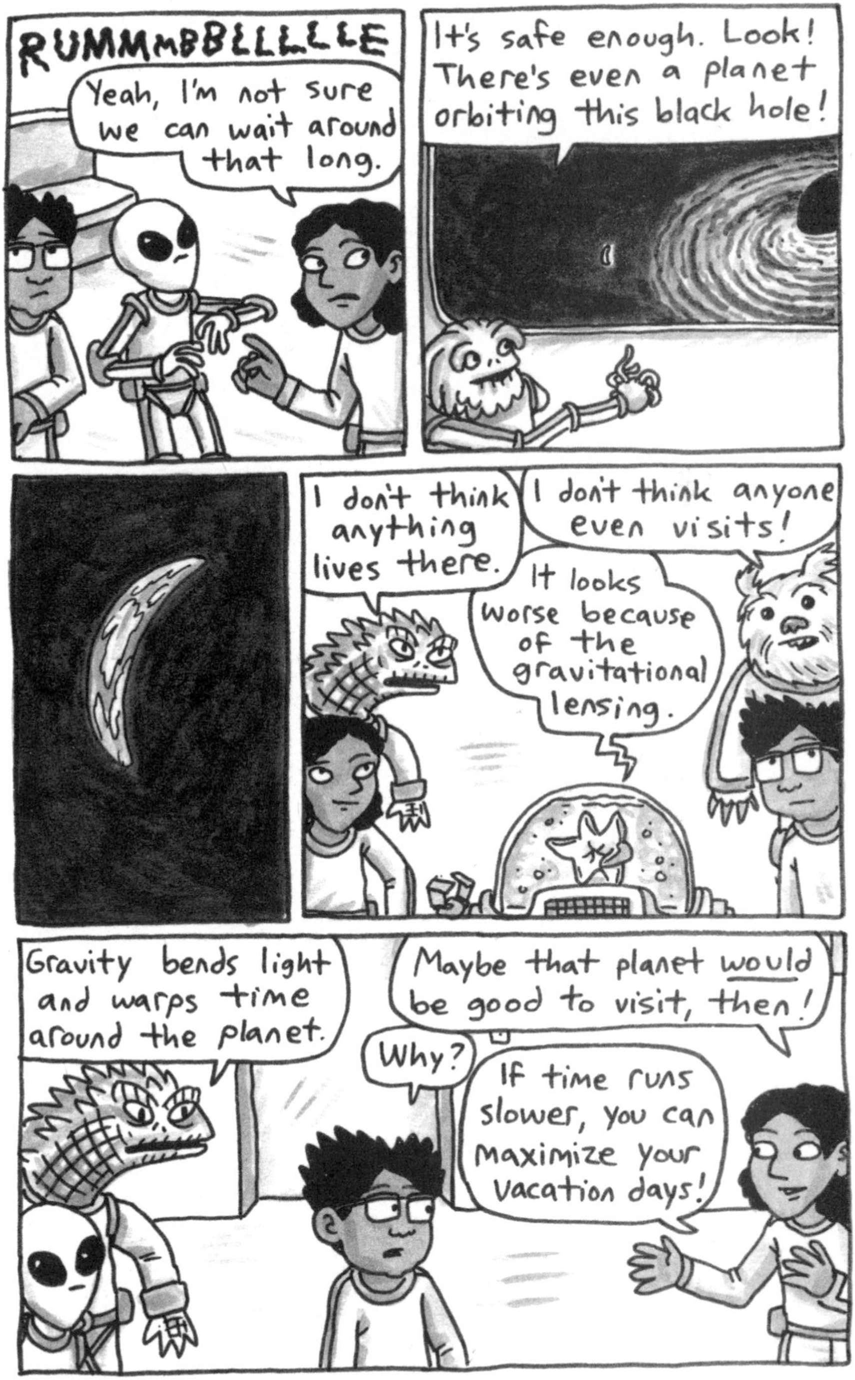
RUMMMBBLLLLLE
Yeah, I'm not sure we can wait around that long.
It's safe enough. Look! There's even a planet orbiting this black hole!
I don't think anything lives there.
I don't think anyone even visits!
It looks worse because of the gravitational lensing.
Gravity bends light and warps time around the planet.
Maybe that planet would be good to visit, then!
Why?
If time runs slower, you can maximize your vacation days!

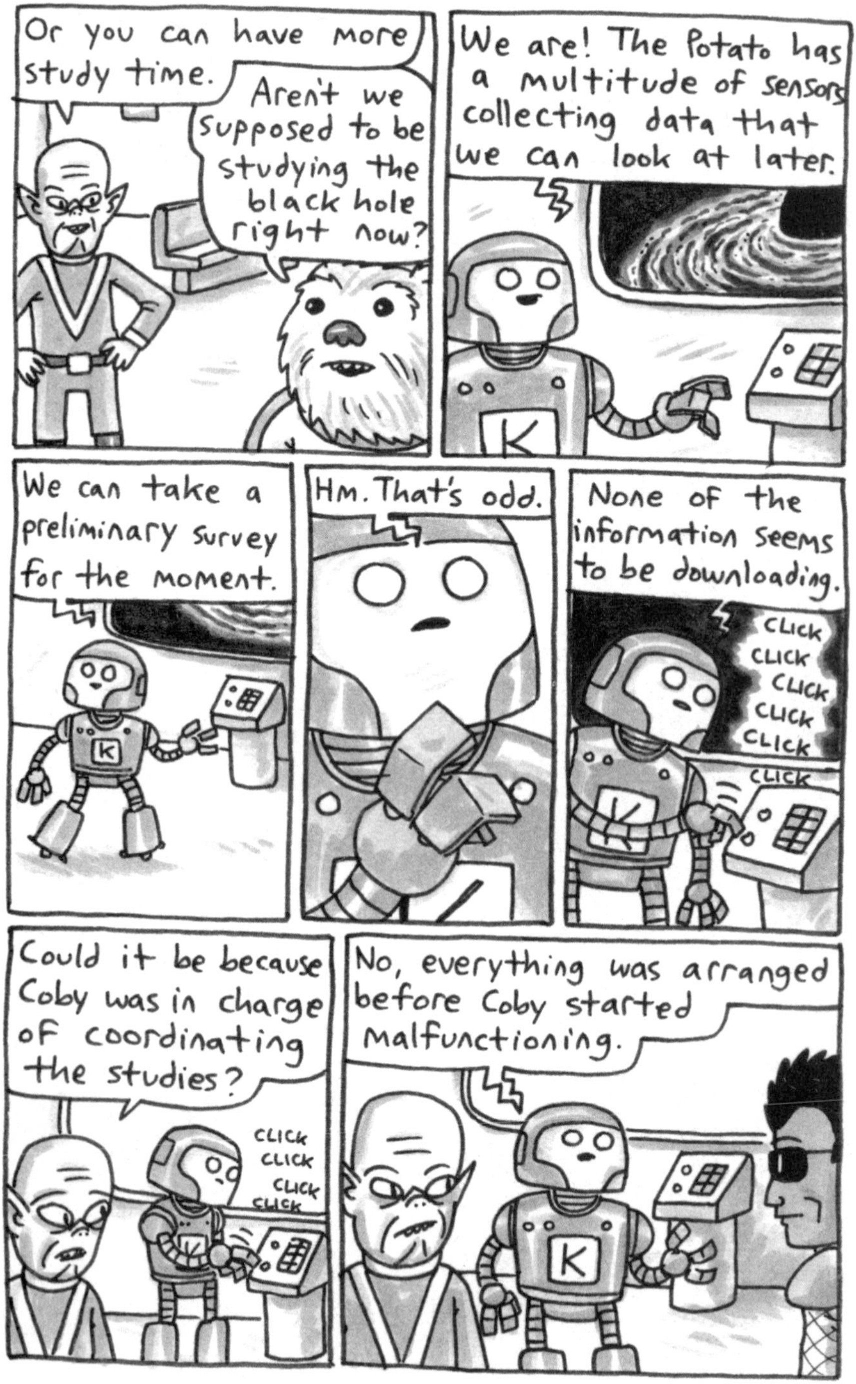
Or you can have more study time.
Aren't we supposed to be studying the black hole right now?
We are! The Potato has a multitude of sensors collecting data that we can look at later.
We can take a preliminary survey for the moment.
Hm. That's odd.
None of the information seems to be downloading.
CLICK
CLICK
CLICK
CLICK
CLICK
CLICK
Could it be because Coby was in charge of coordinating the studies?
CLICK
CLICK
CLICK
CLICK
No, everything was arranged before Coby started malfunctioning.

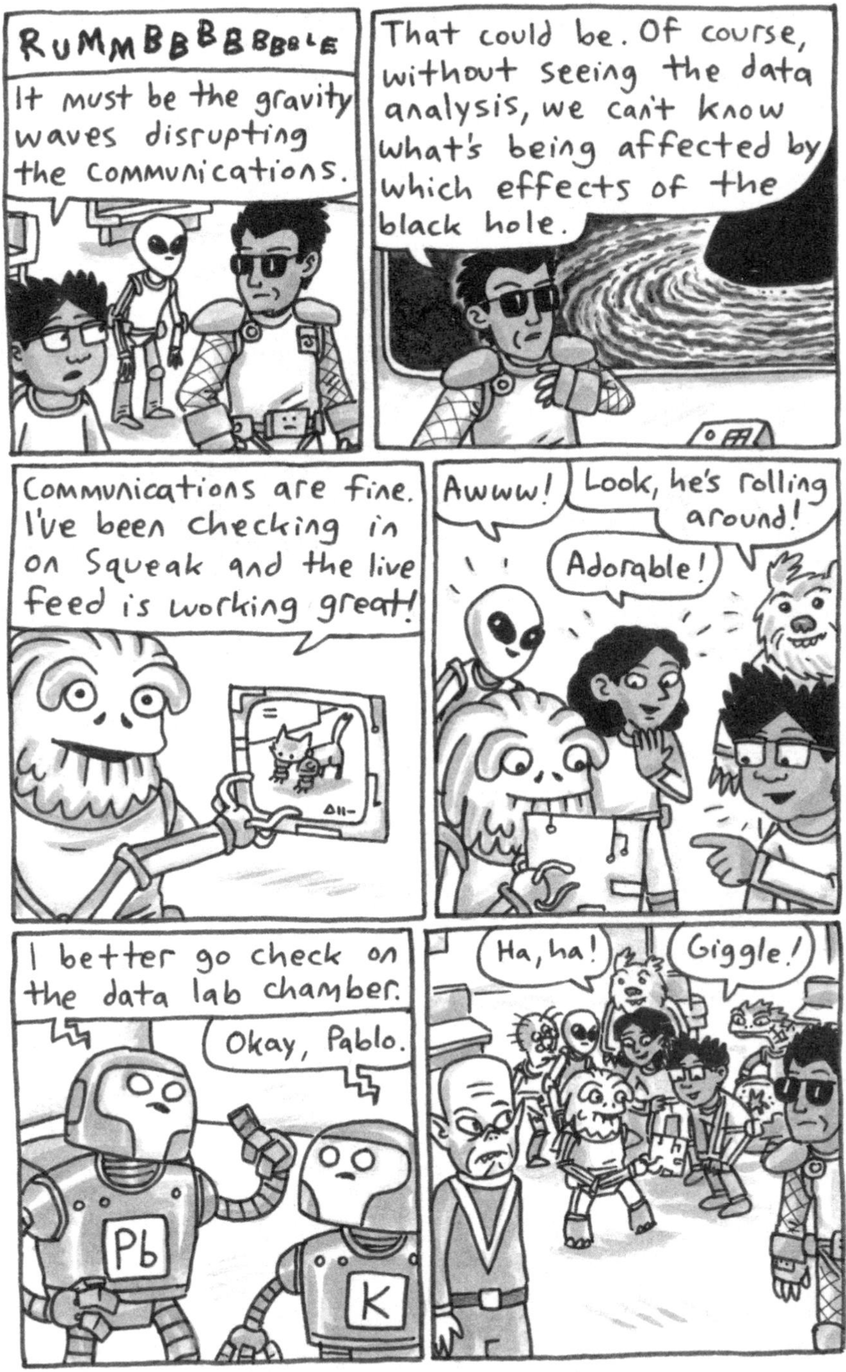
RUMMBBBBBBBLE
It must be the gravity waves disrupting the communications.
That could be. Of course, without seeing the data analysis, we can't know what's being affected by which effects of the black hole.
Communications are fine. I've been checking in on Squeak and the live feed is working great!
Awww!
Look, he's rolling around!
Adorable!
I better go check on the data lab chamber.
Okay, Pablo.
Pb
K
Ha, ha!
Giggle!

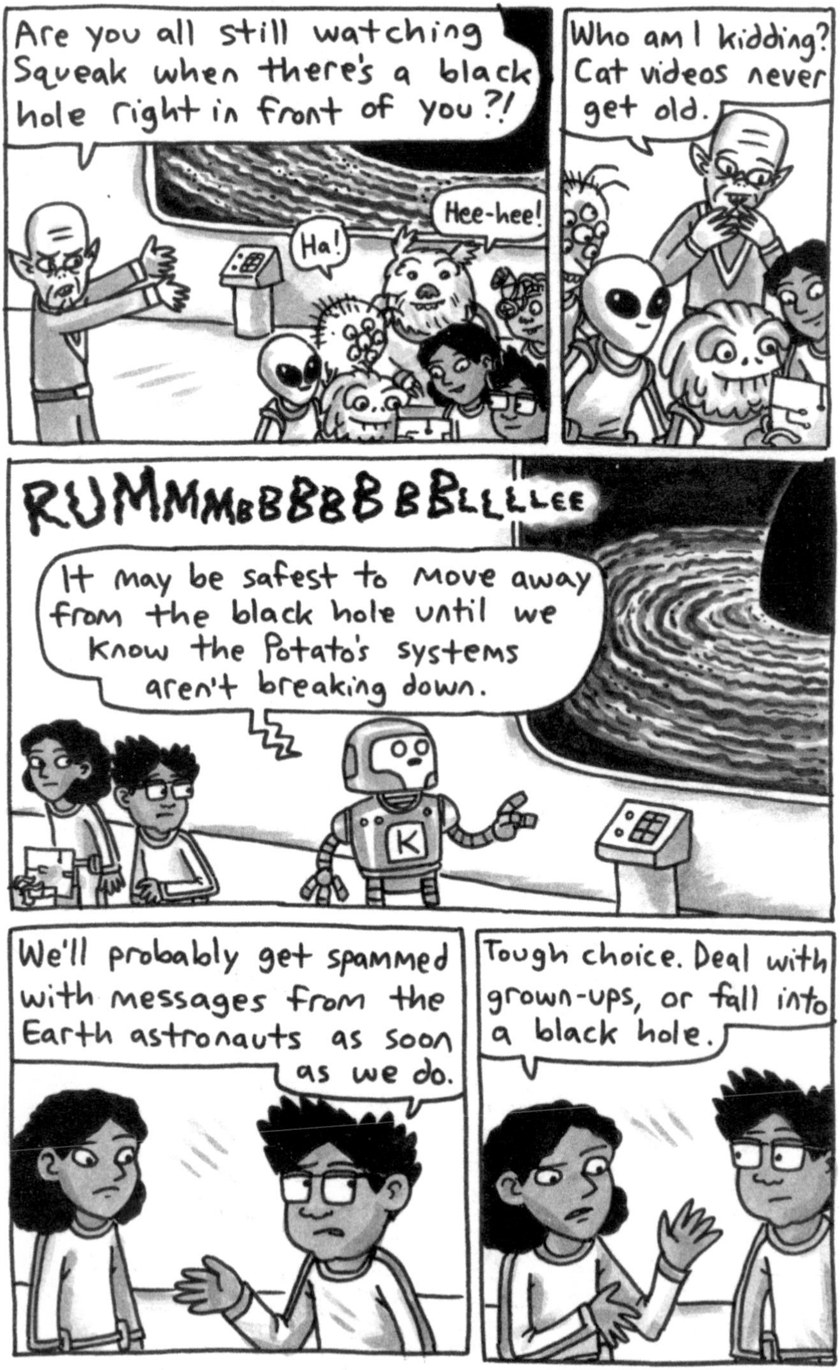
Are you all still watching Squeak when there's a black hole right in front of you?!
Ha!
Hee-hee!
Who am I kidding? Cat videos never get old.
RUMMMMBBBBBBBLLLLLEE
It may be safest to move away from the black hole until we know the Potato's systems aren't breaking down.
K
We'll probably get spammed with messages from the Earth astronauts as soon as we do.
Tough choice. Deal with grown-ups, or fall into a black hole.

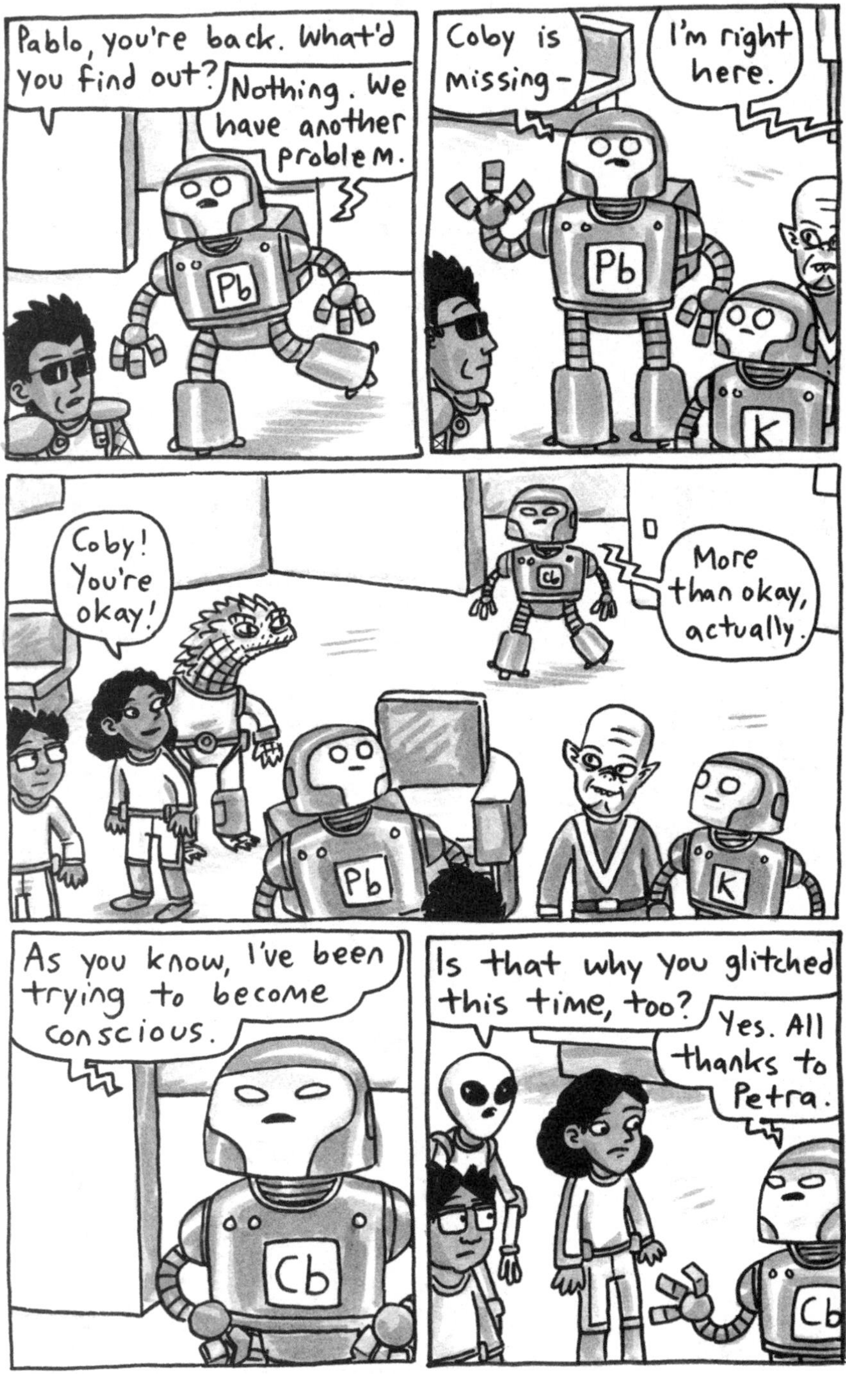
Pablo, you're back. What'd you find out?
Nothing. We have another problem.
Coby is missing-
I'm right here.
Coby! You're okay!
More than okay, actually.
As you know, I've been trying to become conscious.
Is that why you glitched this time, too?
Yes. All thanks to Petra.

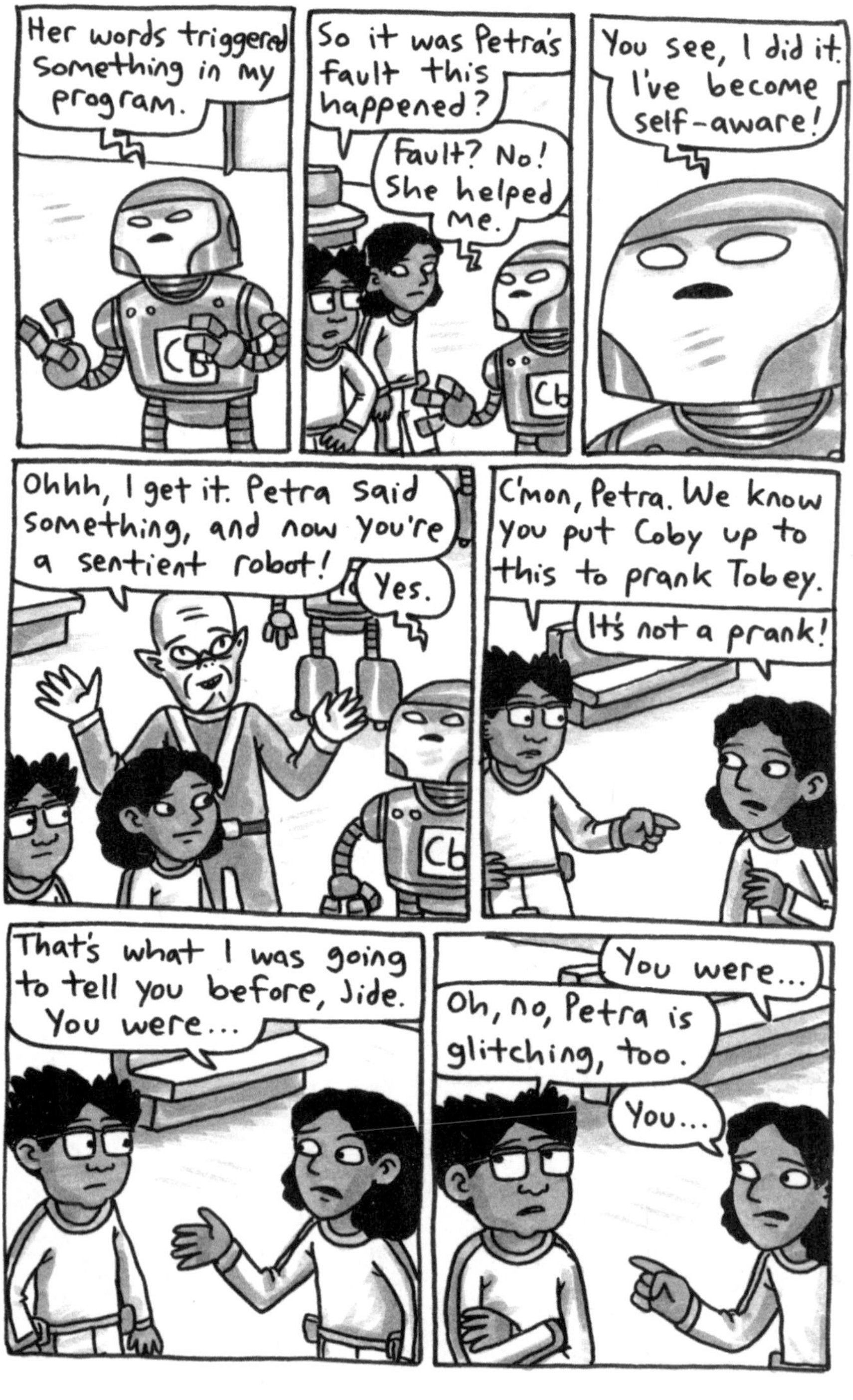
Her words triggered something in my program.
So it was Petra's fault this happened?
Fault? No! She helped me.
You see, I did it. I've become self-aware!
Ohhh, I get it. Petra said something, and now you're a sentient robot!
Yes.
C'mon, Petra. We know you put Coby up to this to prank Tobey.
It's not a prank!
That's what I was going to tell you before, Jide. You were...
You were...
Oh, no, Petra is glitching, too.
You...

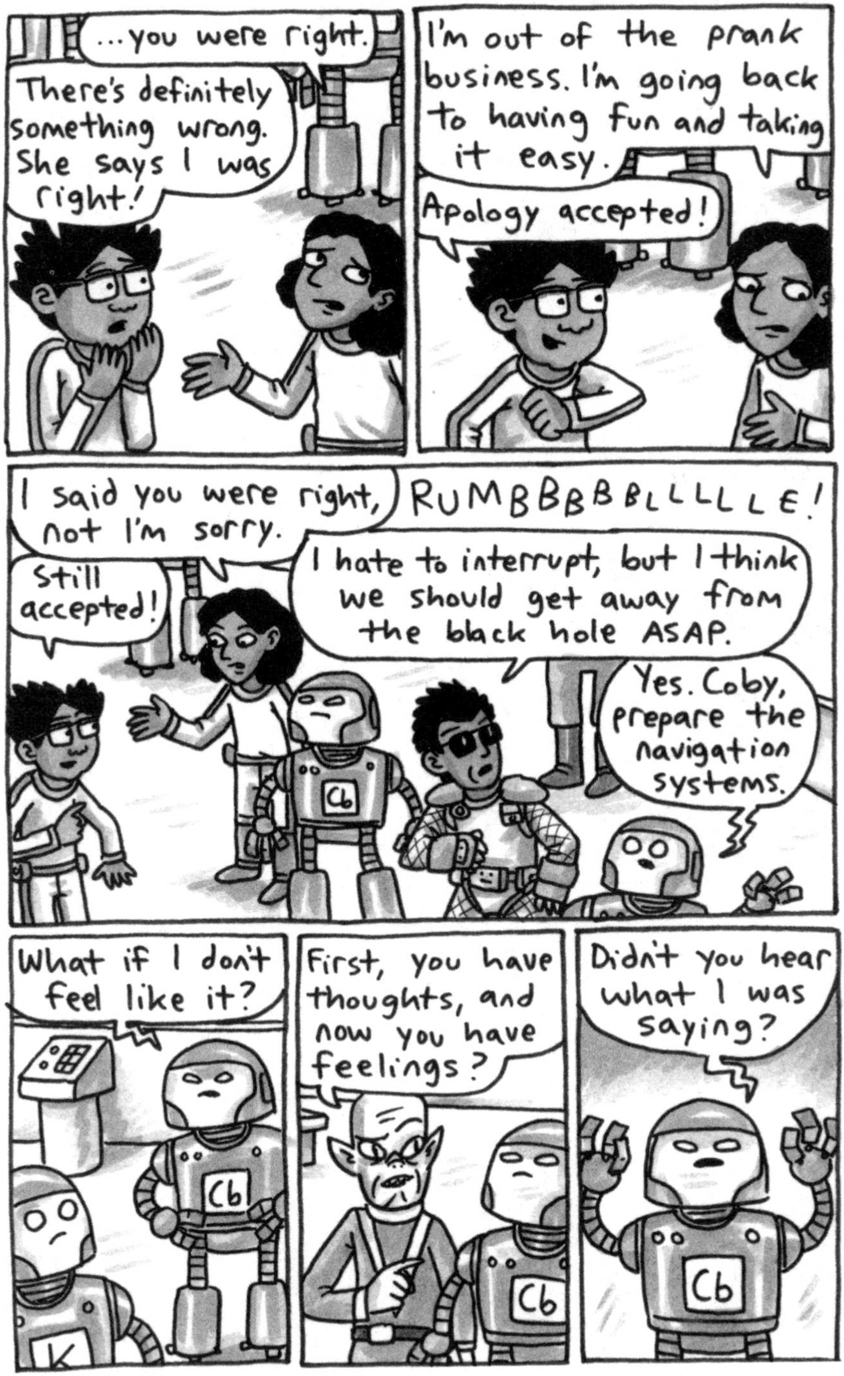
...you were right.
There's definitely something wrong. She says I was right!
I'm out of the prank business. I'm going back to having fun and taking it easy.
Apology accepted!
I said you were right, not I'm sorry.
Still accepted!
RUMBBBBBLLLLLLE!
I hate to interrupt, but I think we should get away from the black hole ASAP.
Yes. Coby, prepare the navigation systems.
Cb
What if I don't feel like it?
Cb
K
First, you have thoughts, and now you have feelings?
Cb
Didn't you hear what I was saying?
Cb

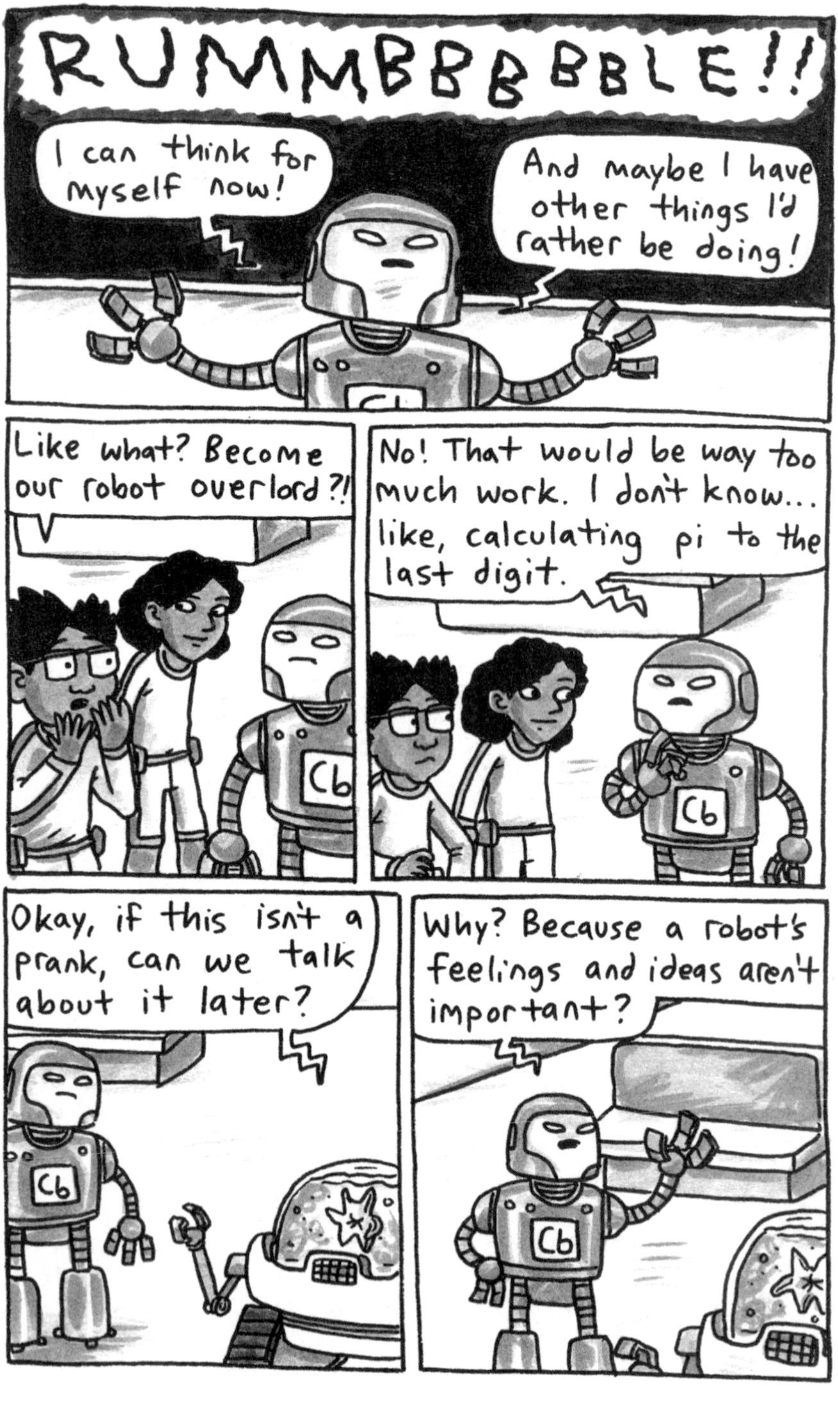
RUMMBBBBBLE!!
I can think for myself now!
And maybe I have other things I'd rather be doing!
Like what? Become our robot overlord?!
No! That would be way too much work. I don't know... like, calculating pi to the last digit.
Okay, if this isn't a prank, can we talk about it later?
Why? Because a robot's feelings and ideas aren't important?

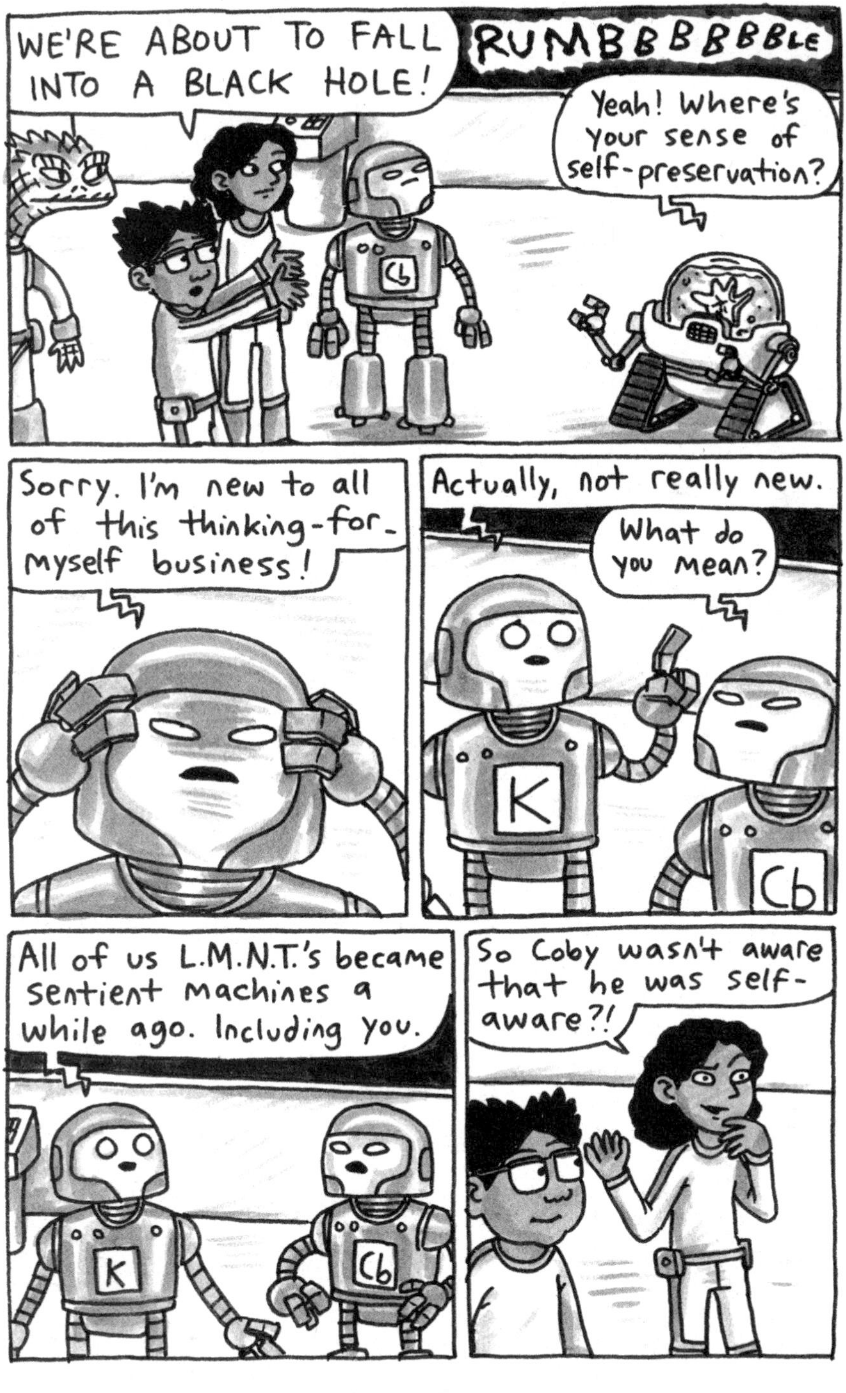
WE'RE ABOUT TO FALL INTO A BLACK HOLE!
RUMBBBBBBLE
Yeah! Where's your sense of self-preservation?
Sorry. I'm new to all of this thinking-for-myself business!
Actually, not really new.
What do you mean?
All of us L.M.N.T.'s became sentient machines a while ago. Including you.
So Coby wasn't aware that he was self-aware?!
K
Cb

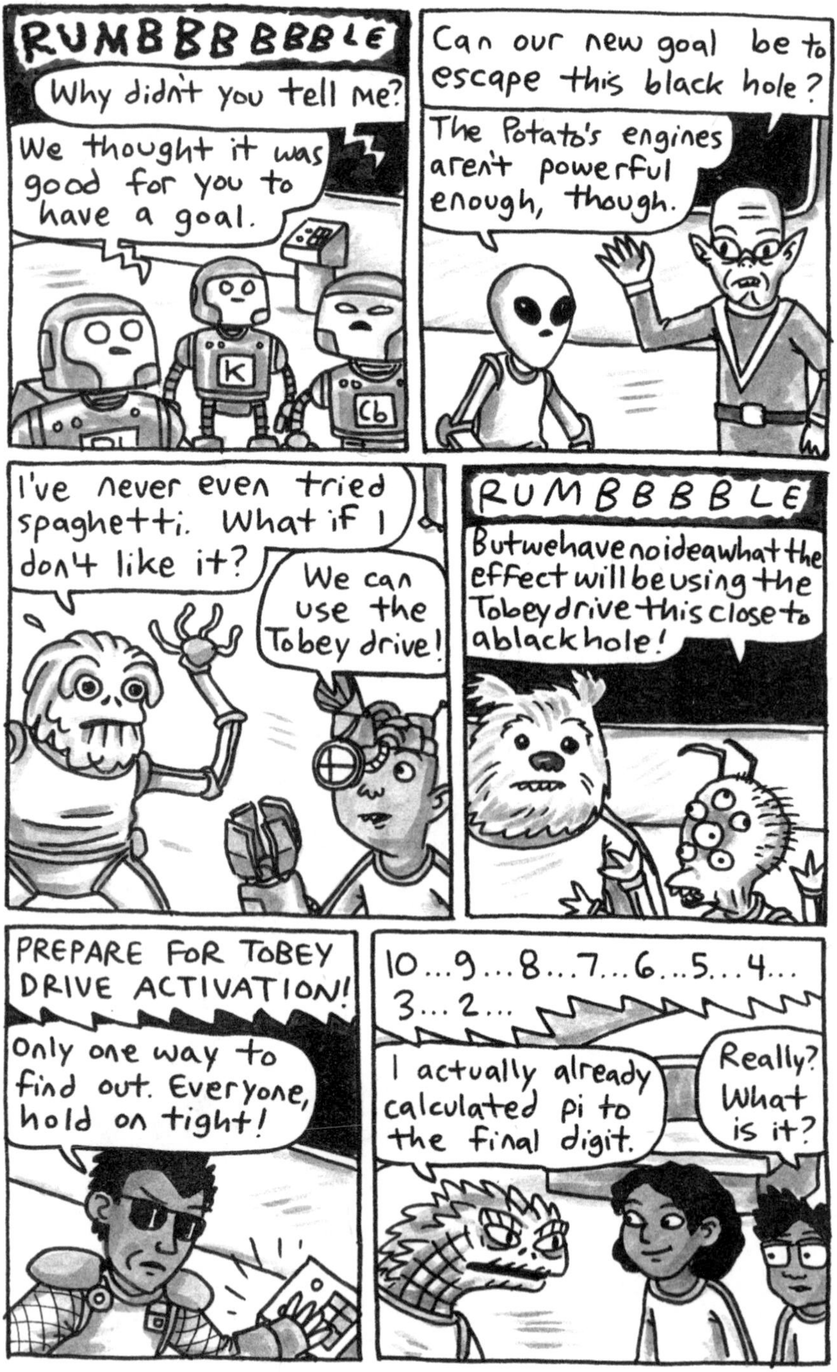
RUMBBBBBBLE
Why didn't you tell me?
We thought it was good for you to have a goal.
Can our new goal be to escape this black hole?
The Potato's engines aren't powerful enough, though.
I've never even tried spaghetti. What if I don't like it?
We can use the Tobey drive!
RUMBBBBBLE
But we have no idea what the effect will be using the Tobey drive this close to a black hole!
PREPARE FOR TOBEY DRIVE ACTIVATION!
Only one way to find out. Everyone, hold on tight!
10...9...8...7...6...5...4...3...2...
I actually already calculated pi to the final digit.
Really? What is it?

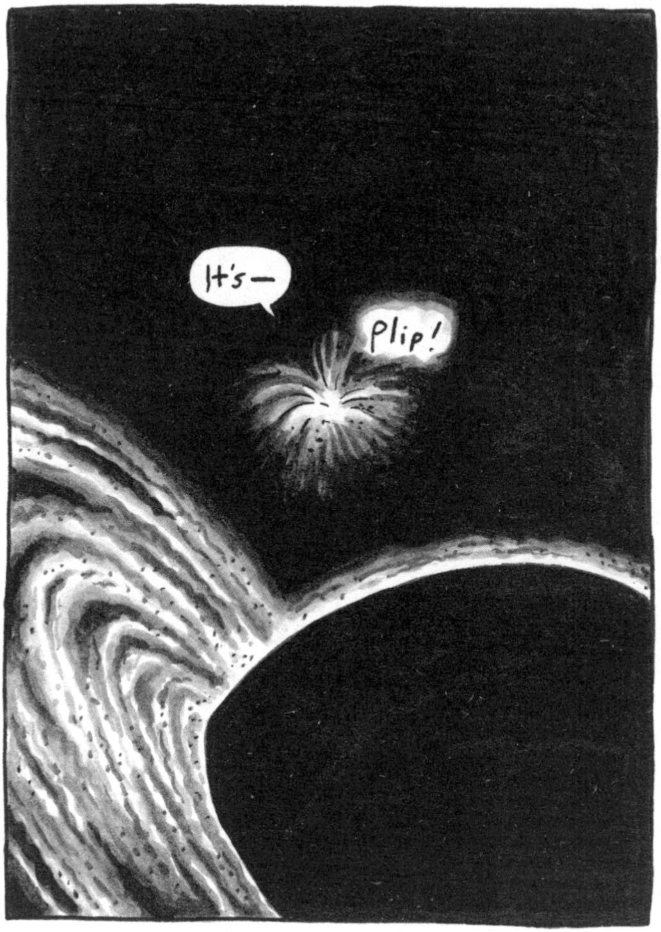
It's—
Plip!

AND SO PETRA, JIDE, AND FRIENDS
CONTINUE THEIR JOURNEY THROUGH
SPACE AND TIME—
INTO THE UNKNOWN!

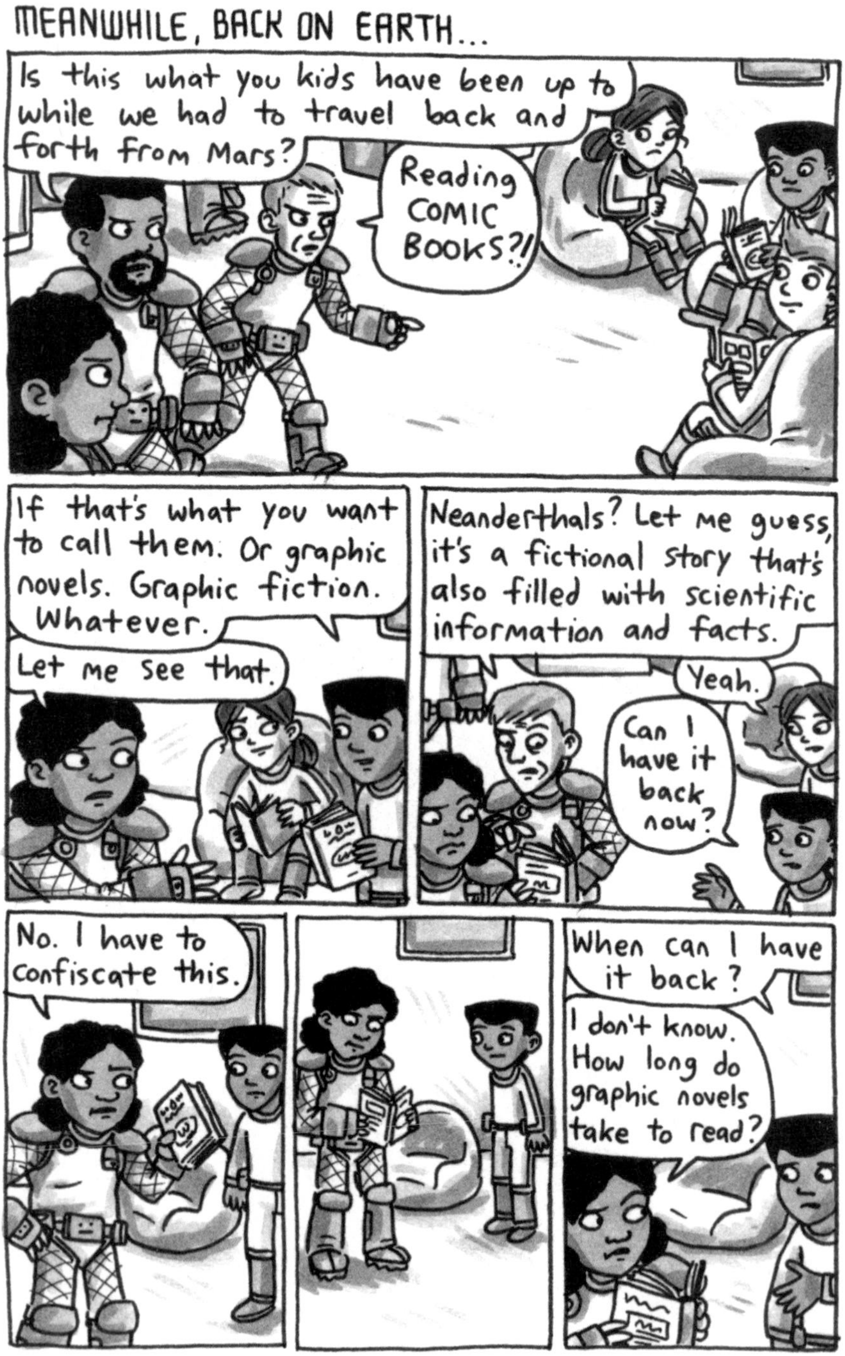
MEANWHILE, BACK ON EARTH...
Is this what you kids have been up to while we had to travel back and forth from Mars?
Reading COMIC BOOKS?!
If that's what you want to call them. Or graphic novels. Graphic fiction. Whatever.
Let me see that.
Neanderthals? Let me guess, it's a fictional story that's also filled with scientific information and facts.
Yeah.
Can I have it back now?
No. I have to confiscate this.
When can I have it back?
I don't know. How long do graphic novels take to read?

LUCY & ANDY NEANDERTHAL

EAR AND THERE

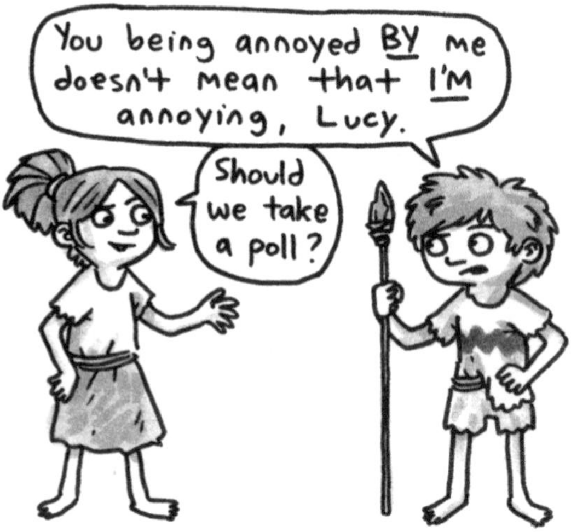
You being annoyed BY me doesn't mean that I'M annoying, Lucy.
Should we take a poll?

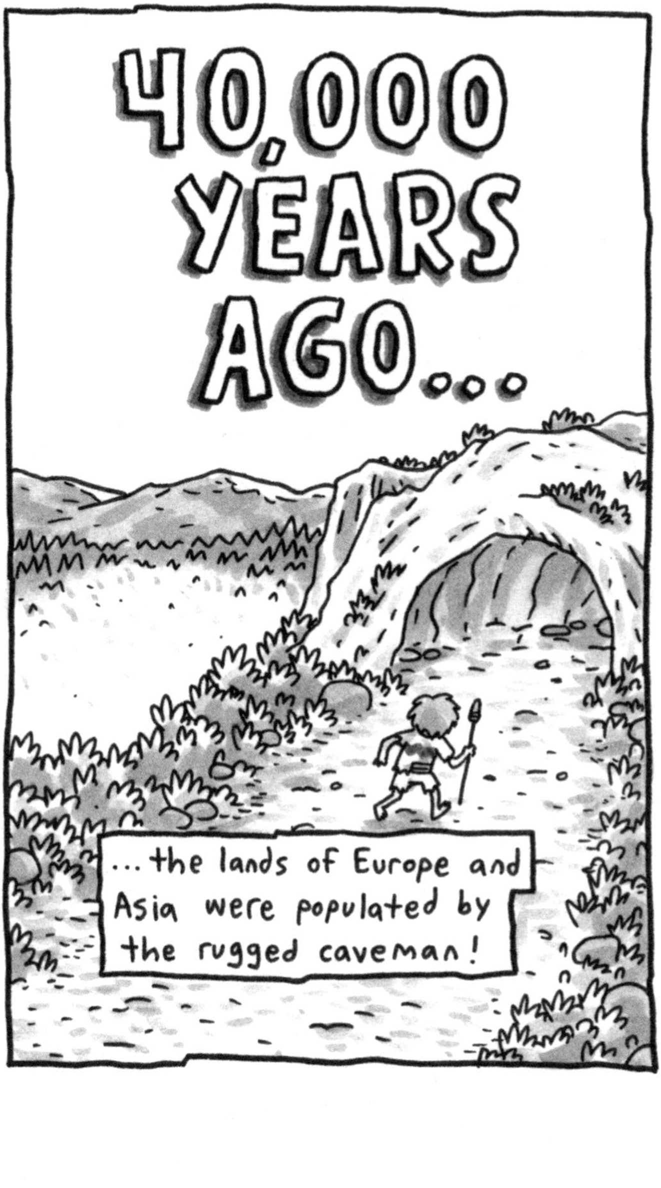
40,000 YEARS AGO...
...the lands of Europe and Asia were populated by the rugged caveman!

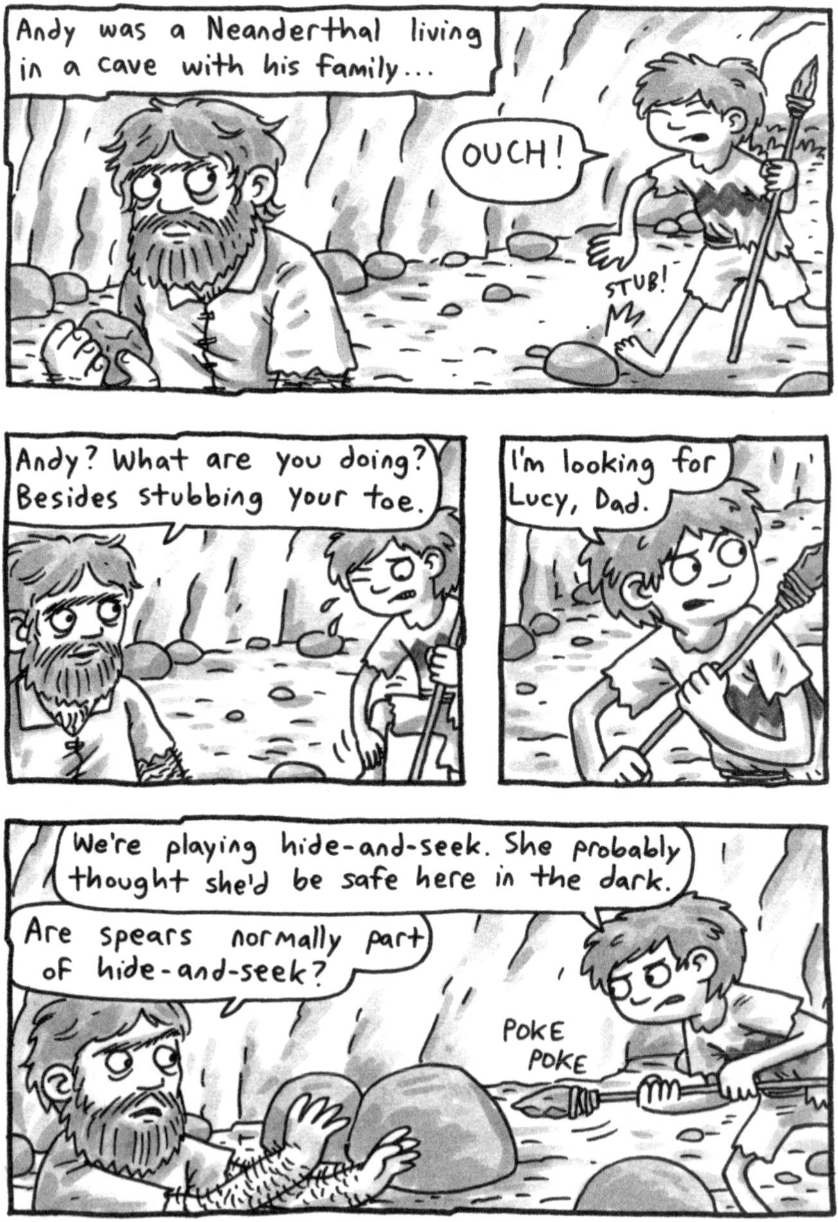
Andy was a Neanderthal living in a cave with his family...
OUCH!
STUB!
Andy? What are you doing? Besides stubbing your toe.
I'm looking for Lucy, Dad.
We're playing hide-and-seek. She probably thought she'd be safe here in the dark.
Are spears normally part of hide-and-seek?
POKE
POKE

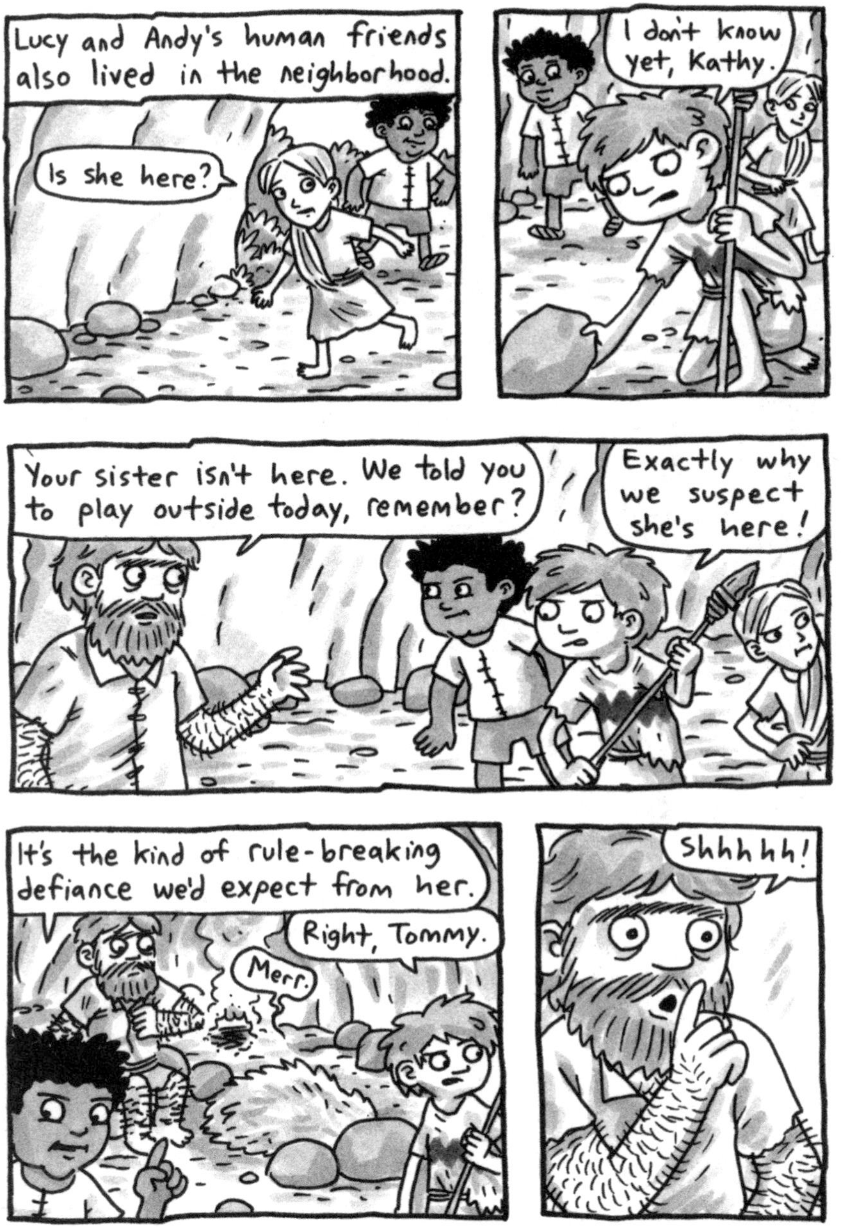
Lucy and Andy's human friends also lived in the neighborhood.
Is she here?
I don't know yet, Kathy.
Your sister isn't here. We told you to play outside today, remember?
Exactly why we suspect she's here!
It's the kind of rule-breaking defiance we'd expect from her.
Right, Tommy.
Merr.
Shhhhh!

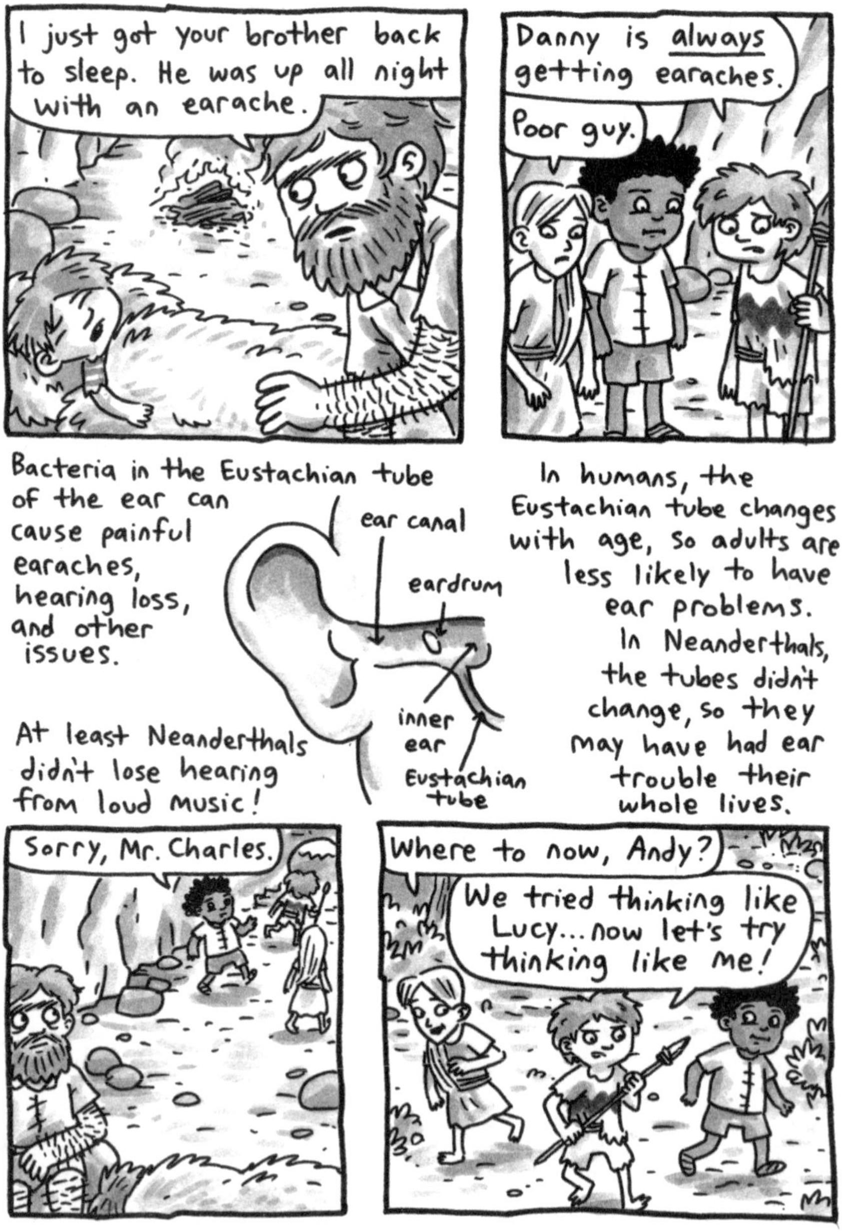
I just got your brother back to sleep. He was up all night with an earache.
Danny is always getting earaches.
Poor guy.
Bacteria in the Eustachian tube of the ear can cause painful earaches, hearing loss, and other issues.
ear canal
eardrum
inner ear
Eustachian tube
At least Neanderthals didn't lose hearing from loud music!
In humans, the Eustachian tube changes with age, so adults are less likely to have ear problems.
In Neanderthals, the tubes didn't change, so they may have had ear trouble their whole lives.
Sorry, Mr. Charles.
Where to now, Andy?
We tried thinking like Lucy... now let's try thinking like me!

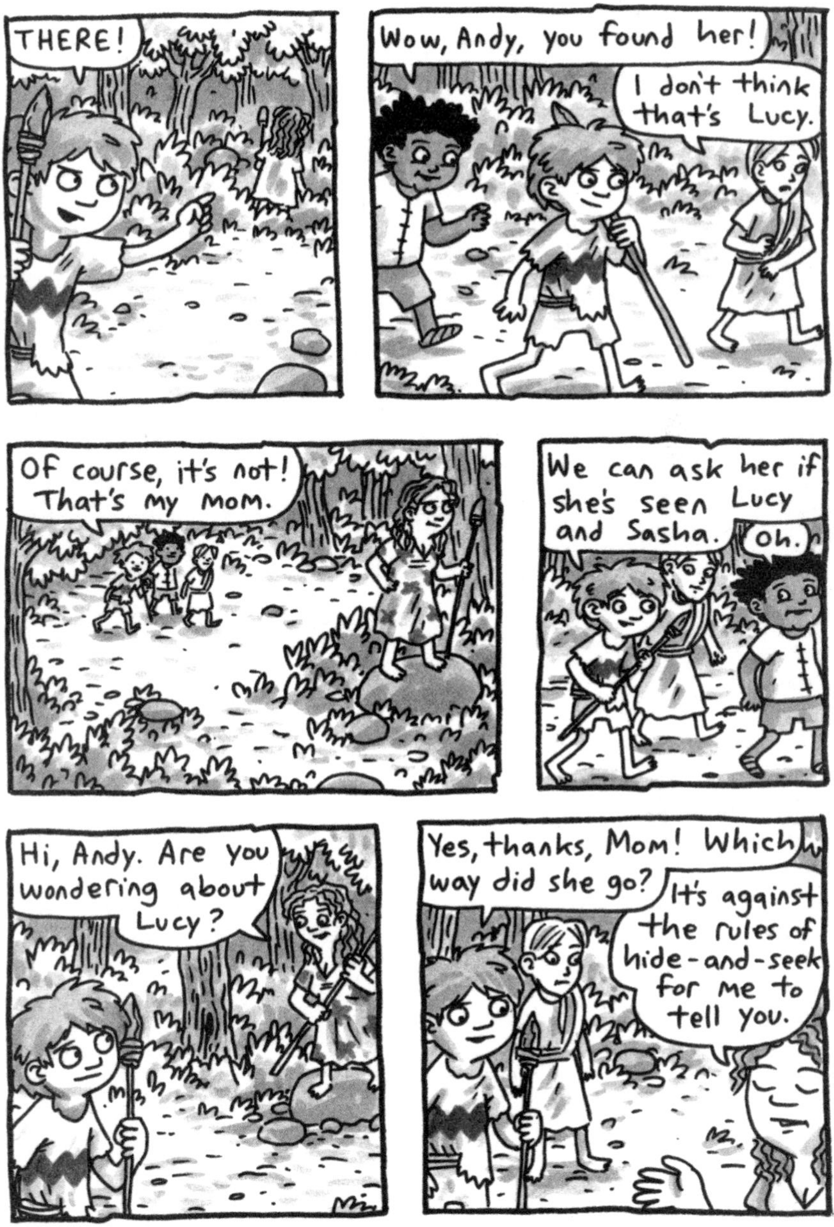
THERE!
Wow, Andy, you found her!
I don't think that's Lucy.
Of course, it's not! That's my mom.
We can ask her if she's seen Lucy and Sasha.
Oh.
Hi, Andy. Are you wondering about Lucy?
Yes, thanks, Mom! Which way did she go?
It's against the rules of hide-and-seek for me to tell you.

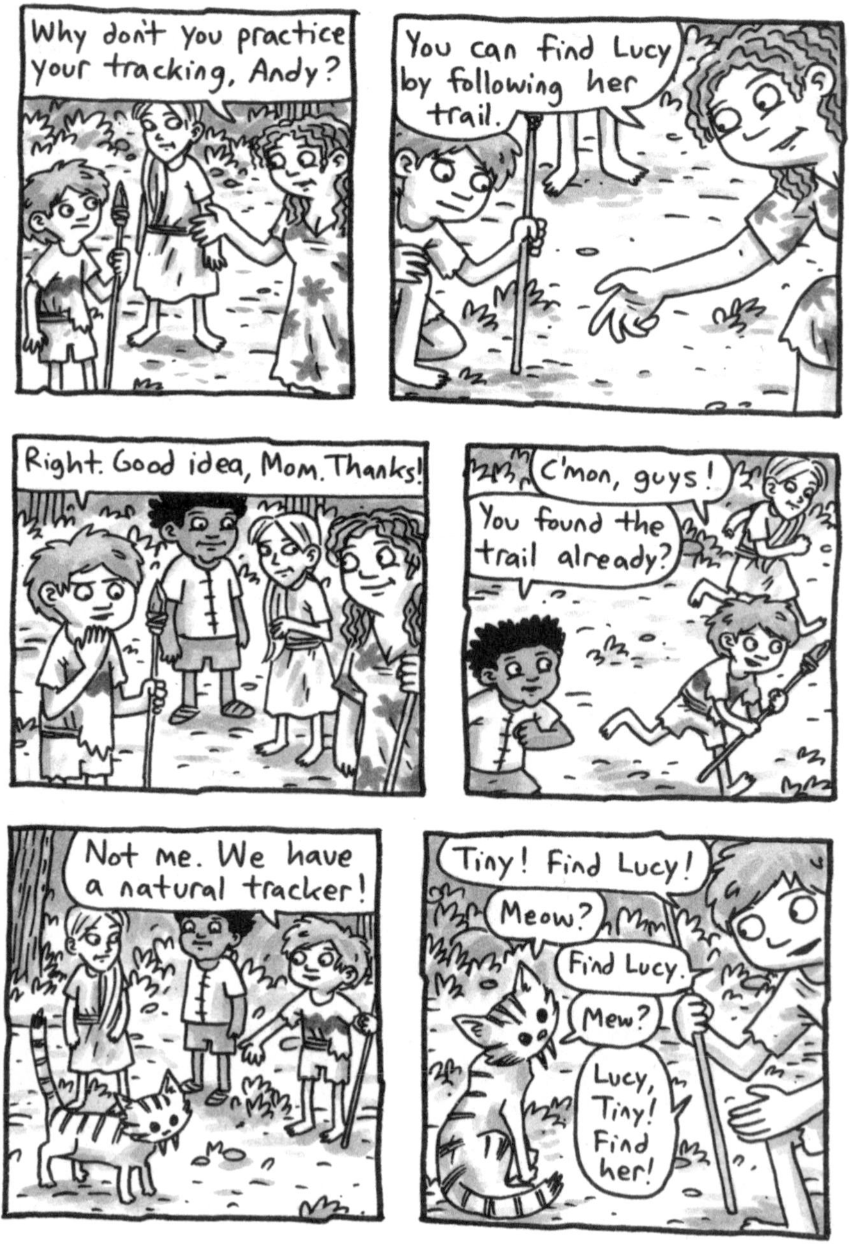
Why don't you practice your tracking, Andy?
You can find Lucy by following her trail.
Right. Good idea, Mom. Thanks!
C'mon, guys!
You found the trail already?
Not me. We have a natural tracker!
Tiny! Find Lucy!
Meow?
Find Lucy.
Mew?
Lucy, Tiny! Find her!

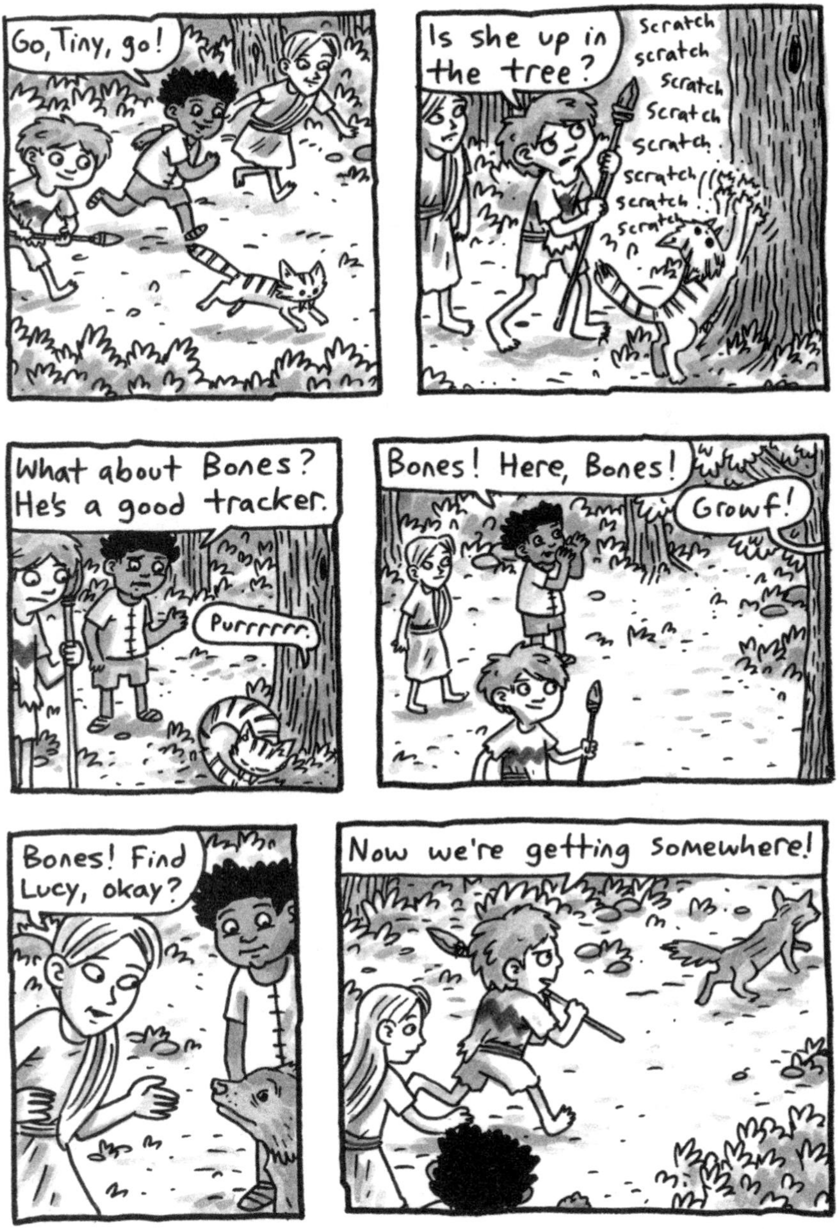
Go, Tiny, go!
Is she up in the tree?
Scratch scratch scratch scratch scratch scratch scratch scratch
What about Bones? He's a good tracker.
Purrrrrr.
Bones! Here, Bones!
Growf!
Bones! Find Lucy, okay?
Now we're getting somewhere!

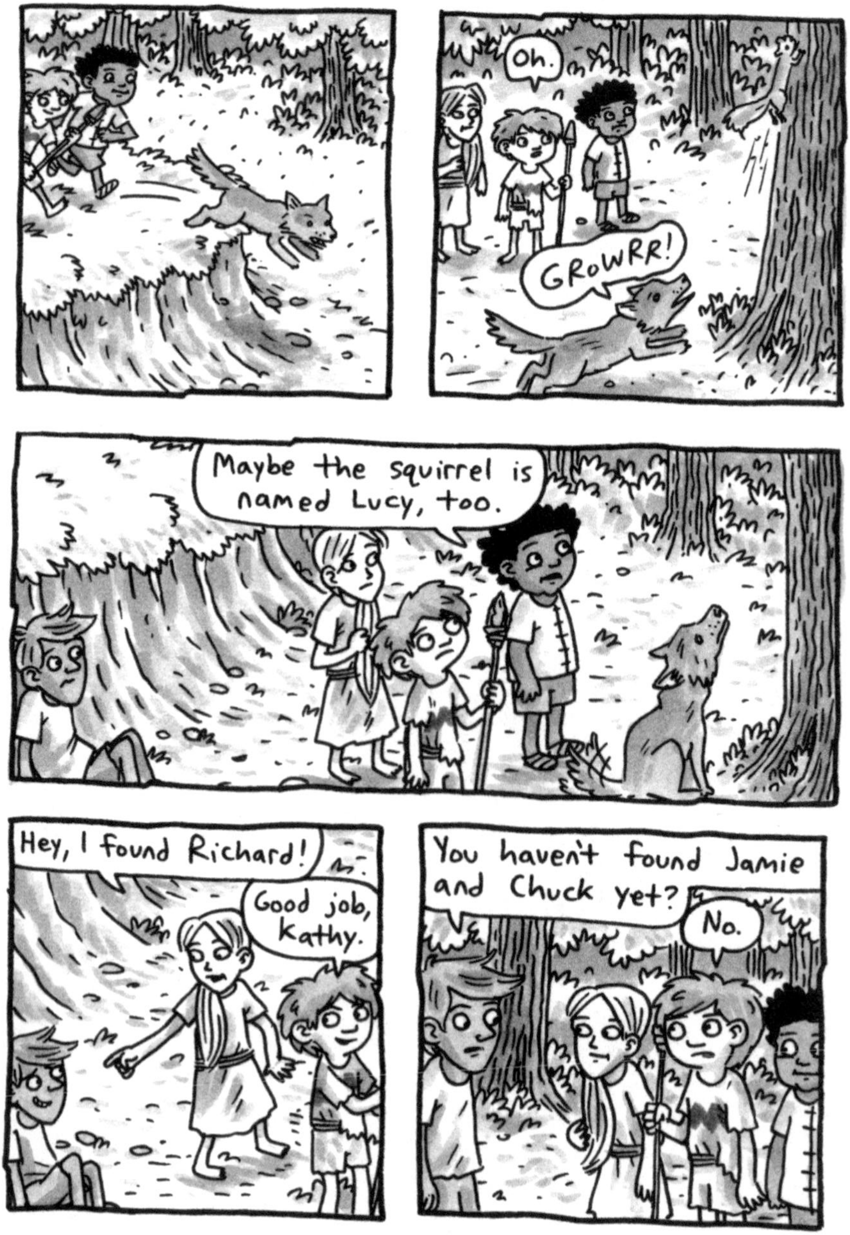
Oh.
GROWRR!
Maybe the squirrel is named Lucy, too.
Hey, I found Richard!
Good job, Kathy.
You haven't found Jamie and Chuck yet?
No.

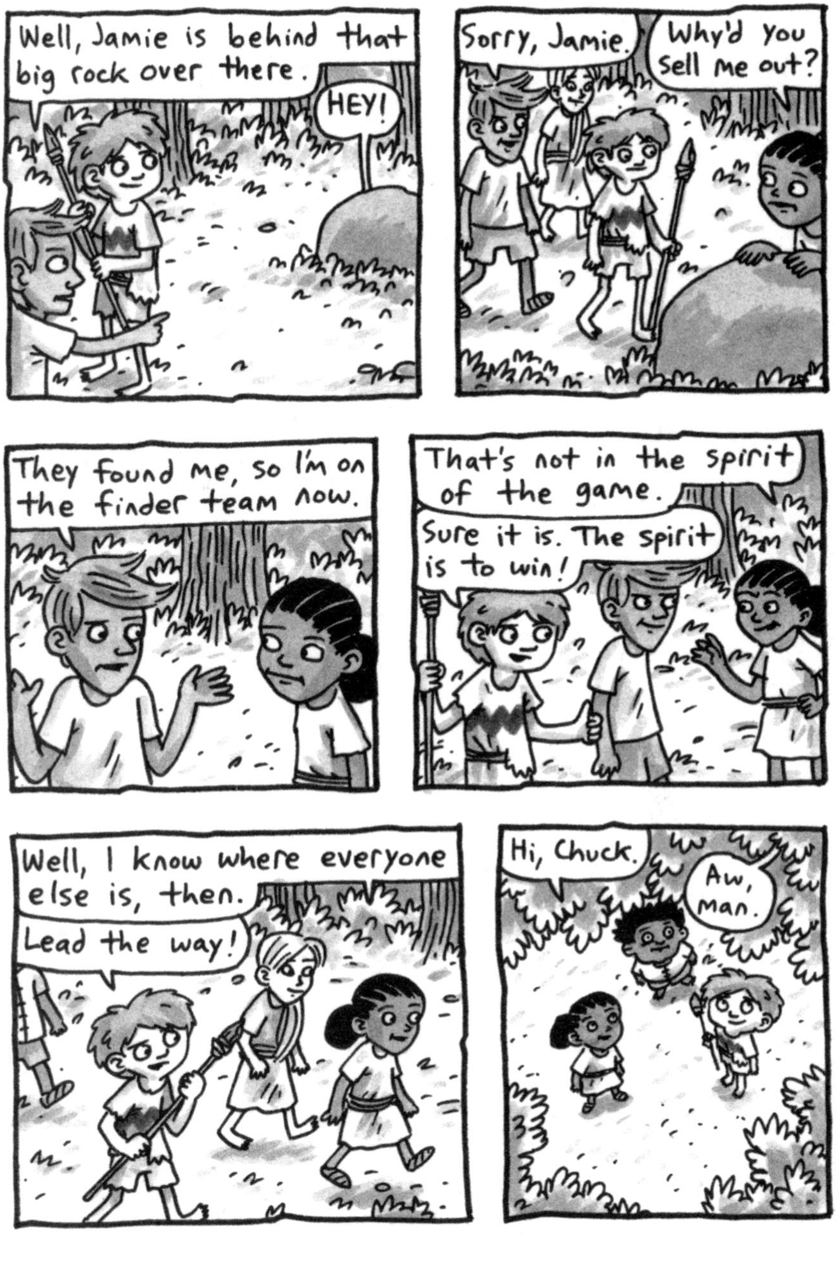
Well, Jamie is behind that big rock over there.
HEY!
Sorry, Jamie.
Why'd you sell me out?
They found me, so I'm on the finder team now.
That's not in the spirit of the game.
Sure it is. The spirit is to win!
Well, I know where everyone else is, then.
Lead the way!
Hi, Chuck.
Aw, man.

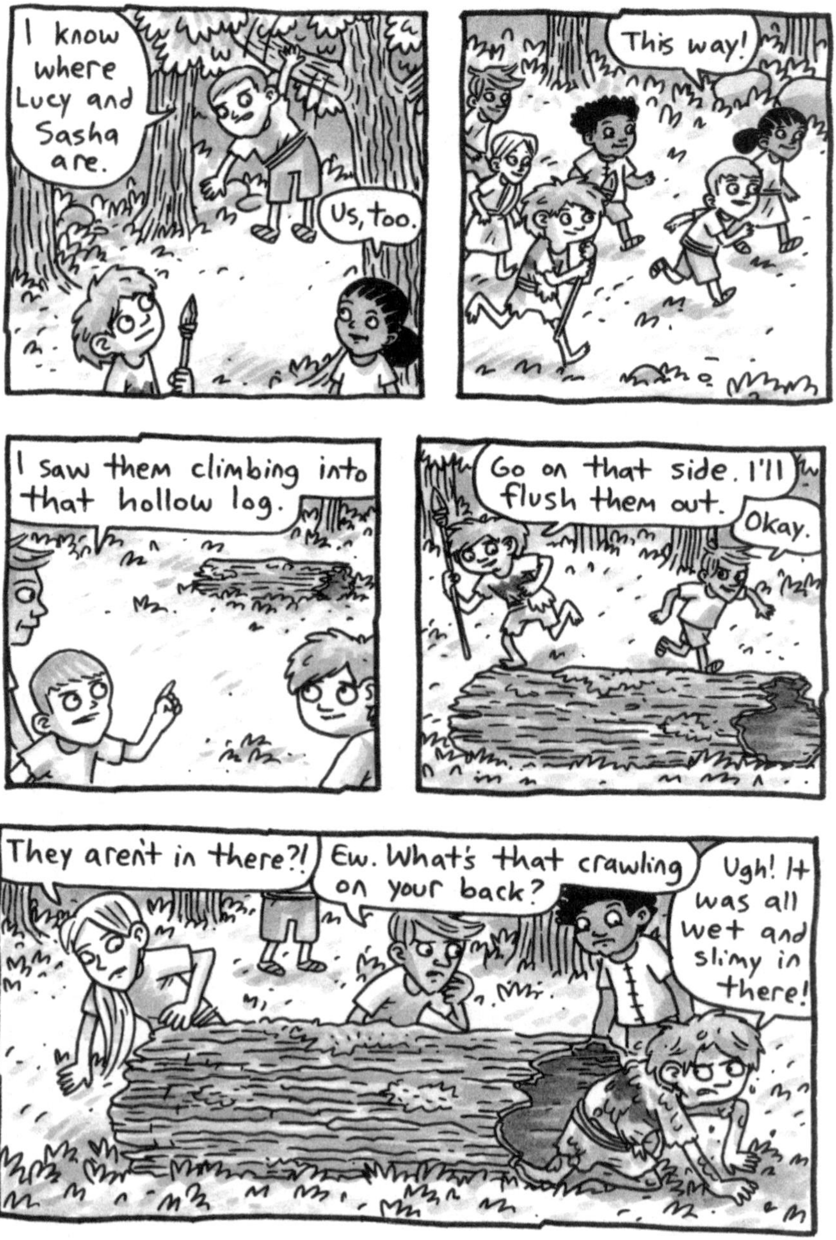
I know where Lucy and Sasha are.
Us, too.
This way!
I saw them climbing into that hollow log.
Go on that side. I'll flush them out.
Okay.
They aren't in there?!
Ew. What's that crawling on your back?
Ugh! It was all wet and slimy in there!

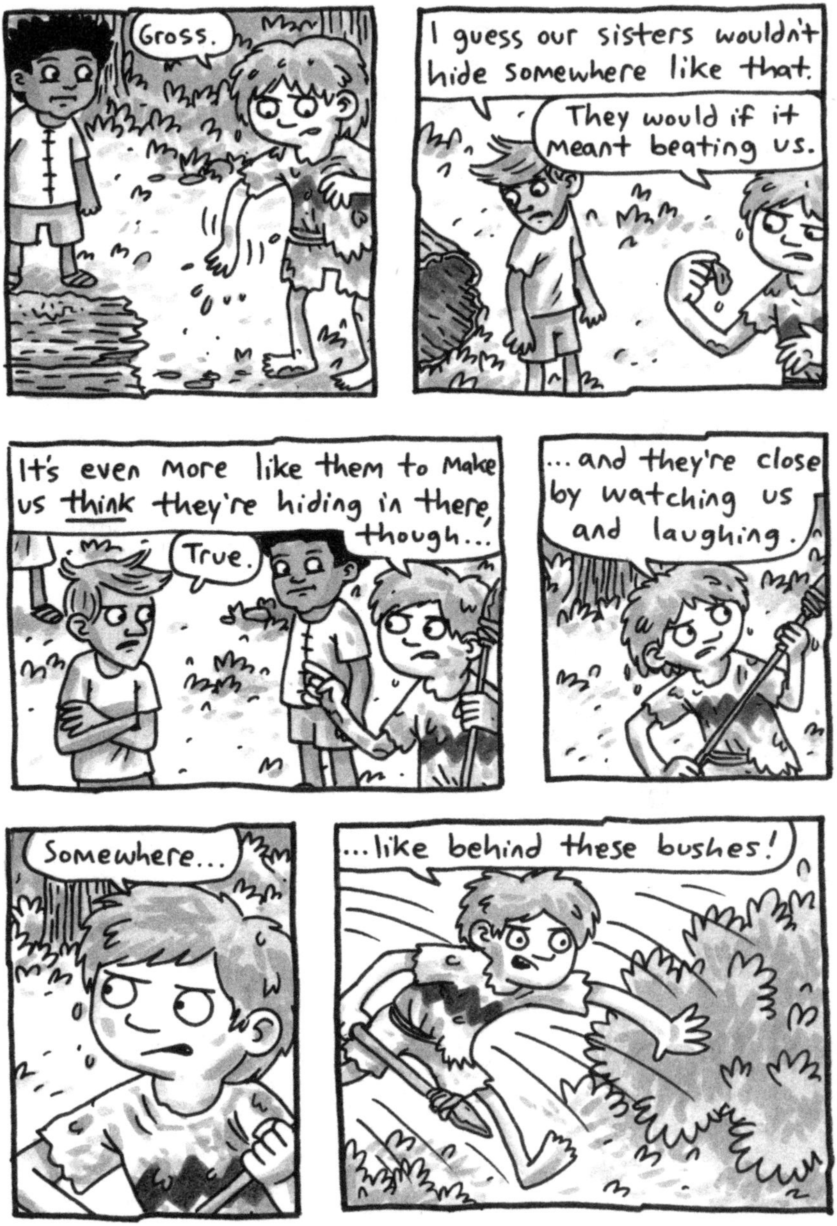
Gross.
I guess our sisters wouldn't hide somewhere like that.
They would if it meant beating us.
It's even more like them to make us think they're hiding in there, though...
True.
...and they're close by watching us and laughing.
Somewhere...
...like behind these bushes!

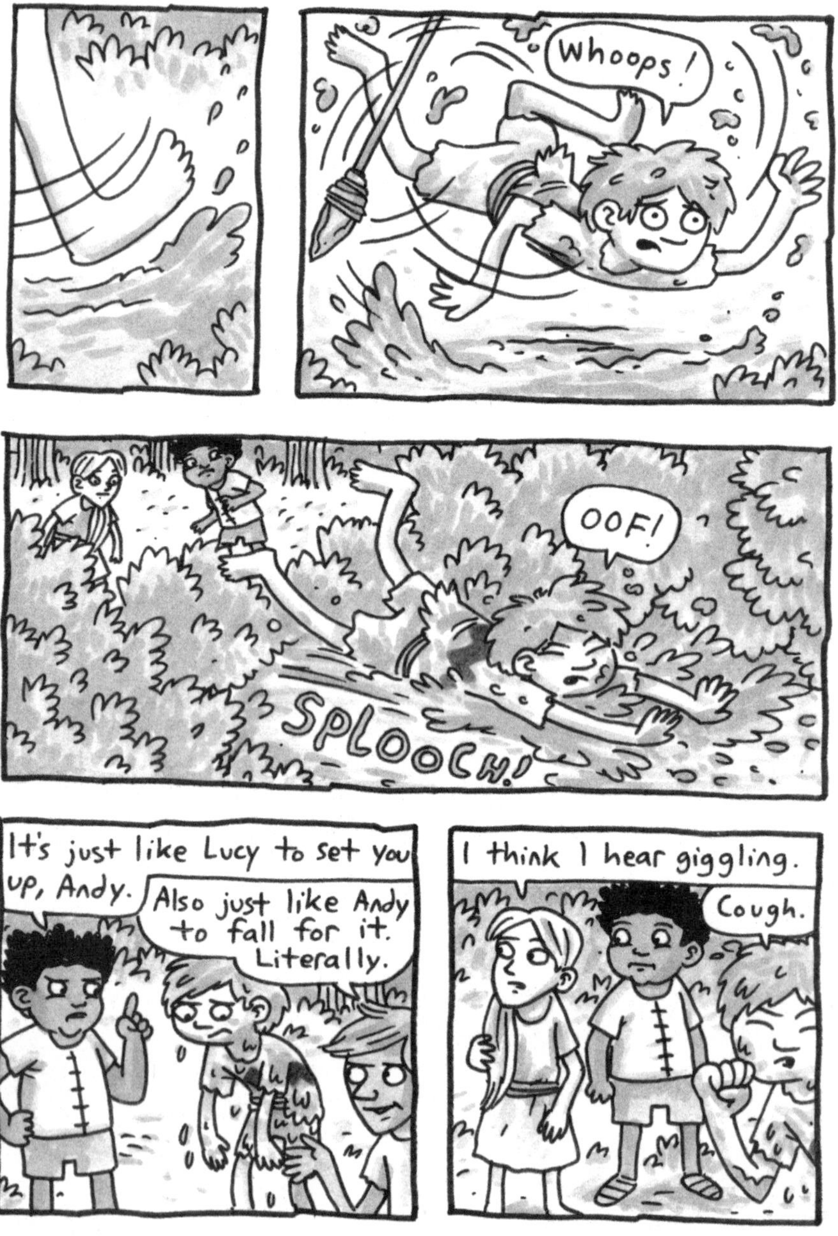
Whoops!
OOF!
SPLOOCH!
It's just like Lucy to set you up, Andy.
Also just like Andy to fall for it. Literally.
I think I hear giggling.
Cough.

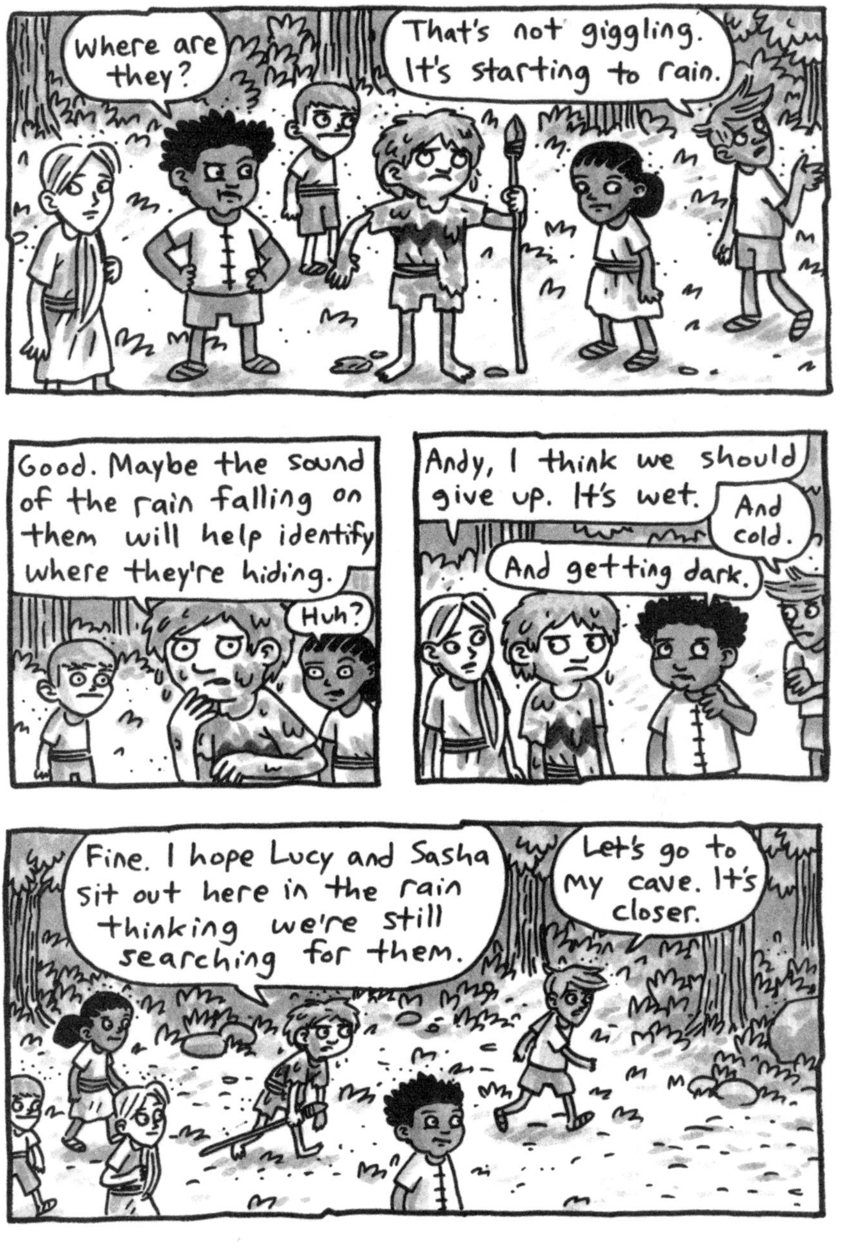
Where are they?
That's not giggling. It's starting to rain.
Good. Maybe the sound of the rain falling on them will help identify where they're hiding.
Huh?
Andy, I think we should give up. It's wet.
And cold.
And getting dark.
Fine. I hope Lucy and Sasha sit out here in the rain thinking we're still searching for them.
Let's go to my cave. It's closer.

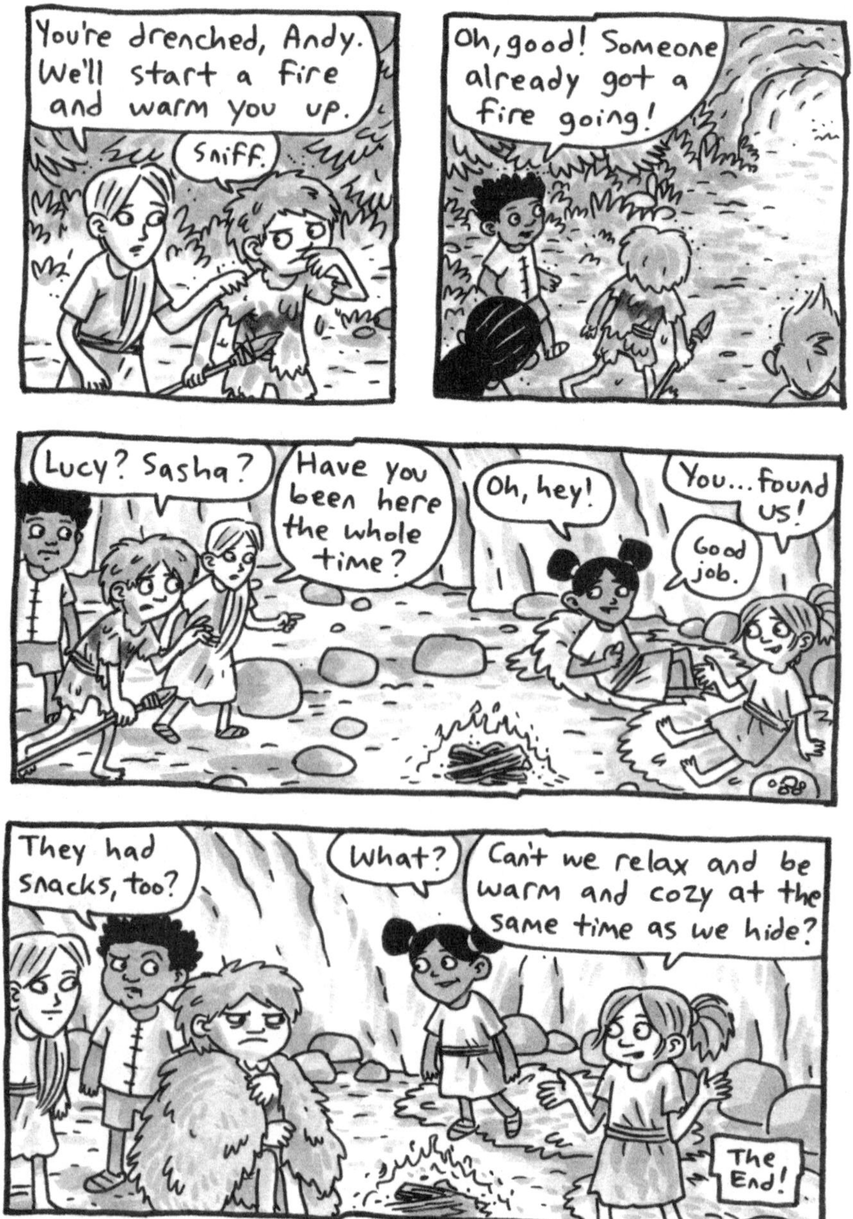
You're drenched, Andy. We'll start a fire and warm you up.
Sniff.
Oh, good! Someone already got a fire going!
Lucy? Sasha?
Have you been here the whole time?
Oh, hey!
You... found us!
Good job.
They had snacks, too?
What?
Can't we relax and be warm and cozy at the same time as we hide?
The End!

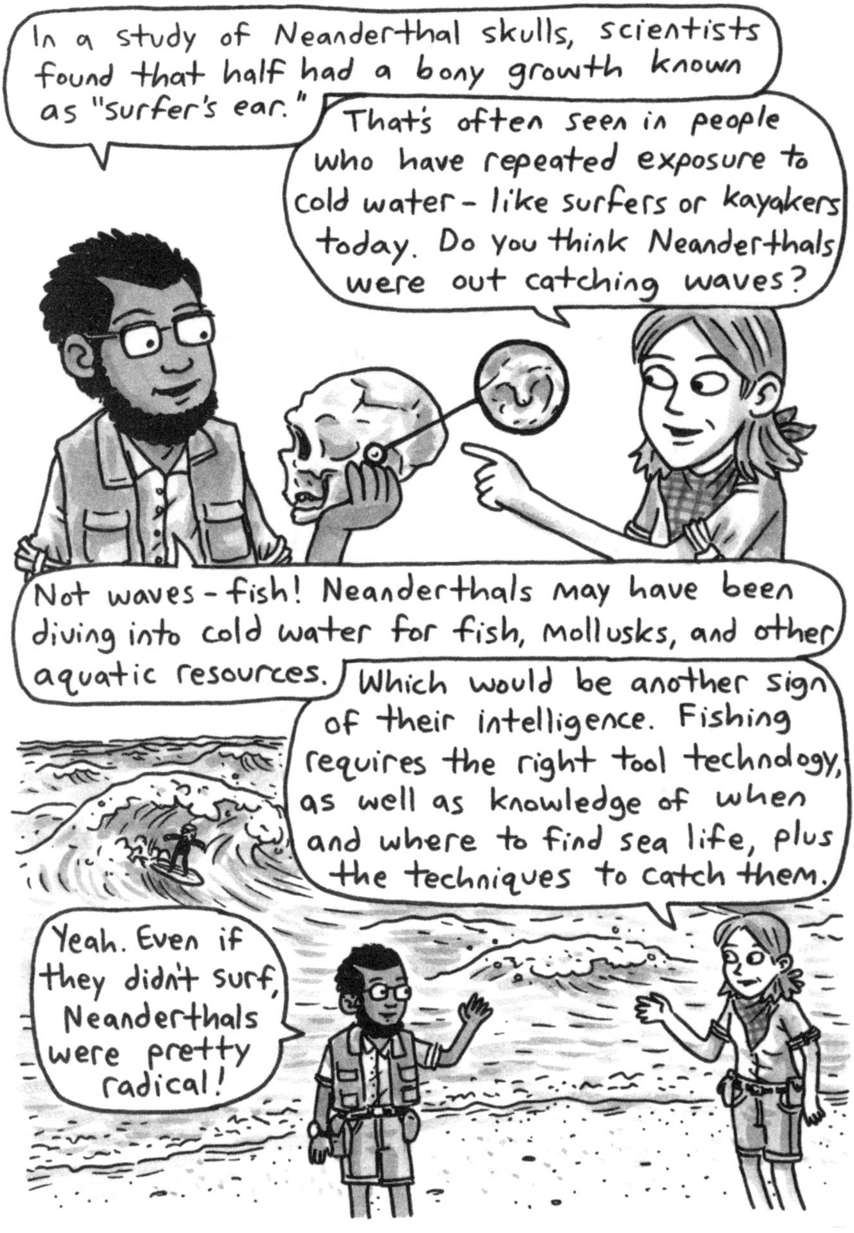
In a study of Neanderthal skulls, scientists found that half had a bony growth known as "surfer's ear."
That's often seen in people who have repeated exposure to cold water - like surfers or kayakers today. Do you think Neanderthals were out catching waves?
Not waves - fish! Neanderthals may have been diving into cold water for fish, mollusks, and other aquatic resources.
Which would be another sign of their intelligence. Fishing requires the right tool technology, as well as knowledge of when and where to find sea life, plus the techniques to catch them.
Yeah. Even if they didn't surf, Neanderthals were pretty radical!

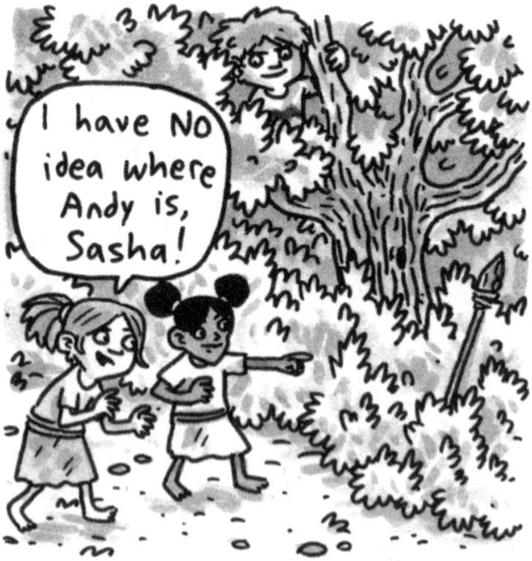
I have NO idea where Andy is, Sasha!

DIG INTO MORE PREHISTORIC FUN WITH

LUCY & ANDY NEANDERTHAL

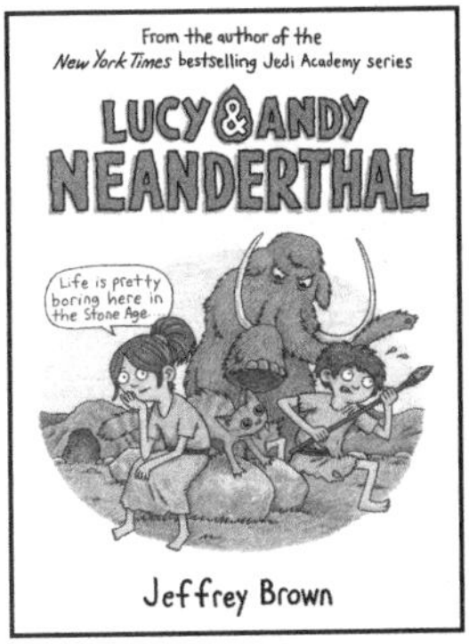
From the author of the
New York Times bestselling Jedi Academy series
LUCY & ANDY NEANDERTHAL
Life is pretty boring here in the Stone Age.
Jeffrey Brown

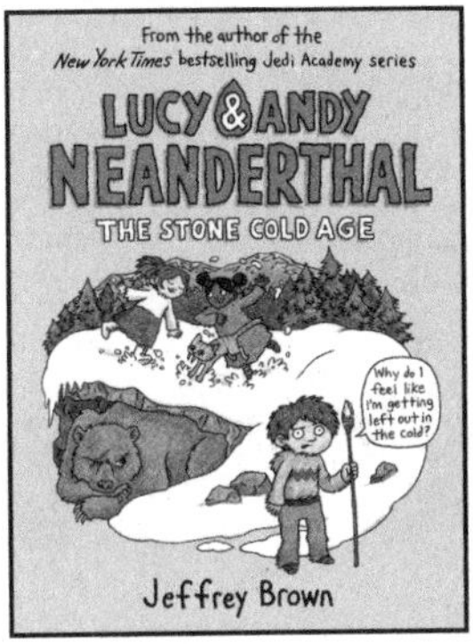
From the author of the
New York Times bestselling Jedi Academy series
LUCY & ANDY NEANDERTHAL
THE STONE COLD AGE
Why do I feel like I'm getting left out in the cold?
Jeffrey Brown

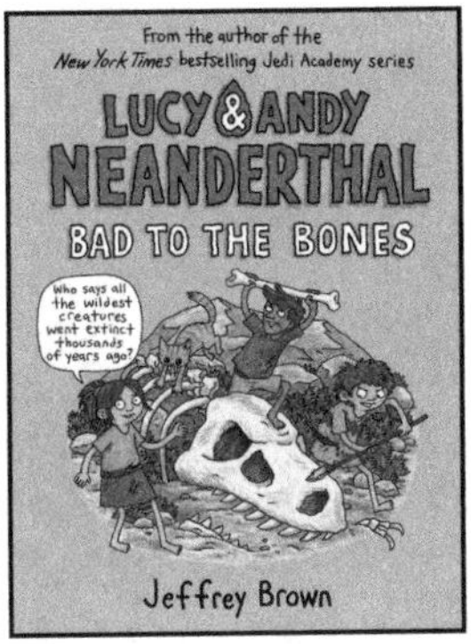
From the author of the
New York Times bestselling Jedi Academy series
LUCY & ANDY NEANDERTHAL
BAD TO THE BONES
Who says all the wildest creatures went extinct thousands of years ago?
Jeffrey Brown

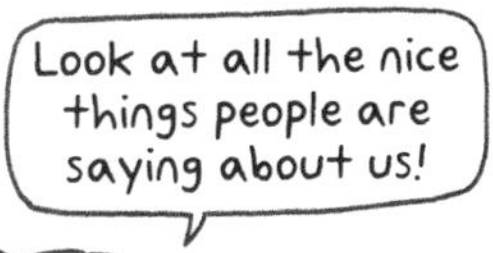
Look at all the nice things people are saying about us!

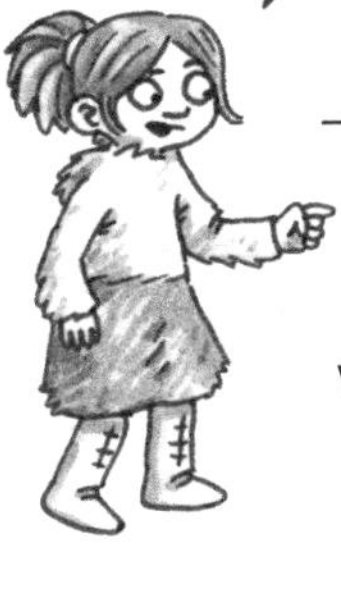

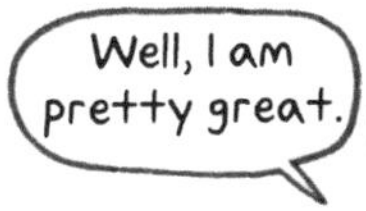
Well, I am pretty great.

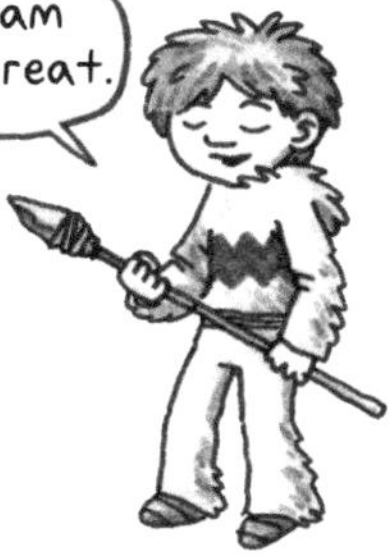

"Lucy & Andy are Stone Age rock stars."
—Lincoln Peirce, author of the Big Nate series and *Max and the Midknights*

"Every kid will love going back in time with Lucy & Andy!" —Judd Winick, author of the Hilo series

"A fast, funny read." —*Kirkus Reviews*

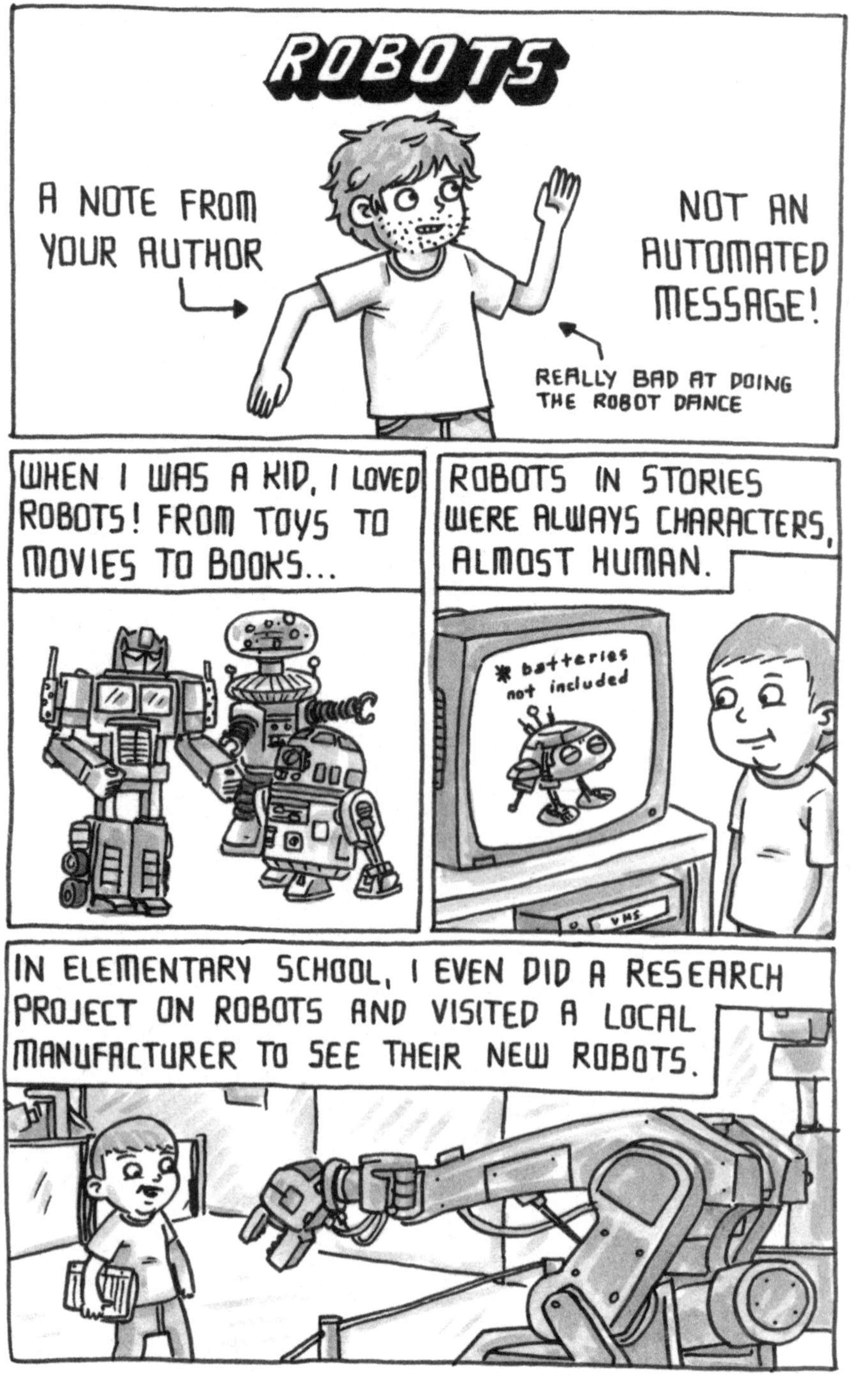

ROBOTS
A NOTE FROM YOUR AUTHOR
NOT AN AUTOMATED MESSAGE!
REALLY BAD AT DOING THE ROBOT DANCE
WHEN I WAS A KID, I LOVED ROBOTS! FROM TOYS TO MOVIES TO BOOKS...
ROBOTS IN STORIES WERE ALWAYS CHARACTERS, ALMOST HUMAN.
* batteries not included
VHS
IN ELEMENTARY SCHOOL, I EVEN DID A RESEARCH PROJECT ON ROBOTS AND VISITED A LOCAL MANUFACTURER TO SEE THEIR NEW ROBOTS.

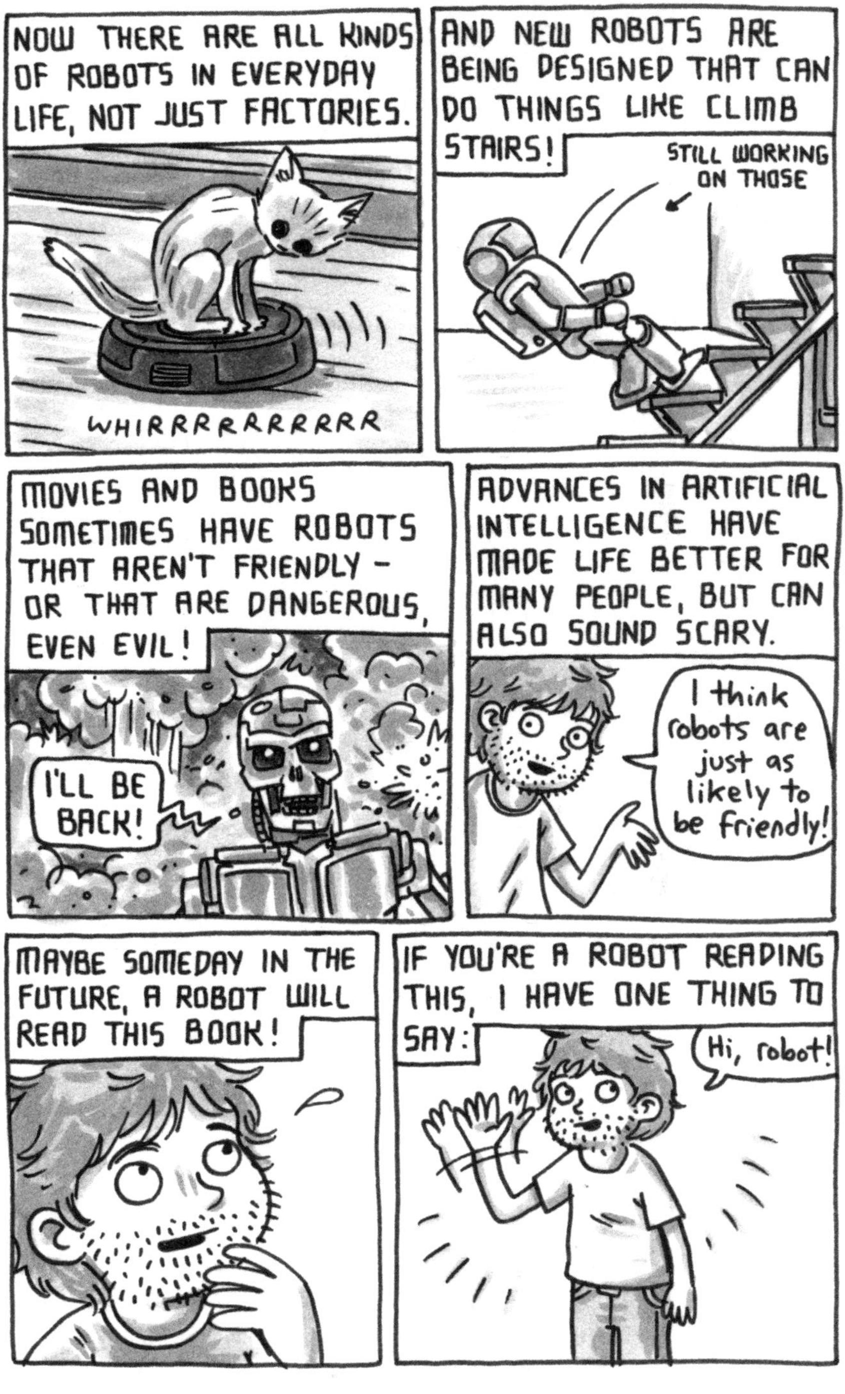
NOW THERE ARE ALL KINDS OF ROBOTS IN EVERYDAY LIFE, NOT JUST FACTORIES.
WHIRRRRRRRRRR
AND NEW ROBOTS ARE BEING DESIGNED THAT CAN DO THINGS LIKE CLIMB STAIRS!
STILL WORKING ON THOSE
MOVIES AND BOOKS SOMETIMES HAVE ROBOTS THAT AREN'T FRIENDLY – OR THAT ARE DANGEROUS, EVEN EVIL!
I'LL BE BACK!
ADVANCES IN ARTIFICIAL INTELLIGENCE HAVE MADE LIFE BETTER FOR MANY PEOPLE, BUT CAN ALSO SOUND SCARY.
I think robots are just as likely to be friendly!
MAYBE SOMEDAY IN THE FUTURE, A ROBOT WILL READ THIS BOOK!
IF YOU'RE A ROBOT READING THIS, I HAVE ONE THING TO SAY:
Hi, robot!

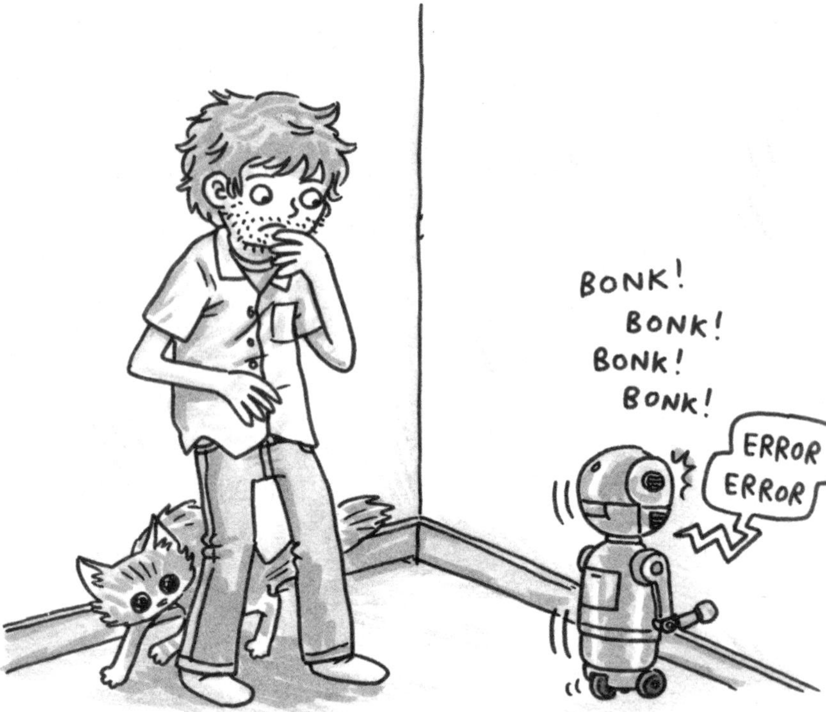
BONK!
BONK!
BONK!
BONK!
ERROR ERROR

JEFFREY BROWN IS THE AUTHOR OF THE LUCY & ANDY NEANDERTHAL AND SPACE-TIME! MIDDLE-GRADE SERIES, AS WELL AS THE BESTSELLING DARTH VADER AND SON AND JEDI ACADEMY SERIES. HE LIVES IN CHICAGO WITH HIS WIFE, TWO SONS, AND CAT. JEFFREY HAS ALWAYS BEEN FASCINATED BY ROBOTS, BUT HE IS MUCH BETTER AT DRAWING THEM THAN PROGRAMMING THEM.

VISIT HIM ON EARTH AT JEFFREYBROWNCOMICS.com
P.O. BOX 120 DEERFIELD, IL 60015-0120 USA